THE
STORIES

Contemporary

Short Fiction

Written

Edited by

in English

Bruce Meyer
Seneca College • University of Toronto

Prentice Hall Canada Inc.
Scarborough, Ontario

Canadian Cataloguing in Publication Data

Main entry under title:

The stories: contemporary short fiction written in English

1. English fiction – 20th century. 2. Short stories, English. I. Meyer, Bruce, 1957–

PN6120.2.S76 1997   823'.0108   C96-930877-9

© 1997 Prentice-Hall Canada Inc., Scarborough, Ontario

Prentice-Hall, Inc., Englewood Cliffs, New Jersey
Prentice-Hall International (UK) Limited, London
Prentice-Hall of Australia, Pty. Limited, Sydney
Prentice-Hall Hispanoamericana, S.A., Mexico City
Prentice-Hall of India Private Limited, New Delhi
Prentice-Hall of Japan, Inc., Tokyo
Simon & Schuster Asia Private Limited, Singapore
Editora Prentice-Hall do Brasil, Ltda., Rio de Janeiro

ISBN 0-13-493107-6

Acquisitions Editor: R. Bersagel
Developmental Editor: K. Sacks
Copy Editor: J. Bates
Production Editor: L. Berland
Production Coordinator: D. Starks
Permissions: M. Leupen
Cover Design: M. Kompter
Cover Image: D. McCormack
Page Layout: D. Fleming

5   WC   01

Printed and bound in Canada

Page 508 constitutes an extension of the copyright page. iiiEvery reasonable effort has been made to obtain permissions for all articles and data used in this edition. If errors or omissions have occurred, they will be corrected in future editions provided written notification has been received by the publisher.

We welcome readers' comments, which can be sent by e-mail to
  phabinfo_pubcanada@prenhall.com

For Kerry, Carolyn, Margaret and Homer

Table of Contents

Alternate Table of Contents

CARIBBEAN—Stories by Caribbean Authors:

CHARACTERIZATION:

CHILDHOOD STORIES:

DISPLACEMENT:

IDENTITY:

IMAGERY:

IRELAND—Stories by Irish Authors:

LOVE:

MOTHER/DAUGHTER RELATIONSHIPS:

SEX:

SHORTER STORIES:

WAR:

WOMEN—Stories About Women

Preface

In recent years, the scope of contemporary courses in the English language tradition has broadened to include a wider and richer range of traditions and cultures. *The Stories* has been designed for courses that have embraced this "new canon."

This anthology is intended as a reader for courses in post-colonial literature, Native North American (First Nations) literature, African and Asian English literature, and contemporary Canadian short fiction, as well as traditional courses in English literature, genre studies, modern American, modern British, modern Canadian, and literature-based composition/rhetoric courses. The key is to place English-language short stories in an international and multifaceted context that supersedes the traditional boundaries of national literatures and illustrates the richness of the language.

The stories themselves have been selected for their strengths in several areas. Readability was the first criterion. Students should feel engaged and entertained as well as stimulated by what they encounter in a story—a text must have clarity, purpose, and accessibility if it is to serve both teachers and students as a didactic instrument.

The second criterion was the manner in which the story speaks not only for itself as an independent work of art, but as a testimonial for the author, an avenue into the larger body of a writer's work—both a tease and a conduit for further exploration.

Third, the issue of national representation was also a key ingredient in the process of choosing a representative selection for *The Stories*. These stories make important statements about their author's countries of origin—as works that are more than mere postcards. The other benefit of including multicultural material is that students, whatever their personal background, will be able to see themselves reflected in the narratives and structures of fiction embraced by the scope of the English language.

A number of important features have been built into this text to make it more adaptable and functional for classroom use than previous texts. Each story is prefaced with an introduction that offers biographical material on the author, a brief discussion of the author's writing with a selected bibliography of important works by that author, and some short comments about the story itself. The story is followed by some topics for discussion to stimulate the exchange of text-oriented readings and to illuminate aspects of the story that underline its significance as a work of art. An alternate table of contents organizes the stories according to theme, region or nationality, and structural or compositional significance.

The Stories begins with an introduction to the structures and characteristics of short fiction, with particular attention to how to read a short story or novella. A glossary lists useful terms for building a solid critical vocabulary. Also included is a list of suggested essay topics that will assist both teachers and students.

The Stories should provide more than literary entertainment and edification, more even than a working knowledge and appreciation of the short story form. The critical introductions, the questions, and the glossary are constructed with the aim of teaching students the skill of close reading, perhaps the most important learning outcome for a literature text. Close reading provides students with the evaluative skills not only to comprehend what they read, but to assimilate, associate, and synthesize that knowledge through analysis and discourse. The aim of *The Stories* is to assist students in the process of becoming critically analytical, qualitatively aware and confident independent readers who remain cautious and curious about what they read even after their institutional learning has come to a conclusion. The intelligent, independent reader, after all, is the desired product of any well-considered literature course.

In the preparation of this anthology several individuals provided invaluable assistance, and their contributions and considerations are gratefully acknowledged: Professor Barry Callaghan of York University for his tough-minded thoughts on fiction and his suggestions on what he has enjoyed teaching and reading; Professor Chelva Kanaganayakam of Trinity College, University of Toronto, for his caring and expert insights into Asian and African literature; Fred Howe of York University for his thorough and sensitive knowledge of Australian and New Zealand literature; Dr. Carolyn Meyer of Seneca College for her expertise in Irish and women's literature; Joseph Bruchac for his suggestions and information on Native American literature; Rebecca Bersagel of Prentice Hall Canada for her wisdom, patience and vision; Karen Sacks of Prentice Hall Canada for the caring, patience and enthusiasm she brought to this project; Lisa Berland of Prentice Hall Canada for her diligence and creativity in matters of production; Marjorie Munro and Allan Gray of Prentice Hall Canada for their challenge and daring; Kerry Johnston, Margaret Meyer and Homer Meyer for their invaluable assistance and support throughout the preparation of this volume.

Bruce Meyer
1997

Introduction: Encountering the Short Story

Our lives are made up of stories: the stories we tell ourselves for amusement, the stories others tell us for information, the stories we attend to when we wish to understand the world around us. When we were very young, stories were read to many of us to teach us and delight us, to give shape and meaning to our world and depth to our ideas and beliefs. We locate ourselves in time by creating histories and chronicles of the events that we feel have been significant to our time and place and to other times and places. We record our lives in our own memories by telling ourselves stories—they are the means by which we comprehend and define ourselves. And even when events or experiences fail to make sense to us, our brains will work overtime to make the absurd plausible by seeking connections, narrative and order among even the most random and coincidental incidents.

For example, here are three statements that may or may not be factual. Picture these ideas in your mind:

i)   I go to baseball games.
ii) I like to eat hot dogs.
iii) I take my cat for walks.

The first statement, *I go to baseball games*, locates the "I" at a baseball stadium. In the second statement, the "I" is eating hot dogs and can easily be pictured in your mind with a red-hot in hand, perhaps in connection with the first statement, sitting in the stands on a sunny day and watching the middle innings of contest. But what is the connection between the third statement, about walking the cat, and the first two? If you pictured the "I" taking the cat for a walk up and down the bleacher seats or through the corridors of the grandstand, then you are probably a natural both for storytelling and story-listening because you made a connection where there was no logical link. You are a born fiction consumer.

But don't worry if you didn't make those connections. Reading fiction requires a great deal of what in literature is known as the "suspension of disbelief," the ability to buy into what the author is saying by allowing the author's statements to stimulate, on your mental movie screens, the mind's eye in your imagination. You are probably still at the stage where you can't be sure whether you should trust the author to lead you in a plausible and comprehensible direction. What you have witnessed, however, is the way in which all writers construct the stories they tell you: they select some ideas or highlights from tangible reality and ask you to make the connections between them to form an overall picture of an event or a person in your mind.

A **narrative** is any sequence of events placed in relationship to one another (juxtaposed) to create the illusion of linkage. In creating a story, an author can give the reader only a selection of the details of life. The astute reader reads a story for *what* the author is depicting, *how* the author is portraying the event, idea or person in the story, *why* the author is choosing to select certain things and not others in the process of relating the information, and the *language and structures* the author has chosen to convey what it is he or she wants the reader to know.

When the reader links all of the selected information presented in a story, he or she gains an impression of the action of the story. The sum total of the action, essentially a tally of what has happened in the course of the narrative, is known as the **plot**. When considering plot, readers should think of the sequence of events as a "play" within their mind—hence the term **dramatic action**. Here the author strives to establish a direct relationship between cause and effect. This cause-and-effect principle, where actions cause reactions and the reactions carry implications, can be traced through a series of steps or identifiable points within the drama of the action.

Conventional stories often start with an **exposition**. Here the author establishes where the story is taking place, who is involved in the story, and some of the major considerations or ideas that will be examined through the process of the story's telling. Often, but not always, the central figure in the story will learn something or act in a certain way that will set the plot in motion and cause the events to unfold through a series of consequences. Having set the events in motion and arranged various dynamic tensions in the story, the author takes the development of the plot another step. In this next step, known as the **conflict**, the individuals in the story come into conflict with one another, with themselves and their various personal concerns (such as their conscience), or with their situations or environments. What the author has done, up to this point, is to arrange for a problem to happen; that problem must now be brought to a head.

The **climax** is the apex or "high point" of the story, the "point of no return" in the dramatic action, often a moment when some important discovery is made, either about the key individual in the story or about those who are challenging that individual. This new information clarifies the problematic issues of the plot and reinforces the need for a resolution.

The pursuit of **resolution** is perhaps one of the main reasons why we read or listen to stories—we desire orderliness, in which the reasons for events are given, and problems and expectations are given plausible explanations and fulfilment. If things were not explained, if our questions and concerns about a story and its focal individuals were not addressed, we would be left with a confused and unsatisfied emptiness, a sense that the story had not delivered what it promised. In a resolution the author answers all or most of the questions and problems that the story has presented in the course of its conflict. Often, but not always, this resolution involves a happy ending in which the focal individual, on whom the reader has focused all of his or her attention and hopes, is allowed a just and fair outcome of the conflict. This pursuit of a satisfying and happy ending is known as **poetic justice**; it can also refer to the meting out of justice to those deserving punishment.

At the conclusion of the story, the author often offers a compensatory statement such as "they lived happily ever after," or presents a new series of lesser problems, or lists the ramifications or complications of the climax in which the context and events of the conflict are finally understood. This aftermath, which often appears at the end of a story where the plot is "unravelled," is called the **denouement**. The denouement has been called "an ingenious untying of the knot of intrigue" or simply a reasonable explanation for all of the events that have unfolded.

More common among contemporary authors in terms of how they construct their endings is the **open ending**, in which the resolution never develops and the reader is left to choose between a range of possibilities rather than settling on a single resolution. In this case, the lack of a resolution is compensated for by the *process* of the story's telling—the focus is on leaving the reader with questions, doubts and problems for consideration. A story may completely upset a reader's expectations about a possible resolution, either by the sudden presentation of new and unexpected information, or by an unexpected turn of events. The *surprise ending* helps make stories interesting, providing the reader with shock, dismay or sudden pleasure.

One of the simpler issues to be addressed when discussing a story is whether it is happy or sad. The difference between a happy and a sad story is essentially the distinction between the age-old literary concepts of **comedy** and **tragedy**. The word comedy is drawn from the Greek word *komus* meaning "a revel." In classical drama, a play that ended with the reconciliation of conflicting parties through the celebration of a marriage was said to be **comic** in its plot. Not only did such dramas end happily (with the opposing sides united in marriage), but humorous interludes involving secondary characters would usually relieve the tension along the way. Our modern term *comedy* takes its origins from this aspect of early stage productions.

Tragedy is also drawn from classical roots. We tend to equate with tragedy any sad story that ends with our expectations for a just resolution being dashed, or with the hero unable to elude an inevitable unhappy fate. The word *tragedy* is taken from the Greek words *tragos* meaning "goat" and *oide* meaning "song." Early tragic poems and

dramas usually dealt with the death of a shepherd, and the songs delivered in honour of the departed herdsman were sad tributes to his worth
in which his loss was lamented. The sense of grief and loss of a focal
individual in a song, drama or poem was meant to evoke in the audience a feeling of emptiness, a despondency over the shattering of hopes
and expectations that the plot had established. This grief caused what
the classical philosopher Aristotle termed "catharsis," an outpouring of
spontaneous emotion as the audience's response to the events. The
meaning of the term tragedy has shifted, and it is now equated with any
story that does not end satisfactorily according to our expectations and
desires.

Several types of plot can be found in a story. One that starts at a
logical beginning or opening, and in which all of the events follow log-
ically and chronologically to the end without major time shifts or backtracks into recollected information or diversions into less consequential
material, is said to have a **linear plot**, a plot that moves more or less in
a straight line from beginning to end. Stories with linear plots usually
have a strong sense of *unity* because the events or individuals being
depicted are located in one place and within a narrow and focused
period of time. When an author backtracks during the progress of the
story by offering up recollected information or laying false trails, the
story is said to have a **digressional plot**.

Usually, when the author digresses from the plot, he or she has
diverged from the unity of the time and the place in which the story is
happening to divulge information to the reader that is not necessarily
part of the immediate circumstances but that the reader needs in order
to gain a more complete understanding of the depicted situation. For
example, if the plot of a story concerns the fact that John is fishing, the
author might digress to tell of previous times when John went fishing,
perhaps relate information about the fish he caught and the ones that
got away, before continuing the story. This plot technique gives the
author the opportunity to create a **story within the story**, the chance
to relay a **subnarrative** that delays the development of the key events
in the story. This delay can be very useful when a writer wishes to add
tension or suspense to the plot.

Events in a story need not be related in the order in which they
happen. An author may decide to tell a story back-to-front, from end to
beginning. This is called a **reverse plot**, which often shifts the focus of
the story from a process of action and reaction to one of blame and
consequence by examining the causes of events through a study of their
effects.

An author may also open a story in the middle of the action, bor-
rowing from the structure of early poetic epics such as Homer's *Odyssey*.
The process of starting in the middle of the story is known as opening
in medias res, or "in the middle of things." This technique allows the

author to suspend the action for dramatic purposes, to introduce a **subplot**, or secondary narrative structure or story line, and to allow for the opportunity to tell a story within the story.

Aside from the ordering of information in a story with regard to "what happens," there are a number of other fundamental issues that readers should consider. *Where* a story takes place is also important. This is called the **setting**. But setting may also refer to the time the action takes place, the manner of living of those individuals who are the focus of the story, and the religious, moral, social and emotional conditions of those involved in the dramatic action of the story. In spatial terms, **setting** can be divided into the **foreground** and the **background**. When an author describes the setting for a story, pay particular attention to what you are being told about the environment and the location. A story may also be set in the mind or memory of an individual. In establishing the setting, an author's focus will converge on various objects. It is possible to examine setting in terms of the depth of detail and even the way in which the author sees. Objects portrayed up close and in detail might suggest a myopic, constricted way of setting the story. (Often, as in Mansfield's "The Garden-Party," objects take on the form of "still lifes" in which they are arranged and portrayed to create a static and artificial impression on the reader.) On the other hand, objects portrayed at a distance lend an expansiveness and a spaciousness to the setting. This aspect of the setting is known as the **field of vision**. In terms of setting, imagine that the author is a director of a movie (in your mind's eye) who is panning, or providing a panoramic view, from shot to shot in order to assist you in locating the story and its details in a visual context.

The setting can also assume a temporal aspect in various ways. The author may choose to locate the story in a specific time and place from the past, thus creating a *historical context* and enlarging the scope of the story by referring to historical events, their implications and known results. Time—when the story is taking place, how long a period the narrative covers, the number of points of **collapsed time**, where the author skips over a period of years in the course of a sentence or two—is also an important expression of setting. Because a story focuses on a selection of depicted incidents rather than reiterating or reporting directly on everything that happens during the period covered by a narrative, authors tend to collapse time. The use of time in a story is known as the *time scheme*.

Culture—the background to the place where the action is happening, the details of how individuals live, their customs, their concerns—is another aspect of setting. With the recent rise of **postcolonial literature** or writing from non-Eurocentric or "emerging" literatures, one of the greatest difficulties for North American readers is adjusting their expectations to what is new, strange and often without precedent in their own experience. Watch for the way housing, food, vegetation and landscape influence stories.

Opening a story by describing a place or an environment, as in the first paragraph of Joyce's "Eveline," is known as **setting the scene**. In much the same way, a script for a play often opens with remarks on where the story is located, details of the scene, the placement of furniture, the time of day and even information on how the scene should be lit. Setting the scene allows readers to build up a picture in their mind's eye of how the world or the situation of the action will look.

As has been stated, writers are constantly feeding us information in their stories that enables us to visualize what it is they are describing. The way in which these descriptions work is through the process of evocation—in effect, the writer is reminding us of what we already know by imparting various verbal clues that we, as readers, "flesh out" in our imaginations by drawing on our own memories and experiences. The mental pictures conjured up by an author are called images. An **image**, in literary terms, is a series of words that bring to mind a picture. For instance, "the red chair" probably causes you to think of a seating device of some sort that is in one of any number of shades of red. If you were asked to draw a detailed picture of that red chair your picture would be different from those drawn by your classmates, because no two people have the same experiences or make use of the same fund of images. An image, although it enables us to visualize an object, has no meaning—or various readings—other than itself.

When an image is repeated several times throughout a narrative, such as darkness in Conrad's "Heart of Darkness," the repeated image is known as a **leitmotif**. Using the device the writer not only keeps the reader entertained and imaginatively stimulated over the course of a narrative, but also creates a visual and imaginative *unity* to the work in which the repeated image reinforces the ideas the author is trying to articulate through the story. A leitmotif need not be just an image; it can also be a repeated action, a repeated phrase or statement, or a recurring idea.

If an author wanted us to interpret an image and assign to it a number of possible meanings or associations, he or she would be creating a **symbol**. The image of the red chair might represent a throne for a king, an altar for a deity, an electric chair for an execution, the seat of a local government, or a special academic position in a college or university. When a universally acknowledged image such as "the sun" is used, then the *symbolic meanings*, or the range of possible associations or readings that the image entails, become much richer. The sun could be a symbol for life, growth, happiness, springtime or summer, eternal life, morning, the Greek god Apollo and so on.

When an image is used in a comparative fashion, when an author is saying "the red chair is *like* a throne" or "the red chair is *like* a horse," and asking us to consider all of the similarities and differences between the two, he or she presents us with a simile. The **simile** is a device that compares two images, and through the process of comparison, or the use of the word "like," leaves the reader with an idea based on a synthesis, amalgam or compromise concept that acts as a third consideration apart from the two things being compared. Similes ask us to acknowledge likeness, and an author who is working hard to activate our visual imaginations will locate a new concept in our minds by reminding us of something we already know.

More complex both for the reader to understand and for the writer to utilize is the metaphor. Where the simile functions in a comparative manner, the **metaphor** functions by *equating* two images. An author who notes that the "red chair *is* a throne" is formulating a metaphor. The metaphor imaginatively identifies one object or image with another, the qualities of the second image being infused into the first. There are two parts to a metaphor: the *vehicle* and the *tenor*. The tenor in "the red chair is a throne" scenario is "the red chair," the central or primary image. The secondary image, whose qualities are being ascribed to the central or primary image, is known as the vehicle.

A metaphor may concern itself with equating one image with another, or can be extended to embrace an entire story in which the plot or the central figure in the narrative represents ideas or larger concerns. For instance, in Faulkner's "A Rose for Emily," Miss Emily Grierson becomes a metaphor for the antebellum or pre–Civil War American South. She is not simply a symbol of longevity or of determined though futile pride, but a metaphor for an entire way of life and civilization; Miss Emily is the tenor, and the vehicle (or that with which she is equated) is the South. This **extended metaphor**, when it assumes a moral message or *moral imperative* (a hard-to-miss association between one thing and another built into the purpose or point of the narrative), is called an **allegory**.

In an allegory, the persons or things that comprise the tenor are associated with larger meanings and concerns that are often outside of the narrative, concerns the story itself may not directly address, but that are so overt and obvious that readers are bound to "get the point" and make the association on their own. Allegories are extremely useful in contemporary fiction because they allow the writer the privilege of making a point without directly stating it—a privilege that, in a world where governments often oppress journalists, allows creative writers the chance to tell the truth without having to spell it out literally.

Literature falls into several categories, such as *poetry, drama, nonfiction* and *fiction*. Most short stories are fiction, narratives composed out of the author's imaginative resources. Hence anything fictional is supposed to be "made up." The term "fictional" is often mistaken for anything that is not true. Herein, however, lies a paradox. One of the functions of literature is to convey universal truths, ideas that can be understood and appreciated by anyone, anywhere, at any time, regardless of their nationality, beliefs or gender; yet these truths, these accepted and unchanging ideas, are conveyed in a medium that uses the imagined, the invented. The question "Did this story really happen?" can usually be answered with a "No," yet what makes the story seem plausible or acceptable to a reader is its sense of verity or truthfulness.

An author establishes *verity* in a story by using information, images, conversations, thoughts and situations that seem believable. The sense of **plausibility**, the idea that the story could have happened just as the author states, is one of the attractions of fiction that makes us want to read on and pursue the narrative to its logical and credible resolution. If a story does not seem plausible, if it inspires a reaction such as "This can't possibly have happened this way," then either the writer has failed in his or her attempt to make the imaginary seem real, or he or she is writing a type of fiction known as fantasy. **Fantasy** is any piece of fiction that obviously and consciously deviates from reality for the purpose of pursuing its narrative. Examples include the fairy tale (a story that uses the supernatural or magic in order to propel the narrative) and futuristic *science fiction* (fantasy that uses scientific facts or conjectures as the basis for its narrative information).

In reading a story, readers should distance themselves from any concerns about whether it is true or not and simply approach it as an entertaining experience in plausibility. To mistake a piece of fiction for a statement of fact (and not to recognize that the structures and elements of fiction discussed in this essay are actively at work in the composition of the story) is a problem known as **literalism**, or assuming that because a story is written it must be true. Fictional stories are simply statements of what might be possible. The reader is left with the task of sorting out the plausible from the implausible, the possible from the impossible—which is half the fun of reading a piece of fiction.

A literalist reading is often the result of mistaken identity—the reader confuses a figure in a story for the author, especially when it is being told from the perspective of a storyteller who is using the pronoun "I." The **narrative voice** is a device authors adopt to separate themselves from the contents of the story (a stance that allows them to function as artists at the controls of an objective creation rather than simply as subjective diary-keepers writing down their life and thoughts). The narrative voice in poetry and classical drama is called the **persona**. In classical drama, an actor would don a mask that would convey to the audience an idea of the individual he was portraying. The Greek word for "mask" is *persona*. In a short story, especially one in which the storyteller is relating his or her direct experience of the events (through the use of the pronoun "I" as in "I did this" or "I saw that" or "this happened to me"), the author is not speaking as the author, but through a persona or masking device, which enables, for example, a female writer to speak as a male or a man to speak as an animal.

Every story, whether fictional or non-fictional, has a narrative voice, which gives the reader the details, ideas and statements that make up the story. Any form of narration has its strengths and its weaknesses, and an astute reader is aware of these when he or she approaches a story. The perspective the narrator offers the reader is called the **point of view**. It is determined by the position of the narrator within the story—as a participant or as a detached, external observer of the events.

An author who tells the story from the perspective of a participant and witness to the events uses the first person pronoun "I." This type of narration is known as first person narration and is related in the first person narrative voice. The narrator is speaking experientially of what he or she has seen, heard or understood. The advantage of this perspective is that the first person narrator has been a participant in, or witness to, the action, often has an emotional connection to the events, a stake in the action, and has a sense of being caught up in the events and ideas that the author is conveying. This lends to the story a sense of immediacy, its firsthand, "I was there" viewpoint drawing the reader into the story. The first person narrative is usually, though not always, subjective, and this subjectivity is both a strength and a weakness. Because the first person narrator is one individual and because no individual can have complete knowledge of an event, his or her perspective is necessarily limited. This limited point of view is further complicated when the credibility of the narrator's testimony of events is called into question. With a first person narrator the reader may be left to speculate uneasily about whether the narrator is telling the truth. Many first person narrators are unreliable—they can't know all of the facts, and the confidence that can be drawn from the narrator's participation in or witnessing of the events is undercut by the biases and prejudices that are part of any subjective interpretation of experience.

An alternative to the first person narrator is the third person narrator. Here the story is told from the perspective of a detached voice, using the third person pronouns "he," "she" or "they." Because the narrator is not a participant in the action and remains external to the events, he or she is said to be omniscient (all-knowing) or all-seeing, able to be in more than one place at a time and observe more than one event at a time. An omniscient or third person narrator can provide the reader with background information, report on simultaneous events, and see into the minds of various figures in a story and discuss what they are thinking. An omniscient narrator allows the reader the privilege of insight, background data, and freedom of both time and space from which to draw information; yet there are limitations to this form also. A third person narrator is weakened by being limited to the stance of observer: because he or she is not a participant in the drama of the narrative, there is often a sense that emotional connection to events has been traded for a more complete knowledge of the situation and a detachment that may tend toward clinical disengagement rather than passionate involvement.

Often an author will step inside the mind of an individual and allow the reader a glimpse of how that person's mind works. The process of narrating the workings of a human mind, the continuous flow of thoughts presented as they flow from one perception to another in response to the ideas or situations with which the individual is involved, is called **stream of consciousness**. The apparent jumble of ideas and thoughts issuing from a person's mind allows an author to dramatize an individual's thought processes.

Thus far, we have spoken of "individuals." The technical name for the participants in a story is characters. Characters can be assigned to varying levels of importance depending on their significance to the outcome or resolution of the events and their participation in the process of the narrative. A character of great importance, in terms of the author's attention and his or her relationship to other characters, is called a **primary character**. Characters who are essential to a subplot but are of secondary importance to the plot are termed **secondary characters**. Figures who make "walk-ons" or minor appearances in the story, to assist in the narrative or simply to aid in the life-like appearance of the events, are called **minor characters**.

The central character, who is the main focus of the action, is known as the **protagonist**, another term borrowed from classical Greek, which is drawn from two words, *proto* meaning "first" and *agonistes* meaning "actor." The protagonist is often, but not always, the hero (or anti-hero) of the story. A character who opposes the actions and aims of the protagonist, and who is often seen as the villain of the story, is called the **antagonist**, that is, "the one who works against the hero."

A character's actions in a story, the **dynamics**, should be viewed with a critical eye, if not complete suspicion. The reader must question why a character behaves in a certain way in a story—this raises the question of motives or *motivation*. In many stories the author will arrange the action of the narrative in order to examine the reasons behind the behaviour of certain characters—that is, their motivation. In the course of a narrative, characters change, grow, learn, respond to events, and gain knowledge and awareness of themselves and their environments from having participated in the dramatic events of the story. This is the process of **character development** and is very important to a story because it locates the narrative as a record of process in which something important is learned or discovered, the suggestion being that knowledge can have a liberating or destructive impact on an individual.

A character is created and defined not only by motives or dynamics, but through the author's *vocabulary* (**diction** or choice of words), issues of morality, or the moral choices a character makes; *points of focus*, or what the character chooses to see or give his or her attention to; as well as habits, appearance and conversations with other characters (**dialogue**).

The way in which characters use language (that is, their diction and vocabulary) tells us a great deal about them. Sophisticated and complex language may suggest that the character is educated and erudite; common language or street slang may carry other connotations regarding the character's background and class. Because language conveys not only information but also emotion, an author constructs a story around the emotional impact of language. The impact the language has on both the characters and the reader is known as **tone**. Authors will evoke a particular tone, reflecting anger, regret, happiness or grief, simply by choosing a vocabulary associated with these emotional states.

Language in a narrative should not be automatically trusted, since it can be used both to express an idea or truth and as a means of masking, hiding or avoiding it. When a narrator or character says one thing yet obviously means another, he or she may be being ironic. **Irony** is one of the more subtle aspects of language, especially when a reader is used to accepting whatever is said by a person as a statement of fact or an expression of honesty. Irony is not lying; irony is the reservation or withholding of meaning (for whatever motive) from a statement by the individual who is making the remark. Irony can be recognized when the reader knows that what is said is not congruent with what is meant. Irony can be extended beyond mere phrases or statements to embrace the whole purpose of a narrative; an entire narrative can be ironic. **Dramatic irony** is being used when a character makes a statement that carries implications for ideas or events of which he or she is unaware but of which the reader is fully informed. It relies on the fact that the reader is more knowledgeable than the character, and this knowledge assists the author in creating tension, anxiety and expectation.

Irony is one of a number of devices that add layers of meaning to apparently straightforward dialogue. *Sarcasm* is being exercised when irony is used to hurt someone emotionally through the use of, say, bitter praise or caustic observation. **Hyperbole** is being used when a narrator or character employs extreme exaggeration for effect, as in a statement such as "My dog is the size of a bus." If, for instance, the speaker wanted to underplay the dog's largeness for the sake of humour or to make the point more emphatically, **understatement** could be used: "My dog is a real mouse." All these devices point up the need for readers to approach the language of a story critically; an author or character may or may not be candid or plain-spoken, and the level of sincerity of a statement is something that good readers will measure for themselves.

Other than action, language is the common thread shared by characters in a story. In dialogue, special attention should be paid to the casualness or formality of the language, as this can be an indicator of the level of familiarity shared by the participants in the dialogue. The use of dialogue also allows the writer to turn the story into a miniature drama. The author then has the opportunity to step back from the process of narration and description, and permits the characters themselves to carry the story forward.

According to the critic Wayne C. Booth in his study *The Rhetoric of Fiction*, there are primarily two types of fiction: **showing** fiction and **telling** fiction. In stories that take the "telling" approach, the author is continually inserting himself or herself as an arbiter in the story, offering explanations for what is going on, observations on the nature of the events, background on the characters, and **segues** (bridges) in both time and space between one event and another. The positive aspects of a "telling" narrative are that the author can skirt issues, be more selective in what information to give the reader, offer opinions and commentary on the actions and choices of the characters, and collapse large periods of time into a few sentences or paragraphs. The drawbacks to a "telling" narrative are that the author is constantly intruding upon the flow of the story, there is an awareness of an authorial presence in the progress of the narrative in which the reader must rely on the (usually omniscient) narrator and trust his or her judgment of the situation, and often there is the sense that the story has been "invaded" by its presenter.

A "showing" narrative is quite different in form and structure in that it is demonstrative where a "telling" narrative is explanatory. In a "showing" narrative, the author steps back from the action and allows the characters to dramatize and enact the events or situations through dialogue, stream of consciousness and minimally narrated action. The advantage of a "showing" approach is that the weight and emphasis of the narrative is placed upon the characters rather than upon the narrator, so the reader is given a profound sense of drama as the events unfold. The negative aspects of "showing" are that the story can take longer to tell and demand more patience from the reader and more awareness of diction and the nuances of action and reaction between characters (their psychology or their intellectual and emotional motivations and responses). Many stories are a mix of both "showing" and "telling" in which the author intrudes as an active presence in the story only when **exegesis** or explanation is absolutely necessary for the smooth progress and speedy development of the narrative.

These aspects of the storytelling process are common to poetry, drama, fiction and non-fiction. In particular, they are attributes and elements of a short story. A **short story** can be defined as any narrative between 500 and 12,000 words in length. It can be non-fictional, but the majority of stories encountered in contemporary literature are fictional. If a short story is longer than 12,000 words it is often called a **novella** (a short novel). Most novellas are between 12,000 and 15,000 words. Novellas tend to be rather more ambitious in scope than short stories. James Baldwin's "Sonny's Blues" and Mavis Gallant's "The Moslem Wife" are examples of the novella form, in which a central theme or idea is developed and extended throughout the narrative. Joseph Conrad's "Heart of Darkness" is an extended novella. In a very short story of less than 500 words, sometimes called a **sketch**, a single idea, confrontation, event or reaction to an event is observed and articulated.

Aside from considerations of narrative voice and showing or telling, the short story comes in various forms. A story can be told in the form of an essay (Frank Moorhouse's "The Drover's Wife") or as **oral history** (Alistair MacLeod's "The Boat"). In this sense, an author will often play with the *form* of the story, and good readers should be aware of how the information in the narrative is being presented as far as its shape and medium are concerned, since form often says a great deal about content.

As a literary expression, the short story has risen in popularity since the last century for a number of reasons. During the nineteenth century, universal education and literacy became a factor in Western society. Because more people could read, there was a greater demand for literary entertainment (in the age before television, movies and radio the printed word played an important role in our entertainment). The short story evolved as a popular form, or **genre**, because it could be read at one sitting (usually within less than an hour) unlike the novel, which demands time, patience, devotion and energy from a reader. Because it developed and articulated a single theme, incident or character, the short story became the genre of the working and newly educated middle class, which had just enough money to buy newspapers and magazines that featured short stories. Because of its popularity, short story writers realized quite early on that they were writing not for an élite audience but for a broad cross-section of the population, and they adjusted their language from the diction and vocabulary of poetry to a more direct, universal way of speaking. The communicability of the short story and its democratic and broad appeal have always made it the "people's choice" among literary forms. As well, early short story writers, particularly the nineteenth-century giants of the form—Edgar Allan Poe in the United States, Guy de Maupassant in France and Anton Chekhov in Russia—frequently published their stories in

magazines and newspapers because of the demand for such publica-
tions. Periodicals could be produced and sold cheaply because of the
nineteenth-century invention of the automated printing press.

The short story, however, has much more ancient roots. The
ancient bards, reciters and singers of long poems such as Homer's *Iliad*
and *Odyssey* could only sing for a certain time before their voices grew
tired. This forced the storytelling process into an *episodic* mode, in
which the larger story contained substories, focused accounts of
selected events linked together by a bridging character or theme. The
episodic quality of many larger works of literature, such as novels and
epic poems, suggests they are actually collections of short stories—a
point not lost on contemporary writers such as William Faulkner,
whose novel *Go Down, Moses* is a series of linked short stories, or Amy
Tan, whose short story "Two Kinds" is one of a series of linked stories
that comprise the novel *The Joy Luck Club*, or Louise Erdrich, whose
"Fleur," originally published as a short story, became a chapter in her
novel *Tracks*.

The fundamental thing to remember about short stories is that they
are written both to inform and to entertain. Authors are speaking to
their readers, their audience, as directly and eloquently as they can.
The short story is an artistic creation, and there is a purpose to everything the author is saying; nothing is there by accident, and every word
serves a purpose. In this introductory essay, you have been given terms,
ideas and concepts that are used in the short story form; an awareness
of these aspects of writing is intended to enrich your enjoyment, not
dampen it. In this selection are stories that have been told, that are
being told and that will continue to be told about the world we live in.
The authors want you to know what they have experienced and imagined. They want to put you in touch with their lives, their environments, their passions, their fears and their dreams. They are allowing
you inside their minds for a glimpse of how they see the world, just as
you allow others into your thoughts when you say to them, "There is
something I need to tell you." That is the purpose of storytelling; it is a
process in which you have been participating all your life.

Jean Arasanayagam

About the Author

Jean Arasanayagam was born in Sri Lanka of Dutch origin. She was educated at the University of Ceylon and the University of Strathclyde in Scotland. She has taught writing at the University of Iowa and has been writer-
in-residence at the University of Exeter in England. She is married to the Sri
Lankan painter Thiagarajah Arasanayagam and lives in Kandy, Sri Lanka.

Critic Chelva Kanaganayakam has noted that in her more recent writing
Arasanayagam addresses the tension "between the need for detachment
and the inability to remain unaffected by the cultural and ethnic conflicts
devastating the country [Sri Lanka]." Much of her work is set against the
backdrop of the social, linguistic, racial and religious strife that has plagued
Sri Lanka in recent years.

Selected Bibliography

Kindura (novel, 1973)
Apocalypse '83 (novel, 1985)
A Colonial Inheritance and Other Poems (1985)
Trial by Terror (poems, 1987)
Reddened Water Flows Clear (poems, 1991)
Fragments of a Journey (short stories, 1992)
All Is Burning (short stories, 1995)

About the Story

The backdrop for this story is the tension between the two major peoples of
Sri Lanka: the Tamils and the Sinhalese. This age-old conflict has manifested itself in recent years in open violence and political strife. In this story,
Arasanayagam locates the action, physically, in a village and psychologically in a state of fearful anxiety and uncertainty, which heightens the violence depicted in the narrative.

The story opens with a quote from the Buddha's "Fire Sermon," which
preaches against violence as a form of ignorance and offers some insight
into the source of hatred and aggression. The idea being conveyed in "The
Fire Sermon" is that the suppression of desire will lead to the extinction of
suffering, a concept that, paradoxically, works against the feelings of the
protagonist and the other women of the village in the story.

All Is Burning

*Bhikkus, all is burning. And what is the all that is burning? Bhikkus, the eye
is burning, visible forms are burning, visual consciousness is burning, visual
impression is burning.... Burning with what? Burning with the fire of lust,
with the fire of hate, with the fire of delusion; I say it is burning with birth,
aging and death, with sorrows, with lamentations, with pains, with griefs,
with despairs.*

— The Buddha's Fire Sermon

She blew out the flame of the bottle lamp, leaving the room in darkness. She took a towel off the line and wrapped it about her shoulders. Seela, her daughter, a young woman in her twenties, sat at the table with her head in her hands.

Night sounds filtered in through the clay walls of the hut. Not just the sounds of insects rasping against the leaves or of wakened birds, but also a vast sighing that rippled through the thick blue-black shadows that lay like welts on the earth.

Seela lifted her head wearily. The weight of melancholy, of despair pressed each image onto her consciousness. She had aged. Felt older than her mother. In the cavern of her being images of dead fish, silver bellies upturned, floated in an inky pool.

"Mother," she whispered. "Mother, shall we go in search of Sena? He may still be alive if he has not been taken away. I'll come with you. You can't go alone. They may still be there, who knows. We can guide each other. It's still not light, we have to search for the path. It may be an unfamiliar one."

Alice was already at the door. She spoke under her breath. "No, you wait. Don't open the door to anyone. Remain in darkness. Don't light the lamp."

"Mother."

"Yes?"

"Don't go alone." Seela rose wearily and dragged her feet to the door.

"No. It is my mission. A journey by myself will be safer. I'll come back here. Don't move. Wait and keep that door barred. Just don't open to any knock."

Alice stepped out, treading softly, warily on her bare feet. It would be easier that way. No sound of any football. She closed the door behind her very quietly. She peered into the darkness with yet its hint of light. Her nerves felt on edge. Her instincts alert, she must let herself be guided, by odours—unusual odours of gunshot, of blood, borne by the slight, chill tremors of wind. There would be that human odour too, of fear, that rank smell of bodies through whose pores fear had breathed.

The sky began to lighten very faintly. Pale innocent streaks of colour appeared before the darker, reddened contusions that bruised the clouds. She walked along in a half-blind, almost groping way, feeling the roughness of tussocks of grass and dislodged stones that trembled beneath her feet.

She still felt her flesh raw, hurt by the events of the night. That sense of peace which came with late evening and the dusk which settled over the river, the trees, the road and their little hamlet had been deceptive. The bathers had returned from the river, they did not linger very long these days. The water, silver shot with ripples of gold, soon turned dark and opaque, vanishing into the dense clumps of trees. The woodsmoke curled up from the huts, spiralling into the sky, a pale wreathing grey.

She had been busy preparing the evening meal. The pot of rice was still on the fire, the fish and vegetables simmering in their pots. Seela, her daughter, was talking to Sena, the young man whom she was going to marry. Alice wanted this marriage for Seela. Her own man had deserted her when she was pregnant, leaving her to bring up the child alone. She had been a servant in so many houses, cooking, minding children, washing piles of linen, dressing her child in the clothes out-grown by other people's children—her mistress's daughter's clothes and those of her friends' children. No more of that for Seela. She had been a bright, intelligent child, had gone to school, passed examinations. She had a future before her. All that was through the efforts, undoubt-edly, that Alice had made.

But it had come to their hamlet too—the *bhishanaya*, the trouble. Yes, it had reached them. There were rumours. The young men in the village, were they too involved in all those happenings? The country was on fire. Everything was on fire. All was burning, burning. Yes, the fires were burning. Fires that burnt down the huts. These and hundreds of other villages burning. The self burning. The unconscious, the visual impressions, burning. The fire of lust and hate, the fire of delusion. The Buddha's Fire Sermon that the villagers heard in the temple—the monk repeated it on the last poya day when they went to hear him, to find some relief for their suffering minds.

"Burning," he said, "with birth, aging and death, with sorrows, with lamentations, with pains, with griefs, with despairs."

And what do we do? Alice thought to herself. Become dispassion-ate, detached? To reach that liberation must I first go out among the dead and their ruined houses? I cannot forget the sound of the vehicles on the road...

They had stopped at the entrance to the village. The darkness had moved like an open door to admit them. And they had entered. The villagers heard the sounds of their boots. The knocking at the doors. The commands.

"Open up."

There was nothing else to do.

Screams. Dying away. Growing fainter. Fainter. She had to go. But not at once. Wait for sometime. Till they heard the sound of the vehi-cles moving off. Then she would go out, in search of Sena, for Seela's sake. She thought of herself. An ordinary woman. Very ordinary. Even the name Alice did not matter to anyone. She knew that she had to do it. Even if there were a vestige of life left she would confront those last moments. And she would have to do it alone.

Seela too had been strong during those last moments. "Mother, our generation, my generation, we know the consequences. We are not afraid."

Now Alice was walking along pathways. They had to lead to the deathspot. Through the grove of trees—wild guava, hard-shelled green belly fruit and straggling palms. A cluster of thambili nestled among some of the thicker fronds, a very pale orange. Her throat felt parched, as if death were already clutching at it. Dry tongued, her belly cavernous and hollow. Out of the trees, out of the grove, she emerged like a sleepwalker into a space where the grass had been trampled and crushed.

Now it was over. The sound of gunshot still echoed in her ears. Yama had visited every house in the village where there were males. They had all been taken away. She had to summon all her strength for this mission. The vision of Yama, the god of death, filled her mind.

I am an ordinary woman, she told herself. I have been a servant in other people's homes for the greater part of my life. Always subservient, obeying orders. Eating after everyone else had eaten. Sleeping on my mat in a corner of a room, seeing that other people were comfortable. And now, now that I had hopes for a different kind of life, now when I thought things would change—but no, things *have* changed, though not for the better. Yet I have to do this for my daughter, look at the faces of the dead and dying. No, Seela couldn't do it. I'll do it for her. I am her mother. Who else has she had all her life? Myself and her grandmother. Two women. There has never been a man to give me strength. I have done things that I never believed possible for a woman to do. No, it will never end for me. My strength grows with each crisis. I've been well trained through the years. There's no one else I can turn to. I'll do it by myself. I can't help it if my mind keeps going back to all the events of the night. I'll relive this experience for ever.

The knocking on all those doors resounded in her ears. She had opened the door. What else could she have done? They wanted Sena. As they did all the males in the village. Behind them she saw that vision—Yama. Yama, the god of death. He too was with them. On whose side was he? He was a constant guest on both fronts these days.

They pointed the guns at Sena. No, he couldn't escape. Nor could all the others. Weeping, shrieking echoed through the night, the night that Alice had thought would be so peaceful. She smelt burning rice. The brands crackled and the fire raced, shedding sparks as it blew up.

Yama, Yama. Was it only she who saw him? Eye for an eye, tooth for a tooth, the men kept saying as they pointed the gun at Sena, prodded him with the butt.

"Don't try to resist," said one of them. "And don't say you are innocent. You want to be martyrs. Then where are the victims? Someone has to be the victim. Who put up all those posters with their violent messages? Who carried off the weapons after the attacks on police stations and the army camps? To use for what purpose? To use against whom? The men of this village—we have proof. The last attack…there were deaths. Now get on, move on.… The fires are spreading all over the country. Come on, hurry up."

Her daughter had fallen at the feet of the men. She had pleaded and wept. "Don't take him away. Don't. Don't." It had all fallen on deaf ears.

There had been so much shouting outside their walls. Commands. Tramp of boots. Sounds of running feet. They had heard the guns. The volley of shots. Went on ceaselessly. Would they ever stop firing?

It seemed a lifetime ago. Alice now smelt the odour of death. Rank. Foetid. Like rotting vegetation. They lay there, clumps of them, their bodies spreadeagled on the earth. Men. Bodies. A mirror of light flickered across her gaze with their distortions, black specks, rust coloured streaks—chiaroscuric images that almost stoned her eyeballs.

She knew she had to go among them. How else would she find Sena? He had to be there. He had to, unless…but could he have had a chance of escaping, in the dark? No, there must have been flashlights. The darkness violated by those coruscating beams. At least if she could find him.… She was a woman who needed certainty. The certainty of truth. It had to be one way or the other. She had never deceived Seela. Nor had she deceived herself. At this moment she did not want the comfort of any human being. This would be her final test, her trial. And Sena, if he still had some life in him, even if he was barely breathing, perhaps he could gasp out a word, perhaps she could even drag him out of this welter of bodies.

She looked at them, almost dispassionately. They were finished. There was nothing more left for them. Their women would have to fend for themselves now. The women were strong enough. And they had their children. They couldn't give up at this stage.

She wiped her face with the edge of her towel. The towel was damp with morning dew. Her face chill and sharp like the edge of a keen blade.

Death walk. That's what this is, she thought. I'll have to turn them over. I have to see the faces. How else can I recognize them? How can I recognize Sena? Men who had belonged to other women. I would never have touched them at any other time.

Her bare feet slid cautiously through the huddle of bodies. They felt so soft. Even the sinewy ones.

She bent over, turned up face after face. All she recognized were the empty faces of men. Men who were all akin, all brothers, husbands, fathers. All gone. To leave life in so unfinished, so haphazard a manner.

She stumbled, almost fell against one of the bodies. I'll have to be careful, she thought. I mustn't jostle them even in death. Perhaps, some of them still have that last breath…the soul that's reluctant to leave the body. No funeral orations for any of them. Individual burials are no longer practicable. It is within our minds that we carry those reminders of what each man was to each woman. Till each one is claimed, if ever they are claimed, they are anonymous. It's happening elsewhere too, perhaps at this very moment…. Soon there'll be no birds left in the village. Startled by gunshot, they'll fly away to another village. Who's going to start life here all over again….

Her movements now became mechanical. But she wove her way through, a searcher who could never give up the search.

Where would the pyres be lit? And where the secret graves? They would be silently carried away, secretly buried. Their names would be mentioned only in whispers. So this was the journey that Yama took daily? Difficult. But she had the strength.

She flicked at a fly with a towel. They were already there, the blue-bottles. The smell of death, it was choking her. She felt suffocated but could not stop. She would go on till she found him.

Could this be Sena…? She peered into a face, called his name softly: "Sena, Sena, Sena." It could be Sena—a young body, but the face all smeared with blood. If she wiped the blood off she might recognize him. She wiped his face gently with the end of her towel and gazed into the face.

No, this was not him. Resembled him…

She stroked his head, caressingly. A woman's gesture. Her towel was sodden. Her clothes felt damp.

He is still warm, she told herself. My towel is soaked with blood. My clothes too—damp, stained. She felt dead, her limbs numbed. She stumbled against yet another body.

There must be so many…so many of them…. Forgive me, son, brother, father, husband, forgive me for touching your sleeping body with my foot, it is not that I mean to insult you…

No, not this one either. Where was he? And such a silence in the village. Where was everybody? Asleep? Awake? Afraid to come out? All the women, the children? Such a silence in the village.

Her head was full of images, strange thoughts…. All the blood must seep into the earth, as if the gods must be propitiated, as if we have had a long drought. What new plants will grow here? Or will it remain a desert, haunted by ghosts and spirits? Shouldn't we leave it this way, to remember them? I must go down to the river, wash my clothes, bathe, watch the water change colour—like my dreams, the dreams that will visit me night after night.

When can I ever complete this journey? Yama told me—some-where—that this is my first journey into the darkness of the under-world.... What's that sound...a groan? Not all are dead then.

She knelt down. Her back ached with so much bending. She felt the man's breath touch the palm of her hand like a slight vapour, a cobweb of mist that faintly wreathed round her fingers.

"I won't leave you alone. I'll stay by you," she said, sitting beside him, wiping his face with the corner of her towel, pushing away the tangled strands of hair from his forehead. She supported his head in her arms.

"Mother," he uttered faintly. His life was ebbing away.

"Mother," he repeated. "Thirsty."

"Wait, I'll bring you a sip of water. I'll go back to my hut. Wait. Don't move."

No, there wasn't time to go back, to fetch water, to give him that drink. Life-giving water? No. It would soon be over. She felt the spasms of his chest, the painful heaving of that wounded breast. She held him until he was still. Her hands were stained with blood. She wiped them slowly but the blood felt sticky, oozing into her skin, her flesh.

That was the end. All she could give him was the hope of that sip of water. And he had called her Mother. That was enough. She was a comfort to him and that was more than all the others had on all the battlefields where they gasped out their lives.

Already, so many bodies and she hadn't found Sena yet.

What could a village do without all its men? We'll have to take their place now, we women, she thought. I'll go back to my daughter. Perhaps there's still hope. They may have taken him away for question-ing. Seela will have to continue living, like all the other women. It won't be the end for us, not while we still have breath.

She rose wearily. She wanted to retch but her mouth was dry, her throat parched.

Two hundred and fifty of them. All the men in the village. Gone. Swept away in that great flood of death. But the women would bear more sons. Life had to, would go on.

Topics for Discussion:

1. What role does violence play in the story? How does it impact upon the reader?

2. How does Arasanayagam convey the violence, both linguistically and imagistically?

3. What role does the epigraph play in setting the mood, scene and tone of the story?

4. Why is fear such an important issue in this story?

5. What is the impact of Arasanayagam's use of sensual imagery and minor detail?

6. How does the supernatural figure in the story, especially the god Yama?

7. Throughout the story there are movements in the narrative structure to internal monologue on the part of the protagonist. How does this enlarge the narrative voice?

Margaret Atwood

About the Author

Canada's pre-eminent writer and person of letters, Margaret Atwood was born in Ottawa in 1939 and spent her summers, until the age of twelve, in the Quebec and Ontario bush country. She received her education at the University of Toronto and Harvard University. Atwood has won numerous literary awards including Governor General's Awards for poetry for *The Circle Game* (1966) and for fiction for *The Handmaid's Tale* (1986). As a literary critic, her study of the relationship between the Canadian environment and characters in Canadian literature, *Survival* (1972), stands as an important statement in Canadian literary theory. She has written novels, collections of poetry, literary criticism and children's books, and has been a major voice as a social activist, particularly with respect to environmental concerns. She has edited a number of anthologies, including *The Oxford Book of Canadian Verse* (1983) and *The Oxford Anthology of Canadian Short Fiction* (1996).

Although it is a seemingly impossible task to sum up Atwood's work in a brief statement, what should be noted is her keen awareness of the environment in which her characters find themselves. With wit and often a skewering sense of satire, Atwood has offered both a vision and a critique of the contemporary world and our relationship to the physical world. Her works often turn on the innate political dynamics within human relationships, from sexual to national politics. Through a probing clarity of vision, she seeks to unmask the charades and illusions at the root of human problems.

Selected Bibliography

The Circle Game (poems, 1966)
The Edible Woman (novel, 1969)
Surfacing (novel, 1972)
Survival: A Thematic Guide to Canadian Literature (criticism, 1972)
Lady Oracle (novel, 1976)
Dancing Girls (short stories, 1977)
Life Before Man (novel, 1979)
Bodily Harm (novel, 1981)
The Handmaid's Tale (novel, 1985)
Wilderness Tips (short stories, 1991)
The Robber Bride (novel, 1993)
Morning in the Burned House (poems, 1995)

About the Story

This story is set, primarily, in northern Ontario at a summer camp for girls. The story opens with Lois, the protagonist, being haunted in her later life by an incident which happened at a summer camp during her childhood. Take note of the way Atwood uses the landscape, the details which she presents, the way it figures in the plot, and the way it is reinterpreted over time by the central character.

The opening paragraphs mention the Group of Seven. This was a gathering of Canadian painters (Tom Thomson, A. Y. Jackson, Arthur Lismer, J. E. H. MacDonald, Lawren Harris, Frederick Varley, Frank Carmichael and A. J. Casson among them) who, in the early years of this century, sought to portray the Canadian wilderness (the bush) from a new, non-Eurocentric vision, by presenting the landscape in all its ruggedness and colour. Their paintings, which now typify the way Canadians perceive their wilderness, contain vistas which are often broken by trees, obstacles and topographical features (lakes, rivers, mountains). Their view of nature is overpowering, raw and unartificial.

David Milne was a later contemporary of the Group of Seven. Milne's paintings are marked by a strange emptiness between colours and objects, a tentative connection between objects in the landscape and between the perceiver and the landscape.

Manitou is the traditional Canadian Indian name for God or the great spirit, which presides over the wilderness. Wampum are strung beads that were carved by Indians from Quohog seashells (a clam-type shell with a blue interior) and were used in trade as a form of currency.

Death by Landscape

Now that the boys are grown up and Rob is dead, Lois has moved to a condominium apartment in one of the newer waterfront developments. She is relieved not to have to worry about the lawn, or about the ivy pushing its muscular little suckers into the brickwork, or the squirrels gnawing their way into the attic and eating the insulation off the wiring, or about strange noises. This building has a security system, and the only plant life is in pots in the solarium.

Lois is glad she's been able to find an apartment big enough for her pictures. They are more crowded together than they were in the house, but this arrangement gives the walls a European look: blocks of pictures, above and beside one another, rather than one over the chesterfield, one over the fireplace, one in the front hall, in the old acceptable manner of sprinkling art around so it does not get too intrusive. This way has more of an impact. You know it's not supposed to be furniture.

None of the pictures is very large, which doesn't mean they aren't valuable. They are paintings, or sketches and drawings, by artists who were not nearly as well known when Lois began to buy them as they are now. Their work later turned up on stamps, or as silk-screen reproductions hung in the principals' offices of high schools, or as jigsaw puzzles, or on beautifully printed calendars sent out by corporations as Christmas gifts, to their less important clients. These artists painted mostly in the twenties and thirties and forties: they painted landscapes. Lois has two Tom Thomsons, three A. Y. Jacksons, a Lawren Harris. She has an Arthur Lismer, she has a J. E. H. MacDonald. She has a David Milne. They are pictures of convoluted tree trunks on an island of pink wave-smoothed stone, with more islands behind; of a lake with rough, bright, sparsely wooded cliffs; of a vivid river shore with a tangle of bush and two beached canoes, one red, one grey; of a yellow autumn woods with the ice-blue gleam of a pond half-seen through the interlaced branches.

It was Lois who'd chosen them. Rob had no interest in art, although he could see the necessity of having something on the walls. He left all the decorating decisions to her, while providing the money, of course. Because of this collection of hers, Lois's friends—especially the men—have given her the reputation of having a good nose for art investments.

But this is not why she bought the pictures, way back then. She bought them because she wanted them. She wanted something that was in them, although she could not have said at the time what it was. It was not peace: she does not find them peaceful in the least. Looking at them fills her with a wordless unease. Despite the fact that there are no people in them or even animals, it's as if there is something, or someone, looking back out.

When she was thirteen, Lois went on a canoe trip. She'd only been on overnights before. This was to be a long one, into the trackless wilderness, as Cappie put it. It was Lois's first canoe trip, and her last.

Cappie was the head of the summer camp to which Lois had been sent ever since she was nine. Camp Manitou, it was called; it was one of the better ones, for girls, though not the best. Girls of her age whose parents could afford it were routinely packed off to such camps, which bore a generic resemblance to one another. They favoured Indian names and had hearty, energetic leaders, who were called Cappie or Skip or Scottie. At these camps you learned to swim well and sail, and paddle a canoe, and perhaps ride a horse or play tennis. When you weren't doing these things you could do Arts and Crafts and turn out dingy, lumpish clay ashtrays for your mother—mothers smoked more, then—or bracelets made of coloured braided string.

Cheerfulness was required at all times, even at breakfast. Loud shouting and the banging of spoons on the tables were allowed, and even encouraged, at ritual intervals. Chocolate bars were rationed, to control tooth decay and pimples. At night, after supper, in the dining hall or outside around a mosquito-infested campfire ring for special treats, there were singsongs. Lois can still remember all the words to "My Darling Clementine," and to "My Bonnie Lies Over the Ocean," with acting-out gestures: a rippling of the hands for "the ocean," two hands together under the cheek for "lies." She will never be able to forget them, which is a sad thought.

Lois thinks she can recognize women who went to these camps, and were good at it. They have a hardness to their handshakes, even now; a way of standing, legs planted firmly and farther apart than usual; a way of sizing you up, to see if you'd be any good in a canoe—the front, not the back. They themselves would be in the back. They would call it the stern.

She knows that such camps still exist, although Camp Manitou does not. They are one of the few things that haven't changed much. They now offer copper enamelling, and functionless pieces of stained glass baked in electric ovens, though judging from the productions of her friends' grandchildren the artistic standards have not improved.

To Lois, encountering it in the first year after the war, Camp Manitou seemed ancient. Its log-sided buildings with the white cement in between the half-logs, its flagpole ringed with whitewashed stones, its weathered grey dock jutting out into Lake Prospect, with its woven rope bumpers and its rusty rings for tying up, its prim round flowerbed of petunias near the office door, must surely have been there always. In truth it dated only from the first decade of the century; it had been founded by Cappie's parents, who'd thought of camping as bracing to the character, like cold showers, and had been passed along to her as an inheritance, and an obligation.

Lois realized, later, that it must have been a struggle for Cappie to keep Camp Manitou going, during the Depression and then the war, when money did not flow freely. If it had been a camp for the very rich, instead of the merely well off, there would have been fewer problems. But there must have been enough Old Girls, ones with daughters, to keep the thing in operation, though not entirely shipshape: furniture was battered, painted trim was peeling, roofs leaked. There were dim photographs of these Old Girls dotted around the dining hall, wearing ample woollen bathing suits and showing their fat, dimpled legs, or standing, arms twined, in odd tennis outfits with baggy skirts.

In the dining hall, over the stone fireplace that was never used, there was a huge moulting stuffed moose head, which looked somehow carnivorous. It was a sort of mascot; its name was Monty Manitou. The older campers spread the story that it was haunted, and came to life in the dark, when the feeble and undependable lights had been turned off or, due to yet another generator failure, had gone out. Lois was afraid of it at first, but not after she got used to it.

Cappie was the same: you had to get used to her. Possibly she was forty, or thirty-five, or fifty. She had fawn-coloured hair that looked as if it was cut with a bowl. Her head jutted forward, jigging like a chicken's as she strode around the camp, clutching notebooks and checking things off in them. She was like their minister in church: both of them smiled a lot and were anxious because they wanted things to go well; they both had the same overwashed skins and stringy necks. But all this disappeared when Cappie was leading a singsong, or otherwise leading. Then she was happy, sure of herself, her plain face almost luminous. She wanted to cause joy. At these times she was loved, at others merely trusted.

There were many things Lois didn't like about Camp Manitou, at first. She hated the noisy chaos and spoon-banging of the dining hall, the rowdy singsongs at which you were expected to yell in order to show that you were enjoying yourself. Hers was not a household that encouraged yelling. She hated the necessity of having to write dutiful letters to her parents claiming she was having fun. She could not complain, because camp cost so much money.

She didn't much like having to undress in a roomful of other girls, even in the dim light, although nobody paid any attention, or sleeping in a cabin with seven other girls: some of whom snored because they had adenoids or colds, some of whom had nightmares, or wet their beds and cried about it. Bottom bunks made her feel closed in, and she was afraid of falling out of top ones; she was afraid of heights. She got homesick, and suspected her parents of having a better time when she wasn't there than when she was, although her mother wrote to her every week saying how much they missed her. All this was when she was nine. By the time she was thirteen she liked it. She was an old hand by then.

Lucy was her best friend at camp. Lois had other friends in winter, when there was school and itchy woollen clothing and darkness in the afternoons, but Lucy was her summer friend.

She turned up the second year, when Lois was ten, and a Bluejay. (Chickadees, Bluejays, Ravens, and Kingfishers—these were the names Camp Manitou assigned to the different age groups, a sort of totemic clan system. In those days, thinks Lois, it was birds for girls, animals for boys: wolves, and so forth. Though some animals and birds were suitable and some were not. Never vultures, for instance; never skunks, or rats.)

Lois helped Lucy to unpack her tin trunk and place the folded clothes on the wooden shelves, and to make up her bed. She put her in the top bunk right above her, where she could keep an eye on her. Already she knew that Lucy was an exception, to a good many rules; already she felt proprietorial.

Lucy was from the United States, where the comic books came from, and the movies. She wasn't from New York or Hollywood or Buffalo, the only American cities Lois knew the names of, but from Chicago. Her house was on the lakeshore and had gates to it, and grounds. They had a maid, all of the time. Lois's family only had a cleaning lady twice a week.

The only reason Lucy was being sent to *this* camp (she cast a look of minor scorn around the cabin, diminishing it and also offending Lois, while at the same time daunting her) was that her mother had been a camper here. Her mother had been a Canadian once, but had married her father, who had a patch over one eye, like a pirate. She showed Lois the picture of him in her wallet. He got the patch in the war. "Shrapnel," said Lucy. Lois, who was unsure about shrapnel, was so impressed she could only grunt. Her own two-eyed unwounded father was tame by comparison.

"My father plays golf," she ventured at last.

"*Everyone* plays golf," said Lucy. "My *mother* plays golf."

Lois's mother did not. Lois took Lucy to see the outhouses and the swimming dock and the dining hall with Monty Manitou's baleful head, knowing in advance they would not measure up.

This was a bad beginning; but Lucy was good-natured, and accepted Camp Manitou with the same casual shrug with which she seemed to accept everything. She would make the best of it, without letting Lois forget that this was what she was doing.

However, there were things Lois knew that Lucy did not. Lucy scratched the tops off all her mosquito bites and had to be taken to the infirmary to be daubed with Ozonol. She took her T-shirt off while sailing, and although the counsellor spotted her after a while and made her put it back on, she burnt spectacularly, bright red, with the X of her bathing-suit straps standing out in alarming white; she let Lois peel the sheets of whispery-thin burned skin off her shoulders. When they sang "Alouette" around the campfire, she did not know any of the French words. The difference was that Lucy did not care about the things she didn't know, whereas Lois did.

During the next winter, and subsequent winters, Lucy and Lois wrote to each other. They were both only children, at a time when this was thought to be a disadvantage, so in their letters they pretended to be sisters, or even twins. Lois had to strain a little over this, because Lucy was so blond, with translucent skin and large blue eyes like a doll's, and Lois was nothing out of the ordinary—just a tallish, thinnish, brownish person with freckles. They signed their letters LL, with the L's entwined together like the monograms on a towel. (Lois and Lucy, thinks Lois. How our names date us. Lois Lane, Superman's girlfriend, enterprising female reporter; "I Love Lucy." Now we are obsolete and it's little Jennifers, little Emilys, little Alexandras and Carolines and Tiffanys.)

They were more effusive in their letters than they ever were in person. They bordered their pages with X's and O's, but when they met again in the summers it was always a shock. They had changed so much, or Lucy had. It was like watching someone grow up in jolts. At first it would be hard to think up things to say.

But Lucy always had a surprise or two, something to show, some marvel to reveal. The first year she had a picture of herself in a tutu, her hair in a ballerina's knot on the top of her head; she pirouetted around the swimming dock, to show Lois how it was done, and almost fell off. The next year she had given that up and was taking horseback riding. (Camp Manitou did not have horses.) The next year her mother and father had been divorced, and she had a new stepfather, one with both eyes, and a new house, although the maid was the same. The next year, when they had graduated from Bluejays and entered Ravens, she got her period, right in the first week at camp. The two of them snitched some matches from their counsellor, who smoked illegally, and made a small fire out behind the farthest outhouse, at dusk, using their flashlights. They could set all kinds of fires by now; they had learned how in Campcraft. On this fire they burned one of Lucy's used sanitary napkins. Lois is not sure why they did this, or whose idea it was. But she can remember the feeling of deep satisfaction it gave her as the white fluff singed and the blood sizzled, as if some wordless ritual had been fulfilled.

They did not get caught, but then they rarely got caught at any of their camp transgressions. Lucy had such large eyes, and was such an accomplished liar.

This year Lucy is different again: slower, more languorous. She is no longer interested in sneaking around after dark, purloining cigarettes from the counsellor, dealing in black-market candy bars. She is pensive, and hard to wake in the mornings. She doesn't like her stepfather, but she doesn't want to live with her real father either, who has a new wife. She thinks her mother may be having a love affair with a doctor; she doesn't know for sure, but she's seen them smooching in his car, out on the driveway, when her stepfather wasn't there. It serves him right. She hates her private school. She has a boyfriend, who is sixteen and works as a gardener's assistant. This is how she met him: in the garden. She describes to Lois what it is like when he kisses her—rubbery at first, but then your knees go limp. She has been forbidden to see him, and threatened with boarding school. She wants to run away from home.

Lois has little to offer in return. Her own life is placid and satisfactory, but there is nothing much that can be said about happiness. "You're so lucky," Lucy tells her, a little smugly. She might as well say *boring* because this is how it makes Lois feel.

Lucy is apathetic about the canoe trip, so Lois has to disguise her own excitement. The evening before they are to leave, she slouches into the campfire ring as if coerced, and sits down with a sigh of endurance, just as Lucy does.

Every canoe trip that went out of camp was given a special send-off by Cappie and the section leader and counsellors, with the whole section in attendance. Cappie painted three streaks of red across each of her cheeks with a lipstick. They looked like three-fingered claw marks. She put a blue circle on her forehead with fountain-pen ink, and tied a twisted bandanna around her head and stuck a row of frazzle-ended feathers around it, and wrapped herself in a red-and-black Hudson's Bay blanket. The counsellors, also in blankets but with only two steaks of red, beat on tom-toms made of round wooden cheese boxes with leather stretched over the top and nailed in place. Cappie was Chief

Cappeosota. they all had to say "How!" when she walked into the circle and stood there with one hand raised.

Looking back on this, Lois finds it disquieting. She knows too much about Indians: this is why. She knows, for instance, that they should not even be called Indians, and that they have enough worries without other people taking their names and dressing up as them. It has all been a form of stealing.

But she remembers too, that she was once ignorant of this. Once she loved the campfire, the flickering of light on the ring of faces, the sound of the fake tom-toms, heavy and fast like a scared heartbeat; she loved Cappie in a red blanket and feathers, solemn, as a chief should be, raising her hand and saying, "Greetings, my Ravens." It was not funny, it was not making fun. She wanted to be an Indian. She wanted to be adventurous and pure, and aboriginal.

⇥⫴⫼⇤

"You go on big water," says Cappie. This is her idea—all their ideas—of how Indians talk. "You go where no man has ever trod. You go many moons." This is not true. They are only going for a week, not many moons. The canoe route is clearly marked, they have gone over it on a map, and there are prepared campsites with names which are used year after year. But when Cappie says this—and despite the way Lucy rolls up her eyes—Lois can feel the water stretching out, with the shores twisting away on either side, immense and a little frightening.

"You bring back much wampum," says Cappie. "Do good in war, my braves, and capture many scalps." This is another of her pretences: that they are boys, and bloodthirsty. But such a game cannot be played by substituting the word "squaw." It would not work at all.

Each of them has to stand up and step forward and have a red line drawn across her cheeks by Cappie. She tells them they must follow in the paths of their ancestors (who most certainly, thinks Lois, looking out the window of her apartment and remembering the family stash of daguerreotypes and sepia-coloured portraits on her mother's dressing table, the stiff-shirted, black-coated, grim-faced men and the beflounced women with their severe hair and their corseted respectability, would never have considered heading off onto an open lake, in a canoe, just for fun).

At the end of the ceremony they all stood and held hands around the circle, and sang taps. This did not sound very Indian, thinks Lois. It sounded like a bugle call at a military post, in a movie. But Cappie was never one to be much concerned with consistency, or with archaeology.

⇥⫴⫼⇤

After breakfast the next morning they set out from the main dock, in four canoes, three in each. The lipstick stripes have not come off completely, and still show faintly pink, like healing burns. They wear their white denim sailing hats, because of the sun, and thin-striped T-shirts, and pale baggy shorts with cuffs rolled up. The middle one kneels, propping her rear end against the rolled sleeping bags. The counsellors going with them are Pat and Kip. Kip is no-nonsense; Pat is easier to wheedle, or fool.

There are puffy clouds and a small breeze. Glints come from the little waves. Lois is in the bow of Kip's canoe. She still can't do a J-stroke very well, and she will have to be in the bow or the middle for the whole trip. Lucy is behind her; her own J-stroke is even worse. She splashes Lois with her paddle, quite a big splash.

"I'll get you back," says Lois.

"There was a stable fly on your shoulder," Lucy says.

Lois turns to look at her, to see if she's grinning. They're in the habit of splashing each other. Back there, the camp has vanished behind the first long point of rock and rough trees.

<hr>

Lois feels as if an invisible rope has broken. They're floating free, on their own, cut loose. Beneath the canoe the lake goes down, deeper and colder than it was a minute before.

"No horsing around in the canoe," says Kip. She's rolled her T-shirt sleeves up to the shoulder; her arms are brown and sinewy, her jaw determined, her stroke perfect. She looks as if she knows exactly what she is doing.

The four canoes keep close together. They sing, raucously and with defiance; they sing "The Quartermaster's Store," and "Clementine," and "Alouette." It is more like bellowing than singing.

After that the wind grows stronger, blowing slantwise against the bows, and they have to put all their energy into shoving themselves through the water.

<hr>

Was there anything important, anything that would provide some sort of reason or clue to what happened next? Lois can remember everything, every detail; but it does her no good.

They stopped at noon for a swim and lunch, and went on in the afternoon. At last they reached Little Birch, which was the first campsite for overnight. Lois and Lucy made the fire, while the others pitched the heavy canvas tents. The fireplace was already there, flat stones piled into a U. A burned tin can and a beer bottle had been left in it. Their fire went out, and they had to restart it. "Hustle your bustle," said Kip. "We're starving."

The sun went down, and in the pink sunset light they brushed their teeth and spat the toothpaste froth into the lake. Kip and Pat put all the food that wasn't in cans into a packsack and slung it into a tree, in case of bears.

Lois and Lucy weren't sleeping in a tent. They'd begged to be allowed to sleep out; that way they could talk without the others hearing. It if rained, they told Kip, they promised not to crawl dripping into the tent over everyone's legs: they would get under the canoes. So they were out on the point.

Lois tried to get comfortable inside her sleeping bag, which smelled of musty storage and of earlier campers, a stale salty sweetness. She curled herself up, with her sweater rolled up under her head for a pillow and her flashlight inside her sleeping bag so it wouldn't roll away. The muscles of her sore arms were making small pings, like rubber bands breaking.

Beside her Lucy was rustling around. Lois could see the glimmering oval of her white face.

"I've got a rock poking into my back," said Lucy.

"So do I," said Lois. "You want to go into the tent?" She herself didn't, but it was right to ask.

"No," said Lucy. She subsided into her sleeping bag. After a moment she said, "It would be nice not to go back."

"To camp?" said Lois.

"To Chicago," said Lucy. "I hate it there."

"What about your boyfriend?" said Lois. Lucy didn't answer. She was either asleep or pretending to be.

There was a moon, and a movement of the trees. In the sky there were stars, layers of stars that went down and down. Kip said that when the stars were bright like that instead of hazy it meant bad weather later on. Out on the lake there were two loons, calling to each other in their insane, mournful voices. At the time it did not sound like grief. It was just background.

The lake in the morning was flat calm. They skimmed along over the glassy surface, leaving V-shaped trails behind them; it felt like flying. As the sun rose higher it got hot, almost too hot. There were stable flies in the canoes, landing on a bare arm or leg for a quick sting. Lois hoped for wind.

They stopped for lunch at the next of the named campsites. Lookout Point. It was called this because, although the site itself was down near the water on a flat shelf of rock, there was a sheer cliff nearby and a trail that led up to the top. The top was the lookout, although what you were supposed to see from there was not clear. Kip said it was just a view.

Lois and Lucy decided to make the climb anyway. They didn't want to hang around waiting for lunch. It wasn't their turn to cook, though they hadn't avoided much by not doing it, because cooking lunch was no big deal, it was just unwrapping the cheese and getting out the bread and peanut butter, but Pat and Kip always had to do their woodsy act and boil up a billy tin for their own tea.

They told Kip where they were going. You had to tell Kip where you were going, even if it was only a little way into the woods to get dry twigs for kindling. You could never go anywhere without a buddy.

"Sure," said Kip, who was crouching over the fire, feeding driftwood into it. "Fifteen minutes to lunch."

"Where are they off to?" said Pat. She was bringing their billy tin of water from the lake.

"Lookout," said Kip.

"Be careful," said Pat. She said it as an afterthought, because it was what she always said.

"They're old hands," Kip said.

Lois looks at her watch; it's ten to twelve. She is the watch-minder; Lucy is careless of time. They walk up the path, which is dry earth and rocks, big rounded pinky-grey boulders or split-open ones with jagged edges. Spindly balsam and spruce trees grow to either side, the lake is blue fragments to the left. The sun is right overhead; there are no shadows anywhere. The heat comes up at them as well as down. The forest is dry and crackly.

It isn't far, but it's a steep climb and they're sweating when they reach the top. They wipe their faces with their bare arms, sit gingerly down on a scorching-hot rock, five feet from the edge but too close for Lois. It's a lookout all right, a sheer drop to the lake and a long view over the water, back the way they've come. It's amazing to Lois that they've travelled so far, over all that water, with nothing to propel them but their own arms. It makes her feel strong. There are all kinds of things she is capable of doing.

"It would be quite a dive off here," says Lucy.

"You'd have to be nuts," says Lois.

"Why?" says Lucy. "It's really deep. It goes straight down." She stands up and takes a step nearer the edge. Lois gets a stab in her midriff, the kind she gets when a car goes too fast over a bump. "Don't," she says.

"Don't what?" says Lucy, glancing around at her mischievously. She knows how Lois feels about heights. But she turns back. "I really have to pee," she says.

"You have toilet paper?" says Lois, who is never without it. She digs in her shorts pocket.

"Thanks," says Lucy.

They are both adept at peeing in the woods: doing it fast so the mosquitoes don't get you, the underwear pulled up between the knees, the squat with the feet apart so you don't wet your legs, facing downhill. The exposed feeling of your bum, as if someone is looking at you from behind. The etiquette when you're with someone else is not to look. Lois stand up and starts to walk down the path, to be out of sight.

"Wait for me?" says Lucy.

Lois climbed down, over and around the boulders, until she could not see Lucy; she waited. She could hear the voices of the others, talking and laughing, down near the shore. One voice was yelling, "Ants! Ants!" Someone must have sat on an ant hill. Off to the side, in the woods, a raven was croaking, a hoarse single note.

She looked at her watch: it was noon. This is when she heard the shout.

She has gone over and over it in her mind since, so many times that the first, real shout has been obliterated, like a footprint trampled by other footprints. But she is sure (she is almost positive, she is nearly certain) that it was not a shout of fear. Not a scream. More like a cry of surprise, cut off too soon. Short, like a dog's bark.

"Lucy?" Lois said. Then she called "Lucy!" By now she was clambering back up, over the stones of the path. Lucy was not up there. Or she was not in sight.

"Stop fooling around," Lois said. "It's lunchtime." But Lucy did not rise from behind a rock or step out, smiling, from behind a tree. The sunlight was all around; the rocks looked white. "This isn't funny!" Lois said, and it wasn't, panic was rising in her, the panic of a small child who does not know where the bigger ones are hidden. She could hear her own heart. She looked quickly around; she lay down on the ground and looked over the edge of the cliff. It made her feel cold. There was nothing.

She went back down the path, stumbling; she was breathing too quickly; she was too frightened to cry. She felt terrible—guilty and dismayed, as if she had done something very bad, by mistake. Something that could never be repaired. "Lucy's gone," she told Kip.

Kip looked up from her fire, annoyed. The water in the billy can was boiling. "What do you mean, gone?" she said. "Where did she go?"

"I don't know," said Lois. "She's just gone."

No one had heard the shout, but then no one had heard Lois calling, either. They had been talking among themselves, by the water.

Kip and Pat went up to the lookout and searched and called, and blew their whistles. Nothing answered.

Then they came back down, and Lois had to tell exactly what had happened. The other girls all sat in a circle and listened to her. Nobody said anything. They all looked frightened, especially Pat and Kip. They were the leaders. You did not just lose a camper like this, for no reason at all.

"Why did you leave her alone?" said Kip.

"I was just down the path," said Lois. "I told you. She had to go to the bathroom." She did not say *pee* in front of people older than herself.

Kip looked disgusted.

"Maybe she just walked off into the woods and got turned around," said one of the girls.

"Maybe she's doing it on purpose," said another.

Nobody believed either of these theories.

They took the canoes and searched around the base of the cliff, and peered down into the water. But there had been no sound of falling rock; there had been no splash. There was no clue, nothing at all. Lucy had simply vanished.

That was the end of the canoe trip. It took them the same two days to go back that it had taken coming in, even though they were short a paddler. They did not sing.

After that, the police went in a motorboat, with dogs; they were the Mounties and the dogs were German shepherds, trained to follow trails in the woods. But it had rained since, and they could find nothing.

Lois is sitting in Cappie's office. Her face is bloated with crying, she's seen that in the mirror. By now she feels numbed; she feels as if she had drowned. She can't stay here. It has been too much of a shock. Tomorrow her parents are coming to take her away. Several of the other girls who were on the canoe trip are also being collected. The others will have to stay, because their parents are in Europe, or cannot be reached.

Cappie is grim. They've tried to hush it up, but of course everyone in camp knows. Soon the papers will know too. You can't keep it quiet, but what can be said? What can be said that makes any sense? "Girl vanishes in broad daylight, without a trace." It can't be believed. Other things, worse things, will be suspected. Negligence, at the very least. But they have always taken such care. Bad luck will gather around Camp Manitou like a fog; parents will avoid it, in favour of other, luckier places. Lois can see Cappie thinking all this, even through her numbness. It's what anyone would think.

Lois sits on the hard wooden chair in Cappie's office, beside the old wooden desk, over which hangs the thumbtacked bulletin board of normal camp routine, and gazes at Cappie through her puffy eyelids. Cappie is now smiling what is supposed to be a reassuring smile. Her manner is too casual: she's after something. Lois has seen this look on Cappie's face when she's sniffing out contraband chocolate bars, hunting down those rumoured to have snuck out of their cabins at night.

"Tell me again," says Cappie, "from the beginning."

Lois has told her story many times by now, to Pat and Kip, to Cappie, to the police, that she knows it word for word. She knows it, but she no longer believes it. It has become a story. "I told you," she said. "She wanted to go to the bathroom. I gave her my toilet paper. I went down the path, I waited for her. I heard this kind of shout..."

"Yes," says Cappie, smiling confidently, "but before that. What did you say to one another?"

Lois thinks. Nobody has asked her this before. "She said you could dive off there. She said it went straight down."

"And what did you say?"

"I said you'd have to be nuts."

"Were you mad at Lucy?" says Cappie, in an encouraging voice.

"No," says Lois. "Why would I be mad at Lucy? I wasn't ever mad at Lucy." She feels like crying again. The times when she has in fact been mad at Lucy have been erased already. Lucy was always perfect.

"Sometimes we're angry when we don't know we're angry," says Cappie, as if to herself. "Sometimes we get really mad and we don't even know it. Sometimes we might do a thing without meaning to, or without knowing what will happen. We lose our tempers."

Lois is only thirteen, but it doesn't take her long to figure out that Cappie is not including herself in any of this. By *we* she means Lois. She is accusing Lois of pushing Lucy off the cliff. The unfairness of this hits her like a slap. "I didn't!" she says.

"Didn't what?" says Cappie softly. "Didn't what, Lois?"

Lois does the worst thing, she begins to cry. Cappie gives her a look like a pounce. She's got what she wanted.

Later, when she was grown up, Lois was able to understand what this interview had been about. She could see Cappie's desperation, her need for a story, a real story with a reason in it; anything but the senseless vacancy Lucy had left for her to deal with. Cappie wanted Lois to supply the reason, to be the reason. It wasn't even for the newspapers or the parents, because she could never make such an accusation without proof. It was for herself: something to explain the loss of Camp Manitou and of all she had worked for, the years of entertaining spoiled children and buttering up parents and making a fool of herself with feathers stuck in her hair. Camp Manitou was in fact lost. It did not survive.

Lois worked all this out, twenty years later. But it was far too late. It was too late even ten minutes afterwards, when she'd left Cappie's office and was walking slowly back to her cabin to pack. Lucy's clothes were still there, folded on the shelves, as if waiting. She felt the other girls in the cabin watching her with speculation in their eyes. *Could she have done it? She must have done it.* For the rest of her life, she has caught people watching her in this way.

Maybe they weren't thinking this. Maybe they were merely sorry for her. But she felt she had been tried and sentenced, and this is what has stayed with her: the knowledge that she had been singled out, condemned for something that was not her fault.

Lois sits in the living room of her apartment, drinking a cup of tea. Through the knee-to-ceiling window she has a wide view of Lake Ontario, with its skin of wrinkled blue-grey light, and of the willows of Centre Island shaken by the wind, which is silent at this distance, and on this side of the glass. When there isn't too much pollution she can see the far shore, the foreign shore; though today it is obscured.

Possibly she could go out, go downstairs, do some shopping; there isn't much in the refrigerator. The boys say she doesn't get out enough. But she isn't hungry, and moving, stirring from this space, is increasingly an effort.

She can hardly remember, now, having her two boys in the hospital, nursing them as babies; she can hardly remember getting married, or what Rob looked like. Even at the time she never felt she was paying full attention. She was tired a lot, as if she was living not one life but two: her own, and another, shadowy life that hovered around her and would not let itself be realized—the life of what would have happened if Lucy had not stepped sideways, and disappeared from time.

She would never go up north, to Rob's family cottage or to any place with wild lakes and wild trees and the calls of loons. She would never go anywhere near. Still, it was as if she was always listening for another voice, the voice of a person who should have been there but was not. An echo.

While Rob was alive, while the boys were growing up, she could pretend she didn't hear it, this empty space in sound. But now there is nothing much left to distract her.

She turns away from the window and looks at her pictures. There is the pinkish island, in the lake, with the intertwisted trees. It's the same landscape they paddled through, that distant summer. She's seen travelogues of this country, aerial photographs; it looks different from above, bigger, more hopeless: lake after lake, random blue puddles in dark green bush, the trees like bristles.

How could you ever find anything there, once it was lost? Maybe if they cut it all down, drained it all away, they might find Lucy's bones, some time, wherever they are hidden. A few bones, some buttons, the buckle from her shorts.

But a dead person is a body; a body occupies space, it exists somewhere. You can see it; you put it in a box and bury it in the ground, and then it's in a box in the ground. But Lucy is not in a box, or in the ground. Because she is nowhere definite, she could be anywhere.

And these paintings are not landscape paintings. Because there aren't any landscapes up there, not in the old, tidy European sense, with a gentle hill, a curving river, a cottage, a mountain in the background, a golden evening sky. Instead there's a tangle, a receding maze, in which you can become lost almost as soon as you step off the path. There are no backgrounds in any of these paintings, no vistas; only a great deal of foreground that goes back and back, endlessly, involving you in its twists and turns of tree and branch and rock. No matter how far back in you go, there will be more. And the trees themselves are hardly trees; they are currents of energy, charged with violent colour.

Who knows how many trees there were on the cliff just before Lucy disappeared? Who counted? Maybe there was one more, afterwards.

Lois sits in her chair and does not move. Her hand with the cup is raised halfway to her mouth. She hears something, almost hears it: a shout of recognition, or of joy.

She looks at the paintings, she looks into them. Every one of them is a picture of Lucy. You can't see her exactly, but she's there, in behind the pink stone island or the one behind that. In the picture of the cliff she is hidden by the clutch of fallen rocks towards the bottom, in the one of the river shore she is crouching beneath the overturned canoe. In the yellow autumn woods she's behind the tree that cannot be seen because of other trees, over beside the blue sliver of pond; but if you walked into the picture and found the tree, it would be the wrong one, because the right one would be farther on.

Everyone has to be somewhere, and this is where Lucy is. She is in Lois's apartment, in the holes that open inwards on the wall, not like windows but like doors. She is here. She is entirely alive.

Topics for Discussion

1. How does Atwood define the relationship between Lois and Lucy?

2. What role does landscape play in the story and how does Atwood show the assimilation of Lucy into the landscape?

3. What sort of comparison is Atwood establishing by making Lucy an American?

4. How does Atwood convey the sense of the passage of time within the story?

5. What point is Atwood making by depicting white people as they attempt to be Indians?

6. Is Lois guilty of killing Lucy? What accounts for Lucy's disappearance? What does the disappearance symbolize?

James Baldwin

About the Author

James Baldwin was born in Harlem, New York City, in 1924, the son of a preacher, whose vocation he practised for a period in his life. He left home at the age of seventeen and worked as handyman, dishwasher, waiter and office boy in New York before travelling abroad and living in France, where he wrote his first novel, *Go Tell It on the Mountain* (1953). He wrote numerous other novels, collections of essays, autobiographies and screenplays. He died in 1987.

Baldwin is perhaps the leading black American male author of this century, a writer who has articulated the pressures, desires and experiences of the African-American community. His most famous short story, "Sonny's Blues," from his collection *Going to Meet the Man* (1965), is considered a classic study in terms of characterization. Its main theme is identity and how one goes about establishing and maintaining it on both individual and racial levels.

Selected Works

Go Tell It on the Mountain (novel, 1953)
Notes of a Native Son (autobiography, 1955)
Giovanni's Room (novel, 1956)
Another Country (novel, 1962)
Going to Meet the Man (short stories, 1965)
Tell Me How Long the Train's Been Gone (novel, 1968)
If Beale Street Could Talk (novel, 1974)
Just Above My Head (novel, 1979)
Jimmy's Blues (poems, 1983)

About the Story

"Sonny's Blues" deals with the life and experiences of a jazz musician and his older brother (the narrator), a high-school mathematics teacher. Baldwin's view, not only of the relationship between the two brothers but also of the world, is a tragic one. He makes the point that suffering is inevitable: what enables some to survive while others are crushed beneath the weight of suffering is the issue of the story, which is conveyed with both empathy and insight.

The blues is a traditional form of African-American music in which the performer acts as a spokesperson and intercessor to express not only his or her own suffering but the sufferings of the group. Related to Sonny's jazz, this spontaneous outpouring of confession, grief, pain and anguish is essentially therapeutic for the audience, so that the blues becomes not only a forum for airing pain but also a celebration of survival.

Sonny's Blues

I read about it in the paper, in the subway, on my way to work. I read it, and I couldn't believe it, and I read it again. Then perhaps I just stared at it, at the newsprint spelling out his name, spelling out the story. I stared at it in the swinging lights of the subway car, and in the faces and bodies of the people, and in my own face, trapped in the darkness which roared outside.

It was not to be believed and I kept telling myself that, as I walked from the subway station to the high school. And at the same time I couldn't doubt it. I was scared, scared for Sonny. He became real to me again. A great block of ice got settled in my belly and kept melting there slowly all day long, while I taught my classes algebra. It was a special kind of ice. It kept melting, sending trickles of ice water all up and down my veins, but it never got less. Sometimes it hardened and seemed to expand until I felt my guts were going to come spilling out or that I was going to choke or scream. This would always be at a moment when I was remembering some specific thing Sonny had once said or done.

When he was about as old as the boys in my classes his face had been bright and open, there was a lot of copper in it; and he'd had wonderfully direct brown eyes, and great gentleness and privacy. I wondered what he looked like now. He had been picked up, the evening before, in a raid on an apartment downtown, for peddling and using heroin.

I couldn't believe it: but what I mean by that is that I couldn't find any room for it anywhere inside me. I had kept it outside me for a long time. I hadn't wanted to know. I had had suspicions, but I didn't name them, I kept putting them away. I told myself that Sonny was wild, but he wasn't crazy. And he'd always been a good boy, he hadn't ever turned hard or evil or disrespectful, the way kids can, so quick, so quick, especially in Harlem. I didn't want to believe that I'd ever see my brother going down, coming to nothing, all that light in his face gone out, in the condition I'd already seen so many others. Yet it had happened and here I was, talking about algebra to a lot of boys who might, every one of them for all I knew, be popping off needles every time they went to the head. Maybe it did more for them than algebra could.

I was sure that the first time Sonny had ever had horse, he couldn't have been much older than these boys were now. These boys, now, were living as we'd been living then, they were growing up with a rush and their heads bumped abruptly against the low ceiling of their actual possibilities. They were filled with rage. All they really knew were two darknesses, the darkness of their lives, which was now closing in on them, and the darkness of the movies, which had blinded them to that other darkness, and in which they now, vindictively, dreamed, at once more together than they were at any other time, and more alone.

When the last bell rang, the last class ended, I let out my breath. It seemed I'd been holding it for all that time. My clothes were wet—I may have looked as though I'd been sitting in a steam bath, all dressed up, all afternoon. I sat alone in the classroom a long time. I listened to the boys outside, downstairs, shouting and cursing and laughing. Their laughter struck me for perhaps the first time. It was not the joyous laughter which—God knows why—one associates with children. It was mocking and insular, its intent was to denigrate. It was disenchanted, and in this, also, lay the authority of their curses. Perhaps I was listening to them because I was thinking about my brother and in them I heard my brother. And myself.

One boy was whistling a tune, at once very complicated and very simple, it seemed to be pouring out of him as though he were a bird, and it sounded very cool and moving through all that harsh, bright air, only just holding its own through all those other sounds.

I stood up and walked over to the window and looked down into the courtyard. It was the beginning of the spring and the sap was rising in the boys. A teacher passed through them every now and again, quickly, as though he or she couldn't wait to get out of that courtyard, to get those boys out of their sight and off their minds. I started collecting my stuff. I thought I'd better get home and talk to Isabel.

The courtyard was almost deserted by the time I got downstairs. I saw this boy standing in the shadow of a doorway, looking just like Sonny. I almost called his name. Then I saw that it wasn't Sonny, but somebody we used to know, a boy from around our block. He'd been Sonny's friend. He'd never been mine, having been too young for me, and, anyway, I'd never liked him. And now, even though he was a grown-up man, he still hung around that block, still spent hours on the street corners, was always high and raggy. I used to run into him from time to time and he'd often work around to asking me for a quarter or fifty cents. He always had some real good excuse, too, and I always gave it to him, I don't know why.

But now, abruptly, I hated him. I couldn't stand the way he looked at me, partly like a dog, partly like a cunning child. I wanted to ask him what the hell he was doing in the school courtyard.

He sort of shuffled over to me, and he said, "I see you got the papers. So you already know about it."

"You mean about Sonny? Yes, I already know about it. How come they didn't get you?"

He grinned. It made him repulsive and it also brought to mind what he'd looked like as a kid. "I wasn't there. I stay away from them people."

"Good for you." I offered him a cigarette and I watched him through the smoke. "You come all the way down here just to tell me about Sonny?"

"That's right." He was sort of shaking his head and his eyes looked strange, as though they were about to cross. The bright sun deadened his damp dark brown skin and it made his eyes look yellow and showed up the dirt in his kinked hair. He smelled funky. I moved a little away from him and I said, "Well, thanks. But I already know about it and I got to get home."

"I'll walk you a little ways," he said. We started walking. There were a couple of kids still loitering in the courtyard and one of them said goodnight to me and looked strangely at the boy beside me.

"What're you going to do?" he asked me. "I mean, about Sonny?"

"Look. I haven't seen Sonny for over a year, I'm not sure I'm going to do anything. Anyway, what the hell *can* I do?"

"That's right," he said quickly, "ain't nothing you can do. Can't much help old Sonny no more, I guess."

It was what I was thinking and so it seemed to me he had no right to say it.

"I'm surprised at Sonny, though," he went on—he had a funny way of talking, he looked straight ahead as though he were talking to himself—"I thought Sonny was a smart boy, I thought he was too smart to get hung."

"I guess he thought so too," I said sharply, "and that's how he got hung. And how about you? You're pretty goddamn smart, I bet."

Then he looked directly at me, just for a minute. "I ain't smart," he said. "If I was smart, I'd have reached for a pistol a long time ago."

"Look. Don't tell *me* your sad story, if it was up to me, I'd give you one." Then I felt guilty—guilty, probably, for never having supposed that the poor bastard *had* a story of his own, much less a sad one, and I asked, quickly, "What's going to happen to him now?"

He didn't answer this. He was off by himself some place. "Funny thing," he said, and from his tone we might have been discussing the quickest way to get to Brooklyn, "when I saw the papers this morning, the first thing I asked myself was if I had anything to do with it. I felt sort of responsible."

I began to listen more carefully. The subway station was on the corner, just before us, and I stopped. He stopped, too. We were in front of a bar and he ducked slightly, peering in, but whoever he was looking for didn't seem to be there. The juke box was blasting away with something black and bouncy and I half watched the barmaid as she danced her way from the juke box to her place behind the bar. And I watched her face as she laughingly responded to something someone said to her, still keeping time to the music. When she smiled one saw the little girl, one sensed the doomed, still-struggling woman beneath the battered face of the semi-whore.

"I never *give* Sonny nothing," the boy said finally, "but a long time ago I come to school high and Sonny asked me how it felt." He paused, I couldn't bear to watch him, I watched the barmaid, and I listened to the music which seemed to be causing the pavement to shake. "I told him it felt great." The music stopped, the barmaid paused and watched the juke box until the music began again. "It did."

All this was carrying me some place I didn't want to go. I certainly didn't want to know how it felt. It filled everything, the people, the houses, the music, the dark, quicksilver barmaid, with menace; and this menace was their reality.

"What's going to happen to him now?" I asked again.

"They'll send him away some place and they'll try to cure him." He shook his head. "Maybe he'll even think he's kicked the habit. Then they'll let him loose"—he gestured, throwing his cigarette into the gutter. "That's all."

"What do you mean, that's *all*?"

But I knew what he meant.

"I *mean*, that's *all*." He turned his head and looked at me, pulling down the corners of his mouth. "Don't you know what I mean?" he asked, softly.

"How the hell *would* I know what you mean?" I almost whispered it, I don't know why.

"That's right," he said to the air, "how would *he* know what I mean?" He turned toward me again, patient and calm, and yet I somehow felt him shaking, shaking as though he were going to fall apart. I felt that ice in my guts again, the dread I'd felt all afternoon; and again I watched the barmaid, moving about the bar, washing glasses, and singing. "Listen. They'll let him out and then it'll just start all over again. That's what I mean."

"You mean—they'll let him out. And then he'll just start working his way back in again. You mean he'll never kick the habit. Is that what you mean?"

"That's right," he said, cheerfully. "*You* see what I mean."

"Tell me," I said at last, "why does he want to die? He must want to die, he's killing himself, why does he want to die?"

He looked at me in surprise. He licked his lips. "He don't want to die. He wants to live. Don't nobody want to die, ever."

Then I wanted to ask him—too many things. He could not have answered, or if he had, I could not have borne the answers. I started walking. "Well, I guess it's none of my business."

"It's going to be rough on old Sonny," he said. We reached the subway station. "This is your station?" he asked. I nodded. I took one step down. "Damn!" he said, suddenly. I looked up at him. He grinned again. "Damn it if I didn't leave all my money home. You ain't got a dollar on you, have you? Just for a couple of days, is all."

All at once something inside gave and threatened to come pouring out of me. I didn't hate him any more. I felt that in another moment I'd start crying like a child.

"Sure," I said. "Don't sweat." I looked in my wallet and didn't have a dollar, I only had a five. "Here," I said. "That hold you?"

He didn't look at it—he didn't want to look at it. A terrible, closed look came over his face, as though he were keeping the number on the bill a secret from him and me. "Thanks," he said, and now he was dying to see me go. "Don't worry about Sonny. Maybe I'll write him or something."

"Sure," I said. "You do that. So long."

"Be seeing you," he said. I went on down the steps.

And I didn't write Sonny or send him anything for a long time. When I finally did, it was just after my little girl died, he wrote me back a letter which made me feel like a bastard.

Here's what he said:

Dear brother,

You don't know how much I needed to hear from you. I wanted to write you many a time but I dug how much I must have hurt you and so I didn't write. But now I feel like a man who's been trying to climb up out of some deep, real deep and funky hole and just saw the sun up there, outside. I got to get outside.

I can't tell you much about how I got here. I mean I don't know how to tell you. I guess I was afraid of something or I was trying to escape from something and you know I have never been very strong in the head (smile). I'm glad Mama and Daddy are dead and can't see what's happened to their son and I swear if I'd known what I was doing I would never have hurt you so, you and a lot of other fine people who were nice to me and who believed in me.

I don't want you to think it had anything to do with me being a musician. It's more than that. Or maybe less than that. I can't get anything straight in my head down here and I try not to think about what's going to happen to me when I get outside again. Sometime I think I'm going to flip and never get outside and sometime I think I'll come straight back. I tell you one thing, though, I'd rather blow my brains out than go through this again. But that's what they all say, so they tell me. If I tell you when I'm coming to New York and if you could meet me, I sure would appreciate it. Give my love to Isabel and the kids and I was sure sorry to hear about little Gracie. I wish I could be like Mama and say the Lord's will be done, but I don't know it seems to me that trouble is the one thing that never does get stopped and I don't know what good it does to blame it on the Lord. But maybe it does some good if you believe it.

Your brother,

Sonny

Then I kept in constant touch with him and I sent him whatever I could and I went to meet him when he came back to New York. When I saw him many things I thought I had forgotten came flooding back to me. This was because I had begun, finally, to wonder about Sonny, about the life that Sonny lived inside. This life, whatever it was, had made him older and thinner and it had deepened the distant stillness in which he had always moved. He looked very unlike my baby brother. Yet, when he smiled, when we shook hands, the baby brother I'd never known looked out from the depths of his private life, like an animal waiting to be coaxed into the light.

"How you been keeping?" he asked me.

"All right. And you?"

"Just fine." He was smiling all over his face. "It's good to see you again."

"It's good to see you."

The seven years' difference in our ages lay between us like a chasm: I wondered if these years would ever operate between us as a bridge. I was remembering, and it made it hard to catch my breath, that I had been there when he was born; and I had heard the first words he had ever spoken. When he started to walk, he walked from our mother straight to me. I caught him just before he fell when he took the first steps he ever took in this world.

"How's Isabel?"

"Just fine. She's dying to see you."

"And the boys?"

"They're fine, too. They're anxious to see their uncle."

"Oh, come on. You know they don't remember me."

"Are you kidding? Of course they remember you."

He grinned again. We got into a taxi. We had a lot to say to each other, far too much to know how to begin.

As the taxi began to move, I asked, "You still want to go to India?"

He laughed. "You still remember that. Hell, no. This place is Indian enough for me."

"It used to belong to them," I said.

And he laughed again. "They damn sure knew what they were doing when they got rid of it."

Years ago, when he was around fourteen, he'd been all hipped on the idea of going to India. He read books about people sitting on rocks, naked, in all kinds of weather, but mostly bad, naturally, and walking barefoot through hot coals and arriving at wisdom. I used to say that it sounded to me as though they were getting away from wisdom as fast as they could. I think he sort of looked down on me for that.

"Do you mind," he asked, "if we have the driver drive alongside the park? On the west side—I haven't seen the city in so long."

"Of course not," I said. I was afraid that I might sound as though I were humoring him, but I hoped he wouldn't take it that way.

So we drove along, between the green of the park and the stony, lifeless elegance of hotels and apartment buildings, toward the vivid, killing streets of our childhood. These streets hadn't changed, though housing projects jutted up out of them now like rocks in the middle of a boiling sea. Most of the houses in which we had grown up had vanished, as had the stores from which we had stolen, the basements in which we had first tried sex, the rooftops from which we had hurled tin cans and bricks. But houses exactly like the houses of our past yet dominated the landscape, boys exactly like the boys we once had been found themselves smothering in these houses, came down into the streets for light and air and found themselves encircled by disaster. Some escaped the trap, most didn't. Those who got out always left something of themselves behind, as some animals amputate a leg and leave it in the trap. It might be said, perhaps, that I had escaped, after all, I was a school teacher; or that Sonny had, he hadn't lived in Harlem for years. Yet, as the cab moved uptown through streets which seemed, with a rush, to darken with dark people, and as I covertly studied Sonny's face, it came to me that what we both were seeking through our separate cab windows was that part of ourselves which had been left behind. It's always at the hour of trouble and confrontation that the missing member aches.

We hit 110th Street and started rolling up Lenox Avenue. And I'd known this avenue all my life, but it seemed to me again, as it had seemed on the day I'd first heard about Sonny's trouble, filled with a hidden menace which was its very breath of life.

"We almost there," said Sonny.

"Almost." We were both too nervous to say anything more.

We live in a housing project. It hasn't been up long. A few days after it was up it seemed uninhabitably new, now, of course, it's already rundown. It looks like a parody of the good, clean, faceless life—God knows the people who live in it do their best to make it a parody. The beat-looking grass lying around isn't enough to make their lives green, the hedges will never hold out the streets, and they know it. The big windows fool no one, they aren't big enough to make space out of no space. They don't bother with the windows, they watch the TV screen instead. The playground is most popular with the children who don't play at jacks, or skip rope, or roller skate, or swing, and they can be found in it after dark. We moved in partly because it's not too far from where I teach, and partly for the kids; but it's really just like the houses in which Sonny and I grew up. The same things happen, they'll have the same things to remember. The moment Sonny and I started into the house I had the feeling that I was simply bringing him back into the danger he had almost died trying to escape.

Sonny has never been talkative. So I don't know why I was sure he'd be dying to talk to me when supper was over the first night. Everything went fine, the oldest boy remembered him, and the youngest boy liked him, and Sonny had remembered to bring something for each of them; and Isabel, who is really much nicer than I am, more open and giving, had gone to a lot of trouble about dinner and was genuinely glad to see him. And she's always been able to tease Sonny in a way that I haven't. It was nice to see her face so vivid again and to hear her laugh and watch her make Sonny laugh. She wasn't, or, anyway, she didn't seem to be, at all uneasy or embarrassed. She chatted as though there were no subject which had to be avoided and she got Sonny past his first, faint stiffness. And thank God she was there, for I was filled with that icy dread again. Everything I did seemed awkward to me, and everything I said sounded freighted with hidden meaning. I was trying to remember everything I'd heard about dope addiction and I couldn't help watching Sonny for signs. I wasn't doing it out of malice. I was trying to find out something about my brother. I was dying to hear him tell me he was safe.

"Safe!" my father grunted, whenever Mama suggested trying to move to a neighborhood which might be safer for children. "Safe, hell! Ain't no place safe for kids, nor nobody."

He always went on like this, but he wasn't, ever, really as bad as he sounded, not even on weekends, when he got drunk. As a matter of fact, he was always on the lookout for "something a little better," but he died before he found it. He died suddenly, during a drunken week-end in the middle of the war, when Sonny was fifteen. He and Sonny hadn't ever got on too well. And this was partly because Sonny was the apple of his father's eye. It was because he loved Sonny so much and was frightened for him, that he was always fighting with him. It doesn't do any good to fight with Sonny. Sonny just moves back, inside himself, where he can't be reached. But the principal reason that they never hit it off is that they were so much alike. Daddy was big and rough and loud-talking, just the opposite of Sonny, but they both had—that same privacy.

Mama tried to tell me something about this, just after Daddy died. I was home on leave from the army.

This was the last time I ever saw my mother alive. Just the same, this picture gets all mixed up in my mind with pictures I had of her when she was younger. The way I always see her is the way she used to be on a Sunday afternoon, say, when the old folks were talking after the big Sunday dinner. I always see her wearing pale blue. She'd be sitting on the sofa. And my father would be sitting in the easy chair, not far from her. And the living room would be full of church folks and relatives. There they sit, in chairs all around the living room, and the night is creeping up outside, but nobody knows it yet. You can see the darkness growing against the windowpanes and you hear the street noises every now and again, or maybe the jangling beat of a tambourine from one of the churches close by, but it's real quiet in the room. For a moment nobody's talking, but every face looks darkening, like the sky outside. And my mother rocks a little from the waist, and my father's eyes are closed. Everyone is looking at something a child can't see. For a minute they've forgotten the children. Maybe a kid is lying on the rug, half asleep. Maybe somebody's got a kid in his lap and is absent-mindedly stroking the kid's head. Maybe there's a kid, quiet and big-eyed, curled up in a big chair in the corner. The silence, the darkness coming, and the darkness in the faces frightens the child obscurely. He hopes that the hand which strokes his forehead will never stop—will never die. He hopes that there will never come a time when the old folks won't be sitting around the living room, talking about where they've come from, and what they've seen, and what's happened to them and their kinfolk.

But something deep and watchful in the child knows that this is bound to end, is already ending. In a moment someone will get up and turn on the light. Then the old folks will remember the children and they won't talk any more that day. And when light fills the room, the child is filled with darkness. He knows that every time this happens he's moved just a little closer to that darkness outside. The darkness outside is what the old folks have been talking about. It's what they've come from. It's what they endure. The child knows that they won't talk any more because if he knows too much about what's happened to *them*, he'll know too much too soon, about what's going to happen to *him*.

The last time I talked to my mother, I remember I was restless. I wanted to get out and see Isabel. We weren't married then and we had a lot to straighten out between us.

There Mama sat, in black, by the window. She was humming an old church song, *Lord, you brought me from a long ways off*. Sonny was out somewhere. Mama kept watching the streets.

"I don't know," she said, "if I'll ever see you again, after you go off from here. But I hope you'll remember the things I tried to teach you."

"Don't talk like that," I said, and smiled. "You'll be here a long time yet."

She smiled, too, but she said nothing. She was quiet for a long time. And I said, "Mama, don't you worry about nothing. I'll be writing all the time, and you be getting the checks...."

"I want to talk to you about your brother," she said, suddenly. "If anything happens to me he ain't going to have nobody to look out for him."

"Mama," I said, "ain't nothing going to happen to you *or* Sonny. Sonny's all right. He's a good boy and he's got good sense."

"It ain't a question of his being a good boy," Mama said, "nor of his having good sense. It ain't only the bad ones, nor yet the dumb ones that gets sucked under." She stopped, looking at me. "Your Daddy once had a brother," she said, and she smiled in a way that made me feel she was in pain. "You didn't never know that, did you?"

"No," I said, "I never knew that," and I watched her face.

"Oh, yes," she said, "your Daddy had a brother." She looked out of the window again. "I know you never saw your Daddy cry. But I did— many a time, through all these years."

I asked her, "What happened to his brother? How come nobody's ever talked about him?"

This was the first time I ever saw my mother look old.

"His brother got killed," she said, "when he was just a little younger than you are now. I knew him. He was a fine boy. He was maybe a little full of the devil, but he didn't mean nobody no harm."

Then she stopped and the room was silent, exactly as it had sometimes been on those Sunday afternoons. Mama kept looking out into the streets.

"He used to have a job in the mill," she said, "and, like all young folks, he just liked to perform on Saturday nights. Saturday nights, him and your father would drift around to different places, go to dances and things like that, or just sit around with people they knew, and your father's brother would sing, he had a fine voice, and play along with himself on his guitar. Well, this particular Saturday night, him and your father was coming home from some place, and they were both a little drunk and there was a moon that night, it was bright like day. Your father's brother was feeling kind of good, and he was whistling to himself, and he had his guitar slung over his shoulder. They was coming down a hill and beneath them was a road that turned off from the highway. Well, your father's brother, being always kind of frisky, decided to run down this hill, and he did, with that guitar banging and clanging behind him, and he ran across the road, and he was making water behind a tree. And your father was sort of amused at him and he was still coming down the hill, kind of slow. Then he heard a car motor and that same minute his brother stepped from behind the tree, into the road, in the moonlight. And he started to cross the road. And your father started to run down the hill, he says he don't know why. This car was full of white men. They was all drunk, and when they seen your father's brother they let out a great whoop and holler and they aimed the car straight at him. They was having fun, they just wanted to scare him, the way they do sometimes, you know. But they was drunk. And I guess the boy, being drunk, too, and scared, kind of lost his head. By the time he jumped it was too late. Your father says he heard his brother scream when the car rolled over him, and he heard the wood of that guitar when it give, and he heard them strings go flying, and he heard them white men shouting, and the car kept on a-going and it ain't stopped till this day. And, time your father got down the hill, his brother weren't nothing but blood and pulp."

Tears were gleaming on my mother's face. There wasn't anything I could say.

"He never mentioned it," she said, "because I never let him mention it before you children. Your Daddy was like a crazy man that night and for many a night thereafter. He says he never in his life seen anything as dark as that road after the lights of that car had gone away. Weren't nothing, weren't nobody on that road, just your Daddy and his brother and that busted guitar. Oh, yes. Your Daddy never did really get right again. Till the day he died he weren't sure but that every white man he saw was the man that killed his brother."

She stopped and took out her handkerchief and dried her eyes and looked at me.

"I ain't telling you all this," she said, "to make you scared or bitter or to make you hate nobody. I'm telling you this because you got a brother. And the world ain't changed."

I guess I didn't want to believe this. I guess she saw this in my face. She turned away from me, toward the window again, searching those streets.

"But I praise my Redeemer," she said at last, "that He called your Daddy home before me. I ain't saying it to throw no flowers at myself, but, I declare, it keeps me from feeling too cast down to know I helped your father get safely through this world. Your father always acted like he was the roughest, strongest man on earth. And everybody took him to be like that. But if he hadn't had *me* there—to see his tears!"

She was crying again. Still, I couldn't move. I said, "Lord, Lord, Mama, I didn't know it was like that."

"Oh, honey," she said, "there's a lot that you don't know. But you are going to find it out." She stood up from the window and came over to me. "You got to hold on to your brother," she said, "and don't let him fall, no matter what it looks like is happening to him and no matter how evil you gets with him. You going to be evil with him many a time. But don't you forget what I told you, you hear?"

"I won't forget," I said. "Don't you worry, I won't forget. I won't let nothing happen to Sonny."

My mother smiled as though she were amused at something she saw in my face. Then, "You may not be able to stop nothing from happening. But you got to let him know you's *there*."

Two days later I was married, and then I was gone. And I had a lot of things on my mind and I pretty well forgot my promise to Mama until I got shipped home on a special furlough for her funeral.

And, after the funeral, with just Sonny and me alone in the empty kitchen, I tried to find out something about him.

"What do you want to do?" I asked him.

"I'm going to be a musician," he said.

For he had graduated, in the time I had been away, from dancing to the juke box to finding out who was playing what, and what they were doing with it, and he had bought himself a set of drums.

"You mean, you want to be a drummer?" I somehow had the feeling that being a drummer might be all right for other people but not for my brother Sonny.

"I don't think," he said, looking at me very gravely, "that I'll ever be a good drummer. But I think I can play a piano."

I frowned. I'd never played the role of the older brother quite so seriously before, had scarcely ever, in fact, asked Sonny a damn thing. I sensed myself in the presence of something I didn't really know how to handle, didn't understand. So I made my frown a little deeper as I asked: "What kind of musician do you want to be?"

He grinned. "How many kinds do you think there are?"

"Be serious," I said.

He laughed, throwing his head back, and then looked at me. "I am serious."

"Well, then, for Christ's sake, stop kidding around and answer a serious question. I mean, do you want to be a concert pianist, you want to play classical music and all that, or—or what?" Long before I finished he was laughing again. "For Christ's sake, Sonny!"

He sobered, but with difficulty. "I'm sorry. But you sound so—scared!" and he was off again.

"Well, you may think it's funny now, baby, but it's not going to be so funny when you have to make your living at it, let me tell you that." I was furious because I knew he was laughing at me and I didn't know why.

"No," he said, very sober now, and afraid, perhaps, that he'd hurt me, "I don't want to be a classical pianist. That isn't what interests me. I mean"—he paused, looking hard at me, as though his eyes would help me to understand, and then gestured helplessly, as though perhaps his hand would help—"I mean, I'll have a lot of studying to do, and I'll have to study everything, but, I mean, I want to play with—jazz musicians." He stopped. "I want to play jazz," he said.

Well, the word had never before sounded as heavy, as real, as it sounded that afternoon in Sonny's mouth. I just looked at him and I was probably frowning a real frown by this time. I simply couldn't see why on earth he'd want to spend his time hanging around nightclubs, clowning around on bandstands, while people pushed each other around a dance floor. It seemed—beneath him, somehow. I had never thought about it before, had never been forced to, but I suppose I had always put jazz musicians in a class with what Daddy called "goodtime people."

"Are you serious?"

"Hell, *yes*, I'm serious."

He looked more helpless than ever, and annoyed, and deeply hurt.

I suggested, helpfully: "You mean—like Louis Armstrong?"

His face closed as though I'd struck him. "No. I'm not talking about none of that old-time, down home crap."

"Well, look, Sonny, I'm sorry, don't get mad. I just don't altogether get it, that's all. Name somebody—you know, a jazz musician you admire."

"Bird."

"Who?"

"Bird! Charlie Parker! Don't they teach you nothing in the goddamn army?"

I lit a cigarette. I was surprised and then a little amused to discover that I was trembling. "I've been out of touch," I said. "You'll have to be patient with me. Now. Who's this Parker character?"

"He's just one of the greatest jazz musicians alive," said Sonny, sullenly, his hands in his pockets, his back to me. "Maybe *the* greatest," he added, bitterly, "that's probably why *you* never heard of him."

"All right," I said, "I'm ignorant. I'm sorry. I'll go out and buy all the cat's records right away, all right?"

"It don't," said Sonny, with dignity, "make any difference to me. I don't care what you listen to. Don't do me no favors."

I was beginning to realize that I'd never seen him so upset before. With another part of my mind I was thinking that this would probably turn out to be one of those things kids go through and that I shouldn't make it seem important by pushing it too hard. Still, I didn't think it would do any harm to ask: "Doesn't all this take a lot of time? Can you make a living at it?"

He turned back to me and half leaned, half sat, on the kitchen table. "Everything takes time," he said, "and—well, yes, sure, I can make a living at it. But what I don't seem to be able to make you understand is that it's the only thing I want to do."

"Well, Sonny," I said, gently, "you know people can't always do exactly what they *want* to do—"

"No, I don't know that," said Sonny, surprising me. "I think people *ought* to do what they want to do, what else are they alive for?"

"You getting to be a big boy," I said desperately, "it's time you started thinking about your future."

"I'm thinking about my future," said Sonny, grimly. "I think about it all the time."

I gave up. I decided, if he didn't change his mind, that we could always talk about it later. "In the meantime," I said, "you got to finish school." We had already decided that he'd have to move in with Isabel and her folks. I knew this wasn't the ideal arrangement because Isabel's folks are inclined to be dicty and they hadn't especially wanted Isabel to marry me. But I didn't know what else to do. "And we have to get you fixed up at Isabel's."

There was a long silence. He moved from the kitchen table to the window. "That's a terrible idea. You know it yourself."

"Do you have a *better* idea?"

He just walked up and down the kitchen for a minute. He was as tall as I was. He had started to shave. I suddenly had the feeling that I didn't know him at all.

He stopped at the kitchen table and picked up my cigarettes. Looking at me with a kind of mocking, amused defiance, he put one between his lips. "You mind?"

"You smoking already?"

He lit the cigarette and nodded, watching me through the smoke. "I just wanted to see if I'd have the courage to smoke in front of you." He grinned and blew a great cloud of smoke to the ceiling. "It was easy." He looked at my face. "Come on, now. I bet you was smoking at my age, tell the truth."

I didn't say anything but the truth was on my face, and he laughed. But now there was something very strained in his laugh. "Sure. And I bet that ain't all you was doing."

He was frightening me a little. "Cut the crap," I said. "We already decided that you was going to go and live at Isabel's. Now what's got into you all of a sudden?"

"*You* decided it," he pointed out. "*I* didn't decide nothing." He stopped in front of me, leaning against the stove, arms loosely folded. "Look, brother. I don't want to stay in Harlem no more, I really don't." He was very earnest. He looked at me, then over toward the kitchen window. There was something in his eyes I'd never seen before, some thoughtfulness, some worry all his own. He rubbed the muscle of one arm. "It's time I was getting out of here."

"Where do you want to *go*, Sonny?"

"I want to join the army. Or the navy, I don't care. If I say I'm old enough, they'll believe me."

Then I got mad. It was because I was so scared. "You must be crazy. You goddamn fool, what the hell do you want to go and join the *army* for?"

"I just told you. To get out of Harlem."

"Sonny, you haven't even finished *school*. And if you really want to be a musician, how do you expect to study if you're in the *army*?"

He looked at me, trapped, and in anguish. "There's ways. I might be able to work out some kind of deal. Anyway, I'll have the G.I. Bill when I come out."

"*If* you come out." We stared at each other. "Sonny, please. Be reasonable. I know the setup is far from perfect. But we got to do the best we can."

"I ain't learning nothing in school," he said. "Even when I go." He turned away from me and opened the window and threw his cigarette out into the narrow alley. I watched his back. "At least, I ain't learning nothing you'd want me to learn." He slammed the window so hard I thought the glass would fly out, and turned back to me. "And I'm sick of the stink of these garbage cans!"

"Sonny," I said, "I know how you feel. But if you don't finish school now, you're going to be sorry later that you didn't." I grabbed him by the shoulders. "And you only got another year. It ain't so bad. And I'll come back and I swear I'll help you do *whatever* you want to do. Just try to put up with it till I come back. Will you please do that? For me?"

He didn't answer and he wouldn't look at me.

"Sonny. You hear me?"

He pulled away. "I hear you. But you never hear anything *I* say."

I didn't know what to say to that. He looked out of the window and then back at me. "OK," he said, and sighed. "I'll try."

Then I said, trying to cheer him up a little, "They got a piano at Isabel's. You can practice on it."

And as a matter of fact, it did cheer him up for a minute. "That's right," he said to himself. "I forgot that." His face relaxed a little. But the worry, the thoughtfulness, played on it still, the way shadows play on a face which is staring into the fire.

But I thought I'd never hear the end of that piano. At first, Isabel would write me, saying how nice it was that Sonny was so serious about his music and how, as soon as he came in from school, or wherever he had been when he was supposed to be at school, he went straight to that piano and stayed there until suppertime. And, after supper, he went back to that piano and stayed there until everybody went to bed. He was at the piano all day Saturday and all day Sunday. Then he bought a record player and started playing records. He'd play one record over and over again, all day long sometimes, and he'd improvise along with it on the piano. Or he'd play one section of the record, one chord, one change, one progression, then he'd do it on the piano. Then back to the record. Then back to the piano.

Well, I really don't know how they stood it. Isabel finally confessed that it wasn't like living with a person at all, it was like living with sound. And the sound didn't make any sense to her, didn't make any sense to any of them—naturally. They began, in a way, to be afflicted by this presence that was living in their home. It was as though Sonny were some sort of god, or monster. He moved in an atmosphere which wasn't like theirs at all. They fed him and he ate, he washed himself, he walked in and out of their door; he certainly wasn't nasty or unpleasant or rude, Sonny isn't any of those things; but it was as though he were all wrapped up in some cloud, some fire, some vision all his own; and there wasn't any way to reach him.

At the same time, he wasn't really a man yet, he was still a child, and they had to watch out for him in all kinds of ways. They certainly couldn't throw him out. Neither did they dare to make a great scene about that piano because even they dimly sensed, as I sensed, from so many thousands of miles away, that Sonny was at that piano playing for his life.

But he hadn't been going to school. One day a letter came from the school board and Isabel's mother got it—there had, apparently, been other letters but Sonny had torn them up. This day, when Sonny came in, Isabel's mother showed him the letter and asked where he'd been spending his time. And she finally got it out of him that he'd been down in Greenwich Village, with musicians and other characters, in a white girl's apartment. And this scared her and she started to scream at him and what came up, once she began—though she denies it to this day—was what sacrifices they were making to give Sonny a decent home and how little he appreciated it.

Sonny didn't play the piano that day. By evening, Isabel's mother had calmed down but then there was the old man to deal with, and Isabel herself. Isabel says she did her best to be calm but she broke down and started crying. She says she just watched Sonny's face. She could tell, by watching him, what was happening with him. And what was happening was that they penetrated his cloud, they had reached him. Even if their fingers had been a thousand times more gentle than human fingers ever are, he could hardly help feeling that they had stripped him naked and were spitting on that nakedness. For he also had to see that his presence, that music, which was life or death to him, had been torture for them and that they had endured it, not at all for his sake, but only for mine. And Sonny couldn't take that. He can take it a little better today than he could then but he's still not very good at it and, frankly, I don't know anybody who is.

The silence of the next few days must have been louder than the sound of all the music ever played since time began. One morning, before she went to work, Isabel was in his room for something and she suddenly realized that all of his records were gone. And she knew for certain that he was gone. And he was. He went as far as the navy would carry him. He finally sent me a postcard from some place in Greece and that was the first I knew that Sonny was still alive. I didn't see him any more until we were both back in New York and the war had long been over.

He was a man by then, of course, but I wasn't willing to see it. He came by the house from time to time, but we fought almost every time we met. I didn't like the way he carried himself, loose and dreamlike all the time, and I didn't like his friends, and his music seemed to be merely an excuse for the life he led. It sounded just that weird and disordered.

Then we had a fight, a pretty awful fight, and I didn't see him for months. By and by I looked him up, where he was living, in a furnished room in the Village, and I tried to make it up. But there were lots of other people in the room and Sonny just lay on his bed, and he wouldn't come downstairs with me, and he treated these other people as though they were his family and I weren't. So I got mad and then he got mad, and then I told him that he might just as well be dead as live the way he was living. Then he stood up and he told me not to worry about him any more in life, that he *was* dead as far as I was concerned. Then he pushed me to the door and the other people looked on as though nothing were happening, and he slammed the door behind me. I stood in the hallway, staring at the door. I heard somebody laugh in the room and then the tears came to my eyes. I started down the steps, whistling to keep from crying, I kept whistling to myself, *You going to need me, baby, one of these cold, rainy days.*

I read about Sonny's trouble in the spring. Little Grace died in the fall. She was a beautiful little girl. But she only lived a little over two years. She died of polio and she suffered. She had a slight fever for a couple of days, but it didn't seem like anything and we just kept her in bed. And we would certainly have called the doctor, but the fever dropped, she seemed to be all right. So we thought it had just been a cold. Then, one day, she was up, playing, Isabel was in the kitchen fixing lunch for the two boys when they'd come in from school, and she heard Grace fall down in the living room. When you have a lot of children you don't always start running when one of them falls, unless they start screaming or something. And, this time, Grace was quiet. Yet, Isabel says that when she heard that *thump* and then that silence, something happened in her to make her afraid. And she ran to the living room and there was little Grace on the floor, all twisted up, and the reason she hadn't screamed was that she couldn't get her breath. And when she did scream, it was the worst sound, Isabel says, that she'd ever heard in all her life, and she still hears it sometimes in her dreams. Isabel will sometimes wake me up with a low, moaning, strangled sound and I have to be quick to awaken her and hold her to me and where Isabel is weeping against me seems a mortal wound.

I think I may have written Sonny the very day that little Grace was buried. I was sitting in the living room in the dark, by myself, and I suddenly thought of Sonny. My trouble made his real.

One Saturday afternoon, when Sonny had been living with us, or, anyway, been in our house, for nearly two weeks, I found myself wandering
aimlessly about the living room, drinking from a can of beer, and trying
to work up the courage to search Sonny's room. He was out, he was
usually out whenever I was home, and Isabel had taken the children to
see their grandparents. Suddenly I was standing still in front of the living room window, watching Seventh Avenue. The idea of searching
Sonny's room made me still. I scarcely dared to admit to myself what
I'd be searching for. I didn't know what I'd do if I found it. Or if I
didn't.

On the sidewalk across from me, near the entrance to a barbecue
joint, some people were holding an old-fashioned revival meeting. The
barbecue cook, wearing a dirty white apron, his conked hair reddish
and metallic in the pale sun, and a cigarette between his lips, stood in
the doorway, watching them. Kids and older people paused in their
errands and stood there, along with some older men and a couple of
very tough-looking women who watched everything that happened on
the avenue, as though they owned it, or were maybe owned by it. Well,
they were watching this, too. The revival was being carried on by three
sisters in black, and a brother. All they had were their voices and their
Bibles and a tambourine. The brother was testifying and while he testi-
fied two of the sisters stood together, seeming to say, amen, and the
third sister walked around with the tambourine outstretched and a couple of people dropped coins into it. Then the brother's testimony ended
and the sister who had been taking up the collection dumped the coins
into her palm and transferred them to the pocket of her long black
robe. Then she raised both hands, striking the tambourine against the
air, and then against one hand, and she started to sing. And the two
other sisters and the brother joined in.

It was strange, suddenly, to watch, though I had been seeing these
street meetings all my life. So, of course, had everybody else down
there. Yet, they paused and watched and listened and I stood still at the
window. "Tis the old ship of Zion," they sang, and the sister with the
tambourine kept a steady, jangling beat, "it has rescued many a thousand!" Not a soul under the sound of their voices was hearing this song
for the first time, not one of them had been rescued. Nor had they seen
much in the way of rescue work being done around them. Neither did
they especially believe in the holiness of the three sisters and the
brother, they knew too much about them, knew where they lived, and
how. The woman with the tambourine, whose voice dominated the air,
whose face was bright with joy, was divided by very little from the
woman who stood watching her, a cigarette between her heavy,
chapped lips, her hair a cuckoo's nest, her face scarred and swollen
from many beatings, and her black eyes glittering like coal. Perhaps
they both knew this, which was why, when, as rarely, they addressed

each other, they addressed each other as Sister. As the singing filled
the air the watching, listening faces underwent a change, the eyes
focusing on something within; the music seemed to soothe a poison out
of them; and time seemed, nearly, to fall away from the sullen, belligerent, battered faces, as though they were fleeing back to their first condition, while dreaming of their last. The barbecue cook half shook his
head and smiled, and dropped his cigarette and disappeared into his
joint. A man fumbled in his pockets for change and stood holding it in
his hand impatiently, as though he had just remembered a pressing
appointment further up the avenue. He looked furious. Then I saw
Sonny, standing on the edge of the crowd. He was carrying a wide, flat
notebook with a green cover, and it made him look, from where I was
standing, almost like a schoolboy. The coppery sun brought out the
copper in his skin, he was very faintly smiling, standing very still. Then
the singing stopped, the tambourine turned into a collection plate
again. The furious man dropped in his coins and vanished, so did a couple of the women, and Sonny dropped some change in the plate, looking directly at the woman with a little smile. He started across the
avenue, toward the house. He has a slow, loping walk, something like
the way Harlem hipsters walk, only he's imposed on this his own half-
beat. I had never really noticed it before.

I stayed at the window, both relieved and apprehensive. As Sonny
disappeared from my sight, they began singing again. And they were
still singing when his key turned in the lock.

"Hey," he said.

"Hey, yourself. You want some beer?"

"No. Well, maybe." But he came up to the window and stood
beside me, looking out. "What a warm voice," he said.

They were singing *If I could only hear my mother pray again!*

"Yes," I said, "and she can sure beat that tambourine."

"But what a terrible song," he said, and laughed. He dropped his
notebook on the sofa and disappeared into the kitchen. "Where's Isabel
and the kids?"

"I think they went to see their grandparents. You hungry?"

"No." He came back into the living room with his can of beer. "You
want to come some place with me tonight?"

I sensed, I don't know how, that I couldn't possibly say no. "Sure.
Where?"

He sat down on the sofa and picked up his notebook and started
leafing through it. "I'm going to sit in with some fellows in a joint in
the Village."

"You mean, you're going to play, tonight?"

"That's right." He took a swallow of his beer and moved back to the
window. He gave me a sidelong look. "If you can stand it."

"I'll try," I said.

He smiled to himself and we both watched as the meeting across the way broke up. The three sisters and the brother, heads bowed, were singing *God be with you till we meet again*. The faces around them were very quiet. Then the song ended. The small crowd dispersed. We watched the three women and the lone man walk slowly up the avenue.

"When she was singing before," said Sonny, abruptly, "her voice reminded me for a minute of what heroin feels like sometimes—when it's in your veins. It makes you feel sort of warm and cool at the same time. And distant. And—and sure." He sipped his beer, very deliberately not looking at me. I watched his face. "It makes you feel—in control. Sometimes you've got to have that feeling."

"Do you?" I sat down slowly in the easy chair.

"Sometimes." He went to the sofa and picked up his notebook again. "Some people do."

"In order," I asked, "to play?" And my voice was very ugly, full of contempt and anger.

"Well"—he looked at me with great, troubled eyes, as though, in fact, he hoped his eyes would tell me things he could never otherwise say—"they *think* so. And *if* they think so—!"

"And what do *you* think?" I asked.

He sat on the sofa and put his can of beer on the floor. "I don't know," he said, and I couldn't be sure if he were answering my question or pursuing his thoughts. His face didn't tell me. "It's not so much to *play*. It's to *stand* it, to be able to make it at all. On any level." He frowned and smiled: "In order to keep from shaking to pieces."

"But these friends of yours," I said, "they seem to shake themselves to pieces pretty goddamn fast."

"Maybe." He played with the notebook. And something told me that I should curb my tongue, that Sonny was doing his best to talk, that I should listen. "But of course you only know the ones that've gone to pieces. Some don't—or at least they haven't *yet* and that's just about all *any* of us can say." He paused. "And then there are some who just live, really, in hell, and they know it and they see what's happening and they go right on. I don't know." He sighed, dropped the notebook, folded his arms. "Some guys, you can tell from the way they play, they on something *all* the time. And you can see that, well, it makes something real for them. But of course," he picked up his beer from the floor and sipped it and put the can down again, "they *want* to, too, you've got to see that. Even some of them that say they don't—*some*, not all."

"And what about you?" I asked—I couldn't help it. "What about you? Do *you* want to?"

He stood up and walked to the window and remained silent for a long time. Then he sighed. "Me," he said. Then: "While I was downstairs before, on my way here, listening to that woman sing, it struck me all of a sudden how much suffering she must have had to go through—to sing like that. It's *repulsive* to think you have to suffer that much."

I said: "But there's no way not to suffer—is there, Sonny?"

"I believe not," he said and smiled, "but that's never stopped anyone from trying." He looked at me. "Has it?" I realized, with this mocking look, that there stood between us, forever, beyond the power of time or forgiveness, the fact that I had held silence—so long!—when he had needed human speech to help him. He turned back to the window. "No, there's no way not to suffer. But you try all kinds of ways to keep from drowning in it, to keep on top of it, and to make it seem—well, like *you*. Like you did something, all right, and now you're suffering for it. You know?" I said nothing. "Well you know," he said, impatiently, "why *do* people suffer? Maybe it's better to do something to give it a reason, *any* reason."

"But we just agreed," I said, "that there's no way not to suffer. Isn't it better, then, just to—take it?"

"But nobody just takes it," Sonny cried, "that's what I'm telling you! *Everybody* tries not to. You're just hung up on the *way* some people try—it's not *your* way!"

The hair on my face began to itch, my face felt wet. "That's not true," I said, "that's not true. I don't give a damn what other people do, I don't even care how they suffer. I just care how *you* suffer." And he looked at me. "Please believe me," I said, "I don't want to see you—die—trying not to suffer."

"I won't," he said, flatly, "die trying not to suffer. At least, not any faster than anybody else."

"But there's no need," I said, trying to laugh, "is there? in killing yourself."

I wanted to say more, but I couldn't. I wanted to talk about will power and how life could be—well, beautiful. I wanted to say that it was all within; but was it? or, rather, wasn't that exactly the trouble? And I wanted to promise that I would never fail him again. But it would all have sounded—empty words and lies.

So I made the promise to myself and prayed that I would keep it.

"It's terrible sometimes, inside," he said, "that's what's the trouble. You walk these streets, black and funky and cold, and there's not really a living ass to talk to, and there's nothing shaking, and there's no way of getting it out—that storm inside. You can't talk it and you can't make love with it, and when you finally try to get with it and play it, you realize *nobody's* listening. So *you've* got to listen. You got to find a way to listen."

And then he walked away from the window and sat on the sofa again, as though all the wind had suddenly been knocked out of him. "Sometimes you'll do *anything* to play, even cut your mother's throat."

He laughed and looked at me. "Or your brother's." Then he sobered. "Or your own." Then: "Don't worry. I'm all right now and I think I'll *be* all right. But I can't forget—where I've been. I don't mean just the physical place I've been, I mean where I've *been*. And *what* I've been."

"What have you been, Sonny?" I asked.

He smiled—but sat sideways on the sofa, his elbow resting on the back, his fingers playing with his mouth and chin, not looking at me. "I've been something I didn't recognize, didn't know I could be. Didn't know anybody could be." He stopped, looking inward, looking help-lessly young, looking old. "I'm not talking about it now because I feel *guilty* or anything like that—maybe it would be better if I did, I don't know. Anyway, I can't really talk about it. Not to you, not to anybody," and now he turned and faced me. "Sometimes, you know, and it was actually when I was most *out* of the world, I felt that I was in it, that I was *with* it, really, and I could play or I didn't really have to *play*, it just came out of me, it was there. And I don't know how I played, thinking about it now, but I know I did awful things, those times, sometimes, to people. Or it wasn't that I *did* anything to them—it was that they weren't real." He picked up the beer can; it was empty; he rolled it between his palms: "And other times—well, I needed a fix, I needed to find a place to lean, I needed to clear a space to *listen*—and I couldn't find it, and I—went crazy, I did terrible things to *me*, I was terrible *for* me." He began pressing the beer can between his hands, I watched the metal begin to give. It glittered, as he played with it, like a knife, and I was afraid he would cut himself, but I said nothing. "Oh well. I can never tell you. I was all by myself at the bottom of something, stinking and sweating and crying and shaking, and I smelled it, you know? *my* stink, and I thought I'd die if I couldn't get away from it and yet, all the same, I knew that everything I was doing was just locking me in with it. And I didn't know," he paused, still flattening the beer can, "I didn't know, I still *don't* know, something kept telling me that maybe it was good to smell your own stink, but I didn't think that *that* was what I'd been trying to do—and—who can stand it?" and he abruptly dropped the ruined beer can, looking at me with a small, still smile, and then rose, walking to the window as though it were the lodestone rock. I watched his face, he watched the avenue. "I couldn't tell you when Mama died—but the reason I wanted to leave Harlem so bad was to get away from drugs. And then, when I ran away, that's what I was running from—really. When I came back, nothing had changed, I hadn't changed, I was just—older." And he stopped, drumming with his fin-gers on the windowpane. The sun had vanished, soon darkness would fall. I watched his face. "It can come again," he said, almost as though speaking to himself. Then he turned to me. "It can come again," he repeated. "I just want you to know that."

"All right," I said, at last. "So it can come again. All right."

He smiled, but the smile was sorrowful. "I had to try to tell you," he said.

"Yes," I said. "I understand that."

"You're my brother," he said, looking straight at me, and not smiling at all.

"Yes," I repeated, "yes. I understand that."

He turned back to the window, looking out. "All that hatred down there," he said, "all that hatred and misery and love. It's a wonder it doesn't blow the avenue apart."

⊱⊰

We went to the only nightclub on a short, dark street, downtown. We squeezed through the narrow, chattering, jam-packed bar to the entrance of the big room, where the bandstand was. And we stood there for a moment, for the lights were very dim in this room and we couldn't see. Then, "Hello, boy," said a voice and an enormous black man, much older than Sonny or myself, erupted out of all that atmospheric lighting and put an arm around Sonny's shoulder. "I been sitting right here," he said, "waiting for you."

He had a big voice, too, and heads in the darkness turned toward us.

Sonny grinned and pulled a little away, and said, "Creole, this is my brother. I told you about him."

Creole shook my hand. "I'm glad to meet you, son," he said, and it was clear that he was glad to meet me *there*, for Sonny's sake. And he smiled, "You got a real musician in *your* family," and he took his arm from Sonny's shoulder and slapped him, lightly, affectionately, with the back of his hand.

"Well. Now I've heard it all," said a voice behind us. This was another musician, and a friend of Sonny's, a coal-black, cheerful-looking man, built close to the ground. He immediately began confiding to me, at the top of his lungs, the most terrible things about Sonny, his teeth gleaming like a lighthouse and his laugh coming up out of him like the beginning of an earthquake. And it turned out that everyone at the bar knew Sonny, or almost everyone; some were musicians, working there, or nearby, or not working, some were simply hangers-on, and some were there to hear Sonny play. I was introduced to all of them and they were all very polite to me. Yet, it was clear that, for them, I was only Sonny's brother. Here, I was in Sonny's world. Or, rather: his kingdom. Here, it was not even a question that his veins bore royal blood.

They were going to play soon and Creole installed me, by myself, at a table in a dark corner. Then I watched them, Creole, and the little black man, and Sonny, and the others, while they horsed around, standing just below the bandstand. The light from the bandstand spilled just a little short of them and, watching them laughing and gesturing and moving about, I had the feeling that they, nevertheless, were being most careful not to step into that circle of light too suddenly: that if they moved into the light too suddenly, without thinking, they would perish in flame. Then, while I watched, one of them, the small, black man, moved into the light and crossed the bandstand and started fooling around with his drums. Then—being funny and being, also, extremely ceremonious—Creole took Sonny by the arm and led him to the piano. A woman's voice called Sonny's name and a few hands started clapping. And Sonny, also being funny and being ceremonious, and so touched, I think, that he could have cried, but neither hiding it nor showing it, riding it like a man, grinned, and put both hands to his heart and bowed from the waist.

Creole then went to the bass fiddle and a lean, very bright-skinned brown man jumped up on the bandstand and picked up his horn. So there they were, and the atmosphere on the bandstand and in the room began to change and tighten. Someone stepped up to the microphone and announced them. Then there were all kinds of murmurs. Some people at the bar shushed others. The waitress ran around, frantically getting in the last orders, guys and chicks got closer to each other, and the lights on the bandstand, on the quartet, turned to a kind of indigo. Then they all looked different there. Creole looked about him for the last time, as though he were making certain that all his chickens were in the coop, and then he—jumped and struck the fiddle. And there they were.

All I know about music is that not many people ever really hear it. And even then, on the rare occasions when something opens within, and the music enters, what we mainly hear, or hear corroborated, are personal, private, vanishing evocations. But the man who creates the music is hearing something else, is dealing with the roar rising from the void and imposing order on it as it hits the air. What is evoked in him, then, is of another order, more terrible because it has no words, and triumphant, too, for that same reason. And his triumph, when he triumphs, is ours. I just watched Sonny's face. His face was troubled, he was working hard, but he wasn't with it. And I had the feeling that, in a way, everyone on the bandstand was waiting for him, both waiting for him and pushing him along. But as I began to watch Creole, I realized that it was Creole who held them all back. He had them on a short rein. Up there, keeping the beat with his whole body, wailing on the fiddle, with his eyes half closed, he was listening to everything, but he was listening to Sonny. He was having a dialogue with Sonny. He wanted Sonny to leave the shoreline and strike out for the deep water. He was Sonny's witness that deep water and drowning were not the same thing—he had been there, and he knew. And he wanted Sonny to know. He was waiting for Sonny to do the things on the keys which would let Creole know that Sonny was in the water.

And, while Creole listened, Sonny moved, deep within, exactly like someone in torment. I had never before thought of how awful the relationship must be between the musician and his instrument. He has to fill it, this instrument, with the breath of life, his own. He has to make it do what he wants it to do. And a piano is just a piano. It's made out of so much wood and wires and little hammers and big ones, and ivory. While there's only so much you can do with it, the only way to find this out is to try; to try and make it do everything.

And Sonny hadn't been near a piano for over a year. And he wasn't on much better terms with his life, not the life that stretched before him now. He and the piano stammered, started one way, got scared, stopped; started another way, panicked, marked time, started again; then seemed to have found a direction, panicked again, got stuck. And the face I saw on Sonny I'd never seen before. Everything had been burned out of it, and, at the same time, things usually hidden were being burned in, by the fire and fury of the battle which was occurring in him up there.

Yet, watching Creole's face as they neared the end of the first set, I had the feeling that something had happened, something I hadn't heard. Then they finished, there was scattered applause, and then, without an instant's warning, Creole started into something else, it was almost sardonic, it was *Am I Blue*. And, as though he commanded, Sonny began to play. Something began to happen. And Creole let out the reins. The dry, low, black man said something awful on the drums, Creole answered, and the drums talked back. Then the horn insisted, sweet and high, slightly detached perhaps, and Creole listened, commenting now and then, dry, and driving, beautiful and calm and old. Then they all came together again, and Sonny was part of the family again. I could tell this from his face. He seemed to have found, right there beneath his fingers, a damn brand-new piano. It seemed that he couldn't get over it. Then, for awhile, just being happy with Sonny, they seemed to be agreeing with him that brand-new pianos certainly were a gas.

Then Creole stepped forward to remind them that what they were playing was the blues. He hit something in all of them, he hit something in me, myself, and the music tightened and deepened, apprehension began to beat the air. Creole began to tell us what the blues were all about. They were not about anything very new. He and his boys up there were keeping it new, at the risk of ruin, destruction, madness, and death, in order to find new ways to make us listen. For, while the tale of how we suffer, and how we are delighted, and how we may triumph is never new, it always must be heard. There isn't any other tale to tell, it's the only light we've got in all this darkness.

And this tale, according to that face, that body, those strong hands on those strings, has another aspect in every country, and a new depth in every generation. Listen, Creole seemed to be saying, listen. Now these are Sonny's blues. He made the little black man on the drums know it, and the bright, brown man on the horn. Creole wasn't trying any longer to get Sonny in the water. He was wishing him Godspeed. Then he stepped back, very slowly, filling the air with the immense suggestion that Sonny speak for himself.

Then they all gathered around Sonny and Sonny played. Every now and again one of them seemed to say, amen. Sonny's fingers filled the air with life, his life. But that life contained so many others. And Sonny went all the way back, he really began with the spare, flat statement of the opening phrase of the song. Then he began to make it his. It was very beautiful because it wasn't hurried and it was no longer a lament. I seemed to hear with what burning he had made it his, with what burning we had yet to make it ours, how we could cease lamenting. Freedom lurked around us and I understood, at last, that he could help us to be free if we would listen, that he would never be free until we did. Yet, there was no battle in his face now. I heard what he had gone through, and would continue to go through until he came to rest in earth. He had made it his: that long line, of which we knew only Mama and Daddy. And he was giving it back, as everything must be given back, so that, passing through death, it can live forever. I saw my mother's face again, and felt, for the first time, how the stones of the road she had walked on must have bruised her feet. I saw the moonlit road where my father's brother died. And it brought something else back to me, and carried me past it, I saw my little girl again and felt Isabel's tears again, and I felt my own tears begin to rise. And I was yet aware that this was only a moment, that the world waited outside, as hungry as a tiger, and that trouble stretched above us, longer than the sky.

Then it was over. Creole and Sonny let out their breath, both soaking wet, and grinning. There was a lot of applause and some of it was real. In the dark, the girl came by and I asked her to take drinks to the bandstand. There was a long pause, while they talked up there in the indigo light and after awhile I saw the girl put a Scotch and milk on top of the piano for Sonny. He didn't seem to notice it, but just before they started playing again, he sipped from it and looked toward me, and nodded. Then he put it back on top of the piano. For me, then, as they began to play again, it glowed and shook above my brother's head like the very cup of trembling.

Topics for Discussion

1. What powers does music have for Sonny?

2. What impact does grief have on the narrator of the story?

3. How does the narrator describe Sonny's addiction?

4. How does Baldwin establish the conflict between the two brothers?

5. How does Baldwin define the concept of the jazz that Sonny plays through the course of the story?

6. In what ways is music a religious experience in the story?

7. What is the role of suffering in the story and in what ways is suffering expressed through the narrative? What avenues are open to the characters in the story to escape their suffering?

8. What is the role of the artist as Baldwin sees it?

9. How does "Sonny's Blues" conform to the idea of the novella? What devices and techniques does Baldwin use to sustain the story for such a duration?

10. What role does prejudice play in the story?

Charles Baxter

About the Author

Charles Baxter was born in Minneapolis, Minnesota, in 1947. He was edu-
cated at Macalester College in St. Paul, Minnesota, before receiving his
Ph.D. from the State University of New York at Buffalo. He has taught at
Wayne State University in Detroit and currently teaches at the University of
Michigan in Ann Arbor.

Baxter's stories focus on the people and the environment of the Detroit
area. He is concerned with how individuals respond to the physical, psychological and spiritual pressures imposed upon them by their surroundings
and their times. In his short story collection *A Relative Stranger*, from which
this story is taken, Baxter examines the failures of the American dream and
the means by which individuals pursue their own spiritual and psychological survival in the midst of urban decay, violence and uncertainty.

Selected Works

Harmony of the World (short stories, 1984)
Through the Safety Net (short stories, 1985)
First Light (novel, 1987)
A Relative Stranger (short stories, 1990)
Shadow Play (novel, 1993)

About the Story

"A Relative Stranger" tells the story of an alcoholic, Oliver Harris, who was
adopted away from his biological family while still a child. The arrival of the
brother he never knew he had upsets his reclusive and isolated life. Baxter,
through the story, explores the ways in which individuals are similar and
dissimilar, and in the process shows the complexities and nuances of characterization.

The Caine Mutiny (1954), a film starring Humphrey Bogart and José
Ferrer, was based on a novel by Herman Wouk (1951) in which the crew of
an American minesweeper during the Second World War seize their ship
from their unstable commanding officer.

A Relative Stranger

I was separated from my biological mother when I was four months
old. Everything from that period goes through the wash of my memory
and comes out clean, blank. The existing snapshots of my mother show
this very young woman holding me, a baby, at arm's length, like a
caught fish, outside in the blaring midday summer sunlight. She's got
clothes up on the clothes-line in the background, little cotton infant
things. In one picture a spotted dog, a mongrel combination of Labrador and Dalmatian, is asleep beside the bassinet. I'd like to know what
the dog's name was, but time has swallowed that information. In
another picture, a half-empty bottle of Grain Belt beer stands on the

lawn near a wading pool. My mother must have figured that if she could have me, at the age of seventeen, she could also have a beer.

My mother's face in these pictures is having a tough time with daylight. It's a struggle for her to bask in so much glare. She squints and smiles, but the smile is all on one side, the right. The left side stays level, except at the edge, where it slips down. Because of the sunlight and the black-and-white film, my mother's face in other respects is bleached, without details, like a sketch for a face. She's a kid in these pictures and she has a kid's face, with hair pulled back with bobby pins and a slight puffiness in the cheeks, which I think must be bubble gum.

She doesn't look like she's ever been used to the outdoors, the poor kid. Sunlight doesn't become her. It's true she smiled, but then she did give me up. I was too much serious work, too much of a squalling load. Her girlish smile was unsteady and finally didn't include me. She gave me away—this is historical record—to my adoptive parents, Harold and Ethel Harris, who were older and more capable of parental love. She also gave them these photographs, the old kind, with soft sawtooth borders, so I'd be sure to know how she had looked when the unfamiliar sunlight hit her in a certain way. I think her teenaged boyfriend, my father, took these pictures. Harold and Ethel Harris were my parents in every respect, in love and in their care of me, except for the fact of these pictures. The other children in the family, also adopted, looked at the snapshots of this backyard lady with curiosity but not much else.

My biological father was never a particle of interest to me compared to my adoptive father, Harold Harris, a man who lived a life of miraculous calm. A piano tuner and occasional jazz saxophonist, Harold liked to sit at home, humming and tapping his fingers in the midst of uproar and riot, kids shouting and plaster falling. He could not be riled; he never made a fist. He was the parental hit of any childhood group, and could drive a car competently with children sitting on his shoulders and banging their hands on the side of his head. Genetic inheritance or not, he gave us all a feeling for pitch. Ask me for an F-sharp, I'll give you one. I get the talent from Harold.

✄◈✄

I went to high school, messed around here and there, did some time in the Navy, and when I was discharged I married my sweetheart of three years, the object of my shipboard love letters, Lynda Claire Norton. We had an apartment. I was clerking at Meijer's Thrifty Acres. I thought we were doing okay. Each night I was sleeping naked next to a sexual angel. At sunrise she would wake me with tender physical comfort, with hair and fingertips. I was working to get a degree from night school. Fourteen months after we were married, right on the day it was due, the baby came. A boy, this was. Jonathan Harold Harris. Then everything went to hell.

I was crazy. Don't ask me to account for it. I have no background or inclination to explain the human mind. Besides, I'm not proud of the way I acted. Lynda moved right out, baby and all, the way any sensible woman would have, and she left me two empty rooms in the apartment in which I could puzzle myself out.

I had turned into the damnedest thing. I was a human monster movie. I'd never seen my daddy shouting the way I had; he had never carried on or made a spectacle of himself. Where had I picked up this terrible craziness that made me yell at a woman who had taken me again and again into her arms? I wrote long letters to the world while I worked at home on my model ships, a dull expression on my face. You will say that liquor was the troublemaker here and you would be correct, but only so far. I had another bad ingredient I was trying to track down. I broke dishes. My mind, day and night, was muzzy with bad intentions. I threw a light bulb against a wall and did not sweep up the glass for days. Food burned on the stove and then I ate it. I was committing outrageous offenses against the spirit. Never, though, did I smash one of the model ships. Give me credit for that.

I love oceans and the ships that move across them. I believe in man-made objects that take their chances on the earth's expanses of water. And so it happened that one weekday afternoon I was watching a rerun of *The Caine Mutiny*, with my workboard set up in front of me with the tiny pieces of my model *Cutty Sark* in separated piles, when the phone rang. For a moment I believed that my wife had had second thoughts about my behavior and was going to give me another chance. To tell the truth, whenever the phone rang, I thought it would be Lynda, announcing her terms for my parole.

"Hello? Is this Oliver Harris?" a man's voice asked.

"This is him," I said. "Who's this?"

"This is your brother." Just like that. Very matter-of-fact. This is your brother. Harold and Ethel Harris had had two other adopted sons, in addition to me, but I knew them. This voice was not them. I gripped the telephone.

Now—and I'm convinced of this—every adopted child fears and fantasizes getting a call like this announcing from out of the blue that someone in the world is a relative and has tracked you down. I know I am not alone in thinking that anyone in the world might be related to me. My biological mother and father were very busy, urgent lovers. Who knows how much procreation they were capable of, together and separately? And maybe they had brothers and sisters, too, as urgent in their own way as my mother and father had been in theirs, filling up the adoption agencies with their offspring. I could never go into a strange city without feeling that I had cousins in it.

Therefore I gripped the telephone, hoping for reason, for the everyday. "This is not my brother," I said.

"Oh yes, it is. Your mother was Alice Barton, right?"

"My mother was Ethel Harris," I said.

"Before that," the voice said, "your mother was Alice Barton. She was my mother, too. This is your brother, Kurt. I'm a couple of years younger than you." He waited. "I know this is a shock," he said.

"You can't find out about me," I said. The room wasn't spinning, but I had an idea that it might. My mouth was open halfway and I was taking short sweaty breaths through it. One shiver took its snaky way down and settled in the lumbar region. "The records are sealed. It's all private, completely secret."

"Not anymore, it isn't," he said. "Haven't you been keeping up? In this country you can find out anything. There are no secrets worth keeping anymore; nobody *wants* privacy, so there isn't any."

He was shoving his pile of ideas at me. My thoughts had left me in great flight, the whole sad flock of them. "Who are you?" I asked.

"Your brother Kurt," he said, repeating himself. "Listen, I won't bore you to explain what I had to do to find you. The fact is that it's possible. Easy, if you have money. You pay someone and someone pays someone and eventually you find out what you want to know. Big surprise, right?" He waited, and when I didn't agree with him, he started up again, this time with small talk. "So I hear that you're married and you have a kid yourself." He laughed. "And I'm an uncle."

"What? No. Now you're only partly right," I said, wanting very hard to correct this man who said he was my brother. "My wife left me. I'm living here alone now."

"Oh. I'm sorry about that." He offered his sympathies in a shallow, masculine way: the compassion offered by princes and salesmen. "But listen," he said, "you're not alone. It's happened before. Couples separate all the time. You'll get back. It's not the end of the world. Oliver?"

"What?"

"Would you be willing to get together and talk?"

"Talk? Talk about what?"

"Well, about being brothers. Or something else. You can talk about anything you please." He waited for me to respond, and I didn't. This was my only weapon—the terrible static of telephone silence. "Look," he said, "this is tough for me. *I'm not a bad person.* I've been sitting by this phone for an hour. I don't know if I'm doing the right thing. My wife...you'll meet her...she hasn't been exactly supportive. She thinks this is a mistake. She says I've gone too far this time. I dialed your number four times before I dialed it to the end. I make hundreds of business calls but this one I could not do. It may be hard for you, also: I mean, I take a little getting used to. I can get obsessive about little things. That's how I found you."

"By being obsessive."

"Yeah. Lucille…that's my wife…she says it's one of my faults. Well, I always wanted a brother, you know, blood-related and everything, but I couldn't have one until I found you. But then I thought you might not like me. It's possible. Are you following me?"

"Yes, I am." I was thinking: here I am in my apartment, recently vacated by my wife, talking to a man who says he's my brother. Isn't there a law against this? Someone help me.

"You don't have to like me," he said, his brusque voice starting to stumble over the consonants. That made me feel better. "But that isn't the point, is it?" Another question I didn't have to answer, so I made him wait. "I can imagine what's in your head. But let's meet. Just once. Let's try it. Not at a house. I only live about twenty miles away. I can meet you in Ann Arbor. We can meet in a bar. I *know* where you live. I drove by your building. I believe I've even seen your car."

"Have you seen me?" This brother had been cruising past my house, taking an interest. Do brothers do that? What *do* they do?

"Well, no, but who cares about looks where brothers are concerned? We'll see each other. Listen, there's this place a couple of miles from you, the Wooden Keg. Could we meet there? Tomorrow at three? Are you off tomorrow?"

"That's a real problem for me," I said. "Booze is my special poison."

"Hell, that's all right," he said. "I'll watch out for you. I'm your brother. Oh. There's one other thing. I lied. I look like you. That's how you'll recognize me. I have seen you."

I held on to the telephone a long time after I hung up. I turned my eyes to the television set. José Ferrer was getting drunk and belligerent at a cocktail party. I switched off the set.

I was in that bar one hour before I said I would be, and my feelings were very grim. I wasn't humming. I didn't want him to be stationed there when I came in. I didn't want to be the one who sauntered in through the door and walked the long distance to the bar stool. I didn't want some strange sibling checking out the way I close the distance or blink behind my glasses while my eyes adjust to the light. I don't like people watching me when they think they're going to get a skeleton key to my character. I'm not a door and I won't be opened that easily.

Going into a bar in the midsummer afternoon takes you out of the steel heat and air-hammer sun; it softens you up until you're all smoothed out. This was one of those wood-sidewall bars with air that hasn't recirculated for fifty years, with framed pictures of thoroughbreds and cars on the walls next to the chrome decorator hubcaps. A man's bar, smelling of cigarettes and hamburger grease and beer. The brown padded light comes down on you from some recessed source, and the leather cushions on those bar stools are as soft as a woman's hand, and before long the bar is one big bed, a bed on a barge eddying down a sluggish river where you've got nothing but good friends lined up on the banks. This is why I am an alcoholic. It wasn't easy drinking Coca-Cola in that place, that dim halfway house between the job and home, and I was about to slide off my wagon and order my first still one when the door cracked open behind me, letting in a trumpet blast of light, and I saw, in the doorframe outline, my brother coming toward me. He was taking his own time. He had on a hat. When the door closed and my eyes adjusted, I got a better look at him, and I saw what he said I would see: I saw instantly that this was my brother. The elves had stolen my shadow and given it to him. A version of my face was fixed on a stranger. From the outdoors came this example of me, wearing a coat and tie.

He took a bar stool next to mine and held out his hand. I held out mine and we shook like old friends, which we were a long way from becoming. "Hey," we both said. He had the eyes, the cheek, and the jaw in a combination I had seen only in the mirror. "Oliver," he said, refusing to let my hand go. "Good to meet you."

"Kurt," I said. "Likewise." Brother or not brother, I wasn't giving away anything too fast. This is America, after all.

"What're you drinking?" he asked.

"Coke."

"Oh. Right." He nodded. When he nodded, the hat nodded. After he saw me looking at it, he said, "Keeps the sun out of my eyes." He took it off and tried to put it on the bar, but there wasn't enough room for it next to the uncleared beer glasses and the ashtrays, so he stood up and dropped it on a hook over by the popcorn machine. There it was, the only hat. He said, "My eyes are sensitive to light. What about yours?" I nodded. Then he laughed, hit the bar with the broad flat of his hand, and said, "Isn't this great?" I wanted to say, yes, it's great, but the true heart of the secret was that no, it was not. It was horrifyingly strange without being eventful. You can't just get a brother off the street. But before I could stop him from doing it, he leaned over and put his right arm, not a large arm but an arm all the same, over my shoulders, and he dropped his head so that it came sliding in toward my chest just under the chin. Here was a man dead set on intimacy. When he straightened up, he said, "We're going to have ourselves a day today, that's for sure." His stutter took some of the certainty out of the words. "You don't have to work this afternoon, right?"

"No," I said. "I'm not scheduled."

"Great," he said. "Let me fill you in on myself."

Instead of giving me his past, he gave me a résumé. He tried to explain his origins. My biological mother, for all the vagueness in her face, had been a demon for good times. She had been passionate and prophylactically carefree. Maybe she had had twenty kids, like old Mother Hubbard. She gave us away like presents to a world that wanted us. This one, this Kurt, she had kept for ten months before he was adopted by some people called Sykes. My brother said that he understood that we—he and I—had two other siblings in Laramie, Wyoming. There might be more he didn't know about. I had a sudden image of Alice Barton as a human stork, flying at tree level and dropping babies into the arms of waiting parents.

Did I relax as my brother's voice took me through his life? Were we related under the skin, and all the way around the block? He talked; I talked. The Sykes family had been bookish types, lawyers, both of them, and Kurt had gone to Michigan State University in East Lansing. He had had certain advantages. No falling plaster or piano tuning. By learning the mysterious dynamics of an orderly life, he had been turned out as a salesman, and now he ran a plastics factory in Southfield, north of Detroit. "A small business," he said in a friendly, smug way. "Just fifteen employees." I heard about his comfortably huge home. I heard about his children, my nephews. From the wallet thick with money and credit cards came the lineup of photos of these beautiful children.

So what was he doing, this successful man, sitting on a bar stool out here, next to his brother, me, the lowly checkout clerk?

"Does anybody have enough friends?" he asked me. "Does anyone have enough *brothers*?" He asked this calmly, but the questions, as questions, were desperate. "Here's what it was," he said. "Two or three times a week I felt like checking in with someone who wasn't a wife and wasn't just a friend. Brothers are a different category, right there in the middle. It's all about *relatedness*, you know what I mean?" I must have scowled. "We can't rush this," he said. "Let's go have dinner somewhere. My treat. And then let's do something."

"Do what?" I asked.

"I've given that a lot of thought," he said. "What do you do the first time out with your brother? You can't just eat and drink. You can't shop; women do that." Then he looked me square in the eye, smiled, and said, "It's summer. Maybe we could go bowling or play some baseball." There was a wild look in his eye. He let out a quick laugh.

We went in his Pontiac Firebird to a German restaurant and loaded up on sauerbraten. I had a vague sense he was lowering himself to my level but did not say so. He ordered a chest-sized decorated stein of beer but I stayed on the cola wagon. I tried to talk about my wife, but it wouldn't come out: all I could say was that I had a problem with myself as a family man. That wasn't me. The crying of babies tore me up. Feeding time gave me inexplicable jitters. I had acted like Godzilla. When I told him this, he nodded hard, like a yes man. It was all reasonable to him.

"Of course," he said. "Of course you were upset and confused." He was understanding me the way I wanted to be understood. I talked some more. Blah blah blah. Outside, it was getting dark. The bill came, and he paid it: out came the thick wallet again, and from a major-league collection of credit cards came the white bank plastic he wanted. I talked more. He agreed with everything I said. He said, "You're exactly right." Then I said something else, and he responded, "Yes, you're exactly right."

That was when I knew I was being conned. In real life people don't say that to you unless they're trying to earn your love in a hurry. But here he was, Kurt Sykes, visibly my brother, telling me I was exactly right. It was hard to resist, but I was holding on, and trying.

"Here's how," he said. He lifted his big stein of beer into the air, and I lifted my glass of Coke. Click. A big blond waitress watched us, her face disciplined into a steel-helmet smile.

After that, it was his idea to go outside and play catch. This activity had all sorts of symbolic meanings for him, but what was I going to do? Go home and watch television? I myself have participated in a few softball leagues and the jock way of life is not alien to me, but I think he believed he could open up if we stayed at my level, throwing something back and forth, grunting and sweating. We drove across town to Buhr Park, where he unloaded his newly purchased baseball, his two brand-new gloves, and a shiny new bat. Baseball was on the agenda. We were going to play ball or die. "We don't have to do any hitting," he said. While I fitted the glove to my left hand—a perfect fit, as if he had measured me—he locked the car. I had never had a car worth locking; it was not a goal.

The sun having set, I jogged out across a field of darkening grass. The sky had that blue tablecloth color it gets at dusk just before the stars come out. I had my jeans, sweatshirt, and sneakers on, my usual day-off drag. I had not dressed up for this event. In fact, I was almost feeling comfortable, except for some growing emotional hot spot I couldn't locate that was making me feel like pushing the baseball into my brother's face. Kurt started to toss the ball toward me and then either noticed his inappropriate dress-for-success formality or felt uncomfortable. He went back to the car and changed into his sweat clothes in the half-dark. He could have been seen, but wasn't, except by me. (My brother could change his clothes out in the open, not even bothering to look around to see who would see. What did this mean?)

Now, dressed down, we started to hustle, keeping the rhythms up. He threw grounders, ineptly, his arm stiff and curious. I bent down, made the imaginary play, and pivoted. He picked up the bat and hit a few high flies toward me. Playing baseball with me was his way of claiming friendship. Fine. Stars came out. We moved across the field,

closer to a floodlit tennis court, so we had a bit of light. I could see fireflies at the edge of where we were playing. On the court to my right, a
high school couple was working their way through their second set.
The girl let out little cries of frustration now and then. They were plea-
surable to hear. Meanwhile, Kurt and I played catch in the near-dark,
following the script that, I could see, he had written through one long
sleepless night after another.

As we threw the ball back and forth, he talked. He continued on in
his résumé. He was married but had two girlfriends. His wife knew
about them both. She did not panic because she expected imperfection
in men. Also, he said, he usually voted Republican. He went to parent-
teacher-organization meetings.

"I suppose you weren't expecting this," he said.

No, I thought, I was *not* expecting you. I glanced at the tennis
court. Clouds of moths and bright bugs swarmed in insect parabolas
around the high-voltage lights. The boy had a white Huron high school
T-shirt on, and white shorts and tennis shoes, and a blue sweatband
around his thick damp hair. The girl was dressed in an odd assortment
of pink and pastel blue clothes. She was flying the colors and was the
better player. He had the force, but she had the accuracy. Between his
heat and her coolness, she piled up the points. I let myself watch her; I
allowed myself that. I was having a harder and harder time keeping my
eyes on my brother.

"You gonna play or look at them?" Kurt asked.

I glanced at him. I thought I'd ignore the question. "You got any
hobbies?" I asked.

He seemed surprised. "Hobbies? No. Unless you count women and
making money."

"How's your pitch?"

"You mean baseball?"

"No. Music. How's your sense of pitch?"

"Don't have one."

"I do," I said. "F-sharp." And I blew it at him.

He leaned back and grimaced. "How do you know that's F-sharp?"

"My daddy taught me," I said. "He taught me all the notes on the
scale. You can live with them. You can become familiar with a note."

"I don't care for music," he said, ending that conversation. We were
still both panting a bit from our exertions. The baseball idea was not
quite working in the way he had planned. He seemed to be considering
the possibility that he might not like me. "What the hell," he said.
"Let's go back to that bar."

Why did I hit my brother in that bar? Gentlemen of the bottle, it is you
I address now. You will understand when I tell you that when my

brother and I entered the bar, cool and smoky and filled with midsummer ballplayers, uniformed men and women, and he thoughtlessly ordered me a Scotch, you will understand that I drank it. Drank it after I saw his wad of money, his credit cards, his wallet-rubbed pictures of the children, my little nephews. He said he would save me from my alcoholism but he did not. Gentlemen, in a state of raw blank irritation I drank down what God and nature have labeled "poison" and fixed with a secret skull and crossbones. He bought me this drink, knowing it was bad for me. My mind withdrew in a snap from my brain. The universe is vast, you cannot predict it. From the great resources of anger I pulled my fund, my honest share. But I do not remember exactly why I said something terrible, and hit my brother in the jaw with my fist. And then again, higher, a punch I had learned in the Navy.

He staggered back, and he looked at me.

His nose was bleeding and my knuckles hurt. I was sitting in the passenger side of his car. My soul ached. My soul was lying facedown. He was taking me back to my apartment, and I knew that my brother would not care to see me from now on. He would reassert his right to be a stranger. I had lost my wife, and now I had lost him, too.

We stumbled into my living room. I wobbled out to the kitchen and, booze-sick, filled a dish towel with ice cubes and brought it to him. My right hand felt swollen. We were going to have ugly bruises, but his were facial and would be worse. Holding the ice to his damaged face, he looked around. Above the ice his eyes flickered on with curiosity. "Ships," he said. Then he pointed at the worktable against the wall. "What's all that?"

"It's my hobby," I said. The words came slow and wormlike out of my puzzled mouth.

He squinted above the ice. "Bottles? And glue?"

"I build ships in bottles." I sounded like a balloon emptying itself of air. I pointed at the decorator shelf on the west wall, where my three-masted clipper ship, the *Thermopylae*, was on display.

"How long have you done this?" he asked.

"So long I can't remember."

"How do you do it?"

He gave me a chance. Even a bad drunk is sometimes forced to seize his life and to speak. So I went over to the worktable. "You need these." I held up the surgical forceps. I could hardly move my fingers for the pain. Alcoholic darkness sat in a corner with its black bag waiting to cover me entirely. I went on talking. "And these. Surgical scissors." Dried specks of glue were stuck to the tips. "Some people cheat and saw off the bottom of the bottle, then glue it back on once the ship is inside. I don't do it that way. It has to grow inside the bottle. You need a challenge. I build the hull inside. I have used prefab hulls. Then you've got to lay the deck down. I like to do it with deck furnishings already in place: you know, the cabin doors and hatch covers and cleats and riding bits already in place on the deck. You put the glue on and then you put the deck in, all in one piece, folded up, through the neck; then you fold it out. With all that glue on, you only have one shot. Then you do the rigging inside the bottle. See these masts? The masts are laid down inside the bottle with the bottom of the mast in a hole."

I pointed to the *Cutty Sark*, which I was working on. I did not care if my hands were broken; I would continue this, the only lecture in my head, even if I sounded like a chattering magpie.

"You see, you pull the mast up inside the bottle with a string attached to the mast, and there's a stop in the hole that'll keep the mast from going too far forward. Then you tie the lines that are already on the mast off on the belaying pins and the bits and the cleats." I stopped. "These are the best things I do. I make ships in bottles better than anything else I do in my life."

"Yes." He had been standing over my worktable, but now he was lying on the sofa again.

"I like ships," I said. "When I was growing up, I had pictures on the wall of yachts. I was the only person in the Harris family who was interested in ships."

"Hmm."

"I like sailboats the most." I was talking to myself. "They're in their own class."

"That's interesting," he said. "That's all very interesting, but I wonder if I could lie down here for a while."

"I think you're already doing it."

"I don't need a pillow or a blanket," Kurt said, covered with sweat. "I can lie here just as is."

"I was going to turn on the air conditioner."

"Good. Put it on low."

I went over to the rattletrap machine and turned it on. The compressor started with a mechanical complaint, a sound like *orrr orrr orrr*, and then faster, *orrorrorr*. By the time I got back into the living room, my brother's eyes were closed.

"You're asleep," I said.

"No," he said, "No, I'm not. My eyes are just closed. I'm bruised and taking a rest here. That's all. Why don't you talk to me for a minute while I lie here with this ice. Say anything."

So I talked against the demons chittering in the corners of the room. I told my brother about being on a carrier in the Navy. I talked about how I watched the blue lifting swells of the Pacific even when I wasn't supposed to and would get my ass kicked for it. I was hypnotized by seawater, the crazy majesty of horizontal lines. I sleepwalked on that ship, I was so happy. I told him about the rolling progress of oceanic storms, and how the cumulonimbus clouds rose up for what looked like three or four miles into the atmosphere. Straight-edged curtains of rain followed us; near the Straits of Gibraltar it once rained for thirty minutes on the forward part of the ship, while the sun burned down on the aft.

I talked about the ship's work, the painting and repairing I did, and I told him about the constant metallic rumble vibrating below decks. I told him about the smell, which was thick with sterile grease stink that stayed in your nostrils, and the smell of working men. Men away from women, men who aren't getting any, go bad, and they start to smell like metal and fur and meat.

Then I told him about the ships I built, the models, and the originals for them, about the masts and sails, and how, in the water, they had been beautiful things.

"What if they fell?" my brother said.

I didn't understand the question, but thought I would try to answer it anyway. It was vague, but it showed he was still awake, still listening. I wanted to ask, fell from where? But I didn't. I said if a man stood on the mainmast lookout, on a whaler, for example, he could lose his balance. If he tumbled from that height, he might slap the water like he was hitting cement. He might be internally damaged, but if he did come up, they'd throw him a lifebuoy, the white ones made out of cork and braided with a square of rope.

I brought one of the ships toward him. "I've got one here," I said, "tiny, the size of your fingernail."

He looked at it, cleated to the ship above the deck. He studied it and then he gazed at me. "Yes," he said. It was the most painful smile I'd ever seen in an adult human being, and it reminded me of me. I thought of the ocean, which I hadn't viewed for years and might not, ever again. "Yes," my brother said from under the icepack. "Now I get it."

Like strangers sitting randomly together in a midnight peeling-gray downtown bus depot smelling of old leather shoes, we talked until four in the morning, and he left, his face bruised dark, carrying one of my ships, the Lightning, under his arm. He came back a week later. We sat in the park this time, not saying much. Then I went to see him, and I met his wife. She's a pleasant woman, a tall blonde who comes fully outfitted with jewels I usually see under glass in display cases. My brother and I know each other better now; we've discovered that we have, in fact, no subjects in common. But it's love, so we have to go on talking, throwing this nonsense into the air, using up the clock. He has apologized for trying to play baseball with me; he admits now that it was a mistake.

When I was small, living with Harold and Ethel Harris and the other Harris children, I knew about my other parents, the aching lovers who had brought me into my life, but I did not miss them. They'd done me my favor and gone on to the rest of their lives. No, the only thing I missed was the world: the oceans, their huge distances, their creatures, the tides, the burning water-light I heard you could see at the equator. I kept a globe nearby my boy's bed. Even though I live here, now, no matter where I ever was, I was always homesick for the rest of the world. My brother does not understand that. He thinks home is where he is now. I show him maps; I tell him about Turkey and the Azores; I have told him about the great variety and beauty of human pigmentation. He listens but won't take me seriously.

When my brother talks now, he fingers his nose, probably to remind me where I hit him. It's a delicate gesture, with a touch of self-pity. With this gesture he establishes a bit of history between us. He wants to look up to me. He's twenty-eight years old, hasn't ever seen Asia, and he says this to me seriously. Have you ever heard the sound of a man's voice from a minaret? I ask him, but he just smiles. He's already called my wife; he has a whole series of happy endings planned, scene by scene. He wants to sit in a chair and see me come into the room, perfected, thanking the past for all it has done for me.

Topics for Discussion

1. What is the purpose of the photograph that the narrator mentions in the opening of the story?

2. How does the first person narrative form influence and shape the plot and the way the story is told?

3. How is Baxter being paradoxical with the title of the story?

4. Why is it important for Oliver Harris to tell the story of his life before he recounts his encounter with his brother?

5. In terms of characterization, how are the brothers different? How does Baxter present those differences to the reader?

6. Why does Oliver Harris wish to remain unknown to his brother and how does he treat the arrival of his sibling in his life?

7. How does Baxter define relationship?

8. Who is Oliver Harris having trouble confronting: himself or his brother? Why does he hit his brother when they go to the bar?

Neil Bissoondath

Neil Bissoondath was born in Trinidad in 1955 and came to Canada in 1973 to study French at York University. Before becoming a full-time writer, he taught English and French as a second language at a private school in Toronto. He now lives in Montreal and appears regularly on Canadian television as a cultural critic and commentator.

Bissoondath is fascinated by that level of tension and violence that lies just below the surface of society, especially in the Caribbean world. His first novel, *A Casual Brutality*, depicts the rift between the First World and the Third World on the imaginary island of Castenada. Like his uncle, V. S. Naipaul, Bissoondath writes about the idea of the modern individual as a displaced person.

Selected Works
Digging Up the Mountains (short stories, 1985)
A Casual Brutality (novel, 1988)
On the Eve of Uncertain Tomorrows (novel, 1991)

About the Story
Culture clash, the process and resulting guilt of fleeing a restrictive background or tradition, the problem of being displaced from one's own culture and finding oneself in a totally new environment—these are problems for growing numbers of individuals in today's world. In an interview with the editor of this book, Bissoondath described some of the sentiments and personal experiences that went into the writing of "The Cage." "I grew up in a culture that restricted me, a culture that imposed its values on me and that had little regard for my personal feelings and desires. From this point of view, I identify with that Japanese girl [in "The Cage"] very closely...the girl can't escape her past.... When I left Trinidad, I knew I was leaving for good.... The girl in this story was incapable of saying that."

The Cage

My father is an architect. Architects are good at designing things: stores, houses, apartments, prisons. For my mother, my father, not an unkind man, designed a house. For me, my father, not a kind man, designed a cage.

My father is a proud man. He traces his ancestry back nine generations. Our family name is well known in Yokohama, not only because of my father's architectural firm but also because of those nine generations: his name is my father's greatest treasure.

It is not mine.

At the Shinto shrine in the backyard my father mumbles the names of his ancestors, calling on them, invoking their presence. With those names he swears, expresses pleasure, offers compliments. He knows those names better than he knows mine.

When I was small, I used to stand at the window of the living room watching my father as he mumbled before the shrine. He almost always wore a grey turtleneck sweater; he suffered from asthma and said that the air that blew in off the sea, over the American warships and docks, came heavy with moisture and oil. On especially damp mornings he would return to the house with the skin under his eyes greyed and his cheeks scarlet. He coughed a great deal, and I could see his chest laboring rhythmically beneath his sweater.

I often wondered why, even on the worst of mornings, with drizzle and a grey mist, he went out to the shrine: couldn't the ancestors wait a day? A few hours? Were they so demanding? One day I asked him why and he just stared back at me in silence. He never answered. Maybe he couldn't. Maybe it was just something he knew deep within him, an urge he bowed to without understanding. Maybe it was to him, as to me, a mystery.

I shall never forget the day he called me Michi, the name of his father's mother. She was the person he loved best in the world, and for many years after her death he would visit her grave, to cry. He called me Michi because he had simply forgotten my name. He became angry when my mother reminded him.

When I was a child he took only occasional notice of me. I was my mother's charge. He was not a bad father. He was just as much of one as he was capable of being. His concerns were less immediate.

His attention grew during the teenage years, for he feared them most. When I was fifteen, I told my parents I no longer wanted to take piano lessons. I saw distress on my mother's face: she had, in her youth, before marriage, wanted to be a concert pianist. When I practised, she would often sit quietly behind me, listening, saying nothing. I could feel her ears reaching out to every key my fingers hit, every sound my touch produced. At times I felt I was playing not for me but for her, giving her through the pain and fatigue in my fingers a skein of memory. But music cannot be a duty. It must come naturally. I am not a musician. I grew bored. My fingers on the piano keys produced a lifeless sound. My father, admitting this, agreed to let me stop. My father, after quietly invoking his ancestors, said it was a bad sign. But he would agree if I accepted the ko-to in place of the piano. I agreed. It gave me my way and allowed him to assert his authority.

However, his distrust of my age continued. One day he searched among my clothes and found a packet of letters. It was a modest collection, three from girlfriends in foreign places, one from a boy I had known briefly in school. His family had moved to Osaka and he had written me this one letter, a friendly letter, a letter to say hello. My father ignored the letters from my girlfriends and handed me the letter from the boy. He demanded that I read it to him: a friendly letter, a silly letter; finally, a humiliating letter. When I finished, he took the letter with him. I never saw it again. At dinner that evening he searched my eyes for signs of crying. He saw none. He exchanged worried glances with my mother.

I hadn't cried. Instead, I had thought; and the lesson I learned was far greater than mere distrust of my father. I learnt, more than anything else, how little of my life was my own, in my father's eyes. It was the horror of this that prevented tears; his claim to my privacy that, finally, caused me to regard him with eyes of ice.

✂✀

I had few friends. My peers and I had little in common. They liked to talk of husbands, babies, houses; boredom was my response. No simple explanation offered itself, nor did I seek one. Maybe it was my age, maybe it was my temperament, but I accepted this situation. Often, in the middle of a gathering of schoolmates, I would slip away home, to my room.

For there, among my school texts, was my favorite companion, a child's book that had been a gift many years before from my father. It was a large book, with hard covers and pages of a thick, velvety paper. It related the story of the first foreigners to come to Japan. Every other page contained an illustration, of the sea, of the ships, of the mountains of Japan, in colors so bright they appeared edible.

The picture that most attracted me presented the first meeting between foreigners and Samurai. They stood, clusters of men, facing one another: foreigners to the right, grotesquely bearded, drab in seafaring leathers; Samurai to the left, resplendent in outfits of patterned and folded color. Behind them, with a purity borne only in the imagination, lay a calm, blue sea tinged here and there by whitecaps of intricate lace. On the horizon, like a dark brown stain on the swept cleanliness of the sky, sat the foreigners' ship.

My father, in giving me the book, had stressed the obvious: the ugliness of the foreigners, the beauty of the Samurai. But my mind was gripped by the roughness, the apparent unpredictability, of the foreigners. The Samurai were of a cold beauty; you knew what to expect of them, and in this my father saw virtue. For me, the foreigners were creatures who could have exploded with a suddenness that was like charm. Looking at them, I wondered about their houses, their food, their families. I wanted to know what they thought and how they felt. This to me was the intrigue of the book, and I would spend many hours struggling with the blank my mind offered when I tried to go beyond the page before me.

I remember one day asking my father to tell me about the foreigners. He was immediately troubled. He said, "They came from Europe." But what did the word "Europe" mean, I asked. Europe: to me, a word without flesh. "This is an unnecessary question," he replied, his eyes regarding the book and me with suspicion. I took the book from his hands and returned to my room.

Not long after this I showed the book to a school friend. We were both about twelve years old at the time and I hoped to find in her companionship of spirit. She looked through the book and handed it back to me, saying nothing. I asked her opinion of it. She said, "It is a very pretty book." And those words, so simple, so empty, created distance between us.

The book has remained in my room ever since, safe, undisplayed.

✖✦✖

At eighteen, when I graduated from high school, my parents tried to marry me off. He was an older man from my father's firm, an architect like my father. They made me wear a kimono to meet him. At first his glances were modest, but as the evening wore on he became bolder. Angered, I returned his searching gazes. He faltered. He became modest once again. Finally, he left.

My behavior had not gone unnoticed. Afterwards my mother scolded me.

I said, "I do not want to marry."

My mother said, "The choice is not yours, it is not any woman's."

My father said nothing. He left the room.

My mother said, "You have made your father very angry."

I said, "I do not want to marry. I want to live with a man."

My mother looked at me as if I had gone mad. "We are sending you to university. You will not waste your education in such a way."

"I want to have a career."

"We are not giving you an education so you can work. Men want educated wives."

"I do not want to be a man's wife."

"Where are you getting such ideas? You associate with the wrong people. Such ideas are foreign to us." Then she too left the room.

The "wrong people" has always been one of my mother's obsessions. I remember inviting a schoolmate to my house. She met my mother. They talked. When my friend left, my mother said, "I do not think you should associate with such people." I was still obedient at the time; I never spoke to the girl again. I understood why my mother took this attitude. The girl's home was in one of the poorer sections of Yokohama, her mother worked as a clerk in a department store. This was the first time my mother was too busy to drive one of my friends home. And for me, guilt came only years later, too late, as with everything in retrospect.

My mother. She once played the piano. She has a degree in opera from Tokyo University. She could have had a career. Instead, she got married. She talks of her life now only to say she is happy. But what is this happiness—who can say? Not I, for I could never be happy in her situation. I maybe know too much. Yet I cannot contradict my mother. I can only say I doubt her. This self-sacrifice—she has given her all to her husband, to her son, to me; she has rejected all possibility of leading her own life, of developing her talent—this self-sacrifice is not for me. She has the ability to put up with things even when she is at odds with them. I suppose this shows strength. Sometimes, though, I wonder if this is not so much strength as a simple lack of choice. My mother does not have the ability to create choice where there is none.

I am, in the end, tangible proof of my mother's failure as a woman.

Once during this same summer that ushered me from high school to university my mother expressed a desire to spend the vacation in Kyoto. My father said he wished to visit Kobe; he was adamant. Later, I heard my father, unaware of my presence, telling my brother to observe his handling of the situation. All along, he said, he had wanted to visit Kyoto but he would let my mother beg a little, cajole him, fawn over him; only then would he agree to visit Kyoto. My mother would think she had won a great victory. And that was the way it worked out. My mother never realized the deception, and my sadness prevented me from revealing it to her. It was too, I knew, part of the game she had long ago accepted.

My mother and women like her, my father and men like him, will tell you that the man's world is in his office, the woman's in her house. But in my parents' house, designed by my father, built by him, his word is law. My mother, if she really believes in the division of domain, lives in a world of illusion.

This facility for seeing the wrong thing, asking the wrong question, already a barrier between acquaintanceship and friendship, made my relations with my brother difficult. I resented having chores to do—washing dishes, making beds, both his and mine, cleaning the house—while his only duty was to protect the family name by staying out of trouble. I resented having my telephone callers interrogated, my letters scanned, my visitors judged, while he was free to socialize with people of his own choosing. I resented the late hours he was permitted to keep while I was forced to spend my evenings practising the ko-to, producing music that bored me to tears and put my father in mind of his ancestors, never far out of reach. I resented my brother's freedom to choose from among the girls he knew while I could meet only those men selected by my father, always architects, always older, always pained by courtship conducted before the boss.

My brother and I have never spoken. He is as much a stranger to me as I am to him. What I know of him I do not like. He is too much like my father. They occasionally pray together at the shrine in the backyard.

I had been accepted at Tokyo University, in dietetics. This field was not my choice, but my father's. From a magazine article he had got the idea that dietetics would be a fine, harmless profession, and one easily dropped for marriage. I would have preferred literature but I had no choice. It was my father's money that afforded me an education, and his connections that brought me entry to prestigious Tokyo University.

I left for Tokyo at the end of the summer, with my mother as temporary chaperone. She settled me in and, after three days, left with the lightest of kisses. She had grown into her role, my mother, and had spent much of her time with me worrying about my father and brother. The moment she left, uncertainty became my sole companion. I was as tentative as a spider's web in wind. I avoided people, grew close to no one. My life was my books, and I emerged from chemistry and anatomy only to attend the occasional gathering organized by the dietetics department. Attendance at these "social evenings" was informally obligatory: even in the wider world, you belonged to a family and owed certain obligations. Nothing exciting ever happened at these parties. You went, you drank a little, ate a little, chatted politely, you left. Little was achieved, save homage to the concept of the group. Maybe occasionally a student would get a low grade raised a little.

It was at one of these gatherings halfway through my first year at university that I met Keisuke, a well-known Japanese poet. I had never heard of him, for my father, probably remembering the childhood incident with my story book, had proscribed literature. So at first I treated Keisuke in an offhand manner. I distrusted his name, Keisuke, a fine old traditional name; it seemed to reflect all the values my father held dear. Nor was he particularly attractive in any way. His physique was undistinguished, tending, if anything, to softness around the middle; and the whites of his eyes were scrawled by a complicated system of red veins, from lack of sleep. At one point in the evening, I heard him say that it was his habit to drop in when he could on the gatherings of the different departments. This declaration, made not to me but to a group that had politely formed around him, scared me a little. It was not something that was done and, although there was a general assent that this was a good idea, I could see the hesitation that preceded the required politeness, the easy discomfort quickly submerged in nods and smiles. And I could see, too, that Keisuke had not missed it. He looked at me and smiled: we shared a secret.

After, when he had left, there were a few whispered comments about how odd he was. One of the professors, a small, balding man, said slyly, "But he's a poet. You know what *they're* like...."

The next day at lunch in the cafeteria, Keisuke appeared at my table and sat down, without asking permission. "So," he said. "Did they find me very odd?"

Flustered at hearing the same word in his mouth as had been used to describe him the previous evening, I instinctively said, "Yes."

For a second there was silence, and then we both began laughing. Our secret, understood by a smile the evening before, was made explicit by the laughter. I became comfortable with him. He asked me to call him "Kay," and he mocked his own name, describing it with the English word "stuffy," which he had to explain to me since my English was not very good at the time.

We talked a great deal. He told me he had lived and studied in America for seven years. His father, an executive with the Panasonic Corporation, had been transferred to New Jersey when Kay was sixteen. Kay knew New York City well, and as he described it—the lights, the noise, the excitement—I wondered why he had returned, after all that time, to Japan.

He smiled at my question. "I am Japanese," he said.

I nodded, but the answer discomforted me. It was my father's explanation of too many things.

Kay and I became friends. He invited me to his apartment not far from the university. It was a small place, and cluttered. On the walls he had hung framed American film posters, all at different heights so that any thought of uniformity was banished. Everywhere—on his desk, on the coffee table, on the kitchen counters—he had stacked books and magazines and papers. We would sit together in a corner on a *tatami*, reading and talking under the yellow light of a wall-lamp.

I told him about my father, my mother, my brother. He showed me some of his poetry. I read it. I understood little. He asked what literature I had read. I told him about my father's prohibition on books and of his final admonition on the night before I left for Tokyo. Stay away, he had said, from books full of fine words. Kawabata, Tanizaki, Mishima would not help my chemistry marks and, besides, writers always had strange ideas anyway, ideas unfit for young female minds.

Kay listened to my story in silence. Then he said, "Your father is a man full of fears." This was like revelation to me.

I confessed that I had read Mishima, for my brother had on the bookshelves in his room the complete works, a gift from our father. I had read them surreptitiously and, at the time, untrained, unaware, I had seized only upon the eroticism. Kay, unsurprised, explained to me what I had missed: the mingling of the sex with blood, and the brooding sense of violence. "Mishima was mad in many respects," he said. "A twentieth-century Samurai. His end was fitting." And now, now that I understand Mishima, I worry about my brother, and I fear him.

One evening, after a light dinner of *sashimi* and warm sake, Kay seduced me. As I write this, I realize what an un-Japanese admission it is. It scares me a little.

After, lying on the *tatami*, smoking my first cigarette and enjoying the warmth and soreness that clasped my body, I felt as if I had been given a precious key, but a key to what I wasn't sure. This too Kay, lying wet next to me, understood. He suggested I read Ibsen and, in the following months as my first year of university drew to a close, he supplied translations to help my shaky English through the Ibsen texts he'd studied in America. We discussed his works, among others, and the more intense our discussions became, the more I found myself articulating thoughts and ideas that would have made my father blue with rage.

Kay, one of those writers with strange ideas whom my father so feared, gave me the ability to put into words what had been for me, until then, ungrasped feelings. With his help, I arrived at last at a kind of self-comprehension, although a confusion—guilt, Kay called it— remained. He said this was so because, although my ideas were coming into focus, their source remained hidden.

However, I do not want to give the impression that I always sailed smoothly. At times, especially after another of the tedious meetings with one of my father's architects—for which I was periodically called home—I felt that the seduction was less a key than a betrayal. As I sat there in my father's spare living room, serving the men, smiling at them, I felt that Kay had heightened my confusion rather than diminished it. But these periods of doubt were shortlived.

The rest of my university career was uneventful. Kay and I continued to see one another from time to time but the intimacy of that first year was never repeated. He had too much work, I had too much work. At least, it was the excuse we used.

I graduated as a dietitian and had no trouble finding a job in a hospital in Yokohama. I worked there for a year, in a profession not of my choosing, counting day after day the calorie intake of patients. Counting calories becomes tedious after a while and the patients soon became little more than mathematical sums in my mind, defining themselves by what they could eat.

At the end of one particularly trying day, I called on a patient, an old woman, chronically ill and querulous, to discuss her rejection of prescribed food. She explained to me in a cross voice that she wanted, of all things, mayonnaise on her food. I told her this was impossible. She became abusive. I became abusive. I hit her with my clipboard. She started to cry, silently, like a child, the tears filling the wrinkles and creases of her crumpled face. It was then, looking at her through my own tears, that I realized I could not continue.

The tedium of the job, living once more in my father's house, smiling at his architects, practising the ko-to, these were all taking their toll on me.

I confronted my parents with my decision. They offered an alternative. They had never been happy about my working; a working wife is in short demand. It would be better, they said, if I were to concentrate on what really mattered. I was getting old, already twenty-three. In five or six years I would be considered an old maid, an also-ran in the race to the conjugal bed. I had better get cracking.

But, as usual, I had my own idea. I had managed to save a tidy sum during my year of work, money my father considered part of a future marriage contract. In Japan, women marry not for love but for security. The man acquires a kind of maid-for-life. For a person with my ideas, marriage means compromise, an affair not of the heart but of the bank account. Therefore, my savings compensated a bit for my advanced age and my father never failed to mention the money when one of the suitors called.

I, however, wanted to travel. My father said it was out of the question; neither he nor my mother could leave Yokohama at the time. I said I wanted to travel alone. My father said this was preposterous, and he called on his ancestors, all nine generations of them, to witness the madness of his daughter.

Kay had once said to me, "Learn from the past but never let it control you." I think it was a line from one of his poems. At that moment the line ran through my mind. If my past would not control me, I decided, then neither would my father's. I told them I was leaving. My father threatened to restrain me physically. He called my brother to help. He came. I did not protest; it would have served no purpose. My father and brother were as one. Even their eyes, black circles trapped behind the same thick lenses, framed by the same black plastic, were indistinguishable. It was these eyes that I saw come at me. As they led me off between them, my mother started crying. But she said nothing. They locked me in my room and told the hospital I was sick.

For a week I lay or sat alone in my room. My mother, silent always, brought me my meals, of which I ate little. I slept a lot, tried to read, spent long hours looking at my picture book: the splendid Samurai, the bearded foreigners. At one point—I no longer remember whether it was day or night; time, after a while, was of no importance—I felt myself slipping into the painting, becoming part of it. I could feel the weight of heavy sea air on my face, the soft tingle of sand beneath my feet; I could hear the broken whisper of softly tumbling surf. I was prepared to surrender myself but something—a voice, a rattle of dishes— tugged me back. For the first time in my captivity, I cried. My tears fell onto the pages of my book and there the stains remain.

They let me out after a week and I returned to work. My father had spoken to the administrator of the hospital, an old friend. Since other members of the staff had complained about the old woman's behavior, no action was taken against me, save a kindly lecture on the virtues of patience.

The next two months were, however, not easy. I was never allowed a moment to myself; my every movement was monitored, every minute accounted for. Even at work, I found out, the administrator asked discreet questions about me. My father had spoken to him about more than my problems with the old woman.

My life became like that of the four song-birds my brother kept in bamboo cages suspended from the ceiling of his room. They would whistle and chirp every morning, each making its own distinct cry, sometimes sounding as if in competition against one another. The birds would sing at precisely the same time every morning, demanding food. I thought they saw this ability to wake him as power, but my brother knew who controlled the food.

One day, with the sense of reserved delight he shared with our father, my brother brought home a new song-bird. It was the smallest of them all, a tiny creature of a blue and a red that sparkled when brushed by the sun. But there was a problem: while the others sang, this new bird remained silent. My brother tried coaxing music out of him, in vain. He tried attacking with a stick, but the bird was unmoved. My brother first tried withholding food, but later when the incentive was offered the bird ignored it, and twice he knocked over his dish, scattering the seed.

The bird uttered only one sound in his week in my brother's bedroom, a pure, shrill whistle. The cry brought my brother, my mother, and me to the room. The bird was lying on the floor of the cage. My brother opened the door and poked the little body with a finger, at first gently, then more roughly. Satisfied it was dead, he picked it up by a wing, took it to the kitchen, and dropped it into the garbage can. He dusted his hands casually and returned to his breakfast. He showed no regret.

I watched my brother with horror. At that moment I hated him. I went to my room and I cried, for the bird, for myself.

He replaced it that evening with a more pliant bird. This one sang easily, and it was fed.

The next day I began playing the traditional daughter. I quit my job, I never complained, I welcomed the architects, smiled at them, hinted to my father of grandchildren: a game, a game for which my real personality had to be hidden away like the pregnant, unwed daughter of a rich family. It was not very difficult, for I discovered in myself a strange determination.

After two months of this, my father, watchful always, put his suspicions aside. He said to my mother, "I have exercised the power of my ancestors. They cannot be resisted." Then he went to visit the grave of Michi, his father's mother.

During this period I grew closer to my mother, for she was most often my guard. One night—it turned out to be my last in my father's house—we sat talking in my room. We had turned off the lights and opened the window. Above the silhouetted trees and roof tops, we could see the sky turning dark, as if expiring. As yet, no stars were visible. The night air was cool and we could hear insects chirping and cluttering in the shrubbery outside. My mother put on a sweater over her kimono, an oddly touching sight, and folded her arms, not sternly as I had once thought, but wearily, like a woman undone. We sat on the bed, I on one side, she on the other, with a great expanse between us.

I asked her, "Have you ever thought of the possibility of leading your own life?"

She sighed. "I used to think of it when I was small but I always knew it would be impossible."

"Why?"

"You are playing games now." She smiled sadly. Without looking at me, she said, "Whatever happens, I am always your mother. Wherever you are, whatever you are doing, you can call me. I will help."

"Who can you call?"

"Your father."

"You once had friends."

"Yes, but your father comes first. Friends just ..." She waved her hands, searching for words. "...just get in the way."

"But you haven't got any friends."

"I am content. I have all I want, all I need. Now say no more about it."

I couldn't see her face. She was all in shadow. But her voice was tender.

The next day, for the first time in many months, she left me alone, unguarded. I packed my bags and called a taxi. The night before, although I hadn't known it, she had been telling me goodbye.

I had always believed I could trust none of my relatives: my father, made in the image of his ancestors; my mother, made in the image of my father; my brother, a stranger. It took me a long time to realize that my mother was my friend. I do not think she really understood me but I was one of those things she put up with even though we were at odds. I hope she can one day understand my attitude but I do not expect this. I can only hope.

I spent two months in Tokyo, in an apartment lent to me by one of Kay's friends. Kay visited me from time to time. We couldn't talk. He seemed uncomfortable with me and, through this, I became uncomfortable with him. We were like polite strangers. This distance, and the silences it brought with it, depressed me; and I, in turn, depressed him.

One evening, after a particularly silent dinner, I asked him to tell me exactly what was wrong.

He said, "Nothing." Then he closed his eyes and said, "I have not been able to write. Your mood affects me. It is not good."

I couldn't reply. There was nothing to say.

He opened his eyes, the whites red-veined, the skin around them reddened, and looked slowly around the apartment. It was very much like his, the film posters, the stacks of books and magazines. He had started a style among his friends.

"There is something else, too," he finally said. "I have been wondering ... well, do you think you did the correct thing in leaving your father's house?"

I looked at him: it was all I could do. The one person of whom I had been sure. I said. "Keisuke. Keisuke."

He left a few minutes later, after putting the dishes into the kitchen sink.

His visits grew less frequent and finally stopped altogether. Without him, I found myself enmeshed in the freedom I had sought, friendless, guideless, at liberty to choose my own way. "Without him": the irony does not escape me.

I found a job, again ironically, playing the piano in a bar. I eventually moved into my own little apartment and developed a small circle of friends, all connected in one way or the other with the bar. One night the owner, an overweight man who dressed in flashy American clothes, tried to pressure me into sleeping with him. I never went back to the bar and so had yet another place to avoid, another place to run from.

In Tokyo, anonymity was easy to obtain: it is not difficult to be alone in a crowd of thousands. Privacy came more easily in large, over-populated Tokyo than in the smaller, relatively slow-paced Yokohama. Tokyo, the least traditional, most western, of our cities is, for me, the safest.

But it was still Japan. I was invited to parties. Japanese parties, like marriages, are business occasions in disguise. Men go to a party to get a promotion or to clinch a deal. The women smile and serve. The men drink and talk. When they have drunk enough, they talk sex and arrange package tours to Korea, where they enjoy the prostitutes of a people they detest.

I felt I had to get away. My first thought was: Europe. But I quickly realized there were yet other places I had to avoid, the usual Japanese destinations: much of Europe, much of America, especially Boston or Philadelphia or New York. So I changed my money to traveller's cheques and bought a plane ticket to Toronto. It was new space. I expected nothing.

⌇⌇⌇

Many Japanese think of snow and bears and wonderful nature like Niagara Falls when they think of Canada. But Toronto, a big city, bigger than Tokyo, less crowded, with more trees and flowers, did not surprise me. I do not know if it was Toronto or me. Probably me.

I rented a room in a big house across from a park. My landlady, Mrs. Harris, lived on the first floor with her sister, Mrs. Duncan, and her cat, Ginger. She was a small woman of about fifty, with hair too blonde for her age. "We are all widows," she said with a smile the first time I went to the house. "Ginger's Tom died last week. A car, poor dear." I thought her a strange woman but she smiled often, the skin on her face stretching into congruent wrinkles.

The second floor was rented to people I never saw. But they liked rock music. Their stereo worked every day, from early morning to late at night. I rarely heard the music but I was always aware of it because of the thump of the bass beneath my feet, like a beating through the worn green carpet.

The third floor was divided into two small rooms. It was one of these that I took. The ceiling followed the contours of the roof, and the walls were painted a white that reflected the little sunlight that came in through the small window. The furniture was sparse: a bed, an easy chair, a table with a lamp. My window overlooked the tops of trees and, to the left, fenced-in tennis courts. Sometimes, on a clear day, I could see Lake Ontario on the horizon, a thin ribbon of blue barely distinguishable from the sky.

I did little in my first weeks in Toronto. I walked. I visited the tourist sights. I learned my way around the city. The last heat of the summer exploded down from the sky every day. It exhausted me, and I spent much time sleeping. My memories of the time are dull, everything seems to have rounded corners, everything seems somehow soft.

On weekends, many people came to the park across the street, to walk, to eat, to talk. I would sit at my window observing them, many forms in blue denim or shades of brown, the occasional red or yellow or purple: glimpses of lives I would never touch, for I stayed at my window.

Looking. Looking. Looking.

⌇⌇⌇

One hot afternoon, returning groggy from my walk, I came across my third-floor neighbor sitting in the small front porch. She was a tall lady with red hair and very white skin. Perspiration slicked her forehead. She wore a thin white T-shirt and shorts. In her right hand she held an open beer bottle.

"Hello," she said as I walked up the stairs. "Hot, isn't it."

I said, "Yes," reaching for the doorknob. It was no cooler in the porch than it had been in the sun, only the heat was different. Out there, the sunlight burned like an open flame; here, it was like steam. I was exhausted. I did not want to deplete the last of my energy by talking. English was still a strain.

"It's like a goddam oven up there," she said, pushing a chair towards me. "Hell, it's like a goddam oven down here. But at least it's open."

I sat down. We had seen each other twice before but each time she had been in a hurry. I had been shy. We had just said hello.

"You from Hong Kong?" she asked.

"No, I am from Tokyo. I am Japanese." Across the street, the browned grass of the park cowered in the shadow of the trees.

"Oh." She sipped from her beer. "What are you doing here?"

"I plan to take English lessons." My words surprised me. It had been something to say, an excuse for being there, but as I heard myself I thought it a good idea.

"Oh." Then there was silence. On the road a car sped by in a spasm of loud music.

"What do you do?" I finally asked; it took courage.

"I dance. I'm a dancer. My name is Sherry."

"Ballet? Jazz?"

"Table."

"Table?"

"I work in a strip joint."

"What is 'strip joint,' please?"

She laughed. "It's a place where ladies like me take off their clothes. For men."

"*Hai.* Yes. I see." The heavy air wrapped itself around my skin like a steamed napkin, and for a second I smelled the oily brine of the Yokohama harbor. "Excuse me, please," I said getting up. The smell, as brief and as powerful as vision, had frightened me.

She watched me open the door. "Like a goddam oven," she said.

The next day I checked the Yellow Pages for a school and went down to their office. It was on the edge of the Yorkville area, a place of expensive stores and restaurants. The sidewalks were crowded: many young people with perfect hair and clothes; many old people trying to look like the young people. On one corner a young man with a clown's face juggled colored balls for a small crowd. On another, a young couple in tuxedos played violins while people hurried by.

I was uncomfortable among these people: their numbers didn't offer anonymity. It was just the opposite, in fact. The people, by their dress, by their extravagance of behavior, demanded to be noticed; they were on display. I walked quickly to the office building where the school was located, into the lobby of marble that created echo in the fall of my footsteps, into the elevator that at last brought relief.

Behind the green door that carried only a number, a man with grey hair and glasses was sitting at a desk. In front of him were a telephone, an ashtray so full that the ashes formed a little mountain, and a messy pile of papers. He was playing Scrabble when I walked in, a rack with tiles at either side of the board. No one else was in the office; he was playing against himself, right hand against left hand.

"Good morning," he said, standing up. "Can I help you?" His suit, of a dark blue, showed chalk smudges at the pockets and on the right shoulder.

"Yes, please, I wish to improve my English language."

He offered me a seat and went to another room to get coffee. The walls of the office were bare; in the far corner a large climbing plant, green leaves dulled by dust, clung weakly to its wooden staff.

He returned with two Styrofoam cups of coffee. He placed one on the desk in front of me, the other on the Scrabble board. As he sat down he asked me if I was from Hong Kong. Then he told me about himself. He spoke some French, some Spanish, some German. He had lived and worked in many places. He didn't like Greek food, cats, and American cigarettes. Finally, after an hour, he told me about the school and we managed to arrange private English lessons for me.

I began the following week. My teacher, a tall, nervous young man with a moustache, was a student at the University of Toronto. He dressed poorly, and was so thin and white that at times, under the fluorescent light of the classroom—desk, chairs, walls bare but for the black rectangle of the chalk board—I thought I could see through him. He said he was a vegetarian.

He wanted to talk about Japan and *hara-kiri*, although he knew nothing about Japan or *hara-kiri*. We discussed food. He insisted that I, being a Japanese person, never ate bread, only rice and vegetables and raw fish and nothing else. He would not believe that I had tasted my first Big Mac in Tokyo.

At one point he said, "Ahh, yes, I understand. American imperialism."

"No," I replied. "Good taste."

He did not appreciate my attempt at humor. He became angry and drilled me severely on grammar and vocabulary, refusing to discuss anything.

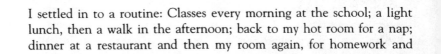

I settled in to a routine: Classes every morning at the school; a light lunch, then a walk in the afternoon; back to my hot room for a nap; dinner at a restaurant and then my room again, for homework and reading. It was an easy, uncomplicated life. For the first time I knew what it was to anticipate the next day without tension.

Sometimes I saw Sherry, my third-floor neighbor. We would exchange a few words of politeness. Once she asked my opinion of a perfume she had bought. Another time she help up to herself a new blouse. Through these brief encounters, I grew comfortable with her, even to like her a little.

My one shadow was a nightmare, Gentle and vivid, it came again and again, at first sporadically, later with greater frequency: my father and Keisuke, both in the dress of Samurai, standing on a beach, swords unsheathed, while behind them the sea wept with the voice of my mother. I would awake with the sound of sobbing in my ears and I would have to speak to myself: *I am in Toronto. I am in Toronto.*

Toronto: a place where my personality could be free, it was not a city of traditions in a country of traditions. It was America, in the best implication that word held for us Japanese: bright, clean, safe, new. Life experienced without the constraints of an overwhelming past. I shall never forget my joy when, awaking one night in a sweat from the nightmare, I realized that here I was a young person and not almost an old maid, that by a simple plane flight I had found rejuvenation.

For two months I lived with a joy I had never imagined possible, the joy of an escape that did not demand constant confrontation with the past.

At the school, the director's hands continued to challenge one another to Scrabble. My teacher grew thinner, shaved his moustache, grew it back, added a beard. I practised grammar, vocabulary, sentence structure.

I was so comfortable I even wrote a short note to my mother, to let her know I was all right.

Summer began signalling its end. The trees across the street lost some of their green; the heat of the day was less severe and at night my room cooled enough that I needed to cover myself with a sheet. At school, I got a new teacher. The first had come in one morning with the shaved head and salmon robes of a religious cult, and had spent much of one class trying to convince me to drop English in favor of Hindi. He was fired.

One evening I saw Sherry in the restaurant where I had dinner. I was surprised, for she usually worked in the evenings.

"How's your English?" she said loudly, motioning me to her table.

"Fine, thank you. I have learnt much. How are you?" I sat down. She had already eaten. The plate before her was empty but for smeared ketchup.

"Not so great. Can't work."

"I am sorry. Are you sick?"

"Not quite. I had an operation."

"It is not serious, I hope."

She laughed. "No. I had a tit job."

"Pardon me, I do not understand."

"They cut my breasts open. Cleaned 'em out. Put in bags of water. Size makes money."

"*Hai.* Yes. I see." Suddenly I was no longer hungry. My eyes swept involuntarily from her face to the table.

She pushed her chair back and picked up her cigarettes. "It hurts," she said softly, a look of pain on her face. "I better go." She stood up. Her face turned into the light. I saw bags under her eyes, wrinkles I had not noticed before, and I realized I had never before seen her without makeup. The light shone through her curled hair, thinning it like an old person's. "See you," she said.

"Yes, sleep well." I watched her go, feeling her take some of my joy with her.

Two weeks later, as I was doing my homework late at night, I was disturbed by noises from Sherry's room. I put my book down and listened. At first there was nothing. Then I heard a quiet groan. I became worried. I went to my door and listened again. Another groan. I opened my door, put my head into the corridor, and said, "Sherry, what is it, please?" I listened. There was no answer, no sound. Uncertain, I closed my door and went back to my books. A few minutes later, Sherry's door slammed and heavy footsteps hurried down the stairs. The front door slammed.

My door flew open. Sherry walked in slowly. She was wearing a bathrobe. "Well, little Miss Jap, you pleased with your work?" She was calm, but it was the calm of anger, the same restraint my father and my brother displayed in times of emotion.

"I am sorry?" I put down my book.

"You just cost me two hundred dollars."

"I do not understand."

"'*What is it please, Sherry?*'" she mimicked me. "The john went soft on me. You think I got paid? Eh? That's two hundred dollars I'm out of, lady."

"Who is John, please?"

"Jesus Christ! What are they teaching you at that school, anyways?"

I was very confused. I said, "I am sorry. Please explain."

"What are you? Some kinda moron?" Then she turned and walked back to her room. Her door slammed.

I got up and closed my door. It was getting cold in the room. I shut the window and got into bed, pulling the sheet tightly up to my neck. That night my nightmare came again: my father, Keisuke, and my mother weeping like the sea.

When I came in from school the next day, Mrs. Harris the landlady called me into the kitchen. She was sitting at the dining table with Mrs. Duncan, Ginger the cat on her lap. The little television next to the fridge was on but the sound was turned down.

Mrs. Harris said, "About last night, my dear, I just wanted to let you know it won't happen again. Sherry's gone. I asked her to leave this morning."

"What happened last night, please? I do not understand." I had tried to seek an explanation from my teacher at the school but, upon hearing the story, she had grown uneasy and talked about the English subjunctive.

"Oh dear," said Mrs. Harris. She glanced at Mrs. Duncan. "Well, you see, dear, she was a stripper. Do you know what that means?"

"I know. She told me." Mrs. Duncan held out a plate of cookies to me. I took one.

"And sometimes, quite often in fact I found out this morning, she brought men back to her room with her. They paid her, you see. To ... well, you know."

"Hai. Yes. I see." I understood now, with horror, the two hundred dollars.

"But she's gone now, thank God."

I went up to my room, the cookie growing moist where the tips of my fingers pressed into it. The door to Sherry's room was open, the bed stripped, the dresser and table cleared of the cosmetics and perfumes Sherry collected. Beneath my feet, the neighbors' stereo beat in its steady palpitation. I felt very alone.

<hr>

The weather in Toronto grew cold. The trees outside my window turned gold and brown, and in one night of wind lost all sign of life. The lake in the distance became a sliver of silver beneath a heavy sky. Now, no one came to the park. The view from my window was of desolation, of bared trees and deadened grass. I rarely looked out. My afternoon walks came to an end. Instead I went directly home from school, to my room.

I talked from time to time with Mrs. Harris and Mrs. Duncan. They spent almost every afternoon in the kitchen. They would drink coffee and eat cookies and talk about the boyfriends they had when they were young. How different from my mother, who could never acknowledge past boyfriends and could not even have a friend to talk to.

At four o'clock every afternoon Mrs. Harris would put on the little television and they would smoke and look at a soap opera. Sometimes they cried a little. I often felt, watching them blow their noses into tissues, that they were crying not for the people in the show but for themselves, for the people they might have been and the people they were.

Their own lives were not so interesting as those they saw on television at four o'clock every afternoon.

I found it strange that they never told me their first names. It was as if they had lost them. One cold, rainy afternoon, an afternoon on which shadows became airborne and floated about in the air, I asked Mrs. Harris why she called herself by her husband's name.

Stroking the cat, she thought for a minute. "It's tradition, dear. Christian tradition."

"Yes, dear," Mrs. Duncan said, "it's as simple as that. It's what women have always done."

"And what do you do with your own names? Are they no longer of importance?"

"A name is a name is a name," Mrs. Harris said. She lit a cigarette and the cat leapt from her lap with a growl.

I saw that Mrs. Harris did not like my questions.

Mrs. Duncan said, "Poor Ginger. She doesn't purr any more."

Mrs. Harris said, "She's gone off her food too." There was worry in her voice.

I went to my room. Through the window, the park hunched gloomily against the rain and cold. I thought of Ginger, and of my mother and Mrs. Harris and Mrs. Duncan, and I remembered the bird that would not sing.

That night my nightmare came again, but now I sensed my own presence, and I no longer knew from whom—my mother or myself— came the sound of the weeping sea.

⋈

Two days later I received an envelope from my mother. I left it unopened for several hours: I feared it, feared what it might say and, more, what it might not. Finally, I ripped it open.

It was a short letter. In it, my mother told me that my father, on discovering my disappearance, had said nothing, had done nothing. He hadn't even called on his ancestors. She said that my father never mentions me. She then explained, briefly, the mystery of myself to me. She spoke of Michi, the idol of my father. Michi had been, my mother said, a strong and independent woman, a woman with her own ideas. She had been beaten into submission by my great-grandfather and was left, in the end, with little but her grandson, my father, as outlet for her sense of life. It was all my mother knew but she hoped the knowledge would help me.

The letter brought me once more directly before the life I had managed to ignore during these months in Toronto. It reminded me that I faced nothing here, that this life of freedom was one without foundation, that it would all inevitably end with a twenty-hour plane flight. That night I did not have my nightmare, for I did not sleep. I spent the night crying, and I could not understand why it was the memory of my father coughing before the Shinto shrine that caused me the greatest sadness.

Depression: the English word is inadequate to describe that which seized me, which took hold of my heart, my lungs, my intestines. This was more like a sickness, a sickness of the soul.

Two nights later it snowed. My coats were too thin for the climate. Instead of buying a new coat, I took out my return plane ticket.

When I arrived in Tokyo, it was raining.

I now work as a language teacher, instructing foreigners, mostly Americans, in Japanese. In return, one of them practises my English with me.

It has been over a year since I left my father's house. Since my return to Japan, I have telephoned my mother once, just to hear her voice. We both cried on the phone, but I did not tell her where I live. No yet.

The sea no longer weeps in my dreams. Instead, some mornings I wake up with wet cheeks and a damp pillow. I do not know why.

Or maybe I do.

There is an English expression, "No man is an island." Or woman. Expressions always contain a grain of truth and this is an expression I wish I had never learned, for it brings into too bright a light what I have come to understand: I am a woman, I am a Japanese woman—I still look to the east when I take medicine—and the ties of tradition still bind me the way they bound Michi. To understand oneself is insufficient. Keisuke has yet to realize that his precept of refusing to let the past impede the future applies, in my country, but to one sex. This is, perhaps, why I failed to understand his poetry when I first read it; it was too alien in too many ways. Keisuke to one side, my father and brother to the other, but it is always the men. For them all, the common sentence: I am Japanese.

There is, as one of my businessmen students puts it, no leadership potential in me. I do not lead, I never have. I have only practised avoidance.

Accepting my father's values would make life easier for me. But I cannot do this automatically. I am not a clock. As a first step, therefore, I am taking a course in flower arranging, a small step, but important in its own way.

For I shall, I fear, return one day soon to my father's house, to the ko-to, to the architects; for I have learned that the corollary of tradition's pride is tradition's guilt. Keisuke was right: I feel guilty for having betrayed my father's name and his nine generations of ancestors. Keisuke helped me recognize my guilt but he did not equip me to deal with it. In this, and not in the seduction, lay the real betrayal.

Tradition designed my cage. My father built it. Keisuke locked it. In returning to my father's house, I betray my mother's faith but the load is lighter on my shoulders than that of the nine generations.

I shall pack away my picture book: it is a child's book. I shall save it for my children, my daughters and my sons. It is to them that I bequeath my dreams.

And in the meantime, I continue to arrange my flowers. Even a cage needs decoration.

Topics for Discussion

1. How does Bissoondath define the idea of "culture clash"?

2. How does Bissoondath convey the idea of dislocation?

3. How important is a person's culture and what does culture (background, upbringing, experience) do to create an individual?

4. Does the protagonist suffer a defeat at the end of the story?

5. What does Bissoondath mean at the end of the story when the protagonist says, "I have learned that the corollary of tradition's pride is tradition's guilt"?

Dionne Brand

About the Author

Dionne Brand was born in Trinidad in 1953 and came to Canada to attend the University of Toronto in the 1970s. Known as an activist, poet and, most recently, novelist, Brand has established herself as a major voice among women writers in Canada, as both a socialist poet and a feminist writer. She has published several books of poetry, a novel and the collection of short stories, *Sans Souci* (1989), from which this story is taken. She was nominated for the Governor General's Award for Poetry in 1990 for her collection *No Language Is Neutral*.

Brand is conscious in her stories of the impact of various forms of history — personal, public, national and racial — on the individual. The story "Photograph" is drawn from her experiences of poverty and endurance in her early years in Trinidad. In all of her writing, she underscores the strength of women not only to endure but to overcome whatever obstacles are put in their way, to provide positive models for children and other women.

Selected Works

'Fore Day Morning (poems, 1978)
Earth Magic (poems, 1980)
Primitive Offensive (poems, 1982)
Winter Epigrams and Epigrams to Ernesto Cardenal in Defense of Claudia (poems, 1983)
Chronicles of the Hostile Sun (poems, 1984)
Sans Souci (short stories, 1989)
In Another Place, Not Here (novel, 1996)

About the Story

This story is part of a contemporary current in Canadian literature that focuses on the use of photographs as essential documents. In novels such as Joy Kogawa's *Obasan* or Timothy Findley's *The Wars*, photographs not only articulate a sense of the past as historical fact but act as artifacts to underscore and regenerate the life within the past. The grandmother's identity card becomes a testament to her existence, a document that triggers a whole series of memories and responses on the part of the narrator. In this story, Brand examines the role of childhood, memory and womanhood.

Photograph

My grandmother has left no trace, no sign of her self. There is no photograph, except one which she took with much trouble for her identity card. I remember the day that she had to take it. It was for voting, when we got Independence; and my grandmother, with fear in her eyes, woke up that morning, got dressed, put on her hat, and left. It was the small beige hat with the lace piece for the face. There was apprehension in the house. My grandmother, on these occasions, the rare ones when she left the house, patted her temples with limacol. Her smelling salts were placed in her purse. The little bottle with the green crystals and liquid had a pungent odour and a powerful aura for me until I was much older. She never let us touch it. She kept it in her purse, now held tightly in one hand, the same hand which held her one embroidered handkerchief.

That morning we all woke up and were put to work getting my grandmother ready to go to the identity card place.

One of us put the water to boil for my grandmother's bath. My big sister combed her hair, and the rest of us were dispatched to get shoes, petticoat, or stockings. My grandmother's mouth moved nervously as these events took place and her fingers hardened over ours each time our clumsy efforts crinkled a pleat or spilled scent.

We were an ever-growing bunch of cousins, sisters, and brothers. My grandmother's grandchildren. Children of my grandmother's daughters. We were seven in all, from time to time more, given to my grandmother for safekeeping. Eula, Kat, Ava, and I were sisters. Eula was the oldest. Genevieve, Wil, and Dri were sister and brothers and our cousins. Our mothers were away. Away-away or in the country-away. That's all we knew of them except for their photographs which we used tauntingly in our battles about whose mother was prettier.

Like the bottle of smelling salts, all my grandmother's things had that same aura. We would wait until she was out of sight, which only meant that she was in the kitchen since she never left the house, and then we would try on her dresses or her hat, or open the bottom drawer of the wardrobe where she kept sheets, pillowcases, and underwear, candles and candlesticks, boxes of matches, pieces of cloth for headties and dresses and curtains, black cake and wafers, rice and sweet bread, in pillowcases, just in case of an emergency. We would unpack my grandmother's things down to the bottom of the drawer, where she kept camphor balls, and touch them over and over again. We would wrap ourselves in pieces of cloth, pretending we were African queens; we would put on my grandmother's gold chain, pretending we were rich. We would pinch her black cakes until they were down to nothing and then we would swear that we never touched them and never saw who did. Often, she caught us and beat us, but we were always on the lookout for the next chance to interfere in my grandmother's sacred things. There was always something new there. Once, just before Christmas, we found a black doll. It caused commotion and rare dissension among us. All of us wanted it, so, of course, my grandmother discovered us. None of us, my grandmother said, deserved it and on top of that she threatened that there would be no Santa Claus for us. She kept the doll at the head of her bed until she relented and gave it to Kat, who was the littlest.

We never knew how anything got into the drawer because we never saw things enter the house. Everything in the drawer was pressed and ironed and smelled of starch and ironing and newness and oldness. My grandmother guarded them often more like burden than treasure. Their depletion would make her anxious; their addition would pose problems of space in our tiny house.

As she rarely left the house, my grandmother felt that everyone on the street where we lived would be looking at her, going to take her picture for her identity card. We felt the same, too, and worried as she left, stepping heavily yet shakily down the short hill that lead to the savannah, at the far end of which was the community centre. My big sister held her hand. We could see the curtains moving discreetly in the houses next to ours as my grandmother walked, head up, face hidden behind her veil. We prayed that she would not fall. She had warned us not to hang out of the windows looking at her. We, nevertheless, hung out of the windows gawking at her, along with the woman who lived across the street, whom my grandmother thought lived a scandalous life and had scandalous children and a scandalous laugh which could be heard all the way up the street when the woman sat old blagging with her friends on her veranda. We now hung out of the windows keeping company with Tante, as she was called, standing with her hands on her massive hips looking and praying for my grandmother. She did not stop, nor did she turn back to give us her look. But we knew that the minute she returned our ears would be burning because we had joined Tante in disgracing my grandmother.

The photograph from that outing is the only one we have of my grandmother, and it is all wrinkled and chewed up, even after my grandmother hid it from us and warned us not to touch it. Someone retrieved it when my grandmother was taken to the hospital. The laminate was now dull, and my grandmother's picture was gray and creased and distant.

As my grandmother turned the corner with my sister, the rest of us turned to lawlessness, eating sugar from the kitchen and opening the new refrigerator as often as we wanted and rummaging through my grandmother's things. Dressed up in my grandmother's clothes and splashing each other with her limacol, we paraded outside the house where she had distinctly told us not to go. We waved at Tante, mincing along in my grandmother's shoes. After a while, we grew tired and querulous; assessing the damage we had done to the kitchen, the sugar bowl, and my grandmother's wardrobe, we began assigning blame. We all decided to tell on each other. Who had more sugar than whom and who was the first to open the cabinet drawer where my grandmother kept our birth certificates.

We liked to smell our birth certificates. Their musty smell and yellowing water-marked coarse paper was proof that my grandmother owned us. She had made such a fuss to get them from our mothers.

A glum silence descended when we realized that it was useless quarrelling. We were all implicated and my grandmother always beat everyone, no matter who committed the crime.

When my grandmother returned we were too chastened to protest her beating. We began to cry as soon as we saw her coming around the corner with my sister. By the time she hit the doorstep we were weeping buckets and the noise we made sounded like a wake, groaning in unison and holding onto each other. My grandmother, too tired from her ordeal at the identity card place, looked at us scornfully and sat down. There was a weakness in her eyes which we recognized. It meant that our beating would be postponed for hours, maybe days, until she could regain her strength. She had been what seemed like hours at the identity card place. My grandmother had to wait, leaning on my sister and having people stare at her, she said. All that indignity, and the pain which always appeared in her back at these moments, had made her barely able to walk back to the house. We, too, had been so distraught that we did not even stand outside the house jumping up and down and shouting that she was coming. So at least she was spared that embarrassment. For the rest of the day we quietly went about our chores, without being told to do them, and walked lightly past my grandmother's room, where she lay resting in a mound, under the pink chenille.

We had always lived with my grandmother. None of us could recollect our mothers, except as letters from England or occasional visits from women who came on weekends and made plans to take us, eventually, to live with them. The letters from England came every two weeks and at Christmas with a brown box full of foreign-smelling clothes. The clothes smelled of a good life in a country where white people lived and where bad-behaved children like us would not be tolerated. All this my grandmother said. There, children had manners and didn't play in mud and didn't dirty everything and didn't cry if there wasn't any food and didn't run under the mango trees, grabbing mangoes when the wind blew them down and walked and did not run through the house like *warrahoons* and did not act like little old *niggers*. Eula, my big sister, would read the letters to my grandmother who, from time to time, would let us listen. Then my grandmother would urge us to grow up and go away too and live well. When she came to the part about going away, we would feel half-proud and half-nervous. The occasional visits made us feel as precarious as the letters. When we misbehaved, my grandmother often threatened to send us away-away, where white men ate Black children, or to quite-too-quite in the country.

Passing by my grandmother's room, bunched up under the spread, with her face tight and hollow-cheeked, her mouth set against us, the spectre of quite-to-quite and white cannibals loomed brightly. It was useless trying to "dog back" to her, she said, when one of my cousins sat close to her bed, inquiring if she would like us to pick her gray hairs out. That was how serious this incident was. Because my grandmother loved us to pick her gray hairs from her head. She would promise us a penny for every ten which we could get by the root. If we broke a hair, that would not count, she said. And, if we threw the little balls of her hair out into the yard for the wind, my grandmother became quite upset since that meant that birds would fly off with her hair and send her mad, send her mind to the four corners of the earth, or they would build a nest with her hair and steal her brain. We never threw hair in the yard for the wind, at least not my grandmother's hair, and we took on her indignant look when we chastised each other for doing it with our own hair. My cousin Genevieve didn't mind though. She chewed her long front plait when she sucked on her thumb and saved balls of hair to throw to the birds. Genevieve made mudpies under the house, which we bought with leaf money. You could get yellow mudpies or brown mudpies or red mudpies. This depended on the depth of the hole under the house and the wash water which my grandmother threw there on Saturdays. We took my grandmother's word that having to search the four corners of the earth for your mind was not an easy task, but Genevieve wondered what it would be like.

There's a photograph of Genevieve and me and two of my sisters someplace. We took it to send to England. My grandmother dressed us up, put my big sister in charge of us, giving her 50 cents tied up in a handkerchief and pinned to the waistband of her dress, and warned us not to give her any trouble. We marched to Wong's Studio on the Coffee, the main road in our town, and fidgeted as Mr. Wong fixed us in front of a promenade scene to take our picture. My little sister cried through it all and sucked her fingers. Nobody knows that it's me in the photograph, but my sisters and Genevieve look like themselves.

Banishment from my grandmother's room was torture. It was her room, even though three of us slept beside her each night. It was a small room with two windows kept shut most of the time, except every afternoon when my grandmother would look out of the front window, her head resting on her big arms, waiting for us to return from school. There was a bed in the room with a headboard where she kept the bible, a bureau with a round mirror, and a washstand with a jug and basin. She spent much of her time here. We, too, sitting on the polished floor under the front window talking to her or against the foot of the bed, if we were trying to get back into her favour or beg her for money. We knew the smell of the brown varnished wood of her bed intimately.

My grandmother's room was rescue from pursuit. Anyone trying to catch anyone would pull up straight and get quiet, if you ducked into her room. We read under my grandmother's bed and, playing catch, we hid from each other behind the bulk of her body.

We never received that licking for the photograph day, but my grandmother could keep a silence that was punishment enough. The photograph now does not look like her. It is gray and pained. In real, she was round and comfortable. When we knew her she had a full lap and beautiful arms; her cocoa brown skin smelled of wood smoke and familiar.

My grandmother never thought that people should sleep on Saturdays. She woke us up *peepee au jour*, as she called it, which meant before it was light outside, and set us to work. My grandmother said that she couldn't stand a lazy house, full of lazy children. The washing had to be done and dried before three o'clock on Saturday when the baking would begin and continue until the evening. My big sister and my grandmother did the washing, leaning over the scrubbing board and the tub, and when we others grew older we scrubbed the clothes out, under the eyes of my grandmother. We had to lay the soap-scrubbed clothes out on the square pile of stones so that the sun would bleach them clean, then pick them up and rinse and hang them to dry. We all learned to bake from the time that our chins could reach the table, and we washed dishes standing on the bench in front of the sink. In the rainy season, the washing was done on the sunniest days. A sudden shower of rain and my grandmother would send us flying to collect the washing off the lines. We would sit for hours watching the rain gush through the drains which we had dug, in anticipation, around the flower garden in front of the house. The yellow-brown water lumbered unsteadily through the drains rebuilding the mud and forming a lake at the place where our efforts were frustrated by a large stone.

In the rainy season, my big sister planted corn and pigeon peas on the right side of the house. Just at the tail end of the season, we planted the flower garden. Zinnias and jump-up-and-kiss-me, which grew easily, and xora and roses, which we could never get to grow. Only the soil on one side of the front yard was good for growing flowers or food. On the other side a soup-sop tree and an almond tree sucked the soil of everything, leaving the ground sandy and thin, and pushed up their roots, ridging the yard into a hill. The almond tree, under the front window, fed a nest of ants which lived in one pillar of our house. A line of small red ants could be seen making their way from pillar to almond tree, carrying bits of leaves and bark.

One Saturday evening, I tried to stay outside playing longer than allowed by my grandmother, leaning on the almond tree and ignoring her calls. "Laugh and cry live in the same house," my grandmother warned, threatening to beat me when I finally came inside. At first I only felt the bite of one ant on my leg but, no sooner, my whole body was invaded by thousands of little red ants biting my skin blue crimson. My sisters and cousins laughed, my grandmother, looking at me pitiably, sent me to the shower; but the itching did not stop and the pains did not subside until the next day.

I often polished the floor on Saturdays. At first, I hated the brown polish-dried rag with which I had to rub the floors, creeping on my hands and knees. I hated the corners of the room which collected fluff and dust. If we tried to polish the floor without first scrubbing it, my grandmother would make us start all over again. My grandmother supervised all these activities when she was ill, sitting on the bed. She saw my distaste for the rag and therefore insisted that I polish over and over again some spot which I was sure that I had gone over. I learned to look at the rag, to notice its layers of brown polish, its waxy shine in some places, its wetness when my grandmother made me mix the polish with kerosene to stretch its use. It became a rich object, all full of continuous ribbing and working, which my grandmother insisted that I do with my hands and no shortcuts of standing and doing it with the heel of my foot. We poor people had to get used to work, my grandmother said. After polishing, we would shine the floor with more rags. Up and down, until my grandmother was satisfied. Then the morris chairs, whose slats fell off every once in a while with our jumping, had to be polished and shined, and the cabinet, and all put back in their place.

She wasted nothing. Everything turned into something else when it was too old to be everything. Dresses turned into skirts and then into underwear. Shoes turned into slippers. Corn, too hard for eating, turned into meal. My grandmother herself never wore anything new, except when she went out. She had two dresses and a petticoat hanging in the wardrobe for those times. At home, she dressed in layers of old clothing, half-slip over dress, old socks, because her feet were always cold, and slippers, cut out of old shoes. A safety pin or two, anchored to the front of her dress or the hem of her skirt, to pin up our falling underwear or ruined zippers.

My grandmother didn't like it when we changed the furniture around. She said that changing the furniture around was a sign to people that we didn't have any money. Only people with no money changed their furniture around and around all the time. My grandmother had various lectures on money, to protect us from the knowledge that we had little or none. At night, we could not drop pennies on the floor, for thieves might be passing and think that we did have money and come to rob us.

My grandmother always said that money ran through your hands like water, especially when you had so many mouths to feed. Every two or three weeks money would run out of my grandmother's hands. These times were as routine as our chores or going to school or the games which we played. My grandmother had stretched it over stewed chicken, rice, provisions, and macaroni pie on Sundays, split peas soup on Mondays, fish and bake on Tuesdays, corn meal and dumplings and salt cod on Wednesday, okra and rice on Thursdays, split peas, salt cod, and rice on Fridays, and pelau on Saturdays. By the time the third week of the month came around my grandmother's stretching would become apparent. She carried a worried look on her face and was more silent than usual. We understood this to be a sign of lean times and times when we could not bother my grandmother or else we would get one of her painful explanations across our ears. Besides it really hurt my grandmother not to give us what we needed, as we all settled with her into a depressive hungry silence.

At times we couldn't help but look accusingly at her. Who else could we blame for the gnawing pain in our stomachs and the dry corners of our mouths? We stared at my grandmother hungrily, while she avoided our eyes. We would all gather around her as she lay in bed, leaning against her or sitting on the floor beside the bed, all in silence. We devoted these silences to hope—hope that something would appear to deliver us, perhaps my grandfather, with provisions from the country—and to wild imagination that we would be rich some day and be able to buy pounds of sugar and milk. But sweet water, a thin mixture of water and sugar, was all the balm for our hunger. When even that did not show itself in abundance, our silences were even deeper. We drank water, until our stomachs became distended and nautical.

My little sister, who came along a few years after we had grown accustomed to the routine of hunger and silence, could never grasp the importance of these moments. We made here swear not to cry for food when there wasn't any and, to give her credit, she did mean it when she promised. But the moment the hungry silence set in, she began to cry, begging my grandmother for sweet water. She probably cried out of fear that we would never eat again, and admittedly our silences were somewhat awesome, mixtures of despair and grief made potent by the weakness which the heavy, hot sun brought on in our bodies.

We resented my little sister for these indiscretions. She reminded us that we were hungry, a thought we had been transcending in our growing asceticism, and we felt sorry for my grandmother having to answer her cries. Because it was only then that my grandmother relented and sent one of us to borrow a cup of sugar from the woman across the street. One of us suffered the indignity of crossing the road and repeating haltingly whatever words my grandmother had told her to say.

My grandmother always sent us to Tante, never to Mrs. Sommard who was a religious woman and our next-door neighbour, nor to Mrs. Benjamin who had money and was our other next-door neighbour. Mrs. Sommard only had prayers to give and Mrs. Benjamin, scorn. But Tante, with nothing, like us, would give whatever she could manage.

Mrs. Sommard was a Seventh Day Adventist, and the only time my grandmother sent one of us to beg a cup of something, Mrs. Sommard sent back a message to pray. My grandmother took it quietly and never sent us there again and told us to have respect for Mrs. Sommard because she was a religious woman and believed that God would provide.

Mrs. Sommard's husband, Mr. Sommard, took two years to die. For the two years that he took to die the house was always brightly lit. Mr. Sommard was so afraid of dying that he could not sleep and didn't like it when darkness fell. He stayed awake all night and all day for two years and kept his wife and daughter awake too. My grandmother said he pinched them if they fell asleep and told them that if he couldn't sleep, they shouldn't sleep either. How this ordeal squared with Mrs. Sommard's religiousness, my grandmother was of two minds about. Either the Lord was trying Mrs. Sommard's faith, or Mrs. Sommard had done some wickedness that the Lord was punishing her for.

The Benjamins, on the other side, we didn't know where they got their money from, but they seemed to have a lot of it. For Mrs. Benjamin sometimes told our friend Patsy not to play with us. Patsy lived with Mrs. Benjamin, her grandmother; Miss Lena, her aunt, and her grandfather, Mr. Benjamin. We could always smell chicken that Miss Lena was cooking from their pot, even when our house fell into silence.

The Benjamins were the reason that my grandmother didn't like us running down into the backyard to pick up mangoes when the wind blew them down. She felt ashamed that we would show such hunger in the eyes of people who had plenty. The next thing was that the Benjamins' rose mango tree was so huge; it spread half its body over their fence into our yard. We felt that this meant that any mangoes that dropped on our side belonged to us, and Patsy Benjamin and her family thought that it belonged to them. My grandmother took their side, not because she thought that they were right, but she thought that if they were such greedy people, they should have the mangoes. Let them kill themselves on it, she said. So she made us call to Mrs. Benjamin and give them all the rose mangoes that fell in our yard. Mrs. Benjamin thought that we were doing this out of respect for their status and so she would often tell us with superiority to keep the mangoes, but my grandmother would decline. We, grudgingly, had to do the same and, as my grandmother warned us, without a sad look on our faces. From time to time we undermined my grandmother's pride by pretending not to find any rose mangoes on the ground, and hid them in a stash under the house or deep in the backyard under leaves. Since my grandmother never ventured from the cover and secrecy of the walls of the house, or that area in the yard hidden by the walls, she was never likely to discover our lie.

Deep in the backyard, over the drain which we called the canal, we were out of range of my grandmother's voice, since she refused to shout, and the palms of her hands, but not her eyes. We were out of reach of her broomstick which she flung at our fleeing backs or up into one of the mango trees where one of us was perched, escaping her beatings.

Deep in the back of the yard, we smoked sponge wood and danced in risqué fashion and uttered the few cuss words that we knew and made up calypsos. There, we pretended to be big people with children. We put our hands on our hips and shook our heads, as we had seen big people do, and complained about having so much children, children, children to feed.

My grandmother showed us how to kill a chicken, holding its body in the tub and placing the scrubbing board over it leaving the neck exposed, then with a sharp knife quickly cut the neck, leaving the scrubbing board over the tub. Few of us became expert at killing a chicken. The beating of the dying fowl would frighten us and the scrubbing board would slip whereupon the headless bird would escape, its warm blood still gushing, propelling its body around and around the house. My grandmother would order us to go get the chicken, which was impossible since the direction that the chicken took and the speed with which it ran were indeterminate. She didn't like us making our faces up in distaste at anything that had to do with eating or cleaning or washing. So, whoever let the chicken escape or whoever refused to go get it would have to stand holding it for five minutes until my grandmother made a few turns in the house, then they would have to pluck it and gut it and wrap the feathers and innards in newspaper, throwing it in the garbage. That person may well have to take the garbage out for a week. If you can eat, my grandmother would say, you can clean and you shouldn't scorn life.

One day we found a huge balloon down in the backyard. It was the biggest balloon we'd ever had and it wasn't even around Christmas time. Patsy Benjamin, who played through her fence with us, hidden by the rose mango tree from her Aunt Lena, forgot herself and started shouting that it was hers. She began crying and ran complaining to her aunt that we had stolen her balloon. Her aunt dragged her inside, and we ran around our house fighting and pulling at each other, swearing that the balloon belonged to this one or that one. My grandmother grabbed one of us on the fourth or fifth round and snatched the balloon away. We never understood the cause for this since it was such a find, and never quite understood my grandmother muttering something about Tante's son leaving his "nastiness" everywhere. Tante, herself, had been trying to get our attention as we raced round and round the house. This was our first brush with what was called "doing rudeness." Later, when my big sister began to menstruate and stopped hanging around with us, we heard from our classmates that men menstruated too, and so we put two and two together and figured that Tante's son's nastiness must have to do with his menstruation.

On our way home from school one day, a rumour blazed its way through all the children just let out from school that there was a male sanitary napkin at the side of the road near the pharmacy on Royal Road. It was someone from the Catholic girl's school who started it, and troupe after troupe of school children hurried to the scene to see it. The rumour spread back and forth, along the Coffee, with school children corroborating and testifying that they had actually seen it. By the time we got there, we only saw an empty brown box which we skirted, a little frightened at first, then pressed in for a better view. There really wasn't very much more to see and we figured that someone must have removed it before we got there. Nevertheless, we swore that we had seen it and continued to spread the rumour along the way, until we got home, picking up the chant which was building as all the girls whipped their fingers at the boys on the street singing, "Boys have periods TOOOOOO!" We couldn't ask my grandmother if men had periods, but it was the source of weeks of arguing back and forth.

When my period came, it was my big sister who told me what to do. My grandmother was not there. By then, my mother had returned from England and an unease had fallen over us. Anyway, when I showed my big sister, she shoved a sanitary napkin and two pins at me and told me not to play with boys anymore and that I couldn't climb the mango tree anymore and that I shouldn't fly around the yard anymore either. I swore everyone not to tell my mother when she got home from work, but they all did anyway and my mother with her air, which I could never determine since I never looked her in the face, said nothing.

My mother had returned. We had anticipated her arrival with a mixture of pride and fear. These added to an uncomfortable sense that things would not be the same, because in the weeks preceding her arrival my grandmother revved up the old warning about us not being able to be rude or disobey anymore, that we would have to be on our best behaviour to be deserving of this woman who had been to England, where children were not like us. She was my grandmother's favourite daughter too, so my grandmother was quite proud of her. When she arrived, some of us hung back behind our grandmother's skirt, embarrassing her before my mother who, my grandmother said, was expecting to meet well-brought-up children who weren't afraid of people.

To tell the truth, we were expecting a white woman to come through the door, the way my grandmother had described my mother and the way the whole street that we lived on treated the news of my mother's return, as if we were about to ascend in their respect. The more my grandmother pushed us forward to say hello to my mother, the more we clung to her skirts, until she finally had to order us to say hello. In the succeeding months, my grandmother tried to push us toward my mother. She looked at us with reproach in her eyes that we did not acknowledge my mother's presence and her power. My mother brought us wieners and fried eggs and mashed potatoes, which we had never had before, and said that she longed for kippers, which we did not know. We enjoyed her strangeness but we were uncomfortable under her eyes. Her suitcase smelled strange and foreign, and for weeks despite our halting welcome of her, we showed off in the neighborhood that we had someone from away.

Then she began ordering us about and the wars began.

Those winters in England, when she must have bicycled to Hampstead General Hospital from which we once received a letter and a postcard with her smiling to us astride a bicycle, must have hardened the smile which my grandmother said that she had and which was dimly recognizable from the photograph. These winters, which she wrote about and which we envied as my sister read them to us, she must have hated. And the thought of four ungrateful children who deprived her of a new dress or stockings to travel to London, made my mother unmerciful on her return.

We would run to my grandmother, hiding behind her skirt, or dive for the sanctuary of my grandmother's room. She would enter, accusing my grandmother of interfering in how she chose to discipline "her" children. We were shocked. Where my mother acquired this authority we could not imagine. At first my grandmother let her hit us, but finally she could not help but intervene and ask my mother if she thought that she was beating animals. Then my mother would reply that my grandmother had brought us up as animals. This insult would galvanize us all against my mother. A back answer would fly from the child in question who would, in turn, receive a slap from my grandmother, whereupon my grandmother would turn on my mother with the length of her tongue. When my grandmother gave someone the length of her tongue, it was given in a low, intense, and damning tone, punctuated by chest beating and the biblical, "I have nurtured a viper in my bosom."

My mother often became hysterical and left the house, crying what my grandmother said were crocodile tears. We had never seen an adult cry in a rage before. The sound in her throat was a gagging yet raging sound, which frightened us, but it was the sight of her tall, threatening figure which cowed us. Later, she lost hope that we would ever come around to her and she began to think and accuse my grandmother of setting her children against her. I recall her shoes mostly, white and thick, striding across the tiny house.

These accusations increased, and my grandmother began to talk of dying and leaving us. Once or twice, my mother tried to intervene on behalf of one or the other of us in a dispute with my grandmother. There would be silence from both my grandmother and us, as to the strangeness of this intervention. It would immediately bring us on side to my grandmother's point of view and my mother would find herself in the company of an old woman and some children who had a life of their own—who understood their plays, their dances, gestures, and signals, who were already intent on one another. My mother would find herself standing outside these gestures into which her inroads were abrupt and incautious. Each foray made our dances more secretive, our gestures subterranean.

Our life stopped when she entered the door of the house, conversations closed in mid-sentence, and elegant gestures with each other turned to sharp asexual movements.

My mother sensed these closures since, at first, we could not hide these scenes fast enough to escape her jealous glance. In the end, we closed our scenes ostentatiously in her presence. My grandmother's tongue lapping over a new story or embellishing an old one would become brusque in "Tell your mother good evening." We, telling my grandmother a story or receiving her assurance that when we get rich, we would buy a this or a that, while picking out her gray hairs, would fall silent. We longed for when my mother stayed away. Most of all we longed for when she worked nights. Then we could sit all evening in the grand darkness of my grandmother's stories.

When the electricity went out and my grandmother sat in the rocking chair, the wicker seat bursting from the weight of her hips, the stories she spun, no matter how often we heard them, languished over the darkness whose thickness we felt, rolling in and out of the veranda. Some nights the darkness, billowing about us, would be suffused by the perfume of lady-of-the-night, a white, velvet, yellow, orchid-like flower which grew up the street in a neighbour's yard. My grandmother's voice, brown and melodic, about how my grandfather, "Yuh Papa, one dark night, was walking from Ortoire to Guayguayare...."

The road was dark and my grandfather walked alone with his torchlight pointed toward his feet. He came to a spot in the road which suddenly chilled him. Then, a few yards later, he came to a hot spot in the road, which made him feel for a shower of rain. Then, up ahead, he saw a figure and behind him he heard its footsteps. He kept walking, the footsteps pursued him dragging a chain, its figure ahead of him. If he had stopped, the figure, which my grandfather knew to be a *legaboo*, would take his soul; so my grandfather walked steadily, shining his torchlight at his feet and repeating psalm twenty-three, until he passed the bridge by the sea wall and passed the savannah, until he arrived at St. Mary's, where he lived with my grandmother.

It was in the darkness of the veranda, in the honey chuckle back of my grandmother's throat, that we learned how to catch a *soucouyant* and a *lajabless* and not to answer to the "hoop! hoop! hoop!" of *duennes*, the souls of dead children who were not baptized, come to call living children to play with them. To catch a soucouyant, you had to either find the barrel of rain water where she had left her skin and throw pepper in it, or sprinkle salt or rice on your doorstep so that when she tried to enter the house to take your blood, she would have to count every grain of salt or rice before entering. If she dropped just one grain or miscounted, she would have to start all over again her impossible task, and in the mornings she would be discovered, distraught and without her skin, on the doorstep.

When we lived in the country before moving to the street, my grandmother had shown us, walking along the beach in back of the house, how to identify a duenne foot. She made it with her heel in the sand and then, without laying the ball of her foot down, imprinted her toes in the front of the heel print.

Back in the country, my grandmother walked outside and up and down the beach and cut coconut with a cutlass and dug chip-chip on the beach and slammed the kitchen window one night just as a mad man leapt to it to try to get into the house. My grandmother said that as a child in the country, my mother had fallen and hit her head, ever since which she had been pampered and given the best food to eat and so up to this day she was very moody and could go off her head at the slightest. My mother took this liberty whenever she returned home, skewing the order of our routines in my grandmother.

It seemed that my grandmother had raised more mad children than usual, for my uncle was also mad, and one time he held up a gas station which was only the second time that my grandmother had to leave the house, again on the arm of my big sister. We readied my grandmother then, and she and my big sister and I went to the courthouse on the Promenade to hear my uncle's case. They didn't allow children in, but they allowed my big sister as my grandmother had to lean on her. My uncle's case was not heard that morning, so we left the court and walked up to the Promenade. We had only gone a few steps when my grandmother felt faint. My sister held the smelling salts at her nostrils, as we slowly made our way as inconspicuously as we could to a bench near the bandstand. My grandmother cried, mopping her eyes with the handkerchief, and talked about the trouble her children had caused her. We, all three, sat on the bench on the Promenade near the bandstand, feeling stiff and uncomfortable. My grandmother said my uncle had allowed the public to wash their mouth in our family business. She was tired by then, and she prayed that my mother would return and take care of us so that she would be able to die in peace.

Soon after, someone must have written my mother to come home, for we received a letter saying that she was finally coming.

We had debated what to call my mother over and over again and came to no conclusions. Some of the words sounded insincere and disloyal, since they really belonged to my grandmother, although we never called her by those names. But when we tried them out for my mother, they hung so cold in the throat that we were discouraged immediately. Calling my mother by her given name was too presumptuous, even though we had always called all our aunts and uncles by theirs. Unable to come to a decision, we abandoned each other to individual choices. In the end, after our vain attempts to form some word, we never called my mother by any name. If we needed to address her, we stood about until she noticed that we were there and then we spoke. Finally, we never called my mother.

All of the words which we knew belonged to my grandmother. All of them, a voluptuous body of endearment, dependence, comfort, and infinite knowing. We were all full of my grandmother, she had left us full and empty of her. We dreamed in my grandmother and we woke up in her, bleary-eyed and gesturing for her arm, her elbows, her smell. We jockeyed with each other, lied to each other, quarrelled with each other and with her for the boon of lying close to her, sculpting ourselves around the roundness of her back. Braiding her hair and oiling her feet. We dreamed in my grandmother and we woke up in her, bleary-eyed and gesturing for her lap, her arms, her elbows, her smell, the fat flesh of her arms. We fought, tricked each other for the crook between her thighs and calves. We anticipated where she would sit and got there before her. We bought her achar and paradise plums.

My mother had walked the streets of London, as the legend went, with one dress on her back for years, in order to send those brown envelops, the stamps from which I saved in an old album. But her years of estrangement had left her angry and us cold to her sacrifice. She settled into fits of fury. Rage which raised welts on our backs, faces, and thin legs. When my grandmother had turned away, laughing from us, saying there was no place to beat, my mother found room.

Our silences which once warded off hunger now warded off her blows. She took to mean impudence, and her rages whipped around our silences more furiously than before. I, the most ascetic of us all, sustained the most terrible moments of her rage. The more enraged she grew, the more silent I became, the harder she hit, the more wooden, I. I refined this silence into a jewel of the most sacred sandalwood, finely grained, perfumed, mournful yet stoic. I became the only inhabitant of a cloistered place carrying my jewel of fullness and emptiness, voluptuousness and scarcity. But she altered the silences profoundly.

Before, with my grandmother, the silences had company, were peopled by our hope. Now, they were desolate.

She had left us full and empty of her. When someone took the time to check, there was no photograph of my grandmother, no figure of my grandmother in layers of clothing and odd-sided socks, no finger stroking the air in reprimand, no arm under her chin at the front window or crossed over her breasts waiting for us.

My grandmother had never been away from home for more than a couple of hours, and only three times that I could remember. So her absence was lonely. We visited her in the hospital every evening. They had put her in a room with eleven other people. The room was bare. You could see underneath all the beds from the doorway, and the floors were always scrubbed with that hospital-smelling antiseptic which reeked its own sickliness and which I detested for years after. My grandmother lay in one of the beds nearest the door, and I remember my big sister remarking to my grandmother that she should have a better room, but my grandmother hushed her saying that it was alright and anyway she wouldn't be there for long and the nurses were nice to her. From the chair beside my grandmother's bed in the hospital you could see the parking lot on Chancery Lane. I would sit with my grandmother, looking out the window and describing the scene to her. You could also see part of the wharf and the Gulf of Paria, which was murky where it held to the wharf. And St. Paul's church where I was confirmed, even though I did not know the catechism and only mumbled when Canon Fraquar drilled us in it.

Through our talks at the window my grandmother made me swear that I would behave for my mother. We planned, when I grew up and went away, that I would send for my grandmother and that I would grow up to be something good, that she and I and Eula and Ava and Kat and Genevieve would go to Guayaguayare and live there forever. I made her promise that she would not leave me with my mother.

It was a Sunday afternoon, the last time that I spoke with my grandmother. I was describing a bicycle rider in the parking lot and my grandmother promised to buy one for me when she got out of hospital.

My big sister cried and curled herself up beneath the radio when my grandmother died. Genevieve's face was wet with tears, her front braid pulled over her nose, she, sucking her thumb.

When they brought my grandmother home, it was after weeks in the white twelve-storey hospital. We took the curtains down, leaving all the windows and doors bare, in respect for the dead. The ornaments, doilies, and plastic flowers were removed, and the mirrors and furniture covered with white sheets. We stayed inside the house and did not go out to play. We kept the house clean and we fell into our routine of silence when faced with hunger. We felt alone. We did not believe. We thought that it was untrue. In disbelief, we said of my grandmother, "Mama can't be serious!"

The night of the wake, the house was full of strangers. My grandmother would never allow this. Strangers, sitting and talking everywhere, even in my grandmother's room. Someone, a great-aunt, a sister of my grandmother, whom we had never seen before, turned to me sitting on the sewing machine and ordered me in a stern voice to get down. I left the room, slinking away, feeling abandoned by my grand-mother to strangers.

I never cried in public for my grandmother. I locked myself in the bathroom or hid deep in the backyard and wept. I had learned, as my grandmother had taught me, never to show people your private business.

When they brought my grandmother home the next day, we all made a line to kiss her goodbye. My littlest sister was afraid; the others smiled for my grandmother. I kissed my grandmother's face hoping that it was warm.

Topics for Discussion

1. What does the Grandmother represent in the story? What makes her a strong figure?

2. How does Brand use the concept of photographs in the story? Why is it so important for the narrator to have the photograph of the Grandmother?

3. How does poverty figure in the story? What role does it play in the shaping of the narrator's outlook?

4. What is the relationship between the mothers and their daughters, and how is the connection, however tentative, established and maintained between them?

5. What is the role of folk beliefs and superstitions in the story?

6. How does Brand use silence in the story and what does the silence say?

7. How is childhood depicted in the story?

A.S. Byatt

About the Author

A(ntonia) S(usan) Byatt was born in Sheffield, Yorkshire (England), on August 24, 1936. She is the sister of novelist Margaret Drabble. Educated at Cambridge, Bryn Mawr and Oxford, she has taught at University College, London, worked as a Lecturer for the British Council and served as chairman of the Society of Authors in Great Britain. In 1990 she won the Booker Prize for her novel *Possession*.

Byatt has said that her novels are about "habits of thought and imagination," a trait reflected in the stories of her first collection of short fiction, *Sugar and Other Stories* (1987). In her short stories in particular, Byatt is fascinated by the relationship between past and present and the ways in which one uses fiction to bridge that distance. She makes use of history—personal, national and literary—in order to set the present in the context of an ongoing tradition, a continuum where human traits and individual humanity are understood to be as lasting as art itself.

Selected Works

Shadow of the Sun (novel, 1964)
The Game (novel, 1968)
The Virgin in the Garden (novel, 1979)
Still Life (novel, 1985)
Sugar and Other Stories (short stories, 1987)
Possession (novel, 1990)
Passions of the Mind (essays, 1993)
Angels and Insects (novellas, 1993)
The Matisse Stories (extended short stories, 1993)
The Djinn in the Nightingale's Eye (short stories, 1994)
Babel Tower (novel, 1996)

About the Story

In her collection of short stories *Sugar and Other Stories* (from which this story is taken), Byatt focuses on the nature of storytelling, the ways in which people are connected through time, either by what they tell each other or by those objects into which is read meaning, continuity and sentiment.

The story opens within the mind of the protagonist (Veronica), a middle-aged woman with a daughter (Jane) in her late teens. Veronica daydreams about a tea party. While thinking about the broken sewing machine, an old relic passed from one generation to the next, Veronica reflects on the repetitions of events, feelings and situations that occur in a family over the space of a century.

Rose-Coloured Teacups

There were three women in the room, two sitting in low, oval-backed armchairs, and one on the end of a bed, her pale head lit by a summer window, her face slightly shadowed. They were young women, full of energy; this could be seen in the quick, alert turns of the heads, the movements of hand to mouth, carrying a cigarette in a long holder, a rose-coloured teacup. They wore knee-length shifts, one olive, one russet (sometimes it was a kind of dull crimson), one, belonging to the pale head, a clotted cream or blanket-wool colour. They all had smooth but not shining pale stockings and barred, buttoned shoes, with pointed toes and very small heels. One dark woman, in a chair, had long hair, knotted in the nape of her neck. The other two were shingled. The pale-headed woman, when she turned her head to look out of the window, could be seen to have the most beautiful slanting ledge of shorn silver and gold from the turn of her skull to the fine neck. She had a fine-edged upper lip, still and calm; a composed look, but expectant. The third woman was harder to see; the haircut was decisive and mannish; Veronica had to resist seeing it as she had always known it, pepper and salt.

She could see the chairs very clearly, one with a pale green linen cover, fitted, and one with a creased chintz, covered with large, floppy roses. She could see the little fire, with its dusty coal scuttle and brass fire-irons. Sometimes she saw it burning brightly, but mostly it was dark, because it was summer outside, and through the window, between the rosy chintz curtains, there was the unchanging college garden with its rosebeds and packed herbaceous border, its sunken pool and smell of mown grass. There were leaves coiling into the picture round the outside of the window-frame—a climbing rose, a creeper, what was it? She could see a desk, not very clearly. It was no good straining to see; it was necessary to wait quietly. There was a dark corner containing a piece of furniture she had never managed to see at all—a wardrobe? She could always see the low table, set for tea. There was a little kettle, on a trivet, and a capacious sprigged teapot, a walnut cake, on a plate, slices of malt loaf, six pink lustre teacups, rosily iridescent, with petal-shaped saucers. The lustre glaze streaked the strong pink with cobwebs of blue-grey and white-gold. And little butter knives with blunt ends and ivory handles there would be, there were, and a little cut glass dish of butter. And one of jam, yes, with a special flat jam spoon. The women talked to each other. They were waiting for someone. She could not hear their conversation or their occasional laughter. She could see the tablecloth, white linen with a drawn threadwork border, and thick embroidered flowers spilling in swags round its edges, done in that embroidery silk that is dyed in deepening and paler shades of the same colour. She mostly saw the flowers as roses, though many of them, looked at more closely, were hybrid or imaginary creations. She was overdoing the pink.

Her daughter Jane called from upstairs, peremptory and wailing. Jane was unusually at home because of some unexpected hiatus in her very busy social life, which flowed and overflowed from house to house, from friend's kitchen to friend's kitchen, loud with rock, pungent with illegal smoke, vigorous-voiced. Jane had decided to sew something. The sewing-machine was in the spare bedroom. She appeared to be slicing up a pillowcase and reconstructing it into the curiously formed bandeaux and rag-ribbons that went with certain versions of her hair. The sewing-machine had given up, Jane said, it was a stupid thing. She sat at the sewing-table and gave the machine a decisive slap, looking up with her extravagant face surrounded by a rayed sooty star of erect and lacquered hair, a jagged work of art. She had her father's big black eyes, outlined in kohl, and Veronica's father's wide and shapely mouth, painted a glossy magenta. She was big and compact, round and slender, very much alive, a woman and a cross child. It wouldn't *pick up*, the needle, Jane said, rattling the wheel round and round, clattering antique pistons and hinges. It was the tension. The tension had gone to pot. She pulled furiously at the pieces of rag and thread whirred out of the underparts of the machine where the shuttle bustled and nattered. The top thread was snapped. Veronica's mother had had the machine as a wedding present in 1930; it had been second-hand then. Veronica had had it since 1960, when Jane's elder sister had been born. She had made baby clothes on it and nightdresses. Only simple things. She was no seamstress. Her mother had been only moderately efficient with the thing, though she had used it to make do in the war, turning collars, cutting down trousers, making coats into skirts, and curtains into dungarees. Her mother's mother had been a dressmaker in the 1890s. And had also done hand-embroidery, cushions and handtowels, handkerchiefs and "runners" for dresser-tops.

Jane tugged at her multiple earrings, coils of gold wire and little glass beads. I had a go at the tension, she said. I can't get it to go back. Jane was forthright and attacking with many things Veronica had her generation's classic inadequacy about: machines, group living, authority. Jane inhabited a mechanical world. She walked the pavements with a pendant black box, she lived amongst a festoon of electricity, hi-fi, hairdryer, tape-deck, curling-tongs, crimper. She had undone the tension-gauge on the elderly Swan Vickers and spattered various metal discs over the sewing-table. She had become irritated with the irregular coil of fine wire, with its needle-eye hook at the end, on which the thread bobs jerkily and peacefully when the machine is in running order. She had tugged and jerked at it, teasing it out of its coil so that it now protruded, a wavering, threatening, disconnected spike, pointing out nowhere.

Veronica felt rage. She said, "But that is a coiled *spring*, Jane—" and heard in her mind's ear a preliminary ghost of her own voice about to embark on a howling plaint, how *could* you, have you no feelings, my mother kept that machine all her life, I always looked after it, it was cared for ...

And abruptly remembered her own mother's voice in the 1950s, unrestrained, wailing, interminable, how could you, how could you, and saw briefly the pair of them, her mother with her miserable disappointed face, the mouth set in a down-droop, and her own undergraduate self, sugar-petticoated, smooth-skinned, eye-lined and passionate, staring at the shards of pink lustre teacups in a road-delivered teachest. The teacups had been given by her mother's old college friend, to take back a new generation to the college. She had not liked the teacups. She did not like pink, and the floral shape of the saucers was most unfashionable. She and her friends drank Nescafé from stone mugs or plain cylinders in primary colours. She had left folded in her drawer the tablecloth embroidered for her by her grandmother, whose style of embroidery was now exemplified by the cloth, so stiff and clean and brilliant, in the visionary teaparty she had taken to imagining since her mother died. It was a curious form of mourning, but compulsive, and partly comforting. It seemed to be all she was capable of. The force of her mother's rage against the house and housewifery that trapped her and, by extension, against her clever daughters, who had all partly evaded that trap, precluded wholehearted mourning. The silence of her absence was like coming in out of a storm. Or like the silence of that still little room, in its bright expectancy, one or any afternoon in the late 1920s.

She could not reproduce that fury against Jane. She repeated, "It's a spring, you can't uncoil it" and Jane said half-heartedly that she didn't see why not, and they sat down together to try to make sense of the scattered parts of the tension-regulator.

Veronica remembered packing the pink cups. Something had been terribly wrong. She remembered moving around her college room in a daze of defeat and anguish barely summoning up the strength to heap the despised crockery, all anyhow, into the crate, thinking that there should have been newspaper to wrap things in and that she didn't have any. And that the effort of finding any was beyond her. But although she could remember the fine frenzy in which the fate of the teacups had seemed immaterial, the cause was gone. Had she lost a lover? Missed a part in a university play? Said something and regretted it? Feared pregnancy? Or had it been merely vaguer fears of meaninglessness and inertia which had assailed her then, when she was lively, and had been replaced now by the stiffer and more precise fears of death and never getting things done? The girl in her memory of that passively miserable day's packing seemed discontinuous with herself—looked in on, as much as the imaginary teaparty. She could remember vividly taking a furtive look through a door in the part of the college where her mother's room had been, and seeing two low chairs and a bed under a window. The chairs in her constructed vision were draped anachronistically in the loose covers they had worn in her brief, half-reluctant glimpse of them. Her mother had wanted her to be at the college and had felt excluded, then, by her daughter's presence there, from her own memories of the place. The past had been made into the past, discontinuous from the present. It had been a fantasy that Veronica would sit in the same chairs, in the same sunlight and drink from the same cups. No one steps into the same river twice. Jane's elder sister, Veronica's elder daughter, had also gone to the college, and Veronica, forewarned, had watched her assert her place in it, her here and now.

The telephone rang. Jane said that would be Barnaby and her cross lassitude fell away. At the door on the way out, she turned and said to Veronica, "I'm sorry about the machine. I'm sure it'll mend. And anyway it's geriatric." She could be heard singing on the stairs, on the way to the telephone, to take up her life again. She sang beautifully in a large clear voice, inherited from her father, who could sing, and not from Veronica and her mother who scraped tunelessly. She was singing in the Brahms Requiem in the school choir. She rolled out joyfully, "Lord make me to know mine end, and the measure of my days, what it is; that I may know, that I may know how frail I am."

The three women sat in the little room, imagined not remembered. Veronica detected in her mother's cream-coloured dress just a touch of awkwardness, her grandmother's ineptness at a trade for which she was not wholly suited, a shoulder out of true, a cuff awry, as so many buttons and cuffs and waistbands had been during the making-do in the time of austerity. This awkwardness in her mother was lovable and vulnerable. The other shingled woman raised the teapot and poured amber tea into rosy teacups. Two of these cups and one saucer, what was salvaged, stood now on Veronica's dresser, useless and, Veronica thought, exquisitely pretty. Her mother raised her pale head expectantly, lifting that fine lip, fixing her whole attention on the door, through which they came— Veronica could see so much—the young men in blazers and wide flannels, college scarves and smoothed hair, smiling decorously. Veronica saw him smile with the wide and shapely smile that had just reappeared, deprecating and casual, on Jane's different, darker face. She saw the little, blonde, pretty face in the window lit with pure pleasure, pure hope, almost content. She could never see any further: from there, it always began again, chairs, tablecloth, sunny window, rosy teacups, a safe place.

Topics for Discussion

1. What does the sewing machine represent?

2. What point is Byatt trying to make by tracing the connection between generations?

3. How does the story open and what is the purpose of that scene?

4. How does Byatt define history in this story? What is history?

5. Who are the participants at the tea party? Where, other than a room at Oxford, does the tea party take place?

Barry Callaghan

About the Author

Barry Callaghan was born in Toronto in 1937 and educated at the University of Toronto. He has worked as a reporter and editor for newspapers and magazines, as a television journalist and foreign correspondent, and as a publisher of his own literary magazine and publishing house (*Exile* and Exile Editions). He is currently a Professor of English at York University's Atkinson College in Toronto.

Callaghan's work in *The Black Queen Stories* and his latest volume, *A Kiss Is Still a Kiss* (from which "Our Thirteenth Summer" is taken), draws upon his familiarity with and passion for his native city of Toronto. He seeks out irony and absurdity in simple human situations and is fascinated by how individuals react when confronted with the inexplicable, the unusual and the oppressive.

Selected Works

The Hogg Poems and Drawings (poems, 1978)
As Close as We Came (poems, 1982)
The Black Queen Stories (short stories, 1982)
Stone Blind Love (poems, 1988)
The Way the Angel Spreads Her Wings (novel, 1989)
When Things Get Worst (novel, 1993)
A Kiss Is Still a Kiss and Other Stories (short stories, 1995)

About the Story

"Our Thirteenth Summer" is set in Toronto's Annex district during the Second World War. The young protagonist becomes aware of the Jewish children on his street, and the unnamed fears that surrounded their families. In the Holocaust, unfolding in Europe during these years, about six million European Jews and countless other minorities were being slaughtered in Nazi concentration camps.

The story is a study in the way children interrelate, the influence adults have on those relationships, and the ways in which the persecuted attempt to protect themselves during times of crisis.

Our Thirteenth Summer

This is a story that comes out of my childhood when I saw what I saw and said what was done and did what I was told.

I was a child during the war and we lived on the upper floor of a duplex in what was then called a railroad apartment, which was a living room at the front end and a sunroom at the back end and a long hall with rooms running off the hall in between. The apartment below was the same. "The same," my father said, "but not exactly the same." A chemist and his family lived there. He was an expert in explosives, working with the war department. He was not old but his hair was white. He told my mother that he was working on "a bomb so big that when it hit, when it blew, the war would end up on Mars."

He was called George Reed. He was a chain smoker and his teeth were yellow and irregular. He had a portwine stain on the back of his left hand. He often kept his left hand in his suitcoat pocket. He didn't talk much. He seemed to be shy and reticent but I always felt that he disapproved of me, disapproved of all of us, but he didn't want to be forced to say so, and so he hid how he felt behind his shyness. Sometimes his left hand fluttered in his pocket, and sometimes he couldn't stop it fluttering, not once it got going. "It's like he's got a trapped bird in there," my mother said. As for his wife, I heard my mother tell my father once that "she looks like someone who's been swept over by sadness and has gone strange."

She was from Vienna. That's what she had told my mother and father. I didn't know where Vienna was. "That's where it all began," my father told me, "Hitler's town, except she's Jewish." She was short and had thick black hair. When she talked she got excited. She leaned down and breathed into my face, she peered into my eyes, like she was looking for something that was way beyond me, beyond my mother and father, like she didn't know what she was looking for and yet she was sure it was out there, whatever it was, long gone and lost. And one day, she breathed in my face and said, "I'm not Jewish," and her son Bobbie told me the same thing. "My father's English and nobody's Jewish." Bobbie and I played together on the front lawn. He had his father's wine stain on his neck, just below his left ear. We played war games with soldiers and tin tanks in the rockery. There were no flowers in the rockery, only mud and stones because the landlord refused to spend money on flowers. He said money was too scarce because of the war. But Bobbie and I didn't want any flowers. We wanted the mud and the stones. We could spend a whole afternoon shifting our soldiers from ledge to ledge, country to country. We took turns being the enemy. Whenever he had to be the Germans, even though they always lost, he always said, "Don't tell my mother, don't let my grandfather hear us."

Every day at ten-thirty in the morning and at four in the afternoon his grandfather came out of their sunroom which was below my bedroom. Bobbie said he slept there and studied his books there with the shades down and then he would come out and take one of his walks, shuffling in his slippers from our house to the end of the street and back. He never spoke to Bobbie. He never spoke to me. He was dressed all in black, in a black suit. He had a long pale face and a long blade nose. He sometimes wore a black broad-brimmed hat and sometimes a shiny black skull cap, and he had long curls of hair that hung down beside his ears. He didn't wear shoes, he wore his black leather slippers.

"If he isn't Jewish, I don't know who is," my mother said.

"We're not Jewish," Bobbie told me.

"Sure you are, you gotta be," I said.

He punched me as hard as he could in the chest. When I got my breath, when I wiped away the tears that had come to my eyes from the punch, I told Bobbie to put up his dukes. My father had taught me how to box. He had bought me boxing gloves, and kneeling down in front of me, he had sparred with me, teaching me how to jab and hook, and how to block punches and take a punch. He'd hit me really hard two or three times. "That's so he'll understand that getting hit never hurts as much as he thinks it's going to hurt," he told my mother. "Once you know that then you won't worry about getting hurt and you can learn how to hit and hit real good."

Bobbie put up his fists. I flicked a left jab in his face. He didn't know what I was doing. He didn't look scared. He looked bewildered, helpless as he tried to duck his head. I hit him with a left hook. His nose began to bleed. He tasted his blood, he looked astonished, and then when he saw blood all over his shirt, he was terrified. "My mother will kill me." He began to bawl, but he was afraid to run into the house. His mother came running out. Her black hair was loose and long and flying all about her head. She screamed and pulled Bobbie behind her, to protect him, but I didn't want to hit him again. I felt sorry. I wished he hadn't hit me and I hadn't hit him.

"Why?" she screamed.

"Because he said I was Jewish," Bobbie said.

"Because he's Jewish ... He's not Jewish," and she swung and hit me in the head, knocking me down. She hauled Bobbie into the house. I looked up from where I was, lying flat on my back, and the old grandfather, who was wearing his skull cap, was standing by their open front window, staring at me, twisting one of his long curls in his fingers.

Later, when I told my father what had happened he said to my mother, "I know they're terrified, I know they're from Vienna, but that's not the point," and he went downstairs and stood very close to Mr. Reed and said through his teeth, "If either one of you ever hits my boy again, I don't care how big your bomb is, I'll knock your block off."

There was a Jewish family up the street, just north of us. Mrs. Asch was plump, almost fat. She wasn't too fat because she didn't waddle, but she had a huge bosom and she would hold my head to her chest. Mr. Asch worked with furriers. He was, my father said, "A cutter." It sounded dangerous, like he should be on *Inner Sanctum Mystery* radio. But he didn't look dangerous. He was small, had pasty-colored skin, a round closely-cropped head, and always wore his skull cap, even under his hat. He came home every evening at six-thirty, sat down looking sullen, ate cold chicken that was shiny and pimpled in its boiled white skin, and drank Coca-Cola. We never drank Coca-Cola in our house. "Rotgut," my mother called it, so I drank Hires Root Beer, telling my friend, my pal, Nathan Asch, that it was a kind of real beer. He didn't believe me but sometimes we put aspirins in it to give it a boost and he

drank it with me and usually he said, "This is living," and we got a
headache that we called a hangover.

Nathan, who was plump like his mother, had one leg shorter than
the other. He wore an ox-blood boot with a double-thick sole and heel.
He couldn't run very fast and he could hardly skate at all, and so,
because I wanted to be a baseball pitcher, he was my catcher. His sister,
who was a lot older and very pretty and worked in a fur salon modelling
coats, had bought him a big round catcher's glove. It was the best glove
anybody on the street had and Nathan knew it and he was proud to be
a catcher and I was proud that he was my catcher because he was good
at blocking any curve balls I threw into the dirt.

On the weekends when Bobbie Reed's mother and grandfather
walked up the street together to the grocery store on Dupont Road,
they would pass the Asch house and most of the time in the summer
the Asches would be sitting out on the front porch listening to Mel
Allen broadcast the Yankee games on WBEN Buffalo, or Ruth the
daughter would have her portable record player set up by the porch
stairs, playing Frankie Lane singing:

> My heart goes where the wild goose goes,
> wild goose, mother goose,
> which is best,
> a wandering fool or a heart at rest ...

and the old man dressed in black would sometimes get a hitch in his
step and hesitate and glance up the walk to the porch. He always wore
some kind of white tasselled cloth under his suitcoat that looked like a
piece of torn sail. If Mr. Asch was sitting on the porch, he'd glower at
the old man and if Mrs. Reed looked at him, then Nathan's father
would get up, still small no matter how tall he tried to stand, and he'd
push his chin out and down and spit. This seemed awful to me, particularly because Mr. Asch was no good at spitting and whatever he hocked
out of his mouth it always went splat and sat there on his own porch
stairs. I didn't understand why he was so angry and why he was spitting
at a woman and I didn't understand spitting on your own stairs. I didn't
understand any of this at all. The second time it happened, I asked
Nathan and he said, "It's because Bobbie and the whole bunch of them
tell everybody they're not Jewish. My father hates them for that."

"I never heard the old man say he wasn't Jewish," I said.

"He don't say nothing," and Nathan shouted, "You don't say nothing," hoping the old man would hear him. "You might as well be from
Mars."

I watched Mrs. Reed thrust out her chin and quicken her stride as
the old man unbuttoned and then buttoned his suitcoat, shuffling away
from us, and he looked bonier and sharper in the shoulder blades than
I'd thought he was, but then, I'd always thought of him as slumped

through the shoulders and he wasn't slumped. His shoulders were very straight, though he did push his feet along the sidewalk like he was tired when he walked.

"Just look at him like he's not there," my mother said. "That's best."

"But he is there," I said.

"So you say," she said and laughed.

About two months after Nathan shouted at the old man it was time for Nathan's birthday. August was always a big month for the kids on the street. August was the last month of the summer holidays and Nathan's birthday was at the beginning of the month and Bobbie's birthday was at the end and all of us were always invited to wear paper hats and blow whistles and bob for apples and eat cake and play hide-and-seek down the alleys between the houses after dark, before we went to bed. I didn't like my birthday because it was in February and it was too cold to play outside. But this year, Nathan's party was different. It was smaller. There were kids there that I didn't know and the kids I knew and expected to see weren't there. Nathan told me that this wasn't going to be his real birthday party, his real birthday party was going to be his *bar mitzvah* because he was turning thirteen and he was going to be a man. After we ate the cake and his mother's cookies, when I said goodbye to him at the door and he thanked me for my gift, a Yankee baseball cap my father had brought from New York, he said, "I can't see you so much anymore."

"What?"

"My father says I can't see you so much, not now that I'm a man."

"Why?"

"'Cause you're a *goi.*"

"What's that?"

"One of the *goyim*, you eat unclean food so you got unclean hearts."

When I came home early, surprising my mother, she was standing alone out on the sidewalk under a street lamp that had just come on. I was crying quietly, not quite sure why because I had done nothing wrong, or maybe it was because Mrs. Asch was never going to hold my head against her big bosom again. The Reed front windows were open and there was loud music coming from the windows as I told my mother what had happened with Nathan and she folded me into her arms and said, "There, there, there's nothing you can do with some people." She sounded very sad but I could tell she was also very angry. As we walked up to our door into the duplex I could hear the music and see the Reeds spinning and twirling, Mrs. Reed with her head thrown back, laughing, and I asked my mother, "What's that they're doing?"

"Waltzing," she said. "That's the way they dance in Vienna, they waltz."

"Like that?"

"It can be very beautiful," she said.

At the end of August, Bobbie turned thirteen, too. I was playing more and more by myself. Once or twice I lay on my bedroom floor with my ear to the floor to see if I could hear Bobbie in the old man's bedroom below me but I never did hear him. Sometimes I heard the old man complaining and singing a kind of moan and once, as he was going out walking, he paused beside the rockery and looked down at me as I lined up two Lancasters at the bottom of the stones. I looked up and he looked down. "Bombers," I said, and another time I had my baseball and my glove beside me and I asked, "Hey, you wanta play catch?" He looked startled and then he laughed. Not a loud laugh, but quiet, like a chuckle. "You speak English?" I asked. He took two steps away and then stopped, turned around, and said in a voice that seemed to be as much heavy breathing as it was a voice, "Of course," and then he kept on walking without looking back.

I asked Bobbie if he was going to have a *bar mitzvah*, too. He sneered at me and said, "Of course not. What d'you think I am?" Then I realized that every night, just before supper, Bobbie and his father were putting on boxing gloves in their living room and Mr. Reed, who probably didn't know anything about boxing, was trying to teach Bobbie how to box. One late afternoon as I stood out on the lawn watching their heads and shoulders duck and weave, I realized that the old man was standing near me and he was watching, too.

"Hi," I said.

He just looked at me, a strange look, like for a minute he thought I was someone else that he was surprised to see, but he didn't say anything. He sighed and went into their house.

Two days before his birthday, Bobbie's mother stopped my mother. Usually they said something nice to each other without meaning it, but this time Bobbie's mother didn't bother. She said, "From now on, nobody calls Bobbie Bobbie anymore. His name is Robin. A man's name. Robin Reed." Bobbie looked kind of mopey, so I said, "Well Robin, I don't hardly see you anymore, not even on the weekend."

"I go with my father on Saturdays now."

"Where?"

"To his lab. He takes me to his lab."

"What for?"

"To teach me chemistry, to teach me what he does."

"Terrific," I said. "He makes bombs."

"He doesn't let me make bombs," he said. "Not yet."

On the afternoon of his birthday, I was all alone. My father was away again and my mother was out shopping. Mr. Reed came home early, his head down, his left hand in his suitcoat pocket, fluttering. I thought he was home to get ready for the party, but not long after, Robin came out on to the front lawn wearing boxing gloves and carrying another pair for me. I thought it was really strange, the gloves were the exact same color as the wine stain on his neck. He said his father had told him that he had to box me before there could be any party. "He says I'm turning thirteen, you know."

For the first time in my life I just suddenly felt all tired, like my whole body was tired. And sad. I was laughing while the two of us stood there with great big gloves hanging off the ends of our arms, but I felt so sad I was almost sick, and though I could tell right away, as soon as Robin put up his gloves, that he was still the same old Bobbie, that he didn't know how to box at all, I only remembered the last time I'd hit him, the blood, and how sorry I felt, and I was half leaning toward him while I was thinking about that and he swung a wild looping left that caught me behind the ear and knocked me down. I wasn't hurt, and he didn't know that I knew he couldn't hurt me no matter how hard he hit me because my father had taught me how to take a really hard punch and not to be afraid. So I got up and pawed the air around Robin, trying not to let him hit me, not really punching him because I felt too tired even if I had wanted to punch him, and then he cuffed me a couple of times, but he didn't know how to punch off the weight of his back leg, so I staggered a little and I saw that Mr. Reed was standing in their front window, his hands flat on the glass, a great big glad smile on his face, but the old grandfather had come out on to the cement stoop beside the rockery. He had on his broad-brimmed black hat and he stood with his arms folded across his chest, the torn sail hanging out from under his arms. He was silent and intent. I let Robin take a bang at my body. I was glad my father wasn't home. He'd have been ashamed and angry and I would have had to fight, had to really beat up Robin or Bobbie or whoever he was. Instead, I wanted to cry. Not because I was hurt. I just wanted it all to be over so that I could cry and so I sat down on the lawn and stayed there because no one I loved could see me, no one I loved was there to make me do anything I didn't want to do, and at last, Robin, totally astonished, turned and ran into the house, ran into his father's arms.

I got up and went down the lawn to the sidewalk and sat on the curb and slowly undid the laces to the boxing gloves with my teeth and pulled the gloves off. I wasn't really sniffling. The Reeds were crazy if they thought I was going to get up and go to Robin's birthday party, but I didn't know why they were actually crazy. Then I heard shuffling leather slippers behind me. I thought he'd gone into the house, too, to be with them, but he was standing close behind me, and when I turned and looked up I was almost angry at him but he was smiling, looking down from under the wide brim of his hat and shaking his head with a kind of bent sorrowful smile.

"It's not so easy to hurt you," he said.

"Nope," I said.

"You would make a good Jew," he said.

"How would you know," I said, real sharp, "you're not Jewish."

"No, that's right," he said, smiling a little more, and then he leaned down and whispered, "I'm the man from Mars."

Topics for Discussion

1. How does Callaghan treat the subject of childhood in the story?

2. What impact does the war have on the events of the story and how does Callaghan use history to inform the events?

3. Why do Bobbie Reed and his mother deny their backgrounds? What is Callaghan saying about the experience of anti-Semitism and the issue of fear?

4. What is Callaghan saying about the nature of identity?

5. What is the significance of turning thirteen? Why is this a demarcation or a moment of passage for these boys?

6. What is the significance of the final boxing match?

7. How do culture and adults influence the relationships between children?

Joseph Conrad

About the Author

Joseph Conrad is one of the most studied yet enigmatic authors in English literature. The subject of countless critical studies, Conrad's works are benchmarks in twentieth-century literature for their style and their treatment of great themes, such as death, honour, courage, history, mystery, paranoia, psychology and a plethora of other issues. His voluminous works in prose fiction make him one of the major novelists and story writers of the English language.

Joseph Conrad was born Jozef Teodor Konrad Korzeniowski in Berdyczow, Poland, in 1857. His first language was Polish; his second, French. He did not learn English until he was twenty, when he immersed himself in the tongue. He was orphaned at the age of eleven (his father was a Polish writer and an exiled nationalist). In 1874 he went to Marseilles, France, where he joined the French Merchant Marine; four years later he joined the crew of a British freighter. By 1886, after serving in the East (mainly the Pacific and the Indian Ocean), he earned his Master's Certificate and became a British citizen. After the publication of *Almayer's Folly* (his first novel) in 1895, he devoted himself full-time to writing and gave up the sea. He died in England in 1924.

"Heart of Darkness," a story about a trip up the Congo River in central Africa, is a reworking of material Conrad attempted in his first novel.

Selected Works

Almayer's Folly (novel, 1895)
An Outcast of the Islands (novel, 1896)
The Nigger of the "Narcissus" (novel, 1898)
Lord Jim (novel, 1900)
Youth and Other Stories (including "Heart of Darkness") (short stories, 1902)
Nostromo (novel, 1904)
The Secret Agent (novel, 1907)
Chance (novel, 1913)
Victory: An Island Tale (novel, 1915)

About the Story

In this quest story, Marlow, an experienced sailor, relates the story of his journey up an African river to retrieve a renegade trader named Kurtz. In the process of journeying through both a physical and psychological landscape, Marlow both deifies and vilifies the object of his journey, the elusive Mr. Kurtz, and examines the nature of evil in all its ramifications and manifestations.

When reading this novella, try to keep track of all the ways in which Conrad expresses "darkness" — both in the sense of darkness as evil and in the sense of darkness as negation.

Heart of Darkness

The *Nellie*, a cruising yawl, swung to her anchor without a flutter of the sails, and was at rest. The flood had made, the wind was nearly calm, and being bound down the river, the only thing for it was to come to and wait for the turn of the tide.

The sea-reach of the Thames stretched before us like the beginning of an interminable waterway. In the offing the sea and the sky were welded together without a joint, and in the luminous space the tanned sails of the barges drifting up with the tide seemed to stand still in red clusters of canvas sharply peaked, with gleams of varnished spirit. A haze rested on the low shores that ran out to sea in vanishing flatness. The air was dark above Gravesend, and farther back still seemed condensed into a mournful gloom, brooding motionless over the biggest, and the greatest, town on earth.

The Director of Companies was our captain and our host. We four affectionately watched his back as he stood in the bows looking to seaward. On the whole river there was nothing that looked half so nautical. He resembled a pilot, which to a seaman is trustworthiness personified. It was difficult to realize his work was not out there in the luminous estuary, within the brooding gloom.

Between us there was, as I have already said somewhere, the bond of the sea. Besides holding our hearts together through long periods of separation, it had the effect of making us tolerant of each other's yarns—and even convictions. The Lawyer—the best of old fellows—had, because of his many years and many virtues, the only cushion on deck, and was lying on the only rug. The Accountant had brought out already a box of dominoes, and was toying architecturally with the bones. Marlow sat cross-legged right aft, leaning against the mizzenmast. He had sunken cheeks, a yellow complexion, a straight back, an ascetic aspect, and, with his arms dropped, the palms of hands outwards, resembled an idol. The director, satisfied the anchor had good hold, made his way aft and sat down amongst us. We exchanged a few words lazily. Afterwards there was silence on board the yacht. For some reason or other we did not begin that game of dominoes. We felt meditative, and fit for nothing but placid staring. The day was ending in a serenity of still and exquisite brilliance. The water shone pacifically; the sky, without a speck, was a benign immensity of unstained light; the very mist on the Essex marshes was like a gauzy and radiant fabric, hung from the wooded rises inland, and draping the low shores in diaphanous folds. Only the gloom to the west, brooding over the upper reaches, became more sombre every minute, as if angered by the approach of the sun.

And at last, in its curved and imperceptible fall, the sun sank low, and from glowing white changed to a dull red without rays and without heat, as if about to go out suddenly, stricken to death by the touch of that gloom brooding over a crowd of men.

Forthwith a change came over the waters, and the serenity became less brilliant but more profound. The old river in its broad reach rested unruffled at the decline of day, after ages of good service done to the race that peopled its banks, spread out in the tranquil dignity of a waterway leading to the uttermost ends of the earth. We looked at the venerable stream not in the vivid flush of a short day that comes and departs for ever, but in the august light of abiding memories. And indeed nothing is easier for a man who has, as the phrase goes, "followed the sea" with reverence and affection, than to evoke the great spirit of the past upon the lower reaches of the Thames.

The tidal current runs to and fro in its unceasing service, crowded with memories of men and ships it had borne to the rest of home or to the battles of the sea. It had known and served all the men of whom the nation is proud, from Sir Francis Drake to Sir John Franklin, knights all, titled and untitled—the great knights-errant of the sea. It had borne all the ships whose names are like jewels flashing in the night of time, from the *Golden Hind* returning with her round flanks full of treasure, to be visited by the Queen's Highness and thus pass out of the gigantic tale, to the *Erebus* and *Terror*, bound on other conquests—and that never returned. It had known the ships and the men. They had sailed from Deptford, from Greenwich, from Erith—the adventurers and the settlers; kings' ships and the ships of men on 'Change; captains, admirals, the dark "interlopers" of the Eastern trade, and the commissioned "generals" of East India fleets. Hunters for gold or pursuers of fame, they all had gone out on that stream, bearing the sword, and often the torch, messengers of the might within the land, bearers of a spark from the sacred fire. What greatness had not floated on the ebb of that river into the mystery of an unknown earth! . . . The dreams of men, the seed of commonwealths, the germs of empires.

The sun set; the dusk fell on the stream, and lights began to appear along the shore. The Chapman lighthouse, a three-legged thing erect on a mud-flat, shone strongly. Lights of ships moved in the fairway—a great stir of lights going up and going down. And farther west on the upper reaches the place of the monstrous town was still marked ominously on the sky, a brooding gloom in sunshine, a lurid glare under the stars.

"And this also," said Marlow suddenly, "has been one of the dark places of the earth."

He was the only man of us who still "followed the sea." The worst that could be said of him was that he did not represent his class. He was a seaman, but he was a wanderer, too, while most seamen lead, if one may so express it, a sedentary life. Their minds are of the stay-at-home order, and their home is always with them—the ship; and so is their country—the sea. One ship is very much like another, and the sea is always the same. In the immutability of their surroundings the foreign shores, the foreign faces, the changing immensity of life, glide past, veiled not by a sense of mystery but by a slightly disdainful ignorance; for there is nothing mysterious to a seaman unless it be the sea itself, which is the mistress of his existence and as inscrutable as Destiny. For the rest, after his hours of work, a casual stroll or a casual spree on shore suffices to unfold for him the secret of a whole continent, and generally he finds the secret not worth knowing. The yarns of seamen have a direct simplicity, the whole meaning of which lies within the shell of a cracked nut. But Marlow was not typical (if his propensity to spin yarns be excepted), and to him the meaning of an episode was not inside like a kernel but outside, enveloping the tale which brought it out only as a glow brings out a haze, in the likeness of one of these misty halos that sometimes are made visible by the spectral illumination of moonshine.

His remark did not seem at all surprising. It was just like Marlow. It was accepted in silence. No one took the trouble to grunt even; and presently he said, very slow—

"I was thinking of very old times, when the Romans first came here, nineteen hundred year ago—the other day. . . . Light came out of this river since—you say Knights? Yes; but it is like a running blaze on a plain, like a flash of lightning in the clouds. We live in the flicker— may it last as long as the old earth keeps rolling! But darkness was here yesterday. Imagine the feelings of a commander of a fine—what d'ye call 'em?—trireme in the Mediterranean, ordered suddenly to the north; run overland across the Gauls in a hurry; put in charge of one of these craft the legionaries—a wonderful lot of handy men they must have been, too—used to build, apparently by the hundred, in a month or two, if we may believe what we read. Imagine him here—the very end of the world, a sea the colour of lead, a sky the colour of smoke, a kind of ship about as rigid as a concertina—and going up this river with stores, or orders, or what you like. Sand-banks, marshes, forests, savages,—precious little to eat fit for a civilized man, nothing but Thames water to drink. No Falernian wine here, no going ashore. Here and there a military camp lost in a wilderness, like a needle in a bundle of hay—cold, fog, tempests, disease, exile, and death—death skulking in the air, in the water, in the bush. They must have been dying like flies here. Oh, yes—he did it. Did it very well, too, no doubt, and without thinking much about it either, except afterwards to brag of what he had done through his time, perhaps. They were men enough to face the darkness. And perhaps he was cheered by keeping his eye on a chance of promotion to the fleet at Ravenna by-and-by, if he had good friends in Rome and survived the awful climate. Or think of a decent young citizen in a toga—perhaps too much dice, you know—coming out here in the train of some prefect, or tax-gatherer, or trader even, to mend his fortunes. Land in a swamp, march through the woods, and in some inland post feel the savagery, the utter savagery, had closed round him—all that mysterious life of the wilderness that stirs in the forest, in the jungles, in the hearts of wild men. There's no initiation either into such mysteries. He has to live in the midst of the incomprehensible, which is also detestable. And it has a fascination, too, that goes to work upon him. The fascination of the abomination—you know, imagine the growing regrets, the longing to escape, the powerless disgust, the surrender, the hate."

He paused.

"Mind," he began again, lifting one arm from the elbow, the palm of the hand outwards, so that, with his legs folded before him, he had the pose of a Buddha preaching in European clothes and without a lotus-flower—"Mind, none of us would feel exactly like this. What saves us is efficiency—the devotion of efficiency. But these chaps were not much account, really. They were no colonists; their administration was merely a squeeze, and nothing more, I suspect. They were conquer-ors, and for that you want only brute force—nothing to boast of, when you have it, since your strength is just an accident arising from the weakness of others. They grabbed what they could get for the sake of what was to be got. It was just robbery with violence, aggravated mur-der on a great scale, and men going at it blind—as is very proper for those who tackle a darkness. The conquest of the earth, which mostly means the taking it away from those who have a different complexion or slightly flatter noses than ourselves, is not a pretty thing when you look into it too much. What redeems it is the idea only. An idea at the back of it; not a sentimental pretence but an idea; and an unselfish belief in the idea—something you can set up, and bow down before, and offer a sacrifice to. . . ."

He broke off. Flames glided in the river, small green flames, red flames, white flames, pursuing, overtaking, joining, crossing each other—then separating slowly or hastily. The traffic of the great city went on in the deepening night upon the sleepless river. We looked on, waiting patiently—there was nothing else to do till the end of the flood; but it was only after a long silence, when he said, in a hesitating voice, "I suppose you fellows remember I did once turn fresh-water sailor for a bit," that we knew we were fated, before the ebb began to run, to hear about one of Marlow's inconclusive experiences.

"I don't want to bother you much with what happened to me per-sonally," he began, showing in this remark the weakness of many tellers of tales who seem so often unaware of what their audience would best like to hear; "yet to understand the effect of it on me you ought to know how I got out there, what I saw, how I went up that river to the place where I first met the poor chap. It was the farthest point of navi-gation and the culminating point of my experience. It seemed some-how to throw a kind of light on everything about me—and into my thoughts. It was sombre enough, too—and pitiful—not extraordinary in any way—not very clear either. No, not very clear. And yet it seemed to throw a kind of light.

"I had then, as you remember, just returned to London after a lot of Indian Ocean, Pacific, China Seas—a regular dose of the East—six years or so, and I was loafing about, hindering you fellows in your work and invading your homes, just as though I had got a heavenly mission to civilize you. It was very fine for a time, but after a bit I did get tired of resting. Then I began to look for a ship—I should think the hardest work on earth. But the ships wouldn't even look at me. And I got tired of that game, too.

"Now when I was a little chap I had a passion for maps. I would look for hours at South America, or Africa, or Australia, and lose myself in all the glories of exploration. At that time there were many blank spaces on the earth, and when I saw one that looked particulary inviting on a map (but they all look that) I would put my finger on it and say, When I grow up I will go there. The North Pole was one of these places, I remember. Well, I haven't been there yet, and shall not try now. The glamour's off. Other places were scattered about the Equator, and in every sort of latitude all over the two hemispheres. I have been in some of them, and . . . well, we won't talk about that. But there was one yet—the biggest, the most blank, so to speak—that I had a hankering after.

"True, by this time it was not a blank space any more. It had got filled since my boyhood with rivers and lakes and names. It had ceased to be a blank space of delightful mystery—a white patch for a boy to dream gloriously over. It had become a place of darkness. But there was in it one river especially, a mightily big river, that you could see on the map, resembling an immense snake uncoiled, with its head in the sea, its body at rest curving afar over a vast country, and its tail lost in the depths of the land. And as I looked at the map of it in a shop-window, it fascinated me as a snake would a bird—a silly little bird. Then I remembered there was a big concern, a Company for trade on that river. Dash it all! I thought to myself, they can't trade without using some kind of craft on that lot of fresh water—steamboats! Why shouldn't I try to get charge of one? I went on along Fleet Street, but could not shake off the idea. The snake had charmed me.

"You understand it was a Continental concern, that Trading society; but I have a lot of relations living on the Continent, because it's cheap and not so nasty as it looks, they say.

"I am sorry to own I began to worry them. This was already a fresh departure for me. I was not used to get things that way, you know. I always went my own road and on my own legs where I had a mind to go. I wouldn't have believed it of myself; but, then—you see—I felt somehow I must get there by hook or by crook. So I worried them. The men said 'My dear fellow,' and did nothing. Then—would you believe it?—I tried the women. I, Charlie Marlow, set the women to work—to get a job. Heavens! Well, you see, the notion drove me. I had an aunt, a dear enthusiastic soul. She wrote: 'It will be delightful. I am ready to do anything, anything for you. It is a glorious idea. I know the wife of a very high personage in the Administration, and also a man who has lots of influence with,' etc., etc. She was determined to make no end of fuss to get me appointed skipper of a river steamboat, if such was my fancy.

"I got my appointment—of course; and I got it very quick. It appears the Company had received news that one of their captains had been killed in a scuffle with the natives. This was my chance, and it made me the more anxious to go. It was only months and months afterwards, when I made the attempt to recover what was left of the body, that I heard the original quarrel arose from a misunderstanding about some hens. Yes, two black hens. Fresleven—that was the fellow's name, a Dane—thought himself wronged somehow in the bargain, so he went ashore and started to hammer the chief of the village with a stick. Oh, it didn't surprise me in the least to hear this, and at the same time to be told that Fresleven was the gentlest, quietest creature that ever walked on two legs. No doubt he was; but he had been a couple of years already out there engaged in the noble cause, you know, and he probably felt the need at last of asserting his self-respect in some way. Therefore he whacked the old nigger mercilessly, while a big crowd of his people watched him, thunderstruck, till some man—I was told the chief's son—in desperation at hearing the old chap yell, made a tentative jab with a spear at the white man—and of course it went quite easy between the shoulder-blades. Then the whole population cleared into the forest, expecting all kinds of calamities to happen, while, on the other hand, the steamer Fresleven commanded left also in a bad panic, in charge of the engineer, I believe. Afterwards nobody seemed to trouble much about Fresleven's remains, till I got out and stepped into his shoes. I couldn't let it rest, though; but when an opportunity offered at last to meet my predecessor, the grass growing through his ribs was tall enough to hide his bones. They were all there. The supernatural being had not been touched after he fell. And the village was deserted, the huts gaped black, rotting, all askew within the fallen enclosures. A calamity had come on it, sure enough. The people had vanished. Mad terror had scattered them, men, women, and children, through the bush, and they had never returned. What became of the hens I don't know either. I should think the cause of progress got them, anyhow. However, through this glorious affair I got my appointment, before I had fairly begun to hope for it.

"I flew around like mad to get ready, and before forty-eight hours I was crossing the Channel to show myself to my employers, and sign the contract. In a very few hours I arrived in a city that always makes me think of a whited sepulchre. Prejudice no doubt. I had no difficulty in finding the Company's offices. It was the biggest thing in the town, and everybody I met was full of it. They were going to run an over-sea empire, and make no end of coin by trade.

"A narrow and deserted street in deep shadow, high houses, innumerable windows with venetian blinds, a dead silence, grass sprouting between the stones, imposing carriage archways right and left, immense double doors standing ponderously ajar. I slipped through one of these cracks, went up a swept and ungarnished staircase, as arid as a desert, and opened the first door I came to. Two women, one fat and the other slim, sat on straw-bottomed chairs, knitting black wool. The slim one got up and walked straight at me—still knitting with downcast eyes—and only just as I began to think of getting out of her way, as you would for a somnambulist, stood still, and looked up. Her dress was as plain as an umbrella-cover, and she turned round without a word and preceded me into a waiting-room. I gave my name, and looked about. Deal table in the middle, plain chairs all round the walls, on one end a large shining map, marked with all the colours of a rainbow. There was a vast amount of red—good to see at any time, because one knows that some real work is done in there, a deuce of a lot of blue, a little green, smears of orange, and, on the East Coast, a purple patch, to show where the jolly pioneers of progress drink the jolly lager-beer. However, I wasn't going into any of these. I was going into the yellow. Dead in the centre. And the river was there—fascinating—deadly—like a snake. Ough! A door opened, a white-haired secretarial head, but wearing a compassionate expression, appeared, and a skinny forefinger beckoned me into the sanctuary. Its light was dim, and a heavy writing-desk squatted in the middle. From behind that structure came out an impression of pale plumpness in a frock-coat. The great man himself. He was five feet six, I should judge, and had his grip on the handle-end of ever so many millions. He shook hands, I fancy, murmured vaguely, was satisfied with my French. *Bon voyage.*

"In about forty-five seconds I found myself again in the waiting-room with the compassionate secretary, who, full of desolation and sympathy, made me sign some document. I believe I undertook amongst other things not to disclose any trade secrets. Well, I am not going to.

"I began to feel slightly uneasy. You know I am not used to such ceremonies, and there was something ominous in the atmosphere. It was just as though I had been let into some conspiracy—I don't know—something not quite right; and I was glad to get out. In the outer room the two women knitted black wool feverishly. People were arriving, and the younger one was walking back and forth introducing them. The old one sat on her chair. Her flat cloth slippers were propped up on a foot-warmer, and a cat reposed on her lap. She wore a starched white affair on her head, had a wart on one cheek, and silver-rimmed spectacles hung on the tip of her nose. She glanced at me above the glasses. The swift and indifferent placidity of that look troubled me. Two youths with foolish and cheery countenances were being

piloted over, and she threw at them the same quick glance of unconcerned wisdom. She seemed to know all about them and about me, too.
An eerie feeling came over me. She seemed uncanny and fateful. Often
far away there I thought of these two, guarding the door of Darkness,
knitting black wool as for a warm pall, one introducing, introducing
continuously to the unknown, the other scrutinizing the cheery and
foolish faces with unconcerned old eyes. *Ave!* Old knitter of black
wool. *Morituri te salutant.* Not many of those she looked at ever saw her
again—not half, by a long way.

"There was yet a visit to the doctor. 'A simple formality,' assured
me the secretary, with an air of taking an immense part in all my sorrows. Accordingly a young chap wearing his hat over the left eyebrow,
some clerk I suppose—there must have been clerks in the business,
though the house was as still as a house in a city of the dead—came
from somewhere upstairs, and led me forth. He was shabby and careless,
with ink-stains on the sleeves of his jacket, and his cravat was large and
billowy, under a chin shaped liked the toe of an old boot. It was a little
too early for the doctor, so I proposed a drink, and thereupon he developed a vein of joviality. As we sat over our vermuths he glorified the
Company's business, and by-and-by I expressed casually my surprise at
him not going out there. He became very cool and collected all at
once. 'I am not such a fool as I look, quoth Plato to his disciples,' he
said sententiously, emptied his glass with great resolution, and we rose.

"The old doctor felt my pulse, evidently thinking of something else
the while. 'Good, good for there,' he mumbled, and then with a certain
eagerness asked me whether I would let him measure my head. Rather
surprised, I said Yes, when he produced a thing like calipers and got the
dimensions back and front and every way, taking notes carefully. He
was an unshaven little man in a threadbare coat like a gaberdine, with
his feet in slippers, and I thought him a harmless fool. 'I always ask
leave, in the interests of science, to measure the crania of those going
out there,' he said. 'And when they come back, too?' I asked. 'Oh, I
never see them,' he remarked; 'and, moreover, the changes take place
inside, you know.' He smiled, as if at some quiet joke. 'So you are going
out there. Famous. Interesting, too.' He gave me a searching glance,
and made another note. 'Ever any madness in your family?' he asked, in
a matter-of-fact tone. I felt very annoyed. 'Is that question in the interests of science, too?' 'It would be,' he said, without taking notice of my
irritation, 'interesting for science to watch the mental changes of individuals, on the spot, but . . .' 'Are you an alienist?' I interrupted. 'Every
doctor should be—a little,' answered that original, imperturbably. 'I
have a little theory which you Messieurs who go out there must help
me to prove. This is my share in the advantages my country shall reap
from the possession of such a magnificent dependency. The mere
wealth I leave to others. Pardon my questions, but you are the first

hman coming under my observation . . .' I hastened to assure him
not in the least typical. 'If I were,' said I, 'I wouldn't be talking
like this with you.' 'What you say is rather profound, and probably erro-
neous,' he said, with a laugh. 'Avoid irritation more than exposure to
the sun. Adieu. How do you English say, eh? Good-bye. Ah! Good-bye.
Adieu. In the tropics one must before everything keep calm.' . . . He
lifted a warning forefinger. . . . 'Du calme, du calme. Adieu.'

"One thing more remained to do—say good-bye to my excellent
aunt. I found her triumphant. I had a cup of tea—the last decent cup of
tea for many days—and in a room that most soothingly looked just as
you would expect a lady's drawing-room to look, we had a long quiet
chat by the fireside. In the course of these confidences it became quite
plain to me I had been represented to the wife of the high dignitary,
and goodness knows to how many more people besides, as an exceptional and gifted creature—a piece of good fortune for the Company—
a man you don't get hold of every day. Good heavens! and I was going
to take charge of a two-penny-half-penny river-steamboat with a penny
whistle attached! It appeared, however, I was also one of the Workers,
with a capital—you know. Something like an emissary of light, something like a lower sort of apostle. There had been a lot of such rot let
loose in print and talk just about that time, and the excellent woman,
living right in the rush of all that humbug, got carried off her feet. She
talked about 'weaning those ignorant millions from their horrid ways,'
till, upon my word, she made me quite uncomfortable. I ventured to
hint that the Company was run for profit.

"'You forget, dear Charlie, that the labourer is worthy of his hire,'
she said, brightly. It's queer how out of touch with truth women are.
They live in a world of their own, and there had never been anything
like it, and never can be. It is too beautiful altogether, and if they were
to set it up it would go to pieces before the first sunset. Some confounded fact we men have been living contentedly with ever since the
day of creation would start up and knock the whole thing over.

"After this I got embraced, told to wear flannel, be sure to write
often, and so on—and I left. In the street—I don't know why—a queer
feeling came to me that I was an impostor. Odd thing that I, who used
to clear out for any part of the world at twenty-four hours' notice, with
less thought than most men give to the crossing of a street, had a
moment—I won't say of hesitation, but of startled pause, before this
commonplace affair. The best way I can explain it to you is by saying
that, for a second or two, I felt as though, instead of going to the centre
of a continent, I were about to set off for the centre of the earth.

"I left in a French steamer, and she called in every blamed port they
have out there, for, as far as I could see, the sole purpose of landing soldiers and custom-house officers. I watched the coast. Watching a coast
as it slips by the ship is like thinking about an enigma. There it is

before you—smiling, frowning, inviting, grand, mean, insipid, or savage, and always mute with an air of whispering, Come and find out. This one was almost featureless, as if still in the making, with an aspect of monotonous grimness. The edge of a colossal jungle, so dark-green as to be almost black, fringed with white surf, ran straight, like a ruled line, far, far away along a blue sea whose glitter was blurred by a creeping mist. The sun was fierce, the land seemed to glisten and drip with steam. Here and there greyish-whitish specks showed up clustered inside the white surf, with a flag flying above them perhaps. Settlements some centuries old, and still no bigger than pinheads on the untouched expanse of their background. We pounded along, stopped, landed soldiers; went on, landed custom-house clerks, presumably. Some, I heard, got drowned in the surf; but whether they did or not, nobody seemed particularly to care. They were just flung out there, and on we went. every day the coast looked the same, as though we had not moved; but we passed various places—trading places—with names like Gran' Bassam, Little Popo; names that seemed to belong to some sordid farce acted in front of a sinister back-cloth. The idleness of a passenger, my isolation amongst all these men with whom I had no point of contact, the oily and languid sea, the uniform sombreness of the coast, seemed to keep me away from the truth of things, within the toil of a mournful and senseless delusion. The voice of the surf now and then was a positive pleasure, like the speech of a brother. It was something natural, that had its reason, that had a meaning. Now and then a boat from the shore gave one a momentary contact with reality. It was paddled by black fellows. You could see from afar the white of their eyeballs glistening. They shouted, sang; their bodies streamed with perspiration; they had faces like grotesque masks—these chaps; but they had bone, muscle, a wild vitality, and intense energy of movement, that was as natural and true as the surf along their coast. They wanted no excuse for being there. They were a great comfort to look at. For a time I would feel I belonged still to a world of straight-forward facts; but the feeling would not last long. Something would turn up to scare it away. Once, I remember, we came upon a man-of-war anchored off the coast. There wasn't even a shed there, and she was shelling the bush. It appears the French had one of their wars going on thereabouts. Her ensign dropped limp like a rag; the muzzles of the long six-inch guns stuck out all over the low hull; the greasy, slimy swell swung her up lazily and let her down, swaying her thin masts. In the empty immensity of earth, sky, and water, there she was, incomprehensible, firing into a continent. Pop, would go one of the six-inch guns; a small flame would dart and vanish, a little white smoke would disappear, a tiny projectile would give a feeble screech—and nothing happened. Nothing could happen. There was a touch of insanity in the proceeding, a sense of lugubrious drollery in the sight; and it was not dissipated by somebody on board assuring me earnestly there was a camp of natives—he called them enemies!—hidden out of sight somewhere.

"We gave her her letters (I heard the men in that lonely ship were dying of fever at the rate of three a-day) and went on. We called at some more places with farcical names, where the merry dance of death and trade goes on in a still and earthy atmosphere as of an overheated catacomb; all along the formless coast bordered by dangerous surf, as if Nature herself had tried to ward off intruders; in and out of rivers, streams of death in life, whose banks were rotting into mud, whose waters, thickened into slime, invaded the contorted mangroves, that seemed to writhe at us in the extremity of an impotent despair. Nowhere did we stop long enough to get a particularized impression, but the general sense of vague and oppressive wonder grew upon me. It was like a weary pilgrimage amongst hints for nightmares.

"It was upward of thirty days before I saw the mouth of the big river. We anchored off the seat of the government. But my work would not begin till some two hundred miles farther on. So as soon as I could I made a start for a place thirty miles higher up.

"I had my passage on a little sea-going steamer. Her captain was a Swede, and knowing me for a seaman, invited me on the bridge. He was a young man, lean, fair, and morose, with lanky hair and a shuffling gait. As we left the miserable little wharf, he tossed his head contemptuously at the shore. 'Been living there?' he asked. I said, 'Yes.' 'Fine lot these government chaps—are they not?' he went on, speaking English with great precision and considerable bitterness. 'It is funny what some people will do for a few francs a-month. I wonder what becomes of that kind when it goes up country?' I said to him I expected to see that soon. 'So-o-o!' he exclaimed. He shuffled athwart, keeping one eye ahead vigilantly. 'Don't be too sure,' he continued. 'The other day I took up a man who hanged himself on the road. He was a Swede, too.' 'Hanged himself! Why, in God's name?' I cried. He kept on looking out watchfully. 'Who knows? The sun too much for him, or the country perhaps.'

"At last we opened a reach. A rocky cliff appeared, mounds of turned-up earth by the shore, houses on a hill, others with iron roofs, amongst a waste of excavations, or hanging to the declivity. A continuous noise of the rapids above hovered over this scene of inhabited devastation. A lot of people, mostly black and naked, moved about like ants. A jetty projected into the river. A blinding sunlight drowned all this at times in a sudden recrudescence of glare. 'There's your Company's station,' said the Swede, pointing to three wooden barrack-like structures on the rocky slope. 'I will send your things up. Four boxes did you say? So. Farewell.'

"I came upon a boiler wallowing in the grass, then found a path leading up the hill. It turned aside for the boulders, and also for an undersized railway-truck lying there on its back with its wheels in the air. One was off. The thing looked as dead as the carcass of some animal. I came upon more pieces of decaying machinery, a stack of rusty rails. To the left a clump of trees made a shady spot, where dark things seemed to stir feebly. I blinked, the path was steep. A horn tooted to the right, and I saw the black people run. A heavy and dull detonation shook the ground, a puff of smoke came out of the cliff, and that was all. No change appeared on the face of the rock. They were building a railway. The cliff was not in the way or anything; but this objectless blasting was all the work going on.

"A slight clinking behind me made me turn my head. Six black men advanced in a file, toiling up the path. They walked erect and slow, balancing small baskets full of earth on their heads, and the clink kept time with their footsteps. Black rags were wound round their loins, and the short ends behind waggled to and fro like tails. I could see every rib, the joints of their limbs were like knots in a rope; each had an iron collar on his neck, and all were connected together with a chain whose bights swung between them, rhythmically clinking. Another report from the cliff make me think suddenly of that ship of war I had seen firing into a continent. It was the same kind of ominous voice; but these men could by no stretch of imagination be called enemies. They were called criminals, and the outraged law, like the bursting shells, had come to them, an insoluble mystery from the sea. All their meagre breasts panted together, the violently dilated nostrils quivered, the eyes stared stonily uphill. They passed me within six inches, without a glance, with that complete, deathlike indifference of unhappy savages. Behind this raw matter one of the reclaimed, the product of the new forces at work, strolled despondently, carrying a rifle by its middle. He had a uniform jacket with one button off, and seeing a white man on the path, hoisted his weapon to his shoulder with alacrity. This was simple prudence, white men being so much alike at a distance that he could not tell who I might be. He was speedily reassured, and with a large, white, rascally grin, and a glance at his charge, seemed to take me into partnership in his exalted trust. After all, I also was a part of the great cause of these high and just proceedings.

"Instead of going up, I turned and descended to the left. My idea was to let that chain-gang get out of sight before I climbed the hill. You know I am not particularly tender; I've had to strike and to fend off. I've had to resist and to attack sometimes—that's only one way of resisting—without counting the exact cost, according to the demands of such sort of life as I had blundered into. I've seen the devil of violence, and the devil of greed, and the devil of hot desire; but, by all the stars! these were strong, lusty, red-eyed devils, that swayed and drove men—men, I tell you. But as I stood on this hillside, I foresaw that in the blinding sunshine of that land I would become acquainted with a flabby, pretending, weak-eyed devil of a rapacious and pitiless folly. How insidious he could be, too, I was only to find out several months later and a thousand miles farther. For a moment I stood appalled, as though by a warning. Finally I descended the hill, obliquely, towards the trees I had seen.

"I avoided a vast artificial hole somebody had been digging on the slope, the purpose of which I found it impossible to divine. It wasn't a quarry or a sandpit, anyhow. It was just a hole. It might have been connected with the philanthropic desire of giving the criminals something to do. I don't know. Then I nearly fell into a very narrow ravine, almost no more than a scar in the hillside. I discovered that a lot of imported drainage-pipes for the settlement had been tumbled in there. There wasn't one that was not broken. It was a wanton smash-up. At last I got under the trees. My purpose was to stroll into the shade for a moment; but no sooner within than it seemed to me I had stepped into the gloomy circle of some Inferno. The rapids were near, and an uninterrupted, uniform, headlong, rushing noise filled the mournful stillness of the grove, where not a breath stirred, not a leaf moved, with a mysterious sound—as though the tearing pace of the launched earth had suddenly become audible.

"Black shapes crouched, lay, sat between the trees leaning against the trunks, clinging to the earth, half coming out, half effaced within the dim light, in all the attitudes of pain, abandonment, and despair. Another mine on the cliff went off, followed by a slight shudder of the soil under my feet. The work was going on. The work! And this was the place where some of the helpers had withdrawn to die.

"They were dying slowly—it was very clear. They were not enemies, they were not criminals, they were nothing earthly now—nothing but black shadows of disease and starvation, lying confusedly in the greenish gloom. Brought from all the recesses of the coast in all the legality of time contracts, lost in uncongenial surroundings, fed on unfamiliar food, they sickened, became inefficient, and were then allowed to crawl away and rest. These moribund shapes were free as air—and nearly as thin. I began to distinguish the gleam of the eyes under the trees. Then, glancing down, I saw a face near my hand. The black bones reclined at full length with one shoulder against the tree, and slowly the eyelids rose and the sunken eyes looked up at me, enormous and vacant, a kind of blind, white flicker in the depths of the orbs, which died out slowly. The man seemed young—almost a boy—but you know with them it's hard to tell. I found nothing else to do but to offer him one of my good Swede's ship's biscuits I had in my pocket. The fingers closed slowly on it and held—there was no other movement and no other glance. He had tied a bit of white worsted round his neck—Why? Where did he get it? Was it a badge—an ornament—a charm—a propitiatory act? Was there any idea at all connected with it?

It looked startling round his black neck, this bit of white thread from beyond the seas.

"Near the same tree two more bundles of acute angles sat with their legs drawn up. One, with his chin propped on his knees, stared at nothing, in an intolerable and appalling manner: his brother phantom rested its forehead, as if overcome with a great weariness; and all about others were scattered in every pose of contorted collapse, as in some picture of a massacre or a pestilence. While I stood horror-struck, one of these creatures rose to his hands and knees, and went off on all-fours towards the river to drink. He lapped out of his hand, then sat up in the sunlight, crossing his shins in front of him, and after a time let his woolly head fall on his breastbone.

"I didn't want any more loitering in the shade, and I made haste towards the station. When near the buildings I met a white man, in such an unexpected elegance of get-up that in the first moment I took him for a sort of vision. I saw a high starched collar, white cuffs, a light alpaca jacket, snowy trousers, a clear necktie, and varnished boots. No hat. Hair parted, brushed, oiled, under a green-lined parasol held in a big white hand. He was amazing, and had a penholder behind his ear.

"I shook hands with this miracle, and I learned he was the Company's chief accountant, and that all the bookkeeping was done at this station. He had come out for a moment, he said, 'to get a breath of fresh air.' The expression sounded wonderfully odd, with its suggestion of sedentary desk-life. I wouldn't have mentioned the fellow to you at all, only it was from his lips that I first heard the name of the man who is so indissolubly connected with the memories of that time. Moreover, I respected the fellow. Yes; I respected his collars, his vast cuffs, his brushed hair. His appearance was certainly that of a hairdresser's dummy; but in the great demoralization of the land he kept up his appearance. That's backbone. His starched collars and got-up shirt-fronts were achievements of character. He had been out nearly three years; and later, I could not help asking him how he managed to sport such linen. He had just the faintest blush, and said modestly, 'I've been teaching one of the native women about the station. It was difficult. She had a distaste for the work.' Thus this man had verily accomplished something. And he was devoted to his books, which were in apple-pie order.

"Everything else in the station was in a muddle—heads, things, buildings. Strings of dusty niggers with splay feet arrived and departed; a stream of manufactured goods, rubbishy cottons, beads, and brass-wire sent into the depths of darkness, and in return came a precious trickle of ivory.

"I had to wait in the station for ten days—an eternity. I lived in a hut in the yard, but to be out of the chaos I would sometimes get into the accountant's office. It was built of horizontal planks, and so badly put together that, as he bent over his high desk, he was barred from neck to heels with narrow strips of sunlight. There was no need to open the big shutters to see. It was hot there, too; big flies buzzed fiendishly, and did not sting, but stabbed. I sat generally on the floor, while, of faultless appearance (and even slightly scented), perching on a high stool, he wrote. Sometimes he stood up for exercise. When a truckle-bed with a sick man (some invalid agent from up-country) was put in there, he exhibited a gentle annoyance. 'The groans of this sick person,' he said, 'distract my attention. And without that it is extremely difficult to guard against clerical errors in this climate.'

"One day he remarked, without lifting his head, 'In the interior you will no doubt meet Mr. Kurtz.' On my asking who Mr. Kurtz was, he said he was a first-class agent; and seeing my disappointment at this information, he added slowly, laying down his pen, 'He is a very remarkable person.' Further questions elicited from him that Mr. Kurtz was at present in charge of a trading post, a very important one, in the true ivory-country, at 'the very bottom of there. Sends in as much ivory as all the others put together . . .' He began to write again. The sick man was too ill to groan. The flies buzzed in a great peace.

"Suddenly there was a growing murmur of voices and a great tramping of feet. A caravan had come in. A violent babble of uncouth sounds burst out on the other side of the planks. All the carriers were speaking together, and in the midst of the uproar the lamentable voice of the chief agent was heard 'giving it up' tearfully for the twentieth time that day. . . . He rose slowly. 'What a frightful row,' he said. He crossed the room gently to look at the sick man, and returning, said to me, 'He does not hear.' 'What! Dead!' I asked, startled. 'No, not yet,' he answered, with great composure. Then, alluding with a toss of the head to the tumult in the station-yard, 'When one has got to make correct entries, one comes to hate those savages—hate them to the death.' He remained thoughtful for a moment. 'When you see Mr. Kurtz,' he went on, 'tell him from me that everything here'—he glanced at the desk—'is very satisfactory. I don't like to write to him—with those messengers of ours you never know who may get hold of your letter—at that Central Station.' He stared at me for a moment with his mild, bulging eyes. 'Oh, he will go far, very far,' he began again. 'He will be a somebody in the Administration before long. They, above—the Council in Europe, you know—mean him to be.'

"He turned to his work. The noise outside had ceased, and presently in going out I stopped at the door. In the steady buzz of flies the homeward-bound agent was lying flushed and insensible; the other, bent over his books, was making correct entries of perfectly correct transactions; and fifty feet below the doorstep I could see the still tree-tops of the grove of death.

"Next day I left that station at last, with a caravan of sixty men, for a two-hundred-mile tramp.

"No use telling you much about that. Paths, paths, everywhere; a stamped-in network of paths spreading over the empty land, through long grass, through burnt grass, through thickets, down and up chilly ravines, up and down stony hills ablaze with heat; and a solitude, a solitude, nobody, not a hut. The population had cleared out a long time ago. Well, if a lot of mysterious niggers armed with all kinds of fearful weapons suddenly took to travelling on the road between Deal and Gravesend, catching the yokels right and left to carry heavy loads for them, I fancy every farm and cottage thereabouts would get empty very soon. Only here the dwellings were gone, too. Still I passed through several abandoned villages. There's something pathetically childish in the ruins of grass walls. Day after day, with the stamp and shuffle of sixty pair of bare feet behind me, each pair under a 60-lb. load. Camp, cook, sleep, strike camp, march. Now and then a carrier dead in harness, at rest in the long grass near the path, with an empty water-gourd and his long staff lying by his side. A great silence around and above. Perhaps on some quiet night the tremor of far-off drums, sinking, swelling, a tremor vast, faint; a sound weird, appealing, suggestive, and wild—and perhaps with as profound a meaning as the sound of bells in a Christian country. Once a white man in an unbuttoned uniform, camping on the path with an armed escort of lank Zanzibaris, very hospitable and festive—not to say drunk. Was looking after the upkeep of the road, he declared. Can't say I saw any road or any upkeep, unless the body of a middle-aged negro, with a bullet-hole in the forehead, upon which I absolutely stumbled three miles farther on, may be considered as a permanent improvement. I had a white companion, too, not a bad chap, but rather too fleshy and with the exasperating habit of fainting on the hot hillsides, miles away from the least bit of shade and water. Annoying, you know, to hold your own coat like a parasol over a man's head while he is coming-to. I couldn't help asking him once what he meant by coming there at all. 'To make money, of course. What do you think?' he said, scornfully. Then he got fever, and had to be carried in a hammock slung under a pole. As he weighed sixteen stone I had no end of rows with the carriers. They jibbed, ran away, sneaked off with their loads in the night—quite a mutiny. So, one evening, I made a speech in English with gestures, not one of which was lost to the sixty pairs of eyes before me, and the next morning I started the hammock off in front all right. An hour afterwards I came upon the whole concern wrecked in a bush—man, hammock, groans, blankets, horrors. The heavy pole had skinned his poor nose. He was very anxious for me to kill somebody, but there wasn't the shadow of a carrier near. I remembered the old doctor—'It would be interesting for science to watch the mental changes of individuals, on the spot.' I felt I

was becoming scientifically interesting. However, all that is to no purpose. On the fifteenth day I came in sight of the big river again, and
hobbled into the Central Station. It was on a back water surrounded by
scrub and forest, with a pretty border of smelly mud on one side, and on
the three others enclosed by a crazy fence of rushes. A neglected gap
was all the gate it had, and the first glance at the place was enough to
let you see the flabby devil was running that show. White men with
long staves in their hands appeared languidly from amongst the buildings, strolling up to take a look at me, and then retired out of sight
somewhere. One of them, a stout, excitable chap with black moustaches, informed me with great volubility and many digressions, as soon
as I told him who I was, that my steamer was at the bottom of the river.
I was thunderstruck. What, how, why? Oh, it was 'all right.' The 'manager himself' was there. All quite correct. 'Everybody had behaved
splendidly! splendidly!'—'You must,' he said in agitation, 'go and see
the general manager at once. He is waiting!'

"I did not see the real significance of that wreck at once. I fancy I
see it now, but I am not sure—not at all. Certainly the affair was too
stupid—when I think of it—to be altogether natural. Still . . . But at
the moment it presented itself simply as a confounded nuisance. The
steamer was sunk. They had started two days before in a sudden hurry
up the river with the manager on board, in charge of some volunteer
skipper, and before they had been out three hours they tore the bottom
out of her on stones, and she sank near the south bank. I asked myself
what I was to do there, now my boat was lost. As a matter of fact, I had
plenty to do in fishing my command out of the river. I had to set about
it the very next day. That, and the repairs when I brought the pieces to
the station, took some months.

"My first interview with the manager was curious. He did not ask
me to sit down after my twenty-mile walk that morning. He was commonplace in complexion, in feature, in manners, and in voice. He was
of middle size and of ordinary build. His eyes, of the usual blue, were
perhaps remarkably cold, and he certainly could make his glance fall on
one as trenchant and heavy as an axe. But even at these times the rest
of his person seemed to disclaim the intention. Otherwise there was
only an indefinable, faint expression of his lips, something stealthy—a
smile—not a smile—I remember it, but I can't explain. It was unconscious, this smile was, though just after he had said something it got
intensified for an instant. It came at the end of his speeches like a seal
applied on the words to make the meaning of the commonest phrase
appear absolutely inscrutable. He was a common trader, from his youth
up employed in these parts—nothing more. He was obeyed, yet he
inspired neither love nor fear, nor even respect. He inspired uneasiness.
That was it! Uneasiness. Not a definite mistrust—just uneasiness—
nothing more. You have no idea how effective such a . . . a . . . faculty

can be. He had no genius for organizing, for initiative, or for order even. That was evident in such things as the deplorable state of the station. He had no learning, and no intelligence. His position had come to him—why? Perhaps because he was never ill . . . He had served three terms of three years out there . . . Because triumphant health in the general rout of constitutions is a kind of power in itself. When he went home on leave he rioted on a large scale—pompously. Jack ashore— with a difference—in externals only. This one could gather from his casual talk. He originated nothing, he could keep the routine going— that's all. But he was great. He was great by this little thing that it was impossible to tell what could control such a man. He never gave that secret away. Perhaps there was nothing within him. Such a suspicion made one pause—for out there there were no external checks. Once when various tropical diseases had laid low almost every 'agent' in the station, he was heard to say, 'Men who come out here should have no entrails.' He sealed the utterance with that smile of his, as though it had been a door opening into a darkness he had in his keeping. You fancied you had seen things—but the seal was on. When annoyed at meal-times by the constant quarrels of the white men about precedence, he ordered an immense round table to be made, for which a special house had to be built. This was the station's mess-room. Where he sat was the first place—the rest were nowhere. One felt this to be his unalterable conviction. He was neither civil nor uncivil. He was quiet. He allowed his 'boy'—an overfed young Negro from the coast—to treat the white men, under his very eyes, with provoking insolence.

"He began to speak as soon as he saw me. I had been very long on the road. He could not wait. Had to start without me. The up-river stations had to be relieved. There had been so many delays already that he did not know who was dead and who was alive, and how they got on— and so on, and so on. He paid no attention to my explanations, and, playing with a stick of sealing-wax, repeated several times that the situation was 'very grave, very grave.' There were rumours that a very important station was in jeopardy, and its chief, Mr. Kurtz, was ill. Hoped it was not true. Mr. Kurtz was . . . I felt weary and irritable. Hang Kurtz, I thought. I interrupted him by saying I had heard of Mr. Kurtz on the coast. 'Ah! So they talk of him down there,' he murmured to himself. Then he began again, assuring me Mr. Kurtz was the best agent he had, an exceptional man, of the greatest importance to the Company; therefore I could understand his anxiety. He was, he said, 'very, very uneasy.' Certainly he fidgeted on his chair a good deal, exclaimed, 'Ah, Mr. Kurtz!', broke the stick of sealing-wax and seemed dumbfounded by the accident. Next thing he wanted to know 'how long it would take to' . . . I interrupted him again. Being hungry, you know, and kept on my feet, too, I was getting savage. 'How could I tell?' I said. 'I hadn't even seen the wreck yet—some months, no doubt.' All this talk seemed to me so futile. 'Some months,' he said. 'Well, let us say three months before we can make a start. Yes. That ought to do the affair.' I flung out of his hut (he lived all alone in a clay hut with a sort of verandah) muttering to myself my opinion of him. He was a chattering idiot. Afterwards I took it back when it was borne in upon me startlingly with what extreme nicety he had estimated the time requisite for the 'affair.'

"I went to work the next day, turning, so to speak, my back on that station. In that way only it seemed to me I could keep my hold on the redeeming facts of life. Still, one must look about sometimes; and then I saw this station, these men strolling aimlessly about in the sunshine of the yard. I asked myself sometimes what it all meant. They wandered here and there with their absurd long staves in their hands, like a lot of faithless pilgrims bewitched inside a rotten fence. The word 'ivory' rang in the air, was whispered, was sighed. You would think they were praying to it. A taint of imbecile rapacity blew through it all, like a whiff from some corpse. By Jove! I've never seen anything so unreal in my life. And outside, the silent wilderness surrounding this cleared speck on the earth struck me as something great and invincible, like evil or truth, waiting patiently for the passing away of this fantastic invasion.

"Oh, these months! Well, never mind. Various things happened. One evening a grass shed full of calico, cotton print, beads, and I don't know what else, burst into a blaze so suddenly that you would have thought the earth had opened to let an avenging fire consume all that trash. I was smoking my pipe quietly by my dismantled steamer, and saw them all cutting capers in the light, with their arms lifted high, when the stout man with moustaches came tearing down to the river, a tin pail in his hand, assured me that everybody was 'behaving splendidly, splendidly,' dipped about a quart of water and tore back again. I noticed there was a hole in the bottom of his pail.

"I strolled up. There was no hurry. You see the thing had gone off like a box of matches. It had been hopeless from the very first. The flame had leaped high, driven everybody back, lighted up everything—and collapsed. The shed was already a heap of embers glowing fiercely. A nigger was being beaten near by. They said he had caused the fire in some way; be that as it may, he was screeching most horribly. I saw him, later, for several days, sitting in a bit of shade looking very sick and trying to recover himself: afterwards he arose and went out—and the wilderness without a sound took him into its bosom again. As I approached the glow from the dark I found myself at the back of two men, talking. I heard the name of Kurtz pronounced, then the words, 'take advantage of this unfortunate accident.' One of the men was the manager. I wished him a good evening. 'Did you ever see anything like it—eh? it is incredible,' he said, and walked off. The other man remained. He was a first-class agent, young, gentlemanly, a bit reserved, with a forked little beard and a hooked nose. He was stand-offish with the other agents, and they on their side said he was the manager's spy upon them. As to me, I had hardly ever spoken to him before. We got into talk, and by-and-by we strolled away from the hissing ruins. Then he asked me to his room, which was in the main building of the station. He struck a match, and I perceived that this young aristocrat had not only a silver-mounted dressing-case but also a whole candle all to himself. Just at that time the manager was the only man supposed to have any right to candles. Native mats covered the clay walls; a collection of spears, assegais, shields, knives was hung up in trophies. The business entrusted to this fellow was the making of bricks—so I had been informed; but there wasn't a fragment of a brick anywhere in the station, and he had been there more than a year—waiting. It seems he could not make bricks without something. I don't know what—straw maybe. Anyway, it could not be found there, and as it was not likely to be sent from Europe, it did not appear clear to me what he was waiting for. An act of special creation perhaps. However, they were all waiting—all the sixteen or twenty pilgrims of them—for something; and upon my word it did not seem an uncongenial occupation, from the way they took it, though the only thing that ever came to them was disease—as far as I could see. They beguiled the time by backbiting and intriguing against each other in a foolish kind of way. There was an air of plotting about that station, but nothing came of it, of course. It was as unreal as everything else—as the philanthropic pretence of the whole concern, as their talk, as their government, as their show of work. The only real feeling was a desire to get appointed to a trading-post where ivory was to be had, so that they could earn percentages. They intrigued and slandered and hated each other only on that account—but as to effectually lifting a little finger—oh, no. By heavens! there is something after all in the world allowing one man to steal a horse while another must not look at a halter. Steal a horse straight out. Very well. He has done it. Perhaps he can ride. But there is a way of looking at a halter that would provoke the most charitable of saints into a kick.

"I had no idea why he wanted to be sociable, but as we chatted in there it suddenly occurred to me the fellow was trying to get at something—in fact, pumping me. He alluded constantly to Europe, to the people I was supposed to know there—putting leading questions as to my acquaintances in the sepulchral city, and so on. His little eyes glittered like mica discs—with curiosity—though he tried to keep up a bit of superciliousness. At first I was astonished, but very soon I became awfully curious to see what he would find out from me. I couldn't possibly imagine what I had in me to make it worth his while. It was very pretty to see how he baffled himself, for in truth my body was full only of chills, and my head had nothing in it but that wretched steamboat business. It was evident he took me for a perfectly shameless prevaricator. At last he got angry, and to conceal a movement of furious annoyance, he yawned. I rose. Then I noticed a small sketch in oils, on a panel, representing a woman, draped and blindfolded, carrying a lighted torch. The background was sombre—almost black. The movement of the woman was stately, and the effect of the torch-light on the face was sinister.

"It arrested me, and he stood by civilly, holding an empty half-pint champagne bottle (medical comforts) with the candle stuck in it. To my question he said Mr. Kurtz had painted this—in this very station more than a year ago—while waiting for means to go to his trading-post. 'Tell me, pray,' said I, 'who is this Mr. Kurtz?'

"'The chief of the Inner Station,' he answered in a short tone, looking away. 'Much obliged,' I said, laughing. 'And you are the brickmaker of the Central Station. Everyone knows that.' He was silent for a while. 'He is a prodigy,' he said at last. 'He is an emissary of pity, and science, and progress, and devil knows what else. We want,' he began to declaim suddenly, 'for the guidance of the cause entrusted to us by Europe, so to speak, higher intelligence, wide sympathies, a singleness of purpose.' 'Who says that?' I asked. 'Lots of them,' he replied. 'Some even write that; and so *he* comes here, a special being, as you ought to know.' 'Why ought I to know?' I interrupted, really surprised. He paid no attention. 'Yes. Today he is chief of the best station, next year he will be assistant-manager, two years more and . . . but I daresay you know what he will be in two years' time. You are of the new gang—the gang of virtue. The same people who sent him specially also recommended you. Oh, don't say no. I've my own eyes to trust.' Light dawned upon me. My dear aunt's influential acquaintances were producing an unexpected effect upon that young man. I nearly burst into a laugh. 'Do you read the Company's confidential correspondence?' I asked. He hadn't a word to say. It was great fun. 'When Mr. Kurtz,' I continued, severely, 'is General Manager, you won't have the opportunity.'

"He blew the candle out suddenly, and we went outside. The moon had risen. Black figures strolled about listlessly, pouring water on the glow, whence proceeded a sound of hissing; steam ascended in the moonlight, the beaten nigger groaned somewhere. 'What a row the brute makes!' said the indefatigable man with the moustaches, appearing near us. 'Serve him right. Transgression—punishment—bang! Pitiless, pitiless. That's the only way. This will prevent all conflagrations for the future. I was just telling the manager . . .' He noticed my companion, and became crestfallen all at once. 'Not in bed yet,' he said, with a kind of servile heartiness; 'it's so natural. Ha! Danger—agitation.' He vanished. I went on to the riverside, and the other followed me. I heard a scathing murmur at my ear, 'Heap of muffs—go to.' The pilgrims could be seen in knots gesticulating, discussing. Several had still their staves in their hands. I verily believe they took these sticks to bed with them. Beyond the fence the forest stood up spectrally in the moonlight, and through the dim stir, through the faint sounds of that lamentable courtyard, the silence of the land went home to one's very heart—its mystery, its greatness, the amazing reality of its concealed life. The hurt nigger moaned feebly somewhere near by, and then fetched a deep sigh that made me mend my pace away from there. I felt a hand introducing itself under my arm. 'My dear sir,' said the fellow, 'I don't want to be misunderstood, and especially by you, who will see Mr. Kurtz long before I can have that pleasure. I wouldn't like him to get a false idea of my disposition. . . .'

"I let him run on, this papier-maché Mephistopheles, and it seemed to me that if I tried I could poke my forefinger through him, and would find nothing inside but a little loose dirt, maybe. He, don't you see, had been planning to be assistant-manager by-and-by under the present man, and I could see that the coming of that Kurtz had upset them both not a little. He talked precipitately, and I did not try to stop him. I had my shoulders against the wreck of my steamer, hauled up on the slope like a carcass of some big river animal. The smell of mud, of primeval mud, by Jove! was in my nostrils, the high stillness of primeval forest was before my eyes; there were shiny patches on the black creek. The moon had spread over everything a thin layer of silver—over the rank grass, over the mud, upon the wall of matted vegetation standing higher than the wall of a temple, over the great river I could see through a sombre gap glittering, glittering, as it flowed broadly by without a murmur. All this was great, expectant, mute, while the man jabbered about himself. I wondered whether the stillness on the face of the immensity looking at us two were meant as an appeal or as a menace. What were we who had strayed in here? Could we handle that dumb thing, or would it handle us? I felt how big, how confoundedly big, was that thing that couldn't talk, and perhaps was deaf as well. What was in there? I could see a little ivory coming out from there, and I had heard Mr. Kurtz was in there. I had heard enough about it, too—God knows! Yet somehow it didn't bring any image with it—no more than if I had been told an angel or a fiend was in there. I believed it in the same way one of you might believe there are inhabitants in the planet Mars. I knew once a Scotch sailmaker who was certain, dead sure, there were people in Mars. If you asked him for some idea how they looked and behaved, he would get shy and mutter something about 'walking on all fours.' If you as much as smiled, he would—though a man of sixty—offer to fight you. I would not have gone so far as to fight for Kurtz, but I went for him near enough to a lie. You know I hate, detest, and can't bear a lie, not because I am straighter than the rest of us, but simply because it appals me. There is a taint of death, a flavour of mortality in lies—which is exactly what I hate and detest in the world—what I want to forget. It makes me miserable and sick, like biting something rotten would do. Temperament, I suppose. Well, I went near enough to it by letting the young fool there believe anything he liked to imagine as to my influence in Europe. I became in an instant as much of a pretence as the rest of the bewitched pilgrims. This simply because I had a notion it somehow would be of help to that Kurtz whom at the time I did not see—you understand. He was just a word for me. I did not see the man in the name any more than you do. Do you see him? Do you see the story? Do you see anything? It seems to me I am trying to tell you a dream—making a vain attempt, because no relations of a dream can convey the dream-sensation, that commingling of absurdity, surprise, and bewilderment in a tremor of struggling revolt, that notion of being captured by the incredible which is of the very essence of dreams. . . ."

He was silent for a while.

". . . No, it is impossible; it is impossible to convey the life-sensation of any given epoch of one's existence—that which makes its truth, its meaning—its subtle and penetrating essence. It is impossible. We live, as we dream—alone. . . ."

He paused again as if reflecting, then added—

"Of course in this you fellows see more than I could then. You see me, whom you know. . . ."

It had become so pitch dark that we listeners could hardly see one another. For a long time already he, sitting apart, had been no more to us than a voice. There was not a word from anybody. The others might have been asleep, but I was awake. I listened, I listened on the watch for the sentence, for the word, that would give me the clue to the faint uneasiness inspired by this narrative that seemed to shape itself without human lips in the heavy night-air of the river.

". . . Yes—I let him run on," Marlow began again, "and think what he pleased about the powers that were behind me. I did! And there was nothing behind me! There was nothing but that wretched, old, mangled steamboat I was leaning against, while he talked fluently about 'the necessity for every man to get on.' 'And when one comes out here, you conceive, it is not to gaze at the moon.' Mr. Kurtz was a 'universal genius,' but even a genius would find it easier to work with 'adequate tools—intelligent men.' He did not make bricks—why, there was a physical impossibility in the way—as I was well aware; and if he did secretarial work for the manager, it was because 'no sensible man rejects wantonly the confidence of his superiors.' Did I see it? I saw it. What more did I want? What I really wanted was rivets, by heaven! Rivets. To get on with the work—to stop the hole. Rivets I wanted. There were cases of them down at the coast—cases—piled up—burst— split! You kicked a loose rivet at every second step in that station yard on the hillside. Rivets had rolled into the grove of death. You could fill your pockets with rivets for the trouble of stooping down—and there wasn't one rivet to be found where it was wanted. We had plates that would do, but nothing to fasten them with. And every week the messenger, a lone negro, letter-bag on shoulder and staff in hand, left our station for the coast. And several times a week a coast caravan came in with trade goods—ghastly glazed calico that made you shudder only to look at it, glass beads value about a penny a quart, confounded spotted cotton handkerchiefs. And no rivets. Three carriers could have brought all that was wanted to set that steamboat afloat.

"He was becoming confidential now, but I fancy my unresponsive attitude must have exasperated him at last, for he judged it necessary to inform me he feared neither God nor devil, let alone any mere man. I said I could see that very well, but what I wanted was a certain quantity of rivets—and rivets were what really Mr. Kurtz wanted, if he had only known it. Now letters went to the coast every week. . . . 'My dear sir,' he cried, 'I write from dictation.' I demanded rivets. There was a way—for an intelligent man. He changed his manner; became very cold, and suddenly began to talk about a hippopotamus; wondered whether sleeping on board the steamer (I stuck to my salvage night and day) I wasn't disturbed. There was an old hippo that had the bad habit of getting out on the bank and roaming at night over the station grounds. The pilgrims used to turn out in a body and empty every rifle they could lay hands on at him. Some even had sat up o' nights for him. All this energy was wasted, though. 'That animal has a charmed life,' he said; 'but you can say this only of brutes in this country. No man—you apprehend me?—no man here bears a charmed life.' He stood there for a moment in the moonlight with his delicate hooked nose set a little askew, and his mica eyes glittering without a wink, then, with a curt Good-night, he strode off. I could see he was disturbed and considerably puzzled, which made me feel more hopeful than I had been for days. It was a great comfort to turn from that chap to my influential friend, the battered, twisted, ruined, tin-pot steamboat. I clambered on board. She rang under my feet like an empty Huntley & Palmers biscuit-tin kicked along a gutter; she was nothing so solid in make, and rather less pretty in shape, but I had expended enough hard work on her to make me love her. No influential friend would have served me better. She had given me a chance to come out a bit—to find out what I could do. No, I don't like work. I had rather laze about and think of all the fine things that can be done. I don't like work—no man does—but I like what is in the work—the chance to find yourself. Your own reality—for yourself, not for others—what no other man can ever know. They can only see the mere show, and never can tell what it really means.

"I was not surprised to see somebody sitting aft, on the deck, with his legs dangling over the mud. You see I rather chummed with the few mechanics there were in that station, whom the other pilgrims naturally despised—on account of their imperfect manners, I suppose. This was the foreman—a boiler-maker by trade—a good worker. He was a lank, bony, yellow-faced man, with big intense eyes. His aspect was worried, and his head was as bald as the palm of my hand; but his hair in falling seemed to have stuck to his chin, and had prospered in the new locality, for his beard hung down to his waist. He was a widower with six young children (he had left them in charge of a sister of his to come out there), and the passion of his life was pigeon-flying. He was an enthusiast and a connoisseur. He would rave about pigeons. After work hours he used sometimes to come over from his hut for a talk about his children and his pigeons; at work, when he had to crawl in the mud under the bottom of the steamboat, he would tie up that beard of his in a kind of white serviette he brought for the purpose. It had loops to go over his ears. In the evening he could be seen squatted on the bank rinsing that wrapper in the creek with great care, then spreading it solemnly on a bush to dry.

"I slapped him on the back and shouted 'We shall have rivets!' He scrambled to his feet exclaiming 'No! Rivets!' as though he couldn't believe his ears. Then in a low voice, 'You . . . eh?' I don't know why we behaved like lunatics. I put my finger to the side of my nose and nodded mysteriously. 'Good for you!' he cried, snapped his fingers above his head, lifting one foot. I tried to jig. We capered on the iron deck. A frightful clatter came out of that hulk, and the virgin forest on the other bank of the creek sent it back in a thundering roll upon the sleeping station. It must have made some of the pilgrims sit up in their hovels. A dark figure obscured the lighted doorway of the manager's hut, vanished, then, a second or so after, the doorway itself vanished, too. We stopped, and the silence driven away by the stamping of our feet flowed back again from the recesses of the land. The great wall of vegetation, an exuberant and entangled mass of trunks, branches, leaves, boughs, festoons, motionless in the moonlight, was like a rioting invasion of soundless life, a rolling wave of plants, piled up, crested, ready to topple over the creek, to sweep every little man of us out of his little existence. And it moved not. A deadened burst of mighty splashes and snorts reached us from afar, as though an ichthyosaurus had been taking a bath of glitter in the great river. 'After all,' said the boiler-maker in a reasonable tone, 'why shouldn't we get the rivets?' Why not, indeed! I did not know of any reason why we shouldn't. 'They'll come in three weeks,' I said, confidently.

"But they didn't. Instead of rivets there came an invasion, an infliction, a visitation. It came in sections during the next three weeks, each section headed by a donkey carrying a white man in new clothes and tan shoes, bowing from that elevation right and left to the impressed pilgrims. A quarrelsome band of footsore sulky niggers trod on the heels of the donkey; a lot of tents, camp-stools, tin boxes, white cases, brown bales would be shot down in the courtyard, and the air of mystery would deepen a little over the muddle of the station. Five such instalments came, with their absurd air of disorderly flight with the loot of innumerable outfit shops and provision stores, that, one would think, they were lugging, after a raid, into the wilderness for equitable division. It was an inextricable mess of things decent in themselves but that human folly made look like spoils of thieving.

"This devoted band called itself the Eldorado Exploring Expedition, and I believe they were sworn to secrecy. Their talk, however, was the talk of sordid buccaneers: it was reckless without hardihood, greedy without audacity, and cruel without courage; there was not an atom of foresight or of serious intention in the whole batch of them, and they did not seem aware these things are wanted for the work of the world. To tear treasure out of the bowels of the land was their desire, with no more moral purpose at the back of it than there is in burglars breaking into a safe. Who paid the expenses of the noble enterprise I don't know; but the uncle of our manager was leader of that lot.

"In exterior he resembled a butcher in a poor neighbourhood, and his eyes had a look of sleepy cunning. He carried his fat paunch with ostentation on his short legs, and during the time his gang infested the station spoke to no one but his nephew. You could see these two roaming about all day long with their heads close together in an everlasting confab.

"I had given up worrying about the rivets. One's capacity for that kind of folly is more limited than you would suppose. I said Hang!— and let things slide. I had plenty of time for meditation, and now and then I would give some thought to Kurtz. I wasn't very interested in him. No. Still, I was curious to see whether this man, who had come out equipped with moral ideas of some sort, would climb to the top after all and how he would set about his work when there."

II
"One evening as I was lying flat on the deck of my steamboat, I heard voices approaching—and there were the nephew and the uncle strolling along the bank. I laid my head on my arm again, and had nearly lost myself in a doze, when somebody said in my ear, as it were: 'I am as harmless as a little child, but I don't like to be dictated to. Am I the manager—or am I not? I was ordered to send him there. It's incredible.' . . . I became aware that the two were standing on the shore alongside the forepart of the steamboat, just below my head. I did not move; it did not occur to me to move: I was sleepy. 'It is unpleasant,' grunted the uncle. 'He has asked the Administration to be sent there,' said the other, 'with the idea of showing what he could do; and I was instructed accordingly. Look at the influence that man must have. Is it not fright-

ful?' They both agreed it was frightful, then made several bizarre remarks: 'Make rain and fine weather—one man—the Council—by the nose'—bits of absurd sentences that got the better of my drowsiness, so that I had pretty near the whole of my wits about me when the uncle said, 'The climate may do away with this difficulty for you. Is he alone there?' 'Yes,' answered the manager; 'he sent his assistant down the river with a note to me in these terms: 'Clear this poor devil out of the country, and don't bother sending more of that sort. I had rather be alone than have the kind of men you can dispose of with me.' It was more than a year ago. Can you imagine such impudence!' 'Anything since then?' asked the other, hoarsely. 'Ivory,' jerked the nephew; 'lots of it—prime sort—lots—most annoying, from him.' 'And with that?' questioned the heavy rumble. 'Invoice,' was the reply fired out, so to speak. Then silence. They had been talking about Kurtz.

"I was broad awake by this time, but, lying perfectly at ease, remained still, having no inducement to change my position. 'How did that ivory come all this way?' growled the elder man, who seemed very vexed. The other explained that it had come with a fleet of canoes in charge of an English half-caste clerk Kurtz had with him; that Kurtz had apparently intended to return himself, the station being by that time bare of goods and stores, but after coming three hundred miles, had suddenly decided to go back, which he started to do alone in a small dugout with four paddlers, leaving the half-caste to continue down the river with the ivory. The two fellows there seemed astounded at anybody attempting such a thing. They were at a loss for an adequate motive. As to me, I seemed to see Kurtz for the first time. It was a distinct glimpse: the dugout, four paddling savages, and the lone white man turning his back suddenly on the headquarters, on relief, on thoughts of home—perhaps; setting his face towards the depths of the wilderness, towards his empty and desolate station. I did not know the motive. Perhaps he was just simply a fine fellow who stuck to his work for its own sake. His name, you understand, had not been pronounced once. He was 'that man.' The half-caste, who, as far as I could see, had conducted a difficult trip with great prudence and pluck, was invariably alluded to as 'that scoundrel.' The 'scoundrel' had reported that the 'man' had been very ill—had recovered imperfectly. . . . The two below me moved away then a few paces, and strolled back and forth at some little distance. I heard: 'Military post—doctor—two hundred miles—quite alone now—unavoidable delays—nine months—no news—strange rumours.' They approached again, just as the manager was saying, 'No one, as far as I know, unless a species of wandering trader—a pestilential fellow, snapping ivory from the natives.' Who was it they were talking about now? I gathered in snatches that this was some man supposed to be in Kurtz's district, and of whom the manager did not approve. 'We will not be free from unfair competition till one of these fellows is hanged for an example,' he said. 'Certainly,' grunted the other; 'get him hanged! Why not? Anything—anything can be done in this country. That's what I say; nobody here, you understand, *here*, can endanger your position. And why? You stand the climate—you outlast them all. The danger is in Europe; but there before I left I took care to—' They moved off and whispered, then their voices rose again. 'The extraordinary series of delays is not my fault. I did my best.' The fat man sighed. 'Very sad.' 'And the pestiferous absurdity of his talk,' continued the other; 'he bothered me enough when he was here. 'Each station should be like a beacon on the road towards better things, a centre for trade of course, but also for humanizing, improving, instructing.' Conceive you—that ass! And he wants to be manager! No, it's—' Here he got choked by excessive indignation, and I lifted my head the least bit. I was surprised to see how near they were—right under me. I could have spat upon their hats. They were looking on the ground, absorbed in thought. The manager was switching his leg with a slender twig: his sagacious relative lifted his head. 'You have been well since you came out this time?' he asked. The other gave a start. 'Who? I? Oh! Like a charm—like a charm. But the rest—oh, my goodness! All sick. They die so quick, too, that I haven't the time to send them out of the country—it's incredible!' 'H'm. Just so,' grunted the uncle. 'Ah! my boy, trust to this—I say, trust to this.' I saw him extend his short flipper of an arm for a gesture that took in the forest, the creek, the mud, the river—seemed to beckon with a dishonouring flourish before the sunlit face of the land a treacherous appeal to the lurking death, to the hidden evil, to the profound darkness of its heart. It was so startling that I leaped to my feet and looked back at the edge of the forest, as though I had expected an answer of some sort to that black display of confidence. You know the foolish notions that come to one sometimes. The high stillness confronted these two figures with its ominous patience, waiting for the passing away of a fantastic invasion.

"They swore aloud together—out of sheer fright, I believe—then pretending not to know anything of my existence, turned back to the station. The sun was low; and leaning forward side by side, they seemed to be tugging painfully uphill their two ridiculous shadows of unequal length, that trailed behind them slowly over the tall grass without bending a single blade.

"In a few days the Eldorado Expedition went into the patient wilderness, that closed upon it as the sea closes over a diver. Long afterwards the news came that all the donkeys were dead. I know nothing as to the fate of the less valuable animals. They, no doubt, like the rest of us, found what they deserved. I did not inquire. I was then rather excited at the prospect of meeting Kurtz very soon. When I say very soon I mean it comparatively. It was just two months from the day we left the creek when we came to the bank below Kurtz's station.

"Going up that river was like travelling back to the earliest beginnings of the world, when vegetation rioted on the earth and the big trees were kings. An empty stream, a great silence, an impenetrable forest. The air was warm, thick, heavy, sluggish. There was no joy in the brilliance of sunshine. The long stretches of the waterway ran on, deserted, into the gloom of overshadowed distances. On silvery sandbanks hippos and alligators sunned themselves side by side. The broadening waters flowed through a mob of wooded islands; you lost your way on that river as you would in a desert, and butted all day long against shoals, trying to find the channel, till you thought yourself bewitched and cut off for ever from everything you had known once—somewhere—far away—in another existence perhaps. There were moments when one's past came back to one, as it will sometimes when you have not a moment to spare to yourself; but it came in the shape of an unrestful and noisy dream, remembered with wonder amongst the overwhelming realities of this strange world of plants, and water, and silence. And this stillness of life did not in the least resemble a peace. It was the stillness of an implacable force brooding over an inscrutable intention. It looked at you with a vengeful aspect. I got used to it afterwards; I did not see it any more; I had no time. I had to keep guessing at the channel; I had to discern, mostly by inspiration, the signs of hidden banks; I watched for sunken stones; I was learning to clap my teeth smartly before my heart flew out, when I shaved by a fluke some infernal sly old snag that would have ripped the life out of the tin-pot steamboat and drowned all the pilgrims; I had to keep a look-out for the signs of dead wood we could cut up in the night for next day's steaming. When you have to attend to things of that sort, to the mere incidents of the surface, the reality—the reality, I tell you—fades. The inner truth is hidden—luckily, luckily. But I felt it all the same; I felt often its mysterious stillness watching me at my monkey tricks, just as it watches you fellows performing on your respective tight-ropes for—what is it? half-a-crown a tumble—"

"Try to be civil, Marlow," growled a voice, and I knew there was at least one listener awake besides myself.

"I beg your pardon. I forgot the heartache which makes up the rest of the price. And indeed what does the price matter, if the trick be well done? You do your tricks very well. And I didn't do badly either, since I managed not to sink that steamboat on my first trip. It's a wonder to me yet. Imagine a blindfolded man set to drive a van over a bad road. I sweated and shivered over that business considerably, I can tell you. After all, for a seaman, to scrape the bottom of the thing that's supposed to float all the time under his care is the unpardonable sin. No one may know of it, but you never forget the thump—eh? A blow on the very heart. You remember it, you dream of it, you wake up at night and think of it—years after—and go hot and cold all over. I don't pre-

tend to say that steamboat floated all the time. More than once she had
to wade for a bit, with twenty cannibals splashing around and pushing.
We had enlisted some of these chaps on the way for a crew. Fine fellows—cannibals—in their place. They were men one could work with,
and I am grateful to them. And, after all, they did not eat each other
before my face: they had brought along a provision of hippo-meat
which went rotten, and made the mystery of the wilderness stink in my
nostrils. Phoo! I can sniff it now. I had the manager on board and three
or four pilgrims with their staves—all complete. Sometimes we came
upon a station close by the bank, clinging to the skirts of the unknown,
and the white men rushing out of a tumbledown hovel, with great gestures of joy and surprise and welcome, seemed very strange—had the
appearance of being held there captive by a spell. The word ivory
would ring in the air for a while—and on we went again into the
silence, along empty reaches, round the still bends, between the high
walls of our winding way, reverberating in hollow claps the ponderous
beat of the stern-wheel. Trees, trees, millions of trees, massive,
immense, running up high; and at their foot, hugging the bank against
the stream, crept the little begrimed steamboat, like a sluggish beetle
crawling on the floor of a lofty portico. It made you feel very small, very
lost, and yet it was not altogether depressing, that feeling. After all, if
you were small, the grimy beetle crawled on—which was just what you
wanted it to do. Where the pilgrims imagined it crawled to I don't
know. To some place where they expected to get something, I bet! For
me it crawled towards Kurtz—exclusively; but when the steam-pipes
started leaking we crawled very slow. The reaches opened before us and
closed behind, as if the forest had stepped leisurely across the water to
bar the way for our return. We penetrated deeper and deeper into the
heart of darkness. It was very quiet there. At night sometimes the roll
of drums behind the curtain of trees would run up the river and remain
sustained faintly, as if hovering in the air high over our heads, till the
first break of day. Whether it meant war, peace, or prayer we could not
tell. The dawns were heralded by the descent of a chill stillness; the
wood-cutters slept, their fires burned low; the snapping of a twig would
make you start. We were wanderers on prehistoric earth, on an earth
that wore the aspect of an unknown planet. We could have fancied
ourselves the first of men taking possession of an accursed inheritance,
to be subdued at the cost of profound anguish and of excessive toil. But
suddenly, as we struggled round a bend, there would be a glimpse of
rush walls, of peaked grass-roofs, a burst of yells, a whirl of black limbs,
a mass of hands clapping, of feet stamping, of bodies swaying, of eyes
rolling, under the droop of heavy and motionless foliage. The steamer
toiled along slowly on the edge of a black and incomprehensible frenzy.
The prehistoric man was cursing us, praying to us, welcoming us—who
could tell? We were cut off from the comprehension of our surround-

ings; we glided past like phantoms, wondering and secretly appalled, as sane men would be before an enthusiastic outbreak in a madhouse. We could not understand because we were too far and could not remember, because we were travelling in the night of first ages, of those ages that are gone, leaving hardly a sign—and no memories.

"The earth seemed unearthly. We are accustomed to look upon the shackled form of a conquered monster, but there—there you could look at a thing monstrous and free. It was unearthly, and the men were—No, they were not inhuman. Well, you know, that was the worst of it—this suspicion of their not being inhuman. It would come slowly to one. They howled and leaped, and spun, and made horrid faces; but what thrilled you was just the thought of their humanity—like yours—the thought of your remote kinship with this wild and passionate uproar. Ugly. Yes, it was ugly enough; but if you were man enough you would admit to yourself that there was in you just the faintest trace of a response to the terrible frankness of that noise, a dim suspicion of there being a meaning in it which you—you so remote from the night of first ages—could comprehend. And why not? The mind of man is capable of anything—because everything is in it, all the past as well as all the future. What was there after all? Joy, fear, sorrow, devotion, valour, rage—who can tell?—but truth—truth stripped of its cloak of time. Let the fool gape and shudder—the man knows, and can look on without a wink. But he must at least be as much of a man as these on the shore. He must meet that truth with his own true stuff—with his own inborn strength. Principles won't do. Acquisitions, clothes, pretty rags—rags that would fly off at the first good shake. No; you want a deliberate belief. An appeal to me in this fiendish row—is there? Very well; I hear; I admit, but I have a voice, too, and for good or evil mine is the speech that cannot be silenced. Of course, a fool, what with sheer fright and fine sentiments, is always safe. Who's that grunting? You wonder I didn't go ashore for a howl and a dance? Well, no—I didn't. Fine sentiments, you say? Fine sentiments, be hanged! I had no time. I had to mess about with white-lead and strips of woollen blanket helping to put bandages on those leaky steam-pipes—I tell you. I had to watch the steering, and circumvent those snags, and get the tin-pot along by hook or by crook. There was surface-truth enough in these things to save a wiser man. And between whiles I had to look after the savage who was fireman. He was an improved specimen; he could fire up a vertical boiler. He was there below me, and, upon my word, to look at him was as edifying as seeing a dog in parody of breeches and a feather hat, walking on his hind legs. A few months of training had done for that really fine chap. He squinted at the steam-gauge and at the water-gauge with an evident effort of intrepidity—and he had filed teeth, too, the poor devil, and the wool of his pate shaved into queer patterns, and three ornamental scars on each of his cheeks. He ought to have been clapping his hands and stamping his feet on the bank, instead of which he was hard at work, a thrall to strange witchcraft, full of improving knowledge. He was useful because he had been instructed; and what he knew was this—that should the water in that transparent thing disappear, the evil spirit inside the boiler would get angry through the greatness of his thirst, and take a terrible vengeance. So he sweated and fired up and watched the glass fearfully (with an impromptu charm, made of rags, tied to his arm, and a piece of polished bone, a big as a watch, stuck flatways through his lower lip), while the wooded banks slipped past us slowly, the short noise was left behind, the interminable miles of silence—and we crept on, towards Kurtz. But the snags were thick, the water was treacherous and shallow, the boiler seemed indeed to have a sulky devil in it, and thus neither that fireman nor I had any time to peer into our creepy thoughts.

"Some fifty miles below the Inner Station we came upon a hut of reeds, an inclined and melancholy pole, with the unrecognizable tatters of what had been a flag of some sort flying from it, and a neatly stacked wood-pile. This was unexpected. We came to the bank, and on the stack of firewood found a flat piece of board with some faded pencil-writing on it. When deciphered it said: 'Wood for you. Hurry up. Approach cautiously.' There was a signature, but it was illegible—not Kurtz—a much longer word. Hurry up. Where? Up the river? 'Approach cautiously.' We had not done so. But the warning could not have been meant for the place where it could be only found after approach. Something was wrong above. But what—and how much? That was the question. We commented adversely upon the imbecility of that telegraphic style. The bush around said nothing, and would not let us look very far, either. A torn curtain of red twill hung in the door-way of the hut, and flapped sadly in our faces. The dwelling was dis-mantled; but we could see a white man had lived there not very long ago. There remained a rude table—a plank on two posts; a heap of rub-bish reposed in a dark corner, and by the door I picked up a book. It had lost its covers, and the pages had been thumbed into a state of extremely dirty softness; but the back had been lovingly stitched afresh with white cotton thread, which looked clean yet. It was an extraordi-nary find. Its title was, An Inquiry into some Points of Seamanship, by a man, Tower, Towson—some such name—Master in His Majesty's Navy. The matter looked dreary reading enough, with illustrative dia-grams and repulsive tables of figures, and the copy was sixty years old. I handled this amazing antiquity with the greatest possible tenderness, lest it should dissolve in my hands. Within, Towson or Towser was inquiring earnestly into the breaking strain of ships' chains and tackle, and other such matters. Not a very enthralling book; but at the first glance you could see there a singleness of intention, an honest concern for the right way of going to work, which made these humble pages, thought out so many years ago, luminous with another than a professional light. The simple old sailor, with his talk of chains and purchases, made me forget the jungle and the pilgrims in a delicious sensation of having come upon something unmistakably real. Such a book being there was wonderful enough; but still more astounding were the notes pencilled in the margin, and plainly referring to the text. I couldn't believe my eyes! They were in cipher! Yes, it looked like cipher. Fancy a man lugging with him a book of that description into this nowhere and studying it—and making notes—in cipher at that! It was an extravagant mystery.

"I had been dimly aware for some time of a worrying noise, and when I lifted my eyes I saw the wood-pile was gone, and the manager, aided by all the pilgrims, was shouting at me from the river-side. I slipped the book into my pocket. I assure you to leave off reading was like tearing myself away from the shelter of an old and solid friendship.

"I started the lame engine ahead. 'It must be this miserable trader—this intruder,' exclaimed the manager, looking back malevolently at the place we had left. 'He must be English,' I said. 'It will not save him from getting into trouble if he is not careful,' muttered the manager darkly. I observed with assumed innocence that no man was safe from trouble in this world.

"The current was more rapid now, the steamer seemed at her last gasp, the stern-wheel flopped languidly, and I caught myself listening on tiptoe for the next beat of the boat, for in sober truth I expected the wretched thing to give up every moment. It was like watching the last flickers of a life. But still we crawled. Sometimes I would pick out a tree a little way ahead to measure our progress towards Kurtz by, but I lost it invariably before we got abreast. To keep the eyes so long on one thing was too much for human patience. The manager displayed a beautiful resignation. I fretted and fumed and took to arguing with myself whether or no I would talk openly with Kurtz; but before I could come to any conclusion it occurred to me that my speech or my silence, indeed any action of mine, would be a mere futility. What did it matter what any one knew or ignored? What did it matter who was manager? One gets sometimes such a flash of insight. The essentials of this affair lay deep under the surface, beyond my reach, and beyond my power of meddling.

"Towards the evening of the second day we judged ourselves about eight miles from Kurtz's station. I wanted to push on; but the manager looked grave, and told me the navigation up there was so dangerous that it would be advisable, the sun being very low already, to wait where we were till next morning. Moreover, he pointed out that if the warning to approach cautiously were to be followed, we must approach in daylight—not at dusk, or in the dark. This was sensible enough. Eight miles meant nearly three hours' steaming for us, and I could also see suspicious ripples at the upper end of the reach. Nevertheless, I was annoyed beyond expression at the delay, and most unreasonably, too, since one night more could not matter much after so many months. As we had plenty of wood, and caution was the word, I brought up in the middle of the stream. The reach was narrow, straight, with high sides like a railway cutting. The dusk came gliding into it long before the sun had set. The current ran smooth and swift, but a dumb immobility sat on the banks. The living trees, lashed together by the creepers and every living bush of the undergrowth, might have been changed into stone, even to the slenderest twig, to the lightest leaf. It was not sleep—it seemed unnatural, like a state of trance. Not the faintest sound of any kind could be heard. You looked on amazed, and began to suspect yourself of being deaf—then the night came suddenly, and struck you blind as well. About three in the morning some large fish leaped, and the loud splash made me jump as though a gun had been fired. When the sun rose there was a white fog, very warm and clammy, and more blinding than the night. It did not shift or drive; it was just there, standing all round you like something solid. At eight or nine, perhaps, it lifted as a shutter lifts. We had a glimpse of the towering multitude of trees, of the immense matted jungle, with the blazing little ball of the sun hanging over it—all perfectly still—and then the white shutter came down again, smoothly, as if sliding in greased grooves. I ordered the chain, which we had begun to heave in, to be paid out again. Before it stopped running with a muffled rattle, a cry, a very loud cry, as of infinite desolation, soared slowly in the opaque air. It ceased. A complaining clamour, modulated in savage discords, filled our ears. The sheer unexpectedness of it made my hair stir under my cap. I don't know how it struck the others: to me it seemed as though the mist itself had screamed, so suddenly, and apparently from all sides at once, did this tumultuous and mournful uproar arise. It culminated in a hurried outbreak of almost intolerably excessive shrieking, which stopped short, leaving us stiffened in a variety of silly attitudes, and obstinately listening to the nearly as appalling and excessive silence. 'Good God! What is the meaning—' stammered at my elbow one of the pilgrims—a little fat man, with sandy hair and red whiskers, who wore side-spring boots, and pink pyjamas tucked into his socks. Two others remained open-mouthed a whole minute, then dashed into the little cabin, to rush out incontinently and stand darting scared glances, with Winchester at 'ready' in their hands. What we could see was just the steamer we were on, her outlines blurred as though she had been on the point of dissolving, and a misty strip of water, perhaps two feet broad, around her—and that was all. The rest of the world was nowhere, as far as our eyes and ears were concerned. Just nowhere. Gone, disappeared; swept off without leaving a whisper or a shadow behind.

"I went forward, and ordered the chain to be hauled in short, so as to be ready to trip the anchor and move the steamboat at once if necessary. 'Will they attack?' whispered an awed voice. 'We will all be butchered in this fog,' murmured another. The faces twitched with the strain, the hands trembled slightly, the eyes forgot to wink. It was very curious to see the contrast of expressions of the white men and of the black fellows of our crew, who were as much strangers to that part of the river as we, though their homes were only eight hundred miles away. The whites, of course greatly discomposed, had besides a curious look of being painfully shocked by such an outrageous row. The others had an alert, naturally interested expression; but their faces were essentially quiet, even those of the one or two who grinned as they hauled at the chain. Several exchanged short, grunting phrases, which seemed to settle the matter to their satisfaction. Their headman, a young, broad-chested black, severely draped in dark-blue fringed cloths, with fierce nostrils and his hair all done up artfully in oily ringlets, stood near me. 'Aha!' I said, just for good fellowship's sake. 'Catch 'im,' he snapped, with a bloodshot widening of his eyes and a flash of sharp teeth—'catch 'im. Give 'im to us.' 'To you, eh?' I asked; 'what would you do with them?' 'Eat 'im!' he said, curtly, and, leaning his elbow on the rail, looked out into the fog in a dignified and profoundly pensive attitude. I would no doubt have been properly horrified, had it not occurred to me that he and his chaps must be very hungry: that they must have been growing increasingly hungry for at least this month past. They had been engaged for six months (I don't think a single one of them had any clear idea of time, as we at the end of countless ages have. They still belonged to the beginnings of time—had no inherited experience to teach them as it were), and of course, as long as there was a piece of paper written over in accordance with some farcical law or other made down the river, it didn't enter anybody's head to trouble how they would live. Certainly they had brought with them some rotten hippo-meat, which couldn't have lasted very long, anyway, even if the pilgrims hadn't, in the midst of a shocking hullabaloo, thrown a considerable quantity of it overboard. It looked like a high-handed proceeding; but it was really a case of legitimate self-defence. You can't breathe dead hippo waking, sleeping, and eating, and at the same time keep your precarious grip on existence. Besides that, they had given them every week three pieces of brass wire, each about nine inches long; and the theory was they were to buy their provisions with that currency in river-side villages. You can see how *that* worked. There were either no villages, or the people were hostile, or the directors, who like the rest of us fed out of tins, with an occasional old he-goat thrown in, didn't want to stop the steamer for some more or less recondite reason. So, unless they swallowed the wire itself, or made loops of it to snare the fishes with, I don't see what good their extravagant salary could be to them. I must say it was paid with a regularity worthy of a large and honourable trading company. For the rest, the only thing to eat—though it didn't look eatable in the least—I saw in their possession was a few lumps of some stuff like half-cooked dough, of a dirty lavender colour, they kept wrapped in leaves, and now and then swallowed a piece of, but so small that it seemed done more for the looks of the thing than for any serious purpose of sustenance. Why in the name of all the gnawing devils of hunger they didn't go for us—they were thirty to five—and have a good tuck in for once, amazes me now when I think of it. They were big powerful men, with not much capacity to weigh the consequences, with courage, with strength, even yet, though their skins were no longer glossy and their muscles no longer hard. And I saw that something restraining, one of those human secrets that baffle probability, had come into play there. I looked at them with a swift quickening of interest—not because it occurred to me I might be eaten by them before very long, though I own to you that just then I perceived—in a new light, as it were—how unwholesome the pilgrims looked, and I hoped, yes, I positively hoped, that my aspect was not so—what shall I say?—so—unappetizing: a touch of fantastic vanity which fitted well with the dream-sensation that pervaded all my days at that time. Perhaps I had a little fever, too. One can't live with one's finger everlastingly on one's pulse. I had often 'a little fever,' or a little touch of other things—the playful paw-strokes of the wilderness, the preliminary trifling before the more serious onslaught which came in due course. Yes; I looked at them as you would on any human being, with a curiosity of their impulses, motives, capacities, weaknesses, when brought to the test of an inexorable physical necessity. Restraint! What possible restraint? Was it superstition, disgust, patience, fear—or some kind of primitive honour? No fear can stand up to hunger, no patience can wear it out, disgust simply does not exist where hunger is; and as to superstition, beliefs, and what you may call principles, they are less than chaff in a breeze. Don't you know the devilry of lingering starvation, its exasperating torment, its black thoughts, its sombre and brooding ferocity? Well, I do. It takes a man all his inborn strength to fight hunger properly. It's really easier to face bereavement, dishonour, and the perdition of one's soul—than this kind of prolonged hunger. Sad, but true. And these chaps, too, had no earthly reason for any kind of scruple. Restraint! I would just as soon have expected restrain from a hyena prowling amongst the corpses of a battlefield. But there was the fact facing me—the fact dazzling, to be seen, like the foam on the depths of the sea, like a ripple on an unfathomable enigma, a mystery greater—when I thought of it—than the curious, inexplicable note of desperate grief in this savage clamour that had swept by us on the river-bank, behind the blind whiteness of the fog.

"Two pilgrims were quarrelling in hurried whispers as to which bank. 'Left.' 'No, no; how can you? Right, right, of course.' 'It is very serious,' said the manager's voice behind me; 'I would be desolated if anything should happen to Mr. Kurtz before we came up.' I looked at him, and had not the slightest doubt he was sincere. He was just the kind of man who would wish to preserve appearances. That was his restraint. But when he muttered something about going on at once, I did not even take the trouble to answer him. I knew, and he knew, that it was impossible. Were we to let go our hold of the bottom, we would be absolutely in the air—in space. We wouldn't be able to tell where we were going to—whether up or down stream, or across—till we fetched against one bank or the other—and then we wouldn't know at first which it was. Of course I made no move. I had no mind for a smash-up. You couldn't imagine a more deadly place for a shipwreck. Whether drowned at once or not, we were sure to perish speedily in one way or another. 'I authorize you to take all the risks,' he said, after a short silence. 'I refuse to take any,' I said, shortly; which was just the answer he expected, though its tone might have surprised him. 'Well, I must defer to your judgement. You are captain,' he said, with marked civility. I turned my shoulder to him in sign of my appreciation, and looked into the fog. How long would it last? It was the most hopeless look-out. The approach to this Kurtz grubbing for ivory in the wretched bush was beset by as many dangers as though he had been an enchanted princess sleeping in a fabulous castle. 'Will they attack, do you think?' asked the manager, in a confidential tone.

"I did not think they would attack, for several obvious reasons. The thick fog was one. If they left the bank in their canoes they would get lost in it, as we would be if we attempted to move. Still, I had also judged the jungle of both banks quite impenetrable—and yet eyes were in it, eyes that had seen us. The river-side bushes were certainly very thick; but the undergrowth behind was evidently penetrable. However, during the short lift I had seen no canoes anywhere in the reach—certainly not abreast of the steamer. But what made the idea of attack inconceivable to me was the nature of the noise—of the cries we had heard. They had not the fierce character boding of immediate hostile intention. Unexpected, wild, and violent as they had been, they had given me an irresistible impression of sorrow. The glimpse of the steamboat had for some reason filled those savages with unrestrained grief. The danger, if any, I expounded, was from our proximity to a great human passion let loose. Even extreme grief may ultimately vent itself in violence—but more generally takes the form of apathy. . . .

"You should have seen the pilgrims stare! They had no heart to grin, or even to revile me: but I believe they thought me gone mad—with fright, maybe. I delivered a regular lecture. My dear boys, it was no good bothering. Keep a look-out? Well, you may guess I watched the fog for the signs of lifting as a cat watches a mouse; but for anything else our eyes were of no more use to us than if we had been buried miles deep in a heap of cotton-wool. It felt like it, too—choking, warm, stifling. Besides, all I said, though it sounded extravagant, was absolutely true to fact. What we afterwards alluded to as an attack was really an attempt at repulse. The action was very far from being aggressive—it was not even defensive, in the usual sense: it was undertaken under the stress of desperation, and in its essence was purely protective.

"It developed itself, I should say, two hours after the fog lifted, and its commencement was at a spot, roughly speaking, about a mile and a half below Kurtz's station. We had just floundered and flopped round a bend, when I saw an inlet, a mere grassy hummock of bright green, in the middle of the stream. It was the only thing of the kind; but as we opened the reach more, I perceived it was the head of a long sandbank, or rather of a chain of shallow patches stretching down the middle of the river. They were discoloured, just awash, and the whole lot was seen just under the water, exactly as a man's backbone is seen running down the middle of his back under the skin. Now, as far I did see, I could go to the right or to the left of this. I didn't know either channel, of course. The banks looked pretty well alike, the depth appeared the same; but as I had been informed the station was on the west side, I naturally headed for the western passage.

"No sooner had we fairly entered it than I became aware it was much narrower than I had supposed. To the left of us there was the long uninterrupted shoal, and to the right a high, steep bank heavily overgrown with bushes. Above the bush the trees stood in serried ranks. The twigs overhung the current thickly, and from distance to distance a large limb of some tree projected rigidly over the stream. It was then well on in the afternoon, the face of the forest was gloomy, and a broad strip of shadow had already fallen on the water. In this shadow we steamed up—very slowly, as you may imagine. I sheered her well inshore—the water being deepest near the bank, as the sounding-pole informed me.

"One of my hungry and forbearing friends was sounding in the bows just below me. This steamboat was exactly like a decked scow. On the deck, there were two little teak-wood houses, with doors and windows. The boiler was in the fore-end, and the machinery right astern. Over the whole there was a light roof, supported on stanchions. The funnel projected through that roof, and in front of the funnel a small cabin built of light planks served for a pilot-house. It contained a couch, two camp-stools, a loaded Martini-Henry leaning in one corner, a tiny table, and the steering-wheel. It had a wide door in front and a broad shutter at each side. All these were always thrown open, of course. I spent my days perched up there on the extreme fore-end of that roof, before the door. At night I slept, or tried to, on the couch. An athletic black belonging to some coast tribe, and educated by my poor predecessor, was the helmsman. He sported a pair of brass earrings, wore a blue cloth wrapper from the waist to the ankles, and thought all the world of himself. He was the most unstable kind of fool I had ever seen. He steered with no end of a swagger while you were by; but if he lost sight of you, he became instantly the prey of an abject funk, and would let that cripple of a steamboat get the upper hand of him in a minute.

"I was looking down at the sounding-pole, and feeling much annoyed to see at each try a little more of it stick out of that river, when I saw my poleman give up the business suddenly, and stretch himself flat on the deck, without even taking the trouble to haul his pole in. He kept hold on it though, and it trailed in the water. At the same time the fireman, whom I could also see below me, sat down abruptly before his furnace and ducked his head. I was amazed. Then I had to look at the river mighty quick, because there was a snag in the fairway. Sticks, little sticks, were flying about—thick: they were whizzing before my nose, dropping below me, striking behind me against my pilot-house. All this time the river, the shore, the woods, were very quiet—perfectly quiet. I could only hear the heavy splashing thump of the stern-wheel and the patter of these things. We cleared the snag clumsily. Arrows, by Jove! We were being shot at! I stepped in quickly to close the shutter on the land-side. That fool-helmsman, his hands on the spokes, was lifting his knees high, stamping his feet, champing his mouth, like a reined-in horse. Confound him! And we were staggering within ten feet of the bank. I had to lean right out to swing the heavy shutter, and I saw a face amongst the leaves on the level with my own, looking at me very fierce and steady and then suddenly, as though a veil had been removed from my eyes, I made out, deep in the tangled gloom, naked breasts, arms, legs, glaring eyes—the bush was swarming with human limbs in movement, glistening, of bronze colour. The twigs shook, swayed, and rustled, the arrows flew out of them, and then the shutter came to. 'Steer her straight,' I said to the helmsman. He held his head rigid, face forward; but his eyes rolled, he kept on, lifting and setting down his feet gently, his mouth foamed a little. 'Keep quiet!' I said in a fury. I might just as well have ordered a tree not to sway in the wind. I darted out. Below me there was a great scuffle of feet on the iron deck; confused exclamations; a voice screamed, 'Can you turn back?' I caught sight of a V-shaped ripple on the water ahead. What? Another snag! A fusillade burst out under my feet. The pilgrims had opened with their Winchesters, and were simply squirting lead into that bush. A deuce of a lot of smoke came up and drove slowly forward. I swore at it. Now I couldn't see the ripple or the snag either. I stood in the doorway, peering, and the arrows came in swarms. They might have been poisoned, but they looked as though they wouldn't kill a cat. The bush began to howl. Our wood-cutters raised a warlike whoop; the

report of a rifle just at my back deafened me. I glanced over my shoulder, and the pilot-house was yet full of noise and smoke when I made a
dash at the wheel. The fool-nigger had dropped everything, to throw
the shutter open and let off that Martini-Henry. He stood before the
wide opening, glaring, and I yelled at him to come back, while I
straightened the sudden twist out of that steamboat. There was no
room to turn even if I had wanted to, the snag was somewhere very
near ahead in that confounded smoke, there was no time to lose, so I
just crowded her into the bank—right into the bank, where I knew the
water was deep.

"We tore slowly along the overhanging bushes in a whirl of broken
twigs and flying leaves. The fusillade below stopped short, as I had fore-
seen it would when the squirts got empty. I threw my head back to a
glinting whizz that traversed the pilot-house, in at one shutterhole and
out at the other. Looking past that mad helmsman, who was shaking
the empty rifle and yelling at the shore, I saw vague forms of men running bent double, leaping, gliding, distinct, incomplete, evanescent.
Something big appeared in the air before the shutter, the rifle went
overboard, and the man stepped back swiftly, looked at me over his
shoulder in an extraordinary, profound, familiar manner, and fell upon
my feet. The side of his head hit the wheel twice, and the end of what
appeared a long cane clattered round and knocked over a little camp-
stool. It looked as though after wrenching that thing from somebody
ashore he had lost his balance in the effort. The thin smoke had blown
away, we were clear of the snag, and looking ahead I could see that in
another hundred yards or so I would be free to sheer off, away from the
bank; but my feet felt so very warm and wet that I had to look down.
The man had rolled on his back and stared straight up at me; both his
hands clutched that cane. It was the shaft of a spear that, either thrown
or lunged through the opening, had caught him in the side just below
the ribs; the blade had gone in out of sight, after making a frightful
gash; my shoes were full; a pool of blood lay very still, gleaming dark-
red under the wheel; his eyes shone with an amazing lustre. The fusillade burst out again. He looked at me anxiously, gripping the spear like
something precious, with an air of being afraid I would try to take it
away from him. I had to make an effort to free my eyes from his gaze
and attend to the steering. With one hand I felt above my head for the
line of the steam whistle, and jerked out screech after screech hurriedly. The tumult of angry and warlike yells were checked instantly,
and then from the depths of the woods went out such a tremulous and
prolonged wail of mournful fear and utter despair as may be imagined to
follow the flight of the last hope from the earth. There was a great commotion in the bush; the shower of arrows stopped, a few dropping shots
rang out sharply—then silence, in which the languid beat of the stern-
wheel came plainly to my ears. I put the helm hard a-starboard at the

moment when the pilgrim in pink pyjamas, very hot and agitated, appeared in the doorway. 'The manager sends me—' he began in an official tone, and stopped short. 'Good God!' he said, glaring at the wounded man.

"We two whites stood over him, and his lustrous and inquiring glance enveloped us both. I declare it looked as though he would presently put to us some question in an understandable language; but he died without uttering a sound, without moving a limb, without twitching a muscle. Only in the very last moment, as though in response to some sign we could not see, to some whisper we could not hear, he frowned heavily, and that frown gave to his black death-mask an inconceivably sombre, brooding, and menacing expression. The lustre of inquiring glance faded swiftly into vacant glassiness. 'Can you steer?' I asked the agent eagerly. He looked very dubious; but I made a grab at his arm, and he understood at once I meant him to steer whether or no. To tell you the truth, I was morbidly anxious to change my shoes and socks. 'He is dead,' murmured the fellow, immensely impressed. 'No doubt about it,' said I, tugging like mad at the shoe-laces. 'And by the way, I suppose Mr. Kurtz is dead as well by this time.'

"For the moment that was the dominant thought. There was a sense of extreme disappointment, as though I had found out I had been striving after something altogether without a substance. I couldn't have been more disgusted if I had travelled all this way for the sole purpose of talking with Mr. Kurtz. Talking with . . . I flung one shoe overboard, and became aware that that was exactly what I had been looking forward to—a talk with Kurtz. I made the strange discovery that I had never imagined him as doing, you know, but as discoursing. I didn't say to myself, 'Now I will never see him,' or 'Now I will never shake him by the hand,' but, 'now I will never hear him.' The man presented himself as a voice. Not of course that I did not connect him with some sort of action. Hadn't I been told in all the tones of jealousy and admiration that he had collected, bartered, swindled, or stolen more ivory than all the other agents together? That was not the point. The point was in his being a gifted creature, and that of all his gifts the one that stood out pre-eminently, that carried with it a sense of real presence, was his ability to talk, his words—the gift of expression, the bewildering, the illuminating, the most exalted and the most contemptible, the pulsating stream of light, or the deceitful flow from the heart of an impenetrable darkness.

"The other shoe went flying unto the devil-god of that river. I thought, By Jove! it's all over. We are too late; he has vanished—the gift has vanished, by means of some spear, arrow, or club. I will never hear that chap speak after all—and my sorrow had a startling extravagance of emotion, even such as I had noticed in the howling sorrow of these savages in the bush. I couldn't have felt more of lonely desolation somehow, had I been robbed of a belief or had missed my destiny in life. . . . Why do you sigh in this beastly way, somebody? Absurd? Well, absurd. Good Lord! mustn't a man ever—Here, give me some tobacco." . . .

There was a pause of profound stillness, then a match flared, and Marlow's lean face appeared, worn, hollow, with downward folds and dropped eyelids, with an aspect of concentrated attention; and as he took vigorous draws at his pipe, it seemed to retreat and advance out of the night in the regular flicker of the tiny flame. The match went out.

"Absurd!" he cried. "This is the worst of trying to tell. . . . Here you all are, each moored with two good addresses, like a hulk with two anchors, a butcher round one corner, a policeman round another, excellent appetites, and temperature normal—you hear—normal from year's end to year's end. And you say, Absurd! Absurd be—exploded! Absurd! My dear boys, what can you expect from a man who out of sheer nervousness had just flung overboard a pair of new shoes! Now I think of it, it is amazing I did not shed tears. I am, upon the whole, proud of my fortitude. I was cut to the quick at the idea of having lost the inestimable privilege of listening to the gifted Kurtz. Of course I was wrong. The privilege was waiting for me. Oh, yes, I heard more than enough. And I was right too. A voice. He was very little more than a voice. And I heard—him—it—this voice—other voices—all of them were so little more than voices—and the memory of that time itself lingers around me, impalpable, like a dying vibration of one immense jabber, silly, atrocious, sordid, savage, or simply mean, without any kind of sense. Voices, voices—even the girl herself—now—"

He was silent for a long time.

"I laid the ghost of his gifts at last with a lie," he began, suddenly. "Girl! What? Did I mention a girl? Oh, she is out of it—completely. They—the women I mean—are out of it—should be out of it. We must help them to stay in that beautiful world of their own, lest ours gets worse. Oh, she had to be out of it. You should have heard the disinterred body of Mr. Kurtz saying, 'My Intended.' You would have perceived directly then how completely she was out of it. And the lofty frontal bone of Mr. Kurtz! They say the hair goes on growing sometimes, but this—ah—specimen, was impressively bald. The wilderness had patted him on the head, and, behold, it was like a ball—an ivory ball; it had caressed him, and—lo!—he had withered; it had taken him, loved him, embraced him, got into his veins, consumed his flesh, and sealed his soul to its own by the inconceivable ceremonies of some devilish initiation. He was its spoiled and pampered favourite. Ivory? I should think so. Heaps of it, stacks of it. The old mud shanty was bursting with it. You would think there was not a single tusk left either above or below the ground in the whole country. 'Mostly fossil,' the manager had remarked, disparagingly. It was no more fossil than I am;

but they call it fossil when it is dug up. It appears these niggers do bury the tusks sometimes—but evidently they couldn't bury this parcel deep enough to save the gifted Mr. Kurtz from his fate. We filled the steamboat with it, and had to pile a lot on the deck. Thus he could see and enjoy as long as he could see, because the appreciation of this favour had remained with him to the last. You should have heard him say, 'My ivory.' Oh yes, I heard him. 'My Intended, my ivory, my station, my river, my—' everything belonged to him. It made me hold my breath in expectation of hearing the wilderness burst into a prodigious peal of laughter that would shake the fixed stars in their places. Everything belonged to him—but that was a trifle. The thing was to know what he belonged to, how many powers of darkness claimed him for their own. That was the reflection that made you creepy all over. It was impossible—it was not good for one either—trying to imagine. He had taken a high seat amongst the devils of the land—I mean literally. You can't understand. How could you?—with solid pavement under your feet, surrounded by kind neighbours ready to cheer you or to fall on you, stepping delicately between the butcher and the policeman, in the holy terror of scandal and gallows and lunatic asylums—how can you imagine what particular region of the first ages a man's untrammelled feet may take him into by the way of solitude—utter solitude without a policeman—by the way of silence—utter silence, where no warning voice of a kind neighbour can be heard whispering of public opinion? These little things make all the great difference. When they are gone you must fall back upon your own innate strength, upon your own capacity for faithfulness. Of course you may be too much of a fool to go wrong—too dull even to know you are being assaulted by the powers of darkness. I take it, no fool ever made a bargain for his soul with the devil: the fool is too much of a fool, or the devil too much of a devil—I don't know which. Or you may be such a thunderingly exalted creature as to be altogether deaf and blind to anything but heavenly sights and sounds. Then the earth for you is only a standing place—and whether to be like this is your loss or your gain I won't pretend to say. But most of us are neither one nor the other. The earth for us is a place to live in, where we must put up with sights, with sounds, with smells, too, by Jove!—breathe dead hippo, so to speak, and not be contaminated. And there, don't you see? your strength comes in, the faith in your ability for the digging of unostentatious holes to bury the stuff in—your power of devotion, not to yourself, but to an obscure, back-breaking business. And that's difficult enough. Mind, I am not trying to excuse or even explain—I am trying to account to myself for—for—Mr. Kurtz—for the shade of Mr. Kurtz. This initiated wraith from the back of Nowhere honoured me with its amazing confidence before it vanished altogether. This was because it could speak English to me. The original Kurtz had been educated partly in England, and—as he was good enough to say himself—his sympathies were in the right place. His mother was half-English, his father was half-French. All Europe contributed to the making of Kurtz; and by-and-by I learned that, most appropriately, the International Society for the Suppression of Savage Customs had entrusted him with the making of a report, for its future guidance. And he had written it, too. I've seen it. I've read it. It was eloquent, vibrating with eloquence, but too high-strung, I think. Seventeen pages of close writing he had found time for! But this must have been before his—let us say—nerves, went wrong, and caused him to preside at certain midnight dances ending with unspeakable rites, which—as far as I reluctantly gathered from what I heard at various times—were offered up to him—do you understand?—to Mr. Kurtz himself. But it was a beautiful piece of writing. The opening paragraph, however, in the light of later information, strikes me now as ominous. He began with the argument that we whites, from the point of development we had arrived at, 'must necessarily appear to them [savages] in the nature of supernatural beings—we approach them with the might as of a deity,' and so on, and so on. 'By the simple exercise of our will we can exert a power for good practically unbounded,' etc. etc. From that point he soared and took me with him. The peroration was magnificent, though difficult to remember, you know. It gave me the notion of an exotic Immensity ruled by an august Benevolence. It made me tingle with enthusiasm. This was the unbounded power of eloquence—of words—of burning noble words. There were no practical hints to interrupt the magic current of phrases, unless a kind of note at the foot of the last page, scrawled evidently much later, in an unsteady hand, may be regarded as the exposition of a method. It was very simple, and at the end of that moving appeal to every altruistic sentiment it blazed at you, luminous and terrifying, like a flash of lightning in a serene sky: 'Exterminate all the brutes!' The curious part was that he had apparently forgotten all about that valuable postscriptum, because, later on, when he in a sense came to himself, he repeatedly entreated me to take good care of 'my pamphlet' (he called it), as it was sure to have in the future a good influence upon his career. I had full information about all these things, and, besides, as it turned out, I was to have the care of his memory. I've done enough for it to give me the indisputable right to lay it, if I choose, for an everlasting rest in the dust-bin of progress, amongst all the sweepings and, figuratively speaking, all the dead cats of civilization. But then, you see, I can't choose. He won't be forgotten. Whatever he was, he was not common. He had the power to charm or frighten rudimentary souls into an aggravated witch-dance in his honour; he could also fill the small souls of the pilgrims with bitter misgivings: he had one devoted friend at least, and he had conquered one soul in the world that was neither rudimentary nor tainted with self-seeking. No; I can't forget him, though I am not prepared to affirm the fellow was exactly worth the life we lost in getting to him. I missed my late helmsman awfully—I missed him even while his body was still lying in the pilot-house. Perhaps you will think it passing strange this regret for a savage who was no more account than a grain of sand in a black Sahara. Well, don't you see, he had done something, he had steered; for months I had him at my back—a help—an instrument. It was a kind of partnership. He steered for me—I had to look after him, I worried about his deficiencies, and thus a subtle bond had been created, of which I only became aware when it was suddenly broken. And the intimate profundity of that look he gave me when he received his hurt remains to this day in my memory—like a claim of distant kinship affirmed in a supreme moment.

"Poor fool! If he had only left that shutter alone. He had no restraint, no restraint—just like Kurtz—a tree swayed by the wind. As soon as I had put on a dry pair of slippers, I dragged him out, after first jerking the spear out of his side, which operation I confess I performed with my eyes shut tight. His heels leaped together over the little door-step; his shoulders were pressed to my breast; I hugged him from behind desperately. Oh! he was heavy, heavy; heavier than any man on earth, I should imagine. Then without more ado I tipped him overboard. The current snatched him as though he had been a wisp of grass, and I saw the body roll over twice before I lost sight of it for ever. All the pilgrims and the manager were then congregated on the awning-deck about the pilot-house, chattering at each other like a flock of excited magpies, and there was a scandalized murmur at my heartless promptitude. What they wanted to keep that body hanging about for I can't guess. Embalm it, maybe. But I had also heard another, and a very ominous, murmur on the deck below. My friends the wood-cutters were likewise scandalized, and with a better show of reason—though I admit that the reason itself was quite inadmissible. Oh, quite! I had made up my mind that if my late helmsman was to be eaten, the fishes alone should have him. He had been a very second-rate helmsman while alive, but now he was dead he might have become a first-class temptation, and possibly cause some startling trouble. Besides, I was anxious to take the wheel, the man in pink pyjamas showing himself a hopeless duffer at the business.

"This I did directly the simple funeral was over. We were going half-speed, keeping right in the middle of the stream, and I listened to the talk about me. They had given up Kurtz, they had given up the station; Kurtz was dead, and the station had been burnt—and so on—and so on. The red-haired pilgrim was beside himself with the thought that at least this poor Kurtz had been properly avenged. 'Say! We must have made a glorious slaughter of them in the bush. Eh? What do you think? Say?' He positively danced, the bloodthirsty little gingery beggar. And he had nearly fainted when he saw the wounded man! I could not help saying, 'You made a glorious lot of smoke, anyhow.' I had seen, from the way the tops of the bushes rustled and flew, that almost all the shots had gone too high. You can't hit anything unless you take aim and fire from the shoulder; but these chaps fired from the hip with their eyes shut. The retreat, I maintained—and I was right—was caused by the screeching of the steam-whistle. Upon this they forgot Kurtz, and began to howl at me with indignant protests.

"The manager stood by the wheel murmuring confidentially about the necessity of getting well away down the river before dark at all events, when I saw in the distance a clearing on the river-side and the outlines of some sort of building. 'What's this?' I asked. He clapped his hands in wonder. 'The station!' he cried. I edged in at once, still going half-speed.

"Through my glasses I saw the slope of a hill interspersed with rare trees and perfectly free from undergrowth. A long decaying building on the summit was half buried in the high grass; the large holes in the peaked roof gaped black from afar; the jungle and the woods made a background. There was no enclosure or fence of any kind; but there had been one apparently, for near the house half-a-dozen slim posts remained in a row, roughly trimmed, and with their upper ends orna-mented with round carved balls. The rails, or whatever there had been between, had disappeared. Of course the forest surrounded all that. The river-bank was clear, and on the water side I saw a white man under a hat like a cart-wheel beckoning persistently with his whole arm. Exam-ining the edge of the forest above and below, I was almost certain I could see movements—human forms gliding here and there. I steamed past prudently, then stopped the engines and let her drift down. The man on the shore began to shout, urging us to land. 'We have been attacked,' screamed the manager. 'I know—I know. It's all right,' yelled back the other, as cheerful as you please. 'Come along. It's all right. I am glad.'

"His aspect reminded me of something I had seen—something funny I had seen somewhere. As I manoeuvred to get alongside, I was asking myself, 'What does this fellow look like?' Suddenly I got it. He looked like a harlequin. His clothes had been made of some stuff that was brown holland probably, but it was covered with patches all over, with bright patches, blue, red, and yellow—patches on the back, patches on the front, patches on elbows, on knees; coloured binding around his jacket, scarlet edging at the bottom of his trousers; and the sunshine made him look extremely gay and wonderfully neat withal, because you could see how beautifully all this patching had been done. A beardless, boyish face, very fair, no features to speak of, nose peeling, little blue eyes, smiles and frowns chasing each other over that open countenance like sunshine and shadow on a wind-swept plain. 'Look out, captain!' he cried; 'there's a snag lodged in here last night.' What! Another snag? I confess I swore shamefully. I had nearly holed my cripple, to finish off that charming trip. The harlequin on the bank turned his little pug-nose up to me. 'You English?' he asked, all smiles. 'Are you?' I shouted from the wheel. The smiles vanished, and he shook his head as if sorry for my disappointment. Then he brightened up. 'Never mind!' he cried, encouragingly. 'Are we in time?' I asked. 'He is up there,' he replied, with a toss of the head up the hill, and becoming gloomy all of a sudden. His face was like the autumn sky, overcast one moment and bright the next.

"When the manager, escorted by the pilgrims, all of them armed to the teeth, had gone to the house this chap came on board. 'I say, I don't like this. These natives are in the bush,' I said. He assured me earnestly it was all right. 'They are simple people,' he added; 'well, I am glad you came. It took me all my time to keep them off.' 'But you said it was all right,' I cried. 'Oh, they meant no harm,' he said; and as I stared he corrected himself, 'Not exactly.' Then vivaciously, 'My faith, your pilot-house wants a clean-up!' In the next breath he advised me to keep enough steam on the boiler to blow the whistle in case of any trouble. 'One good screech will do more for you than all your rifles. They are simple people,' he repeated. He rattled away at such a rate he quite overwhelmed me. He seemed to be trying to make up for lots of silence, and actually hinted, laughing, that such was the case. 'Don't you talk with Mr. Kurtz?' I said. 'You don't talk with that man—you listen to him.' he exclaimed with severe exaltation. 'But now—' He waved his arm, and in the twinkling of an eye was in the uttermost depths of despondency. In a moment he came up again with a jump, possessed himself of both my hands, shook them continuously, while he gabbled: 'Brother sailor . . . honour . . . pleasure . . . delight . . . introduce myself . . . Russian . . . son of an arch-priest . . . Government of Tambov . . . What? Tobacco! English tobacco; the excellent English tobacco! Now, that's brotherly. Smoke? Where's a sailor that does not smoke?'

"The pipe soothed him, and gradually I made out he had run away from school, had gone to sea in a Russian ship; ran away again; served some time in English ships; was now reconciled with the arch-priest. He made a point of that. 'But when one is young one must see things, gather experience, ideas; enlarge the mind.' 'Here!' I interrupted. 'You can never tell! Here I met Mr. Kurtz,' he said, youthfully solemn and reproachful. I held my tongue after that. It appears he had persuaded a Dutch trading-house on the coast to fit him out with stores and goods, and had started for the interior with a light heart, and no more idea of what would happen to him than a baby. He had been wandering about that river for nearly two years alone, cut off from everybody and everything. 'I am not so young as I look. I am twenty-five,' he said. 'At first old Van Shuyten would tell me to go to the devil,' he narrated with keen enjoyment; 'but I stuck to him, and talked and talked, till at last he got afraid I would talk the hind-leg off his favourite dog, so he gave me some cheap things and a few guns, and told me he hoped he would never see my face again. Good old Dutchman, Van Shuyten. I sent him one small lot of ivory a year ago, so that he can't call me a little thief when I get back. I hope he got it. And for the rest I don't care. I had some wood stacked for you. That was my old house. Did you see?'

"I gave him Towson's book. He made as though he would kiss me, but restrained himself. 'The only book I had left, and I thought I had lost it,' he said, looking at it ecstatically. 'So many accidents happen to a man going about alone, you know. Canoes get upset sometimes—and sometimes you've got to clear out so quick when the people get angry.' He thumbed the pages. 'You made notes in Russian?' I asked. He nodded. 'I thought they were written in cipher,' I said. He laughed, then became serious. 'I had lots of trouble to keep these people off,' he said. 'Did they want to kill you?' I asked. 'Oh, no!' he cried, and checked himself. 'Why did they attack us?' I pursued. He hesitated, then said shamefacedly, 'They don't want him to go.' 'Don't they?' I said, curiously. He nodded a nod full of mystery and wisdom. 'I tell you,' he cried, 'this man has enlarged my mind.' He opened his arms wide, staring at me with his little blue eyes that were perfectly round."

III

"I looked at him, lost in astonishment. There he was before me, in motley, as though he had absconded from a troupe of mimes, enthusiastic, fabulous. His very existence was improbable, inexplicable, and altogether bewildering. He was an insoluble problem. It was inconceivable how he had existed, how he had succeeded in getting so far, how he had managed to remain—why he did not instantly disappear. 'I went a little farther,' he said, 'then still a little farther—till I had gone so far that I don't know how I'll ever get back. Never mind. Plenty time. I can manage. You take Kurtz away quick—quick—I tell you.' The glamour of youth enveloped his parti-coloured rags, his destitution, his loneliness, the essential desolation of his futile wanderings. For months—for years—his life hadn't been worth a day's purchase; and there he was gallantly, thoughtlessly alive, to all appearance indestructible solely by the virtue of his few years and of his unreflecting audacity. I was seduced into something like admiration—like envy. Glamour urged him on, glamour kept him unscathed. He surely wanted nothing from the wilderness but space to breathe in and to push on through. His need was to exist, and to move onwards at the greatest possible risk, and with a maximum of privation. If the absolutely pure, uncalculating, unpractical spirit of adventure had ever ruled a human being, it ruled this be-patched youth. I almost envied him the possession of this modest and clear flame. It seemed to have consumed all thought of self so completely, that even while he was talking to you, you forgot that it was he—the man before your eyes—who had gone through these things. I did not envy him his devotion to Kurtz, though. He had not meditated over it. It came to him, and he accepted it with a sort of eager fatalism. I must say that to me it appeared about the most danger-ous thing in every way he had come upon so far.

"They had come together unavoidably, like two ships becalmed near each other, and lay rubbing sides at last. I suppose Kurtz wanted an audience, because on a certain occasion, when encamped in the forest, they had talked all night, or more probably Kurtz had talked. 'We talked of everything,' he said, quite transported at the recollection. 'I forgot there was such a thing as sleep. The night did not seem to last an hour. Everything! Everything! . . . Of love, too.' 'Ah, he talked to you of love!' I said, much amused. 'It isn't what you think,' he cried, almost passionately. 'It was in general. He made me see things—things.'

"He threw his arms up. We were on deck at the time, and the head-man of my wood-cutters, lounging near by, turned upon him his heavy and glittering eyes. I looked around, and I don't know why, but I assure you that never, never before, did this land, this river, this jungle, the very arch of this blazing sky, appear to me so hopeless and so dark, so impenetrable to human thought, so pitiless to human weakness. 'And ever since, you have been with him, of course?' I said.

"On the contrary. It appears their intercourse had been very much broken by various causes. He had as he informed me proudly, managed to nurse Kurtz through two illnesses (he alluded to it as you would to some risky feat), but as a rule Kurtz wandered alone, far in the depths of the forest. 'Very often coming to this station, I had to wait days and days before he would turn up,' he said. 'Ah, it was worth waiting for!—sometimes.' 'What was he doing? exploring or what?' I asked. 'Oh, yes, of course'; he had discovered lots of villages, a lake, too—he did not know exactly in what direction; it was dangerous to inquire too much—but mostly his expeditions had been for ivory. 'But he had no goods to trade with by that time,' I objected. 'There's a good lot of car-tridges left even yet,' he answered, looking away. 'To speak plainly, he raided the country,' I said. He nodded. 'Not alone, surely!' He muttered something about the villages round that lake. 'Kurtz got the tribe to fol-low him, did he?' I suggested. He fidgeted a little. 'They adored him,' he said. The tone of these words was so extraordinary that I looked at him searchingly. It was curious to see his mingled eagerness and reluctance to speak of Kurtz. The man filled his life, occupied his thoughts, swayed his emotions. 'What can you expect?' he burst out; 'he came to them with thunder and lightning, you know—and they had never seen any-thing like it—and very terrible. He could be very terrible. You can't judge Mr. Kurtz as you would an ordinary man. No, no, no! Now—just to give you an idea—I don't mind telling you, he wanted to shoot me, too, one day—but I don't judge him.' 'Shoot you!' I cried. 'What for?' 'Well, I had a small lot of ivory the chief of that village near my house gave me. You see I used to shoot game for them. Well, he wanted it, and wouldn't hear reason. He declared he would shoot me unless I gave him the ivory and then cleared out of the country, because he could do so, and had a fancy for it, and there was nothing on earth to prevent him killing whom he jolly well pleased. And it was true, too. I gave him the ivory. What did I care! But I didn't clear out. No, no. I couldn't leave him. I had to be careful, of course, till we got friendly again for a time. He had his second illness then. Afterwards I had to keep out of the way; but I didn't mind. He was living for the most part in those villages on the lake. When he came down to the river, sometimes he would take to me, and sometimes it was better for me to be careful. This man suffered too much. He hated all this, and somehow he couldn't get away. When I had a chance I begged him to try and leave while there was time; I offered to go back with him. And he would say yes, and then he would remain; go off on another ivory hunt; disappear for weeks; forget himself amongst these people—forget himself—you know.' 'Why! he's mad,' I said. He protested indignantly. Mr. Kurtz couldn't be mad. If I had heard him talk, only two days ago, I wouldn't dare hint at such a thing. . . . I had taken up my binoculars while we talked, and was looking at the shore, sweeping the limit of the forest at each side and at the back of the house. The consciousness of there being people in that bush, so silent, so quiet—as silent and quiet as the ruined house on the hill—made me uneasy. There was no sign on the face of nature of this amazing tale that was not so much told as suggested to me in desolate exclamations, completed by shrugs, in interrupted phrases, in hints ending in deep sighs. The woods were unmoved, like a mask—heavy, like the closed door of a prison—they looked with their air of hidden knowledge, of patient expectation, of unapproachable silence. The Russian was explaining to me that it was only lately that Mr. Kurtz had come down to the river, bringing along with him all the fighting men of that lake tribe. He had been absent for several months—getting himself adored, I suppose—and had come down unexpectedly, with the intention to all appearance of making a raid either across the river or down stream. Evidently the appetite for more ivory had got the better of the—what shall I say?—less material aspirations. However, he had got much worse suddenly. 'I heard he was lying helpless, and so I came up—took my chance,' said the Russian. 'Oh, he is bad, very bad.' I directed my glass to the house. There were no signs of life, but there was the ruined roof, the long mud wall peeping above the grass, with three little square window-holes, no two the same size: all this brought within reach of my hand, as it were. And then I made a brusque movement, and one of the remaining posts of that vanished fence leaped up in the field of my glass. You remember I told you I had been struck at the distance by certain attempts at ornamentation, rather remarkable in the ruinous aspect of the place. Now I had suddenly a nearer view, and its first result was to make me throw my head back as if before a blow. Then I went carefully from post to post with my glass, and I saw my mistake. These round knobs were not ornamental but symbolic; they were expressive and puzzling, striking and disturbing—food for thought and also for the vultures if there had been any looking down from the sky; but at all events for such ants as were industrious enough to ascend the pole. They would have been even more impressive, those heads on the stakes, if their faces had not been turned to the house. Only one, the first I had made out, was facing my way. I was not so shocked as you may think. The start back I had given was really nothing but a movement of surprise. I had expected to see a knob of wood there, you know. I returned deliberately to the first I had seen—and there it was, black, dried, sunken, with closed eyelids—a head that seemed to sleep at the top of that pole, and, with the shrunken dry lips showing a narrow white line of the teeth, was smiling, too, smiling continuously at some endless and jocose dream of that eternal slumber.

"I am not disclosing any trade secrets. In fact, the manager said afterwards that Mr. Kurtz's methods had ruined the district. I have no opinion on that point, but I want you clearly to understand that there was nothing exactly profitable in these heads being there. They only showed that Mr. Kurtz lacked restraint in the gratification of his various lusts, that there was something wanting in him—some small matter which, when the pressing need arose, could not be found under his magnificent eloquence. Whether he knew of this deficiency himself I can't say. I think the knowledge came to him at last—only at the very last. But the wilderness had found him out early, and had taken on him a terrible vengeance for the fantastic invasion. I think it had whispered to him things about himself which he did not know, things of which he had no conception till he took counsel with this great solitude—and the whisper had proved irresistibly fascinating. It echoed loudly within him because he was hollow at the core. . . . I put down the glass, and the head that had appeared near enough to be spoken to seemed at once to have leaped away from me into inaccessible distance.

"The admirer of Mr. Kurtz was a bit crestfallen. In a hurried, indistinct voice he began to assure me he had not dared to take these—say, symbols—down. He was not afraid of the natives; they would not stir till Mr. Kurtz gave the word. His ascendancy was extraordinary. The camps of these people surrounded the place, and the chiefs came every day to see him. They would crawl . . . 'I don't want to know anything of the ceremonies used when approaching Mr. Kurtz,' I shouted. Curious, this feeling that came over me that such details would be more intolerable than those heads drying on the stakes under Mr. Kurtz's windows. After all, that was only a savage sight, while I seemed at one bound to have been transported into some lightless region of subtle horrors, where pure, uncomplicated savagery was a positive relief, being something that had a right to exist—obviously—in the sunshine. The young man looked at me with surprise. I suppose it did not occur to him that Mr. Kurtz was no idol of mine. He forgot I hadn't heard any of these splendid monologues on, what was it? on love, justice, conduct of life— or what not. If it had come to crawling before Mr. Kurtz, he crawled as much as the veriest savage of them all. I had no idea of the conditions, he said: these heads were the heads of rebels. I shocked him excessively by laughing. Rebels! What would be the next definition I was to hear? There had been enemies, criminals, workers—and these were rebels. Those rebellious heads looked very subdued to me on their sticks. 'You don't know how such a life tries a man like Kurtz,' cried Kurtz's last disciple. 'Well, and you?' I said. 'I! I am a simple man. I have no great thoughts. I want nothing from anybody. How can you compare me to . . . ?' His feelings were too much for speech, and suddenly he broke down. 'I don't understand,' he groaned. 'I've been doing my best to keep him alive, and that's enough. I had no hand in all this. I have no abilities. There hasn't been a drop of medicine or a mouthful of invalid food for months here. He was shamefully abandoned. A man like this, with such ideas. Shamefully! Shamefully! I—I—haven't slept for the last ten nights. . . .'

"His voice lost itself in the calm of the evening. The long shadows of the forest had slipped downhill while we talked, had gone far beyond the ruined hovel, beyond the symbolic row of stakes. All this was in the gloom, while we down there were yet in the sunshine, and the stretch of the river abreast of the clearing glittered in a still and dazzling splendour, with a murky and overshadowed bend above and below. Not a living soul was seen on the shore. The bushes did not rustle.

"Suddenly round the corner of the house a group of men appeared, as though they had come up from the ground. They waded waist-deep in the grass, in a compact body, bearing an improvised stretcher in their midst. Instantly, in the emptiness of the landscape, a cry arose whose shrillness pierced the still air like a sharp arrow flying straight to the very heart of the land; and, as if by enchantment, streams of human beings—of naked human beings—with spears in their hands, with bows, with shields, with wild glances and savage movements, were poured into the clearing by the dark-faced and pensive forest. The bushes shook, the grass swayed for a time, and then everything stood still in attentive immobility.

"'Now, if he does not say the right thing to them we are all done for,' said the Russian at my elbow. The knot of men with the stretcher had stopped, too, halfway to the steamer, as if petrified. I saw the man on the stretcher sit up, lank and with an uplifted arm, above the shoulders of the bearers. 'Let us hope that the man who can talk so well of love in general will find some particular reason to spare us this time,' I said. I resented bitterly the absurd danger of our situation, as if to be at the mercy of that atrocious phantom had been a dishonouring necessity. I could not hear a sound, but through my glasses I saw the thin arm extended commandingly, the lower jaw moving, the eyes of that apparition shining darkly far in its bony head that nodded with grotesque jerks. Kurtz—Kurtz—that means short in German—don't it? Well, the name was as true as everything else in his life—and death. He looked at least seven feet long. His covering had fallen off, and his body emerged from it pitiful and appalling as from a winding-sheet. I could see the cage of his ribs all astir, the bones of his arm waving. It was as though an animated image of death carved out of old ivory had been shaking its hand with menaces at a motionless crowd of men made of dark and glittering bronze. I saw him open his mouth wide—it gave him a weirdly voracious aspect, as though he had wanted to swallow all the air, all the earth, all the men before him. A deep voice reached me faintly. He must have been shouting. He fell back suddenly. The stretcher shook as the bearers staggered forward again, and almost at the same time I noticed that the crowd of savages was vanishing without any perceptible movement of retreat, as if the forest that had ejected these beings so suddenly had drawn them in again as the breath is drawn in a long aspiration.

"Some of the pilgrims behind the stretcher carried his arms—two shot-guns, a heavy rifle, and a light revolver-carbine—the thunderbolts of that pitiful Jupiter. The manager bent over him murmuring as he walked beside his head. They laid him down in one of the little cabins—just a room for a bedplace and a camp-stool or two, you know. We had brought his belated correspondence, and a lot of torn envelopes and open letters littered his bed. His hand roamed feebly amongst these papers. I was struck by the fire of his eyes and the composed languor of his expression. It was not so much the exhaustion of disease. He did not seem in pain. This shadow looked satiated and calm, as though for the moment it had had its fill of all the emotions.

"He rustled one of the letters, and looking straight in my face said, 'I am glad.' Somebody had been writing to him about me. These special recommendations were turning up again. The volume of tone he emitted without effort, almost without the trouble of moving his lips, amazed me. A voice! a voice! It was grave, profound, vibrating, while the man did not seem capable of a whisper. However, he had enough strength in him—factitious no doubt—to very nearly make an end of us, as you shall hear directly.

"The manager appeared silently in the doorway; I stepped out at once and he drew the curtain after me. The Russian, eyed curiously by the pilgrims, was staring at the shore. I followed the direction of his glance.

"Dark human shapes could be made out in the distance, flitting indistinctly against the gloomy border of the forest, and near the river two bronze figures, leaning on tall spears, stood in the sunlight under fantastic head-dresses of spotted skins, warlike and still in statuesque repose. And from right to left along the lighted shore moved a wild and gorgeous apparition of a woman.

"She walked with measured steps, draped in striped and fringed cloths, treading the earth proudly, with a slight jingle and flash of barbarous ornaments. She carried her head high; her hair was done in the shape of a helmet; she had brass leggings to the knees, brass wire gauntlets to the elbow, a crimson spot on her tawny cheek, innumerable necklaces of glass beads on her neck; bizarre things, charms, gifts of witch-men, that hung about her, glittered and trembled at every step. She must have had the value of several elephant tusks upon her. She was savage and superb, wild-eyed and magnificent; there was something ominous and stately in her deliberate progress. And in the hush that had fallen suddenly upon the whole sorrowful land, the immense wilderness, the colossal body of the fecund and mysterious life seemed to look at her, pensive, as though it had been looking at the image of its own tenebrous and passionate soul.

"She came abreast of the steamer, stood still, and faced us. Her long shadow fell to the water's edge. Her face had a tragic and fierce aspect of wild sorrow and of dumb pain mingled with the fear of some struggling, half-shaped resolve. She stood looking at us without a stir, and like the wilderness itself, with an air of brooding over an inscrutable purpose. A whole minute passed, and then she made a step forward. There was a low jingle, a glint of yellow metal, a sway of fringed draperies, and she stopped as if her heart had failed her. The young fellow by my side growled. The pilgrims murmured at my back. She looked at us all as if her life had depended upon the unswerving steadiness of her glance. Suddenly she opened her bared arms and threw them up rigid above her head, as though in an uncontrollable desire to touch the sky, and at the same time the swift shadows darted out on the earth, swept around on the river, gathering the steamer into a shadowy embrace. A formidable silence hung over the scene.

"She turned away slowly, walked on, following the bank, and passed into the bushes on the left. Once only her eyes gleamed back at us in the dusk of the thickets before she disappeared.

"'If she had offered to come aboard I really think I would have tried to shoot her,' said the man of patches, nervously. 'I had been risking my life every day for the last fortnight to keep her out of the house. She got in one day and kicked up a row about those miserable rags I picked up in the storeroom to mend my clothes with. I wasn't decent. At least it must have been that, for she talked like a fury to Kurtz for an hour, pointing at me now and then. I don't understand the dialect of this tribe. Luckily for me, I fancy Kurtz felt too ill that day to care, or there would have been mischief. I don't understand. . . . No—it's too much for me. Ah, well, it's over now.'

"At this moment I heard Kurtz's deep voice behind the curtain: 'Save me!—save the ivory, you mean. Don't tell me. Save *me*! Why, I've had to save you. You are interrupting my plans now. Sick! Sick! Not so sick as you would like to believe. Never mind. I'll carry my ideas out yet—I will return. I'll show you what can be done. You with your little peddling notions—you are interfering with me. I will return. I . . .'

"The manager came out. He did me the honour to take me under the arm and lead me aside. 'He is very low, very low,' he said. He considered it necessary to sigh, but neglected to be consistently sorrowful. 'We have done all we could for him—haven't we? But there is no disguising the fact, Mr. Kurtz has done more harm than good to the Company. He did not see the time was not ripe for vigorous action. Cautiously, cautiously—that's my principle. We must be cautious yet. The district is closed to us for a time. Deplorable! Upon the whole, the trade will suffer. I don't deny there is a remarkable quantity of ivory— mostly fossil. We must save it, at all events—but look how precarious the position is—and why? Because the method is unsound.' 'Do you,' said I, looking at the shore, 'call it 'unsound method'?' 'Without doubt,' he exclaimed, hotly. 'Don't you?' . . . 'No method at all,' I murmured after a while. 'Exactly,' he exulted. 'I anticipated this, Shows a complete want of judgement. It is my duty to point it out in the proper quarter.' 'Oh,' said I, 'that fellow—what's his name?—the brickmaker, will make a readable report for you.' He appeared confounded for a moment. It seemed to me I had never breathed an atmosphere so vile, and I turned mentally to Kurtz for relief—positively for relief. 'Nevertheless I think Mr. Kurtz is a remarkable man,' I said with emphasis. He started, dropped on me a cold heavy glance, said very quietly, 'He *was*,' and turned his back on me. My hour of favour was over; I found myself lumped along with Kurtz as a partisan of methods for which the time was not ripe: I was unsound! Ah! but it was something to have at least a choice of nightmares.

"I had turned to the wilderness really, not to Mr. Kurtz, who, I was ready to admit, was as good as buried. And for a moment it seemed to me as if I also were buried in a vast grave full of unspeakable secrets. I felt an intolerable weight oppressing my breast, the smell of the damp earth, the unseen presence of victorious corruption, the darkness of an impenetrable night. . . . The Russian tapped me on the shoulder. I heard him mumbling and stammering something about 'brother seaman—couldn't conceal—knowledge of matters that would affect Mr. Kurtz's reputation.' I waited. For him evidently Mr. Kurtz was not in his grave; I suspect that for him Mr. Kurtz was one of the immortals.

'Well!' said I at last, 'speak out. As it happens, I am Mr. Kurtz's friend—in a way.'

"He stated with a good deal of formality that had we not been 'of the same profession,' he would have kept the matter to himself without regard to consequences. 'He suspected there was an active ill will towards him on the part of these white men that—' 'You are right,' I said, remembering a certain conversation I had overheard. 'The manager thinks you ought to be hanged.' He showed a concern at this intelligence which amused me at first. 'I had better get out of the way quietly,' he said, earnestly. 'I can do no more for Kurtz now, and they would soon find some excuse. What's to stop them? There's a military post three hundred miles from here.' 'Well, upon my word,' said I, 'perhaps you had better go if you have any friends amongst the savages near by.' 'Plenty,' he said. 'They are simple people—and I want nothing, you know.' He stood biting his lip, then: 'I don't want any harm to happen to these whites here, but of course I was thinking of Mr. Kurtz's reputation—but you are a brother seaman and—' 'All right,' said I, after a time. 'Mr. Kurtz's reputation is safe with me.' I did not know how truly I spoke.

"He informed me, lowering his voice, that it was Kurtz who had ordered the attack to be made on the steamer. 'He hated sometimes the idea of being taken away—and then again . . . But I don't understand these matters. I am a simple man. He thought it would scare you away—that you would give it up, thinking him dead. I could not stop him. Oh, I had an awful time of it this last month.' 'Very well,' I said. 'He is all right now.' 'Ye-e-es,' he muttered, not very convinced apparently. 'Thanks,' said I; 'I shall keep my eyes open.' 'But quiet—eh?' he urged, anxiously. 'It would be awful for his reputation if anybody here—' I promised a complete discretion with great gravity. 'I have a canoe and three black fellows waiting not very far. I am off. Could you give me a few Martini-Henry cartridges?' I could, and did, with proper secrecy. He helped himself, with a wink at me, to a handful of my tobacco. 'Between sailors—you know—good English tobacco.' At the door of the pilot-house he turned round—'I say, haven't you a pair of shoes you could spare?' He raised one leg. 'Look.' The soles were tied with knotted strings sandal-wise under his bare feet. I rooted out an old pair, at which he looked with admiration before tucking it under his left arm. One of his pockets (bright red) was bulging with cartridges, from the other (dark blue) peeped 'Townson's Inquiry,' etc., etc. He seemed to think himself excellently well equipped for a renewed encounter with the wilderness. 'Ah! I'll never, never meet such a man again. You ought to have heard him recite poetry—his own, too, it was, he told me. Poetry!' He rolled his eyes at the recollection of these delights. 'Oh, he enlarged my mind!' 'Good-bye,' said I. He shook hands and vanished in the night. Sometimes I ask myself whether I had ever really seen him—whether it was possible to meet such a phenome-non! . . .

"When I woke up shortly after midnight his warning came to my mind with its hint of danger that seemed, in the starred darkness, real enough to make me get up for the purpose of having a look round. On the hill a big fire burned, illuminating fitfully a crooked corner of the station-house. One of the agents with a picket of a few of our blacks, armed for the purpose, was keeping guard over the ivory; but deep within the forest, red gleams that wavered, that seemed to sink and rise from the ground amongst confused columnar shapes of intense black-ness, showed the exact position of the camp where Mr. Kurtz's adorers were keeping their uneasy vigil. The monotonous beating of a big drum filled the air with muffled shocks and a lingering vibration. A steady droning sound of many men chanting each to himself some weird incantation came out from the black, flat wall of the woods as the hum-ming of bees comes out of a hive, and had a strange narcotic effect upon my half-awake senses. I believe I dozed off leaning over the rail, till an abrupt burst of yells, an overwhelming outbreak of a pent-up and mysterious frenzy, woke me up in a bewildered wonder. It was cut short all at once, and the low droning went on with an effect of audible and soothing silence. I glanced casually into the little cabin. A light was burning within, but Mr. Kurtz was not there.

"I think I would have raised an outcry if I had believed my eyes. But I didn't believe them at first—the thing seemed so impossible. The fact is I was completely unnerved by a sheer blank fright, pure abstract ter-ror, unconnected with any distinct shape of physical danger. What made this emotion so overpowering was—how shall I define it?—the moral shock I received, as if something altogether monstrous, intolera-ble to thought and odious to the soul, had been thrust upon me unex-pectedly. This lasted of course the merest fraction of a second, and then the usual sense of commonplace, deadly danger, the possibility of a sud-den onslaught and massacre, or something of the kind, which I saw impending, was positively welcome and composing. It pacified me, in fact, so much, that I did not raise an alarm.

"There was an agent buttoned up inside an ulster and sleeping on a chair on deck within three feet of me. The yells had not awakened him; he snored very slightly; I left him to his slumbers and leaped ashore. I did not betray Mr. Kurtz—it was ordered I should never betray him—it was written I should be loyal to the nightmare of my choice. I was anxious to deal with this shadow by myself alone—and to this day I don't know why I was so jealous of sharing with any one the peculiar blackness of the experience.

"As soon as I got on the bank I saw a trail—a broad trail through the grass. I remember the exultation with which I said to myself, 'He can't walk—he is crawling on all-fours—I've got him.' The grass was wet with dew. I strode rapidly with clenched fists. I fancy I had some vague notion of falling upon him and giving him a drubbing. I don't know. I had some imbecile thoughts. The knitting old woman with the cat obtruded herself upon my memory as a most improper person to be sitting at the other end of such an affair. I saw a row of pilgrims squirting lead in the air out of Winchesters held to the hip. I thought I would never get back to the steamer, and imagined myself living alone and unarmed in the woods to an advanced age. Such silly things—you know. And I remember I confounded the beat of the drum with the beating of my heart, and was pleased at its calm regularity.

"I kept to the track though—then stopped to listen. The night was very clear; a dark blue space, sparkling with dew and starlight, in which black things stood very still. I thought I could see a kind of motion ahead of me. I was strangely cocksure of everything that night. I actually left the track and ran in a wide semicircle (I verily believe chuckling to myself) so as to get in front of that stir, of that motion I had seen—If indeed I had seen anything. I was circumventing Kurtz as though it had been a boyish game.

"I came upon him, and, if he had not heard me coming, I would have fallen over him, too, but he got up in time. He rose, unsteady, long, pale indistinct, like a vapour exhaled by the earth, and swayed slightly, misty and silent before me; while at my back the fires loomed between the trees, and the murmur of many voices issued from the forest. I had cut him off cleverly; but when actually confronting him I seemed to come to my senses, I saw the danger in its right proportion. It was by no means over yet. Suppose he began to shout? Though he could hardly stand, there was still plenty of vigour in his voice. 'Go away—hide yourself,' he said, in that profound tone. It was very awful. I glanced back. We were within thirty yards from the nearest fire. A black figure stood up, strode on long black legs, waving long black arms, across the glow. It had horns—antelope horns, I think—on its head. Some sorcerer, some witch-man, no doubt: it looked fiend-like enough. 'Do you know what you are doing?' I whispered. 'Perfectly,' he answered, raising his voice for that single word: it sounded to me far off and yet loud, like a hail through a speaking-trumpet. If he makes a row we are lost, I thought to myself. This clearly was not a case for fisticuffs, even apart from the very natural aversion I had to beat that Shadow—this wandering and tormented thing. 'You will be lost,' I said—'utterly lost.' One gets sometimes such a flash of inspiration, you know. I did say the right thing, though indeed he could not have been more irretrievably lost than he was at this very moment, when the foundations of our intimacy were being laid—to endure—to endure—even to the end—even beyond.

"'I had immense plans,' he muttered irresolutely. 'Yes,' said I; 'but if you try to shout I'll smash your head with—' There was not a stick or a stone near. 'I will throttle you for good,' I corrected myself. 'I was on the threshold of great things,' he pleaded, in a voice of longing, with a wistfulness of tone that made my blood run cold. 'And now for this stupid scoundrel—' 'Your success in Europe is assured in any case,' I affirmed, steadily. I did not want to have the throttling of him, you understand—and indeed it would have been very little use for any practical purpose. I tried to break the spell—the heavy, mute spell of the wilderness—that seemed to draw him to its pitiless breast by the awakening of forgotten and brutal instincts, by the memory of gratified and monstrous passions. This alone, I was convinced, had driven him out to the edge of the forest, to the bush, towards the gleam of fires, the throb of drums, the drone of weird incantations; this alone had beguiled his unlawful soul beyond the bounds of permitted aspirations. And, don't you see, the terror of the position was not in being knocked on the head—though I had a very lively sense of that danger, too—but in this, that I had to deal with a being to whom I could not appeal in the name of anything high or low. I had, even like the niggers, to invoke him—himself—his own exalted and incredible degradation. There was nothing either above or below him, and I knew it. He had kicked himself loose of the earth. Confound the man! he had kicked the very earth to pieces. He was alone, and I before him did not know whether I stood on the ground or floated in the air. I've been telling you what we said—repeating the phrases we pronounced—but what's the good? They were common everyday words—the familiar, vague sounds exchanged on every waking day of life. But what of that? They had behind them, to my mind, the terrific suggestiveness of words heard in dreams, of phrases spoken in nightmares. Soul! If anybody had ever struggled with a soul, I am the man. And I wasn't arguing with a lunatic either. Believe me or not, his intelligence was perfectly clear—concentrated, it is true, upon himself with horrible intensity, yet clear; and therein was my only chance—barring, of course, the killing him there and then, which wasn't so good, on account of unavoidable noise. But his soul was mad. Being alone in the wilderness, it had looked within itself, and, by heavens! I tell you, it had gone mad. I had—for my sins, I suppose—to go through the ordeal of looking into it myself. No eloquence could have been so withering to one's belief in mankind as his final burst of sincerity. He struggled with himself, too. I saw it—I heard it. I saw the inconceivable mystery of a soul that knew no restraint, no faith, and no fear, yet struggling blindly with itself. I kept my head pretty well; but when I had him at last stretched on the couch, I wiped my forehead, while my legs shook under me as though I had carried half a ton on my back down that hill. And yet I had only supported him, his bony arm clasped round my neck—and he was not much heavier than a child.

"When next day we left at noon, the crowd, of whose presence behind the curtain of trees I had been acutely conscious all the time, flowed out of the woods again, filled the clearing, covered the slope with a mass of naked, breathing, quivering, bronze bodies. I steamed up a bit, then swung downstream, and two thousand eyes followed the evolutions of the splashing, thumping, fierce river-demon beating the water with its terrible tail and breathing black smoke into the air. In front of the first rank, along the river, three men, plastered with bright red earth from head to foot, strutted to and fro restlessly. When we came abreast again, they faced the river, stamped their feet, nodded their horned heads, swayed their scarlet bodies; they shook towards the fierce river-demon a bunch of black feathers, a mangy skin with a pendent tail—something that looked like a dried gourd; they shouted periodically together strings of amazing words that resembled no sounds of human language; and the deep murmurs of the crowd, interrupted suddenly, were like the responses of some satanic litany.

"We had carried Kurtz into the pilot-house: there was more air there. Lying on the couch, he stared through the open shutter. There was an eddy in the mass of human bodies, and the woman with helmeted head and tawny cheeks rushed out to the very brink of the stream. She put out her hands, shouted something, and all that wild mob took up the shout in a roaring chorus of articulated, rapid, breathless utterance.

"'Do you understand this?' I asked.

"He kept on looking out past me with fiery, longing eyes, with a mingled expression of wistfulness and hate. He made no answer, but I saw a smile, a smile of indefinable meaning, appear on his colourless lips that a moment after twitched convulsively. 'Do I not?' he said slowly, gasping, as if the words had been torn out of him by a supernatural power.

"I pulled the string of the whistle, and I did this because I saw the pilgrims on deck getting out their rifles with an air of anticipating a jolly lark. At the sudden screech there was a movement of abject terror through that wedged mass of bodies. 'Don't! don't you frighten them away,' cried someone on deck disconsolately. I pulled the string time after time. They broke and ran, they leaped, they crouched, they swerved, they dodged the flying terror of the sound. The three red chaps had fallen flat, face down on the shore, as though they had been shot dead. Only the barbarous and superb woman did not so much as flinch and stretched tragically her bare arms after us over the sombre and glittering river.

"And then that imbecile crowd down on the deck started their little fun, and I could see nothing more for smoke.

"The brown current ran swiftly out of the heart of darkness, bearing us down towards the sea with twice the speed of our upward progress; and Kurtz's life was running swiftly, too, ebbing, ebbing out of his heart into the sea of inexorable time. The manager was very placid, he had no vital anxieties now, he took us both in with a comprehensive and satisfied glance: the 'affair' had come off as well as could be wished. I saw the time approaching when I would be left alone of the party of 'unsound method.' The pilgrims looked upon me with disfavour. I was, so to speak, numbered with the dead. It is strange how I accepted this unforeseen partnership, this choice of nightmares forced upon me in the tenebrous land invaded by these mean and greedy phantoms.

"Kurtz discoursed. A voice! a voice! It rang deep to the very last. It survived his strength to hide in the magnificent folds of eloquence the barren darkness of his heart. Oh, he struggled! he struggled! The wastes of his weary brain were haunted by shadowy images now—images of wealth and fame revolving obsequiously round his unextinguishable gift of noble and lofty expression. My Intended, my station, my career, my ideas—these were the subjects for the occasional utterances of elevated sentiments. The shade of the original Kurtz frequented the bedside of the hollow sham, whose fate it was to be buried presently in the mould of primeval earth. But both the diabolic love and the unearthly hate of the mysteries it had penetrated fought for the possession of that soul satiated with primitive emotions, avid of lying fame, of sham distinction, of all appearances of success and power.

"Sometimes he was contemptibly childish. He desired to have kings meet him at railway-stations on his return from some ghastly Nowhere, where he intended to accomplish great things. 'You show them you have in you something that is really profitable, and then there will be no limits to the recognition of your ability,' he would say. 'Of course you must take care of the motives—right motives—always.' The long reaches that were like one and the same reach, monotonous bends that were exactly alike, slipped past the steamer with their multitude of secular trees looking patiently after this grimy fragment of another world, the forerunner of change, of conquest, of trade, of massacres, of blessings. I looked ahead—piloting. 'Close the shutters,' said Kurtz suddenly one day; 'I can't bear to look at this.' I did so. There was a silence. 'Oh, but I will wring your heart yet!' he cried at the invisible wilderness.

"We broke down—as I had expected—and had to lie up for repairs at the head of an island. This delay was the first thing that shook Kurtz's confidence. One morning he gave me a packet of papers and a photograph—the lot tied together with a shoe-string. 'Keep this for me,' he said. 'This noxious fool' (meaning the manager) 'is capable of prying into my boxes when I am not looking.' In the afternoon I saw him. He was lying on his back with closed eyes, and I withdrew quietly, but I heard him mutter, 'Live rightly, die, die . . .' I listened. There was nothing more. Was he rehearsing some speech in his sleep, or was it a fragment of a phrase from some newspaper article? He had been writing for the papers and meant to do so again, 'for the furthering of my ideas. It's a duty.'

"His was an impenetrable darkness. I looked at him as you peer down at a man who is lying at the bottom of a precipice where the sun never shines. But I had not much time to give him, because I was help-ing the engine-driver to take to pieces the leaky cylinders, to straighten a bent connecting-rod, and in other such matters. I lived in an infernal mess of rust, filings, nuts, bolts, spanners, hammers, ratchet-drills— things I abominate, because I don't get on with them. I tended the lit-tle forge we fortunately had aboard; I toiled wearily in a wretched scrap-heap—unless I had the shakes too bad to stand.

"One evening coming in with a candle I was startled to hear him say a little tremulously, 'I am lying here in the dark waiting for death.' The light was within a foot of his eyes. I forced myself to murmur, 'Oh, nonsense!' and stood over him as if transfixed.

"Anything approaching the change that came over his features I have never seen before, and hope never to see again. Oh, I wasn't touched. I was fascinated. It was as though a veil had been rent. I saw on that ivory face the expression of sombre pride, of ruthless power, of craven terror—of an intense and hopeless despair. Did he live his life again in every detail of desire, temptation, and surrender during that supreme moment of complete knowledge? He cried in a whisper at some image, at some vision—he cried out twice, a cry that was no more than a breath—

"'The horror! The horror!'

"I blew the candle out and left the cabin. The pilgrims were dining in the mess-room, and I took my place opposite the manager, who lifted his eyes to give me a questioning glance, which I successfully ignored. He leaned back, serene, with that peculiar smile of his sealing the unexpressed depths of his meanness. A continuous shower of small flies streamed upon the lamp, upon the cloth, upon our hands and faces. Suddenly the manager's boy put his insolent black head in the doorway, and said in a tone of scathing contempt—

"'Mister Kurtz—he dead.'

"All the pilgrims rushed out to see. I remained, and went on with my dinner. I believe I was considered brutally callous. However, I did not eat much. There was a lamp in there—light, don't you know—and outside it was so beastly, beastly dark. I went no more near the remark-able man who had pronounced a judgement upon the adventures of his soul on this earth. The voice was gone. What else had been there? But I am of course aware that next day the pilgrims buried something in a muddy hole.

"And then they very nearly buried me.

"However, as you see, I did not go to join Kurtz there and then. I did not. I remained to dream the nightmare out to the end, and to show my loyalty to Kurtz once more. Destiny. My destiny! Droll thing life is—that mysterious arrangement of merciless logic for a futile pur-pose. The most you can hope from it is some knowledge of yourself— that comes too late—a crop of unextinguishable regrets. I have

wrestled with death. It is the most unexciting contest you can imagine.
It takes place in an impalpable greyness, with nothing underfoot, with
nothing around, without spectators, without clamour, without glory,
without the great desire of victory, without the great fear of defeat, in a
sickly atmosphere of tepid scepticism, without much belief in your own
right, and still less in that of your adversary. If such is the form of ultimate wisdom, then life is a greater riddle than some of us think it to be.
I was within a hair's-breadth of the last opportunity for pronounce-
ment, and I found with humiliation that probably I would have nothing to say. This is the reason why I affirm that Kurtz was a remarkable
man. He had something to say. He said it. Since I had peeped over the
edge myself, I understand better the meaning of his stare, that could
not see the flame of the candle, but was wide enough to embrace the
whole universe, piercing enough to penetrate all the hearts that beat in
the darkness. He had summed up—he had judged. 'The horror!' He was
a remarkable man. After all, this was the expression of some sort of
belief; it had candour, it had conviction, it had a vibrating note of
revolt in its whisper, it had the appalling face of a glimpsed truth—the
strange commingling of desire and hate. And it is not my own extremity I remember best—a vision of greyness without form filled with physical pain, and a careless contempt for the evanescence of all things—
even of this pain itself. No! It is his extremity that I seem to have lived
through. True, he had made that last stride, he had stepped over the
edge, while I had been permitted to draw back my hesitating foot. And
perhaps in this is the whole difference; perhaps all the wisdom, and all
truth, and all sincerity, are just compressed into that inappreciable
moment of time in which we step over the threshold of the invisible.
Perhaps! I like to think my summing-up would not have been a word of
careless contempt. Better his cry—much better. It was an affirmation, a
moral victory, paid for by innumerable defeats, by abominable terrors,
by abominable satisfactions. But it was a victory! That is why I have
remained loyal to Kurtz to the last, and even beyond, when a long time
after I heard once more, not his own voice, but the echo of his magnificent eloquence thrown to me from a soul as translucently pure as a cliff
of crystal.

"No, they did not bury me, though there is a period of time which I
remember mistily, with a shuddering wonder, like a passage through
some inconceivable world that had no hope in it and no desire. I found
myself back in the sepulchral city resenting the sight of people hurrying
through the streets to filch a little money from each other, to devour
their infamous cookery, to gulp their unwholesome beer, to dream their
insignificant and silly dreams. They trespassed upon my thoughts. They
were intruders whose knowledge of life was to me an irritating pretence, because I felt so sure they could not possibly know the things I
knew. Their bearing, which was simply the bearing of commonplace

individuals going about their business in the assurance of perfect safety, was offensive to me like the outrageous flauntings of folly in the face of a danger it is unable to comprehend. I had no particular desire to enlighten them, but I had some difficulty in restraining myself from laughing in their faces, so full of stupid importance. I daresay I was not very well at that time. I tottered about the streets—there were various affairs to settle—grinning bitterly at perfectly respectable persons. I admit my behaviour was inexcusable, but then my temperature was seldom normal in these days. My dear aunt's endeavours to 'nurse up my strength' seemed altogether beside the mark. It was not my strength that wanted nursing, it was my imagination that wanted soothing. I kept the bundle of papers given me by Kurtz, not knowing exactly what to do with it. His mother had died lately, watched over, as I was told, by his Intended. A clean-shaved man, with an official manner and wearing gold-rimmed spectacles, called on me one day and made inquiries, at first circuitous, afterwards suavely pressing, about what he was pleased to denominate certain 'documents.' I was not surprised, because I had had two rows with the manager on the subject out there. I had refused to give up the smallest scrap out of that package, and I took the same attitude with the spectacled man. He became darkly menacing at last, and with much heat argued that the Company had the right to every bit of information about its 'territories.' And said he, 'Mr. Kurtz's knowledge of unexplored regions must have been necessarily extensive and peculiar—owing to his great abilities and to the deplorable circumstances in which he had been placed: therefore—' I assured him Mr. Kurtz's knowledge, however extensive, did not bear upon the problems of commerce or administration. He invoked then the name of science. 'It would be an incalculable loss if,' etc., etc. I offered him the report on the 'Suppression of Savage Customs,' with the postscriptum torn off. He took it up eagerly, but ended by sniffing at it with an air of contempt. 'This is not what we had a right to expect,' he remarked. 'Expect nothing else,' I said. 'There are only private letters.' He withdrew upon some threat of legal proceedings, and I saw him no more; but another fellow, calling himself Kurtz's cousin, appeared two days later, and was anxious to hear all the details about his dear relative's last moments. Incidentally he gave me to understand that Kurtz had been essentially a great musician. 'There was the making of an immense success,' said the man, who was an organist, I believe, with lank grey hair flowing over a greasy coat-collar. I had no reason to doubt his statement; and to this day I am unable to say what was Kurtz's profession, whether he ever had any—which was the greatest of his talents. I had taken him for a painter who wrote for the papers, or else for a journalist who could paint—but even the cousin (who took snuff during the interview) could not tell me what he had been—exactly. He was a universal genius—on that point I agreed with the old chap, who thereupon blew his nose noisily into a large cotton handkerchief and withdrew in senile agitation, bearing off some family letters and memoranda without importance. Ultimately a journalist anxious to know something of the fate of his 'dear colleague' turned up. This visitor informed me Kurtz's proper sphere ought to have been politics 'on the popular side.' He had furry straight eyebrows, bristly hair cropped short, an eye-glass on a broad ribbon, and, becoming expansive, confessed his opinion that Kurtz really couldn't write a bit—'but heavens! how that man could talk. He electrified large meetings. He had faith—don't you see?—he had the faith. He could get himself to believe anything—anything. He would have been a splendid leader of an extreme party.' 'What party?' I asked. 'Any party,' answered the other. 'He was an—an—extremist.' Did I not think so? I assented. Did I know, he asked, with a sudden flash of curiosity, 'what it was that had induced him to go out there?' 'Yes,' said I, and forthwith handed him the famous Report for publication, if he thought fit. He glanced through it hurriedly, mumbling all the time, judged 'it would do,' and took himself off with this plunder.

"Thus I was left at last with a slim packet of letters and the girl's portrait. She struck me as beautiful—I mean she had a beautiful expression. I know that the sunlight can be made to lie, too, yet one felt that no manipulation of light and pose could have conveyed the delicate shade of truthfulness upon those features. She seemed ready to listen without mental reservation, without suspicion, without a thought for herself. I concluded I would go and give her back her portrait and those letters myself. Curiosity? Yes; and also some other feelings perhaps. All that had been Kurtz's had passed out of my hands: his soul, his body, his station, his plans, his ivory, his career. There remained only his memory and his Intended—and I wanted to give that up, too, to the past, in a way—to surrender personally all that remained of him with me to that oblivion which is the last word of our common fate. I don't defend myself. I had no clear perception of what it was I really wanted. Perhaps it was an impulse of unconscious loyalty, or a fulfilment of one of these ironic necessities that lurk in the facts of human existence. I don't know. I can't tell. But I went.

"I thought his memory was like the other memories of the dead that accumulate in every man's life—a vague impress on the brain of shadows that had fallen on it in their swift and final passage; but before the high and ponderous door, between the tall houses of a street as still and decorous as a well-kept alley in a cemetery, I had a vision of him on the stretcher, opening his mouth voraciously, as if to devour all the earth with all its mankind. He lived then before me; he lived as much as he had ever lived—a shadow insatiable of splendid appearances, of frightful realities; a shadow darker than the shadow of the night, and draped nobly in the folds of a gorgeous eloquence. The vision seemed to enter the house with me—the stretcher, the phantom-bearers, the wild crowd of obedient worshippers, the gloom of the forests, the glitter of the reach between the murky bends, the beat of the drum, regular and muffled like the beating of a heart—the heart of a conquering darkness. It was a moment of triumph for the wilderness, an invading and vengeful rush which, it seemed to me, I would have to keep back alone for the salvation of another soul. And the memory of what I had heard him say afar there, with the horned shapes stirring at my back, in the glow of fires, within the patient woods, those broken phrases came back to me, were heard again in their ominous and terrifying simplicity. I remembered his abject pleading, his abject threats, the colossal scale of his vile desires, the meanness, the torment, the tempestuous anguish of his soul. And later on I seemed to see his collected languid manner, when he said one day, 'This lot of ivory now is really mine. The Company did not pay for it. I collected it myself at a very great personal risk. I am afraid they will try to claim it as theirs though. H'm. It is a difficult case. What do you think I ought to do—resist? Eh? I want no more than justice.' . . . He wanted no more than justice—no more than justice. I rang the bell before a mahogany door on the first floor, and while I waited he seemed to stare at me out of the glassy panel—stare with that wide and immense stare embracing, condemning, loathing all the universe. I seemed to hear the whispered cry, 'The horror! The horror!'

"The dusk was falling. I had to wait in a lofty drawing-room with three long windows from floor to ceiling that were like three luminous and bedraped columns. The bent gilt legs and backs of the furniture shone in indistinct curves. The tall marble fireplace had a cold and monumental whiteness. A grand piano stood massively in a corner; with dark gleams on the flat surfaces like a sombre and polished sarcophagus. A high door opened—closed. I rose.

"She came forward, all in black, with a pale head, floating towards me in the dusk. She was in mourning. It was more than a year since his death, more than a year since the news came; she seemed as though she would remember and mourn for ever. She took both my hands in hers and murmured, 'I had heard you were coming.' I noticed she was not very young—I mean not girlish. She had a mature capacity for fidelity, for belief, for suffering. The room seemed to have grown darker, as if all the sad light of the cloudy evening had taken refuge on her forehead. This fair hair, this pale visage, this pure brow, seemed surrounded by an ashy halo from which the dark eyes looked out at me. Their glance was guileless, profound, confident, and trustful. She carried her sorrowful head as though she were proud of that sorrow, as though she would say, I—I alone know how to mourn for him as he deserves. But while we were still shaking hands, such a look of awful desolation came upon her face that I perceived she was one of those creatures that are not the playthings of Time. For her he had died only yesterday. And, by Jove!

the impression was so powerful that for me, too, he seemed to have died only yesterday—nay, this very minute. I saw her and him in the same instant of time—his death and her sorrow—I saw her sorrow in the very moment of his death. Do you understand? I saw them together—I heard them together. She had said, with a deep catch of the breath, 'I have survived'; while my strained ears seemed to hear distinctly, min-gled with her tone of despairing regret, the summing-up whisper of his eternal condemnation. I asked myself what I was doing there, with a sensation of panic in my heart as though I had blundered into a place of cruel and absurd mysteries not fit for a human being to behold. She motioned me to a chair. We sat down. I laid the packet gently on the little table, and she put her hand over it. . . . 'You knew him well,' she murmured, after a moment of mourning silence.

"'Intimacy grows quickly out there,' I said. 'I knew him as well as it is possible for one man to know another.'

"'And you admired him,' she said. 'It was impossible to know him and not to admire him. Was it?'

"'He was a remarkable man,' I said, unsteadily. Then before the appealing fixity of her gaze, that seemed to watch for more words on my lips, I went on. 'It was impossible not to—'

"'Love him,' she finished eagerly, silencing me into an appalled dumbness. 'How true! how true! But when you think that no one knew him so well as I! I had all his noble confidence. I knew him best.'

"'You knew him best,' I repeated. And perhaps she did. But with every word spoken the room was growing darker, and only her fore-head, smooth and white, remained illuminated by the unextinguishable light of belief and love.

"'You were his friend,' she went on. 'His friend,' she repeated, a little louder. 'You must have been, if he had given you this, and sent you to me. I feel I can speak to you—and oh! I must speak. I want you—you who have heard his last words—to know I have been worthy of him. . . . It is not pride. . . . Yes! I am proud to know I understood him better than any one on earth—he told me so himself. And since his mother died I have had no one—no one—to—to—'

"I listened. The darkness deepened. I was not even sure whether he had given me the right bundle. I rather suspect he wanted me to take care of another batch of his papers which, after his death, I saw the manager examining under the lamp. And the girl talked, easing her pain in the certitude of my sympathy; she talked as thirsty men drink. I had heard that her engagement with Kurtz had been disapproved by her people. He wasn't rich enough or something. And indeed I don't know whether he had not been a pauper all his life. He had given me some reason to infer that it was his impatience of comparative poverty that drove him out there.

"'. . . Who was not his friend who had heard him speak once?' she was saying. 'He drew men towards him by what was best in them.' She looked at me with intensity. 'It is the gift of the great,' she went on, and the sound of her low voice seemed to have the accompaniment of all the other sounds, full of mystery, desolation, and sorrow, I had ever heard—the ripple of the river, the soughing of the trees swayed by the wind, the murmurs of the crowds, the faint ring of incomprehensible words cried from afar, the whisper of a voice speaking from beyond the threshold of an eternal darkness. 'But you have heard him! You know!' she cried.

"'Yes, I know,' I said with something like despair in my heart, but bowing my head before the faith that was in her, before that great and saving illusion that shone with an unearthly glow in the darkness, in the triumphant darkness from which I could not have defended her—from which I could not even defend myself.

"'What a loss to me—to us!'—she corrected herself with beautiful generosity; then added in a murmur, 'To the world.' By the last gleams of twilight I could see the glitter of her eyes, full of tears—of tears that would not fall.

"'I have been very happy—very fortunate—very proud,' she went on. 'Too fortunate. Too happy for a little while. And now I am unhappy for—for life.'

"She stood up; her fair hair seemed to catch all the remaining light in a glimmer of gold. I rose, too.

"'And of all this,' she went on, mournfully, 'of all his promise, and of all his greatness, of his generous mind, of his noble heart, nothing remains—nothing but a memory. You and I—'

"'We shall always remember him,' I said, hastily.

"'No!' she cried. 'It is impossible that all this should be lost—that such a life should be sacrificed to leave nothing—but sorrow. You know what vast plans he had. I knew of them, too—I could not perhaps understand—but others knew of them. Something must remain. His words, at least, have not died.'

"'His words will remain,' I said.

"'And his example,' she whispered to herself. 'Men looked up to him—his goodness shone in every act. His example—'

"'True,' I said; 'his example, too. Yes, his example. I forgot that.'

"'But I do not. I cannot—I cannot believe—not yet. I cannot believe that I shall never see him again, that nobody will see him again, never, never, never.'

"She put out her arms as if after a retreating figure, stretching them back and with clasped pale hands across the fading and narrow sheen of the window. Never see him! I saw him clearly enough then. I shall see this eloquent phantom as long as I live, and I shall see her, too, a tragic and familiar Shade, resembling in this gesture another one, tragic also, and bedecked with powerless charms, stretching bare brown arms over the glitter of the infernal stream, the stream of darkness. She said suddenly very low, 'He died as he lived.'

"'His end,' said I, with dull anger stirring in me, 'was in every way worthy of his life.'

"'And I was not with him,' she murmured. My anger subsided before a feeling of infinite pity.

"'Everything that could be done—' I mumbled.

"'Ah, but I believed in him more than any one on earth—more than his own mother, more than—himself. He needed me! Me! I would have treasured every sigh, every word, every sign, every glance.'

"I felt like a chill grip on my chest. 'Don't,' I said, in a muffled voice.

"'Forgive me. I—I—have mourned so long in silence—in silence . . . You were with him—to the last? I think of his loneliness. Nobody near to understand him as I would have understood. Perhaps no one to hear . . .'

"'To the very end,' I said, shakily. 'I heard his very last words. . . .' I stopped in fright.

"'Repeat them,' she murmured in a heart-broken tone. 'I want—I want—something—something—to—to live with.'

"I was on the point of crying at her, 'Don't you hear them?' The dusk was repeating them in a persistent whisper all around us, in a whisper that seemed to swell menacingly like the first whisper of a rising wind. 'The horror! the horror!'

"'His last word—to live with,' she insisted. 'Don't you understand I loved him—I loved him—I loved him!'

"I pulled myself together and spoke slowly.

"'The last word he pronounced was—your name.'

"I heard a light sigh and then my heart stood still, stopped dead short by an exulting and terrible cry, by the cry of inconceivable triumph and of unspeakable pain. 'I knew it—I was sure!' . . . She knew. She was sure. I heard her weeping; she had hidden her face in her hands. It seemed to me that the house would collapse before I could escape, that the heavens would fall upon my head. But nothing happened. The heavens do not fall for such a trifle. Would they have fallen, I wonder, if I had rendered Kurtz that justice which was his due? Hadn't he said he wanted only justice? But I couldn't. I could not tell her. It would have been too dark—too dark altogether. . . ."

Marlow ceased, and sat apart, indistinct and silent, in the pose of a meditating Buddha. Nobody moved for a time. "We have lost the first of the ebb," said the Director, suddenly. I raised my head. The offing was barred by a black bank of clouds, and the tranquil waterway leading to the uttermost ends of the earth flowed sombre under an overcast sky—seemed to lead into the heart of an immense darkness.

Topics for Discussion:

1. According to Conrad's use of darkness, how would one define a *leitmotif?*
2. How does Conrad define evil? What various forms of evil are found in the novella?
3. What is the symbolic significance of the rivers mentioned in the narrative? How does Conrad use setting to convey ideas other than place?
4. Why is Marlow so fascinated by Kurtz?
5. How does Conrad convey the various ideas of death?
6. What is the purpose of the scene on the deck of the *Nellie* at the beginning and the ending of the story?
7. What role does Kurtz's "intended" play in the story?
8. Why does Conrad relate Marlow's narrative to the history of Roman exploration of England? What role does history play in the story?
9. What is the significance of the two women knitting in the Company office?
10. Why does Kurtz set himself up as a deity to the natives and why do they defend and worship him?
11. How does Marlow express the sense of going back in time during his journey up the river? Why does Conrad make the jungle setting so primordial?
12. Why does Marlow lie to Kurtz's intended? What is the purpose of legend-making and why does Marlow reinvent Kurtz in his mind even before their meeting?
13. What does Kurtz represent?

Jose Y. Dalisay, Jr.

About the Author
Jose Y(ap) Dalisay, Jr. was born in Romblon island in the Philippines in 1954. He was educated at the University of the Philippines, the University of Michigan and the University of Wisconsin. He was winner of a Fulbright Fellowship. He was arrested and spent seven months in prison for his political activities in 1973 when President Marcos declared martial law. Dalisay now teaches English and creative writing at the University of the Philippines in Quezon City.

Considered one of the leading short story writers in the Philippines, Dalisay writes with a keen awareness of the history of his country, particularly the history of American involvement since the Second World War. "Spy Story" is taken from *Oldtimer and Other Stories*.

Selected Works
Oldtimer and Other Stories (short stories, 1984)
Sarcophagus and Other Stories (short stories, 1992)
Killing Time in a Warm Place (novel, 1992)

About the Story
"Spy Story" is set during the Cold War—a period of intensely paranoid international relations between the Soviet Union (now Russia) and the United States, when both sides eschewed open warfare in favour of political brinkmanship and espionage. In the background of this period, the Vietnam War raged. American spies were particularly active in Southeast Asia during this period because the U.S. government feared that the fall of Vietnam would trigger the "domino effect," according to which one nation after another would fall under Communist domination.

The story is set in a bar in the Philippines where Fred, a Filipino who works as a chauffeur for the United States Embassy, is busy entertaining an American government representative whom he reinvents as a spy.

Spy Story

He didn't like it the first half-hour because he was just as uptight as the girls were. The Guadarrama was a new place for him; he knew neither the bartender nor the Mama-san and he felt useless, a feeling he was even less accustomed to.

He sipped his beer and held it close, and it helped him stay on this side of the cool while the girls kept to their side of the fence. Whatever cool was and wherever the fence was; it was hopeless to define anything exactly after three beers, in the eerie blackness of the ultraviolet lamp they turned on, or "off," as the case could have been every time the Guadarrama's in-house band took a restroom break. Mantovani came on over the speakers and a fan of Mozart in the next table groaned.

A big fat American in a hula shirt and plaid pants was waddling towards him, flashing a fluorescent grin, and he realized with a start that he knew the man and was, in fact, the man's host, or guest, depending on either whose country it was, or who ended up paying the bill. He was even more surprised to see that this man McCord had one of the natives in tow, a slip of a girl, chosen from among the half-dozen in the left-corner lot. The girl's hand was trapped in the crook of McCord's elbow, and seemed to stick out of his body like an odd growth. Two tapered stripes meant the girl had just her bikini on and was probably angling for business before the room lights came on and McCord saw other sights.

"Fred!" It was the first time in something like forty-five minutes that he'd heard his name called and Fred remembered that McCord was supposed to be Luke, or Lucas, or Lew.

"Fred, you gotta meet Yaw-lee. Yaw-lee, is it? Yaw-lee, say hello to Fred, a great friend of mine."

Yoly nodded to Fred, chose quickly from what must have been a thin repertoire of thin smiles and gave one to him. "Hi, Fred. Are you Indonesian?"

"No. Filipino. *Kumusta?*"

Her for-Indonesians-only smile vanished and McCord laughed as he settled in his chair and propped Yoly up on his lap and laid a fat palm across *her* lap, all in one continuous motion. He laughed like a burst balloon—no "hee-haws" or "ha-has," just one long "heeee."

"Whatsamatter, Yaw-lee? Can't recognize one of your own? Heee. . . . Gotta little confession of my own to make, though. Been to 'Nam, Bangkok, Bali, 'n all those places, on business, ya know, and I still can't tell which is which. I don't mean the places, friend, I mean you and our Asian brothers. Whatszat Confucius say? Ya seen one, ya seen them all! Heeee. . . ." Fred shuddered as McCord's left hand was still on Yoly's lap like a hairy lizard asleep on a rock and with his free hand he whipped out his handkerchief expertly as though he'd practiced it all his life. Yoly took the handkerchief even more deftly from McCord's hand. The American frowned for a split second at the thought that Yoly was stealing his Hong Kong-made handkerchief right under his nose, then relaxed and played old Daddy as Yoly went to work on his steaming forehead.

"It's okay, dear, I do this for you, free, okay? Just for you." Yoly ran a hankie-covered finger across McCord's wet lips and purred "I like you." McCord seemed stunned to hear this, glanced at Fred with the look of a man with five minutes to live, and said softly to Yoly's ear "I like you, too, Yaw-lee."

Fred gagged, rose and said "Restroom." "John," he thought, was probably easier, he's heard that a lot more often at the office, but it seemed confusing just then and Fred brooded over his English on the way to the Men's room.

A pair of hands grabbed at Fred's neck the moment he leaned against the restroom wall to piss. He had just begun to close his eyes and he thought Oh my God the last thing I saw alive was green paint and my fly was open. He smelled alcohol; the hands were washed in alcohol; they were kneading him. It felt good. He turned and recognized his masseur as a brown blur with an exotic dash of red across the mouth. The fellow also used eye make-up and Fred noticed that he-she was smiling but his-her eyes were looking to do murder.

"Okay, boss?"

Fred zipped up and pressed a coin to the masseur's palm and the red lips mimicked a pout but Fred was out before they broke apart in a winner's grin.

Fred picked his way across the tables to where he'd left McCord and Yoly and saw even from afar that the scene and the mood had changed. Yoly was now in his seat across from McCord and they were holding hands under the tale, looking into each other's eyes and whispering. A fresh beer and rum coke had been brought up and forgotten, as he probably was by Luke, Lucas or Lewis McCord.

Fred slipped onto a vacant stool in the bar, between two other couples, ordered his own beer and began to think of Marlene.

Now Marlene was *his* kind of girl in *his* kind of place, Fred said, and if it hadn't been for this date with McCurdy—or, rather, McCord—he would've been at Marlene's that very minute. Marlene was white and pink and smooth and luscious and was even worth the conversation, sometimes. She was cool. She was a dream he could live with. Marlene never "went out," too, not that he knew of, anyway.

He checked McCord and saw the man's head making little nods from side to side. McCord was talking and Yoly had her listening act pat, from the unblinking eyes and the half-opened mouth and the chin-knuckles-and-elbows set-up, down to the curled toes, just in case McCord dropped his pen. There wasn't a girl in the world with a more obvious fascination for tractors, the Pittsburgh Steelers and grains futures than Yaw-lee. There were even times, Fred thought, that Marlene looked much too much like that, even though he had a much more interesting line-up of topics that invariable included basketball, limousines, life in the States and the antics of the men he'd heard about that life from, over at the Embassy. McCord would be up for verbal vivisection next week but he didn't seem to promise much of a story, at least not the sort of story that Marlene liked. Marlene saw all of Fred's visiting friends as being just half a notch below the American bald-eagle Presidency, the way Fred told things, and sometimes Fred even spoke in clipped, hushed tones behind a dark green pair of American Optical aviator's glasses as though *he*, too, had to protect his anonymity. Marlene, of course, never really *saw* Fred's friends, not yet, although he kept promising that he would bring one of them over to Marlene's beer-and-goat-stew joint one day, just for show and then only for maybe ten minutes of their precious time.

⤬

Luscious Lucius McCord was an agricultural engineer, the first of his specialty to fall into Fred's hands. McCord had liked him instantly as soon as they'd driven off from the airport and by the time they'd gotten to McCord's hotel Fred had him down as another of his fast friends.

"Geez, man, does this thing have *brakes*? Heeee!..." McCord had said from the backseat and Fred saw in the mirror that McCord had both hands glued onto the backrest of the empty seat beside Fred. McCord was grinning. Running into some heavy traffic, Fred tipped his cap, gunned the shift stick forward, stepped on the gas and squeezed the horn ring. The big white Bonneville punched a six-foot-wide hole between the Volks and the Colt ahead of it by sheer force of terror and slid through. McCord almost clapped.

That, plus his English, plus the impression he somehow projected of being in on every little secret the city had, endeared him to Sparks. Mr. Sparks worked over at the Cultural Affairs office, signing little vellum-paper notes with RSVPs. Fred dropped them every now and then at the same tired addresses around Manila, often as not handing them over personally, like a special envoy from the White House, to some giggling uniformed maid. If he was lucky he got to use the flashy El Dorado from the car pool—Sparks signed *anything* in the cause of culture—and if he wasn't, well, the Bonneville wasn't too bad, either. The important thing was to cruise around with "US EMB" plates because they took you to some very special places just any old "H," or even "RP" or "DC," couldn't. When he had to get to somewhere *fast*, like 120 KPH on a 40 KPH MAX road, Fred wore his best frantic, wild-eyed "I've-got-*him*-in-the-backseat" look. Him who? "The Ambassador-that's-who-and-get-out-of-my-way-Geronimo!"

After five, however, Fred slipped incognito behind the wheel of a metallic brown, fully-loaded, "B"-plated '73 Toyota that was legally his—though he had had to lay everything on the block, just that *once*, ten years' good service to the US government, fidelity, friendship and the RP-US Mutual Assistance Pact and all that, for a small personal loan from his boss, Andrew V. Sparks, just to get the deal on the car nailed down with the Indian ex-diplomat who was selling it cheap but for dollars US, no rupees please, thank you.

Sparks had coughed a bit and Fred began walking backwards to the door, eyes on the floor, when Sparks quite casually said "Sure thing" and Fred threw his cap to the ceiling.

Since then, however, and despite the fact that he had long paid Mr. Sparks back, black-market-dollar-by-black-market-dollar plus a new size-"XL" *barong* for the favor, Fred never quite felt that the Toyota was truly and totally his own, especially when Sparks began gifting him, or *it*, with a perfectly serviceable air conditioner "that Harry was going to throw to the junk heap, Chrissakes," a set of run-away "radials the kids were going to use for swings" and even a fancy US Bicentennial sticker from the Philadelphia Tourist Bureau. From his own money, Fred covered the dashboard with fake fuzz of pale pink that made Sparks wince when he saw it, and Fred thought that he knew he should have bought the orange one instead.

⬥

It wasn't long after the radials came that Sparks put in his first gee-I'm-in-a-fix "personal request" for Fred to show a visiting history professor named Zabusky "the sights." Almost as an afterthought, Sparks slipped him three hundred-notes "for the gas and whatever." Man oh man, that was a *lot* of gas and whatever.

"You mean the Folk Art Theater and the Metropolitan Museum, Mr. Sparks?" Fred had asked, proud of his with-it-ness, but Sparks had laughed and said "Hell, no!"

He didn't get to use the El Dorado or even the Bonneville, either, Sparks pleading "after-hours regulations," but then Fred had his Toyota and an always-full tank, courtesy of a four-foot length of garden hose and the Bonneville Gas Co. He wondered if Sparks knew about *that*.

Zabusky was short, gruff and had a tic in his left eye but turned out to be a regular cocktail-lounge dreamboat, charming the ladies with what Fred overheard to be "coochiecoos" and pinches in the right places at the right time. It must've helped, too, that the professor tried to pay their first drinks off with a genuine C-note, sorry, no change here either, but then Fred suddenly felt very hospitably Filipino with his first guest and dove for the bill and peeled off his own local hundred-note from Sparks' "whatever" fund and paid and immediately felt foolish afterwards. It occurred to Fred the next morning that Zabusky's C-note had looked as though it had seen a lot of the same use—always flashed, never changed—but what the hell, the night had been fun, ending at a motel where Fred had played *cara y cruz* with the roomboys while Zabusky coochie-cooed it upstairs with an ethnic Venus named Vheng. Fred didn't mind the wait; he cleared two hundred-plus for the bother and won P3.50 from the roomboys.

The visiting professor was followed by half-a-dozen others over as many months, and Fred found that he enjoyed the extra business despite the fact that Sparks was still calling them "requests," "favors" and "I-owe-you-ones" and actually seemed anxious that Fred would turn him down every time he asked. Just as smoothly, Fred put on his own little show of almost, almost having a reason to say no before saying "but just for you . . ." in the second act.

Baggio was a Detroit cop on loan as a consultant to the city's traffic division; despite this being *his* country, Fred felt obliged to make the El Dorado crawl. Housman was a limnologist, whatever that was; Fellows was an amateur golfer; and the three Smiths—just like that, all at once, a statistical freak—were plain civil servants. One of them, Jim Smith, was even just another chauffeur on some visiting Congressman's staff and true to calling insisted on taking the wheel when Fred picked him up in the Toyota. Fred wondered why, between colleagues in the profession, Jim Smith had to go through Sparks to get the thing set up, and even more so why Sparks seemed so concerned for the well-being of his government's chauffeurs. Fred drove convoy with Jim Smith the next day when the Congressman called at Malacañang and Sparks decided to come along for the ride, wearing his most rumpled and worried look, but nothing passed between Sparks and Smith, not even the most perfunctory "How ya doin'."

It was a dripping wet day in July when Fred looked up from the old copy of *Newsweek* he'd been thumbing through in the backseat of a Ford wagon in the maintenance shed and stared at his own eyes in the mirror as though to confirm how shocked he really was at his one-plus-one discovery. The back issue had an uncharacteristically flippant story on spies, spooks and saboteurs—in the movies, it turned out—but Fred was no fool to miss the connections, and when he emerged form the shed he glanced left, right and backward before making for the cafeteria. He'd nearly finished his coffee when he saw Sparks stride in with Mrs. Loewe from Visas and they were chatting about something having to do with ballet. She couldn't be, Fred decided and Sparks detached himself for a while from the old lady still smiling just a sec and kept his smile on as he passed Fred a note jotted down on the back of a visa-denial form. Maybe *she* was in it after all.

"Oh there you are that's all right nothing's up except this—uh—call I got from Jerry you know Jerry the new guy in Waite's office. Asked me if I could spare you for a little chore this afternoon and hell I couldn't say no he's not a bad guy so —" Sparks paused and shrugged. "Name's McCord CX 319 that's Hong Kong 4 pm there won't be anyone else from Waite's or ours so make a sign and smile and bring him to the Tropicana. It's all there," Sparks added helpfully, nodding at the note that Fred was trying to make some sense of. "Grab something from the car pool I'll sign for it but get it back here before five the Old Man's been up in arms about US EMB cars all over the —" Sparks stopped there and Fred nodded profoundly. So Jerry and Mr. Waite—Economic Affairs—were in it, too.

"The 'usual,' sir?" Fred asked, and just in time because Sparks had already turned to rejoin Mrs. Loewe.

Sparks barely looked back and said, smiling, "Uh-huh." US Emb. Reg. 47.03 Official Transport Para. (b) was quite clear enough about the point. Be back soon.

Fred wanted to ask a few more things and wondered why Sparks had said nothing about "gas and whatever" this time since he would be using the Toyota after five but he shut up, concluding that Sparks had found out his little Bonneville Gas Co. racket but was keeping mum— as a friendly favor, and as wisely bought insurance. As for the balance, well, there was a lot of time tomorrow to attend to that giggle-giggle-little detail. If Sparks signed anything, he would reimburse anything.

"McCord, Lucius T."

He was another one of them. Somehow Fred didn't feel too excited about that, not anymore, and that was good. You had to keep cool and casual to survive in the business, and Fred was resolved to become not only the friendliest and most efficient but also the coolest, more casual and longest surviving chauffeur the "CIA, Manila Station" ever had.

CIA HQS. Calling FRED. "Your mission, should you decide to accept it, is to personally arrange and supervise the R & R requirements of executives detailed to the MLA Station. . ." Pick-Up MCCORD LT. S/S. Show him the sights. Over. Fred felt dizzy.

"Where'dya learn to speak English?" McCord had demanded at the Customs area, thinking Fred was too good to be true and was, therefore, a professional con man in the US Embassy chauffeur's disguise. McCord had just spent weeks in Chiang Mai to push local research along on a new poppy-flower-killing device which he promptly nicknamed the Poppycock, but no one seemed to know enough English to appreciate the subtle humor of the thing.

"In school." Fred said dryly, not totally impressed by this new arrival. "Most of us speak English here."

"Heeeeh!..." McCord said, his eyes twinkling. "Never could make any sense out of that goddamn Spanish phrase-book anyway." And then McCord leaned closer, confidentially, and said "But I'll bet your girls speak French! Most girls do, heeee!. . ." and slapped Fred flat across the back. Right away Fred thought God they sure picked a joker for this job but strangely enough he felt McCord was somebody he could get to like; McCord, at least, was a relief from the no-smiles Foggy Bottom Type A's he's been driving around lately and legitimately. These were Mr. Jessup's Political Affairs people but sometimes Sparks loaned him out to *that* section, too.

⋙⧓⋘

"Won't you take me to—Funky Town! Won't you take me to—Funky Town!"

His head snapped back up sharply and Fred realized that he had been asleep for some time. It seemed a long time, but he knew that that was only because he was half-drunk. Or half-sober.

The five-piece band was back onstage with "Funky Town" and the two-piece dancers were back in their proper places. The dancefloor lights had also been switched back from UV black to red but visibility stayed pretty much at the same murky level except where the dancers shook it. All the girls had made-to-order crocheted bikinis with their names lettered lovingly across the bottoms—JOYCE, ANNA, BABES—Fred looked higher on up and smiled. He looked still *higher* up, and scratched his chin, wondering to himself why fellows like McCord who had their choice of Playmates, Pets and Honeys back home preferred the sunbaked, curly-top, buck-toothed types that A. Mabini had in the hundreds to uncommonly creamy chinitas like Marlene who was the closest thing Fred had to a Playmate, Far Eastern edition.

McCord. Fred remembered McCord and nearly knocked over an Australian sailor when he swiveled to where McCord and the girl had been. "Ey, mate!"

"Sorry," Fred mumbled. There were three of the sailors and while they all glared at him he knew they would think him too much of a zero, a nothing, to waste the effort of a fight for. It was the same way the girls saw him in every Mabini bar and while it *did* hurt a bit at first it was something he soon learned to expect, even cherish, because indifference kept him cool, casual and anonymous.

McCord and—who was it? Yaw-lee—Yoly were still there all right but again Fred sensed that things had passed on to something else: McCord had both of Yoly's hands in his, up close to his chest, but Yoly herself sagged back in her chair looking all of being deathly bored by McCord. Yoly had dropped all pretenses of listening and McCord was in love and kept on talking and wasn't being listened to and was, degree by dark degree, becoming desperate. The Mama-san passed by their table and without looking at McCord gave a hand sign that only Yoly understood.

So *that*, Fred thought, was McCord's little pot of jam—McCord like falling in love, over and over again like a movie fan, and it was even better if the ladies fell in love with him likewise. He was a sucker for the soft touch, the yours-only endearment, the bittersweet mush. Yoly had said "I like you" but it was the brow-mopping and lip-touching thing before that that had pushed a button and set a bomb ticking. Baggio the cop was McCord's antithesis—he liked things bad and bruising at first, and only then turned angelic.

Yoly's glances began to turn to another foreign-looking fellow seated alone at a corner table and McCord had to be stoneblind not to notice that; but this time he was doing the pretending and showed nothing. The foreigner was about Fred's own local-medium size and was black-haired and bearded and was puffing at a thin dark cigarette. The man had deep-set eyes and they were trained at Yoly. Fred felt at some loss at being unable to tell the man's nationality right off—it was a game he was fairly good at—and saw that McCord was having the same problems. The man could've been Albanian, Czech or Mongolian— although Fred had never seen a live Mongolian before—but the one thing Fred was sure of was that the man exuded an almost palpable From-Behind-the-Curtain effect. The only thing you had to do was to have a look at the man's passport to make a positive ID, but Fred realized that even that wasn't foolproof because passports could be faked if you were in the right business. The man was a *spy*. He'd latched on to McCord one way or another—could've been there all the time for all he or even McCord knew, from Bangkok to HK to Manila—but the relevant info was that he'd shown up there, much too visibly for an eye like Fred's to miss.

The Cold War had blown over across the Russian steppes and the China Sea to the Guadarrama and Fred moved slowly and deliberately to McCord's table so the mystery man could make no mistake telling which side *he* was on.

"Fred, can you believe that this honey has *two* little ones? I love kids, I just love kids," McCord was saying sweetly.

"Luke—"

The Mama-san cruised within sour-grinning range. McCord felt Yoly's hands stiffen in his. "Tell me how much you love me, Yaw-lee. Tell me just one more time, just so's my friend Fred can share the pleasure of knowing —"

"*Putangina, pare, sabihin mo sa kaibigan mo, magbayad na siya ng bar fine para makalabas na 'ko habang maaga-aga pa. Kung ayaw niya, sasama ako sa iba!*" Yoly hissed sideways to Fred but he forgave her for not seeing the geopolitical implications of the thing. The Curtain-crosser smirked and Fred understood perfectly why.

"Whatszat? What's she saying, Fred?"

"She says you're okay."

"I'll drink to that! Heeee!... Hey! —"

McCord let go of a hand of Yoly's to raise his for a waiter and Yoly took advantage of this to try and make a break for it as nicely as possible if at all possible; and she'd half-stood up but then McCord brought his palm down flat on the table again whammo no dice no deal and Yoly flinched and seemed all set to cry but she sat back down instead, trembling. McCord glared at his ladylove for about five seconds of pure unadulterated rage and let go of Yoly's other hand, wet and warped.

"Something wrong, Yaw-lee?" McCord was smiling again.

Yoly shook her head as she nursed one hand in the other, alternately, and said to Fred: "*Tanungin mo nga siya kung ano 'ng gusto niya, ibibigay ko na matapos lang.*"

Fred managed another "Luke –" and stopped right there when the Mama-san came over and this was bad because Fred had seen her arguing with a smile with Mr. Freeze or whatever the man's *nom de guerre* was. The stakes were getting higher and the scene was turning uglier faster than Fred could anticipate anything. Now Mr. Freeze had wired the Mama-san up may-I-inconvenience-you-with-a-little-bomb and sent her shuffling down Oneway Street to his target McCord.

The Mama-san let out her most patience-nearly-exhausted laugh and touched McCord lightly on the shoulder. McCord's jaw turned to stone and the Mama-san took her hand back more swiftly than McCord could've lunged at it and bitten it off.

"Is there *something* you want, darling, anything?" The Mama-san waited sweetly but McCord said nothing, keeping his eyes on Yoly. The Mama-san turned to Fred and dispensing with pleasantries said, "*Nalulugi kami sa bata mo, pare. Ikaw na 'ng kumausap, magkano ba 'ng gusto mo?*"

As frostily as he could, Fred looked at Mama-san straight in the eye to make it clear to her that he was no cheap pimp, hustler or fixer. He was an educated escort trusted by no less than Station Chief Sparks but of course it was impossible to tell her that. The two beers and rum coke came and Fred swiped his straight off the tray contemptuously. He wondered how much Mr. Freeze was offering on the other side and he realized that the man's mission was contraposed not to McCord's but to *his*. Calling "Volga" CTR, "Operation Anti-R&R" now on the board and moving, over. The man was probably mumbling something to that effect right that very minute over a mike disguised as a martini olive.

Fred took a sip of ice-cold beer. McCord planted the rum coke in Yoly's hand, raised that hand and wound his right hand which had his beer around Yoly's wrist—it seemed too terribly complicated to work—and McCord said "To us" blowing the words softly across to Yoly as though they were rose petals fit to swim on the surface of her rum coke. Things became even more difficult when McCord tried to drink his beer *from around* Yoly's wrist but he had to give up it didn't work.

The evening could have cooled off and flashed a big "M" for "mellow" in the sky at that point if the Mama-san had had more respect for men with missions. Instead she said, "*Hey* mister *sorry* but you *talk* with Yoly for two hours now no? You *want* Yoly some *more*? Our bar fine is cheap, only one-fifty for you, *okay?*"

"She's enjoyin' her drink, lady," McCord said too casually Fred thought and the Mama-san gave up.

"No drinks, no more drinks nonono. See that guy, yah, that one? He also *like* Yoly, like Yoly *more* and will pay our bar fine so what can we *do*, hah? *Di ba? Bisnis 'to e!*"

Yoly slunk back farther and lower in her seat feeling very very uncomfortable and didn't even notice or worry that her strap had come loose and that her bubbies were giving the Australians a hard time. The Albanian/Czech/Mongolian spook was playing it very very low-profile now that he'd gotten his game going; he gazed at no one and nothing that Fred could identify and lit up another dark brown cigarette. And that little diversion nearly cost the Mama-san her life because Fred was watching him and not McCord who had risen in the meanwhile with a slow deep rumble like the Incredible Hulk twice enraged and McCord had his hands around the lady's neck before she could even shriek. So Yoly did what shrieking had to be done and the night's 1 AM Bar War began in earnest with Fred diving for cover as the bartender rushed to the table with a bat featuring the signatures of the USS Roanoake baseball team.

"Luke out!" Fred screamed, mixing up his English thoroughly and effectively and Luke McCord spun just in time without letting go of the Mama-san's neck and the bat crashed down on the table, sending hickory splinters and sailors' names flying in all directions. Yoly finally remembered her two feet and ran and Fred saw that she had pink high heels on, the same shade as his dashboard fuzz. But Yoly did the next-worst thing in the house by running straight in the direction of Mr. Freeze and Mr. Freeze froze and said "putangina" when he saw McCord beating a path to him.

"Putangina" Fred said just as quickly and passed out the moment the bartender's stump of a bat touched his skull, a stump was enough for a stupid duck who kept looking elsewhere. Oh my God his soul whispered the last thing I saw was a lost Pinoy with a bad bad mouth.

Sparks finally lived up to his name at the Precinct 5 station which he was familiar with, he assured the sergeant who called, only because he passed it on his way to work every morning. This time he even had a reason for that worried and rumpled look that was an emotional plateau he got *down* and not for once *up* to. What also amazed Fred when he heard Sparks come in and saw him turn around the corner to his billet was the fact that Sparks had a light blue tie on very properly for an unscheduled but sufficiently frantic 2 AM police station invitation, Respondez S'il Vous Plait. He wondered what Sparks did for his evenings.

Sparks said this and said that, to him and then to the precinct major and then to him again. The Cultural Affairs Specialist was very very upset and was very very upset because Fred was smiling blissfully despite the huge livid lump on his crown. Fred heard something about an X-ray and an administrative something and a what-the-fucking-station-are-you-talk-ing-about-we're-in-the-*precinct*-station-if-you-want-to-know and Fred realized that he'd been talking about *the* Station and shut up and smiled. Of course Sparks under the circumstances was quite understandably obliged to disavow anything.

McCord was nowhere to be seen, neither at the precinct station nor in the Toyota that Sparks helped him recover outside the Guadarrama. Fred stayed in Sparks's Rambler while Sparks took his key and strode casually to the Toyota like it was his own and even chatted up a never-say-die late-working transvestite about a white man in a hula shirt. The Guadarrama's door hung loose on a broken hinge and was kept in place only because a man who looked to Sparks like an Indian or a Ceylonese had leaned against it and had fallen asleep. The place seemed dead.

Sparks drove the Toyota around the block and parked it with the motor running behind the Rambler and said to Fred "He's gone maybe he got the girl or he could be dead serves the SOB right the man says he saw a big something bobbing in the bay coulda been a man or a whale or whatever I don't care. Call the Tropicana in the morning, will you? McCord's got three meetings set for the AgTech thing and...."

They switched cars and Sparks drove off. But of course McCord wasn't there or at the station or anywhere, Fred chuckled, they would've had a back-up team just for McCord. Calling MCCORD LT EXITEXITEXIT Situation Red. At least, Fred whistled as he shifted to 1st, Mr. Freeze was one of *his* own and therefore his cover was safe and hadn't been blown otherwise the KGB...but that was thinking too far afield for a night's action.

Reimburse reimburse reimburse, he reminded himself instead, driving up the street and passing places with names like St. Moritz-Lovebirds-Romeo's-Old Vienna-Kiss-New-Bangkok-Bee Club-Den Rose-China Coast-Zuri Inn.

If he survived the morning, Fred resolved, he would go to Marlene's while the story was still fresh and he had the lump to show for proof and maybe even take McCord along if the man was alive and God these places but for the names were all the same. Fred sighed, shifted to 4th and thought truetruetrue ya seen one ya seen them all.

Topics for Discussion

1. How does Dalisay initially present McCord? Why does Dalisay make McCord an American?

2. What does being American mean to the characters in the story, especially Fred and McCord?

3. What is McCord's response to Fred's knowledge of English? What role does language, especially specialized terms and short forms, play in the story?

4. What role does the Cold War play in the story?

5. What are the differences between the way McCord is treated by the locals and the way they treat Fred?

6. What is Dalisay suggesting by the presence of the dark foreigner in the bar?

7. Is Mr. Freeze really a KGB (Russian secret police) agent? Is there any suggestion on Dalisay's part that McCord is a spy?

8. What is the relationship between the title and the plot of the story? Is the espionage real or imagined?

Anita Desai

About the Author

Anita Desai was born Anita Mazumbar in Mussoorie, India, in 1937 of a German mother and an Indian father, and was educated at the University of Delhi. She began writing at the age of seven and has been a professional writer throughout her life. According to Desai, "writing is my way of plunging to the depths and exploring...underlying truth." Her work, as she notes, is an effort to "discover, to underline and convey the true significance of things."

Like those of Katherine Mansfield, her stories are penetrations of small, often overlooked events, ideas and objects, which are magnified by the attention given to them and made all the more important by the desire and passion her characters bring to those observations and situations. She has stressed that her work is not about India per se, but about the details of life that touch on simple human emotions and concerns. She uses her idiom to address accessible, universal problems and ideas.

Selected Works

Cry, The Peacock (novel, 1963)
Voices in the City (novel, 1965)
Bye-Bye, Blackbird (novel, 1971)
Where Shall We Go This Summer? (novel, 1975)
Fire on the Mountain (novel, 1977)
Games at Twilight (short stories, 1978)
Clear Light of Day (novel, 1980)
In Custody (novel, 1984)
Baumgartner's Bombay (novel, 1988)
Journey to Ithaca (novel, 1995)

About the Story

"Pineapple Cake," from Desai's *Games at Twilight*, is set at a Christian wedding in India where a young boy, Victor, has accompanied his mother to the ceremony. He behaves himself because he has been promised a piece of pineapple cake.

Take special note of the way Desai communicates a great deal of information and detail in a very short, poignant way. Look at the way Desai depicts the relationship between the child and his mother, and the way the mother appears to compare boys with girls in her thoughts. Much is implied in this story that is not said directly. This sense of ellipsis, of implying an idea without putting it into words, enriches the variety of readings that can be made of this brief vignette.

Pineapple Cake

Victor was a nervous rather than rebellious child. But it made no difference to his mother: she had the same way of dealing with nerves and rebels.

"You like pineapple cake, don't you? Well, come along, get dressed quickly—yes, yes, the velvet shorts—the new shoes, yes—hurry—pineapple cake for good boys...."

So it had gone all afternoon and, by holding out the bait of pineapple cake, his favourite, Mrs. Fernandez had the boy dressed in his new frilled shirt and purple velvet shorts and new shoes that bit his toes and had him sitting quietly in church right through the long ceremony. Or so she thought, her faith in pineapple cake being matched only by her faith in Our Lady of Mount Mary, Bandra Hill, Bombay. Looking at Victor, trying hard to keep his loud breathing bottled inside his chest and leaning down to see what made his shoes so vicious, you might have thought she had been successful, but success never satisfies and Mrs. Fernandez sighed to think how much easier it would have been if she had had a daughter instead. Little girls love weddings, little girls play at weddings, little girls can be dressed in can-can petticoats and frocks like crêpe-paper bells of pink and orange, their oiled and ringleted hair crowned with rustling wreaths of paper flowers. She glanced around her rather tiredly to hear the church rustling and crepitating with excited little girls, dim and dusty as it was, lit here and there by a blazing afternoon window of red and blue glass, a flare of candles or a silver bell breathless in the turgid air. This reminded her how she had come to this church to pray and light candles to Our Lady when she was expecting Victor, and it made her glance down at him and wonder why he was perspiring so. Yes, the collar of the frilled shirt was a bit tight and the church was airless and stuffy but it wasn't very refined of him to sweat so. Of course all the little boys in her row seemed to be in the same state—each one threatened or bribed into docility, their silence straining in their chests, soundlessly clamouring. Their eyes were the eyes of prisoners, dark and blazing at the ignominy and boredom and injustice of it all. When they shut their eyes and bowed their heads in prayer, it was as if half the candles in church had gone out, and it was darker.

Relenting, Mrs. Fernandez whispered, under cover of the sonorous prayer led by the grey padre in faded purple, "Nearly over now, Victor. In a little while we'll be going to tea—pineapple cake for you."

Victor hadn't much faith in his mother's promises. They had a way of getting postponed or cancelled on account of some small accidental lapse on his part. He might tear a hole in his sleeve—no pocket money. Or stare a minute too long at Uncle Arthur who was down on a visit from Goa and had a wen on the back of his bald head—no caramel custard for pudding. So he would not exchange looks with her but stared stolidly down at his polished shoes, licked his dry lips and wondered if there would be Fanta or Coca-Cola at tea.

Then the ceremony came to an end. How or why, he could not tell, sunk so far below eye-level in that lake of breathless witnesses to the marriage of Carmen Maria Braganza of Goa and George de Mello of Byculla, Bombay. He had seen nothing of it, only followed, disconsolately and confusedly, the smells and sounds of it, like some underground creature, an infant mole, trying to make out what went on outside its burrow, and whether it was alarming or enticing. Now it was over and his mother was digging him in the ribs, shoving him out, hurrying him by running into his heels, and now they were streaming out with the tide. At the door he made out the purple of the padre's robes, he was handed a pink paper flower by a little girl who held a silver basket full of them and whose face gleamed with fanatic self-importance, and then he was swept down the stairs, held onto by his elbow and, once on ground level, his mother was making a din about finding a vehicle to take them to the reception at Green's. "The tea will be at Green's, you know," she had been saying several times a day for weeks now. "Those de Mellos must have money—they can't be so badly off— tea at Green's, after all."

It was no easy matter, she found, to be taken care of, for although there was a whole line of cabs at the kerb, they all belonged to the more important members of the de Mello and Braganza families. When Mrs. Fernandez realized this, she set her lips together and looked dangerously wrathful, and the party atmosphere began quickly to dissolve in the acid of bad temper and the threat to her dignity. Victor stupidly began a fantasy of slipping out of her hold and breaking into a toy shop for skates and speeding ahead of the whole caravan on a magic pair, to arrive at Green's before the bride, losing his mother on the way ... But she found two seats, in the nick of time, in a taxi that already contained a short, broad woman in a purple net frock and a long thin man with an adam's apple that struggled to rise above his polka-dotted bow tie and then slipped down again with an audible croak. The four of them sat squeezed together and the women made little remarks about how beautiful Carmen Maria had looked and how the de Mellos couldn't be badly off, tea at Green's, after all. "Green's," the woman in the purple net frock yelled into the taxi driver's ear and gave her bottom an important shake that knocked Victor against the door. He felt that he was being shoved out, he was not wanted, he had no place here. This must have made him look peaked for his mother squeezed his hand and whispered, "You've been a good boy—pineapple cake for you." Victor sat still, not breathing. The man with the adam's apple stretched his neck longer and longer, swivelled his head about on the top of it and said nothing, but the frog in his throat gurgled to itself.

Let out of the taxi, Victor looked about him at the wonders of Bombay harbour while the elders tried to be polite and yet not pay the taxi. Had his father brought him here on a Sunday outing, with a ferry boat ride and a fresh coconut drink for treats, he would have enjoyed the Arab dhows with their muddy sails, the ships and tankers and seagulls and the Gateway of India like a coloured version of the photograph in his history book, but it was too unexpected. He had been promised pineapple cake at Green's, sufficiently overwhelming in itself—he hadn't the wherewithal to cope with the Gateway of India as well.

Instinctively he put out his hand to find his mother's and received another shock—she had slipped on a pair of gloves, dreadfully new ones of crackling nylon lace, like fresh bandages on her purple hands. She squeezed his hand, saying "If you want to do soo-soo, tell me, I'll find the toilet. Don't you go and wet your pants, man." Horrified, he pulled away but she caught him by the collar and led him into the hotel and up the stairs to the tea room where refreshments were to be served in celebration of Carmen Maria's and George de Mello's wedding. The band was still playing "Here Comes The Bride" when Victor and his mother entered.

Here there was a repetition of the scene over the taxi: this time it was seats at a suitable table that Mrs. Fernandez demanded, could not find, then spotted, was turned away from and, finally, led to two others by a slippery-smooth waiter used to such scenes. The tables had been arranged in the form of the letter E, and covered with white cloths. Little vases marched up the centres of the tables, sprouting stiff zinnias and limp periwinkles. The guests, chief and otherwise, seemed flustered by the arrangements, rustled about, making adjustments and readjustments, but the staff showed no such hesitations over protocol. They seated the party masterfully, had the tables laid out impeccably and, when the band swung into the "Do Re Mi" song from *The Sound of Music*, brought in the wedding cake. Everyone craned to see Carmen Maria cut it, and Victor's mother gave him a pinch that made him half-rise from his chair, whispering, "Stand up if you can't see, man, stand up to see Carmen Maria cut the cake." There was a burst of laughter, applause and raucous congratulation with an undertone of ribaldry that unnerved Victor and made him sink down on his chair, already a bit sick.

The band was playing a lively version of "I am Sixteen, Going on Seventeen" when Victor heard a curious sound, as of a choked drain being forced. Others heard it too for suddenly chairs were being scraped back, people were standing up, some of them stepped backwards and nearly fell on top of Victor who hastily got off his chair. The mother of the bride, in her pink and silver gauzes, ran up, crying "Oh no, oh no, no, nó!"

Two seats down sat the man with the long, thin neck in which an adam's apple rose and fell so lugubriously. Only he was no longer sitting. He was sprawled over his chair, his head hanging over the back in a curiously unhinged way, as though dangling at the end of a rope. The woman in the purple net dress was leaning over him and screaming

"Aub, Aub, my darling Aubrey! Help my darling Aubrey!" Victor gave a shiver and stepped back and back till someone caught and held him.

Someone ran past—perhaps one of those confident young waiters who knew all there was to know—shouting "Phone for a doctor, quick! Call Dr. Patel," and then there was a long, ripping groan all the way down the tables which seemed to come from the woman in the purple net dress or perhaps from the bride's mother, Victor could not tell— "Oh, why did it have to happen *today?* Couldn't he have gone into another day?" Carmen Maria, the bride, began to sob frightenedly. After that someone grasped the long-necked old man by his knees and armpits and carried him away, his head and his shoes dangling like stuffed paper bags. The knot of guests around him loosened and came apart to make way for what was obviously a corpse.

Dimly, Victor realized this. The screams and sobs of the party-dressed women underlined it. So did the slow, stunned way in which people rose from the table, scraped back their chairs and retreated to the balcony, shaking their heads and muttering, "An omen, I tell you, it must be an omen." Victor made a hesitant move towards the balcony—perhaps he would see the hearse arrive.

But Victor's mother was holding him by the arm and she gave it an excited tug. "Sit *down*, man," she whispered furtively, "here comes the pineapple cake," and, to his amazement, a plate of pastries was actually on the table now—iced, coloured and gay. "Take it, take the pineapple cake," she urged him, pushing him towards the plate, and when the boy didn't move but stared down at the pastry dish as though it were the corpse on the red rexine sofa, her mouth gave an impatient twitch and she reached out to fork the pineapple cake onto her own plate. She ate it quickly. Wiping her mouth primly, she said, "I think we'd better go now."

Topics for Discussion

1. How does Desai portray the child and what is she saying about the nature of childhood?

2. What is the role of desire in the story?

3. How does Desai define and convey faith and belief in the story?

4. How does Desai create and convey the atmosphere of the wedding?

5. What happens at the wedding to cast a pall of seriousness over the event?

6. What impact does Desai create by ending the story without the boy receiving his promised piece of pineapple cake?

7. How does Desai convey the idea of manipulation?

8. What does the pineapple cake represent?

Louise Erdrich

About the Author

Louise Erdrich, one of the rising new voices of contemporary North American Native literature, was born in Little Falls, Minnesota, in 1954 and grew up in Wahpeton, North Dakota. She received her education at Dartmouth College and Johns Hopkins University, and has won a number of major American literary awards including a Guggenheim Fellowship. She belongs to the Turtle Mountain Band of the Chippewa Nation and is married to novelist and historian Michael Dorris.

In Erdrich's novels and stories, she "celebrates Native American survival." Conscious of the spiritual values inherent in the traditional ways of life, she balances this cultural awareness against the realities and hardships of the contemporary North American Native experience, always aware that transcendence of these problems, both through language and experience, is the primary aim of her writing. For Erdrich, North American Native culture is still evolving, despite its history of suppression by the dominant Eurocentric culture.

Selected Works

Jacklight (poems, 1984)
Love Medicine (novel, 1984)
Tracks (novel, 1988)
Baptism of Desire (novel, 1989)
The Crown of Columbus (with Michael Dorris, novel, 1991)

About the Story

Originally published as a short story, "Fleur" appears as a chapter in Erdrich's novel *Tracks* (1988). Narrated by a young woman named Pauline, the story deals with issues such as luck, superstition and coincidence (illustrated by gambling and card games).

The character Fleur is "twice born." A number of cultures have traditional beliefs that those who are brought back from death, literally born a second time, are invested with special supernatural powers that allow them to survive all manner of deadly experiences.

Fleur

The first time she drowned in the cold and glassy waters of Matchimanito, Fleur Pillager was only a child. Two men saw the boat tip, saw her struggle in the waves. They rowed over to the place she went down, and jumped in. When they lifted her over the gunwales, she was cold to the touch and stiff, so they slapped her face, shook her by the heels, worked her arms and pounded her back until she coughed up lake water. She shivered all over like a dog, then took a breath. But it wasn't long afterward that those two men disappeared. The first wandered off and the other, Jean Hat, got himself run over by his own surveyor's cart.

It went to show, the people said. It figured to them all right. By saving Fleur Pillager, those two had lost themselves.

The next time she fell in the lake, Fleur Pillager was fifteen years old and no one touched her. She washed on shore, her skin a dull dead gray, but when George Many Women bent to look closer, he saw her chest move. Then her eyes spun open, clear black agate, and she looked at him. "You take my place," she hissed. Everybody scattered and left her there, so no one knows how she dragged herself home. Soon after that we noticed Many Women changed, grew afraid, wouldn't leave his house and would not be forced to go near water or guide the mappers back into the bush. For his caution, he lived until the day that his sons brought him a new tin bathtub. Then the first time he used it he slipped, got knocked out, and breathed water while his wife stood in the other room frying breakfast.

Men stayed clear of Fleur Pillager after the second drowning. Even though she was good-looking, nobody dared to court her because it was clear that Misshepeshu, the water man, the monster, wanted her for himself. He's a devil, that one, love hungry with desire and maddened for the touch of young girls, the strong and daring especially, the ones like Fleur.

Our mothers warn us that we'll think he's handsome, for he appears with green eyes, copper skin, a mouth tender as a child's. But if you fall into his arms, he sprouts horns, fangs, claws, fins. His feet are joined as one and his skin, brass scales, rings to the touch. You're fascinated, cannot move. He casts a shell necklace at your feet, weeps gleaming chips that harden into mica on your breasts. He holds you under. Then he takes the body of a lion, a fat brown worm, or a familiar man. He's made of gold. He's made of beach moss. He's a thing of dry foam, a thing of death by drowning, the death a Chippewa cannot survive.

Unless you are Fleur Pillager. We all knew she couldn't swim. After the first time, we thought she'd keep to herself, live quiet, stop killing men off by drowning in the lake. We thought she would keep the good ways. But then, after the second return, and after old Nanapush nursed her through the sickness, we knew that we were dealing with something much more serious. Alone out there, she went haywire, out of control. She messed with evil, laughed at the old women's advice and dressed like a man. She got herself into some half-forgotten medicine, studied ways we shouldn't talk about. Some say she kept the finger of a child in her pocket and a powder of unborn rabbits in a leather thong around her neck. She laid the heart of an owl on her tongue so she could see at night, and went out, hunting, not even in her own body. We know for sure because the next morning, in the snow or dust, we followed the tracks of her bare feet and saw where they changed, where the claws sprang out, the pad broadened and pressed into the dirt. By night we heard her chuffing cough, the bear cough. By day her silence and the wide grin she threw to bring down our guard made us frightened. Some thought that Fleur Pillager should be driven from the reservation, but not a single person who spoke like that had the nerve. And finally, when people were just about to get together and throw her out, she left on her own and didn't come back all summer. That's what I'm telling about.

During those months, when Fleur lived a few miles south in Argus, things happened. She almost destroyed that town.

When she got down to Argus in the year of 1913, it was just a grid of six streets on either side of the railroad depot. There were two elevators, one central, the other a few miles west. Two stores competed for the trade of the three hundred citizens, and three churches quarreled with one another for their souls. There was a frame building for Lutherans, a heavy brick one for Episcopalians, and a long narrow shingle Catholic church. This last had a slender steeple, twice as high as any building or tree.

No doubt, across the low flat wheat, watching from the road as she came near on foot, Fleur saw that steeple rise, a shadow thin as a needle. Maybe in that raw space it drew her the way a lone tree draws lightning. Maybe, in the end, the Catholics are to blame. For if she hadn't seen that sign of pride, that slim prayer, that marker, maybe she would have just kept walking.

But Fleur Pillager turned, and the first place she went once she came into town was to the back door of the priest's residence attached to the landmark church. She didn't go there for a handout, although she got that, but to ask for work. She got that too, or we got her. It's hard to tell which came out worse, her or the men or the town, although as always Fleur lived.

The men who worked at the butcher's had carved about a thousand carcasses between them, maybe half of that steers and the other half pigs, sheep, and game like deer, elk, and bear. That's not even mentioning the chickens, which were beyond counting. Pete Kozka owned the place, and employed three men: Lily Veddar, Tor Grunewald, and Dutch James.

I got to Argus through Dutch. He was making a mercantile delivery to the reservation when he met my father's sister Regina, a Puyat and then a Kashpaw through her first husband. Dutch didn't change her name right off, that came later. He never did adopt her son, Russell, whose father lived somewhere in Montana now.

During the time I stayed with them, I hardly saw Dutch or Regina look each other in the eye or talk. Perhaps it was because, except for me, the Puyats were known as a quiet family with little to say. We were mixed-bloods, skinners in the clan for which the name was lost. In the spring before the winter that took so many Chippewa, I bothered my father into sending me south, to the white town. I had decided to learn the lace-making trade from nuns.

"You'll fade out there," he said, reminding me that I was lighter than my sisters. "You won't be an Indian once you return."

"Then maybe I won't come back," I told him. I wanted to be like my mother, who showed her half-white. I wanted to be like my grandfather, pure Canadian. That was because even as a child I saw that to hang back was to perish. I saw through the eyes of the world outside of us. I would not speak our language. In English, I told my father we should build an outhouse with a door that swung open and shut.

"We don't have such a thing upon our house." He laughed. But he scorned me when I would not bead, when I refused to prick my fingers with quills, or hid rather than rub brains on the stiff skins of animals.

"I was made for better," I told him. "Send me down to your sister." So he did. But I did not learn to thread and work the bobbins and spools. I swept the floors in a butcher shop, and cared for my cousin Russell.

Every day I took him to the shop and we set to work—sprinkled fresh sawdust, ran a hambone across the street to a customer's beanpot or a package of sausage to the corner. Russell took the greater share of orders, worked the harder. Though young, he was fast, reliable. He never stopped to watch a cloud pass, or a spider secure a fly with the same quick care as Pete wrapped a thick steak for the doctor. Russell and I were different. He never sat to rest, never fell to wishing he owned a pair of shoes like those that passed on the feet of white girls, shoes of hard red leather decorated with cut holes. He never listened to what those girls said about him, or imagined them doubling back to catch him by the hand. In truth, I hardly rinsed through the white girls' thoughts.

That winter, we had no word from my family, although Regina asked. No one knew yet how many were lost, people kept no track. We heard that wood could not be sawed fast enough to build the houses for their graves, and there were so few people strong enough to work, anyway, that by the time they got around to it the brush had grown, obscuring the new-turned soil, the marks of burials. The priests tried to discourage the habit of burying the dead in trees, but the ones they dragged down had no names to them, just scraps of their belongings. Sometimes in my head I had a dream I could not shake. I saw my sisters and my mother swaying in the branches, buried too high to reach, wrapped in lace I never hooked.

I tried to stop myself from remembering what it was like to have companions, to have my mother and sisters around me, but when Fleur came to us that June, I remembered. I made excuses to work next to her, I questioned her, but Fleur refused to talk about the Puyats or about the winter. She shook her head, looked away. She touched my face once, as if by accident, or to quiet me, and said that perhaps my family had moved north to avoid the sickness, as some mixed-bloods did.

I was fifteen, alone, and so poor-looking I was invisible to most customers and to the men in the shop. Until they needed me, I blended into the stained brown walls, a skinny big-nosed girl with staring eyes.

From this, I took what advantage I could find. Because I could fade into a corner or squeeze beneath a shelf I knew everything: how much cash there was in the till, what the men joked about when no one was around, and what they did to Fleur.

Kozka's Meats served farmers for a fifty-mile radius, both to slaughter, for it had a stockpen and chute, and to cure the meat by smoking it or spicing it in sausage. The storage locker was a marvel, made of many thicknesses of brick, earth insulation, and Minnesota timber, lined inside with wood shavings and vast blocks of ice cut from the deepest end of Matchimanito, hauled down from the reservation each winter by horse and sled.

A ramshackle board building, part killing shed, part store, was fixed to the low square of the lockers. That's where Fleur worked. Kozka hired her for her strength. She could lift a haunch or carry a pole of sausages without stumbling, and she soon learned cutting from Fritzie, a string-thin blond who chain-smoked and handled the razor-edged knives with nerveless precision, slicing close to her stained fingers. The two women worked afternoons, wrapping their cuts in paper, and Fleur carried the packages to the lockers. Russell liked to help her. He vanished when I called, took none of my orders, but I soon learned that he could always be found alongside Fleur's hip, one hand gently pinching a fold of her skirt, so delicately that she could pretend not to notice.

Of course, she did. She knew the effect she had on men, even the very youngest of them. She swayed them, sotted them, made them curious about her habits, drew them close with careless ease and cast them off with the same indifference. She was good to Russell, it is true, even fussed about him like a mother, combed his hair with her fingers, and scolded me for kicking or teasing him.

Fleur poked bits of sugar between Russell's lips when we sat for meals, skimmed the cream from the jar when Fritzie's back was turned and spooned it into his mouth. For work, she gave him small packages to carry when she and Fritzie piled cut meat outside the locker's heavy doors, opened only at five p.m. each afternoon, before the men ate supper.

Sometimes Dutch, Tor, and Lily stayed at the lockers after closing, and when they did Russell and I stayed too, cleaned the floors, restocked the fires in the front smokehouse, while the men sat around the squat, cold cast-iron stove spearing slats of herring onto hardtack bread. They played long games of poker, or cribbage on a board made from the planed end of a salt crate. They talked. We ate our bread and the ends of sausages, watched and listened, although there wasn't much to hear since almost nothing ever happened in Argus. Tor was married, Dutch lived with Regina, and Lily read circulars. They mainly discussed the auctions to come, equipment, or women.

Every so often, Pete Kozka came out front to make a whist, leaving Fritzie to smoke her cigarettes and fry raised donuts in the back room. He sat and played a few rounds but kept his thoughts to himself. Fritzie did not tolerate him talking behind her back, and the one book he read was the New Testament. If he said something, it concerned weather or a surplus of wheat. He had a good-luck talisman, the opal-white lens of a cow's eye. Playing rummy, he rubbed it between his fingers. That soft sound and the slap of cards was about the only conversation.

Fleur finally gave them a subject.

Her cheeks were wide and flat, her hands large, chapped, muscular. Fleur's shoulders were broad and curved as a yoke, her hips fishlike, slippery, narrow. An old green dress clung to her waist, worn thin where she sat. Her glossy braids were like the tails of animals, and swung against her when she moved, deliberately, slowly in her work, held in and half-tamed. But only half. I could tell, but the others never noticed. They never looked into her sly brown eyes or noticed her teeth, strong and sharp and very white. Her legs were bare, and since she padded in beadworked moccasins they never saw that her fifth toes were missing. They never knew she'd drowned. They were blinded, they were stupid, they only saw her in the flesh.

And yet it wasn't just that she was a Chippewa, or even that she was a woman, it wasn't that she was good-looking or even that she was alone that made their brains hum. It was how she played cards.

Women didn't usually play with men, so the evening that Fleur drew a chair to the men's table there was a shock of surprise.

"What's this," said Lily. He was fat, with a snake's pale eyes and precious skin, smooth and lily-white, which is how he got his name. Lily had a dog, a stumpy mean little bull of a thing with a belly drum-tight from eating pork rinds. The dog was as fond of the cards as Lily, and straddled his barrel thighs through games of stud, rum poker, *vingt-un*. The dog snapped at Fleur's arm that first night, but cringed back, its snarl frozen, when she took her place.

"I thought," she said, her voice soft and stroking, "you might deal me in."

There was a space between the lead bin of spiced flour and the wall where Russell and I just fit. He tried to inch toward Fleur's skirt, to fit against her. Who knew but that he might have brought her luck like Lily's dog, except I sensed we'd be driven away if the men noticed us and so I pulled him back by the suspenders. We hunkered down, my arm around his neck. Russell smelled of caraway and pepper, of dust and sour dirt. He watched the game with tense interest for a minute or so, then went limp, leaned against me, and dropped his mouth wide. I kept my eyes open, saw Fleur's black hair swing over the chair, her feet solid on the boards of the floor. I couldn't see on the table where the cards slapped, so after they were deep in their game I pressed Russell down and raised myself in the shadows, crouched on a sill of wood.

I watched Fleur's hands stack and riffle, divide the cards, spill them to each player in a blur, rake and shuffle again. Tor, short and scrappy, shut one eye and squinted the other at Fleur. Dutch screwed his lips around a wet cigar.

"Gotta see a man," he mumbled, getting up to go out back to the privy. The others broke, left their cards, and Fleur sat alone in the lamplight that glowed in a sheen across the push of her breasts. I watched her closely, then she paid me a beam of notice for the first time. She turned, looked straight at me, and grinned the white wolf grin a Pillager turns on its victims, except that she wasn't after me.

"Pauline there," she said. "How much money you got?"

We had all been paid for the week that day. Eight cents was in my pocket.

"Stake me." She held out her long fingers. I put the coins on her palm and then I melted back to nothing, part of the walls and tables, twined close with Russell. It wasn't long before I understood something that I didn't know then. The men would not have seen me no matter what I did, how I moved. For my dress hung loose and my back was already stooped, an old woman's. Work had roughened me, reading made my eyes sore, forgetting my family had hardened my face, and scrubbing down bare boards had given me big, reddened knuckles.

When the men came back and sat around the table, they had drawn together. They shot each other small glances, stuck their tongues in their cheeks, burst out laughing at odd moments, to rattle Fleur. But she never minded. They played their *vingt-un*, staying even as Fleur slowly gained. Those pennies I had given her drew nickels and attracted dimes until there was a small pile in front of her.

Then she hooked them with five card draw, nothing wild. She dealt, discarded, drew, and then she sighed and her cards gave a little shiver. Tor's eye gleamed, and Dutch straightened in his seat.

"I'll pay to see that hand," said Lily Veddar.

Fleur showed, and she had nothing there, nothing at all.

Tor's thin smile cracked open, and he threw in his hand too.

"Well, we know one thing," he said, leaning back in his chair, "the squaw can't bluff."

With that I lowered myself into a mound of swept sawdust and slept. I woke during the night, but none of them had moved yet so I couldn't either. Still later, the men must have gone out again, or Fritzie come to break the game, because I was lifted, soothed, cradled in a woman's arms and rocked so quiet that I kept my eyes shut while Fleur rolled first me, then Russell, into a closet of grimy ledgers, oiled paper, balls of string, and thick files that fit beneath us like a mattress.

The game went on after work the next evening. Russell slept, I got my eight cents back five times over, and Fleur kept the rest of the dollar she'd won for a stake. This time they didn't play so late, but they played regular, and then kept going at it. They stuck with poker, or variations, for one solid week and each time Fleur won exactly one dollar, no more and no less, too consistent for luck.

By this time, Lily and the other men were so lit with suspense that they got Pete to join the game. They concentrated, the fat dog tense in Lily Veddar's lap, Tor suspicious, Dutch stroking his huge square brow, Pete steady. It wasn't that Fleur won that hooked them in so, because she lost hands too. It was rather that she never had a freak deal or even anything above a straight. She only took on her low cards, which didn't sit right. By chance, Fleur should have gotten a full or a flush by now. The irritating thing was she beat with pairs and never bluffed, because she couldn't, and still she ended each night with exactly one dollar. Lily couldn't believe, first of all, that a woman could be smart enough to play cards, but even if she was, that she would then be stupid enough to cheat for a dollar a night. By day I watched him turn the problem over, his lard-white face dull, small fingers probing at his knuckles, until he finally thought he had Fleur figured as a bit-time player, caution her game. Raising the stakes would throw her.

More than anything now, he wanted Fleur to come away with something but a dollar. Two bits less or ten more, the sum didn't matter just so he broke her streak.

Night after night she played, won her dollar, and left to stay in a place that only Russell and I knew about. Fritzie had done two things of value for Fleur. She had given her a black umbrella with a stout handle and material made to shed water, and also let her board on the premises. Every night, Fleur bathed in the slaughtering tub, then slept in the unused brick smokehouse behind the lockers, a windowless place tarred on the inside with scorched fats. When I brushed against her skin I noticed that she smelled of the walls, rich and woody, slightly burnt. Since that night she put me in the closet, I was no longer jealous or afraid of her, but followed her close as Russell, closer, stayed with her, became her moving shadow that the men never noticed, the shadow that could have saved her.

August, the month that bears fruit, closed around the shop and Pete and Fritzie left for Minnesota to escape the heat. A month running, Fleur had won thirty dollars and only Pete's presence had kept Lily at bay. But Pete was gone now, and one payday, with the heat so bad no one could move but Fleur, the men sat and played and waited while she finished work. The cards sweat, limp in their fingers, the table was slick with grease, and even the walls were warm to the touch. The air was motionless. Fleur was in the next room boiling heads.

Her green dress, drenched, wrapped her like a transparent sheet. A skin of lakeweed. Black snarls of veining clung to her arms. Her braids were loose, half unraveled, tied behind her neck in a thick loop. She stood in steam, turning skulls through a vat with a wooden paddle. When scraps boiled to the surface, she bent with a round tin sieve and scooped them out. She'd filled two dishpans.

"Ain't that enough now?" called Lily. "We're waiting." The stump of a dog trembled in his lap, alive with rage. It never smelled me or noticed me above Fleur's smoky skin. The air was heavy in the corner, and pressed Russell and me down. Fleur sat with the men.

"Now what do you say?" Lily asked the dog. It barked. That was the signal for the real game to start.

"Let's up the ante," said Lily, who had been stalking this night for weeks. He had a roll of money in his pocket. Fleur had five bills in her dress. Each man had saved his full pay that the bank officer had drawn from the Kozkas' account.

"Ante a dollar then," said Fleur, and pitched hers in. She lost, but they let her scrape along, a cent at a time. And then she won some. She played unevenly, as if chance were all she had. She reeled them in. The game went on. The dog was stiff now, poised on Lily's knees, a ball of vicious muscle with its yellow eyes slit in concentration. It gave advice, seemed to sniff the lay of Fleur's cards, twitched and nudged. Fleur was up, then down, saved by a scratch. Tor dealt seven cards, three down. The pot grew, round by round, until it held all the money. Nobody folded. Then it all rode on one last card and they went silent. Fleur picked hers up and drew a long breath. The heat lowered like a bell. Her card shook, but she stayed in.

Lily smiled and took the dog's head tenderly between his palms.

"Say Fatso," he said, crooning the words. "You reckon that girl's bluffing?"

The dog whined and Lily laughed. "Me too," he said. "Let's show." He tossed his bills and coins into the pot and then they turned their cards over.

Lily looked once, looked again, then he squeezed the dog like a fist of dough and slammed it on the table.

Fleur threw out her arms and swept the money close, grinning that same wolf grin that she'd used on me, the grin that had them. She jammed the bills inside her dress, scooped the coins in waxed white paper that she tied with string.

"Another round," said Lily, his voice choked with burrs. But Fleur opened her mouth and yawned, then walked out back to gather slops for the big hog that was waiting in the stockpen to be killed.

The men sat still as rocks, their hands spread on the oiled wood table. Dutch had chewed his cigar to damp shreds, Tor's eye was dull. Lily's gaze was the only one to follow Fleur. Russell and I didn't breathe. I felt them gathering, saw Dutch's veins, the ones in his forehead that stood out in anger. The dog rolled off the table and curled in a knot below the counter, where none of the men could touch him.

Lily rose and stepped to the closet of ledgers where Pete kept his private stock. He brought back a bottle, uncorked and tipped it between his fingers. The lump in his throat moved, then he passed it on. They drank, steeped in the whiskey's fire, and planned with their eyes things they couldn't say aloud.

When they left, I grabbed Russell by the arm, dragged him along. We followed, hid in the clutter of broken boards and chicken crates beside the stockpen, where the men settled. Fleur could not be seen at first, and then the moon broke and showed her, slipping cautiously along the rough board chute with a bucket in her hand. Her hair fell wild and coarse to her waist, and her dress was a floating patch in the dark. She made a pig-calling sound, rang the tin pail lightly against the wood, paused suspiciously. But too late. In the sound of the ring Lily moved, fat and nimble, stepped right behind Fleur and put out his creamy hands. Russell strained foward and I stopped his mouth with both fists before he yelled. At Lily's first touch, Fleur whirled and doused him with the bucket of sour slops. He pushed her against the big fence and the package of coins split, went clinking and jumping, winked against the wood. Fleur rolled over once and vanished into the yard.

The moon fell behind a curtain of ragged clouds, and Lily followed into the dark muck. But he tripped, pitched over the huge flank of the pig, who lay mired to the snout, heavily snoring. Russell and I sprang from the weeds and climbed the boards of the pen, stuck like glue. We saw the sow rise to her neat, knobby knees, gain her balance and sway, curious, as Lily stumbled forward. Fleur had backed into the angle of splintered wood just beyond and when Lily tried to jostle past, the sow raised her powerful neck and suddenly struck, quick and hard as a snake. She plunged at Lily's thick waist and snatched a mouthful of shirt. She lunged again, caught him lower so that he grunted in pained surprise. He seemed to ponder, breathing deep. Then he launched his huge bulk in a swimmer's dive.

The sow screamed as his body smacked over hers. She rolled, striking out with her knife-sharp hooves and Lily gathered himself upon her, took her foot-long face by the ears, and scraped her snout and cheeks against the trestles of the pen. He hurled the sow's tight skull against an iron post, but instead of knocking her dead, he woke her from her dream.

She reared, shrieked, and then he squeezed her so hard that they leaned into each other and posed in a standing embrace. They bowed jerkily, as if to begin. Then his arms swung and flailed. She sank her black fangs into his shoulder, clasping him, dancing him forward and backward through the pen. Their steps picked up pace, went wild. The two dipped as one, box-stepped, tripped one another. She ran her split foot through his hair. He grabbed her kinked tail. They went down and came up, the same shape and then the same color until the men couldn't tell one from the other in that light and Fleur was able to vault the gates, swing down, hit gravel.

The men saw, yelled, and chased her at a dead run to the smoke-house. And Lily too, once the sow gave up in disgust and freed him. That is when I should have gone to Fleur, saved her, thrown myself on Dutch the way Russell did once he unlocked my arms. He stuck to his stepfather's leg as if he'd been flung there. Dutch dragged him for a few steps, his leg a branch, then cuffed Russell off and left him shouting and bawling in the sticky weeds. I closed my eyes and put my hands on my ears, so there is nothing more to describe but what I couldn't block out: those yells from Russell, Fleur's hoarse breath, so loud it filled me, her cry in the old language and our names repeated over and over among the words.

The heat was still dense the next morning when I entered slowly through the side door of the shop. Fleur was gone and Russell slunk along the woodwork like a beaten dog. The men were slack-faced, hungover. Lily was paler and softer than ever, as if his flesh had steamed on his bones. They smoked, took pulls off a bottle. It wasn't yet noon. Russell disappeared outside to sit by the stock gate, to hold his own knees and rock back and forth. I worked awhile, waiting shop and sharpening steel. But I was sick, I was smothered, I was sweating so hard that my hands slipped on the knives and I wiped my fingers clean of the greasy touch of the customers' coins. Lily opened his mouth and roared once, not in anger. There was no meaning to the sound. His terrier dog, sprawled limp beside his foot, never lifted its head. Nor did the other men.

They didn't notice when I stepped outdoors to call Russell. And then I forgot the men because I realized that we were all balanced, ready to tip, to fly, to be crushed as soon as the weather broke. The sky was so low that I felt the weight of it like a door. Clouds hung down, witch teats, a tornado's green-brown cones, and as I watched, one flicked out and became a delicate probing thumb. Even as Russell ran to me, the wind blew suddenly, cold, and then came blinding rain.

Inside, the men had vanished and the whole place was trembling as if a huge hand was pinched at the rafters, shaking it. We ran straight through, screaming for Dutch or for any of them. Russell's fingers were clenched in my skirt. I shook him off once, but he darted after and held me close in terror when we stopped. He called for Regina, called for Fleur. The heavy doors of the lockers, where the men had surely taken shelter without us, stood shut. Russell howled. They must have heard him, even above the driving wind, because the two of us could hear, from inside, the barking of that dog. A moment, and everything went still. We didn't dare move in that strange hush of suspension. I listened, Russell too. Then we heard a cry building in the wind, faint at first, a whistle and then a shrill scream that tore through the walls and gathered around the two of us, and at last spoke plain.

It was Russell, I am sure, who first put his arms on the bar, thick iron that was made to slide along the wall and fall across the hasp and lock. He strained and shoved, too slight to move it into place, but he did not look to me for help. Sometimes, thinking back, I see my arms lift, my hands grasp, see myself dropping the beam into the metal grip. At other times, that moment is erased. But always I see Russell's face the moment after, as he turned, as he ran for the door—a peaceful look of complicit satisfaction.

Then the wind plucked him. He flew as though by wires in the seat of his trousers, with me right after, toward the side wall of the shop that rose grand as a curtain, spilling us forward as the building toppled.

Outside, the wind was stronger, a hand held against us. We struggled forward. The bushes tossed, rain battered, the awning flapped off a storefront, the rails of porches rattled. The odd cloud became a fat snout that nosed along the earth and sniffled, jabbed, picked at things, sucked them up, blew them apart, rooted around as if it was following a certain scent, then stopped behind us at the butcher shop and bored down like a drill.

I pitched head over heels along the dirt drive, kept moving and tumbling in such amazement that I felt no fear, past Russell, who was lodged against a small pine. The sky was cluttered. A herd of cattle flew through the air like giant birds, dropping dung, their mouths opened in stunned bellows. A candle, still lighted, blew past, and tables, napkins, garden tools, a whole school of drifting eyeglasses, jackets on hangers, hams, a checkerboard, a lampshade, and at last the sow from behind the lockers, on the run, her hooves a blur, set free, swooping, diving, screaming as everything in Argus fell apart and got turned upside down, smashed, and thoroughly wrecked.

Days passed before the town went looking for the men. Lily was a bachelor, after all, and Tor's wife had suffered a blow to the head that made her forgetful. Understandable. But what about Regina? That would always remain a question in people's minds. For she said nothing about her husband's absence to anyone. The whole town was occupied with digging out, in high relief because even though the Catholic steeple had been ripped off like a peaked cap and sent across five fields, those huddled in the cellar were unhurt. Walls had fallen, windows were demolished, but the stores were intact and so were the bankers and shop owners who had taken refuge in their safes or beneath their cash registers. It was a fair-minded disaster, no one could be said to have suffered much more than the next, except for Kozka's Meats.

When Pete and Fritzie came home, they found that the boards of the front building had been split to kindling, piled in a huge pyramid, and the shop equipment was blasted far and wide. Pete paced off the distance the iron bathtub had been flung, a hundred feet. The glass candy case went fifty, and landed without so much as a cracked pane. There were other surprises as well, for the back rooms where Fritzie and Pete lived were undisturbed. Fritzie said the dust still coated her china figures, and upon her kitchen table, in the ashtray, perched the last cigarette she'd put out in haste. She lit and finished it, looking through the window. From there, she could see that the old smokehouse Fleur had slept in was crushed to a reddish sand and the stockpens were completely torn apart, the rails stacked helter-skelter. Fritzie asked for Fleur. People shrugged. Then she asked about the others, and suddenly, the town understood that three men were missing.

There was a rally of help, a gathering of shovels and volunteers. We passed boards from hand to hand, stacked them, uncovered what lay beneath the pile of jagged two-by-fours. The lockers, full of meat that was Pete and Fritzie's investment, slowly came into sight, still intact. When enough room was made for a man to stand on the roof, there were calls, a general urge to hack through and see what lay below. But Fritzie shouted that she wouldn't allow it because the meat would spoil. And so the work continued, board by board, until at last the solid doors of the freezer were revealed and people pressed to the entry. It was locked from the outside, someone shouted, wedged down, a tornado's freak whim. Regina stood in the crowd, clutching Russell's collar, trying to hold him against her short, tough body. Everyone wanted to be the first to enter, but only Russell and I were quick enough to slip through beside Pete and Fritzie as they shoved into the sudden icy air.

Pete scraped a match on his boot, lit the lamp Fritzie held, and then the four of us stood in its circle. Light glared off the skinned and hanging carcasses, the crates of wrapped sausages, the bright and cloudy blocks of lake ice, pure as winter. The cold bit into us, pleasant at first, then numbing. We stood there for a moment before we saw the men, or more rightly, the humps of fur, the iced and shaggy hides they wore, the bearskins they had taken down and wrapped about themselves. We stepped closer and Fritzie tilted the lantern beneath the flaps of fur into their faces. The dog was there, perched among them, heavy as a doorstop. The three had hunched around a barrel where the game was still laid out, and a dead lantern and an empty bottle too. But they had thrown down their last hands and hunkered tight, clutching one another, knuckles raw from beating at the door they had also attacked with hooks. Frost stars gleamed off their eyelashes and the stubble of their beards. Their faces were set in concentration, mouths open as if to speak some careful thought, some agreement they'd come to in each other's arms.

Only after they were taken out and laid in the sun to thaw did someone think to determine whether they were all entirely dead, frozen solid. That is when Dutch James's faint heartbeat was discovered.

≍⤓►

Power travels in the bloodlines, handed out before birth. It comes down through the hands, which in the Pillagers are strong and knotted, big, spidery and rough, with sensitive fingertips good at dealing cards. It comes through the eyes, too, belligerent, darkest brown, the eyes of those in the bear clan, impolite as they gaze directly at a person.

In my dreams, I look straight back at Fleur, at the men. I am no longer the watcher on the dark sill, the skinny girl.

The blood draws us back, as if it runs through a vein of earth. I left Argus, left Russell and Regina back there with Dutch. I came home and, except for talking to my cousins, live a quiet life. Fleur lives quiet too, down on Matchimanito with her boat. Some say she married the water man, Misshepeshu, or that she lives in shame with white men or windigos, or that she's killed them all. I am about the only one here who ever goes to visit her. That spring, I went to help out in her cabin when she bore the child, whose green eyes and skin the color of an old penny have made more talk, as no one can decide if the child is mixed blood or what, fathered in a smokehouse, or by a man with brass scales, or by the lake. The girl is bold, smiling in her sleep, as if she knows what people wonder, as if she hears the old men talk, turning the story over.

It comes up different every time, and has no ending, no beginning. They get the middle wrong too. They only know they don't know anything.

Topics for Discussion

1. What is the relationship between gambling and magic?
2. What are the effects, dramatic or otherwise, of setting the story in a butcher's shop?
3. How does Erdrich make use of mythology and beliefs in the story?

4. What is the role of the first person narrator in the story? How does her personal experience influence the events and how does her perspective shape the telling process?

5. How does the description of the card game resemble that of a sporting event?

6. What is the role of jealousy in the story?

7. What is the impact of Erdrich's use of "butcher's terminology" in the story?

William Faulkner

About the Author

Novelist, story writer, poet and screenwriter, William Faulkner was born in New Albany, Mississippi, in 1897 and spent a year attending the University of Mississippi before joining the Royal Flying Corps in Canada during the First World War (he lived briefly in Toronto). After the war he spent a short time at Oxford. He then worked at various odd jobs before becoming a full-time writer on the advice of writer Sherwood Anderson.

Faulkner's novels rarely became bestsellers during his lifetime and in order to support himself he worked as a screenwriter for a number of films including *Paths of Glory* and *The Big Sleep*. He was awarded the Nobel Prize for Literature in 1950. In his famous address to the Swedish Academy he stated, "Man will not only endure, he will prevail," which in many ways sums up the philosophy he brought to his work.

Most of Faulkner's novels are set in the imaginary Yoknapatawpha County, in the state of Mississippi, into which he weaves the history of the American South using a series of recurring characters, motifs and themes. Against this backdrop, Faulkner sets what he terms the essential human virtues of "courage and honour and hope and pride and compassion and pity and sacrifice which have been the glory of the past."

William Faulkner died in 1962.

Selected Works

The Marble Faun (poetry, 1924)
Soldiers' Pay (novel, 1926)
Mosquitoes (novel, 1927)
Sartoris (novel, 1929)
The Sound and the Fury (novel, 1929)
As I Lay Dying (novel, 1930)
Sanctuary (novel, 1931)
Light in August (novel, 1932)
Absalom, Absalom! (novel, 1936)
Go Down, Moses (novel of linked stories, 1942)
Intruder in the Dust (novel, 1948)
Collected Stories (1950)
Requiem for a Nun (novel, 1951)
The Reivers (novel, 1962)

About the Story

This story is set in Jefferson, the central town of Yoknapatawpha County, Mississippi. It focuses on the character of Emily Grierson, a spinster who is the last member of a once great family. Emily Grierson is used by Faulkner as a metaphor for the South, an assemblage of archaic beliefs and social practices, remnants of the antebellum period before the Civil War (1861–1865), which the South lost.

Note Faulkner's use of vernacular language. Many nowadays consider his use of the word "nigger" offensive. Faulkner did not intend it to be so. In the period he was chronicling, "nigger" was not considered a derogatory term. What he did was to portray the language habits of the time and place in which he was writing. Such derogatory language reflected the tension between the races, and Faulkner was not a writer to shy away from the realities of language, place or history.

As a writer, Faulkner was sympathetic to the plight of African-Americans. He wrote an appendix for Malcolm Cowley's *The Portable Faulkner* (1946) in which he sketched out the characters from his novel *The Sound and the Fury;* beside Dilsey, the Compsons' nursemaid, he wrote succinctly, "They endured." Faulkner depicted Yoknapatawpha County as a place where the races mixed peacefully (as in stories such as "The Bear" in *Go Down, Moses*). He saw African-Americans as the inheritors not only of the land but of the history and values of the place. The fear and tension between races, according to Faulkner's reading of history, emerged from the Civil War and the end of slavery in the American South.

Faulkner's narrative contains some of the elements of classical tragedy — tragic revelation at the conclusion of the narrative, a solitary figure who clings stubbornly to self-destructive beliefs and ideals, and a "chorus" of townspeople who offer opinions and commentary on the dramatic action of the story.

A Rose for Emily

When Miss Emily Grierson died, our whole town went to her funeral: the men through a sort of respectful affection for a fallen monument, the women mostly out of curiosity to see the inside of her house, which no one save an old manservant—a combined gardener and cook—had seen in at least ten years.

It was a big, squarish frame house that had once been white, decorated with cupolas and spires and scrolled balconies in the heavily lightsome style of the seventies, set on what had once been our most select street. But garages and cotton gins had encroached and obliterated even the august names of that neighborhood; only Miss Emily's house was left, lifting its stubborn and coquettish decay above the cotton wagons and the gasoline pumps—an eyesore among eyesores. And now Miss Emily had gone to join the representatives of those august names where they lay in the cedar-bemused cemetery among the ranked and anonymous graves of Union and Confederate soldiers who fell at the battle of Jefferson.

Alive, Miss Emily had been a tradition, a duty, and a care; a sort of hereditary obligation upon the town, dating from that day in 1894 when Colonel Sartoris, the mayor—he who fathered the edict that no Negro woman should appear on the streets without an apron—remitted her taxes, the dispensation dating from the death of her father on into perpetuity. Not that Miss Emily would have accepted charity. Colonel Sartoris invented an involved tale to the effect that Miss Emily's father had loaned money to the town, which the town, as a matter of business, preferred this way of repaying. Only a man of Colonel Sartoris' generation and thought could have invented it, and only a woman could have believed it.

When the next generation, with its more modern ideas, became mayors and aldermen, this arrangement created some little dissatisfaction. On the first of the year they mailed her a tax notice. February came, and there was no reply. They wrote her a formal letter, asking her to call at the sheriff's office at her convenience. A week later the mayor wrote her himself, offering to call or to send his car for her, and received in reply a note on paper of an archaic shape, in a thin, flowing calligraphy in faded ink, to the effect that she no longer went out at all. The tax notice was also enclosed, without comment.

They called a special meeting of the Board of Aldermen. A deputation waited upon her, knocked at the door through which no visitor had passed since she ceased giving china-painting lessons eight or ten years earlier. They were admitted by the old Negro into a dim hall from which a stairway mounted into still more shadow. It smelled of dust and disuse—a close, dank smell. The Negro led them into the parlor. It was furnished in heavy, leather-covered furniture. When the Negro opened the blinds of one window, they could see that the leather was cracked; and when they sat down, a faint dust rose sluggishly about their thighs, spinning with slow motes in the single sun-ray. On a tarnished gilt easel before the fireplace stood a crayon portrait of Miss Emily's father.

They rose when she entered—a small, fat woman in black, with a thin gold chain descending to her waist and vanishing into her belt, leaning on an ebony cane with a tarnished gold head. Her skeleton was small and spare; perhaps that was why what would have been merely plumpness in another was obesity in her. She looked bloated, like a body long submerged in motionless water, and of that pallid hue. Her eyes, lost in the fatty ridges of her face, looked like two small pieces of coal pressed into a lump of dough as they moved from one face to another while the visitors stated their errand.

She did not ask them to sit. She just stood in the door and listened quietly until the spokesman came to a stumbling halt. Then they could hear the invisible watch ticking at the end of the gold chain.

Her voice was dry and cold. "I have no taxes in Jefferson. Colonel Sartoris explained it to me. Perhaps one of you can gain access to the city records and satisfy yourselves."

"But we have. We are the city authorities, Miss Emily. Didn't you get a notice from the sheriff, signed by him?"

"I received a paper, yes," Miss Emily said. "Perhaps he considers himself the sheriff ... I have no taxes in Jefferson."

"But there is nothing on the books to show that, you see. We must go by the—"

"See Colonel Sartoris. I have no taxes in Jefferson."

"But, Miss Emily—"

"See Colonel Sartoris." (Colonel Sartoris had been dead almost ten years.) "I have no taxes in Jefferson. Tobe!" The Negro appeared. "Show these gentlemen out."

II

So she vanquished them, horse and foot, just as she had vanquished their fathers thirty years before about the smell. That was two years after her father's death and a short time after her sweetheart—the one we believed would marry her—had deserted her. After her father's death she went out very little; after her sweetheart went away, people hardly saw her at all. A few of the ladies had the temerity to call, but were not received, and the only sign of life about the place was the Negro man—a young man then—going in and out with a market basket.

"Just as if a man—any man—could keep a kitchen properly," the ladies said; so they were not surprised when the smell developed. It was another link between the gross, teeming world and the high and mighty Griersons.

A neighbor, a woman, complained to the mayor, Judge Stevens, eighty years old.

"But what will you have me do about it, madam?" he said.

"Why, send her word to stop it," the woman said. "Isn't there a law?"

"I'm sure that won't be necessary," Judge Stevens said. "It's probably just a snake or a rat that nigger of hers killed in the yard. I'll speak to him about it."

The next day he received two more complaints, one from a man who came in diffident deprecation. "We really must do something about it, Judge. I'd be the last one in the world to bother Miss Emily, but we've got to do something." That night the Board of Aldermen met—three graybeards and one younger man, a member of the rising generation.

"It's simple enough," he said. "Send her word to have her place cleaned up. Give her a certain time to do it in, and if she don't ..."

"Dammit, sir," Judge Stevens said, "will you accuse a lady to her face of smelling bad?"

So the next night, after midnight, four men crossed Miss Emily's lawn and slunk about the house like burglars, sniffing along the base of the brickwork and at the cellar openings while one of them performed a regular sowing motion with his hand out of a sack slung from his shoulder. They broke open the cellar door and sprinkled lime there, and in all the outbuildings. As they recrossed the lawn, a window that had been dark was lighted and Miss Emily sat in it, the light behind her, and her upright torso motionless as that of an idol. They crept quietly across the lawn and into the shadow of the locusts that lined the street. After a week or two the smell went away.

That was when people had begun to feel really sorry for her. People in our town, remembering how old lady Wyatt, her great-aunt, had gone completely crazy at last, believed that the Griersons held themselves a little too high for what they really were. None of the young men were quite good enough for Miss Emily and such. We had long thought of them as a tableau, Miss Emily a slender figure in white in the background, her father a spraddled silhouette in the foreground, his back to her and clutching a horsewhip, the two of them framed by the back-flung front door. So when she got to be thirty and was still single, we were not pleased exactly, but vindicated; even with insanity in the family she wouldn't have turned down all of her chances if they had really materialized.

When her father died, it got about that the house was all that was left to her; and in a way, people were glad. At last they could pity Miss Emily. Being left alone, and a pauper, she had become humanized. Now she too would know the old thrill and the old despair of a penny more or less.

The day after his death all the ladies prepared to call at the house and offer condolence and aid, as is our custom. Miss Emily met them at the door, dressed as usual and with no trace of grief on her face. She told them that her father was not dead. She did that for three days, with the ministers calling on her, and the doctors, trying to persuade her to let them dispose of the body. Just as they were about to resort to law and force, she broke down, and they buried her father quickly.

We did not say she was crazy then. We believed she had to do that. We remembered all the young men her father had driven away, and we knew that with nothing left, she would have to cling to that which had robbed her, as people will.

III

She was sick for a long time. When we saw her again, her hair was cut short, making her look like a girl, with a vague resemblance to those angels in colored church windows—sort of tragic and serene.

The town had just let the contracts for paving the sidewalks, and in the summer after her father's death they began the work. The construction company came with niggers and mules and machinery, and a foreman named Homer Barron, a Yankee—a big, dark, ready man, with a big voice and eyes lighter than his face. The little boys would follow in groups to hear him cuss the niggers, and the niggers singing in time to the rise and fall of picks. Pretty soon he knew everybody in town. Whenever you heard a lot of laughing anywhere about the square, Homer Barron would be in the center of the group. Presently we began to see him and Miss Emily on Sunday afternoons driving in the yellow-wheeled buggy and the matched team of bays from the livery stable.

At first we were glad that Miss Emily would have an interest, because the ladies all said, "Of course a Grierson would not think seriously of a

Northerner, a day laborer." But there were still others, older people, who said that even grief could not cause a real lady to forget *noblesse oblige*—without calling it *noblesse oblige*. They just said, "Poor Emily. Her kinsfolk should come to her." She had some kin in Alabama; but years ago her father had fallen out with them over the estate of old lady Wyatt, the crazy woman, and there was no communication between the two families. They had not even been represented at the funeral.

And as soon as the old people said, "Poor Emily," the whispering began. "Do you suppose it's really so?" they said to one another. "Of course it is. What else could ..." This behind their hands; rustling of craned silk and satin behind jalousies closed upon the sun of Sunday afternoon as the thin, swift clop-clop-clop of the matched team passed: "Poor Emily."

She carried her head high enough—even when we believed that she was fallen. It was as if she demanded more than ever the recognition of her dignity as the last Grierson; as if it had wanted that touch of earthiness to reaffirm her imperviousness. Like when she bought the rat poison, the arsenic. That was over a year after they had begun to say "Poor Emily," and while the two female cousins were visiting her.

"I want some poison," she said to the druggist. She was over thirty then, still a slight woman, though thinner than usual, with cold, haughty black eyes in a face the flesh of which was strained across the temples and about the eye-sockets as you imagine a lighthouse-keeper's face ought to look. "I want some poison," she said.

"Yes, Miss Emily. What kind? For rats and such? I'd recom—"

"I want the best you have. I don't care what kind."

The druggist named several. "They'll kill anything up to an elephant. But what you want is—"

"Arsenic," Miss Emily said. "Is that a good one?"

"Is ... arsenic? Yes, ma'am. But what you want—"

"I want arsenic."

The druggist looked down at her. She looked back at him, erect, her face like a strained flag. "Why, of course," the druggist said. "If that's what you want. But the law requires you to tell what you are going to use it for."

Miss Emily just stared at him, her head tilted back in order to look him eye for eye, until he looked away and went and got the arsenic and wrapped it up. The Negro delivery boy brought her the package; the druggist didn't come back. When she opened the package at home there was written on the box, under the skull and bones: "For rats."

IV

So the next day we all said, "She will kill herself"; and we said it would be the best thing. When she had first begun to be seen with Homer Barron, we had said, "She will marry him." Then we said, "She will persuade him yet," because Homer himself had remarked—he liked men, and it was known that he drank with the younger men in the Elks' Club—that he was not a marrying man. Later we said, "Poor Emily" behind the jalousies as they passed on Sunday afternoon in the glittering buggy, Miss Emily with her head high and Homer Barron with his hat cocked and a cigar in his teeth, reins and whip in a yellow glove.

Then some of the ladies began to say that it was a disgrace to the town and a bad example to the young people. The men did not want to interfere, but at last the ladies forced the Baptist minister—Miss Emily's people were Episcopal—to call upon her. He would never divulge what happened during that interview, but he refused to go back again. The next Sunday they again drove about the streets, and the following day the minister's wife wrote to Miss Emily's relations in Alabama.

So she had blood-kin under her roof again and we sat back to watch developments. At first nothing happened. Then we were sure that they were to be married. We learned that Miss Emily had been to the jeweler's and ordered a man's toilet set in silver, with the letters H. B. on each piece. Two days later we learned that she had bought a complete outfit of men's clothing, including a nightshirt, and we said, "They are married." We were really glad. We were glad because the two female cousins were even more Grierson than Miss Emily had ever been.

So we were not surprised when Homer Barron—the streets had been finished some time since—was gone. We were a little disappointed that there was not a public blowing-off, but we believed that he had gone on to prepare for Miss Emily's coming, or to give her a chance to get rid of the cousins. (By that time it was a cabal, and we were all Miss Emily's allies to help circumvent the cousins.) Sure enough, after another week they departed. And, as we had expected all along, within three days Homer Barron was back in town. A neighbor saw the Negro man admit him at the kitchen door at dusk one evening.

And that was the last we saw of Homer Barron. And of Miss Emily for some time. The Negro man went in and out with the market basket, but the front door remained closed. Now and then we would see her at a window for a moment, as the men did that night when they sprinkled the lime, but for almost six months she did not appear on the streets. Then we knew that this was to be expected too; as if that quality of her father which had thwarted her woman's life so many times had been too virulent and too furious to die.

When we next saw Miss Emily, she had grown fat and her hair was turning gray. During the next few years it grew grayer and grayer until it attained an even pepper-and-salt iron-gray, when it ceased turning. Up to the day of her death at seventy-four it was still that vigorous iron-gray, like the hair of an active man.

From that time on her front door remained closed, save for a period of six or seven years, when she was about forty, during which she gave lessons in china-painting. She fitted up a studio in one of the downstairs rooms, where the daughters and granddaughters of Colonel Sartoris' contemporaries were sent to her with the same regularity and in the same spirit that they were sent to church on Sundays with a twenty-five-cent piece for the collection plate. Meanwhile her taxes had been remitted.

Then the newer generation became the backbone and the spirit of the town, and the painting pupils grew up and fell away and did not send their children to her with boxes of color and tedious brushes and pictures cut from the ladies' magazines. The front door closed upon the last one and remained closed for good. When the town got free postal delivery, Miss Emily alone refused to let them fasten the metal numbers above her door and attach a mailbox to it. She would not listen to them.

Daily, monthly, yearly we watched the Negro grow grayer and more stooped, going in and out with the market basket. Each December we sent her a tax notice, which would be returned by the post office a week later, unclaimed. Now and then we would see her in one of the downstairs windows—she had evidently shut up the top floor of the house—like the carven torso of an idol in a niche, looking or not looking at us, we could never tell which. Thus she passed from generation to generation—dear, inescapable, impervious, tranquil, and perverse.

And so she died. Fell ill in the house filled with dust and shadows, with only a doddering Negro man to wait on her. We did not even know she was sick; we had long since given up trying to get any information from the Negro. He talked to no one, probably not even to her, for his voice had grown harsh and rusty, as if from disuse.

She died in one of the downstairs rooms, in a heavy walnut bed with a curtain, her gray head propped on a pillow yellow and moldy with age and lack of sunlight.

V

The Negro met the first of the ladies at the front door and let them in, with their hushed, sibilant voices and their quick, curious glances, and then he disappeared. He walked right through the house and out the back and was not seen again.

The two female cousins came at once. They held the funeral on the second day, with the town coming to look at Miss Emily beneath a mass of bought flowers, with the crayon face of her father musing profoundly above the bier and the ladies sibilant and macabre; and the very old men—some in their brushed Confederate uniforms—on the porch and the lawn, talking of Miss Emily as if she had been a contemporary of theirs, believing that they had danced with her and courted her perhaps, confusing time with its mathematical progression, as the old do, to whom all the past is not a diminishing road but, instead, a huge meadow which no winter ever quite touches, divided from them now by the narrow bottle-neck of the most recent decade of years.

Already we knew that there was one room in that region above stairs which no one had seen in forty years, and which would have to be forced. They waited until Miss Emily was decently in the ground before they opened it.

The violence of breaking down the door seemed to fill this room with pervading dust. A thin, acrid pall as of the tomb seemed to lie everywhere upon this room decked and furnished as for a bridal: upon the valance curtains of faded rose color, upon the rose-shaded lights, upon the dressing table, upon the delicate array of crystal and the man's toilet things backed with tarnished silver, silver so tarnished that the monogram was obscured. Among them lay a collar and tie, as if they had just been removed, which, lifted, left upon the surface a pale crescent in the dust. Upon a chair hung the suit, carefully folded; beneath it the two mute shoes and the discarded socks.

The man himself lay in the bed.

For a long while we just stood there, looking down at the profound and fleshless grin. The body had apparently once lain in the attitude of an embrace, but now the long sleep that outlasts love, that conquers even the grimace of love, had cuckolded him. What was left of him, rotted beneath what was left of the nightshirt, had become inextricable from the bed in which he lay; and upon him and upon the pillow beside him lay that even coating of the patient and biding dust.

Then we noticed that in the second pillow was the indentation of a head. One of us lifted something from it, and leaning forward, that faint and invisible dust dry and acrid in the nostrils, we saw a long strand of iron-gray hair.

Topics for Discussion

1. In what way is Emily Grierson a monument and what does she represent in the story? How does Faulkner go about making her into a symbol?

2. What function do the townspeople serve in the story as reflections of audience opinion or as assistants in the narrative process?

3. How does Faulkner create the surprise ending and how does the ending impact upon the story?

4. How does Faulkner use history in the story?

5. What role does Emily Grierson's father play in the story?

6. How does Faulkner define chivalry and what role does it play in the story?

7. What is Faulkner suggesting about the nature of social change by comparing the older generation with the new generation of townspeople?

8. How does the first person narrative form influence the way the story is told and the way we read the story?

Mavis Gallant

About the Author

Mavis Gallant was born in Montreal in 1922 and educated at various schools in Canada and the United States. She worked as a reporter for the *Montreal Standard* during the 1940s. She left the newspaper world when she discovered that she was not paid as much as men for doing the same job. Since the 1950s she has been a full-time writer and has lived in Europe, chiefly in Paris, although she has steadfastly maintained her Canadian citizenship. Her short stories frequently appear in *The New Yorker*. She won the Governor General's Award for Fiction in 1981 for her collection of short stories *Home Truths*.

Particularly in the collection of stories from which the novella "The Moslem Wife" is drawn, *From the Fifteenth District* (1979), Gallant's work is concerned with the way the civilizing values of European culture became weakened in the wake of the Second World War. Her stories are often nostalgic for the *fin-de-siècle* world of elegance and artifice that reached its nadir in the first decade of the twentieth century. Her female protagonists often act as "keepers of the flame" of European civilization and values— guardians of a culture constantly threatened by the transient values and superficiality of a disposable society that honours neither tradition nor excellence. For Gallant, as she stated in her essay "What Is Style?" (in *Paris Notebooks*), style is "the distillation of a lifetime of reading and listening, of selection and rejection," and Gallant has consciously sought to locate her stories, verbally, stylistically and contextually, within the traditions established by such European literary giants as Marcel Proust and the short story writer Colette.

Selected Works

The Other Paris (short stories, 1956)
Green Water, Green Sky (novel, 1959)
My Heart Is Broken (short stories, 1964)
A Fairly Good Time (novel, 1970)
The Pegnitz Junction (short stories, 1973)
From the Fifteenth District (short stories, 1979)
Home Truths: Selected Canadian Stories (short stories, 1981)
Overhead in a Balloon: Stories of Paris (short stories, 1985)
Paris Notebooks: Essays and Reviews (criticism, 1988)

About the Story

Gailant sets "The Moslem Wife" in the twilight of the *fin-de-siècle* world of grand tours and high artifice that marked the end of the nineteenth and the beginning of the twentieth century in Europe. Netta's hotel is located in the south of France in what was, and still is, a popular summer tourist area for northern Europeans.

These Mediterranean resort hotels offered a retreat from the humdrum world where everything was done for the guests, where they could abdicate their responsibilities and concerns for a world of sensory and aesthetic enjoyment. The modern four-star hotel is modelled on the late-nineteenth-century idea of a retreat into artifice, security and comfort, rather than just a place to stay, a way station on a journey.

Netta Ross's world is that of English expatriates who have fled, for reasons of health or wealth, to the warm climate of the south of France, a world filled with aromatic plants and flowers that in Gallant's descriptions evoke traditional concepts of paradise. The story covers the decline of the hotel during the period from the end of the First World War, through the German Occupation during the Second World War, to the aftermath of the liberation, a scope which embodies a history of the twentieth century as told through the impact of events on a single protagonist.

The Moslem Wife

In the south of France, in the business room of a hotel quite near to the house where Katherine Mansfield (whom no one in this hotel had ever heard of) was writing "The Daughters of the Late Colonel," Netta Asher's father announced that there would never be a man-made catastrophe in Europe again. The dead of that recent war, the doomed nonsense of the Russian Bolsheviks had finally knocked sense into European heads. What people wanted now was to get on with life. When he said "life," he meant its commercial business.

Who would have contradicted Mr. Asher? Certainly not Netta. She did not understand what he meant quite so well as his French solicitor seemed to, but she did listen with interest and respect, and then watched him signing papers that, she knew, concerned her for life. He was renewing the long lease her family held on the Hotel Prince Albert and Albion. Netta was then eleven. One hundred years should at least see her through the prime of her life, said Mr. Asher, only half jokingly, for of course he thought his seed was immortal.

Netta supposed she might easily live to be more than a hundred—at any rate, for years and years. She knew that her father did not want her to marry until she was twenty-six and that she was then supposed to have a pair of children, the elder a boy. Netta and her father and the French lawyer shook hands on the lease, and she was given her first glass of champagne. The date on the bottle was 1909, for the year of her birth. Netta bravely pronounced the wine delicious, but her father said she would know much better vintages before she was through.

Netta remembered the handshake but perhaps not the terms. When the lease had eighty-eight years to run, she married her first cousin, Jack Ross, which was not at all what her father had had in mind. Nor would there be the useful pair of children—Jack couldn't abide them. Like Netta he came from a hotelkeeping family where the young were like blight. Netta had up to now never shown a scrap of maternal feeling over anything, but Mr. Asher thought Jack might have made an amiable parent—a kind one, at least. She consoled Mr. Asher on one count, by taking the hotel over in his lifetime. The hotel was, to Netta, a natural life; and so when Mr. Asher, dying, said, "She behaves as I wanted her to," he was right as far as the drift of Netta's behavior was concerned but wrong about its course.

The Ashers' hotel was not down on the seafront, though boats and sea could be had from the south-facing rooms.

Across a road nearly empty of traffic were handsome villas, and behind and to either side stood healthy olive trees and a large lemon grove. The hotel was painted a deep ochre with white trim. It had white awnings and green shutters and black iron balconies as lacquered and shiny as Chinese boxes. It possessed two tennis courts, a lily pond, a sheltered winter garden, a formal rose garden, and trees full of nightingales. In the summer dark, *belles-de-nuit* glowed pink, lemon, white, and after their evening watering they gave off a perfume that varied from plant to plant and seemed to match the petals' coloration. In May the nights were dense with stars and fireflies. From the rose garden one might have seen the twin pulse of cigarettes on a balcony, where Jack and Netta sat drinking a last brandy-and-soda before turning in. Most of the rooms were shuttered by then, for no traveller would have dreamed of being south except in winter. Jack and Netta and a few servants had the whole place to themselves. Netta would hire workmen and have the rooms that needed it repainted—the blue cardroom, and the red-walled bar, and the white dining room, where Victorian mirrors gave back glossy walls and blown curtains and nineteenth-century views of the Ligurian coast, the work of an Asher great-uncle. Everything upstairs and down was soaked and wiped and polished, and even the pictures were relentlessly washed with soft cloths and ordinary laundry soap. Netta also had the boiler overhauled and the linen mended and new monograms embroidered and the looking glasses resilvered and the shutters taken off their hinges and scraped and made spruce green again for next year's sun to fade, while Jack talked about decorators and expert gardeners and even wrote to some, and banged tennis balls against the large new garage. He also read books and translated poetry for its own sake and practiced playing the clarinet. He had studied music once, and still thought that an important life, a musical life, was there in the middle distance. One summer, just to see if he could, he translated pages of St. John Perse, which were as blank as the garage wall to Netta, in any tongue.

Netta adored every minute of her life, and she thought Jack had a good life too, with nearly half the year for the pleasures that suited him. As soon as the grounds and rooms and cellar and roof had been put to rights, she and Jack packed and went travelling somewhere. Jack made plans. He was never so cheerful as when buying Baedekers and dragging out their stickered trunks. But Netta was nothing of a traveller. She would have been glad to see the same sun rising out of the same sea from the window every day until she died. She loved Jack, and what she liked best after him was the hotel. It was a place where, once, people had come to die of tuberculosis, yet it held no trace or feeling of danger. When Netta walked with her workmen through sheeted summer rooms, hearing the cicadas and hearing Jack start, stop, start some deeply alien music (alien even when her memory automatically gave her a composer's name), she was reminded that here the dead had never been allowed to corrupt the living; the dead had been dressed for an outing and removed as soon as their first muscular stiffness relaxed. Some were wheeled out in chairs, sitting, and some reclined on portable cots, as if merely resting.

That is why there is no bad atmosphere here, she would say to herself. Death has been swept away, discarded. When the shutters are closed on a room, it is for sleep or for love. Netta could think this easily because neither she nor Jack was ever sick. They knew nothing about insomnia, and they made love every day of their lives—they had married in order to be able to.

Spring had been the season for dying in the old days. Invalids who had struggled through the dark comfort of winter took fright as the night receded. They felt without protection. Netta knew about this, and about the difference between darkness and brightness, but neither affected her. She was not afraid of death or of the dead—they were nothing but cold, heavy furniture. She could have tied jaws shut and weighted eyelids with native instinctiveness, as other women were born knowing the temperature of an infant's milk.

"There are no ghosts," she could say, entering the room where her mother, then her father had died. "If there were, I would know."

Netta took it for granted, now she was married, that Jack felt as she did about light, dark, death, and love. They were as alike in some ways (none of them physical) as a couple of twins, spoke much the same language in the same accents, had the same jokes—mostly about other people—and had been together as much as their families would let them for most of their lives. Other men seemed dull to Netta—slower, perhaps, lacking the spoken shorthand she had with Jack. She never mentioned this. For one thing, both of them had the idea that, being English, one must not say too much. Born abroad, they worked hard at an Englishness that was innocently inaccurate, rooted mostly in attitudes. Their families had been innkeepers along this coast for a century, even before Dr. James Henry Bennet had discovered "the Genoese Rivieras." In one of his guides to the region, a "Mr. Ross" is mentioned as a hotel owner who will accept English bank checks, and there is a "Mr. Asher," reliable purveyor of English groceries. The most trustworthy shipping agents in 1860 are the Montale brothers, converts to the Anglican Church, possessors of a British *laissez-passer* to Malta and Egypt. These families, by now plaited like hair, were connections of Netta's and Jack's and still in business from beyond Marseilles to Genoa. No wonder that other men bored her, and that each thought the other both familiar and unique. But of course they were unalike too. When once someone asked them, "Are you related to Montale, the poet?" Netta answered, "What poet?" and Jack said, "I wish we were."

There were no poets in the family. Apart from the great-uncle who had painted landscapes, the only person to try anything peculiar had been Jack, with his music. He had been allowed to study, up to a point; his father had been no good with hotels—had been a failure, in fact, bailed out four times by his cousins, and it had been thought, for a time, that Jack Ross might be a dunderhead too. Music might do him; he might not be fit for anything else.

Information of this kind about the meaning of failure had been gleaned by Netta years before, when she first became aware of her little cousin. Jack's father and mother—the commercial blunderers—had come to the Prince Albert and Albion to ride out a crisis. They were somewhere between undischarged bankruptcy and annihilation, but one was polite: Netta curtsied to her aunt and uncle. Her eyes were on Jack. She could not read yet, though she could sift and classify attitudes. She drew near him, sucking her lower lip, her hands behind her back. For the first time she was conscious of the beauty of another child. He was younger than Netta, imprisoned in a portable-fence arrangement in which he moved tirelessly, crabwise, hanging on a barrier he could easily have climbed. He was as fair as his Irish mother and sunburned a deep brown. His blue gaze was not a baby's—it was too challenging. He was naked except for shorts that were large and seemed to fall down. The sunburn, the undress were because his mother was reckless and rather odd. Netta—whose mother was perfect—wore boots, stockings, a longsleeved frock, and a white sun hat. She heard the adults laugh and say that Jack looked like a prizefighter. She walked around his prison, staring, and the blue-eyed fighter stared back.

The Rosses stayed a long time, while the family sent telegrams and tried to raise money for them. No one looked after Jack much. He would lie on a marble step of the staircase watching the hotel guests going into the cardroom or the dining room. One night, for a reason that remorse was to wipe out in a minute, Netta gave him such a savage kick (though he was not really in her way) that one of his legs remained paralyzed for a long time.

"Why did you do it?" her father asked her—this in the room where she was shut up on bread and water. Netta didn't know. She loved Jack, but who would believe it now? Jack learned to walk, then to run, and in time to ski and play tennis; but her lifelong gift to him was a loss of balance, a sudden lopsided bend of a knee. Jack's parents had meantime been given a small hotel to run at Bandol. Mr. Asher, responsible for a bank loan, kept an eye on the place. He went often, in a hotel car with a chauffeur, Netta perched beside him. When, years later, the families found out that the devoted young cousins had become lovers, they separated them without saying much. Netta was too independent to be dealt with. Besides, her father did not want a rift; his wife had died, and he needed Netta. Jack, whose claim on music had been the subject of teasing until now, was suddenly sent to study in England. Netta saw that he was secretly dismayed. He wanted to be almost anything as long as it was impossible, and then only as an act of grace. Netta's father did think it was his duty to tell her that marriage was, at its best, a parched arrangement, intolerable without a flow of golden guineas and fresh blood. As cousins, Jack and Netta could not bring each other anything except stale money. Nothing stopped them: they were married four months after Jack became twenty-one. Netta heard someone remark at her wedding, "She doesn't need a husband," meaning perhaps the practical, matter-of-fact person she now seemed to be. She did have the dry, burned-out look of someone turned inward. Her dark eyes glowed out of a thin face. She had the shape of a girl of fourteen. Jack, who was large, and fair, and who might be stout at forty if he wasn't careful, looked exactly his age, and seemed quite ready to be married.

Netta could not understand why, loving Jack as she did, she did not look more like him. It had troubled her in the past when they did not think exactly the same thing at almost the same time. During the secret meetings of their long engagement she had noticed how even before a parting they were nearly apart—they had begun to "unmesh," as she called it. Drinking a last drink, usually in the buffet of a railway station, she would see that Jack was somewhere else, thinking about the next-best thing to Netta. The next-best thing might only be a book he wanted to finish reading, but it was enough to make her feel exiled. He often told Netta, "I'm not holding on to you. You're free," because he thought it needed saying, and of course he wanted freedom for himself. But to Netta "freedom" had a cold sound. Is that what I do want, she would wonder. Is that what I think he should offer? Their partings were often on the edge of parting forever, not just because Jack had said or done or thought the wrong thing but because between them they generated the high sexual tension that leads to quarrels. Barely ten minutes after agreeing that no one in the world could possibly know what they knew, one of them, either one, could curse the other out over something trivial. Yet they were, and remained, much in love, and when they were apart Netta sent him letters that were almost despairing with enchantment.

Jack answered, of course, but his letters were cautious. Her exploration of feeling was part of an unlimited capacity she seemed to have for passionate behavior, so at odds with her appearance, which had been dry and sardonic even in childhood. Save for an erotic sentence or two near the end (which Netta read first) Jack's messages might have been meant for any girl cousin he particularly liked. Love was memory, and he was no good at the memory game; he needed Netta there. The instant he saw her he knew all he had missed. But Netta, by then, felt forgotten, and she came to each new meeting aggressive and hurt, afflicted with the physical signs of her doubts and injuries—cold sores, rashes, erratic periods, mysterious temperatures. If she tried to discuss it he would say, "We aren't going over all that again, are we?" Where Netta was concerned he had settled for the established faith, but Netta who had a wilder, more secret God, wanted a prayer a minute, not to speak of unending miracles and revelations.

When they finally married, both were relieved that the strain of partings and of tense disputes in railway stations would come to a stop. Each privately blamed the other for past violence, and both believed that once they could live openly, without interference, they would never have a disagreement again. Netta did not want Jack to regret the cold freedom he had vainly tried to offer her. He must have his liberty, and his music, and other people, and, oh, anything he wanted—whatever would stop him from saying he was ready to let her go free. The first thing Netta did was to make certain they had the best room in the hotel. She had never actually owned a room until now. The private apartments of her family had always been surrendered in a crisis: everyone had packed up and moved as beds were required. She and Jack were hopelessly untidy, because both had spent their early years moving down hotel corridors, trailing belts and raincoats, with tennis shoes hanging from knotted strings over their shoulders, their arms around books and sweaters and gray flannel bundles. Both had done lessons in the corners of lounges, with cups and glasses rattling, and other children running, and English voices louder than anything. Jack, who had been vaguely educated, remembered his boarding schools as places where one had a permanent bed. Netta chose for her marriage a south-facing room with a large balcony and an awning of dazzling white. It was furnished with lemonwood that had been brought to the Riviera by Russians for their own villas long before. To the lemonwood Netta's mother had added English chintzes; the result, in Netta's eyes, was not bizarre but charming. The room was deeply mirrored; when the shutters were closed on hot afternoons a play of light became as green as a forest on the walls, and as blue as seawater in the glass. A quality of suspension, of disbelief in gravity, now belonged to Netta. She became tidy, silent, less introspective, as watchful and as reflective as her bedroom mirrors. Jack stayed as he was, luckily; any alteration would have worried her, just as a change in an often-read story will trouble a small child. She was intensely, almost unnaturally happy.

One day she overheard an English doctor, whose wife played bridge every afternoon at the hotel, refer to her, to Netta, as "the little Moslem wife." It was said affectionately, for the doctor liked her. She wondered if he had seen through walls and had watched her picking up the clothing and the wet towels Jack left strewn like clues to his presence. The phrase was collected and passed from mouth to mouth in the idle English colony. Netta, the last person in the world deliberately to eavesdrop (she lacked that sort of interest in other people), was sharp of hearing where her marriage was concerned. She had a special antenna for Jack, for his shades of meaning, secret intentions, for his innocent contradictions. Perhaps "Moslem wife" meant several things, and possibly it was plain to anyone with eyes that Jack, without meaning a bit of harm by it, had a way with women. Those he attracted were a puzzling lot, to Netta. She had already catalogued them—elegant elderly parties with tongues like carving knives; gentle, clever girls who flourished on the unattainable; untouchable-daughter types, canny about their virginity, wondering if Jack would be father enough to justify the sacrifice. There was still another kind—tough, sunburned, clad in dark colors—who made Netta think in the vocabulary of horoscopes: Her gem—diamonds. Her color—black. Her language—worse than Netta's. She noticed that even when Jack had no real use for a woman he never made it apparent; he adopted anyone who took a liking to him. He assumed—Netta thought—a tribal, paternal air that was curious in so young a man. The plot of attraction interested him, no matter how it turned out. He was like someone reading several novels at once, or like someone playing simultaneous chess.

Netta did not want her marriage to become a world of stone. She said nothing except, "Listen, Jack, I've been at this hotel business longer than you have. It's wiser not to be too pally with the guests." At Christmas the older women gave him boxes of expensive soap. "They must think someone around here wants a good wash," Netta remarked. Outside their fenced area of private jokes and private love was a landscape too open, too light-drenched, for serious talk. And then, when? Jack woke up quickly and early in the morning and smiled as naturally as children do. He knew where he was and the day of the week and the hour. The best moment of the day was the first cigarette. When something bloody happened, it was never before six in the evening. At night he had a dark look that went with a dark mood, sometimes. Netta would tell him that she could see a cruise ship floating on the black horizon like a piece of the Milky Way, and she would get that look for an answer. But it never lasted. His memory was too short to let him sulk, no matter what fragment of night had crossed his mind. She knew, having heard other couples all her life, that at least she and Jack never made the conjugal sounds that passed for conversation and that might as well have been bow-wow and quack quack.

If, by chance, Jack found himself drawn to another woman, if the tide of attraction suddenly ran the other way, then he would discover in himself a great need to talk to his wife. They sat out on their balcony for much of one long night and he told her about his Irish mother. His mother's eccentricity—"Vera's dottiness," where the family was concerned—had kept Jack from taking anything seriously. He had been afraid of pulling her mad attention in his direction. Countless times she had faked tuberculosis and cancer and announced her own imminent death. A telephone call from a hospital had once declared her lost in a car crash. "It's a new life, a new life," her husband had babbled, coming away from the phone. Jack saw his father then as beautiful. Women are beautiful when they fall in love, said Jack; sometimes the glow will last a few hours, sometimes even a day or two.

"You know," said Jack, as if Netta knew, "the look of amazement on a girl's face…"

Well, that same incandescence had suffused Jack's father when he thought his wife had died, and it continued to shine until a taxi deposited dotty Vera with her cheerful announcement that she had certainly brought off a successful April Fool. After Jack's father died she became violent. "Getting away from her was a form of violence in me," Jack said. "But I did it." That was why he was secretive; that was why he was independent. He had never wanted any woman to get her hands on his life.

Netta heard this out calmly. Where his own feelings were concerned she thought he was making them up as he went along. The garden smelled coolly of jasmine and mimosa. She wondered who his new girl was, and if he was likely to blurt out a name. But all he had been working up to was that his mother—mad, spoiled, devilish, whatever she was—would need to live with Jack and Netta, unless Netta agreed to giving her an income. An income would let her remain where she was—at the moment, in a Rudolf Steiner community in Switzerland, devoted to medieval gardening and to getting the best out of Goethe. Netta's father's training prevented even the thought of spending the money in such a manner.

"You won't regret all you've told me, will you?" she asked. She saw that the new situation would be her burden, her chain, her mean little joke sometimes. Jack scarcely hesitated before saying that where Netta mattered he could never regret anything. But what really interested him now was his mother.

"Lifts give her claustrophobia," he said. "She mustn't be higher than the second floor." He sounded like a man bringing a legal concubine into his household, scrupulously anxious to give all his women equal rights. "And I hope she will make friends," he said. "It won't be easy, at her age. One can't live without them." He probably meant that he had none. Netta had been raised not to expect to have friends: you could not run a hotel and have scores of personal ties. She expected people to be polite and punctual and to mean what they said, and that was the end of it. Jack gave his friendship easily, but he expected considerable diversion in return.

Netta said dryly, "If she plays bridge, she can play with Mrs. Blackley." This was the wife of the doctor who had first said "Moslem wife."

He had come down here to the Riviera for his wife's health; the two belonged to a subcolony of flat-dwelling expatriates. His medical practice was limited to hypochondriacs and rheumatic patients. He had time on his hands: Netta often saw him in the hotel reading room, standing, leafing—he took pleasure in handling books. Netta, no reader, did not like touching a book unless it was new. The doctor had a trick of speech Jack loved to imitate: he would break up his words with an extra syllable, some words only, and at that not every time. "It is all a matter of stu-hyle," he said, for "style," or, Jack's favorite, "Oh, well, in the end it all comes down to su-hex." "Uh-hebb and flo-ho of hormones" was the way he once described the behavior of saints—Netta had looked twice at him over that. He was a firm agnostic and the first person from whom Netta heard there existed a magical Dr. Freud. When Netta's father had died of pneumonia, the doctor's "I'm su-horry, Netta" had been so heartfelt she could not have wished it said another way.

His wife, Georgina, could lower her blood pressure or stop her heartbeat nearly at will. Netta sometimes wondered why Dr. Blackley had brought her to a soft climate rather than to the man at Vienna he so admired. Georgina was well enough to play fierce bridge, with Jack and anyone good enough. Her husband usually came to fetch her at the end of the afternoon when the players stopped for tea. Once, because he was obliged to return at once to a patient who needed him, she said, "Can't you be competent about anything?" Netta thought she understood, then, his resigned repetition of "It's all su-hex." "Oh, don't explain. You bore me," said his wife, turning her back.

Netta followed him out to his car. She wore an Indian shawl that had been her mother's. The wind blew her hair; she had to hold it back. She said, "Why don't you kill her?"

"I am not a desperate person," he said. He looked at Netta, she looking up at him because she had to look up to nearly everyone except children, and he said. "I've wondered why we haven't been to bed."

"Who?" said Netta. "You and your wife? Oh. You mean me." She was not offended, she just gave the shawl a brusque tug and said, "Not a hope. Never with a guest," though of course that was not the reason.

"You might have to, if the guest were a maharaja," he said, to make it all harmless. "I am told it is pu-hart of the courtesy they expect."

"We don't get their trade," said Netta. This has not stopped her liking the doctor. She pitied him, rather, because of his wife, and because he wasn't Jack and could not have Netta.

"I do love you," said the doctor, deciding finally to sit down in his car. "Ee-nee-ormously." She watched him drive away as if she loved him too, and might never see him again. It never crossed her mind to mention any of this conversation to Jack.

That very spring, perhaps because of the doctor's words, the hotel did get some maharaja trade—three little sisters with ebony curls, men's eyebrows, large heads, and delicate hands and feet. They had four rooms, one for their governess. A chauffeur on permanent call lodged elsewhere. The governess, who was Dutch, had a perfect triangle of a nose and said "whom" for "who," pronouncing it "whum." The girls were to learn French, tennis, and swimming. The chauffeur arrived with a hairdresser, who cut their long hair; it lay on the governess's carpet, enough to fill a large pillow. Their toe- and fingernails were filed to points and looked like a kitten's teeth. They came smiling down the marble staircase, carrying new tennis racquets, wearing blue linen skirts and navy blazers. Mrs. Blackley glanced up from the bridge game as they went by the cardroom. She had been one of those opposed to their having lessons at the English Lawn Tennis Club, for reasons that were, to her, perfectly evident.

She said, loudly, "They'll have to be in white."

"End whay, pray?" cried the governess, pointing her triangle nose.

"They can't go on the courts except in white. It is a private club. Entirely white."

"Whum do they all think they are?" the governess asked, prepared to stalk on. But the girls, with their newly cropped heads, and their vulnerable necks showing, caught the drift and refused to go.

"Whom indeed," said Georgina Blackley, fiddling with her bridge hand and looking happy.

"My wife's seamstress could run up white frocks for them in a minute," said Jack. Perhaps he did not dislike children all that much.

"Whom could," muttered Georgina.

But it turned out that the governess was not allowed to choose their clothes, and so Jack gave the children lessons at the hotel. For six weeks they trotted around the courts looking angelic in blue, or hopelessly foreign, depending upon who saw them. Of course they fell in love with Jack, offering him a passionate loyalty they had nowhere else to place. Netta watched the transfer of this gentle, anxious gift. After they departed, Jack was bad-tempered for several evenings and then never spoke of them again; they, needless to say, had been dragged from him weeping.

When this happened the Rosses had been married nearly five years. Being childless but still very loving, they had trouble deciding which of the two would be the child. Netta overheard "He's a darling, but she's a sergeant major and no mistake. And so *mean*." She also heard "He's a lazy bastard. He bullies her. She's a fool." She searched her heart again about children. Was it Jack or had it been Netta who had first said no? The only child she had ever admired was Jack, and not as a child but as a fighter, defying her. She and Jack were not the sort to have animal children, and Jack's dotty mother would probably soon be child enough for any couple to handle. Jack still seemed to adopt, in a tribal sense of his, half the women who fell in love with him. The only woman who resisted adoption was Netta—still burned-out, still ardent, in a manner of speaking still fourteen. His mother had turned up meanwhile, getting down from a train wearing a sly air of enjoying her own jokes, just as she must have looked on the day of the April Fool. At first she was no great trouble, though she did complain about an ulcerated leg. After years of pretending, she at last had something real. Netta's policy of silence made Jack's mother confident. She began to make a mockery of his music: "All that money gone for nothing!" Or else, "The amount we wasted on schools! The hours he's thrown away with his nose in a book. All that reading—if at least it had got him somewhere." Netta noticed that he spent more time playing bridge and chatting to cronies in the bar now. She thought hard, and decided not to make it her business. His mother had once been pretty; perhaps he still saw her that way. She came of a ramshackle family with a usable past; she spoke of the Ashers and the Rosses as if she had known them when they were tinkers. English residents who had a low but solid barrier with Jack and Netta were fences-down with his mad mother: they seemed to take her at her own word when it was about herself. She began then to behave like a superior sort of guest, inviting large parties to her table for meals, ordering special wines and dishes at inconvenient hours, standing endless rounds of drinks in the bar.

Netta told herself, Jack wants it this way. It is his home too. She began to live a life apart, leaving Jack to his mother. She sat wearing her own mother's shawl, hunched over a new, modern adding machine, punching out accounts. "Funny couple," she heard now. She frowned, smiling in her mind; none of these people knew what bound them, or how tied they were. She had the habit of dodging out of her mother-in-law's parties by saying, "I've got such an awful lot to do." It made them laugh, because they thought this was Netta's term for slave-driving the servants. They thought the staff did the work, and that Netta counted the profits and was too busy with bookkeeping to keep an eye on Jack—who now, at twenty-six, was as attractive as he ever would be.

A woman named Iris Cordier was one of Jack's mother's new friends. Tall, loud, in winter dully pale, she reminded Netta of a blond penguin. Her voice moved between a squeak and a moo, and was a mark of the distinguished literary family to which her father belonged. Her mother, a Frenchwoman, had been in and out of nursing homes for years. The Cordiers haunted the Riviera, with Iris looking after her parents and watching their diets. Now she lived in a flat somewhere in Roquebrune with the survivor of the pair—the mother, Netta believed. Iris paused and glanced in the business room where Mr. Asher had signed the hundred-year lease. She was on her way to lunch—Jack's mother's guest, of course.

"I say, aren't you Miss Asher?"

"I was." Iris, like Dr. Blackley, was probably younger than she looked. Out of her own childhood Netta recalled a desperate adolescent Iris with middle-aged parents clamped like handcuffs on her life. "How is your mother?" Netta had been about to say "How is Mrs. Cordier?" but it sounded servile.

"I didn't know you knew her."

"I remember her well. Your father too. He was a nice person."

"And still his," said Iris, sharply. "He lives with me, and he always will. French daughters don't abandon their parents." No one had ever sounded more English to Netta. "And your father and mother?"

"Both dead now. I'm married to Jack Ross."

"Nobody told me," said Iris, in a way that made Netta think, Good Lord, Iris too? Jack could not possibly seem like a patriarchal figure where she was concerned; perhaps this time the game was reversed and Iris played at being tribal and maternal. The idea of Jack, or of any man, flinging himself on that iron bosom made Netta smile. As if startled, Iris covered her mouth. She seemed to be frightened of smiling back.

Oh, well, and what of it, Iris too, said Netta to herself, suddenly turning back to her accounts. As it happened, Netta was mistaken (as she never would have been with a bill). That day Jack was meeting Iris for the first time.

The upshot of these errors and encounters was an invitation to Roquebrune to visit Iris's father. Jack's mother was ruthlessly excluded, even though Iris probably owed her a return engagement because of the lunch. Netta supposed that Iris had decided one had to get past Netta to reach Jack—an inexactness if ever there was one. Or perhaps it was Netta Iris wanted. In that case the error became a farce. Netta had almost no knowledge of private houses. She looked around at something that did not much interest her, for she hated to leave her own home, and saw Iris's father, apparently too old and shaky to get out of his armchair. He smiled and he nodded, meanwhile stroking an aged cat. He said to Netta, "You resemble your mother. A sweet woman. Obliging and quiet. I used to tell her that I longed to live in her hotel and be looked after."

Not by me, thought Netta.

Iris's amber bracelets rattled as she pushed and pulled everyone through introductions. Jack and Netta had been asked to meet a young American Netta had often seen in her own bar, and a couple named Sandy and Sandra Braunsweg, who turned out to be Anglo-Swiss and twins. Iris's long arms were around them as she cried to Netta, "Don't you know these babies?" They were, like the Rosses, somewhere in their twenties. Jack looked on, blue-eyed, interested, smiling at everything new. Netta supposed that she was now seeing some of the rather

hard-up snobbish—snobbish what? "Intelligumhen-sia," she imagined
Dr. Blackley supplying. Having arrived at a word, Netta was ready to go
home; but they had only just arrived. The American turned to Netta.
He looked bored, and astonished by it. He needs the word for "bored,"
she decided. Then he can go home, too. The Riviera was no place for
Americans. They could not sit all day waiting for mail and the daily
papers and for the clock to show a respectable drinking time. They
made the best of things when they were caught with a house they'd
been rash enough to rent unseen. Netta often had them then *en pension*
for meals: a hotel dining room was one way of meeting people. They
paid a fee to use the tennis courts, and they liked the bar. Netta would
notice then how Jack picked up any accent within hearing.

Jack was now being attentive to the old man, Iris's father. Though
this was none of Mr. Cordier's business, Jack said, "My wife and I are
first cousins, as well as second cousins twice over."

"You don't look it."

Everyone began to speak at once, and it was a minute or two before
Netta heard Jack again. This time he said, "We are from a family of
great..." It was lost. What now? Great innkeepers? Worriers? Skin-
flints? Whatever it was, old Mr. Cordier kept nodding to show he
approved.

"We don't see nearly enough of young men like you," he said.

"True!" said Iris loudly. "We live in a dreary world of ill women
down here." Netta thought this hard on the American, on Mr. Cordier,
and on the male Braunsweg twin, but none of them looked offended.
"I've got no time for women," said Iris. She slapped down a glass of
whiskey so that it splashed, and rapped on a table with her knuckles.
"Shall I tell you why? Because women don't tick over. They just simply
don't tick over." No one disputed this. Iris went on: Women were
underinformed. One could have virile conversations only with men.
Women were attached to the past through fear, whereas men had a
fearless sense of history. "Men tick," she said, glaring at Jack.

"I am not attached to a past," said Netta, slowly. "The past holds no
attractions." She was not used to general conversation. She thought
that every word called for consideration and for an answer. "Nothing
could be worse than the way we children were dressed. And our mothers—the hard waves of their hair, the white lips. I think of those pale
profiles and I wonder if those women were ever young."

Poor Netta, who saw herself as profoundly English, spread conster-
nation by being suddenly foreign and gassy. She talked the English of
expatriate children, as if reading aloud. The twins looked shocked. But
she had appealed to the American. He sat beside her on a scuffed velvet sofa. He was so large that she slid an inch or so in his direction
when he sat down. He was Sandra Braunsweg's special friend: they had
been in London together. He was trying to write.

"What do you mean?" said Netta. "Write what?"

"Well—a novel, to start," he said. His father had staked him to one year, then another. He mentioned all that Sandra had borne with, how she had actually kicked and punched him to keep him from being too American. He had embarrassed her to death in London by asking a waitress, "Miss, where's the toilet?"

Netta said, "Didn't you mind being corrected?"

"Oh, no. It was just friendly."

Jack meanwhile was listening to Sandra telling about her English forebears and her English education. "I had many years of undeniably excellent schooling," she said. "Mitten Todd."

"What's that?" said Jack.

"It's near Bristol. I met excellent girls from Italy, Spain. I took *him* there to visit," she said, generously including the American. "I said, 'Get a yellow necktie.' He went straight out and bought one. I wore a little Schiaparelli. Bought in Geneva but still a real...A yellow jacket over a gray...Well, we arrived at my excellent old school, and even though the day was drizzly I said, 'Put the top of the car back.' He did so at once, and then he understood. The interior of the car harmonized perfectly with the yellow and gray." The twins were orphaned. Iris was like a mother.

"When Mummy died we didn't know where to put all the Chippendale," said Sandra, "Iris took a lot of it."

Netta thought, She is so silly. How can he respond? The girl's dimples and freckles and soft little hands were nothing Netta could have ever described: she had never in her life thought a word like "pretty." People were beautiful or they were not. Her happiness had always been great enough to allow for despair. She knew that some people thought Jack was happy and she was not.

"And what made you marry your young cousin?" the old man boomed at Netta. Perhaps his background allowed him to ask impertinent questions; he must have been doing so nearly forever. He stroked his cat; he was confident. He was spokesman for a roomful of wondering people.

"Jack was a moody child and I promised his mother I would look after him," said Netta. In her hopelessly un-English way she believed she had said something funny.

At eleven o'clock the hotel car expected to fetch the Rosses was nowhere. They trudged home by moonlight. For the last hour of the evening Jack had been skewered on virile conversations, first with Iris, then with Sandra, to whom Netta had already given "Chippendale" as a private name. It proved that Iris was right about concentrating on men and their ticking—Jack even thought Sandra rather pretty.

"Prettier than me?" said Netta, without the faintest idea what she meant, but aware she had said something stupid.

"Not so attractive," said Jack. His slight limp returned straight out of childhood. *She* had caused his accident.

"But she's not always clear," said Netta. "Mitten Todd, for example."

"Who're you talking about?"

"Who are *you?*"

"Iris, of course."

As if they had suddenly quarrelled they fell silent. In silence they entered their room and prepared for bed. Jack poured a whiskey, walked on the clothes he had dropped, carried his drink to the bathroom. Through the half-shut door he called suddenly, "Why did you say that asinine thing about promising to look after me?"

"It seemed so unlikely, I thought they'd laugh." She had a glimpse of herself in the mirrors picking up his shed clothes.

He said, "Well, is it true?"

She was quiet for such a long time that he came to see if she was still in the room. She said, "No, your mother never said that or anything like it."

"We shouldn't have gone to Roquebrune," said Jack. "I think those bloody people are going to be a nuisance. Iris wants her father to stay here, with the cat, while she goes to England for a month. How do we get out of that?"

"By saying no."

"I'm rotten at no."

"I told you not to be too pally with women," she said, as a joke again, but jokes were her way of having floods of tears.

Before this had a chance to heal, Iris's father moved in, bringing his cat in a basket. He looked at his room and said, "Medium large." He looked at his bed and said, "Reasonably long." He was, in short, daft about measurements. When he took books out of the reading room, he was apt to return them with "This volume contains about 70,000 words" written inside the back cover.

Netta had not wanted Iris's father, but Jack had said yes to it. She had not wanted the sick cat, but Jack had said yes to that too. The old man, who was lost without Iris, lived for his meals. He would appear at the shut doors of the dining room an hour too early, waiting for the menu to be typed and posted. In a voice that matched Iris's for carrying power, he read aloud, alone: "Consommé. Good Lord, again? Is there a choice between the fish and the cutlet? I can't possibly eat all of that. A bit of salad and a boiled egg. That's all I could possibly want." That was rubbish, because Mr. Cordier ate the menu and more, and if there were two puddings, or a pudding and ice cream, he ate both and asked for pastry, fruit, and cheese to follow. One day, after Dr. Blackley had attended him for faintness, Netta passed a message on to Iris, who had been back from England for a fortnight now but seemed in no hurry to take her father away.

"Keith Blackley thinks your father should go on a diet."

"He can't," said Iris. "Our other doctor says dieting causes cancer."

"You can't have heard that properly," Netta said.

"It is like those silly people who smoke to keep their figures," said Iris. "Dieting."

"Blackley hasn't said he should smoke, just that he should eat less of everything."

"My father has never smoked in his life," Iris cried. "As for his diet, I weighed his food out for years. He's not here forever. I'll take him back as soon as he's had enough of hotels."

He stayed for a long time, and the cat did too, and a nuisance they both were to the servants. When the cat was too ailing to walk, the old man carried it to a path behind the tennis courts and put it down on the gravel to die. Netta came out with the old man's tea on a tray (not done for everyone, but having him out of the way was a relief) and she saw the cat lying on its side, eyes wide, as if profoundly thinking. She saw unlicked dirt on its coat and ants exploring its paws. The old man sat in a garden chair, wearing a panama hat, his hands clasped on a stick. He called, "Oh, Netta, take her away. I am too old to watch anything die. I know what she'll do," he said, indifferently, his voice falling as she came near. "Oh, I know that. Turn on her back and give a shriek. I've heard it often."

Netta disburdened her tray onto a garden table and pulled the tray cloth under the cat. She was angered at the haste and indecency of the ants. "It would be polite to leave her," she said. "She doesn't want to be watched."

"I always sit here," said the old man.

Jack, making for the courts with Chippendale, looked as if the sight of the two conversing amused him. Then he understood and scooped up the cat and tray cloth and went away with the cat over his shoulder. He laid it in the shade of a Judas tree, and within an hour it was dead. Iris's father said, "I've got no one to talk to here. That's my trouble. That shroud was too small for my poor Polly. Ask my daughter to fetch me."

Jack's mother said that night, "I'm sure you wish that I had a devoted daughter to take me away too." Because of the attention given the cat she seemed to feel she had not been nuisance enough. She had taken to saying, "My leg is dying before I am," and imploring Jack to preserve her leg, should it be amputated, and make certain it was buried with her. She wanted Jack to be close by at nearly any hour now, so that she could lean on him. After sitting for hours at bridge she had trouble climbing two flights of stairs; nothing would induce her to use the lift.

"Nothing ever came of your music," she would say, leaning on him. "Of course, you have a wife to distract you now. I needed a daughter. Every woman does." Netta managed to trap her alone, and forced her to sit while she stood over her. Netta said, "Look, Aunt Vera, I forbid you, I absolutely forbid you, do you hear, to make a nurse of Jack, and I shall strangle you with my own hands if you go on saying nothing came of his music. You are not to say it in my hearing or out of it. Is that plain?"

Jack's mother got up to her room without assistance. About an hour later the gardener found her on a soft bed of wallflowers. "An inch to the left and she'd have landed on a rake," he said to Netta. She was still alive when Netta knelt down. In her fall she had crushed the plants, the yellow minted *giroflées de Nice*. Netta thought that she was now, at last, for the first time, inhaling one of the smells of death. Her aunt's arms and legs were turned and twisted; her skirt was pulled so that her swollen leg showed. It seemed that she had jumped carrying her walking stick—it lay across the path. She often slept in an armchair, afternoons, with one eye slightly open. She opened that eye now and, seeing she had Netta, said, "My son." Netta was thinking, I have never known her. And if I knew her, then it was Jack or myself I could not understand. Netta was afraid of giving orders, and of telling people not to touch her aunt before Dr. Blackley could be summoned, because she knew that she had always been mistaken. Now Jack was there, propping his mother up, brushing leaves and earth out of her hair. Her head dropped on his shoulder. Netta thought from the sudden heaviness that her aunt had died, but she sighed and opened that one eye again, saying this time, "Doctor?" Netta left everyone doing the wrong things to her dying—no, her murdered—aunt. She said quite calmly into a telephone, "I am afraid that my aunt must have jumped or fallen from the second floor."

Jack found a letter on his mother's night table that began, "Why blame Netta? I forgive." At dawn he and Netta sat at a card table with yesterday's cigarettes still not cleaned out of the ashtray, and he did not ask what Netta had said or done that called for forgiveness. They kept pushing the letter back and forth. He would read it and then Netta would. It seemed natural for them to be silent. Jack had sat beside his mother for much of the night. Each of them then went to sleep for an hour, apart, in one of the empty rooms, just as they had done in the old days when their parents were juggling beds and guests and double and single quarters. By the time the doctor returned for his second visit Jack was neatly dressed and seemed wide awake. He sat in the bar drinking black coffee and reading a travel book of Evelyn Waugh's called *Labels*. Netta, who looked far more untidy and underslept, wondered if Jack wished he might leave now, and sail from Monte Carlo on the Stella Polaris.

Dr. Blackley said, "Well, you are a dim pair. She is not in pu-hain, you know." Netta supposed this was the roundabout way doctors have of announcing death, very like "Her sufferings have ended." But Jack, looking hard at the doctor, had heard another meaning. "Jumped or fell," said Dr. Blackley. "She neither fell nor jumped. She is up there enjoying a damned good thu-hing."

Netta went out and through the lounge and up the marble steps. She sat down in the shaded room on the chair where Jack had spent most of the night. Her aunt did not look like anyone Netta knew, not even like Jack. She stared at the alien face and said, "Aunt Vera, Keith Blackley says there is nothing really the matter. You must have made a mistake. Perhaps you fainted on the path, overcome by the scent of wallflowers. What would you like me to tell Jack?"

Jack's mother turned on her side and slowly, tenderly, raised herself on an elbow. "Well, Netta," she said, "I daresay the fool is right. But as I've been given a lot of sleeping stuff, I'd as soon stay here for now."

Netta said, "Are you hungry?"

"I should very much like a ham sandwich on English bread, and about that much gin with a lump of ice."

She began coming down for meals a few days later. They knew she had crept down the stairs and flung her walking stick over the path and let herself fall hard on a bed of wallflowers—had even plucked her skirt up for a bit of accuracy; but she was also someone returned from beyond the limits, from the other side of the wall. Once she said, "It was like diving and suddenly realizing there was no water in the sea." Again, "It is not true that your life rushes before your eyes. You can see the flowers floating up to you. Even a short fall takes a long time."

Everyone was deeply changed by this incident. The effect on the victim herself was that she got religion hard.

"We are all hopeless nonbelievers!" shouted Iris, drinking in the bar one afternoon. "At least, I hope we are. But when I see you, Vera, I feel there might be something in religion. You look positively temperate."

"I am allowed to love God, I hope," said Jack's mother.

Jack never saw or heard his mother anymore. He leaned against the bar, reading. It was his favorite place. Even on the sunniest of afternoons he read by the red-shaded light. Netta was present only because she had supplies to check. Knowing she ought to keep out of this, she still said, "Religion is more than love. It is supposed to tell you why you exist and what you are expected to do about it."

"You have no religious feelings at all?" This was the only serious and almost the only friendly question Iris was ever to ask Netta.

"None," said Netta. "I'm running a business."

"I love God as Jack used to love music," said his mother. "At least he said he did when we were paying for lessons."

"Adam and Eve had God," said Netta. "They had nobody *but* God. A fat lot of good that did them." This was as far as their dialectic went. Jack had not moved once except to turn pages. He read steadily but cautiously now, as if every author had a design on him. That was one effect of his mother's incident. The other was that he gave up bridge and went back to playing the clarinet. Iris hammered out an accompaniment on the upright piano in the old music room, mostly used for listening to radio broadcasts. She was the only person Netta had ever heard who could make Mozart sound like an Irish jig. Presently Iris began to say that it was time Jack gave a concert. Before this could turn into a crisis Iris changed her mind and said what he wanted was a holiday. Netta thought he needed something: he seemed to be exhausted by love, friendship, by being a husband, someone's son, by trying to make a world out of reading and sense out of life. A visit to England to meet some stimulating people, said Iris. To help Iris with her tiresome father during the journey. To visit art galleries and bookshops and go to concerts. To meet people. To talk.

This was a hot, troubled season, and many persons were planning journeys—not to meet other people but for fear of a war. The hotel had emptied out by the end of March. Netta, whose father had known there would never be another catastrophe, had her workmen come in, as usual. She could hear the radiators being drained and got ready for painting as she packed Jack's clothes. They had never been separated before. They kept telling each other that it was only for a short holiday—for three or four weeks. She was surprised at how neat marriage was, at how many years and feelings could be folded and put under a lid. Once, she went to the window so that he would not see her tears and think she was trying to blackmail him. Looking out, she noticed the American, Chippendale's lover, idly knocking a tennis ball against the garage, as Jack had done in the early summers of their life; he had come round to the hotel looking for a partner, but that season there were none. She suddenly knew to a certainty that if Jack were to die she would search the crowd of mourners for a man she could live with. She would not return from the funeral alone.

Grief and memory, yes, she had said to herself, but what about three o'clock in the morning?

By June nearly everyone Netta knew had vanished, or, like the Blackleys, had started to pack. Netta had new tablecloths made, and ordered new white awnings, and two dozen rosebushes from the nursery at Cap Ferrat. The American came over every day and followed her from room to room, talking. He had nothing better to do. The Swiss twins were in

England. His father, who had been backing his writing career until now, had suddenly changed his mind about it—now, when he needed money to get out of Europe. He had projects for living on his own, but they required a dose of funds. He wanted to open a restaurant on the Riviera where nothing but chicken pie would be served. Or else a vast and expensive café where people would pay to make their own sandwiches. He said that he was seeing the food of the future, but all that Netta could see was customers asking for their money back. He trapped her behind the bar and said he loved her; Netta made other women look like stuffed dolls. He could still remember the shock of meeting her, the attraction, the brilliant answer she had made to Iris about attachments to the past.

Netta let him rave until he asked for a loan. She laughed and wondered if it was for the chicken-pie restaurant. No—he wanted to get on a boat sailing from Cannes. She said, quite cheerfully, "I can't be Venus and Barclays Bank. You have to choose."

He said, "Can't Venus ever turn up with a letter of credit?"

She shook her head. "Not a hope."

But when it was July and Jack hadn't come back, he cornered her again. Money wasn't in it now: his father had not only relented but had virtually ordered him home. He was about twenty-two, she guessed. He could still plead successfully for parental help and for indulgence from women. She said, no more than affectionately, "I'm going to show you a very pretty room."

A few days later Dr. Blackley came alone to say goodbye.

"Are you really staying?" he asked.

"I am responsible for the last eighty-one years of this lease," said Netta. "I'm going to be thirty. It's a long tenure. Besides, I've got Jack's mother and she won't leave. Jack has a chance now to visit America. It doesn't sound sensible to me, but she writes encouraging him. She imagines him suddenly very rich and sending for her. I've discovered the limit of what you can feel about people. I've discovered something else," she said abruptly. "It is that sex and love have nothing in common. Only a coincidence, sometimes. You think the coincidence will go on and so you get married. I suppose that is what men are born knowing and women learn by accident."

"I'm su-horry."

"For God's sake, don't be. It's a relief."

She had no feeling of guilt, only of amazement. Jack, as a memory, was in a restricted area—the tennis courts, the cardroom, the bar. She saw him at bridge with Mrs. Blackley and pouring drinks for temporary friends. He crossed the lounge jauntily with a cluster of little dark-haired girls wearing blue. In the mirrored bedroom there was only Netta. Her dreams were cleansed of him. The looking glasses still held their blue-and-silver-water shadows, but they lost the habit of giving back the moods and gestures of a Moslem wife.

━✠━

About five years after this, Netta wrote to Jack. The war had caught him in America, during the voyage his mother had so wanted him to have. His limp had kept him out of the Army. As his mother (now dead) might have put it, all that reading had finally got him some-where: he had spent the last years putting out a two-pager on aspects of European culture—part of a scrupulous effort Britain was making for the West. That was nearly all Netta knew. A Belgian Red Cross official had arrived, apparently in Jack's name, to see if she was still alive. She sat in her father's business room, wearing a coat and a shawl because there was no way of heating any part of the hotel now, and she tried to get on with the letter she had been writing in her head, on and off, for many years.

"In June, 1940, we were evacuated," she started, for the tenth or eleventh time. "I was back by October. Italians had taken over the hotel. They used the mirror behind the bar for target practice. Oddly enough it was not smashed. It is covered with spiderwebs, and the bul-let hole is the spider. I had great trouble over Aunt Vera, who disap-peared and was found finally in one of the attic rooms.

"The Italians made a pet of her. Took her picture. She enjoyed that. Everyone who became thin had a desire to be photographed, as if knowing they would use this intimidating evidence against those loved ones who had missed being starved. Guilt for life. After an initial period of hardship, during which she often had her picture taken at her request, the Italians brought food and looked after her, more than any-one. She was their mama. We were annexed territory and in time we had the same food as the Italians. The thin pictures of your mother are here on my desk.

"She buried her British passport and would never say where. Per-haps under the Judas tree with Mr. Cordier's cat, Polly. She remained just as mad and just as spoiled, and that became dangerous when life stopped being ordinary. She complained about me to the Italians. At that time a complaint was a matter of prison and of death if it was made to the wrong person. Luckily for me, there was also the right person to take the message.

"A couple of years after that, the Germans and certain French took over and the Italians were shut up in another hotel without food or water, and some people risked their well-being to take water to them (for not everyone preferred the new situation, you can believe me). When she was dying I asked her if she had a message for one Italian officer who had made such a pet of her and she said, 'No, why?' She died without a word for anybody. She was buried as 'Rossini,' because the Italians had changed people's names. She had said she was French, a Frenchwoman named Ross, and so some peculiar civil status was created for us—the two Mrs. Rossinis.

"The records were topsy-turvy; it would have meant going to the Germans and explaining my dead aunt was British, and of course I thought I would not. The death certificate and permission to bury are for a Vera Rossini. I have them here on my desk for you with her pictures.

"You are probably wondering where I have found all this writing paper. The Germans left it behind. When we were being shelled I took what few books were left in the reading room down to what used to be the wine cellar and read by candlelight. You are probably wondering where the candles came from. A long story. I even have paint for the radiators, large buckets that have never been opened.

"I live in one room, my mother's old sitting room. The business room can be used but the files are gone. When the Italians were here your mother was their mother, but I was not their Moslem wife, although I still had respect for men. One yelled 'Luce, luce,' because your mother was showing a light. She said, 'Bugger you, you little toad.' He said, 'Granny, I said "luce," not "Duce."'

"Not long ago we crept out of our shelled homes, looking like cave dwellers. When you see the hotel again, it will be functioning. I shall have painted the radiators. Long shoots of bramble come in through the cardroom windows. There are drifts of leaves in the old music room and I saw scorpions and heard their rustling like the rustle of death. Everything that could have been looted has gone. Sheets, bedding, mattresses. The neighbors did quite a lot of that. At the risk of their lives. When the Italians were here we had rice and oil. Your mother, who was crazy, used to put out grains to feed the mice.

"When the Germans came we had to live under Vichy law, which meant each region lived on what it could produce. As ours produces nothing, we got quite thin again. Aunt Vera died plump. Do you know what it means when I say she used to complain about me?

"Send me some books. As long as they are in English. I am quite sick of the three other languages in which I've heard so many threats, such boasting, such a lot of lying.

"For a time I thought people would like to know how the Italians left and the Germans came in. It was like this: They came in with the first car moving slowly, flying the French flag. The highest-ranking French official in the region. Not a German. No, just a chap getting his job back. The Belgian Red Cross people were completely uninterested and warned me that no one would ever want to hear.

"I suppose that you already have the fiction of all this. The fiction must be different, oh very different, from Italians sobbing with homesickness in the night. The Germans were not real, they were especially got up for the events of the time. Sat in the white dining room, eating with whatever plates and spoons were not broken or looted, ate soups that were mostly water, were forbidden to complain. Only in retreat did they develop faces and I noticed then that some were terrified and many were old. A radio broadcast from some untouched area advised the local population not to attack them as they retreated, it would make wild animals of them. But they were attacked by some young boys shooting out of a window and eight hostages were taken, including the son of the man who cut the maharaja's daughters' black hair, and they were shot and left along the wall of a café on the more or less Italian side of the border. And the man who owned the café was killed too, but later, by civilians—he had given names to the Gestapo once, or perhaps it was something else. He got on the wrong side of the right side at the wrong time, and he was thrown down the deep gorge between the two frontiers.

"Up in one of the hill villages Germans stayed till no one was alive. I was at that time in the former wine cellar, reading books by candlelight.

"The Belgian Red Cross team found the skeleton of a German deserter in a cave and took back the helmet and skull to Knokke-le-Zoute as souvenirs.

"My war has ended. Our family held together almost from the Napoleonic adventures. It is shattered now. Sentiment does not keep families whole—only mutual pride and mutual money."

This true story sounded so implausible that she decided never to send it. She wrote a sensible letter asking for sugar and rice and for new books; nothing must be older than 1940.

Jack answered at once: there were no new authors (he had been asking people). Sugar was unobtainable, and there were queues for rice. Shoes had been rationed. There were no women's stockings but lisle, and the famous American legs looked terrible. You could not find butter or meat or tinned pineapple. In restaurants, instead of butter you were given miniature golf balls of cream cheese. He supposed that all this must sound like small beer to Netta.

A notice arrived that a CARE package awaited her at the post office. It meant that Jack had added his name and his money to a mailing list. She refused to sign for it; then she changed her mind and discovered it was not from Jack but from the American she had once taken to such a pretty room. Jack did send rice and sugar and delicious coffee but he forgot about books. His letters followed; sometimes three arrived in a morning. She left them sealed for days. When she sat down to answer, all she could remember were implausible things.

Iris came back. She was the first. She had grown puffy in England— the result of drinking whatever alcohol she could get her hands on and grimly eating her sweets allowance: there would be that much less gin and chocolate for the Germans if ever they landed. She put her now wide bottom on a comfortable armchair—one of the few chairs the first wave of Italians had not burned with cigarettes or idly hacked at with daggers—and said Jack had been living with a woman in America and to spare the gossip had let her be known as his wife. Another Mrs. Ross? When Netta discovered it was dimpled Chippendale, she laughed aloud.

"I've seen them," said Iris. "I mean I saw them together. King Charles and a spaniel. Jack wiped his feet on her."

Netta's feelings were of lightness, relief. She would not have to tell Jack about the partisans hanging by the neck in the arches of the Place Masséna at Nice. When Iris had finished talking, Netta said, "What about his music?"

"I don't know."

"How can you not know something so important."

"Jack had a good chance at things, but he made a mess of everything," said Iris. "My father is still living. Life really is too incredible for some of us."

A dark girl of about twenty turned up soon after. Her costume, a gray dress buttoned to the neck, gave her the appearance of being in uniform. She unzipped a military-looking bag and cried, in an unplaceable accent, "Hallo, hallo, Mrs. Ross? A few small gifts for you," and unpacked a bottle of Haig, four tins of corned beef, a jar of honey, and six pairs of American nylon stockings, which Netta had never seen before, and were as good to have under a mattress as gold. Netta looked up at the tall girl.

"Remember? I was the middle sister. With," she said gravely, "the typical middle-sister problems." She scarcely recalled Jack, her beloved. The memory of Netta had grown up with her. "I remember you laughing," she said, without loving that memory. She was a severe, tragic girl. "You were the first adult I ever heard laughing. At night in bed I could hear it from your balcony. You sat smoking with, I suppose, your handsome husband. I used to laugh just to hear you."

She had married an Iranian journalist. He had discovered that political prisoners in the United States were working under lamentable conditions in tin mines. President Truman had sent them there. People from all over the world planned to unite to get them out. The girl said she had been to Germany and to Austria, she had visited camps, they were all alike, and that was already the past, and the future was the prisoners in the tin mines.

Netta said, "In what part of the country are these mines?"

The middle sister looked at her sadly and said, "Is there more than one part?"

For the first time in years, Netta could see Jack clearly. They were silently sharing a joke; he had caught it too. She and the girl lunched in a corner of the battered dining room. The tables were scarred with initials. There were no tablecloths. One of the great-uncle's paintings still hung on a wall. It showed the Quai Laurenti, a country road alongside the sea. Netta, who had no use for the past, was discovering a past she could regret. Out of a dark, gentle silence—silence imposed by the impossibility of telling anything real—she counted the cracks in the walls. When silence failed she heard power saws ripping into olive trees and a lemon grove. With a sense of deliverance she understood that soon there would be nothing left to spoil. Her great-uncle's picture, which ought to have changed out of sympathetic magic, remained faithful. She regretted everything now, even the three anxious little girls in blue linen. Every calamitous season between then and now seemed to descend directly from Georgina Blackley's having said "white" just to keep three children in their place. Clad in buttoned-up gray, the middle sister now picked at corned beef and said she had hated her father, her mother, her sisters, and most of all the Dutch governess.

"Where is she now?" said Netta.

"Dead, I hope." This was from someone who had visited camps. Netta sat listening, her cheek on her hand. Death made death casual: she had always known. Neither the vanquished in their flight nor the victors returning to pick over rubble seemed half so vindictive as a tragic girl who had disliked her governess.

Dr. Blackley came back looking positively cheerful. In those days men still liked soldiering. It made them feel young, if they needed to feel it, and it got them away from home. War made the break few men could make on their own. The doctor looked years younger, too, and very fit. His wife was not with him. She had survived everything, and the hardships she had undergone had completely restored her to health—which had made it easy for her husband to leave her. Actually, he had never gone back, except to wind up the matter.

"There are things about Georgina I respect and admire," he said, as husbands will say from a distance. His war had been in Malta. He had come here, as soon as he could, to the shelled, gnawed, tarnished coast (as if he had not seen enough at Malta) to ask Netta to divorce Jack and to marry him, or live with him—anything she wanted, on any terms.

But she wanted nothing—at least, not from him.

"Well, one can't defeat a memory," he said. "I always thought it was mostly su-hex between the two of you."

"So it was," said Netta. "So far as I remember."

"Everyone noticed. You would vanish at odd hours. Dis-huppear."

"Yes, we did."

"You can't live on memories," he objected. "Though I respect you for being faithful, of course."

"What you are talking about is something of which one has no specific memory," said Netta. "Only of reasons. Places. Rooms. It is as abstract to remember as to read about. That is why it is boring in talk except as a joke, and boring in books except for poetry."

"You never read poetry."

"I do now."

"I guessed that," he said.

"That lack of memory is why people are unfaithful, as it is so curiously called. When I see closed shutters I know there are lovers behind them. That is how the memory works. The rest is just convention and small talk."

"Why lovers? Why not someone sleeping off the wine he had for lunch?"

"No. Lovers."

"A middle-aged man cutting his toenails in the bathtub," he said with unexpected feeling. "Wearing bifocal lenses so that he can see his own feet."

"No, lovers. Always."

He said, "Have you missed him?"

"Missed who?"

"Who the bloody hell are we talking about?"

"The Italian commander billeted here. He was not a guest. He was here by force. I was not breaking a rule. Without him I'd have perished in every way. He may be home with his wife now. Or in that fortress near Turin where he sent other men. Or dead." She looked at the doctor and said, "Well, what would you like me to do? Sit here and cry?"

"I can't imagine you with a brute."

"I never said that."

"Do you miss him still?"

"The absence of Jack was like a cancer which I am sure has taken root, and of which I am bound to die," said Netta.

"You'll bu-hury us all," he said, as doctors tell the condemned.

"I haven't said I won't." She rose suddenly and straightened her skirt, as she used to do when hotel guests became pally. "Conversation over," it meant.

"Don't be too hard on Jack," he said.

"I am hard on myself," she replied.

After he had gone he sent her a parcel of books, printed on grayish paper, in warped wartime covers. All of the titles were, to Netta, unknown. There was *Fireman Flower* and *The Horse's Mouth* and *Four Quartets* and *The Stuff to Give the Troops* and *Better Than a Kick in the Pants* and *Put Out More Flags*. A note added that the next package would contain Henry Green and Dylan Thomas. She guessed he would not want to be thanked, but she did so anyway. At the end of her letter was "Please remember, if you mind to much, that I said no to you once before." Leaning on the bar, exactly as Jack used to, with a glass of the middle sister's drink at hand, she opened *Better Than a Kick in the Pants* and read, "...two Fascists came in, one of them tall and thin and tough looking, the other smaller, with only one arm and an empty sleeve pinned up to his shoulder. Both of them were quite young and wore black shirts."

Oh, thought Netta, I am the only one who knows all this. No one will ever realize how much I know of the truth, the truth, the truth, and she put her head on her hands, her elbows on the scarred bar, and let the first tears of her after-war run down her wrists.

⌦⫘⌫

The last to return was the one who should have been first. Jack wrote that he was coming down from the north as far as Nice by bus. It was a common way of travelling and much cheaper than by train. Netta guessed that he was mildly hard up and that he had saved nothing from his war job. The bus came in at six, at the foot of the Place Masséna. There was a deep-blue late-afternoon sky and pale sunlight. She could hear birds from the public gardens nearby. The Place was as she had always seen it, like an elegant drawing room with a blue ceiling. It was nearly empty. Jack looked out on this sunlighted, handsome space and said, "Well, I'll just leave my stuff at the bus office, for the moment"— perhaps noticing that Netta had not invited him anywhere. He placed his ticket on the counter, and she saw that he had not come from far away: he must have been moving south by stages. He carried an aura of London pub life; he had been in London for weeks.

A frowning man hurrying to wind things up so he could have his first drink of the evening said, "The office is closing and we don't keep baggage here."

"People used to be nice," Jack said.

"Bus people?"

"Just people."

She was hit by the sharp change in his accent. As for the way of speaking, which is something else again, he was like the heir to great estates back home after a Grand Tour. Perhaps the estates had run down in his absence. She slipped the frowning man a thousand francs, a new pastel-tinted bill, on which the face of a calm girl glowed like an opal. She said, "We shan't be long."

She set off over the Place, walking diagonally—Jack beside her, of course. He did not ask where they were headed, though he did make her smile by saying, "Did you bring a car?," expecting one of the hotel cars to be parked nearby, perhaps with a driver to open the door; perhaps with cold chicken and wine in a hamper, too. He said, "I'd forgotten about having to tip for every little thing." He did not question his destination, which was no farther than a café at the far end of the square. What she felt at that instant was intense revulsion. She thought, I don't want him, and pushed away some invisible flying thing—a bat or a blown paper. He looked at her with surprise. He must have been wondering if hardship had taught Netta to talk in her mind.

This is it, the freedom he was always offering me, she said to herself, smiling up at the beautiful sky.

They moved slowly along the nearly empty square, pausing only when some worn-out Peugeot or an old bicycle, finding no other target, made a swing in their direction. Safely on the pavement, they walked under the arches where partisans had been hanged. It seemed to Netta the bodies had been taken down only a day or so before. Jack, who knew about this way of dying from hearsay, chose a café table nearly under a poor lad's bound, dangling feet.

"I had a woman next to me on the bus who kept a hedgehog all winter in a basketful of shavings," he said. "He can drink milk out of a wineglass." He hesitated. "I'm sorry about the books you asked for. I was sick of books by then. I was sick of rhetoric and culture and patriotic crap."

"I suppose it is all very different over there," said Netta.

"God, yes."

He seemed to expect her to ask questions, so she said, "What kind of clothes do they wear?"

"They wear quite a lot of plaids and tartans. They eat at peculiar hours. You'll see them eating strawberries and cream just when you're thinking of having a drink."

She said, "Did you visit the tin mines, where Truman sends his political prisoners?"

"*Tin* mines?" said Jack. "No."

"Remember the three little girls from the maharaja trade?"

Neither could quite hear what the other had to say. They were partially deaf to each other.

Netta continued softly, "Now, as I understand it, she first brought an American to London, and then she took an Englishman to America."

He had too much the habit of women, he was playing too close a game, to waste points saying, "Who? What?"

"It was over as fast as it started," he said. "But then the war came and we were stuck. She became a friend," he said. "I'm quite fond of her"—which Netta translated as, "It is a subterranean river that may yet come to light." "You wouldn't know her," he said. "She's very different now. I talked so much about the south, down here, she finally found some land going dirt cheap at Bandol. The major arranged for her to have an orchard next to her property, so she won't have neighbors. It hardly cost her anything. He said to her, 'You're very pretty.'"

"No one ever had a bargain in property because of a pretty face," said Netta.

"Wasn't it lucky," said Jack. He could no longer hear himself, let alone Netta. "The war was unsettling, being in America. She minded not being active. Actually she was using the Swiss passport, which made it worse. Her brother was killed over Bremen. She needs security now. In a way it was sorcerer and apprentice between us, and she suddenly grew up. She'll be better off with a roof over her head. She writes a little now. Her poetry isn't bad," he said, as if Netta had challenged its quality.

"Is she at Bandol now, writing poetry?"

"Well, no." He laughed suddenly. "There isn't a roof yet. And, you know, people don't sit writing that way. They just think they're going to."

"Who has replaced you?" said Netta. "Another sorcerer?"

"Oh, he...he looks like George II in a strong light. Or like Queen Anne. Queen Anne and Lady Mary, somebody called them." Iris, that must have been. Queen Anne and Lady Mary wasn't bad—better than King Charles and his spaniel. She was beginning to enjoy his story. He saw it, and said lightly, "I was too preoccupied with you to manage another life. I couldn't see myself going on and on away from you. I didn't want to grow middle-aged at odds with myself."

But he had lost her; she was enjoying a reverie about Jack now, wearing one of those purple sunburns people acquire at golf. She saw him driving an open car, with large soft freckles on his purple skull. She saw his mistress's dog on the front seat and the dog's ears flying like pennants. The revulsion she felt did not lend distance but brought a dreamy reality closer still. He must be thirty-four now, she said to herself. A terrible age for a man who has never imagined thirty-four.

"Well, perhaps you have made a mess of it," she said, quoting Iris.

"What mess? I'm here. *He*—"

"Queen Anne?"

"Yes, well, actually Gerald is his name; he wears nothing but brown. Brown suit, brown tie, brown shoes. I said, '*He* can't go to Mitten Todd. He won't match.'"

"Harmonize," she said.

"That's it. Harmonize with the—"

"What about Gerald's wife? I'm sure he has one."

"Lucretia."

"No, really?"

"On my honor. When I last saw them they were all together, talking."

Netta was remembering what the middle sister had said about laughter on the balcony. She couldn't look at him. The merest crossing of glances made her start laughing rather wildly into her hands. The hysterical quality of her own laughter caught her in midair. What were they talking about? He hitched his chair nearer and dared to take her wrist.

"Tell me, now," he said as if they were to be two old confidence men getting their stories straight. "What about you? Was there ever..." The glaze of laughter had not left his face and voice. She saw that he would make her his business, if she let him. Pulling back, she felt another clasp, through a wall of fog. She groped for this other, invisible hand, but it dissolved. It was a lost, indifferent hand; it no longer recognized her warmth. She understood: He is dead...Jack, closed to ghosts, deaf to their voices, was spared this. He would be spared everything, she saw. She envied him his imperviousness, his true unhysterical laughter.

Perhaps that's why I kicked him, she said. I was always jealous. Not of women. Of his short memory, his comfortable imagination. And I am going to be thirty-seven and I have a dark, an accurate, a deadly memory.

He still held her wrist and turned it another way, saying, "Look, there's paint on it."

"Oh, God, where is the waiter?" she cried, as if that were the one important thing. Jack looked his age, exactly. She looked like a burned-out child who had been told a ghost story. Desperately seeking the waiter, she turned to the café behind them and saw the last light of the long afternoon strike the mirror above the bar—a flash in a tunnel; hands juggling with fire. That unexpected play, at a remove, borne indoors, displayed to anyone who could stare without blinking, was a complete story. It was the brightness on the looking glass, the only part of a life, or a love, or a promise, that could never be concealed, changed, or corrupted.

Not a hope, she was trying to tell him. He could read her face now. She reminded herself, If I say it, I am free. I can finish painting the radiators in peace. I can read every book in the world. If I had relied on my memory for guidance, I would never have crept out of the wine cellar. Memory is what ought to prevent you from buying a dog after the first dog dies, but it never does. It should at least keep you from saying yes twice to the same person.

"I've always loved you," he chose to announce—it really was an announcement, in a new voice that stated nothing except facts.

The dark, the ghosts, the candlelight, her tears on the scarred bar—*they* were real. And still, whether she wanted to see it or not, the light of imagination danced all over the square. She did not dare to turn again to the mirror, lest she confuse the two and forget which light was real. A pure white awning on a cross street seemed to her to be of indestructible beauty. The window it sheltered was hollowed with sadness and shadow. She said with the same deep sadness, "I believe you." The wave of revulsion receded, sucked back under another wave—a powerful adolescent craving for something simple, such as true love.

Her face did not show this. It was set in adolescent stubbornness, and this was one of their old, secret meetings when, sullen and hurt, she had to be coaxed into life as Jack wanted it lived. It was the same voyage, at the same rate of speed. The Place seemed to her to be full of invisible traffic—first a whisper of tires, then a faint, high screeching, then a steady roar. If Jack heard anything, it could be only the blood in the veins and his loud, happy thought. To a practical romantic like Jack, dying to get Netta to bed right away, what she was hearing was only the uh-hebb and flo-ho of hormones, as Dr. Blackley said. She caught a look of amazement on his face: *Now* he knew what he had been deprived of. *Now* he remembered. It had been Netta, all along.

Their evening shadows accompanied them over the long square. "I still have a car," she remarked. "But no petrol. There's a train." She did keep on hearing a noise, as of heavy traffic rushing near and tearing away. Her own quiet voice carried across it, saying, "Not a hope." He must have heard that. Why, it was as loud as a shout. He held her arm lightly. He was as buoyant as morning. This *was* his morning—the first light on the mirror, the first cigarette. He pulled her into an archway where no one could see. What could I do, she asked her ghosts, but let my arm be held, my steps be guided?

Later, Jack said that the walk with Netta back across the Place Masséna was the happiest event of his life. Having no reliable counter-event to put in its place, she let the memory stand.

Topics for Discussion

1. How does Gallant sustain the narrative for such an extended period in the novella? How does this story relate to the definition of a novella?

2. What is the role of the hotel in the story? How does Gallant define a hotel?

3. What are the differences between the pre-war world and the post-war world as defined in the story?

4. How does Gallant convey the concept of lushness that is associated with the hotel, and what impact does the demise of the hotel have, not only on Netta but on the world of the resort area?

5. In what ways does Gallant define tradition, and what role do these concepts of tradition play in the story?

6. What contrasts does Gallant establish by conveying the differences between the characters Jack and Netta?

7. What is the impact of Gallant's style, her sentence structure (syntax), and her use of descriptive and often elaborate vocabulary (diction)?

8. How does Gallant convey the passage of time? What is the impact of history and how is Gallant defining the nature of the twentieth century through the narrative of the story?

Nadine Gordimer

About the Author

Nadine Gordimer was born in Springs, Transvaal, South Africa, in 1923 and was educated at the University of Witwatersrand in Johannesburg. She has taught at Harvard, Princeton, Northwestern and the University of Michigan. For years she lived under constant threat of death from those who felt that her writing was inimical to the apartheid government. As a chronicler of her times in South Africa, a period during which apartheid was eventually overthrown, Gordimer was an influential voice for morality. In her essay "A Writer's Freedom" (from *The Essential Gesture*), she stressed that the role of the writer is to observe without becoming politically entangled, and to express what he or she sees and feels from the standpoint of the moral observer and educated artist. She won the 1993 Nobel Prize for Literature.

Gordimer's work is located in the idiom and environment of her native South Africa. Writing from a white perspective, her stories often speak with deep sympathy of the difficulties facing the black majority in South Africa, and focus on the human issues during that period of struggle. As a writer of fiction she had the privilege of being able to say things that others could not about the oppressive regime—which supports the paradox that fiction (essentially that which is "concocted" or "made up") is a powerful vehicle for truth. As Gordimer noted in the introductory essay to her *Selected Stories* (1983), from which "Six Feet of the Country" is taken, a writer's task is a difficult one, especially in the context of a politicized environment: "The tension between standing apart and being fully involved: that is what makes a writer... Fiction is a way of exploring possibilities present but undreamt of in the living of a single life."

Selected Works

The Lying Days (novel, 1953)
A World of Strangers (novel, 1958)
Occasion for Loving (novel, 1963)
The Late Bourgeois World (novel, 1966)
A Guest of Honour (novel, 1970)
The Conservationist (novel, 1974)
Burger's Daughter (novel, 1979)
July's People (novel, 1981)
Selected Stories (short stories, 1983)
A Sport of Nature (novel, 1987)
The Essential Gesture: Writing, Politics and Places (essays, 1988)
My Son's Story (novel, 1990)

About the Story

The story deals with the problems facing a white farm owner and a black family when a farmhand dies and the family requests the return of his body from the health authorities for burial. In this narrative, Gordimer has established a metaphor for the situation of the oppressed black majority in South Africa during the years of apartheid. The apartheid policy of racial separation was instituted through a series of laws that cemented white supremacy in South Africa at the cost of black freedoms. The Pass Laws and other legislation forbade free movement of blacks throughout the country, established "homelands" or restricted areas where blacks were forced to live (usually in wretched conditions), denied to blacks the opportunity of social and economic advancement, and prohibited interracial relationships and marriages. Apartheid was abolished in 1993 under the leadership of Nelson Mandela.

"Piccanins" is a derogatory term for small black children.

Six Feet of the Country

My wife and I are not real farmers—not even Lerice, really. We bought our place, ten miles out of Johannesburg on one of the main roads, to change something in ourselves, I suppose; you seem to rattle about so much within a marriage like ours. You long to hear nothing but a deep satisfying silence when you sound a marriage. The farm hasn't managed that for us, of course, but it has done other things, unexpected, illogical. Lerice, who I thought would retire there in Chekhovian sadness for a month or two, and then leave the place to the servants while she tried yet again to get a part she wanted and become the actress she would like to be, has sunk into the business of running the farm with all the serious intensity with which she once imbued the shadows in a playwright's mind. I should have given it up long ago if it had not been for her. Her hands, once small and plain and well-kept—she was not the sort of actress who wears red paint and diamond rings—are hard as a dog's pads.

I, of course, am there only in the evenings and at weekends. I am a partner in a travel agency which is flourishing—needs to be, as I tell Lerice, in order to carry the farm. Still, though I know we can't afford it, and though the sweetish smell of the fowls Lerice breeds sickens me, so that I avoid going past their runs, the farm is beautiful in a way I had almost forgotten—especially on a Sunday morning when I get up and go out into the paddock and see not the palm trees and fishpond and imitation-stone bird bath of the suburbs but white ducks on the dam, the lucerne field brilliant as window-dresser's grass, and the little, stocky, mean-eyed bull, lustful but bored, having his face tenderly licked by one of his ladies. Lerice comes out with her hair uncombed, in her hand a stick dripping with cattle dip. She will stand and look dreamily for a moment, the way she would pretend to look sometimes in those plays. "They'll mate tomorrow," she will say. "This is their second day. Look how she loves him, my little Napoleon." So that when people come to see us on Sunday afternoon, I am likely to hear myself saying as I pour out the drinks, "When I drive back home from the city every day past those rows of suburban houses, I wonder how the devil we ever did stand it ... Would you care to look around?" And there I am, taking some pretty girl and her young husband stumbling down to our riverbank, the girl catching her stockings on the mealie-stooks and stepping over cow turds humming with jewel-green flies while she says, ... the *tensions* of the damned city. And you're near enough to get into town to a show, too! I think it's wonderful. Why, you've got it both ways!"

And for a moment I accept the triumph as if I *had* managed it—the impossibility that I've been trying for all my life: just as if the truth was that you could get it "both ways," instead of finding yourself with not even one way or the other but a third, one you had not provided for at all.

But even in our saner moments, when I find Lerice's earthy enthusiasms just as irritating as I once found her histrionical ones, and she finds what she calls my "jealousy" of her capacity for enthusiasm as big a proof of my inadequacy for her as a mate as ever it was, we do believe that we have at least honestly escaped those tensions peculiar to the city about which our visitors speak. When Johannesburg people speak of "tension," they don't mean hurrying people in crowded streets, the struggle for money, or the general competitive character of city life. They mean the guns under the white men's pillows and the burglar bars on the white men's windows. They mean those strange moments on city pavements when a black man won't stand aside for a white man.

Out in the country, even ten miles out, life is better than that. In the country, there is a lingering remnant of the pretransitional stage; our relationship with the blacks is almost feudal. Wrong, I suppose, obsolete, but more comfortable all around. We have no burglar bars, no gun. Lerice's farm boys have their wives and their piccanins living with them on the land. They brew their sour beer without the fear of police raids. In fact, we've always rather prided ourselves that the poor devils have nothing much to fear, being with us; Lerice even keeps an eye on their children, with all the competence of a woman who has never had a child of her own, and she certainly doctors them all—children and adults—like babies whenever they happen to be sick.

It was because of this that we were not particularly startled one night last winter when the boy Albert came knocking at our window long after we had gone to bed. I wasn't in our bed but sleeping in the little dressing-room-cum-linen-room next door, because Lerice had annoyed me and I didn't want to find myself softening towards her simply because of the sweet smell of the talcum powder on her flesh after her bath. She came and woke me up. "Albert says one of the boys is very sick," she said. "I think you'd better go down and see. He wouldn't get us up at this hour for nothing."

"What time is it?"

"What does it matter?" Lerice is maddeningly logical.

I got up awkwardly as she watched me—how is it I always feel a fool when I have deserted her bed? After all, I know from the way she never looks at me when she talks to me at breakfast next day that she is hurt and humiliated at my not wanting her—and I went out, clumsy with sleep.

"Which of the boys is it?" I asked Albert as we followed the dance of my torch.

"He's too sick. Very sick," he said.

"But who? Franz?" I remembered Franz had had a bad cough for the past week.

Albert did not answer; he had given me the path, and was walking along beside me in the tall dead grass. When the light of the torch caught his face, I saw that he looked acutely embarrassed. "What's this all about?" I said.

He lowered his head under the glance of the light. "It's not me, baas. I don't know. Petrus he send me."

Irritated, I hurried him along to the huts. And there, on Petrus's iron bedstead, with its brick stilts, was a young man, dead. On his forehead there was still a light, cold sweat; his body was warm. The boys stood around as they do in the kitchen when it is discovered that someone has broken a dish—uncooperative, silent. Somebody's wife hung about in the shadows, her hands wrung together under her apron.

I had not seen a dead man since the war. This was very different. I felt like the others—extraneous, useless. "What was the matter?" I asked.

The woman patted at her chest and shook her head to indicate the painful impossibility of breathing.

He must have died of pneumonia.

I turned to Petrus. "Who was this boy? What was he doing here?" The light of a candle on the floor showed that Petrus was weeping. He followed me out the door.

When we were outside, in the dark, I waited for him to speak. But he didn't. "Now, come on, Petrus, you must tell me who this boy was. Was he a friend of yours?"

"He's my brother, baas. He came from Rhodesia to look for work."

※

The story startled Lerice and me a little. The young boy had walked down from Rhodesia to look for work in Johannesburg, had caught a chill from sleeping out along the way and had lain ill in his brother Petrus's hut since his arrival three days before. Our boys had been frightened to ask us for help for him because we had never been intended ever to know of his presence. Rhodesian natives are barred from entering the Union unless they have a permit; the young man was an illegal immigrant. No doubt our boys had managed the whole thing successfully several times before; a number of relatives must have walked the seven or eight hundred miles from poverty to the paradise of zoot suits, police raids and black slum townships that is their *Egoli*,

City of Gold—the African name for Johannesburg. It was merely a matter of getting such a man to lie low on our farm until a job could be found with someone who would be glad to take the risk of prosecution for employing an illegal immigrant in exchange for the services of someone as yet untainted by the city.

Well, this was one who would never get up again.

"You would think they would have felt they could tell *us*," said Lerice next morning. "Once the man was ill. You would have thought at least—" When she is getting intense over something, she has a way of standing in the middle of a room as people do when they are shortly to leave on a journey, looking searchingly about her at the most familiar objects as if she had never seen them before. I had noticed that in Petrus's presence in the kitchen, earlier, she had had the air of being almost offended with him, almost hurt.

In any case, I really haven't the time or inclination any more to go into everything in our life that I know Lerice, from those alarmed and pressing eyes of hers, would like us to go into. She is the kind of woman who doesn't mind if she looks plain, or odd; I don't suppose she would even care if she knew how strange she looks when her whole face is out of proportion with urgent uncertainty. I said, "Now I'm the one who'll have to do all the dirty work, I suppose."

She was still staring at me, trying me out with those eyes—wasting her time, if she only knew.

"I'll have to notify the health authorities," I said calmly. "They can't just cart him off and bury him. After all, we don't really know what he died of."

She simply stood there, as if she had given up—simply ceased to see me at all.

I don't know when I've been so irritated. "It might have been something contagious," I said. "God knows." There was no answer.

I am not enamoured of holding conversations with myself. I went out to shout to one of the boys to open the garage and get the car ready for my morning drive to town.

As I had expected, it turned out to be quite a business. I had to notify the police as well as the health authorities, and answer a lot of tedious questions: How was it I was ignorant of the boy's presence? If I did not supervise my native quarters, how did I know that that sort of thing didn't go on all the time? And when I flared up and told them that so long as my natives did their work, I didn't think it my right or concern to poke my nose into their private lives, I got from the coarse, dull-witted police sergeant one of those looks that come not from any thinking process going on in the brain but from that faculty common to all who are possessed by the master-race theory—a look of insanely inane certainty. He grinned at me with a mixture of scorn and delight at my stupidity.

Then I had to explain to Petrus why the health authorities had to take away the body for a post-mortem—and, in fact, what a post-mortem was. When I telephoned the health department some days later to find out the result, I was told that the cause of death was, as we had thought, pneumonia, and that the body had been suitably disposed of. I went out to where Petrus was mixing a mash for the fowls and told him that it was all right, there would be no trouble; his brother had died from that pain in his chest. Petrus put down the paraffin tin and said, "When can we go to fetch him, baas?"

"To fetch him?"

"Will the baas please ask them when we must come?"

I went back inside and called Lerice, all over the house. She came down the stairs from the spare bedrooms, and I said, "Now what am I going to do? When I told Petrus, he just asked calmly when they could go and fetch the body. They think they're going to bury him themselves."

"Well, go back and tell him," said Lerice. "You must tell him. Why didn't you tell him then?"

When I found Petrus again, he looked up politely. "Look, Petrus," I said. "You can't go to fetch your brother. They've done it already—they've *buried* him, you understand?"

"Where?" he said slowly, dully, as if he thought that perhaps he was getting this wrong.

"You see, he was a stranger. They knew he wasn't from here, and they didn't know he had some of his people here so they thought they must bury him." It was difficult to make a pauper's grave sound like a privilege.

"Please, baas, the baas must ask them." But he did not mean that he wanted to know the burial place. He simply ignored the incomprehensible machinery I told him had set to work on his dead brother; he wanted the brother back.

"But, Petrus," I said, "how can I? Your brother is buried already. I can't ask them now."

"Oh, baas!" he said. He stood with his bran-smeared hands uncurled at his sides, one corner of his mouth twitching.

"Good God, Petrus, they won't listen to me! They can't, anyway. I'm sorry, but I can't do it. You understand?"

He just kept on looking at me, out of his knowledge that white men have everything, can do anything; if they don't, it is because they won't.

And then, at dinner, Lerice started. "You could at least phone," she said.

"Christ, what d'you think I am? Am I supposed to bring the dead back to life?"

But I could not exaggerate my way out of this ridiculous responsibility that had been thrust on me. "Phone them up," she went on. "And at least you'll be able to tell him you've done it and they've explained that it's impossible."

She disappeared somewhere into the kitchen quarters after coffee. A little later she came back to tell me, "The old father's coming down from Rhodesia to be at the funeral. He's got a permit and he's already on his way."

Unfortunately, it was not impossible to get the body back. The authorities said that it was somewhat irregular, but that since the hygiene conditions had been fulfilled, they could not refuse permission for exhumation. I found out that, with the undertaker's charges, it would cost twenty pounds. Ah, I thought, that settles it. On five pounds a month, Petrus won't have twenty pounds—and just as well, since it couldn't do the dead any good. Certainly I should not offer it to him myself. Twenty pounds—or anything else within reason, for that matter—I would have spent without grudging it on doctors or medicines that might have helped the boy when he was alive. Once he was dead, I had no intention of encouraging Petrus to throw away, on a gesture, more than he spent to clothe his whole family in a year.

When I told him, in the kitchen that night, he said, "Twenty pounds?"

I said, "Yes, that's right, twenty pounds."

For a moment, I had the feeling, from the look on his face, that he was calculating. But when he spoke again I thought I must have imagined it. "We must pay twenty pounds!" he said in the faraway voice in which a person speaks of something so unattainable it does not bear thinking about.

"All right, Petrus," I said, and went back to the living room.

The next morning before I went to town, Petrus asked to see me. "Please, baas," he said, awkwardly, handing me a bundle of notes. They're so seldom on the giving rather than the receiving side, poor devils, they don't really know how to hand money to a white man. There it was, the twenty pounds, in ones and halves, some creased and folded until they were soft as dirty rags, others smooth and fairly new— Franz's money, I suppose, and Albert's, and Dora the cook's, and Jacob the gardener's, and God knows who else's besides, from all the farms and small holdings round about. I took it in irritation more than in astonishment, really—irritation at the waste, the uselessness of this sacrifice by people so poor. Just like the poor everywhere, I thought, who stint themselves the decencies of life in order to ensure themselves the decencies of death. So incomprehensible to people like Lerice and me, who regard life as something to be spent extravagantly and, if we think about death at all, regard it as the final bankruptcy.

The farm hands don't work on Saturday afternoon anyway, so it was a good day for the funeral. Petrus and his father had borrowed our donkey-cart to fetch the coffin from the city, where, Petrus told Lerice on their return, everything was "nice"—the coffin waiting for them, already sealed up to save them from what must have been a rather unpleasant sight after two weeks' interment. (It had taken all that time for the authorities and the undertaker to make the final arrangements for moving the body.) All morning, the coffin lay in Petrus's hut, awaiting the trip to the little old burial ground, just outside the eastern boundary of our farm, that was a relic of the days when this was a real farming district rather than a fashionable rural estate. It was pure chance that I happened to be down there near the fence when the procession came past; once again Lerice had forgotten her promise to me and had made the house uninhabitable on a Saturday afternoon. I had come home and been infuriated to find her in a pair of filthy old slacks and with her hair uncombed since the night before, having all the varnish scraped from the living-room floor, if you please. So I had taken my No. 8 iron and gone off to practise my approach shots. In my annoyance, I had forgotten about the funeral, and was reminded only when I saw the procession coming up the path along the outside of the fence towards me; from where I was standing, you can see the graves quite clearly, and that day the sun glinted on bits of broken pottery, a lopsided homemade cross, and jam-jars brown with rainwater and dead flowers.

I felt a little awkward, and did not know whether to go on hitting my golf ball or stop at least until the whole gathering was decently past. The donkey-cart creaks and screeches with every revolution of the wheels, and it came along in a slow, halting fashion somehow peculiarly suited to the two donkeys who drew it, their little potbellies rubbed and rough, their heads sunk between the shafts, and their ears flattened back with an air submissive and downcast; peculiarly suited, too, to the group of men and women who came along slowly behind. The patient ass. Watching, I thought, you can see now why the creature became a Biblical symbol. Then the procession drew level with me and stopped, so I had to put down my club. The coffin was taken down off the cart—it was a shiny, yellow-varnished wood, like cheap furniture—and the donkeys twitched their ears against the flies. Petrus, Franz, Albert and the old father from Rhodesia hoisted it on their shoulders and the procession moved on, on foot. It was really a very awkward moment. I stood there rather foolishly at the fence, quite still, and slowly they filed past, not looking up, the four men bent beneath the shiny wooden box, and the straggling troop of mourners. All of them were servants or neighbours' servants whom I knew as casual easygoing gossipers about our lands or kitchen. I heard the old man's breathing.

I had just bent to pick up my club again when there was a sort of jar in the flowing solemnity of their processional mood; I felt it at once, like a wave of heat along the air, or one of those sudden currents of cold catching at your legs in a placid stream. The old man's voice was muttering something; the people had stopped, confused, and they bumped into one another, some pressing to go on, others hissing them to be still. I could see that they were embarrassed, but they could not ignore the voice; it was much the way that the mumblings of a prophet, though not clear at first, arrest the mind. The corner of the coffin the old man carried was sagging at an angle; he seemed to be trying to get out from under the weight of it. Now Petrus expostulated with him.

The little boy who had been left to watch the donkeys dropped the reins and ran to see. I don't know why—unless it was for the same reason people crowd around someone who has fainted in a cinema—but I parted the wires of the fence and went through, after him.

Petrus lifted his eyes to me—to anybody—with distress and horror. The old man from Rhodesia had let go of the coffin entirely, and the three others, unable to support it on their own, had laid it on the ground, in the pathway. Already there was a film of dust lightly wavering up its shiny sides. I did not understand what the old man was saying; I hesitated to interfere. But now the whole seething group turned on my silence. The old man himself came over to me, with his hands outspread and shaking, and spoke directly to me, saying something that I could tell from the tone, without understanding the words, was shocking and extraordinary.

"What is it, Petrus? What's wrong?" I appealed.

Petrus threw up his hands, bowed his head in a series of hysterical shakes, then thrust his face up at me suddenly. "He says, 'My son was not so heavy.'"

Silence. I could hear the old man breathing; he kept his mouth a little open, as old people do.

"My son was young and thin," he said at last, in English.

Again silence. Then babble broke out. The old man thundered against everybody; his teeth were yellowed and few, and he had one of those fine, grizzled, sweeping moustaches one doesn't often see nowadays, which must have been grown in emulation of early Empire-builders. It seemed to frame all his utterances with a special validity. He shocked the assembly; they thought he was mad, but they had to listen to him. With his own hands he began to prise the lid off the coffin and three of the men came forward to help him. Then he sat down on the ground; very old, very weak and unable to speak, he merely lifted a trembling hand towards what was there. He abdicated, he handed it over to them; he was no good any more.

They crowded round to look (and so did I), and now they forgot the nature of this surprise and the occasion of grief to which it belonged, and for a few minutes were carried up in the astonishment of the surprise itself. They gasped and flared noisily with excitement. I even noticed the little boy who had held the donkeys jumping up and down, almost weeping with rage because the backs of the grownups crowded him out of his view.

In the coffin was someone no one had seen before: a heavily built, rather light-skinned native with a neatly stitched scar on his forehead—perhaps from a blow in a brawl that had also dealt him some other, slower-working injury that had killed him.

✦

I wrangled with the authorities for a week over that body. I had the feeling that they were shocked, in a laconic fashion, by their own mistake, but that in the confusion of their anonymous dead they were helpless to put it right. They said to me, "We are trying to find out," and "We are still making inquiries." It was as if at any moment they might conduct me into their mortuary and say, "There! Lift up the sheets; look for him—your poultry boy's brother. There are so many black faces—surely one will do?"

And every evening when I got home, Petrus was waiting in the kitchen. "Well, they're trying. They're still looking. The baas is seeing to it for you, Petrus," I would tell him. "God, half the time I should be in the office I'm driving around the back end of the town chasing after this affair," I added aside, to Lerice, one night.

She and Petrus both kept their eyes turned on me as I spoke, and, oddly, for those moments they looked exactly alike, though it sounds impossible: my wife, with her high, white forehead and her attenuated Englishwoman's body, and the poultry boy, with his horny bare feet below khaki trousers tied at the knee with string and the peculiar rankness of his nervous sweat coming from his skin.

"What makes you so indignant, so determined about this now?" said Lerice suddenly.

I stared at her. "It's a matter of principle. Why should they get away with a swindle? It's time these officials had a jolt from someone who'll bother to take the trouble."

She said, "Oh." And as Petrus slowly opened the kitchen door to leave, sensing that the talk had gone beyond him, she turned away, too.

I continued to pass on assurances to Petrus every evening, but although what I said was the same and the voice in which I said it was the same, every evening it sounded weaker. At last, it became clear that we would never get Petrus's brother back, because nobody really knew where he was. Somewhere in a graveyard as uniform as a housing scheme, somewhere under a number that didn't belong to him, or in the medical school, perhaps, laboriously reduced to layers of muscle and strings of nerve? Goodness knows. He had no identity in this world anyway.

It was only then, and in a voice of shame, that Petrus asked me to try and get the money back.

"From the way he asks, you'd think he was robbing his dead brother," I said to Lerice later. But as I've said, Lerice had got so intense about this business that she couldn't even appreciate a little ironic smile.

I tried to get the money; Lerice tried. We both telephoned and wrote and argued, but nothing came of it. It appeared that the main expense had been the undertaker, and after all he had done his job. So the whole thing was a complete waste, even more of a waste for the poor devils than I had thought it would be.

The old man from Rhodesia was about Lerice's father's size, so she gave him one of her father's old suits, and he went back home rather better off, for the winter, than he had come.

Topics for Discussion

1. What does the story say about the position of black Africans during the apartheid regime?

2. Why is the body treated like a disposable object?

3. How does the narrator react to the death of the man?

4. What does the story say about the nature of South African society during this period?

5. Is this a political story? Does Gordimer allow the story to be "political"? How does one define the term "political"?

6. What are the perceived differences between white society and black society in the story?

7. What role does the first person narrative form play in the telling of the story? Is the narrator involved or detached from the situation? If involved, what is the extent of that involvement?

8. What is the relationship between the title and the events of the story?

Katherine Govier

About the Author

Katherine Govier was born in Edmonton, Alberta, in 1948 and received her education at the University of Alberta and York University. She has worked as a journalist in Canada, England and the United States, and has been writer-in-residence at the University of Alberta. Govier is author of four novels and three collections of short stories. She lives in Toronto.

Much of her fiction is concerned with the roles of women in the contemporary world and the ways in which they attempt to accommodate expanding possibilities in their lives. She is also concerned with the contemporary Canadian urban experience, as in her collection of short stories set in Toronto, *Fables of Brunswick Avenue*. In her introduction to a special Canadian issue of the British literary magazine *Aquarius* (1981), Govier stressed that the Canadian experience is, by virtue of demographics, an urban one rather than a wilderness one.

Selected Bibliography

Random Descent (novel, 1979)
Going Through the Motions (novel, 1982)
Fables of Brunswick Avenue (short stories, 1985)
Between Men (novel, 1987)
Before and After (short stories, 1989)
Hearts of Flame (novel, 1991)
The Immaculate Conception Photography Gallery (short stories, 1994)

About the Story

This story, set in the Italian area of Toronto (roughly bordered by St. Clair Avenue and Dufferin, Jane and College streets) known as "Little Italy," addresses the relationship between truth and lies as they are represented and conveyed through photographs. Like a number of other Canadian writers, including Dionne Brand (see her story "Photograph"), Govier is concerned with the nature of reality as it is conveyed by documentary and seemingly factual evidence.

The "Immaculate Conception" refers to the Christian belief in the miraculous conception of Jesus Christ. Christianity holds that Christ was conceived by the Virgin Mary receiving the Word of God whispered in her ear when the Spirit of God took the form of a dove and entered through her window. Because Christ was not conceived carnally (through sexual intercourse), it is held that the conception was pristine, perfect or immaculate.

The Immaculate Conception Photography Gallery

Sandro named the little photography shop on St. Clair Avenue West, between Lord's Shoes and Bargain Jimmies, after the parish church in the village where he was born. He had hankered after wider horizons, the rippled brown prairies, the hard-edged mountains. But when he reached Toronto he met necessity in the form of a wife and babies, and, never having seen a western sunset, he settled down in Little Italy. He photographed the brides in their fat lacquered curls and imported lace, and their quick babies in christening gowns brought over from home. Blown up to near life size on cardboard cutouts, their pictures filled the windows of his little shop.

Sandro had been there ten years already when he first really saw his sign, and the window. He stood still in front of it and looked. A particularly buxom bride with a lace bodice and cap sleeves cut in little scallops shimmered in a haze of concupiscence under the sign reading Immaculate Conception Photography Gallery. Sandro was not like his neighbours any more, he was modern, a Canadian. He no longer went to church. As he stared, one of the street drunks shuffled into place beside him. Sandro knew them all, they came into the shop in winter. (No one ought to have to stay outside in that cold, Sandro believed.) But he especially knew Becker. Becker was a smart man; he used to be a philosopher at a university.

"Immaculate conception," said Sandro to Becker. "What do you think?"

Becker lifted his eyes to the window. He made a squeezing gesture at the breasts. "I never could buy that story," he said.

Sandro laughed, but he didn't change the sign that year or the next and he got to be forty-five and then fifty and it didn't seem worth it. The Immaculate Conception Photography Gallery had a reputation. Business came in from as far away as Rosedale and North Toronto, because Sandro was a magician with a camera. He also had skill with brushes and lights and paint, he reshot his negatives, he lined them with silver, he had tricks even new graduates of photography school couldn't (or wouldn't) copy.

Sandro was not proud of his tricks. They began in a gradual way, fixing stray hairs and taking wrinkles out of dresses. He did it once, then twice, then people came in asking for it. Perhaps he'd have gone on this way, with small lies, but he met with a situation that was larger than most; it would have started a feud in the old country. During a very large and very expensive wedding party Tony the bridegroom seduced Alicia the bridesmaid in the basketball storage room under the floor of the parish hall. Six months later Tony confessed, hoping perhaps to be released from his vows. But the parents judged it was too late to dissolve the union: Diora was used, she was no longer a virgin, there was a child coming. Tony was reprimanded, Diora consoled, the mothers became enemies, the newly-weds made up. Only Alicia remained to be dealt with. The offence became hers.

In Italy, community ostracism would have been the punishment of choice. But this was Canada, and if no one acknowledged Alicia on the street, if no one visited her mother, who was heavy on her feet and forced to sit on the sofa protesting her daughter's innocence, if no one invited her father out behind to drink home-made wine, Alicia didn't care. She went off to her job behind the till in a drugstore with her chin thrust out much as before. The inlaws perceived that the young woman could not be subdued by the old methods. This being the case, it was better she not exist at all.

Which was why Diora's mother turned up at Sandro's counter with the wedding photos. The pain Alicia had caused! she began. Diora's mother's very own miserable wages, saved these eighteen years, had paid for these photographs! She wept. The money was spent, but the joy was spoiled. When she and Diora's father looked at the row of faces flanking bride and groom there she was—Alicia, the whore! She wiped her tears and made her pitch.

"You can solve our problem, Sandro. I will get a new cake, we will all come to the parish hall. You will take the photographs again. Of course," she added, "we can't pay you again."

Sandro smiled, it was so preposterous. "Even if I could afford to do all that work for nothing, I hate to say it, but Diora's out to here."

"Don't argue with me."

"I wouldn't be so bold," said Sandro. "But I will not take the photographs over."

The woman slapped the photographs where they lay on the counter. "You will! I don't care how you do it!" And she left.

Sandro went to the back and put his negatives on the light box. He brought out his magic solution and his razor blades and his brushes. He circled Alicia's head and shoulders in the first row and went to work. He felt a little badly, watching the bright circle of her face fade and swim, darken down to nothing. But how easily she vanished! He filled in the white spot with a bit of velvet curtain trimmed from the side.

"I'm like a plastic surgeon," he told his wife. "Take that patch of skin from the inner thigh and put it over the scar on the face. Then sand the edges. Isn't that what they do? Only it isn't a face I'm fixing, it's a memory."

His wife stood on two flat feet beside the sink. She shook the carrot she was peeling. "I don't care about Alicia," she said, "but Diora's mother is making a mistake. She is starting them off with a lie in their marriage. And why is she doing it? For her pride! I don't like this, Sandro."

"You're missing the point," said Sandro.

The next day he had another look at his work. Alicia's shoulders and the bodice of her dress were still there, in front of the chest of the uncle of the bride. He couldn't remove them; it would leave a hole in Uncle. Sandro had nothing to fill the hole, no spare male torsos in black tie. He considered putting a head on top, but whose head? There was no such thing as a free face. A stranger would be questioned, a friend would have an alibi. Perhaps Diora's mother would not notice the black velvet space, as where a tooth had been knocked out, between the smiling faces.

Indeed she didn't but kissed his hand fervently and thanked him with tears in her eyes. "Twenty-five thousand that wedding cost me. Twenty-five thousand to get this photograph and you have rescued it."

"Surely you got dinner and a dance too?" said Sandro.

"The wedding was one day. This is forever," said Diora's mother.

"I won't do that again," said Sandro, putting the cloth over his head and looking into his camera lens to do a passport photo. In the community the doctored photograph had been examined and re-examined. Alicia's detractors enjoyed the headless shoulders as evidence of a violent punishment.

"No, I won't do that again at all," said Sandro to himself, turning aside compliments with a shake of his head. But there was another wedding. After the provolone e melone, the veal picata, the many-tiered cake topped with swans, the father of the bride drew Sandro aside and asked for a set of prints with the groom's parents removed.

"My God, why?" said Sandro.

"He's a bastard. A bad man."

"Shouldn't have let her marry his son, then," said Sandro, pulling a cigarette out of the pack in his pocket. These conversations made him nervous.

The father's weathered face was dark, his dinner-jacket did not button around his chest. He moaned and ground his lower teeth against his uppers. "You know how they are, these girls in Canada. I am ashamed to say it, but I couldn't stop her."

Sandro said nothing.

"Look, I sat here all night long, said nothing, did nothing. I don't wanna look at him for the next twenty years."

Sandro drew in a long tube of smoke.

"I paid a bundle for this night. I wanna remember it nice-like."

The smoke made Sandro nauseous. He dropped his cigarette and ground it into the floor with his toe, damning his own weakness. "So what am I going to do with the table?"

The father put out a hand like a tool, narrowed his eyes, and began to saw, where the other man sat.

"And leave it dangling, no legs?"

"So make new legs."

"I'm a photographer, not a carpenter," said Sandro. "I don't make table legs."

"Where you get legs is your problem," said the father. "I'm doing well here. I've got ten guys working for me. You look like you could use some new equipment."

And what harm was it after all, it was only a photograph, said Sandro to himself. Then too there was the technical challenge. Waiting until they all got up to get their bonbonnière, he took a shot of the head table empty. Working neatly with his scalpel, he cut the table from this second negative, removed the inlaws and their chairs from the first one, stuck the empty table-end onto the table in the first picture, blended over the join neatly, and printed it. Presto! Only one set of inlaws.

"I don't mind telling you, it gives me a sick feeling," said Sandro to his wife. "I was there. I saw them. We had a conversation. They smiled for me. Now ..." he shrugged. "An empty table. Lucky I don't go to church any more."

"Let the man who paid good money to have you do it confess, not you," she said. "A photograph is a photograph."

"That's what I thought too," said Sandro.

The next morning Sandro went to the Donut House, got himself a take-out coffee and stood on the street beside his window.

"Why do people care about photographs so much?" he asked Becker. Becker had newspaper stuffed in the soles of his shoes. He had on a pair of stained brown pants tied up at the waist with a paisley necktie. His bottle was clutched in a paper bag gathered around the neck.

"You can put them on your mantel," said Becker. "They don't talk back."

"Don't people prefer life?" said Sandro.

"People prefer things," said Becker.

"Don't they want their memories to be true?"

"No," said Becker.

"Another thing. Are we here just to get our photograph taken? Do we have a higher purpose?"

Becker pulled one of the newspapers out of his shoe. There were Brian and Mila Mulroney having a gloaty kiss. They were smeared by muddy water and depressed by the joint in the ball of Becker's foot.

"I mean real people," said Sandro. "Have we no loyalty to the natural?"

"These are existential questions, Sandro," said Becker. "Too many more of them and you'll be out here on the street with the rest of us."

Sandro drained the coffee from his cup, pitched it in the bin painted "Keep Toronto Clean" and went back into his gallery. The existential questions nagged. But he did go out and get the motor drive for the camera. In the next few months he eradicated a pregnancy from a wedding photo, added a daughter-in-law who complained of being left out of the Christmas shots, and made a groom taller. Working in the darkroom, he was hit by vertigo. He was on a slide, beginning a descent. He wanted to know what the bottom felt like.

After a year of such operations a man from the Beaches came in with a tiny black and white photo of a long-lost brother. He wanted it coloured and fitted into a family shot around a picnic table on Centre Island.

"Is this some kind of joke?" said Sandro. It was the only discretion he practised now: he wanted to talk about it before he did it.

"No. I'm going to send it to Mother. She thinks Christopher wrote us all off."

"Did he?" said Sandro.

"Better she should not know."

Sandro neglected to ask if Christopher was fat or thin. He ended up taking a medium-sized pair of shoulders from his own cousin and propping them up behind a bush, with Christopher's head on top. Afterward, Sandro lay sleepless in his bed. Suppose that in the next few months Christopher should turn up dead, say murdered. Then Mother would produce the photograph stamped Immaculate Conception Photography Gallery, 1816 St. Clair Avenue West. Sandro would be implicated. The police might come.

"I believe adding people is worse than taking them away," he said to his wife.

"You say yes to do it, then you do it. You think it's wrong, you say no."

"Let me try this on you, Becker," said Sandro the next morning. "To take a person out is only half a lie. It proves nothing except that he was not in that shot. To add a person is a whole lie: it proves that he was there, when he was not."

"You haven't proven a thing, you're just fooling around with celluloid. Have you got a buck?" said Becker.

"It is better to be a murderer than a creator. I am playing God, outplaying God at His own game." He was smarter than Becker now. He knew it was the photographs that lasted, not the people. In the end the proof was in the proof. Though he hadn't prayed in thirty years, Sandro began to pray. It was like riding a bicycle: he got the hang of it again instantly. "Make me strong," he prayed, "strong enough to resist the new equipment that I might buy, strong enough to resist the temptation to expand the gallery, to buy a house in the suburbs. Make me say no to people who want alterations."

But Sandro's prayers were not answered. When people offered him money to dissolve an errant relative, he said yes. He said yes out of curiosity. He said yes out of a desire to test his skills. He said yes out of greed. He said yes out of compassion. "What is the cost of a little happiness?" he said. "Perhaps God doesn't count photographs. After all, they're not one of a kind."

Sandro began to be haunted, in slow moments behind the counter in the Immaculate Conception, by the faces of those whose presence he had tampered with. He kept a file—Alicia the lusty bridesmaid, Antonia and Marco, the undesired inlaws. Their heads, their shoes and their hands, removed from the scene with surgical precision, he saved for the moment when, God willing, a forgiving relative would ask him to replace them. But the day did not come. Sandro was not happy.

"Becker," he said, for he had a habit now of buying Becker a coffee first thing in the morning and standing out if it was warm, or in if it was cold, for a chat. "Becker, let's say it's a good service I'm doing. It makes people happy, even if it tells lies."

"Sandro," said Becker, who enjoyed his coffee, "these photographs, doctored by request of the subjects, reflect back the lives they wish to have. The unpleasant bits are removed, the wishes are added. If you didn't do it, someone else would. Memory would. It's a service."

"It's also money," said Sandro. He found Becker too eager to make excuses now. He liked him better before.

"You're like Tintoretto, painting in his patron, softening his greedy profile, lifting the chin of his fat wife. It pays for the part that's true art."

"Which part is that?" said Sandro, but Becker didn't answer. He was still standing there when Diora came in. She'd matured, she'd gained weight, and her twins, now six years old, were handsome and strong. Sandro's heart flew up in his breast. Perhaps she had made friends with Alicia, perhaps Diora had come to have her bridesmaid reinstated.

"The long nightmare is over," said Diora. "I've left him."

The boys were running from shelf to shelf lifting up the photographs with their glass frames and putting them down again. Sandro watched them with one eye. He knew what she was going to say.

"I want you to take him out of those pictures," she said.

"You'd look very foolish as a bride with no groom," he said severely.

"No, no, not those," she said. "I mean the kids' birthday shots."

They had been particularly fine, those shots, taken only two weeks ago, Tony tall and dark, Diora and the children radiant and blond.

"Be reasonable, Diora," he said. "I never liked him myself. But he balances the portrait. Besides, he was there."

"He was not there!" cried Diora. Her sons went on turning all the pictures to face the walls. "He was never there. He was running around, in his heart he was not with me. I was alone with my children."

"I'll take another one," said Sandro. "Of you and the boys. Whenever you like. This one stays like it is."

"We won't pay."

"But Diora," said Sandro, "everyone knows he's their father."

"They have no father," said Diora flatly.

"It's immaculate conception," said Becker gleefully.

But Diora did not hear. "It's our photograph, and we want him out. You do your job. The rest of it's none of your business." She put one hand on the back of the head of each of her twins and marched them out the door.

Sandro leaned on his counter idly flipping the pages of a wedding album. He had a vision of a great decorated room, with a cake on the table. Everyone had had his way, the husband had removed the wife, the wife the husband, the bridesmaid her parents, and so forth. There was no one there.

"We make up our lives out of the people around us," he said to Becker. "When they don't live up to standard, we can't just wipe them out."

"Don't ask me," said Becker. "I just lit out for the streets. Couldn't live up to a damn thing." Then he too went out the door.

"Lucky bugger," said Sandro.

Alone, he went to his darkroom. He opened his drawer of bits and pieces. His disappeared ones, the inconvenient people. His body parts, his halves of torsos, tips of shiny black shoes. Each face, each item of clothing punctured him a little. He looked at his negatives stored in drawers. They were scarred, pathetic things. I haven't the stomach for it, not any more, thought Sandro.

As he walked home, St. Clair Avenue seemed very fine. The best part was, he thought, there were no relationships. Neither this leaning drunk nor that window-shopper was so connected to any other as to endanger his, or her, existence. The tolerance of indifference, said Sandro to himself, trying to remember it so that he could tell Becker.

But Sandro felt ill at ease in his own home, by its very definition a dangerous and unreliable setting. His wife was stirring something, with her lips tight together. His children, almost grown up now, bred secrets as they looked at television. He himself only posed in the doorway, looking for hidden seams and the faint hair-lines of an airbrush.

That night he stood exhausted by his bed. His wife lay on her side with one round shoulder above the sheet. Behind her on the wall was the photo he'd taken of their village before he left Italy. He ought to reshoot it, take out that gas station and clean up the square a little. His pillow had an indentation, as if a head had been erased. He slept in a chair.

In the morning he went down to the shop. He got his best camera and set up a tripod on the sidewalk directly across the street. He took several shots in the solid bright morning light. He locked the door and placed the CLOSED sign in the window. In the darkroom he developed the film, floating the negatives in the pungent fluid until the row of shop fronts came through clearly, the flat brick faces, the curving concrete trim, the two balls on the crowns. Deftly he dissolved each brick of his store, the window and the sign. Deftly he reattached each brick of the store on the west side to the bricks of the store to the east.

I have been many things in my life, thought Sandro, a presser of shutters, a confessor, a false prophet. Now I am a bricklayer, and a good one. He taped the negatives together and developed them. He touched up the join and then photographed it again. He developed this second negative and it was perfect. Number 1812, Lord's Shoes, joined directly to 1820, Bargain Jimmies: the Immaculate Conception Photography Gallery at 1816 no longer existed. Working quickly, because he wanted to finish before the day was over, he blew it up to two feet by three feet. He cleared out his window display of brides and babies and stood up this new photograph—one of the finest he'd ever taken, he thought. Then he took a couple of cameras and a bag with the tripod and some lenses. He turned out the light, pulling the door shut behind him, and began to walk west.

Topics for Discussion

1. Are photographs documentary records or simply works of art? What is the difference between a work of art and a document?

2. Is removing people's images from photographs a form of lying?

3. What is the role of Becker in the story?

4. Why does Sandro close up his shop and walk away at the end of the story? What is the significance of his final photograph?

5. What is the relationship between the title of the story and the story itself?

6. What is the relationship between the setting and the story?

7. What is Govier saying about the nature of miracles in the modern world?

Graham Greene

About the Author

One of England's foremost novelists of the twentieth century, Graham Greene was born in 1904 in Berkhamsted, England, where his father was headmaster of the school he attended. As a youth he attempted suicide and played Russian roulette to ease his boredom. In 1926 he joined the Catholic Church, a major concern in many of his important novels. He trained as a newspaperman and worked as an editor with *The Times* and the *Spectator* before joining the Foreign Office in 1941. After the war, he worked as a screenwriter (including the film script to *The Third Man*, which starred Joseph Cotten and Orson Welles), and travelled throughout the world. He died in 1991 in the south of France.

Greene examines important questions of the spirit and of human character, such as the meaning of faith (*The End of the Affair, The Power and the Glory*), from the perspective of highly personal and individual narrators. One of the chief problems experienced by his narrators/protagonists is their struggle to come to an understanding of themselves, especially their inner selves. The conflict usually ensues from the tension between the temporal world of time and place and appearance and the extemporal world of abstract considerations, belief and personal philosophy.

Selected Works

Brighton Rock (novel, 1938)
The Power and the Glory (novel, 1940)
The Heart of the Matter (novel, 1948)
The End of the Affair (novel, 1951)
The Quiet American (novel, 1955)

About the Story

This story describes how a man goes for a weekend to the country with a prostitute he has picked up in a London bar. He decides to hold his tryst in his old hometown, a place he has not returned to for many years. The town is Bishop's Hendron, in Hertfordshire, north of London.

The Innocent

It was a mistake to take Lola there. I knew it the moment we alighted from the train at the small country station. On an autumn evening one remembers more of childhood than at any other time of year, and her bright veneered face, the small bag which hardly pretended to contain our things for the night, simply didn't go with the old grain warehouses across the small canal, the few lights up the hill, the posters of an ancient film. But she said, "Let's go into the country," and Bishop's Hendron was, of course, the first name which came into my head. Nobody would know me there now, and it hadn't occurred to me that it would be I who remembered.

Even the old porter touched a chord. I said, "There'll be a four-wheeler at the entrance," and there was, though at first I didn't notice it, seeing the two taxis and thinking, "The old place is coming on." It was very dark, and the thin autumn mist, the smell of wet leaves and canal water were deeply familiar.

Lola said, "But why did you choose this place? It's grim." It was no use explaining to her why it wasn't grim to me, that that sand heap by the canal had always been there (when I was three I remember thinking it was what other people meant by the seaside). I took the bag (I've said it was light; it was simply a forged passport of respectability) and said we'd walk. We came up over the little humpbacked bridge and passed the alms-houses. When I was five I saw a middle-aged man run into one to commit suicide; he carried a knife and all the neighbours pursued him up the stairs. She said, "I never thought the country was like *this*." They were ugly alms-houses, little grey stone boxes, but I knew them as I knew nothing else. It was like listening to music, all that walk.

But I had to say something to Lola. It wasn't her fault that she didn't belong here. We passed the school, the church, and came round into the old wide High Street and the sense of the first twelve years of life. If I hadn't come, I shouldn't have known that sense would be so strong, because those years hadn't been particularly happy or particularly miserable; they had been ordinary years, but now with the smell of wood fires, of the cold striking up from the dark damp paving stones, I thought I knew what it was that held me. It was the smell of innocence.

I said to Lola, "It's a good inn, and there'll be nothing here, you'll see, to keep us up. We'll have dinner and drinks and go to bed." But the worst of it was that I couldn't help wishing that I were alone. I hadn't been back all these years; I hadn't realized how well I remembered the place. Things I'd quite forgotten, like that sand heap, were coming back with an effect of pathos and nostalgia. I could have been very happy that night in a melancholy autumnal way, wandering about the little town, picking up clues to that time of life when, however miserable we are, we have expectations. It wouldn't be the same if I came back again, for then there would be the memories of Lola, and Lola meant just nothing at all. We had happened to pick each other up at a bar the day before and liked each other. Lola was all right, there was no one I would rather spend the night with, but she didn't fit in with *these* memories. We ought to have gone to Maidenhead. That's country too.

The inn was not quite where I remembered it. There was the Town Hall, but they had built a new cinema with a Moorish dome and a café, and there was a garage which hadn't existed in my time. I had forgotten too the turning to the left up a steep villaed hill.

"I don't believe that road was there in my day," I said.

"Your day?" Lola asked.

"Didn't I tell you? I was born here."

"You must get a kick out of bringing me here," Lola said. "I suppose you used to think of nights like this when you were a boy."

"Yes," I said, because it wasn't her fault. She was all right. I liked her scent. She used a good shade of lipstick. It was costing me a lot, a fiver for Lola and then all the bills and fares and drinks, but I'd have thought it money well spent anywhere else in the world.

I lingered at the bottom of that road. Something was stirring in the mind, but I don't think I should have remembered what, if a crowd of children hadn't come down the hill at that moment into the frosty lamplight, their voices sharp and shrill, their breath fuming as they passed under the lamps. They all carried linen bags, and some of the bags were embroidered with initials. They were in their best clothes and a little self-conscious. The small girls kept to themselves in a kind of compact beleaguered group, and one thought of hair ribbons and shining shoes and the sedate tinkle of a piano. It all came back to me: they had been to a dancing lesson, just as I used to go, to a small square house with a drive of rhododendrons half-way up the hill. More than ever I wished that Lola were not with me, less than ever did she fit, as I thought "something's missing from the picture," and a sense of pain glowed dully at the bottom of my brain.

We had several drinks at the bar, but there was half an hour before they would agree to serve dinner. I said to Lola, "You don't want to drag round this town. If you don't mind, I'll just slip out for ten minutes and look at a place I used to know." She didn't mind. There was a local man, perhaps a schoolmaster, at the bar simply longing to stand her a drink. I could see how he envied me, coming down with her like this from town just for a night.

※彡

I walked up the hill. The first houses were all new. I resented them. They hid such things as fields and gates I might have remembered. It was like a map which had got wet in the pocket and pieces had stuck together; when you opened it there were whole patches hidden. But half-way up, there the house really was, the drive; perhaps the same old lady was giving lessons. Children exaggerate age. She may not in those days have been more than thirty-five. I could hear the piano. She was following the same routine. Children under eight, 6–7 p.m. Children eight to thirteen, 7–8. I opened the gate and went in a little way. I was trying to remember.

I don't know what brought it back. I think it was simply the autumn, the cold, the wet frosting leaves, rather than the piano, which had played different tunes in those days. I remembered the small girl as well as one remembers anyone without a photograph to refer to. She was a year older than I was: she must have been just on the point of eight. I loved her with an intensity I have never felt since, I believe, for anyone. At least I have never made the mistake of laughing at children's love. It has a terrible inevitability of separation because there *can* be no satisfaction. Of course one invents tales of houses on fire, of war and forlorn charges which prove one's courage in her eyes, but never of marriage. One knows without being told that that can't happen, but the knowledge doesn't mean that one suffers less. I remembered all the games of blind-man's buff at birthday parties when I vainly hoped to catch her, so that I might have the excuse to touch and hold her, but I never caught her; she always kept out of my way.

But once a week for two winters I had my chance: I danced with her. That made it worse (it was cutting off our only contact) when she told me during one of the last lessons of the winter that next year she would join the older class. She liked me too, I knew it, but we had no way of expressing it. I used to go to her birthday parties and she would come to mine, but we never even ran home together after the dancing class. It would have seemed odd; I don't think it occurred to us. I had to join my own boisterous teasing male companions, and she the besieged, the hustled, the shrilly indignant sex on the way down the hill.

I shivered there in the mist and turned my coat collar up. The piano was playing a dance from an old C. B. Cochran revue. It seemed a long journey to have taken to find only Lola at the end of it. There *is* something about innocence one is never quite resigned to lose. Now when I am unhappy about a girl, I can simply go and buy another one. Then the best I could think of was to write some passionate message and slip it into a hole (it was extraordinary how I began to remember everything) in the woodwork of the gate. I had once told her about the hole, and sooner or later I was sure she would put in her fingers and find the message. I wondered what the message could have been. One wasn't able to express much, I thought, in those days; but because the expression was inadequate, it didn't mean that the pain was shallower than what one sometimes suffered now. I remembered how for days I had felt in the hole and always found the message there. Then the dancing lessons stopped. Probably by the next winter I had forgotten.

As I went out of the gate I looked to see if the hole existed. It was there. I put in my finger, and, in its safe shelter from the seasons and the years, the scrap of paper rested yet. I pulled it out and opened it. Then I struck a match, a tiny glow of heat in the mist and dark. It was a shock to see by its diminutive flame a picture of crude obscenity. There could be no mistake; there were my initials below the childish inaccurate sketch of a man and woman. But it woke fewer memories than the fume of breath, the linen bags, a damp leaf, or the pile of sand. I didn't recognize it; it might have been drawn by a dirty-minded stranger on a lavatory wall. All I could remember was the purity, the intensity, the pain of that passion.

I felt at first as if I had been betrayed. "After all," I told myself, "Lola's not so much out of place here." But later that night, when Lola turned away from me and fell asleep, I began to realize the deep innocence of that drawing. I had believed I was drawing something with a meaning and beautiful; it was only now after thirty years of life that the picture seemed obscene.

Topics for Discussion

1. How does Greene define "innocence"?

2. What is the relationship between memory and environment and how does Greene establish this?

3. What triggers his memories? How does Greene narrate and relate the idea of nostalgia? What is the impact of nostalgia?

4. What is the relationship between the adult and the child within the adult, according to Greene? Does age corrupt an individual?

5. How does Greene convey the idea of love and how does he define the various concepts of love in the story?

6. How does the narrator's relationship to the town of his childhood compare with your relationship to the place where you grew up?

James Joyce

About the Author

James Joyce was born in Dublin in 1882 and died in Zurich, Switzerland, in 1941. He was educated at University College, Dublin, and moved to the Continent (Trieste, Paris and Zurich), where he did much of his major writing. During his lifetime, he established himself as one of the leading voices of the Modernist movement in literature. His collection of stories, *Dubliners*, from which "Eveline" is taken, went largely unnoticed when it was released on the eve of the First World War.

A Portrait of the Artist as a Young Man established Joyce as a major literary voice. This novel, which is largely intertextual (that is, it refers to other texts) and frequently alludes to the politics and cultural tensions of his time (the tug of Irish nationalism on one hand and of continentalism and universal artistic values on the other), defines the ideas of escape that Joyce explored in *Dubliners*, especially in the story "Eveline." In telling the story of the protagonist, Stephen Dedalus, using the approach of a *Bildungsroman* (a novel which traces the imaginative and intellectual growth and development of a character from childhood into adulthood), Joyce defines the role of the artist in the modern world as creator of the "uncreated conscience of my race" and arbiter of artistic values in danger of being perverted by the temporal world.

His next major work, *Ulysses*, is a retelling, through parody and stream-of-consciousness narrative, of Homer's classical Greek epic *The Odyssey*, set in Dublin on a single day in June 1904. Through protagonist Leopold Bloom's travels around Dublin, Joyce mirrors the events of the classical precursor. In the end, Stephen Dedalus (also the protagonist of Joyce's earlier novel) finds a father figure in Bloom.

Joyce's final masterwork, *Finnegans Wake* (for which the dramatist Samuel Beckett acted as Joyce's amanuensis), is a dream-vision written in a strange amalgam of linguistic jokes and literary allusions, and takes as its central theme the Christian concepts of the Fall and Resurrection.

Selected Works

Dubliners (short stories, 1914)
A Portrait of the Artist as a Young Man (novel, 1916)
Exiles (drama, 1918)
Ulysses (novel, 1922)
Finnegans Wake (novel, 1939)

About the Story

The thirteen stories and one novella ("The Dead") in *Dubliners* are connected by Joyce's use of a common setting (the city of Dublin), the use of repeated *leitmotifs* such as coins, images of the Eucharist (the Catholic ritual in which bread and wine are transformed by the act of transubstantiation into the blood and body of Christ for the purpose of celebrating communion, or a ritual repetition of the Last Supper), and through the recurring themes of paralysis and a desire to flee from Ireland. Watch for references to the Eucharist, such as the burnt toast (the host) and the ringing bell (which marks the moment at which the bread and wine are transformed).

"Eveline" is the first story in *Dubliners* to be written in the third person narrative voice. Note that Joyce makes this change when the focus of the stories shifts from childhood (first person, subjective narratives) to adulthood (third person, objective narratives).

Also note Joyce's poetic use of language. Each sentence is crammed with meaning and a wide range of subtle linguistic allusions, such as in the opening lines where evening "invades the avenue." These resonances are part of the depth of the story.

Eveline

She sat at the window watching the evening invade the avenue. Her head was leaned against the window curtains and in her nostrils was the odour of dusty cretonne. She was tired.

Few people passed. The man out of the last house passed on his way home; she heard his footsteps clacking along the concrete pavement and afterwards crunching on the cinder path before the new red houses. One time there used to be a field there in which they used to play every evening with other people's children. Then a man from Belfast bought the field and built houses in it—not like their little brown houses but bright brick houses with shining roofs. The children of the avenue used to play together in that field—the Devines, the Waters, the Dunns, little Keogh the cripple, she and her brothers and sisters. Ernest, however, never played: he was too grown up. Her father used often to hunt them in out of the field with his blackthorn stick; but usually little Keogh used to keep *nix* and call out when he saw her father coming. Still they seemed to have been rather happy then. Her father was not so bad then; and besides, her mother was alive. That was a long time ago; she and her brothers and sisters were all grown up; her mother was dead. Tizzie Dunn was dead, too, and the Waters had gone back to England. Everything changes. Now she was going to go away like the others, to leave her home.

Home! She looked round the room, reviewing all its familiar objects which she had dusted once a week for so many years, wondering where on earth all the dust came from. Perhaps she would never see again those familiar objects from which she had never dreamed of being divided. And yet during all those years she had never found out the name of the priest whose yellowing photograph hung on the wall above the broken harmonium beside the coloured print of the promises made to Blessed Margaret Mary Alacoque. He had been a school friend of her father. Whenever he showed the photograph to a visitor her father used to pass it with a casual word:

—He is in Melbourne now.

She had consented to go away, to leave her home. Was that wise? She tried to weigh each side of the question. In her home anyway she had shelter and food; she had those whom she had known all her life about her. Of course she had to work hard both in the house and at business. What would they say of her in the Stores when they found out that she had run away with a fellow? Say she was a fool, perhaps; and her place would be filled up by advertisement. Miss Gavan would be glad. She had always had an edge on her, especially whenever there were people listening.

—Miss Hill, don't you see these ladies are waiting?

—Look lively, Miss Hill, please.

She would not cry many tears at leaving the Stores.

But in her new home, in a distant unknown country, it would not be like that. Then she would be married—she, Eveline. People would treat her with respect then. She would not be treated as her mother had been. Even now, though she was over nineteen, she sometimes felt herself in danger of her father's violence. She knew it was that that had given her the palpitations. When they were growing up he had never gone for her, like he used to go for Harry and Ernest, because she was a girl; but latterly he had begun to threaten her and say what he would do to her only for her dead mother's sake. And now she had nobody to protect her. Ernest was dead and Harry, who was in the church decorating business, was nearly always down somewhere in the country. Besides, the invariable squabble for money on Saturday nights had begun to weary her unspeakably. She always gave her entire wages— seven shillings—and Harry always sent up what he could but the trouble was to get any money from her father. He said she used to squander the money, that she had no head, that he wasn't going to give her his hard-earned money to throw about the streets, and much more, for he was usually fairly bad of a Saturday night. In the end he would give her the money and ask her had she any intention of buying Sunday's dinner. Then she had to rush out as quickly as she could and do her marketing, holding her black leather purse tightly in her hand as she elbowed her way through the crowds and returning home late under her load of provisions. She had hard work to keep the house together and to see that the two young children who had been left to her charge went to school regularly and got their meals regularly. It was hard work—a hard life—but now that she was about to leave it she did not find it a wholly undesirable life.

She was about to explore another life with Frank. Frank was very kind, manly, open-hearted. She was to go away with him by the night-boat to be his wife and to live with him in Buenos Ayres where he had a home waiting for her. How well she remembered the first time she had seen him; he was lodging in a house on the main road where she used to visit. It seemed a few weeks ago. He was standing at the gate, his peaked cap pushed back on his head and his hair tumbled forward over a face of bronze. Then they had come to know each other. He used to meet her outside the Stores every evening and see her home. He took her to see *The Bohemian Girl* and she felt elated as she sat in an unaccustomed part of the theatre with him. He was awfully fond of music and sang a little. People knew that they were courting and, when he sang about the lass that loves a sailor, she always felt pleasantly confused. He used to call her Poppens out of fun. First of all it had been an excitement for her to have a fellow and then she had begun to like him. He had tales of distant countries. He had started as a deck boy at a pound a month on a ship of the Allan Line going out to Canada. He told her the names of the ships he had been on and the names of the different services. He had sailed through the Straits of Magellan and he told her stories of the terrible Patagonians. He had fallen on his feet in Buenos Ayres, he said, and had come over to the old country just for a holiday. Of course, her father had found out the affair and had forbidden her to have anything to say to him.

—I know these sailor chaps, he said.

One day he had quarrelled with Frank and after that she had to meet her lover secretly.

The evening deepened in the avenue. The white of two letters in her lap grew indistinct. One was to Harry; the other was to her father. Ernest had been her favourite but she liked Harry too. Her father was becoming old lately, she noticed; he would miss her. Sometimes he could be very nice. Not long before, when she had been laid up for a day, he had read her out a ghost story and made toast for her at the fire. Another day, when their mother was alive, they had all gone for a picnic to the Hill of Howth. She remembered her father putting on her mother's bonnet to make the children laugh.

Her time was running out but she continued to sit by the window, leaning her head against the window curtain, inhaling the odour of dusty cretonne. Down far in the avenue she could hear a street organ playing. She knew the air. Strange that it should come that very night to remind her of the promise to her mother, her promise to keep the home together as long as she could. She remembered the last night of her mother's illness; she was again in the close dark room at the other side of the hall and outside she heard a melancholy air of Italy. The organ-player had been ordered to go away and given sixpence. She remembered her father strutting back into the sick-room saying;

—Damned Italians! coming over here!

As she mused the pitiful vision of her mother's life laid its spell on the very quick of her being—that life of commonplace sacrifices closing in final craziness. She trembled as she heard again her mother's voice saying constantly with foolish insistence:

—Derevaun Seraun! Derevaun Seraun!

She stood up in a sudden impulse of terror. Escape! She must escape! Frank would save her. He would give her life, perhaps love, too.

But she wanted to live. Why should she be unhappy? She had a right to happiness. Frank would take her in his arms, fold her in his arms. He would save her.

She stood among the swaying crowd in the station at the North Wall. He held her hand and she knew that he was speaking to her, saying something about the passage over and over again. The station was full of soldiers with brown baggages. Through the wide doors of the sheds she caught a glimpse of the black mass of the boat, lying in beside the quay wall, with illumined portholes. She answered nothing. She felt her cheek pale and cold and, out of a maze of distress, she prayed to God to direct her, to show her what was her duty. The boat blew a long mournful whistle into the mist. If she went, to-morrow she would be on the sea with Frank, steaming towards Buenos Ayres. Their passage had been booked. Could she still draw back after all he had done for her? Her distress awoke a nausea in her body and she kept moving her lips in silent fervent prayer.

A bell clanged upon her heart. She felt him seize her hand:

—Come!

All the seas of the world tumbled about her heart. He was drawing her into them: he would drown her. She gripped with both hands at the iron railing.

—Come!

No! No! No! It was impossible. Her hands clutched the iron in frenzy. Amid the seas she sent a cry of anguish!

—Eveline! Evvy!

He rushed beyond the barrier and called to her to follow. He was shouted at to go on but he still called to her. She set her white face to him, passive, like a helpless animal. Her eyes gave him no sign of love or farewell or recognition.

Topics for Discussion

1. Why does Eveline run away from Frank at the moment of her potential liberation?

2. How does Joyce convey the ideas of fear and anxiety?

3. Why is Eveline afraid?

4. What roles do time and distance play in the story?

5. Why does Joyce repeat certain words, such as "hard," and what impact does this have on the reader's perceptions of the story?

6. How does Joyce incorporate *leitmotifs* into the story?

7. How does Joyce describe the setting of the story?

8. How does the rest of the world compare to Dublin in this story?

Alex La Guma

About the Author

Alex La Guma, a black South African who wrote against the apartheid regime that characterized that nation from 1948 until 1994, was born in the Coloured ghetto of District Six, Cape Town, in 1925. In 1948, the year of the implementation of apartheid, La Guma joined the outlawed Communist Party and officially became an enemy of the state. As a trade union activist and journalist, he was one of 156 defendants in the famous Treason Trial of 1956–60. After his acquittal he was detained for questioning by state authorities for several months before being granted an exit permit in 1966, when he moved to London, England. He later lived in Havana, Cuba, where he was chief representative of the African National Congress in the Caribbean, a post he held until his death in 1985.

La Guma's stories and novels take up the issues that confronted South Africa during this period—political oppression, detentions without bail or hearing, and political death squads. In his hands, the short story becomes an instrument of political expression.

Selected Works

A Walk in the Night (novel, 1962)
And a Threefold Cord (novel, 1964)
The Stone Country (novel, 1967)
A Walk in the Night and Other Stories (short stories, 1967)
In the Fog of the Season's End (novel, 1972)
Time of the Butcherbird (novel, 1979)

About the Story

"The Lemon Orchard," from the collection *A Walk in the Night*, was first published in 1967 while La Guma was in exile. In this story, a group of white men are leading a man (presumably black or "Cape Coloured"—a term applied under the Apartheid regime to those of mixed racial origin) through a lemon orchard under cover of darkness.

The Lemon Orchard

The men came down between two long, regular rows of trees. The winter had not passed completely and there was a chill in the air; and the moon was hidden behind long, high parallels of cloud which hung like suspended streamers of dirty cotton-wool in the sky. All of the men but one wore thick clothes against the coolness of the night. The night and earth was cold and damp, and the shoes of the men sank into the soil and left exact, ridged foot prints, but they could not be seen in the dark.

One of the men walked ahead holding a small cycle lantern that worked from a battery, leading the way down the avenue of trees while the others came behind in the dark. The night close around was quiet now that the crickets had stopped their small noises, but far out others that did not feel the presence of the men continued the monotonous creek-creek-creek. Somewhere, even further, a dog started barking in short high yaps, and then stopped abruptly. The men were walking through an orchard of lemons and the sharp, bitter-sweet citrus smell hung gently on the night air.

"Do not go so fast," the man who brought up the rear of the party called to the man with the lantern. "It's as dark as a kaffir's soul here at the back."

He called softly, as if the darkness demanded silence. He was a big man and wore khaki trousers and laced-up riding boots, and an old shooting jacket with leather patches on the right breast and the elbows.

The shotgun was loaded. In the dark this man's face was invisible except for a blur of shadowed hollows and lighter crags. Although he walked in the rear he was the leader of the party. The lantern-bearer slowed down for the rest to catch up with him.

"Cold?" the man with the shotgun asked, speaking with sarcasm. "Are you colder than this verdomte hotnot, here?" And he gestured in the dark with the muzzle of the gun at the man who stumbled along in their midst and who was the only one not warmly dressed.

This man wore trousers and a raincoat which they had allowed him to pull on over his pyjamas when they had taken him from his lodgings, and he shivered now with chill, clenching his teeth to prevent them from chattering. He had not been given time to tie his shoes and the metal-covered ends of the laces clicked as he moved.

"Are you cold, hotnot," the man with the light jeered.

The coloured man did not reply. He was afraid, but his fear was mixed with a stubbornness which forbade him to answer them.

"He is not cold," the fifth man in the party said. "He is shivering with fear. Is it not so, hotnot?"

The coloured man said nothing, but stared ahead of himself into the half-light made by the small lantern. He could see the silhouette of the man who carried the light, but he did not want to look at the two who flanked him, the one who had complained of the cold, and the one who had spoken of his fear. They each carried a sjambok and every now and then one of them slapped a corduroyed leg with his.

"He is dumb also," the one who had spoken last chuckled.

"No, Andries. Wait a minute," the leader who carried the shotgun said, and they all stopped between the row of trees. The man with the lantern turned and put the light on the rest of the party.

"What is it?" he asked.

"Wag'n oomblikkie. Wait a moment," the leader said, speaking with forced casualness. "He is not dumb. He is a slim hotnot; one of those educated bushmen. Listen, hotnot," he addressed the coloured man, speaking angrily now. "When a baas speaks to you, you answer him. Do you hear?" The coloured man's wrists were tied behind him with a riem and the leader brought the muzzle of the shotgun down, pressing it hard into the small of the man's back above where the wrists met. "Do you hear, hotnot? Answer me or I will shoot a hole through your spine."

The bound man felt the hard round metal of the gun muzzle through the loose raincoat and clenched his teeth. He was cold and tried to prevent himself from shivering in case it should be mistaken for cowardice. He heard the small metallic noise as the man with the gun thumbed back the hammer of the shotgun. In spite of the cold little drops of sweat began to form on his upper lip under the overnight stubble.

"For God's sake, don't shoot him," the man with the light said, laughing a little nervously. "We don't want to be involved in any murder."

"What are you saying, man?" the leader asked. Now with the beam of the battery-lamp on his face the shadows in it were washed away to reveal the mass of tiny wrinkled and deep creases which covered the red-clay complexion of his face like the myriad lines which indicate rivers, streams, roads and railways on a map. They wound around the ridges of his chin and climbed the sharp range of his nose and the peaks of his chin and cheekbones, and his eyes were hard and blue like two frozen lakes.

"This is mos a slim hotnot," he said again. "A teacher in a school for which we pay. He lives off our sweat, and he had the audacity to be cheeky and uncivilized towards a minister of our church and no hotnot will be cheeky to a white man while I live."

"Ja, man," the lantern-bearer agreed. "But we are going to deal with him. There is no necessity to shoot him. We don't want that kind of trouble."

"I will shoot whatever hotnot or kaffir I desire, and see me get into trouble over it. I demand respect from these donders. Let them answer when they're spoken to."

He jabbed the muzzle suddenly into the coloured man's back so that he stumbled struggling to keep his balance. "Do you hear, jong? Did I not speak to you?" The man who had jeered about the prisoner's fear stepped up then, and hit him in the face, striking him on a cheekbone with the clenched fist which still held the sjambok. He was angry over the delay and wanted the man to submit so that they could proceed. "Listen you hotnot bastard," he said loudly. "Why don't you answer?"

The man stumbled, caught himself and stood in the rambling shadow of one of the lemon trees. The lantern-light swung on him and he looked away from the centre of the beam. He was afraid the leader would shoot him in anger and he had no wish to die. He straightened up and looked away from them.

"Well?" demanded the man who had struck him.

"Yes, baas," the bound man said, speaking with a mixture of dignity and contempt which was missed by those who surrounded him.

"Yes there," the man with the light said. "You could save yourself trouble. Next time you'll remember. Now let us get on." The lantern swung forward again and he walked ahead. The leader shoved their prisoner on with the muzzle of the shotgun, and he stumbled after the bobbing lantern with the other men on each side of him.

"The amazing thing about it is that this bliksem should have taken the principal, and the meester of the church before the magistrate and demand payment for the hiding they gave him for being cheeky to them," the leader said to all in general. "This verdomte hotnot. I have never heard of such a thing in all my born days."

"Well, we will give him a better hiding," the man Adries said. "This time we will teach him a lesson, Oom. He won't demand damages from anybody when we're done with him."

"And afterwards he won't be seen around here again. He will pack his things and go and live in the city where they're not so particular about the dignity of the volk. Do you hear, hotnot?" This time they were not concerned about receiving a reply but the leader went on, saying, "We don't want any educated hottentots in our town."

"Neither black Englishmen," added one of the others.

The dog started barking again at the farm house which was invisible on the dark hillside at the other end of the little valley. "It's that Jagter," the man with the lantern said. "I wonder what bothers him. He is a good watch-dog. I offered Meneer Marais five pounds for that dog, but he won't sell. I would like to have a dog like that. I would take great care of such a dog."

The blackness of the night crouched over the orchard and the leaves rustled with a harsh whispering that was inconsistent with the pleasant scent of lemons. The chill in the air had increased, and far-off the creek-creek-creek of the crickets blended into solid strips of high-pitched sound. Then the moon came from behind the banks of cloud and its white light touched the leaves with wet silver, and the perfume of lemons seemed to grow stronger, as if the juice was being crushed from them.

They walked a little way further in the moonlight and the man with the lantern said, "This is as good a place as any, Oom."

They had come into a wide gap in the orchard, a small amphitheatre surrounded by fragrant growth, and they all stopped within it. The moonlight clung for a while to the leaves and the angled branches, so that along their tips and edges the moisture gleamed with the quivering shine of scattered quicksilver.

Topics for Discussion

1. How does La Guma portray violence in the story?

2. How does the story maintain suspense and tension?

3. What is the relationship between the setting and the title of the story?

4. What does the story say about the position of black or Coloured people in South Africa during this period?

5. Is this a political story? If so, what makes it political? How does the story define the ways in which a writer can confront troubling situations?

6. How does the story end? Is the black man murdered?

7. How does La Guma use specialized patterns of speech to convey accents and characters?

Margaret Laurence

About the Author

Margaret Laurence was born Jean Margaret Wemyss in Nepawa, Manitoba, in 1926 and died in Lakefield, Ontario, in 1987. She was educated at the University of Winnipeg and worked as a journalist after her graduation. She lived in Somalia, Ghana and England before returning to Canada where she became a full-time writer. She twice won the Governor General's Award, for *A Jest of God* (1966) and *The Diviners* (1974), and was awarded the Order of Canada in 1971.

Most of Laurence's novels and stories make up the Manawaka cycle, a series of interconnected narratives set in the imaginary small town of Manawaka, Manitoba. The recurring characters, themes and plots encompass a profound sense of the interrelationship between individuals of various classes and racial backgrounds, as well as a sense of interconnectedness between past and present. For Laurence, the world of the memory, of the inner self, is what defines the individual, and her female protagonists are constantly in search of themselves through the process of coming to terms with their own pasts and identities.

Selected Works

This Side Jordan (novel, 1960)
The Tomorrow Tamer (short stories, 1963)
The Prophet's Camel Bell (memoir, 1963)
The Stone Angel (novel, 1964)
A Jest of God (novel, 1966)
The Fire Dwellers (novel, 1969)
A Bird in the House (short stories, 1970)
The Diviners (novel, 1974)
Heart of a Stranger (essays, 1976)

About the Story

"The Loons," from the collection *A Bird in the House*, is an important link in her Manawaka cycle of novels and stories (*The Stone Angel, A Bird in the House, A Jest of God, The Diviners*). The story provides background to the Tonnerres, a family of Métis (part French, part Cree Indian) whose proud past is now little more than a shell of remorse.

The story opens with a brief allusion to the Riel Rebellion of 1885. In 1870 and again in 1885, Louis Riel, a Métis member of Parliament for Manitoba, attempted to establish a nation for his people (and members of other First Nations communities), with its capital first at Winnipeg and later at Batoche in Saskatchewan. These two rebellions were suppressed by the government of Sir John A. Macdonald, the first Canadian Prime Minister. Riel was hanged at Regina, Saskatchewan, in 1886 and today is considered by many a martyr for the indigenous peoples of Canada.

The father of the co-protagonist Piquette Tonnerre is named Lazarus Tonnerre. The name Lazarus is taken from the New Testament. Christ miraculously raised Lazarus from the dead.

The Tonnerres are central to the Manawaka cycle. In the first novel of the cycle, *The Stone Angel*, John Shipley (the son of the protagonist, Hagar

Shipley) steals a kilt pin from his mother and trades it to Lazarus Tonnerre for a knife which Lazarus's father, Rider Tonnerre, used at the Battle of Batoche. Eventually, in *The Diviners* (the final novel of the cycle), Morag Gunn has a child (Pique) by Jules Tonnerre (brother of Piquette from "The Loons"), who inherits both the kilt pin and the knife (which was traded by John Shipley to Morag's adopted father, Christy Logan). Hence, Pique Tonnerre becomes the inheritor of the cultural symbols (the knife for the Métis and the kilt pin for the Scots) of the two principal groups in Manawaka.

The world of Manawaka is organized along ethnic lines into three communities: the ruling class Scots, of which Vanessa MacLeod and her family are members, the immigrant Ukrainians (who figure in *The Diviners* and *The Fire Dwellers*) and the Métis.

Brebeuf was a Jesuit missionary sent to the Georgian Bay region of Ontario in the early seventeenth century. He was martyred by the Indians (who ate his heart) and later canonized for his work in proselytizing among the Indians. Tecumseh was an Indian chief of the Shawnee tribe who assisted the British in the defence of Canada during the War of 1812.

The Loons

Just below Manawaka, where the Wachakwa River ran brown and noisy over the pebbles, the scrub oak and grey-green willow and chokecherry bushes grew in a dense thicket. In a clearing at the centre of the thicket stood the Tonnerre family's shack. The basis of this dwelling was a small square cabin made of poplar poles and chinked with mud, which had been built by Jules Tonnerre some fifty years before, when he came back from Batoche with a bullet in his thigh, the year that Riel was hung and the voices of the Metis entered their long silence. Jules had only intended to stay the winter in the Wachakwa Valley, but the family was still there in the thirties, when I was a child. As the Tonnerres had increased, their settlement had been added to, until the clearing at the foot of the town hill was a chaos of lean-tos, wooden packing cases, warped lumber, discarded car tyres, ramshackle chicken coops, tangled strands of barbed wire and rusty tin cans.

The Tonnerres were French half-breeds, and among themselves they spoke a *patois* that was neither Cree nor French. Their English was broken and full of obscenities. They did not belong among the Cree of the Galloping Mountain reservation, further north, and they did not belong among the Scots-Irish and Ukrainians of Manawaka, either. They were, as my Grandmother MacLeod would have put it, neither flesh, fowl, nor good salt herring. When their men were not working at odd jobs or as section hands on the C.P.R., they lived on relief. In the summers, one of the Tonnerre youngsters, with a face that seemed totally unfamiliar with laughter, would knock at the doors of the town's brick houses and offer for sale a lard-pail full of bruised wild strawberries, and if he got as much as a quarter he would grab the coin and run before the customer had time to change her mind. Sometimes old Jules, or his son Lazarus, would get mixed up in a Saturday-night brawl, and would hit out at whoever was nearest, or howl drunkenly among the offended shoppers on Main Street, and then the Mountie would put them for the night in the barred cell underneath the Court House, and the next morning they would be quiet again.

Piquette Tonnerre, the daughter of Lazarus, was in my class at school. She was older than I, but she had failed several grades, perhaps because her attendance had always been sporadic and her interest in schoolwork negligible. Part of the reason she had missed a lot of school was that she had had tuberculosis of the bone, and had once spent many months in hospital. I knew this because my father was the doctor who had looked after her. Her sickness was almost the only thing I knew about her, however. Otherwise, she existed for me only as a vaguely embarrassing presence, with her hoarse voice and her clumsy limping walk and her grimy cotton dresses that were always miles too long. I was neither friendly nor unfriendly towards her. She dwelt and moved somewhere within my scope of vision, but I did not actually notice her very much until that peculiar summer when I was eleven.

"I don't know what to do about that kid," my father said at dinner one evening. "Piquette Tonnerre, I mean. The damn bone's flared up again. I've had her in hospital for quite a while now, and it's under control all right, but I hate like the dickens to send her home again."

"Couldn't you explain to her mother that she has to rest a lot?" my mother said.

"The mother's not there," my father replied. "She took off a few years back. Can't say I blame her. Piquette cooks for them, and she says Lazarus would never do anything for himself as long as she's there. Anyway, I don't think she'd take much care of herself, once she got back. She's only thirteen, after all. Beth, I was thinking—what about taking her up to Diamond Lake with us this summer? A couple of months rest would give that bone a much better chance."

My mother looked stunned.

"But Ewen—what about Roddie and Vanessa?"

"She's not contagious," my father said. "And it would be company for Vanessa."

"Oh dear," my mother said in distress, "I'll bet anything she has nits in her hair."

"For Pete's sake," my father said crossly, "do you think Matron would let her stay in the hospital for all this time like that? Don't be silly, Beth."

Grandmother MacLeod, her delicately featured face as rigid as a cameo, now brought her mauve-veined hands together as though she were about to begin a prayer.

"Ewen, if that half-breed youngster comes along to Diamond Lake, I'm not going," she announced. "I'll go to Morag's for the summer."

I had trouble in stifling my urge to laugh, for my mother brightened visibly and quickly tried to hide it. If it came to a choice between Grandmother MacLeod and Piquette, Piquette would win hands down, nits or not.

"It might be quite nice for you, at that," she mused. "You haven't seen Morag for over a year, and you might enjoy being in the city for a while. Well, Ewen dear, you do what you think best. If you think it would do Piquette some good, then we'll be glad to have her, as long as she behaves herself."

So it happened that several weeks later, when we all piled into my father's old Nash, surrounded by suitcases and boxes of provisions and toys for my ten-month-old brother, Piquette was with us and Grandmother MacLeod, miraculously, was not. My father would only be staying at the cottage for a couple of weeks, for he had to get back to his practice, but the rest of us would stay at Diamond Lake until the end of August.

Our cottage was not named, as many were, "Dew Drop Inn" or "Bide-a-Wee," or "Bonnie Doon." The sign on the roadway bore in austere letters only our name, MacLeod. It was not a large cottage, but it was on the lakefront. You could look out the windows and see, through the filigree of the spruce trees, the water glistening greenly as the sun caught it. All around the cottage were ferns, and sharp-branched raspberry bushes, and moss that had grown over fallen tree trunks. If you looked carefully among the weeds and grass, you could find wild strawberry plants which were in white flower now and in another month would bear fruit, the fragrant globes hanging like miniature scarlet lanterns on the thin hairy stems. The two grey squirrels were still there, gossiping at us from the tall spruce beside the cottage, and by the end of the summer they would again be tame enough to take pieces of crust from my hands. The broad moose antlers that hung above the back door were a little more bleached and fissured after the winter, but otherwise everything was the same. I raced joyfully around my kingdom, greeting all the places I had not seen for a year. My brother, Roderick, who had not been born when we were here last summer, sat on the car rug in the sunshine and examined a brown spruce cone, meticulously turning it round and round in his small and curious hands. My mother and father toted the luggage from car to cottage, exclaiming over how well the place had wintered, no broken windows, thank goodness, no apparent damage from storm-felled branches or snow.

Only after I had finished looking around did I notice Piquette. She was sitting on the swing, her lame leg held stiffly out, and her other foot scuffing the ground as she swung slowly back and forth. Her long hair hung black and straight around her shoulders, and her broad coarse-featured face bore no expression—it was blank, as though she no longer dwelt within her own skull, as though she had gone elsewhere. I approached her very hesitantly.

"Want to come and play?"

Piquette looked at me with a sudden flash of scorn.

"I ain't a kid," she said.

Wounded, I stamped angrily away, swearing I would not speak to her for the rest of the summer. In the days that followed, however, Piquette began to interest me, and I began to want to interest her. My reasons did not appear bizarre to me. Unlikely as it may seem, I had only just realised that the Tonnerre family, whom I had always heard called half-breeds, were actually Indians, or as near as made no difference. My acquaintance with Indians was not extensive. I did not remember ever having seen a real Indian, and my new awareness that Piquette sprang from the people of Big Bear and Poundmaker, of Tecumseh, of the Iroquois who had eaten Father Brebeuf's heart—all this gave her an instant attraction in my eyes. I was a devoted reader of Pauline Johnson at this age, and sometimes would orate aloud and in an exalted voice, *West Wind, blow from your prairie nest; Blow from the mountains, blow from the west*—and so on. It seemed to me that Piquette must be in some way a daughter of the forest, a kind of junior prophetess of the wilds, who might impart to me, if I took the right approach, some of the secrets which she undoubtedly knew—where the whippoorwill made her nest, how the coyote reared her young, or whatever it was that it said in Hiawatha.

I set about gaining Piquette's trust. She was not allowed to go swimming, with her bad leg, but I managed to lure her down to the beach—or rather, she came because there was nothing else to do. The water was always icy, for the lake was fed by springs, but I swam like a dog, thrashing my arms and legs around at such speed and with such an output of energy that I never grew cold. Finally, when I had had enough, I came out and sat beside Piquette on the sand. When she saw me approaching, her hand squashed flat the sand castle she had been building, and she looked at me sullenly, without speaking.

"Do you like this place?" I asked, after a while, intending to lead on from there into the question of forest lore.

Piquette shrugged. "It's okay. Good as anywhere."

"I love it," I said. "We come here every summer."

"So what?" Her voice was distant, and I glanced at her uncertainly, wondering what I could have said wrong.

"Do you want to come for a walk?" I asked her. "We wouldn't need to go far. If you walk just around the point there, you come to a bay where great big reeds grow in the water, and all kinds of fish hang around there. Want to? Come on."

She shook her head.

"Your dad said I ain't supposed to do no more walking than I got to."

I tried another line.

"I bet you know a lot about the woods and all that, eh?" I began respectfully.

Piquette looked at me from her large dark unsmiling eyes.

"I don't know what in hell you're talkin' about," she replied. "You nuts or somethin'? If you mean where my old man, and me, and all them live, you better shut up, by Jesus, you hear?"

I was startled and my feelings were hurt, but I had a kind of dogged perseverance. I ignored her rebuff.

"You know something, Piquette? There's loons here, on this lake. You can see their nests just up the shore there, behind those logs. At night, you can hear them even from the cottage, but it's better to listen from the beach. My dad says we should listen and try to remember how they sound, because in a few years when more cottages are built at Diamond Lake and more people come in, the loons will go away."

Piquette was picking up stones and snail shells and then dropping them again.

"Who gives a good goddamn?" she said.

It became increasingly obvious that, as an Indian, Piquette was a dead loss. That evening I went out by myself, scrambling through the bushes that overhung the steep path, my feet slipping on the fallen spruce needles that covered the ground. When I reached the shore, I walked along the firm damp sand to the small pier that my father had built, and sat down there. I heard someone else crashing through the undergrowth and the bracken, and for a moment I thought Piquette had changed her mind, but it turned out to be my father. He sat beside me on the pier and we waited, without speaking.

At night the lake was like black glass with a streak of amber which was the path of the moon. All around, the spruce trees grew tall and close-set, branches blackly sharp against the sky, which was lightened by a cold flickering of stars. Then the loons began their calling. They rose like phantom birds from the nests on the shore, and flew out onto the dark still surface of the water.

No one can ever describe that ululating sound, the crying of the loons, and no one who has heard it can ever forget it. Plaintive, and yet with a quality of chilling mockery, those voices belonged to a world separated by aeons from our neat world of summer cottages and the lighted lamps of home.

"They must have sounded just like that," my father remarked, "before any person ever set foot here."

Then he laughed. "You could say the same, of course, about sparrows, or chipmunks, but somehow it only strikes you that way with the loons."

"I know," I said.

Neither of us suspected that this would be the last time we would ever sit here together on the shore, listening. We stayed for perhaps half an hour, and then we went back to the cottage. My mother was reading beside the fireplace. Piquette was looking at the burning birch log, and not doing anything.

"You should have come along," I said, although in fact I was glad she had not.

"Not me," Piquette said. "You wouldn' catch me walkin' way down there jus' for a bunch of squawkin' birds."

Piquette and I remained ill at ease with one another. I felt I had somehow failed my father, but I did not know what was the matter, nor why she would not or could not respond when I suggested exploring the woods or playing house. I thought it was probably her slow and difficult walking that held her back. She stayed most of the time in the cottage with my mother, helping her with the dishes or with Roddie, but hardly ever talking. Then the Duncans arrived at their cottage, and I spent my days with Mavis, who was my best friend. I could not reach Piquette at all, and I soon lost interest in trying. But all that summer she remained as both a reproach and a mystery to me.

That winter my father died of pneumonia, after less than a week's illness. For some time I saw nothing around me, being completely immersed in my own pain and my mother's. When I looked outward once more, I scarcely noticed that Piquette Tonnerre was no longer at school. I do not remember seeing her at all until four years later, one Saturday night when Mavis and I were having Cokes in the Regal Café. The jukebox was booming like tuneful thunder, and beside it, leaning lightly on its chrome and its rainbow glass, was a girl.

Piquette must have been seventeen then, although she looked about twenty. I stared at her, astounded that anyone could have changed so much. Her face, so stolid and expressionless before, was animated now with a gaiety that was almost violent. She laughed and talked very loudly with the boys around her. Her lipstick was bright carmine, and her hair was cut short and frizzily permed. She had not been pretty as a child, and she was not pretty now, for her features were still heavy and blunt. But her dark and slightly slanted eyes were beautiful, and her skin-tight skirt and orange sweater displayed to enviable advantage a soft and slender body.

She saw me, and walked over. She teetered a little, but it was not due to her once-tubercular leg, for her limp was almost gone.

"Hi, Vanessa." Her voice still had the same hoarseness. "Long time no see, eh?"

"Hi," I said. "Where've you been keeping yourself, Piquette?"

"Oh, I been around," she said. "I been away almost two years now. Been all over the place—Winnipeg, Regina, Saskatoon. Jesus, what I could tell you! I come back this summer, but I ain't stayin'. You kids goin' to the dance?"

"No," I said abruptly, for this was a sore point with me. I was fifteen, and thought I was old enough to go to the Saturday-night dances at the Flamingo. My mother, however, thought otherwise.

"Y'oughta come," Piquette said. "I never miss one. It's just about the on'y thing in this jerkwater town that's any fun. Boy, you couldn' catch me stayin' here. I don' give a shit about this place. It stinks."

She sat down beside me, and I caught the harsh over-sweetness of her perfume.

"Listen, you wanna know something, Vanessa?" she confided, her voice only slightly blurred. "Your dad was the only person in Manawaka that ever done anything good to me."

I nodded speechlessly. I was certain she was speaking the truth. I knew a little more than I had that summer at Diamond Lake, but I could not reach her now any more than I had then. I was ashamed, ashamed of my own timidity, the frightened tendency to look the other way. Yet I felt no real warmth towards her—I only felt that I ought to, because of that distant summer and because my father had hoped she would be company for me, or perhaps that I would be for her, but it had not happened that way. At this moment, meeting her again, I had to admit that she repelled and embarrassed me, and I could not help despising the self-pity in her voice. I wished she would go away. I did not want to see her. I did not know what to say to her. It seemed that we had nothing to say to one another.

"I'll tell you something else," Piquette went on. "All the old bitches an' biddies in this town will sure be surprised. I'm gettin' married this fall—my boyfriend, he's an English fella, works in the stockyards in the city there, a very tall guy, got blond wavy hair. Gee, is he ever handsome. Got this real classy name. Alvin Gerald Cummings—some handle, eh? They call him Al."

For the merest instant, then, I saw her. I really did see her, for the first and only time in all the years we had both lived in the same town. Her defiant face, momentarily, became unguarded and unmasked, and in her eyes there was a terrifying hope.

"Gee, Piquette—" I burst out awkwardly, "that's swell. That's really wonderful. Congratulations—good luck—I hope you'll be happy—"

As I mouthed the conventional phrases, I could only guess how great her need must have been, that she had been forced to seek the very things she so bitterly rejected.

When I was eighteen, I left Manawaka and went away to college. At the end of my first year, I came back home for the summer. I spent the first few days in talking non-stop with my mother, as we exchanged all the news that somehow had not found its way into letters—what had happened in my life and what had happened here in Manawaka while I was away. My mother searched her memory for events that concerned people I knew.

"Did I ever write you about Piquette Tonnerre, Vanessa?" she asked one morning.

"No, I don't think so," I replied. "Last I heard of her, she was going to marry some guy in the city. Is she still there?"

My mother looked perturbed, and it was a moment before she spoke, as though she did not know how to express what she had to tell and wished she did not need to try.

"She's dead," she said at last. Then, as I stared at her, "Oh, Vanessa, when it happened, I couldn't help thinking of her as she was that summer—so sullen and gauche and badly dressed. I couldn't help wondering if we could have done something more at that time—but what could we do? She used to be around in the cottage there with me all day, and honestly, it was all I could do to get a word out of her. She didn't even talk to your father very much, although I think she liked him, in her way."

"What happened?" I asked.

"Either her husband left her, or she left him," my mother said. "I don't know which. Anyway, she came back here with two youngsters, both only babies—they must have been born very close together. She kept house, I guess, for Lazarus and her brothers, down in the valley there, in the old Tonnerre place. I used to see her on the street sometimes, but she never spoke to me. She'd put on an awful lot of weight, and she looked a mess, to tell you the truth, a real slattern, dressed any old how. She was up in court a couple of times—drunk and disorderly, of course. One Saturday night last winter, during the coldest weather, Piquette was alone in the shack with the children. The Tonnerres made home brew all the time, so I've heard, and Lazarus said later she'd been drinking most of the day when he and the boys went out that evening. They had an old woodstove there—you know the kind, with exposed pipes. The shack caught fire. Piquette didn't get out, and neither did the children."

I did not say anything. As so often with Piquette, there did not seem to be anything to say. There was a kind of silence around the image in my mind of the fire and the snow, and I wished I could put from my memory the look that I had seen once in Piquette's eyes.

I went up to Diamond Lake for a few days that summer, with Mavis and her family. The MacLeod cottage had been sold after my father's death, and I did not even go to look at it, not wanting to witness my long-ago kingdom possessed now by strangers. But one evening I went down to the shore by myself.

The small pier which my father had built was gone, and in its place there was a large and solid pier built by the government, for Galloping Mountain was now a national park, and Diamond Lake had been renamed Lake Wapakata, for it was felt that an Indian name would have a greater appeal to tourists. The one store had become several dozen, and the settlement had all the attributes of a flourishing resort—hotels, a dance-hall, cafés with neon signs, the penetrating odours of potato chips and hot dogs.

I sat on the government pier and looked out across the water. At night the lake at least was the same as it had always been, darkly shining and bearing within its black glass the streak of amber that was the path of the moon. There was no wind that evening, and everything was quiet all around me. It seemed too quiet, and then I realized that the loons were no longer here. I listened for some time, to make sure, but never once did I hear that long-drawn call, half mocking and half plaintive, spearing through the stillness across the lake.

I did not know what had happened to the birds. Perhaps they had gone away to some far place of belonging. Perhaps they had been unable to find such a place, and had simply died out, having ceased to care any longer whether they lived or not.

I remembered how Piquette had scorned to come along, when my father and I sat there and listened to the lake birds. It seemed to me now that in some unconscious and totally unrecognised way, Piquette might have been the only one, after all, who had heard the crying of the loons.

Topics for Discussion

1. What do the loons symbolize? How does Laurence go about transforming the birds into symbols?

2. Why does Vanessa become fascinated with Piquette? What does she represent to her?

3. How does Laurence depict the changes in the landscape and what is she saying by portraying these changes?

4. What impact does the setting of the story have on the events in the narrative?

5. How does Laurence convey the sense of tragedy at the end of the story?

6. What does Laurence mean at the end of the story when Vanessa notes that only Piquette heard the crying of the loons?

7. What role does history play in the story?

D.H. Lawrence

About the Author

D(avid) H(erbert) Lawrence, one of the leading novelists, poets and critics of the twentieth century, was born in Eastwood, Nottinghamshire, England, in 1885 and was educated at University College, Nottingham. He worked for a short period as a schoolteacher before becoming a full-time writer and artist. He eloped with his French professor's wife, Frieda Weekley (sister of the famous German aviator Baron von Richthofen, "the Red Baron" of the First World War), in 1912, and married her in 1914. During the war, Lawrence and his German wife fell out of public favour in England. They spent much of their life together travelling throughout Europe and the American Southwest (where Lawrence, as a painter, had a profound influence upon the artist community at Taos, New Mexico).

His frank depiction and discussion of matters relating to sexuality, and his fervent attacks on the puritanical attitudes of England during and after the First World War, prompted the banning and even burning of his books by an unenlightened English public.

In 1908 he had developed a lung infection, which developed into tuberculosis and eventually led to his death in France in 1930. Like Katherine Mansfield, with whom he shared both a literary and a passionate relationship, the effects of his disease resulted in a frenzy of literary activity: letters, critical essays, poems, novels, travel accounts and short stories.

Lawrence believed that modern industrialism had perverted man from his roots in an unbridled and unselfconscious nature. In *The Prussian Officer and Other Stories*, from which "Odour of Chrysanthemums" is taken, Lawrence chastised the "mechanistic" way of life that resulted from the overflow of science into human nature. He continued this theme in his novels *The Rainbow* (1915) and *Women in Love* (1920), a sequence of long narratives that traces the history of the Brangwen family from their roots in early industrial England through the eve of the First World War. His desire to relocate man, both physically and philosophically, in the sensual world, was also reflected in the villified *Lady Chatterley's Lover* (1929), which dealt with open sexuality and desire, and, owing to censorship, was not published in its entirety until 1960.

One reason why Lawrence's works took so long to be embraced by a cautious English readership was because he often attempted to use his characters as "mouthpieces" for his own philosophical concerns, many of which dealt with the physical, moral, sensual and intellectual liberation of individuals from constraining and limiting values of the time. He was prone to didactic discourse (known among scholars as "the Lawrentian rant"), focusing the narratives on the level of ideas rather than action.

Selected Works

The White Peacock (novel, 1911)
Sons and Lovers (novel, 1913)
The Prussian Officer and Other Stories (short stories, 1914)
The Rainbow (novel, 1915)
Women In Love (novel, 1920)
Kangaroo (novel, 1923)
Lady Chatterley's Lover (novel, 1929)

About the Story

D. H. Lawrence was born and raised in the industrial Midlands of England, which at the time was in transition from a pastoral, natural environment to an industrialized one. The stories in *The Prussian Officer*, including "Odour of Chrysanthemums," deal with the tensions that arise in individuals who are caught between nature and industrialism. Pay particular attention to the opening of the story, where in his subtle use of detail Lawrence paints a picture of a landscape that combines these opposites, a world of seeming contradictions where human beings are reduced to "engines."

A colliery is a coal mine and those who work in the mine are known as colliers.

In the opening section of the story, and again in the conclusion, Lawrence uses the image of the chrysanthemums. By repeating the image in several places he is establishing a *leitmotif* that unifies the story and through symbolic and personal associations conveys the themes of change, fallen beauty, life, death and the passage of time.

Odour of Chrysanthemums

I

The small locomotive engine, Number 4, came clanking, stumbling down from Selston with seven full waggons. It appeared round the corner with loud threats of speed, but the colt that it startled from among the gorse, which still flickered indistinctly in the raw afternoon, outdistanced it at a canter. A woman, walking up the railway line to Underwood, drew back into the hedge, held her basket aside, and watched the footplate of the engine advancing. The trucks thumped heavily past, one by one, with slow inevitable movement, as she stood insignificantly trapped between the jolting black waggons and the hedge; then they curved away towards the coppice where the withered oak leaves dropped noiselessly, while the birds, pulling at the scarlet hips beside the track, made off into the dusk that had already crept into the spinney. In the open, the smoke from the engine sank and cleaved to the rough grass. The fields were dreary and forsaken, and in the marshy strip that led to the whimsey, a reedy pit-pond, the fowls had already abandoned their run among the alders to roost in the tarred fowl-house. The pit-bank loomed up beyond the pond, flames like red sores licking its ashy sides, in the afternoon's stagnant light. Just beyond rose the tapering chimneys and the clumsy black headstocks of Brinsley Colliery. The two wheels were spinning fast up against the sky, and the winding-engine rapped out its little spasms. The miners were being turned up.

The engine whistled as it came into the wide bay of railway lines beside the colliery, where rows of trucks stood in harbour.

Miners, single, trailing and in groups, passed like shadows diverging home. At the edge of the ribbed level of sidings squat a low cottage, three steps down from the cinder track. A large bony vine clutched at the house, as if to claw down the tiled roof. Round the bricked yard grew a few wintry primroses. Beyond, the long garden sloped down to a bush-covered brook course. There were some twiggy apple trees, winter-crack trees, and ragged cabbages. Beside the path hung dishevelled pink chrysanthemums, like pink cloths hung on bushes. A woman came stooping out of the felt-covered fowl-house, half-way down the garden. She closed and padlocked the door, then drew herself erect, having brushed some bits from her white apron.

She was a tall woman of imperious mien, handsome, with definite black eyebrows. Her smooth black hair was parted exactly. For a few moments she stood steadily watching the miners as they passed along the railway; then she turned towards the brook course. Her face was calm and set, her mouth was closed with disillusionment. After a moment she called:

"John!" There was no answer. She waited, and then said distinctly:

"Where are you?"

"Here!" replied a child's sulky voice from among the bushes. The woman looked piercingly through the dusk.

"Are you at that brook?" she asked sternly.

For answer the child showed himself before the raspberry-canes that rose like whips. He was a small, sturdy boy of five. He stood quite still, defiantly.

"Oh!" said the mother, conciliated. "I thought you were down at that wet brook—and you remember what I told you—"

The boy did not move or answer.

"Come, come on in," she said more gently, "it's getting dark. There's your grandfather's engine coming down the line!"

The lad advanced slowly, with resentful, taciturn movement. He was dressed in trousers and waistcoat of cloth that was too thick and hard for the size of the garments. They were evidently cut down from a man's clothes.

As they went towards the house he tore at the ragged wisps of chrysanthemums and dropped the petals in handfuls along the path.

"Don't do that—it does look nasty," said his mother. He refrained, and she, suddenly pitiful, broke off a twig with three or four wan flowers and held them against her face. When mother and son reached the yard her hand hesitated, and instead of laying the flower aside, she pushed it in her apron-band. The mother and son stood at the foot of the three steps looking across the bay of lines at the passing home of the miners. The trundle of the small train was imminent. Suddenly the engine loomed past the house and came to a stop opposite the gate.

The engine-driver, a short man with round grey beard, leaned out of the cab high above the woman.

"Have you got a cup of tea?" he said in a cheery, hearty fashion.

It was her father. She went in, saying she would mash. Directly, she returned.

"I didn't come to see you on Sunday," began the little grey-bearded man.

"I didn't expect you," said his daughter.

The engine-driver winced; then reassuming his cheery, airy manner, he said:

"Oh, have you heard then? Well, and what do you think—?"

"I think it is soon enough," she replied.

At her brief censure the little man made an impatient gesture, and said coaxingly, yet with dangerous coldness:

"Well, what's a man to do? It's no sort of life for a man of my years, to sit at my own hearth like a stranger. And if I'm going to marry again it may as well be soon as late—what does it matter to anybody?"

The woman did not reply, but turned and went into the house. The man in the engine-cab stood assertive, till she returned with a cup of tea and a piece of bread and butter on a plate. She went up the steps and stood near the footplate of the hissing engine.

"You needn't 'a' brought me bread an' butter," said her father. "But a cup of tea"—he sipped appreciatively—"it's very nice." He sipped for a moment or two, then: "I hear as Walter's got another bout on," he said.

"When hasn't he?" said the woman bitterly.

"I heered tell of him in the Lord Nelson braggin' as he was going to spend that b—— afore he went: half a sovereign that was."

"When?" asked the woman.

"A' Sat'day night—I know that's true."

"Very likely," she laughed bitterly. "He gives me twenty-three shillings."

"Aye, it's a nice thing, when a man can do nothing with his money but make a beast of himself!" said the grey-whiskered man. The woman turned her head away. Her father swallowed the last of his tea and handed her the cup.

"Aye," he sighed, wiping his mouth. "It's a settler, it is—"

He put his hand on the lever. The little engine strained and groaned, and the train rumbled towards the crossing. The woman again looked across the metals. Darkness was settling over the spaces of the railway and trucks; the miners, in grey sombre groups, were still passing home. The winding-engine pulsed hurriedly, with brief pauses. Elizabeth Bates looked at the dreary flow of men, then she went indoors. Her husband did not come.

The kitchen was small and full of firelight; red coals piled glowing up the chimney mouth. All the life of the room seemed in the white, warm hearth and the steel fender reflecting the red fire. The cloth was laid for tea; cups glinted in the shadows. At the back, where the lowest stairs protruded into the room, the boy sat struggling with a knife and a piece of whitewood. He was almost hidden in the shadow. It was half past four. They had but to await the father's coming to begin tea. As the mother watched her son's sullen little struggle with the wood, she saw herself in his silence and pertinacity; she saw the father in the child's indifference to all but himself. She seemed to be occupied by her husband. He had probably gone past his home, slung past his own door, to drink before he came in, while his dinner spoiled and wasted in waiting. She glanced at the clock, then took the potatoes to strain them in the yard. The garden and fields beyond the brook were closed in uncertain darkness. When she rose with the saucepan, leaving the drain steaming into the night behind her, she saw the yellow lamps were lit along the high road that went up the hill away beyond the space of the railway lines and the field.

Then again she watched the men trooping home, fewer now and fewer.

Indoors the fire was sinking and the room was dark red. The woman put her saucepan on the hob, and set a batter pudding near the mouth of the oven. Then she stood unmoving. Directly, gratefully, came quick young steps to the door. Someone hung on the latch a moment, then a little girl entered and began pulling off her outdoor things, dragging a mass of curls, just ripening from gold to brown, over her eyes with her hat.

Her mother chid her for coming late from school, and said she would have to keep her at home the dark winter days.

"Why, mother, it's hardly a bit dark yet. The lamp's not lighted, and my father's not home."

"No, he isn't. But it's a quarter to five! Did you see anything of him?"

The child became serious. She looked at her mother with large, wistful blue eyes.

"No, mother, I've never seen him. Why? Has he come up an' gone past, to Old Brinsley? He hasn't, mother, 'cos I never saw him."

"He'd watch that," said the mother bitterly, "he'd take care as you didn't see him. But you may depend upon it, he's seated in the Prince of Wales. He wouldn't be this late."

The girl looked at her mother piteously.

"Let's have our teas, mother, should we?" said she.

The mother called John to table. She opened the door once more and looked out across the darkness of the lines. All was deserted: she could not hear the winding-engines.

"Perhaps," she said to herself, "he's stopped to get some ripping done."

They sat down to tea. John, at the end of the table near the door, was almost lost in the darkness. Their faces were hidden from each other. The girl crouched against the fender slowly moving a thick piece of bread before the fire. The lad, his face a dusky mark on the shadow, sat watching her who was transfigured in the red glow.

"I do think it's beautiful to look in the fire," said the child.

"Do you?" said her mother. "Why?"

"It's so red, and full of little caves—and it feels so nice, and you can fair smell it."

"It'll want mending directly," replied her mother, "and then if your father comes he'll carry on and say there never is a fire when a man comes home sweating from the pit. A public-house is always warm enough."

There was silence till the boy said complainingly: "Make haste, our Annie."

"Well, I am doing! I can't make the fire do it no faster, can I?"

"She keeps wafflin' it about so's to make'er slow," grumbled the boy.

"Don't have such an evil imagination, child," replied the mother.

Soon the room was busy in the darkness with the crisp sound of crunching. The mother ate very little. She drank her tea determinedly, and sat thinking. When she rose her anger was evident in the stern unbending of her head. She looked at the pudding in the fender, and broke out:

"It is a scandalous thing as a man can't even come home to his dinner! If it's crozzled up to a cinder I don't see why I should care. Past his very door he goes to get to a public-house, and here I sit with his dinner waiting for him—"

She went out. As she dropped piece after piece of coal on the red fire, the shadows fell on the walls, till the room was almost in total darkness.

"I canna see," grumbled the invisible John. In spite of herself, the mother laughed.

"You know the way to your mouth," she said. She set the dustpan outside the door. When she came again like a shadow on the hearth, the lad repeated, complaining sulkily:

"I canna see."

"Good gracious!" cried the mother irritably, "you're as bad as your father if it's a bit dusk!"

Nevertheless she took a paper spill from the sheaf on the mantelpiece and proceeded to light the lamp that hung from the ceiling in the middle of the room. As she reached up, her figure displayed itself just rounding with maternity.

"Oh, mother—!" exclaimed the girl.

"What?" said the woman, suspended in the act of putting the lamp glass over the flame. The copper reflector shone handsomely on her, as she stood with uplifted arm, turning to face her daughter.

"You've got a flower in your apron!" said the child, in a little rapture at this unusual event.

"Goodness me!" exclaimed the woman, relieved. "One would think the house was afire." She replaced the glass and waited a moment before turning up the wick. A pale shadow was seen floating vaguely on the floor.

"Let me smell!" said the child, still rapturously, coming forward and putting her face to her mother's waist.

"Go along, silly!" said the mother, turning up the lamp. The light revealed their suspense so that the woman felt it almost unbearable. Annie was still bending at her waist. Irritably, the mother took the flowers out from her apron-band.

"Oh, mother—don't take them out!" Annie cried, catching her hand and trying to replace the sprig.

"Such nonsense!" said the mother, turning away. The child put the pale chrysanthemums to her lips, murmuring:

"Don't they smell beautiful!"

Her mother gave a short laugh.

"No," she said, "not to me. It was chrysanthemums when I married him, and chrysanthemums when you were born, and the first time they ever brought him home drunk, he'd got brown chrysanthemums in his button-hole."

She looked at the children. Their eyes and their parted lips were wondering. The mother sat rocking in silence for some time. Then she looked at the clock.

"Twenty minutes to six!" In a tone of fine bitter carelessness she continued: "Eh, he'll not come now till they bring him. There he'll stick! But he needn't come rolling in here in his pit-dirt, for I won't wash him. He can lie on the floor—Eh, what a fool I've been, what a fool! And this is what I came here for, to this dirty hole, rats and all, for him to clink past his very door. Twice last week—he's begun now—"

She silenced herself, and rose to clear the table.

While for an hour or more the children played, subduedly intent, fertile of imagination, united in fear of the mother's wrath, and in dread of their father's home-coming. Mrs. Bates sat in her rocking-chair making a "singlet' of thick cream-coloured flannel, which gave a dull wounded sound as she tore off the grey edge. She worked at her sewing with energy, listening to the children, and her anger wearied itself, lay down to rest, opening its eyes from time to time and steadily watching, its ears raised to listen. Sometimes even her anger quailed and shrank, and the mother suspended her sewing, tracing the footsteps that thudded along the sleepers outside; she would lift her head sharply to bid the children "hush," but she recovered herself in time, and the footsteps went past the gate, and the children were not flung out of their play-world.

But at last Annie sighed, and gave in. She glanced at her waggon of slippers, and loathed the game. She turned plaintively to her mother.

"Mother!"—but she was inarticulate.

John crept out like a frog from under the sofa. His mother glanced up.

"Yes," she said, "just look at those shirt-sleeves!"

The boy held them out to survey them, saying nothing. Then somebody called in a hoarse voice away down the line, and suspense bristled in the room, till two people had gone by outside, talking.

"It is time for bed," said the mother.

"My father hasn't come," wailed Annie plaintively. But her mother was primed with courage.

"Never mind. They'll bring him when he does come—like a log." She meant there would be no scene. "And he may sleep on the floor till he wakes himself. I know he'll not go to work tomorrow after this!"

The children had their hands and faces wiped with a flannel. They were very quiet. When they had put on their night-dresses, they said their prayers, the boy mumbling. The mother looked down at them, at the brown silken bush of intertwining curls in the nape of the girl's neck, at the little black head of the lad, and her heart burst with anger at their father who caused all three such distress. The children hid their faces in her skirts for comfort.

When Mrs. Bates came down, the room was strangely empty, with a tension of expectancy. She took up her sewing and stitched for some time without raising her head. Meantime her anger was tinged with fear.

II

The clock struck eight and she rose suddenly, dropping her sewing on her chair. She went to the stairfoot door, opened it, listening. Then she went out, locking the door behind her.

Something scuffled in the yard, and she started, though she knew it was only the rats with which the place was overrun. The night was very dark. In the great bay of railway lines, bulked with trucks, there was no trace of light, only away back she could see a few yellow lamps at the pit-top, and the red smear of the burning pit-bank on the night. She hurried along the edge of the track, then, crossing the converging lines, came to the stile by the white gates, whence she emerged on the road. Then the fear which had led her shrank. People were walking up to New Brinsley; she saw the lights in the houses; twenty yards further on were the broad windows of the Prince of Wales, very warm and bright, and the loud voices of men could be heard distinctly. What a fool she had been to imagine that anything had happened to him! He was merely drinking over there at the Prince of Wales. She faltered. She had never yet been to fetch him, and she never would go. So she continued her walk towards the long straggling line of houses, standing blank on the highway. She entered a passage between the dwellings.

"Mr. Rigley?—Yes! Did you want him? No, he's not in at this minute."

The raw-boned woman leaned forward from her dark scullery and peered at the other, upon whom fell a dim light through the blind of the kitchen window.

"Is it Mrs. Bates?" she asked in a tone tinged with respect.

"Yes. I wondered if your Master was at home. Mine hasn't come yet."

"'Asn't 'e! Oh, Jack's been 'ome an' 'ad 'is dinner an' gone out. 'E's just gone for 'alf an hour afore bedtime. Did you call at the Prince of Wales?"

"No—"

"No, you didn't like—! It's not very nice." The other woman was indulgent. There was an awkward pause. "Jack never said nothink about—about your Mester," she said.

"No!—I expect he's stuck in there!"

Elizabeth Bates said this bitterly, and with recklessness. She knew that the woman across the yard was standing at her door listening, but she did not care. As she turned:

"Stop a minute! I'll go an' ask Jack if 'e knows anythink," said Mrs. Rigley.

"Oh, no—I wouldn't like to put—?"

"Yes, I will, if you'll just step inside an' see as th' childer doesn't come downstairs and set theirselves afire."

Elizabeth Bates, murmuring a remonstrance, stepped inside. The other woman apologized for the state of the room.

The kitchen needed apology. There were little frocks and trousers and childish undergarments on the squab and on the floor, and a litter of playthings everywhere. On the black American cloth of the table were pieces of bread and cake, crusts, slops, and a teapot with cold tea.

"Eh, ours is just as bad," said Elizabeth Bates, looking at the woman, not at the house. Mrs. Rigley put a shawl over her head and hurried out, saying:

"I shanna be a minute."

The other sat, noting with faint disapproval the general untidiness of the room. Then she fell to counting the shoes of various sizes scattered over the floor. There were twelve. She sighed and said to herself, "No wonder!"—glancing at the litter. There came the scratching of two pairs of feet on the yard, and the Rigleys entered. Elizabeth Bates rose. Rigley was a big man, with very large bones. His head looked particularly bony.

Across his temple was a blue scar, caused by a wound got in the pit, a wound in which the coal-dust remained blue like tattooing.

"'Asna 'e come whoam yit?" asked the man, without any form of greeting, but with deference and sympathy. "I couldna say wheer he is—'e's non ower theer!"—he jerked his head to signify the Prince of Wales.

"'E's 'appen gone up to th' Yew," said Mrs. Rigley.

There was another pause. Rigley had evidently something to get off his mind:

"Ah left 'im finishin' a stint," he began. "Loose-all 'ad bin gone about ten minutes when we com'n away, an' I shouted "Are ter comin', Walt?' an' 'e said, 'Go on, Ah shanna be but a'ef a minnit,' se we com'n ter th' bottom, me an' Bowers, thinkin' as 'e wor just behint, an' 'ud come up i' th' next bantle—"

He stood perplexed, as if answering a charge of deserting his mate. Elizabeth Bates, now again certain of disaster, hastened to reassure him:

"I expect 'e's gone up to th' Yew Tree, as you say. It's not the first time. I've fretted myself into a fever before now. He'll come home when they carry him."

"Ay, isn't it too bad!" deplored the other woman.

"I'll just step up to Dick's an' see if 'e *is* theer," offered the man, afraid of appearing alarmed, afraid of taking liberties.

"Oh, I wouldn't think of bothering you that far," said Elizabeth Bates, with emphasis, but he knew she was glad of his offer.

As they stumbled up the entry, Elizabeth Bates heard Rigley's wife run across the yard and open her neighbour's door. At this, suddenly all the blood in her body seemed to switch away from her heart.

"Mind!" warned Rigley. "Ah've said many a time as Ah'd fill up them ruts in this entry, sumb'dy 'll be breakin' their legs yit."

She recovered herself and walked quickly along with the miner.

"I don't like leaving the children in bed, and nobody in the house," she said.

"No, you dunna!" he replied courteously. They were soon at the gate of the cottage.

"Well, I shanna be many minnits. Dunna you be frettin' now, 'e'll be all right," said the butty.

"Thank you very much, Mr. Rigley," she replied.

"You're welcome!" he stammered, moving away. "I shanna be many minnits."

The house was quiet. Elizabeth Bates took off her hat and shawl, and rolled back the rug. When she had finished, she sat down. It was a few minutes past nine. She was startled by the rapid chuff of the winding-engine at the pit, and the sharp whirr of the brakes on the rope as it descended. Again she felt the painful sweep of her blood, and she put her hand to her side, saying aloud, "Good gracious!—it's only the nine o'clock deputy going down," rebuking herself.

She sat still, listening. Half an hour of this, and she was wearied out.

"What am I working myself up like this for?" she said pitiably to herself, "I s'll only be doing myself some damage."

She took out her sewing again.

At a quarter to ten there were footsteps. One person! She watched for the door to open. It was an elderly woman, in a black bonnet and a black woollen shawl—his mother. She was about sixty years old, pale, with blue eyes, and her face all wrinkled and lamentable. She shut the door and turned to her daughter-in-law peevishly.

"Eh, Lizzie, whatever shall we do, whatever shall we do!" she cried.

Elizabeth drew back a little, sharply.

"What is it, mother?" she said.

The elder woman seated herself on the sofa.

"I don't know, child, I can't tell you!"—she shook her head slowly. Elizabeth sat watching her, anxious and vexed.

"I don't know," replied the grandmother, sighing very deeply. "There's no end to my troubles, there isn't. The things I've gone through, I'm sure it's enough—!" She wept without wiping her eyes, the tears running.

"But, mother," interrupted Elizabeth, "what do you mean? What is it?"

The grandmother slowly wiped her eyes. The fountains of her tears were stopped by Elizabeth's directness. She wiped her eyes slowly.

"Poor child! Eh, you poor thing!" she moaned. "I don't know what we're going to do, I don't—and you as you are—it's a thing, it is indeed!"

Elizabeth waited.

"Is he dead?" she asked, and at the words her heart swung violently, though she felt a slight flush of shame at the ultimate extravagance of the question. Her words sufficiently frightened the old lady, almost brought her to herself.

"Don't say so. Elizabeth! We'll hope it's not as bad as that; no, may the Lord spare us that, Elizabeth. Jack Rigley came just as I was sittin" down to a glass afore going to bed, an' 'e said, ''Appen you'll go down th' line, Mrs. Bates. Walt's had an accident. 'Appen you'll go an' sit wi' 'er till we can get him home.' I hadn't time to ask him a word afore he was gone. An' I put my bonnet on an' come straight down, Lizzie. I thought to myself, 'Eh, that poor blessed child, if anybody should come an' tell her of a sudden, there's no knowin' what'll 'appen to 'er.' You mustn't let it upset you, Lizzie—or you know what to expect. How long is it, six months—or is it five, Lizzie? Ay!"—the old woman shook her head—"time slips on, it slips on! Ay!"

Elizabeth's thoughts were busy elsewhere. If he was killed—would she be able to manage on the little pension and what she could earn?—

she counted up rapidly. If he was hurt—they wouldn't take him to the hospital—how tiresome he would be to nurse!—but perhaps she'd be able to get him away from the drink and his hateful ways. She would—while he was ill. The tears offered to come to her eyes at the picture. But what sentimental luxury was this she was beginning? She turned to consider the children. At any rate she was absolutely necessary for them. They were her business.

"Ay!" repeated the old woman, "it seems but a week or two since he brought me his first wages. Ay—he was a good lad, Elizabeth, he was, in his way. I don't know why he got to be such a trouble, I don't. He was a happy lad at home, only full of spirits. But there's no mistake he's been a handful of trouble, he has! I hope the Lord'll spare him to mend his ways. I hope so, I hope so. You've had a sight o' trouble with him, Elizabeth, you have indeed. But he was a jolly enough lad wi' me, he was, I can assure you. I don't know how it is...."

The old woman continued to muse aloud, a monotonous irritating sound, while Elizabeth thought concentratedly, startled once, when she heard the winding-engine chuff quickly, and the brakes skirr with a shriek. Then she heard the engine more slowly, and the brakes made no sound. The old woman did not notice. Elizabeth waited in suspense. The mother-in-law talked, with lapses into silence.

"But he wasn't your son, Lizzie, an' it makes a difference. Whatever he was, I remember him when he was little an' I learned to understand him and to make allowances. You've got to make allowances for them—"

It was half past ten, and the old woman was saying: "But it's trouble from beginning to end; you're never too old for trouble, never too old for that—" when the gate banged back, and there were heavy feet on the steps.

"I'll go, Lizzie, let me go," cried the old woman, rising. But Elizabeth was at the door. It was a man in pit-clothes.

"They're bringin' 'im, Missis," he said. Elizabeth's heart halted a moment. Then it surged on again, almost suffocating her.

"Is he—is it bad?" she asked.

The man turned away, looking at the darkness:

"The doctor says 'e'd been dead hours. 'E saw 'im i' th' lamp-cabin."

The old woman, who stood just behind Elizabeth, dropped into a chair, and folded her hands, crying: "Oh, my boy, my boy!"

"Hush!" said Elizabeth, with a sharp twitch of a frown.

"Be still, mother, don't waken th' children: I wouldn't have them down for anything!"

The old woman moaned softly, rocking herself. The man was drawing away. Elizabeth took a step forward.

"How was it?" she asked.

"Well, I couldn't say for sure," the man replied, very ill at ease. "'E wor finishin' a stint an' th' butties 'ad gone, an' a lot o' stuff come down atop 'n 'im."

"And crushed him?" cried the widow, with a shudder.

"No," said the man, "it fell at th' back of 'im. 'E wor under th' face, an' it niver touched 'im. It shut 'im in. It seems 'e wor smothered."

Elizabeth shrank back. She heard the old woman behind her cry:

"What?—what did 'e say it was?"

The man replied, more loudly: "E wor smothered!"

Then the old woman wailed aloud, and this relieved Elizabeth.

"Oh, mother," she said, putting her hand on the old woman, "don't waken th' children, don't waken th' children."

She wept a little, unknowing, while the old mother rocked herself and moaned. Elizabeth remembered that they were bringing him home, and she must be ready. "They'll lay him in the parlour," she said to herself, standing a moment pale and perplexed.

Then she lighted a candle and went into the tiny room. The air was cold and damp, but she could not make a fire, there was no fireplace. She set down the candle and looked round. The candle-light glittered on the lustre-glasses, on the two vases that held some of the pink chrysanthemums, and on the dark mahogany. There was a cold, deathly smell of chrysanthemums in the room. Elizabeth stood looking at the flowers. She turned away, and calculated whether there would be room to lay him on the floor, between the couch and the chiffonier. She pushed the chairs aside. There would be room to lay him down and to step round him. Then she fetched the old red tablecloth, and another old cloth, spreading them down to save her bit of carpet. She shivered on leaving the parlour; so, from the dresser-drawer she took a clean shirt and put it at the fire to air. All the time her mother-in-law was rocking herself in the chair and moaning.

"You'll have to move from there, mother," said Elizabeth. "They'll be bringing him in. Come in the rocker."

The old mother rose mechanically, and seated herself by the fire, continuing to lament. Elizabeth went into the pantry for another candle, and there, in the little penthouse under the naked tiles, she heard them coming. She stood still in the pantry doorway, listening. She heard them pass the end of the house, and come awkwardly down the three steps, a jumble of shuffling footsteps and muttering voices. The old woman was silent. The men were in the yard.

Then Elizabeth heard Matthews, the manager of the pit, say: "You go in first, Jim. Mind!"

The door came open, and the two women saw a collier backing into the room, holding one end of a stretcher, on which they could see the nailed pit-boots of the dead man. The two carriers halted, the man at the head stooping to the lintel of the door.

"Wheer will you have him?" asked the manager, a short, white-bearded man.

Elizabeth roused herself and came from the pantry carrying the unlighted candle.

"In the parlour," she said.

"In there, Jim!" pointed the manager, and the carriers backed round into the tiny room. The coat with which they had covered the body fell off as they awkwardly turned through the two doorways, and the women saw their man, naked to the waist, lying stripped for work. The old woman began to moan in a low voice of horror.

"Lay th' stretcher at th' side," snapped the manager, "an put 'im on th' cloths. Mind now, mind! Look you now—!"

One of the men had knocked off a vase of chrysanthemums. He stared awkwardly, then they set down the stretcher. Elizabeth did not look at her husband. As soon as she could get in the room, she went and picked up the broken vase and the flowers.

"Wait a minute!" she said.

The three men waited in silence while she mopped up the water with a duster.

"Eh, what a job, what a job, to be sure!" the manager was saying, rubbing his brow with trouble and perplexity. "Never knew such a thing in my life, never! He'd no business to ha' been left. I never knew such a thing in my life! Fell over him clean as a whistle, an' shut him in. Not four foot of space, there wasn't—yet it scarce bruised him."

He looked down at the dead man, lying prone, half naked, all grimed with coal-dust.

"'Sphyxiated," the doctor said. It is the most terrible job I've ever known. Seems as if it was done o' purpose. Clean over him, an' shut 'im in, like a mouse-trap"—he made a sharp, descending gesture with his hand.

The colliers standing by jerked aside their heads in hopeless comment.

The horror of the thing bristled upon them all.

Then they heard the girl's voice upstairs calling shrilly:

"Mother, mother—who is it? Mother, who is it?"

Elizabeth hurried to the foot of the stairs and opened the door:

"Go to sleep!" she commanded sharply. "What are you shouting about? Go to sleep at once—there's nothing—"

Then she began to mount the stairs. They could hear her on the boards, and on the plaster floor of the little bedroom. They could hear her distinctly:

"What's the matter now?—what's the matter with you, silly thing?"—her voice was much agitated, with an unreal gentleness.

"I thought it was some men come," said the plaintive voice of the child. "Has he come?"

"Yes, they've brought him. There's nothing to make a fuss about. Go to sleep now, like a good child."

They could hear her voice in the bedroom, they waited whilst she covered the children under the bedclothes.

"Is he drunk?" asked the girl, timidly, faintly.

"No! No—he's not! He—he's asleep."

"Is he asleep downstairs?"

"Yes—and don't make a noise."

There was silence for a moment, then the men heard the frightened child again:

"What's that noise?"

"It's nothing, I tell you, what are you bothering for?"

The noise was the grandmother moaning. She was oblivious of everything, sitting on her chair rocking and moaning. The manager put his hand on her arm and bade her "Sh—sh!!"

The old woman opened her eyes and looked at him. She was shocked by this interruption, and seemed to wonder.

"What time is it?"—the plaintive thin voice of the child, sinking back unhappily into sleep, asked this last question.

"Ten o'clock," answered the mother more softly. Then she must have bent down and kissed the children.

Matthews beckoned to the men to come away. They put on their caps and took up the stretcher. Stepping over the body, they tiptoed out of the house. None of them spoke till they were far from the wakeful children.

When Elizabeth came down she found her mother alone on the parlour floor, leaning over the dead man, the tears dropping on him.

"We must lay him out," the wife said. She put on the kettle, then returning knelt at the feet, and began to unfasten the knotted leather laces. The room was clammy and dim with only one candle, so that she had to bend her face almost to the floor. At last she got off the heavy boots and put them away.

"You must help me now," she whispered to the old woman. Together they stripped the man.

When they arose, saw him lying in the naïve dignity of death, the women stood arrested in fear and respect. For a few moments they remained still, looking down, the old mother whimpering. Elizabeth felt countermanded. She saw him, how utterly inviolable he lay in himself. She had nothing to do with him. She could not accept it. Stooping, she laid her hand on him, in claim. He was still warm, for the mine was hot where he had died. His mother had his face between her hands, and was murmuring incoherently. The old tears fell in succession as drops from wet leaves; the mother was not weeping, merely her tears flowed. Elizabeth embraced the body of her husband, with cheek and lips. She seemed to be listening, inquiring, trying to get some connexion. But she could not. She was driven away. He was impregnable.

She rose, went into the kitchen, where she poured warm water into a bowl, brought soap and flannel and a soft towel.

"I must wash him," she said.

Then the old mother rose stiffly, and watched Elizabeth as she carefully washed his face, carefully brushing the big blond moustache from his mouth with the flannel. She was afraid with a bottomless fear, so she ministered to him. The old woman, jealous, said:

"Let me wipe him!"—and she kneeled on the other side drying slowly as Elizabeth washed, her big black bonnet sometimes brushing the dark head of her daughter-in-law. They worked thus in silence for a long time. They never forgot it was death, and the touch of the man's dead body gave them strange emotions, different in each of the women; a great dread possessed them both, the mother felt the lie was given to her womb, she was denied; the wife felt the utter isolation of the human soul, the child within her was a weight apart from her.

At last it was finished. He was a man of handsome body, and his face showed no traces of drink. He was blond, full-fleshed, with fine limbs. But he was dead.

"Bless him," whispered his mother, looking always at his face, and speaking out of sheer terror. "Dear lad—bless him!" She spoke in a faint, sibilant ecstasy of fear and mother love.

Elizabeth sank down again to the floor, and put her face against his neck, and trembled and shuddered. But she had to draw away again. He was dead, and her living flesh had no place against his. A great dread and weariness held her; she was so unavailing. Her life was gone like this.

"White as milk he is, clear as a twelve-month baby, bless him, the darling!" the old mother murmured to herself. "Not a mark on him, clear and clean and white, beautiful as ever a child was made," she murmured with pride. Elizabeth kept her face hidden.

"He went peaceful, Lizzie—peaceful as sleep. Isn't he beautiful, the lamb? Ay—he must ha' made his peace, Lizzie. 'Appen he made it all right, Lizzie, shut in there. He'd have time. He wouldn't look like this if he hadn't made his peace. The lamb, the dear lamb. Eh, but he had a hearty laugh. I loved to hear it. He had the heartiest laugh, Lizzie, as a lad—"

Elizabeth looked up. The man's mouth was fallen back, slightly open under the cover of the moustache. The eyes, half shut, did not show glazed in the obscurity. Life with its smoky burning gone from him, had left him apart and utterly alien to her. And she knew what a stranger he was to her. In her womb was ice of fear, because of this separate stranger with whom she had been living as one flesh. Was this what it all meant—utter, intact separateness, obscured by heat of living? In dread she turned her face away. The face was too deadly. There had been nothing between them, and yet they had come together, exchanging their nakedness repeatedly. Each time he had taken her, they had been two isolated beings, far apart as now. He was no more responsible than she. The child was like ice in her womb. For as she looked at the dead man, her mind, cold and detached, said clearly: "Who am I? What have I been doing? I have been fighting a husband who did not exist. He existed all the time. What wrong have I done? What was that I have been living with? There lies the reality, this man." And her soul died in her for fear: she knew she had never seen him, he had never seen her, they had met in the dark and had fought in the dark, not knowing whom they met nor whom they fought. And now she saw, and turned silent in seeing. For she had been wrong. She had said he was something he was not; she had felt familiar with him. Whereas he was apart all the while, living as she never lived, feeling as she never felt.

In fear and shame she looked at his naked body, that she had known falsely. And he was the father of her children. Her soul was torn from her body and stood apart. She looked at his naked body and was ashamed, as if she had denied it. After all, it was itself. It seemed awful to her. She looked at his face, and she turned her own face to the wall. For his look was other than hers, his way was not her way. She had denied him what he was—she saw it now. She had refused him as himself. And this had been her life, and his life. She was grateful to death, which restored the truth. And she knew she was not dead.

And all the while her heart was bursting with grief and pity for him. What had he suffered? What stretch of horror for this helpless man! She was rigid with agony. She had not been able to help him. He had been cruelly injured, this naked man, this other being, and she could make no reparation. There were the children—but the children belonged to life. This dead man had nothing to do with them. He and she were only channels through which life had flowed to issue in the children. She was a mother—but how awful she knew it now to have been a wife. And he, dead now, how awful he must have felt it to be a husband. She felt that in the next world he would be a stranger to her. If they met there, in the beyond, they would only be ashamed of what had been before. The children had come, for some mysterious reason, out of both of them. But the children did not unite them. Now he was dead, she knew how eternally he was apart from her, how eternally he had nothing more to do with her. She saw this episode of her life closed. They had denied each other in life. Now he had withdrawn. An anguish came over her. It was finished then: it had become hopeless between them long before he died. Yet he had been her husband. But how little!

"Have you got his shirt, 'Lizabeth?"

Elizabeth turned without answering, though she strove to weep and behave as her mother-in-law expected. But she could not, she was silenced. She went into the kitchen and returned with the garment.

"It is aired," she said, grasping the cotton shirt here and there to try. She was almost ashamed to handle him; what right had she or anyone to lay hands on him; but her touch was humble on his body. It was hard work to clothe him. He was so heavy and inert. A terrible dread gripped her all the while: that he could be so heavy and utterly inert, unresponsive, apart. The horror of the distance between them was almost too much for her—it was so infinite a gap she must look across.

At last it was finished. They covered him with a sheet and left him lying, with his face bound. And she fastened the door of the little parlour, lest the children should see what was lying there. Then, with peace sunk heavy on her heart, she went about making tidy the kitchen. She knew she submitted to life, which was her immediate master. But from death, her ultimate master, she winced with fear and shame.

Topics for Discussion

1. What do the chrysanthemums represent? What is the significance of the breaking of the vase of chrysanthemums by one of the miners?

2. How does Lawrence establish the setting in the opening sections of the story and what is the relationship between the setting and the plot?

3. What sort of relationship does the wife have with her husband and how does Lawrence convey this relationship?

4. How does Lawrence define life?

5. Why does the woman remain calm after she knows that her husband is dead?

6. In the first part of the story, how does Lawrence sustain the sense of expectation with regard to the husband's late homecoming from the mine?

7. What is the relationship between the mother and her children, especially the unborn child in her womb?

8. What is the ritual significance in the washing of the miner's body?

9. How does Lawrence define "mechanistic" behaviour in the story? What does he mean by "mechanically" when the wife's mother rises from her chair?

SKY Lee

About the Author
SKY Lee was born in Port Alberni, British Columbia, in 1952 and educated at the University of British Columbia and Douglas College in B.C. She has worked as a nurse and children's book illustrator, and lives on the West Coast.

As a feminist and member of the Chinese-Canadian community, Lee has been instrumental in giving a voice to Chinese-Canadian women. Her landmark novel, *The Disappearing Moon Cafe* (1990), chronicled four generations of a Chinese family in Vancouver from the end of the last century through to the present. The plot of that brilliant novel reads like a Greek tragedy as it touches on themes of incest, buried truth, misplaced identity and tragically repeating history. It is related through a succession of ancestral voices, each of whom tell her story—stories in which the same mistakes are repeated, generation after generation, until the final voice, that of the narrator and storyteller, brings order to the chaos of the chronicle by exposing the truth of her forebears' lives.

Selected Works
The Disappearing Moon Cafe (novel, 1990)
Bellydancer (short stories, 1994)

About the Story
Three middle-aged, single Chinese women (half-sisters by the same father and various mothers), tenants of the same Vancouver apartment building, receive eviction notices. While they attempt to extricate themselves from this predicament, the three women share their pasts and family connections. In the course of the story, Lee returns to her theme from *The Disappearing Moon Cafe* of the gulf of power between men and women in the Chinese-Canadian community, and how the women must plot and plan and use their wiles to overcome their relatively weak situations.

The Soong Sisters

Until they got their eviction notices, Sue Mei, May Lynn, and Su-lin were bickering as usual. At the time, the argument was about Su-lin's old beans in the rooftop garden. And that, of course, got batted along to other points of contention, such as May Lynn's good-for-nothing, mangy old carpet of a dog. But none of this was all that serious. May Lynn and Su-lin, who do most of the spatting and batting, still slept with their apartment doors open—the summer evenings being hot and humid, and the Vancouver of 1972, which Sue Mei contemplated from the top of their four-storey apartment building, being quiet and peaceful. Up the street, the many-splendoured neon lights of chinatown were as yet the brightest flowers of the night.

When the notices to evict actually arrived in the post, Sue Mei was sitting at May Lynn's kitchen table, eating the crappiest things for breakfast. Instant coffee. Waffles that tasted like their cardboard box, swimming in a toxic brown puddle of corn syrup, smeared with margarine kept in a greasy, plastic yellow container with its printed label flaking off. And reading the local newspaper, swallowing it like a daily source of disgruntlement. The ink on the newsprint comes off, but the stories decidedly do not, was her predictable complaint. May Lynn sipped herbal tea, reading the *Manchester Guardian*. Her mutt smelled old and doggy. But this was perhaps not the time for Sue Mei to mention that again, because May Lynn paid for all the newspaper subscriptions, and the good ol' morning sun does shine through once in a while.

By the time the notion of eviction arrested their attentions, these grey framed envelopes from the powers-that-be—i.e., governments and banks—were becoming less and less a curiosity. After all, hadn't they all three once successfully tackled the omnipotence of the passport office for their journey back to their ancestral villages near Hoy Saan? Sue Mei claimed that if they could do that, they could do anything. She had done all the talking for them to the perfunctory at the wooden counter, referring to the trip as their travels abroad. A few years ago, that seemed quite the occasion, for which she took her fur coat out of storage and unwrapped her snap-top, black leather purse. (These days, Sue Mei grumbled bitterly about the diminishing quality of life. Woodward's beautiful food floor was kaput. She trudged over to the Dollar Meat Market in worn-out sneakers and tacky sweat pants, and she, too, kept her change purse in a pocket sewn into her waistband.)

"We're being evicted," offered Sue Mei to the everlasting, boring calm of the tiny kitchen nook with its faded yellow arborite, its hobbled and chipped table; to the plastic squeeze bottles; to the cracked cups drying in the drainer, to the ten thousand years of soot on the outside of the window that overlooked the regurgitating garbage bins in the alley.

May Lynn's mouth dropped open. Then they both turned their heads and yelled simultaneously out the door, down the hall to Su-lin's apartment, where she was probably feeding her cagefuls of rats and mice, cooing at the little horrors like beloved children.

"Suuuee weee," they mimicked without giggles this time, "Suee weee." Until they heard Su-lin's slippers shuffling along the creaking linoleum floor, slapping out a slavish rhythm. Until her lovely face popped around, looking for goodies.

But then there was no sense in mentioning the eviction notices until Su-lin got settled. She'd have to test the fading warmth of the teapot, or get an extra plate or sniff at the instant coffee in Sue Mei's cup first. Oh, and here come those leechy cats of hers, thought Sue Mei cattily! Oh, and even better, the snoop from downstairs, nicknamed Madame Cabbage Face!

"Chou Taitai was nice enough to come and visit." Su-lin smiled at Madame Cabbage Face, who had followed her across the threshold, only to be abruptly shoved back out by Sue Mei. But wasn't this kind of brutish behaviour expected of Sue Mei? Chou Taitai and she have had words before. One squawk more or less hardly makes a difference in this shitty henhouse, Sue Mei had once told her in a livid snit, but today she took some pains to be nice.

"Oh, then perhaps Chou Taitai would be kind enough to come back another time? Because we have private business to attend to," she said and closed the door.

"What business?" asked Su-lin, who was looking for pet food and hardly listening. At their feet there were some rumblings because May Lynn's dog did not get along with Su-lin's cats. And Sue Mei was feeling very pressured by now.

"We got eviction notices," blurted out Sue Mei. Aah, finally, the appreciative silence that she very much needed to hear.

Days later, Sue Mei found herself groping through decades of dust in the closet and thinking mournfully, Aah, life is but a passing dream. Nothing fit her any more.

"What on earth do they wear these days?" she asked May Lynn, even though she knew that nothing had really changed except her way of looking at things but, as a result, everything has changed. And, of course, May Lynn was no help.

"Sue Mei, for god's sake," she said, exasperated. "You think it matters to them what you wear? Those greedy buggers are hoping we show up wearing a coffin as soon as is convenient. Anything less is incidental. Hey, if you really want to make a big splash, go naked and fart in their ugly mugs. That ought to get their attention, love. Go as stark raving naked as you seem to feel."

All Sue Mei found was an old suitcase full of her mother's old yellowed magazine clippings, including one that recited that little ditty about the Soong Sisters of China.

One loved money,
the other loved power,
and the third loved China.

She knew that May Lynn was right. Disguise is everything. Only she wished she knew for sure whether it was a disguise of power or a disguise of powerlessness.

"When did I ever say anything that could even be remotely interpreted like that?" disputed May Lynn. But she noticed Sue Mei's disquiet and offered, "We'll go shopping at Sandra's of Vancouver. Nothing but the best will do for my honey."

However, when they got there, they found a health-food store instead. It was another low blow, and Sue Mei seemed to crumple a little more. Just when and where did we get old, she wondered, watching May Lynn wander up and down the plank aisles in sturdy leather walking shoes, looking at vitamins and avocados. Her hair was quite peppery now, but her smile at the clerk in a red gingham apron who handed her a free bag of popcorn was still as fresh as the day they met. Her face was full of fine fret lines though her eyes were amazingly child-like; and she was immensely pleased with herself, searching out Sue Mei to tell her, "That sweet young thing over there informs me that popcorn is a very good source of roughage."

"Well, it constipates the heck out of me," commented Sue Mei rather dryly. Nobody offered her little free samples when she stomped by.

Luckily the little Mozart Tea Shop was still across the street, and they ducked in for tea and cake. But it was crowded, and May Lynn noticed how Sue Mei's face clenched a little more, so she asked ever so sweetly if they could get ahead of the lineup, because her friend was feeling faint. And people, being as kind and generous as she knew them to be, readily agreed.

"Remember when we first met, Meimei? We made a date to meet here for lunch. D'you remember?" May Lynn asked after they were served.

"No, I thought we had lunch in the cafeteria," replied Sue Mei, watching May Lynn circling her upside-down cake with little jabs and pokes.

"This cake is far too rich for me," May Lynn said aside, and Sue Mei knew she would inevitably pass the cake over to her. That was the reason she looked the way she did, and May Lynn looked the way she did.

"Well, yes, we did," May Lynn continued. "The practical side to us took over, as it always does. You only had an hour for lunch. Remember? You were typing in that horrid little—what did you call it?—cess-pool at the university. And I had my little Console back in those days. I had it parked in a special hiding place in the bushes, right next to the library, remember? Those were the good old days when one could still play cat and mouse with the authorities. Anyway, I could have gotten you here and back in an hour. So what if you were a few minutes late? It would have given your supervisors a cheap thrill, and something to gossip about for a few days. They were a dreadful lot. I don't know how you stood it there for fifteen years."

"Seventeen years." Sue Mei sniffed. And yes, of course she remembered the day she glanced up from her Smith Corona typewriter and saw a stylish woman singling her out. She was both surprised and embarrassed to find herself being introduced to Miss May Lynn Merriam, a post-doctorate fellow of the University of Texas who brazenly strode up to her desk at the rear of the typing pool and asked if she was Miss Sue Mei Chong, and would she please have lunch with her soon. Say, one day this week?

"I ... I bring my lunch," Sue Mei had stammered, dumbfounded, as the clacking typewriters around her came to an abrupt and mysterious standstill. May Lynn smiled down at her and made a mockingly loud suggestion that they might have a mutual acquaintance about whom they would need to chat at length.

Sue Mei noticed how tall and slim she was, and how she threw her shoulders back in that way of hers, and how she was not at all chinese until she spoke specifically to Sue Mei. But thereafter she was very much chinese, and not at all intimidated—a young, female, certainly not beautiful but energetic associate professor of asian studies from the United States, where, according to Sue Mei's indignant supervisors, "they have none of our kind of politeness at all."

"Well, I never thought I'd live to see a yellow-eyed chink! Who does she think she is?" Sue Mei heard one of them hiss at the other. And it was true that the colour of her eyes was amazing—the palest green hazel. Since then Sue Mei had always thought of them as golden.

It was a job, and she was lucky to land even that much. Back in those postwar days, they were still very good at the wartime scare tactics. After Beakins gave her the good ol' heave-ho—wait a minute ... first they told her she was the best heavy-duty tractor mechanic they ever had and then they gave her the boot—it took her years to get over the injustice of it all. Sharing dingy little rooms in chinatown with her ailing mother did nothing to lift her spirits. Trolley cars in the sweltering heat of summer, library books with her boxed lunches, runs on the heels of her Woolworth nylons; it wasn't so much the lack of prospects as the dearth of surprises to which Sue Mei could not submit.

May Lynn was a surprise. In fact, she has been the most fabulous surprise after glittering surprise for twenty-four years now.

"Oh you. You always had to be shown how to enjoy yourself," May Lynn has baited more than once.

"Oh you. Things were different for you. You didn't look chinese. And you had all the advantages," Sue Mei would briskly snap back.

May Lynn sat in the tea shop, looked smug and let her eat cake. Admittedly she did enjoy teasing Sue Mei a bit too much, but that was because she liked to think that she understood her. Sue Mei hadn't changed much in all those years. A face that she wore like a paper bag in public; she would never be able to recreate herself with enough contentment or security or even adequacy. However, her one saving grace was that she clearly preferred herself like this.

And whatever Sue Mei prefers May Lynn prefers to let her be. For instance, ages ago, May Lynn used to drive her home after work, and Sue Mei used to gripe about how expensive an automobile was to operate, so May Lynn bought a brand-new shockingly expensive Town and Country convertible.

"But I can afford it now, because I'm moving to a much cheaper place. Really, the rent is going to be incredibly low." She remembered following Sue Mei into Capital Poultry and Fish at Keefer and Gore as she told her this. Sue Mei wasn't intending to buy; she just wanted to harass the cheating old goat in there by telling him he sold his halibut steaks for a good cent more a pound than the Five Star on Carrall.

"Oh? Where are you moving to?" inquired Sue Mei as she poked at the fanlike gills of the codfish on ice.

"Well, the widow Quan upstairs is going to move in with her youngest daughter's family, so I've put in a deposit for her suite with Mrs. Wong of Sunbeam Realty."

"You actually went to see those crooks? Mrs. Quan upstairs in my building?" asked Sue Mei, her eyes intense and black and startled, her complexion apparently too brown, nose too flat and too fleshy, her lips sculpted, hair thick in a full-bodied french roll. And as May Lynn nodded yes, she thought Sue Mei was absolutely gorgeous.

"In my building? Are you crazy?"

"Well, yes and no. I mean, think about it! I'll save both time and money, since I drive you home every day. And I won't have to drive back and forth across town to pick you up whenever we go to the movies or something. I thought that would impress you. And it's almost like the penthouse suite, so I won't lose my social standing or anything like that."

"You don't belong in a falling-down chinatown tenement building full of ... of dumb old women!" yelled Sue Mei, recoiling from the very idea of such a distressing arrangement.

"Well, golly, you don't have to be such a snob about it. An opening like this doesn't come up every day," cried May Lynn to Sue Mei's back because she was already storming out of the fish store.

"Don't you dare!" were Sue Mei's fatally attractive last words on the matter.

"Does this mean ... I'm still invited to dinner, aren't I?" May Lynn called after her.

"Actually it was her mom who invited me," she explained to the cheapskate at Capital Poultry and Fish, "so I better buy some fish or something."

May Lynn knew Sue Mei well enough to know that she would never leave her mother to move in with her, and her mother would never leave chinatown, so May Lynn had to be the one to learn to live with Sue Mei and her dogged inhibitions.

On June 6, 1962, May Lynn was in the middle of publishing a paper titled "A Reinterpretative Study of the Classics of Mountain and Sea." Sue Mei, who had worked by her side all along, knew as much if not more about the subject. They were reading over the proofs in May Lynn's office when they heard a dull and dense thud downstairs. May

Lynn's dog was just a big ol' galloping puppy then, prone to mischief, so May Lynn went downstairs to investigate and was the first to reach Sue Mei's mother, who was laid out in the narrow landing in the hallway. May Lynn gently lifted the old woman's head as her eyes glazed over and her lips turned purplish.

"Yew Sue Mei mama" were her last words, fired off perhaps randomly, perhaps not. Since then, May Lynn had wondered every so often what the old woman had meant to say, but Sue Mei was so devastated by her mother's death that May Lynn just grabbed at their literal meaning. She hadn't even realized this until a few years ago when she began to notice that unfailingly, at the end of supper, Sue Mei served her oolong tea and the gruel made with the fragrant rice stuck on the bottom of the pot, exactly as she had done with her mother. And— wouldn't you guess?—of course May Lynn slurped it all up whether she wanted to or not.

She should have initiated a move immediately after the death, but the years slipped away unnoticed, and Su-lin slipped in unnoticed, and Sue Mei kept having to fix up the place, and so on and so forth. So now that they were being threatened with eviction, May Lynn knew very well that Sue Mei would in fact dig in further and prepare for the fight of their lives.

"May Lynn, I think you may be right." Sue Mei revved up her big motor right there, in the dainty tea shop. "We really shouldn't allow ourselves to get herded along by profit mongers."

May Lynn watched with a wide knowing smile; she couldn't imagine when she had mentioned anything like that, but Sue Mei had a fascinating interpretation of life that was all her own.

"And what about the other tenants—Chou Taitai, the foreigner from China, and Sammy Lee, that bag of bones who never contributes his fair share of work," she ran on.

"And look at old Granny Yen Kwei on the ground floor. What will become of her? She's lived there for fifty-five years, for gosh sakes ..."

"And predicting for the past five, with amazing conviction, that she's going to die for sure," added May Lynn, "with the coming of each first harsh frost. However, it is true that she has never had to predict where, since it is an absolute given that it will be at home, where all the memories are. It's all a part of her inalienable rice. Besides, the rent's unbelievably cheap. So what are we waiting for, dear heart? Let's finish our tea and get out there to start up our earth mover."

"We ... two old bags? We can't even keep up with this damned crazy world, never mind put a dent in it," said Sue Mei, collecting her gloves and purse.

"Shopping bags," contributed May Lynn in another vein. "We're shopping, so we're two old shopping bags."

"Oh you, you can't take anything seriously." But the important thing was that Sue Mei laughed all the way home.

When Sue Mei set out to find the slum landlord responsible for their eviction, she was surprised to be directed to an address in the old working-class neighbourhood of Kitsilano. There she found herself gawking at the mini-skirted, upbeat colours of the law offices of Ward, Wade & Wong. She had to write down the name of Wong Gum Lung for the pretty, perplexed receptionist.

"Is this how you write Danny's name in chinese?" she asked as she swung off her little office perch and tugged at her skintight hot pants. She seems very nice, thought Sue Mei, as she watched the long lime-green nylon legs stride away as the woman took the note in to her boss.

Sue Mei's heart began to thump when she saw her nephew approaching. She wondered if she shouldn't have prepared herself better for this moment, even though deep inside she knew she had been preparing all her life. But even as he approached, and she could see that the man she had feared all her life had become young all over again, she knew that the passing of time had no meaning—never has.

Her nephew, Danny Wong, was the same tall graceful man with confidence in his face and clean lines to his dark conservative suit. He had the very same steadfast blank gaze that she remembered when she was very small and vulnerable, dressed up in a painfully expensive, newly starched dress and pinafore, and she with her mother knelt before her father to humbly beg for a bit, just the tiniest bit of legitimacy. Sue Mei also remembered that her mother did not ever sob except late at night, so she stood up very straight.

He came right up to her, and he was blameless. And he would continue to be a man in the blessed power of his prime, generation after generation, for all eternity. He looked at her, but did not, at first, recognize who she might have been.

"This is my late grandfather's name. You knew him well?" He was smiling affably and reached out his hand casually to her, as his grandfather would have done to his peer. She was flattered and utterly charmed in spite of herself, and, of course, flustered. After all, he seemed to suggest to the dinosaur, times have really quite changed, haven't they? His hand was powdery dry, warm and very masculine.

"Of course," he said, "how do you do, Auntie—?" Danny referred to the eviction notice, "Auntie Sue Mei. And how is your mother?"

"She's been dead ..." uttered Sue Mei, completely startled. Then she clamped her mouth shut, embarrassed at having to tell him for how long.

"Oh, I am so sorry. I must have been thinking of someone else. I see you live in one of our buildings in chinatown." He smiled affably again and waved his hand casually in the direction of his private office with its spectacular waterfront view.

"Of course"—as Sue Mei got into the meat of her story to May Lynn and Su-lin, they all sat down to dinner, savouring every detail, from the wonderful aroma of a clear winter-melon-and-pork-bone broth cooked over low heat, delicately flavoured with dried shrimp, to the enticing texture of beef-flank strips stir-fried in garlic and onions and simmered for just a minute in home-canned tomatoes and the steamed rock cod swimming in a picturesque pond of oil, soy and emerald greens, and finally the tightly packed barbecued duck from Kay Wah on the table in front of them—"he was absolutely ruthless, but he didn't reckon on us being so different from what he imagined we would be. I think he supposed that we would be too terrified or ashamed of our lowlife bastardized selves to make a peep, much less to threaten to yell it out loud for all chinatown to hear. But times have really quite changed, haven't they?"

She picked up her chopsticks triumphantly and lightly touched the white fluffy round mound of rice in her bowl. Su-lin, she had noticed, preferred to press her rice down. May Lynn ignored hers altogether, in favour of the savouries.

"Aw, I betcha he knew you right away then," Su-lin launched in, as Sue Mei and May Lynn stuffed big juicy pieces of duck into their mouths. "I mean, you look just like him, don't you know? And of course Danny must know what a philandering old shit his forefather was. Hah, I betcha he's had to deal with this one more than once, eh?"

"Hard to say how many women the old tyrant ... used like my mother," Sue Mei said, with her mouth awkwardly full.

"Well, I remember that I was shocked when I first laid eyes on you," added Su-lin. "I thought you were one of his real daughters. You looked snotty enough when you came into the Smilin' Buddha, remember, a long time ago. Golly gee whiz, what a dive that place was, but were the tips ever good! All those big burly loggers. Hey, d'ya wanna see where I broke my arm during that big ol' riot? Forty-eight stitches, can you believe it?"

This was one of Su-lin's often repeated gestures, but May Lynn looked at the spot Su-lin pointed to on her arm with the same fresh attention as the first time. Sue Mei smiled to see them friendly again. It helped to have May Lynn's mouth occupied with good food. Su-lin told the same story about how her high heel got caught when she was hurrying to take shelter during a drunken brawl that erupted at her place of work. And she fell against a table full of beer glasses.

However, the tender moment didn't last. May Lynn swallowed hard and challenged Su-lin, "What do you mean 'one of his real daughters'?"

"You know very well what I mean—one of his 'legit' daughters." Su-lin's glare was much deadlier than her verbal jabs.

"Well, then say 'legit,'" demanded May Lynn. "Don't Sue Mei and I look 'real' to you?"

Sue Mei didn't interfere any more, even though she thought May Lynn rode Su-lin unmercifully. After all, Sue Mei had met May Lynn's mother in San Francisco—a dear, sweet, diplomat's wife, long retired with hubby number four who was a sri lankan from London, so she understood that Su-lin and May Lynn would never, ever see eye to eye.

May Lynn's mother had the most amazing mass of flyaway, angelic white hair. She travelled the U.S. extensively, raising "jillions of dollars" for various third-world causes. She still spoke with an enchanting texan drawl and said things like, "Honey, if y'all ever see me getting conservative, do me the supreme favour of delivering a good swift kick to my ass end!"

It was difficult for Sue Mei, who had always thought of herself as a common garden variety of bastard, to imagine this vibrant woman in a clandestine liaison with a chinese man in 1924. Yet apparently May Lynn's mother, as a young audacious student of anthropology from the University of California, thought nothing of turning Wong Golden Dragon, who in his day was a vicious, small-time crook, on his head, or returning home, pregnant with his child. May Lynn grew up as pampered and privileged and unconventional as her mother at her grandparents' cliff-clinging house overlooking the Pacific Ocean on Fanhill Island, just north of San Francisco.

May Lynn's mother proudly asserted that she once spoke three dialects of the chinese language. And she had passed by Vancouver with Henrietta Mertz, the famous anthropologist, who was also a dear old friend of the family, because they were interested in investigating some evidence of an ancient chinese landing on the west coast of North America, way, way before Columbus. And, thank goodness, May Lynn's mother suffered no discombobulation about speaking candidly of her affair with May Lynn's father.

"Well, my dear, that man just about broke my heart to bits. But wasn't I the nincompoop in those days? However, the baby was good. Not just good, she was absolutely perfect."

Yes indeedee, Sue Mei could well appreciate how Su-lin, the middle of seven slave children, a runaway by the time she was fourteen, and one of Wong Gum Lung's common garden variety whores by fifteen, would simply not be able to wrap her small-town redneck sensibilities around that one.

"Now, don't get me wrong. There was not one nasty word exchanged between Mr. Danny and me." Sue Mei drew them back to her story as a wave of well-being washed over her and her full stomach. "It was all so cold-bloodedly slick and smooth. I had only to mention Su-lin's name to our Mr. Danny once." It was a brilliantly deployed statement, because she knew Su-lin thrived on such mentionables.

Sure enough, Su-lin broke into giggles. "Did you show him my proof?" Su-lin asked.

"Oh, no, nothing like that," answered Sue Mei. "He, I'm sure, remembers exactly who you are. No, my basic approach was that we all came from the same seed of the patriarch. And fathers, by their very nature, want all their offspring to thrive, whether we live within his big house or at the weedy edges of his vast lands and estates."

May Lynn chuckled and clapped her hands.

"Then did you tell him to not bother raising the rent for, say, another twenty years?" piped in Su-lin. With the tables turned, there is always the fantasy of power.

"Well, no—not like that. We all know that it's not a good idea to put a man on the defensive. I may have mentioned our retired income not keeping up with the current rate of inflation."

"Too subtle," commented May Lynn.

"No," disagreed Su-lin, "it's smarter to keep to the old 'a Wong is never wrong' trick. Sue Mei knows what she's doing." Su-lin threw a long, admiring smile at Sue Mei and reached for her emptied rice bowl, wanting to refill it, but Sue Mei stopped her.

"You eat" she said. "Your rice has gotten cold."

Su-lin obeyed like a child. She often ate last, and she ate as she has always eaten, hunched over her food like a sorrowful lump of a woman-child, shovelling it down her throat in shame. And Sue Mei had always pretended she didn't notice.

She met Su-lin right after her forty-eight very tender stitches on her arm. At the time Su-lin was staying in the manager's apartment above the strip joint she worked in on East Hastings. Sue Mei had bought her a nice box of chocolates and marvelled at how young she must have been when she dared to go against the grain in chinatown and charged Wong Gum Lung with statutory rape.

Su-lin was overwhelmed by the fact that someone, and another woman at that, would be so kind as to pay her a friendly visit, and she did want so much to be friends. At first Sue Mei was just as happy to have tracked down another of Wong Gum Lung's indiscretions, or should she call them soul debts. Because, in the long run, her efforts certainly paid off. But more important, since then Su-lin had become a dear old friend, and the perfect counterpoint to May Lynn and herself. Together they felt as rich and powerful as the Soong sisters of old China.

"When my mother started to go grey at the edges, I knew she was going to die," Su-lin once confessed to Sue Mei. "I promised myself that I was going to bugger off. I was fourteen then. Old enough!

"Oh, I didn't tell any of my sisters. You never knew when they'd turn on you. Mean and unpredictable, we were. We had to be. My sisters would have finked on me for an extra scrap of salt fish.

"Even the littlest ones had to spend days upon days wheel-barrowing cow manure from this farmer's barnyard to our vegetable garden. The poor white kids used to chuck their trash at us.

"I used to think that my old man beat on me the worst because he couldn't stop me from going to school. By the time I was nine, these white biddies came along and threatened him with jail if he didn't let the younger girls go to school.

"Yep, I surely did run away. Left my old man yelling at my mother's corpse, slapping it around—would you believe that? Well, now when I remember that, I think how horrible. But you know, at the time, I didn't think nothing of it. It was no different from when she was alive, you know what I mean? I guess he was upset that she finally escaped. Jeez, I walked along that pitch-black highway until my feet bled. Got on that CPR ferry at Nanaimo and came right into Vancouver.

"Hah, you know what I found out years later. My sisters weren't so mad that I got away. They were mad because they thought I was self-ish not to think of taking any of them with me. But it wasn't like that. At the time I didn't think that I was going to get anywhere, like I had a future or something. I really believed I was going to die. You know how chinese are always saying 'Go die!'"

One day, a few months later, while cleaning, Sue Mei ran across the eviction notices and finally threw them away since nobody had heard a peep from Danny Wong.

"I'll file one, just for the records," said Sue Mei to May Lynn, "but I really don't think they'll come after us again. Do you?"

"No, absolutely not," answered May Lynn. "I think you set them straight this time."

"I betcha they're hoping that we die off soon," said Sue Mei.

"Well, as long as they don't take it upon themselves to help us along," rejoined May Lynn.

"I wouldn't be at all surprised. They are such go-getters these days, aren't they?" Sue Mei joked.

May Lynn smirked as she turned back to whatever she was reading, but Sue Mei wanted to talk.

"I betcha haven't even noticed how I have changed since my little encounter with Mr. Danny Wong, have you?"

May Lynn took off her reading glasses and gave Sue Mei all her attention. Somehow they have never failed to engage each other's interest.

"Right you are there. I guess I have not, so ... ?" replied May Lynn most companionably.

"Well, for one thing, I am starting to appreciate myself a little. I mean, look at me. I'm fifty-eight years old, with only a bit of a spare tire. I have you and Su-lin, and I don't want for anything. Not a thing. If that doesn't mean that I am content, I don't know what does. And I was thinking how I supported my mom right up until the day she died—in fact, since I was fifteen years old. That's quite something, don't you think? And do you know what else? I have just recently saved the homes of sixteen old ladies who kind of like living with each other, three cranky old men who kind of don't, thirty-three pigeons, five cats, three budgies, two canaries, one very old dog, one cockatiel, ten caged rats and mice and who knows how many loose ones—all in one go!" exclaimed Sue Mei.

"Well, bravo, I say, hear, hear, and absolutely bravo!" exclaimed May Lynn.

"Aannd you know what else? Well, all along, I guess I thought we didn't have much of a life. You know, I felt we—well, not you, but the rest of us—were rejects. In fact, they actually had me believing that I was totally undeserving, and I was supposed to be missing out on even the basics. All my life I felt like that, then felt stupid for feeling like that. You know ... beating myself up over and over again.

"But the last straw was to have that man that day—our ever so legal regal Danny Wong—come along with all his kindhearted, new liberal attitudes to tell me that even our shame is worthless and outdated now. Well, after a whole lifetime, I have grown very attached to our leper status, thank you very much. I realized that if that was all we have in this life—so be it! And that slick hotshot, that symbol of everything I was never allowed to be, was even trying to take that away. Can you imagine?" cried Sue Mei fiercely.

"Hear, hear," agreed May Lynn.

"Greedy buggers! They'll reduce you to rubble if you let them."

"Literally." May Lynn looked at Sue Mei adoringly.

"Off with their heads," gloated Sue Mei in all her glory, but then she leaned closer to May Lynn and whispered, "I gotta tell you a secret, though. Actually, I always wanted a son like our Mr. Danny Wong."

"Whatever for?" yelped May Lynn.

"To be legit, I guess," answered Sue Mei patly.

"You've got to be kidding," demanded May Lynn.

"Well, I guess I've gotten over that one too," decided Sue Mei.

"Well, I should hope so," concluded May Lynn, regaining her composure.

Topics for Discussion

1. How does Lee establish the sisters' different personalities? How are the sisters different from one another?

2. How does Lee communicate the idea that the sisters are living in their own isolated world?

3. What role does conversation play in the telling of the story?

4. What is the role of change in the story? How do the sisters cope with change?

5. What differences does Lee delineate between men and women during the visit by Sue Mei to the legal office of Danny Wong?

6. In what ways is this a feminist story?

7. How do the women emerge victorious from their situation? What understanding do they gain of themselves at the end of the story?

About the Author

Doris Lessing, a prolific and popular writer of novels, stories, plays and other works, was born in 1919 in Kermansha, Persia (now Iran), of British parentage, and in 1924 moved with her family to Southern Rhodesia (now Zimbabwe), where she received her education. Before becoming a professional writer she worked as a telephone operator, a clerk, a typist, an au pair and a journalist in South Africa and London. She has lived in London since 1949. Aside from the selected works in the following list, Lessing has also written two novel cycles, *Children of Violence* (a *Bildungsroman* of five novels dealing with the life, growth and development of a Rhodesian girl who goes to live in London), and *Canopus in Argus: Archives* (a five-novel science-fiction series that traces human history and human relations in the context of the battle between good and evil).

Her fiction covers a broad canvas, exploring the worlds of Africa, Britain and even outer space. Her primary concerns are to chronicle life in the twentieth century, to show the relationship between the individual and his or her world, and to examine the stream of unhappiness that pervades modern culture.

"Casualty" is from her 1992 collection of short stories, *The Real Thing*.

Selected Works

The Grass Is Singing (novel, 1950)
Retreat to Innocence (novel, 1956)
The Golden Notebook (novel, 1962)
African Stories (short stories, 1965)
Briefing for a Descent into Hell (novel, 1971)
The Summer Before the Dark (novel, 1973)
Memoirs of a Survivor (novel, 1975)
The Good Terrorist (novel, 1985)
The Fifth Child (novel, 1988)
The Real Thing (short stories, 1992)

About the Story

"Casualty" is a story about waiting, observing, impatience and the passage of time. "Casualty ward" is the name given in England and some other countries to the emergency room of a hospital, which is where this story is set. The impatient old woman, who is both participant and observer of events in the waiting room, is in many ways a metaphor for the human condition in the modern, bureaucratic world where subjectivity and self-centredness offer a retreat from pain for those caught up in "the system."

Casualty

All of them looking one way, they sat on metal chairs, the kind that are hard and slippery and stack into each other. They kept their attention on the woman behind the reception desk, who was apparently not interested in them now she had their names, addresses, complaints all tidily written down on forms. She was an ample young woman with the rainy violet eyes that seem designed only for laughing or weeping, but now they were full of the stern impartiality of justice. Her name button said she was Nurse Doolan.

It was a large room with walls an uninteresting shade of beige, bare except for the notice, "If You Have Nothing Urgently Wrong Please Go To Your Own Doctor." Evidently the twenty or so people here did not believe their own doctors were as good as this hospital casualty department. Only one of them seemed in urgent need, a dishevelled woman of forty or so with dyed orange hair, who was propping her wrapped left hand on her right shoulder. Everyone knew the wrist was broken because the woman with her had nodded commandingly at them, turning round to do it, and mouthed, "Her *wrist*. She broke it." Satisfied they must all acknowledge precedence, she had placed her charge in the end of the front row nearest to the door that said "No Admittance." They did not challenge her. The broken-wristed one, exhausted with pain, drowsed in her seat, and her face was bluish white, so that with the brush of orange hair she looked like a clown. But Nurse Doolan did not seem to think she deserved more than the others, for when the next name was called it was not the owner of the wrist. "Harkness," said Nurse Doolan and while an apparently fit young man walked into "No Admittance" the poor clown's attendant stood up and complained, "But it is urgent, it is a broken *wrist*."

"Won't be long," said Nurse Doolan, and placidly studied her pile of forms.

"They don't care. They don't care at all," said an old woman in a wheelchair. Her voice was loud and accusing. She was fat and looked like a constipated frog. Her face, full of healthy colour, showed a practised resignation to life's taunts. "I fell down a good six hours ago, and my shoulder's broke, I know that!" The elderly woman sitting with her did not try to engage anyone's sympathy, but rather avoided eyes that had already clearly said, Rather you than me! She said quietly, "It's all right, Auntie, don't go on."

"Don't go on, *she* says," said the old woman, eighty if she was a day, and full of energy. "It's all right for some."

A boy of about twelve emerged from the mysteries behind "No Admittance" with a crutch and a bandaged foot, and was guided through this waiting room to the outside pavement by a nurse who left him there, presumably to be picked up. She came back.

"Nurse," said the old woman, "my shoulder's broke and I've been sitting here for hours . . . ever so long," she added, as her relative murmured, "Not long, Auntie, only half an hour."

This nurse glanced towards Doolan at Reception, who signalled with her violet eyes. Nurse Bates, directed, stopped by the wheelchair and switched on appropriate sympathy. "Let's have a look," she said.

The elderly niece drew back part of a bright pink cardigan from the shoulder which sat there, stoutly and soberly bare, except for a grimy shoulder strap. "You want me naked, I suppose that's it now! For everyone to gape at! that's it, I suppose!" The nurse bent over the shoulder, gently manipulating it, while everybody stared somewhere else, so as not to give the old horror the satisfaction of feeling looked at.

"Owwwww," wailed the old woman.

"You'll live," said the nurse briskly, straightening herself.

"It's broken, isn't it?" urged Auntie.

"You've got a bit of a bruise, but that's about it, I think. They'll find out in X-ray." And she stepped smartly off towards "No Admittance," raising her brows and smiling with her eyes at Nurse Doolan, who smiled with hers.

"They don't care," came the loud voice. "None of them care. How'd you like to be lying on the floor by yourself half the night and no one near you to lift you up?"

The elderly niece, a thin and colourless creature who probably— though for her sake everyone hoped not— devoted her life to this old bully, did not bother to defend herself, but smoothed back the pink cardigan over the shoulder which if you looked hard did have a mauveish shine.

"Day after day, sitting by myself, I might as well be dead."

"Would you like a cup of tea, Auntie?"

"Might as well, if you'll put yourself out. Not that it'll be worth drinking."

The niece allowed her face to show a moment's exhaustion as she turned away from Auntie, but then she smiled and went through the rows of waiting people with "Excuse me, excuse me, please."

"Fanshawe," said Nurse Doolan, apparently in reply to some summons in the ether, for no one had come out.

A man of sixty-five or so, who wore a red leather slipper on one foot, used a stick to heave himself up, and walked slowly to the inner door, careful the stick did not slip.

"You'd think they'd have nonslip floors," came from the wheelchair.

"They *are* nonslip," said Doolan firmly.

"Better be safe than sorry," said Mr. Fanshawe going into "No Admittance" with a wink all round that meant he wasn't going to be associated with that old bitch.

"And what about my sister?" asked the woman who was now cradling the broken-wristed one. Her voice trembled, and she seemed about to weep with indignation.

And indeed the poor clown seemed half conscious, her orange head drooping, then jerking up, then falling forward, and she even groaned. She heard herself groan and embarrassment woke her up. She flashed painful smiles along the front row, and as far as she could turn her head to the back. "I fell," she muttered, confessing it, begging forgiveness. "I fell, you see."

"You're not the only one to fall," came from the wheelchair.

"There's been a bad accident," said Nurse Doolan. "They've been working in there like navvies these last three hours."

"Oh, that's it, is it?" "That's what it is, then!" "Oh well, in that case…" came from the longsuffering crowd.

"Never seen anything like it," said Nurse Doolan, sharing this with them.

It was noticeable that she and some others glanced nervously at the old woman, who decided not to have her say, not this time. And here was her niece with her tea in the plastic foam cup.

"And what did I tell you?" demanded Auntie, taking the cup and at once noisily gulping the tea. "Plastic rubbish and it's cold, you'd think…"

A trundling sound from inside "No Admittance." As the doors opened there emerged the back of a young black porter in his natty uniform, then a steel trolley, and on the trolley a human form rolled in bandages to the waist, but naked above and showing a strong healthy young man's chest. Black. From the neck began a cocoon: a white bandaged head. Alert brown eyes looked out from the cocoon. The trolley disappeared into the interior of the hospital on its way to some ward several floors up.

"The wrist," said Nurse Doolan, "Bisley," and the woman with the broken wrist was urged to her feet by her sister, and stood swaying. Doolan at once pressed a bell which they heard shrilling inside "No Admittance." The same nurse came running out, saw why she had been summoned, and with Nurse Bates on one side and her sister on the other the half-conscious Wrist was supported within.

Now a new addition to the morning's casualties. In came two young women, made up and dressed up as if off to a disco, chattering away and apparently in the best of health. They lowered their voices, sensing that their jollity was not being appreciated, and sat at the very back, whispering and sometimes giggling. What could they be doing in Casualty?

It seemed that at any moment this was what the old woman would start asking, for she was fixing them with a hard, cold, accusing look. "Auntie," said her niece hastily, "would you like another tea? I could do with one myself."

"I don't mind." And she graciously handed over her cup. The niece went out again.

And then, everything changed. A group of young men appeared outside the glass doors to the world where cars came and went, where visitors walked past, where there was ordinariness and health. This group sent waves of urgency and alarm into the waiting room even before the doors opened.

A young workman in white overalls blotched with red stood gripping the edge of a door because over his shoulder lay a body, and it was heavy, as they could all see, being limp and with no fight in it. This body was a young man too, but his white overalls were soaked with a dreadful dark pulsing blood that still welled from somewhere.

"Why didn't you..." began Nurse Doolan, on her way to saying, "You're not supposed to come in at that door, you need a stretcher, this isn't at all how we do things..." Something on these lines, but no one would ever know, for having taken one look at what was before them, she put her thumb down on the bell to make it shrill in the ears of the doctors and nurses working inside out of sight.

Feet and voices, and out came running the same nurse; three doctors—two women and a man—and a porter with a stretcher.

Seeing the group of young men just inside the door these professionals all stopped still, and the main woman doctor waved aside the stretcher.

"He fell off the roof," said the young man who held his mate. "He fell off." He sounded incredulous, appealing to them, the experts, to say that this was impossible and could not have happened. His mate at his elbow, a youth whose sky-blue overalls had no spot or stain, corroborated, "Yes, he fell off. Suddenly he wasn't there. And then..." Another youth, following behind, still held a paint roller in one hand. Orange paint. These three young men were about twenty, certainly not more than twenty-two or twenty-three. They were pale, shocked, and their eyes told everyone they had seen something terrible and could not stop looking at it.

The woman doctor in charge summoned the group forward, and the doctors and nurse stood to one side as the young men went through into "No Admittance." Blood pattered down.

And then they were all able to see the face that hung over the blood-soaked shoulder. It was dull grey, not a colour many of them were likely to have seen on a face. The mouth hung open. The eyes were open. Blue eyes...The professionals followed the young men in, and the doors swung shut.

Nurse Doolan came out from behind the desk with a cloth, and bent to wipe blood off the floor. She too looked sick.

Meanwhile the second cup of tea arrived, and the old woman took it. The niece, feeling that something had happened in the few minutes she had been gone, was looking around, but no one looked at her. They stared at "No Admittance," and their faces were full of news.

"Well," said the old woman loudly, full of gleeful energy. "I haven't done badly at that, have I? I am eighty-five this year and there's plenty more where that came from!"

No one looked at her, and no one said anything.

Topics for Discussion

1. How does Lessing create the character of the old woman?

2. In what ways is the hospital casualty unit a metaphor and what is it a metaphor for?

3. What role does indifference play in the story?

4. Why is the old woman afraid?

5. How does Lessing use detail in describing the various injuries and what impact does this detail have on the reader?

6. What is the old woman's reaction to her perceived lack of importance?

7. What is the relationship between the setting and title and what sort of environment is the casualty ward?

8. How does Lessing define survival?

Catherine Lim

About the Author

Catherine Lim was born in Kulim, Kedah, Malaysia, in 1942 but is a naturalized Singaporean. She received her education in English at the University of Malaya (now the National University of Singapore) and earned an M.A. and a Ph.D. in Linguistics. She has worked as a schoolteacher, as deputy director in the Curriculum Development Institute of Singapore, and as a language specialist with the Regional English Language Centre. She lives in Singapore.

Lim's work reflects the cosmopolitan nature of her city/nation of Singapore through a realistic style and a passion for subtle irony. Her stories often focus on human traits and characteristics such as greed and possessiveness, as in "The Jade Pendant," which is taken from her 1978 collection *Little Ironies*.

Selected Works

Little Ironies: Stories of Singapore (short stories, 1978)
Or Else, the Lightning God and Other Stories (short stories, 1980)
The Serpent's Tooth (novel, 1982)
They Do Return (short stories, 1983)
The Shadow of a Shadow of a Dream: Love Stories of Singapore (short stories, 1987)
O Singapore! Stories in Celebration (short stories, 1989)
Deadline for Love and Other Stories (short stories, 1992)
The Woman's Book of Superlatives (short stories, 1992)
Love's Lonely Impulses (poetry, 1992)

About the Story

In "The Jade Pendant," Lim tells the story of a woman, Mrs. Khoo, who has inherited a valuable piece of jade jewellery (jade is a hard green stone) and for whom the jewel is an essential status symbol, even though she and her husband are in tight financial circumstances. The story also contains a subplot of the relationship between Mrs. Khoo and her servants. In the process of exploring the nature and meaning of possession, Lim also examines the relationship between mother and daughter, which is defined by the succession of the pendant from one generation to the next.

The Jade Pendant

The Jade Pendant had gathered round it a number of myths, some of which were quite absurd, such as the one that it was worth half-a-million dollars, but the reality was astonishing enough to raise gasps of admiration and envy. The jewel, as big as the palm of a child's hand, consisted of a thick circular piece of intricately carved jade of the most brilliant and lucid green, surrounded by innumerable diamonds arranged in floral designs. It was to be worn on a chain round the neck, but the sheer weight of the jewel, not to mention the extreme folly of risking loss or theft, had caused it to be little disturbed in its place in the bank vaults. Mrs. Khoo had worn it only twice—once at a banquet given by a sultan—the jewel had been specially flown, under strict security, to the royal town where it made a stir, even at a function that glittered with fabulous jewels—and again, at the wedding of her nephew. Since then, it had lain safely in the bank vaults, for the myriad weddings and other functions that Mrs. Khoo had subsequently attended were considered too insignificant to justify the presence of this jewel, the like of which nobody had ever seen. But its absence on the broad perfumed bosom of Mrs. Khoo was as likely to provoke comments as its presence: "Ah, you're not wearing the Jade Pendant! That's a disappointment to me, for I had hoped to see it. I've heard so much about it."

To make up for the loss of pleasure that would have been afforded by the sight of the Jade Pendant, Mrs. Khoo would talk about its history—how it had come down to her from her mother who had got it from her own mother, and if its origin was traced far enough, it could be ascertained that the first possessor was a concubine of a Vietnamese emperor of the seventeenth century. Its continuing connections with royalty must be something predestined, for, confided Mrs. Khoo, her mother had once told her that the wife of a sultan who had seen it had wanted to buy it, no matter how great the cost; she had actually sent emissaries to begin the task of negotiation and purchase. It was an extremely difficult thing to do, but the persistent royal lady was at last turned down.

The engrossing question had been: whom would Mrs. Khoo leave the jewel to when she died—her daughter-in-law or her daughter? Mrs. Khoo had actually long settled the matter in favour of her daughter. There was nothing she would not do for Lian Kim, her favourite child. Moreover, she would not wait for her death to hand over the jewel—when Lian Kim got married, the gift would be made. The bride would wear the Jade Pendant at the wedding dinner, for every one of the guests to see.

When Lian Kim was home for the holidays with her fiancé, she had insisted on her mother taking the jewel out of the bank for him to see. He was an Art student whom she had met in London, and the wonder on his face and the long whistle of admiration and incredulity as he looked at the Jade Pendant that Lian Kim had laughingly placed on his artist's begrimed sweater, was a small but definite step toward the mollification of his future mother-in-law whose chagrin, when her daughter wrote to her of being engaged to a foreigner, was great indeed. How vexing, she had thought to herself and later said to her husband, although she would not have dared to say the same to her daughter. How vexing to have a daughter married to a foreigner, and a poor one at that. But there was nothing to be done, once the young people of today made up their minds. Her vexation was increased that day by a very humiliating incident. She had just shown the Jade Pendant to Lian Kim and Ron and was getting ready to put it back in its case of red velvet, when she heard Ah Soh sweeping outside the room. Upon impulse, she called Ah Soh into the room to view the jewel, thinking afterwards, in the generosity of her heart, that even a humble widowed relative who made cakes and puddings for sale in the streets, could be given the pleasure of looking at the jewel. Ah Soh was all gratitude. She left her broom outside, tiptoed in with a great show of respect and awe, and raised her hands in shrill wonderment even before the box was opened to reveal its treasure. She exclaimed, she praised, she was breathless with the effort of pleasing a rich relative who allowed her and her daughter to live in a room at the back of the great house, to eat the food left on the great table, to benefit by the sale of old clothes, beer-bottles and newspapers.

Unfortunately, Ah Soh's daughter, a simple-minded girl of Lian Kim's age, had ambled in then, looking for her mother and on seeing the jewel, had crowed with childish delight, and actually snatched it up and pranced round the room, shrilly parading it on her chest. The terror of her mother who had quickly glanced up to see the look of violent disgust and displeasure on the face of Mrs. Khoo, was itself terrifying to behold. She shrieked at the girl, snatched the jewel back, laid it reverently back in its case and began scolding the erring daughter as vehemently as she could. The insulted pride of the lady whose countenance had taken on a look of extreme hauteur, was to be mollified by no less than a severe thrashing of the offender, which Ah Soh immediately executed, secret anger against her rich relative lending great strength to her thin scrawny arms. The girl who looked no more than a child though she was over twenty, whimpered, and would have been thrashed sick had not Mrs. Khoo intervened by saying stiffly. "That will do, Ah Soh. Do you want to kill the child?" "Better for her to be killed than to insult you in this way!" sobbed Ah Soh.

Mrs. Khoo, who found the incident too disgusting to be mentioned to her husband or daughter, soon forgot it. She spent the three weeks of her daughter's vacation home, in pleasing the young couple as much as she could. She got the servants to cook all kinds of delicacies, and Ah Soh, anxious to pacify her further, helped as much as she could, endlessly. Whenever she could spare the time from her mah-jong, Mrs. Khoo entertained them, not sparing any expense. Mr. Khoo who doted on his youngest daughter was even willing to take time off from his gambling and his race-horses to take the couple round and introduce them proudly to his wide circle of friends. Lian Kim and Ron were to be married by the end of the year. "A sad occasion for the mother, ha! ha! do you know why?" Mr. Khoo would laugh heartily, his round florid face wreathed in smiles. "Because the Jade Pendant will be made over from mother to daughter. Ah, these women! They and their jewels. But

I tell you, that trinket's worth at least—" he would then whisper conspiratorially into the ears of his friend, revelling in the look of amazement on the face of the listener.

It would never have occurred to any of their friends to ask Mr. or Mrs. Khoo about whether they were thinking of selling the Jade Pendant—it would have been an insult too great to be borne. Yet the possibility had occurred to Mrs. Khoo, and the realisation, after some time, that it *would* have to be sold brought a spasm of terror to the lady as she paced about in her room, thinking what a sad state of affairs the family was in financially. The money and the property that had come down to them from their parents and grandparents—almost all dissipated! Mr. Khoo and his gambling and his horses and entertaining, the expensive education of her two sons and her daughter abroad—they were forever writing home for more money.

The immediate worry was the expense of Lian Kim's wedding. It could not, must not, be on a scale less than that of the wedding of her elder brother two years ago, or the wedding of a cousin, for that would be a severe loss of family face. Mrs. Khoo made a quick calculation of the cost of the wedding dress and trousseau, specially ordered from a French house of fashion, the furnishings for the new flat in London to be rented by the couple after their marriage, the wedding dinner for at least five hundred people in the Imperial Hotel—where was she to get the money from? She uttered little cries of agitation and wrung her hands in vexation, as she walked about in her room. She had on one occasion represented the difficulties to her husband, but he had only laughed, pinched her cheek and said, "Now, now, you are always worrying. We are O.K., O.K. and you go and get whatever you like, old girl." She had not dared to speak of her difficulties to Lian Kim—she could not bear to spoil the happiness of her beloved child.

Once she was tempted to approach Ah Soh to borrow some money—she had heard whispers of the immense sum of money that Ah Soh had slowly accumulated over forty years, money she had saved from her sale of cakes and puddings, and from extreme frugality: Ah Soh made her own cigarettes by rolling the tobacco salvaged from thrown-away cigarette ends, in little square pieces of paper, and her simple-minded daughter wore only the cast-off clothes of Lian Kim and other relatives. But she had quickly rejected the idea. What, degrade herself by seeking help from a relative who was no better than a servant? Mrs. Khoo's inherent dislike of Ah Soh was increased by her suspicion that behind all that effusive humility and deference was a shrewdness and alertness that saw everything that was going on, and she even fancied that the little frightened-looking eyes in the thin pallid face sometimes laughed at her. After Lian Kim's wedding I shall no longer tolerate her in the house, thought Mrs. Khoo resentfully. She and that imbecile daughter she dotes on so much can pack up and leave.

The thought of the wedding which should have given so much pleasure to her fond mother's heart distressed her, for again and again she wondered where the money was to come from. Their two houses were already mortgaged; the shares would fetch but little. No matter how hard she tried to avoid it, the conclusion she inevitably reached was: the Jade Pendant had to go. The impact of so awesome a decision caused Mrs. Khoo to have a violent headache. The only consolation she could find in so dismal a situation was the thought that nobody need know that the Jade Pendant had been sold, as she could always give some explanation or other for its not being worn at the wedding, whereas if the wedding celebration were to be scaled down, how dreadful a loss of face that would be!

She then went into urgent and secret family consultation in which her husband finally assented to the sale, stressing that they should get as good a price for such a jewel as they possibly could. It was not so easy to win her daughter round—Lian Kim fretted excessively about the loss of something she had been promised, and it was only after a great deal of sulking that she could consent to the sale. The prospect of a modest wedding celebration was even more appalling than that of having to do without the Jade Pendant, and of the numerous excuses thought up to account for its absence, she at last settled on this one: that the huge old-fashioned jewel would not go nicely with her Dior gown.

The secrecy with which the sale of the Jade Pendant was to be effected became a matter of first importance. Following the very discreet inquiries about potential buyers, an offer came and with conditions that could not but please Mrs. Khoo—the interested party was a very wealthy lady who made her home in another country, she wanted absolute secrecy in the entire proceeding, she would send round a third person to collect the item. Her offer moreover was generous. Insist on cash, said Mr. Khoo. You never know about these so-called rich foreigners. Cash it was, and the Jade Pendant left its place in the bank vaults forever.

With the matter settled, Mrs. Khoo was happy again, and bustled about in the wedding preparations. My daughter has decided not to wear the Jade Pendant, she told her friends. Oh, these young people nowadays, they do not appreciate the beautiful things left them by their ancestors, and they are so intolerant of our old ways! Mrs. Khoo, caught up happily in the whirl of invitations and other preparations, did not, however, forget to tell Ah Soh, but in a kindly voice, "There will be so many guests all dressed grandly and with their jewels, that it is better for you to dress well too. I hope you have bought new clothes for the occasion?" Ah Soh humbly and gratefully assured her that she had.

The wedding dinner and celebration was on a scale as to merit talk for at least the next three days. At least one Minister and three Members of Parliament, together with numerous business tycoons, were present. Mrs. Khoo moved briskly among the guests, and even in the flutters of maternal anxiety and happiness, had the time to hope that that simple-minded daughter of Ah Soh would not do anything to mar the splendour of the occasion. She had wanted, tactfully, to tell Ah Soh not to bring her along, but had decided to be generous and charitable for such an occasion as this—the wedding of her youngest and favourite daughter.

Her gaze swept briefly over the heads in that large resplendent, chandeliered room, and rested on a spot in the far corner, where she could easily pick out Ah Soh, decently dressed for once, sitting with her daughter and some relatives. Mrs. Khoo wondered why the eyes not only of those at that table, but of those from the neighbouring tables were fixed on the imbecile child—people were positively staring at her, and not only staring, but whispering loudly, urgently among themselves. The whispering and the staring spread outwards in widening ripples of mounting excitement and tension. Mrs. Khoo made her way towards this focus of tremulous attention, and she too stared—not at the idiot child-like face but at the jewel that rested awkwardly on the flat, child-like chest. The Jade Pendant! The idiot girl crowed with pleasure, and her mother who sat very near to her, holding her hand affectionately, was nodding to the faces crowding in upon them, the frightened look gone forever from her eyes.

Oh, where is Mr. Khoo! Please do something! shrieked Mrs. Khoo, moving about distractedly, wringing her hands. Oh, what shall we do? How shall we bear it? Lian Kim, she mustn't know, it will kill her to know! And I will kill her for having done this to me! How could she do such a thing to me!

Topics for Discussion

1. How does Lim convey the idea of possessiveness?

2. What does the jade pendant represent in the story?

3. How does Lim establish surprise with the ending of the story?

4. Why is class such an important issue in the story? How does Lim convey class differences in the story?

5. What roles do status and impression play in the story? Why is Mrs. Khoo so determined to impress everyone with the jade pendant?

6. Why is it important for Lian Kim to inherit the jade pendant? What part does inheritance play in the story?

7. How does Lim convey the idea of the pendant increasing in value?

Bernard MacLaverty

About the Author

Bernard MacLaverty was born in Belfast, Northern Ireland, in 1942 and educated at Queen's University, Belfast. He has worked as a medical laboratory
technician and a teacher, and served as writer-in-residence at the University
of Aberdeen (1983–85). His novel *Cal* (1983), a story about the Troubles in
Northern Ireland, was made into a successful feature film. He lives in Glasgow, Scotland.

Selected Works

Lamb (novel, 1980)
A Time to Dance and Other Stories (short stories, 1982)
Cal (novel, 1983)
Secrets and Other Stories (short stories, 1984)
The Great Profundo and Other Stories (short stories, 1988)

About the Story

The story is set in Ireland in the 1950s or 1960s. The narrator's great-aunt, a
woman nearing the end of a long life, is protective of her privacy, especially a
collection of letters and papers she keeps in an old desk, which speak of an
entirely different person from the one the narrator knows. In this story,
MacLaverty is exploring the issue of personal history within the context of
larger events, in this case the First World War. Note how the author integrates
letters into the text of the story.

Secrets

He had been called to be there at the end. His Great Aunt Mary had
been dying for some days now and the house was full of relatives. He
had just left his girlfriend home—they had been studying for "A" levels
together—and had come back to the house to find all the lights spilling
onto the lawn and a sense of purpose which had been absent from the
last few days.

He knelt at the bedroom door to join in the prayers. His knees were
on the wooden threshold and he edged them forward onto the carpet.
They had tried to wrap her fingers around a crucifix but they kept loos-
ening. She lay low on the pillow and her face seemed to have shrunk by
half since he had gone out earlier in the night. Her white hair was
damped and pushed back from her forehead. She twisted her head from
side to side, her eyes closed. The prayers chorused on, trying to cover
the sound she was making deep in her throat. Someone said about her
teeth and his mother leaned over her and said, "That's the pet," and
took her dentures from her mouth. The lower half of her face seemed to
collapse. She half opened her eyes but could not raise her eyelids
enough and showed only crescents of white.

"Hail Mary full of grace . . ." the prayers went on. He closed his hands over his face so that he would not have to look but smelt the trace of his girlfriend's handcream from his hands. The noise, deep and guttural, that his aunt was making became intolerable to him. It was as if she were drowning. She had lost all the dignity he knew her to have. He got up from the floor and stepped between the others who were kneeling and went into her sitting-room off the same landing.

He was trembling with anger or sorrow, he didn't know which. He sat in the brightness of her big sitting-room at the oval table and waited for something to happen. On the table was a cut-glass vase of irises, dying because she had been in bed for over a week. He sat staring at them. They were withering from the tips inward, scrolling themselves delicately, brown and neat. Clearing up after themselves. He stared at them for a long time until he heard the sounds of women weeping from the next room.

━━◅▷◅▷━━

His aunt had been small—her head on a level with his when she sat at her table—and she seemed to get smaller each year. Her skin fresh, her hair white and waved and always well washed. She wore no jewelry except a cameo ring on the third finger of her right hand and, around her neck, a gold locket on a chain. The white classical profile on the ring was almost worn through and had become translucent and indistinct. The boy had noticed the ring when she had read to him as a child. In the beginning fairy tales, then as he got older extracts from famous novels, Lorna Doone, Persuasion, Wuthering Heights and her favourite extract, because she read it so often, Pip's meeting with Miss Havisham from Great Expectations. She would sit with him on her knee, her arms around him and holding the page flat with her hand. When he was bored he would interrupt her and ask about the ring. He loved hearing her tell of how her grandmother had given it to her as a brooch and she had had a ring made from it. He would try to count back to see how old it was. Had her grandmother got it from her grandmother? And if so what had she turned it into? She would nod her head from side to side and say, "How would I know a thing like that?" keeping her place in the closed book with her finger.

"Don't be so inquisitive," she'd say. "Let's see what happens next in the story."

One day she was sitting copying figures into a long narrow book with a dip pen when he came into her room. She didn't look up but when he asked her a question she just said, "Mm?" and went on writing. The vase of irises on the oval table vibrated slightly as she wrote.

"What is it?" She wiped the nib on blotting paper and looked up at him over her reading glasses.

"I've started collecting stamps and Mamma says you might have some."

"Does she now—?"

She got up from the table and went to the tall walnut bureau-book-case standing in the alcove. From a shelf of the bookcase she took a small wallet of keys and selected one for the lock. There was a harsh metal shearing sound as she pulled the desk flap down. The writing area was covered with green leather which had dog-eared at the corners. The inner part was divided into pigeon holes, all bulging with papers. Some of them, envelopes, were gathered in batches nipped at the waist with elastic bands. There were postcards and bills and cash-books. She pointed to the postcards.

"You may have the stamps on those," she said. "But don't tear them. Steam them off."

She went back to the oval table and continued writing. He sat on the arm of the chair looking through the picture postcards—torchlight processions at Lourdes, brown photographs of town centres, dull black and whites of beaches backed by faded hotels. Then he turned them over and began to sort the stamps. Spanish, with a bald man, French with a rooster, German with funny jerky print, some Italian with what looked like a chimney-sweep's bundle and a hatchet.

"These are great," he said. "I haven't got any of them."

"Just be careful how you take them off."

"Can I take them downstairs?"

"Is your mother there?"

"Yes."

"Then perhaps it's best if you bring the kettle up here."

He went down to the kitchen. His mother was in the morning room polishing silver. He took the kettle and the flex upstairs. Except for the dipping and scratching of his aunt's pen the room was silent. It was at the back of the house overlooking the orchard and the sound of traffic from the main road was distant and muted. A tiny rattle began as the kettle warmed up, then it bubbled and steam gushed quietly from its spout. The cards began to curl slightly in the jet of steam but she didn't seem to be watching. The stamps peeled moistly off and he put them in a saucer of water to flatten them.

"Who is Brother Benignus?" he asked. She seemed not to hear. He asked again and she looked over her glasses.

"He was a friend."

His flourishing signature appeared again and again. Sometimes Bro Benignus, sometimes Benignus and once Iggy.

"Is he alive?"

"No, he's dead now. Watch the kettle doesn't run dry."

When he had all the stamps off he put the postcards together and replaced them in the pigeon-hole. He reached over towards the letters but before his hand touched them his aunt's voice, harsh for once, warned.

"A-A-A," she moved her pen from side to side. "Do-not-touch," she said and smiled. "Anything else, yes! That section, no!" She resumed her writing.

The boy went through some other papers and found some photographs. One was of a beautiful girl. It was very old-fashioned but he could see that she was beautiful. The picture was a pale brown oval set on a white square of card. The edges of the oval were misty. The girl in the photograph was young and had dark, dark hair scraped severely back and tied like a knotted rope on the top of her head—high arched eyebrows, her nose straight and thin, her mouth slightly smiling, yet not smiling—the way a mouth is after smiling. Her eyes looked out at him dark and knowing and beautiful.

"Who is that?" he asked.

"Why? What do you think of her?"

"She's all right."

"Do you think she is beautiful?" The boy nodded.

"That's me," she said. The boy was glad he had pleased her in return for the stamps.

Other photographs were there, not posed ones like Aunt Mary's but Brownie snaps of laughing groups of girls in bucket hats like German helmets and coats to their ankles. They seemed tiny faces covered in clothes. There was a photograph of a young man smoking a cigarette, his hair combed one way by the wind against a background of sea.

"Who is that in the uniform?" the boy asked.

"He's a soldier," she answered without looking up.

"Oh," said the boy. "But who is he?"

"He was a friend of mine before you were born," she said. Then added, "Do I smell something cooking? Take your stamps and off you go. That's the boy."

The boy looked at the back of the picture of the man and saw in black spidery ink "John, Aug '15 Ballintoye."

"I thought maybe it was Brother Benignus," he said. She looked at him not answering.

"Was your friend killed in the war?"

At first she said no, but then she changed her mind.

"Perhaps he was," she said, then smiled. "You are far too inquisitive. Put it to use and go and see what is for tea. Your mother will need the kettle." She came over to the bureau and helped tidy the photographs away. Then she locked it and put the keys on the shelf.

"Will you bring me up my tray?"

The boy nodded and left.

⧓

It was a Sunday evening, bright and summery. He was doing his homework and his mother was sitting on the carpet in one of her periodic fits of tidying out the drawers of the mahogany sideboard. On one side of her was a heap of paper scraps torn in quarters and bits of rubbish, on the other the useful items that had to be kept. The boy heard the bottom stair creak under Aunt Mary's light footstep. She knocked and put her head round the door and said that she was walking to Devotions. She was dressed in her good coat and hat and was just easing her fingers into her second glove. The boy saw her stop and pat her hair into place before the mirror in the hallway. His mother stretched over and slammed the door shut. It vibrated, then he heard the deeper sound of the outside door closing and her first few steps on the gravelled driveway. He sat for a long time wondering if he would have time or not. Devotions could take anything from twenty minutes to three quarters of an hour, depending on who was saying it.

Ten minutes must have passed, then the boy left his homework and went upstairs and into his aunt's sitting room. He stood in front of the bureau wondering, then he reached for the keys. He tried several before he got the right one. The desk flap screeched as he pulled it down. He pretended to look at the postcards again in case there were any stamps he had missed. Then he put them away and reached for the bundle of letters. The elastic band was thick and old, brittle almost and when he took it off its track remained on the wad of letters. He carefully opened one and took out the letter and unfolded it, frail, khaki-coloured.

My dearest Mary, it began. I am so tired I can hardly write to you. I have spent what seems like all day censoring letters (there is a howitzer about 100 yds away firing every 2 minutes). The letters are heartrending in their attempt to express what they cannot. Some of the men are illiterate, others almost so. I know that they feel as much as we do, yet they do not have the words to express it. That is your job in the schoolroom to give us generations who can read and write well. They have ...

The boy's eye skipped down the page and over the next. He read the last paragraph.

Mary I love you as much as ever—more so that we cannot be together. I do not know which is worse, the hurt of this war or being separated from you. Give all my love to Brendan and all at home.

It was signed, scribbled with what he took to be John. He folded the paper carefully into its original creases and put it in the envelope. He opened another.

My love, it is thinking of you that keeps me sane. When I get a moment I open my memories of you as if I were reading. Your long dark hair—I always imagine you wearing the blouse with the tiny roses, the white one that opened down the back—your eyes that said so much without words, the way you lowered your head when I said anything that embarrassed you, and the clean nape of your neck.

The day I think about most was the day we climbed the head at Ballycastle. In a hollow, out of the wind, the air full of pollen and the sound of insects, the grass warm and dry and you lying beside me your hair undone, between me and the sun. You remember that that was where I first kissed you and the look of disbelief in your eyes that made me laugh afterwards.

It makes me laugh now to see myself savouring these memories standing alone up to my thighs in muck. It is everywhere, two, three feet deep. To walk ten yards leaves you quite breathless.

I haven't time to write more today so I leave you with my feet in the clay and my head in the clouds. I love you, John.

He did not bother to put the letter back into the envelope but opened another.

My dearest, I am so cold that I find it difficult to keep my hand steady enough to write. You remember when we swam the last two fingers of your hand went the colour and texture of candles with the cold. Well that is how I am all over. It is almost four days since I had any real sensation in my feet or legs. Everything is frozen. The ground is like steel.

Forgive me telling you this but I feel I have to say it to someone. The worst thing is the dead. They sit or lie frozen in the position they died. You can distinguish them from the living because their faces are the colour of slate. God help us when the thaw comes . . . This war is beginning to have an effect on me. I have lost all sense of feeling. The only emotion I have experienced lately is one of anger. Sheer white trembling anger. I have no pity or sorrow for the dead and injured. I thank God it is not me but I am enraged that it had to be them. If I live through this experience I will be a different person.

The only thing that remains constant is my love for you.

Today a man died beside me. A piece of shrapnel had pierced his neck as we were moving under fire. I pulled him into a crater and stayed with him until he died. I watched him choke and then drown in his blood.

I am full of anger which has no direction.

He sorted through the pile and read half some, all of others. The sun had fallen low in the sky and shone directly into the room onto the pages he was reading making the paper glare. He selected a letter from the back of the pile and shaded it with his hand as he read.

Dearest Mary, I am writing this to you from my hospital bed. I hope that you were not too worried about not hearing from me. I have been here, so they tell me, for two weeks and it took another two weeks before I could bring myself to write this letter.

I have been thinking a lot as I lie here about the war and about myself and about you. I do not know how to say this but I feel deeply that I must do something, must sacrifice something to make up for the horror of the past year. In some strange way Christ has spoken to me through the carnage ...

Suddenly the boy heard the creak of the stair and he frantically tried to slip the letter back into its envelope but it crumpled and would not fit. He bundled them all together. He could hear his aunt's familiar puffing on the short stairs to her room. He spread the elastic band wide with his fingers. It snapped and the letters scattered. He pushed them into their pigeon hole and quickly closed the desk flap. The brass screeched loudly and clicked shut. At that moment his aunt came into the room.

"What are you doing, boy?" she snapped.

"Nothing." He stood with the keys in his hand. She walked to the bureau and opened it. The letters sprung out in an untidy heap.

"You have been reading my letters," she said quietly. Her mouth was tight with the words and her eyes blazed. The boy could say nothing. She struck him across the side of the face.

"Get out," she said. "Get out of my room."

The boy, the side of his face stinging and red, put the keys on the table on his way out. When he reached the door she called to him. He stopped, his hand on the handle.

"You are dirt," she hissed, "and always will be dirt. I shall remember this till the day I die."

Even though it was a warm evening there was a fire in the large fireplace. His mother had asked him to light it so that she could clear out Aunt Mary's stuff. The room could then be his study, she said. She came in and seeing him at the table said, "I hope I'm not disturbing you."

"No."

She took the keys from her pocket, opened the bureau and began burning papers and cards. She glanced quickly at each one before she flicked it onto the fire.

"Who was Brother Benignus?" he asked.

His mother stopped sorting and said, "I don't know. Your aunt kept herself very much to herself. She got books from him through the post occasionally. That much I do know."

She went on burning the cards. They built into strata, glowing red and black. Now and again she broke up the pile with the poker, sending showers of sparks up the chimney. He saw her come to the letters. She took off the elastic band and put it to one side with the useful things and began dealing the envelopes into the fire. She opened one and read quickly through it, then threw it on top of the burning pile.

"Mama," he said.

"Yes?"

"Did Aunt Mary say anything about me?"

"What do you mean?"

"Before she died—did she say anything?"

"Not that I know of—the poor thing was too far gone to speak, God rest her." She went on burning, lifting the corners of the letters with the poker to let the flames underneath them.

When he felt a hardness in his throat he put his head down on his books. Tears came into his eyes for the first time since she had died and he cried silently into the crook of his arm for the woman who had been his maiden aunt, his teller of tales, that she might forgive him.

Topics for Discussion

1. Why does the Aunt wish to keep her past a secret?

2. How does MacLaverty establish the distance between youth and age in the story?

3. What is the story saying about curiosity?

4. What feelings is the protagonist left with at the end of the story? How does MacLaverty present this?

5. How does the author maintain and control the sense of suspense and anxiety throughout the story?

Alistair MacLeod

About the Author

Alistair MacLeod was born in North Battleford, Saskatchewan, in 1936. His parents were of Cape Breton origin, and they returned to the Maritimes where he completed his high school education. He worked as a teacher and a miner until he completed his education at St. Francis Xavier University, the University of New Brunswick and Notre Dame University. He currently lives in Windsor, Ontario, where he is Professor of English at the University of Windsor.

A meticulous and slow writer by his own admission, MacLeod is particularly interested in the relationship between the individual and the environment, how people earn their living through the physical life, and how the process of survival influences the choices made in a person's life. Many of his stories deal with the heritage, tradition and preservation of what he perceives to be the dwindling Gaelic culture of Nova Scotia and Newfoundland. His landscapes are bound up with the sea, mining and the themes of dislocation and dispossession.

Selected Works

The Lost Salt Gift of Blood (short stories, 1976)
As Birds Bring Forth the Sun (short stories, 1986)

About the Story

In this story, drawn from his collection *The Lost Salt Gift of Blood*, MacLeod is concerned with the ways in which individuals become separated from their pasts because of the choices they make. The story also makes use of the "oral tradition," the passing down of stories by word of mouth—a tradition as old as storytelling itself.

The fishing rights to certain waters off the coasts of Nova Scotia, Newfoundland and Prince Edward Island are passed from one generation to another, so that, like farmers of the ocean, each family has a particular territory to harvest, which is respected by other fishing families.

The Boat

There are times even now, when I awake at four o'clock in the morning with the terrible fear that I have overslept; when I imagine that my father is waiting for me in the room below the darkened stairs or that the shorebound men are tossing pebbles against my window while blowing their hands and stomping their feet impatiently on the frozen steadfast earth. There are times when I am half out of bed and fumbling for socks and mumbling for words before I realize that I am foolishly alone, that no one waits at the base of the stairs and no boat rides restlessly in the waters by the pier.

At such times only the grey corpses on the overflowing ashtray beside my bed bear witness to the extinction of the latest spark and silently await the crushing out of the most recent of their fellows. And then because I am afraid to be alone with death, I dress rapidly, make a great to-do about clearing my throat, turn on both faucets in the sink and proceed to make loud splashing ineffectual noises. Later I go out and walk the mile to the all-night restaurant.

In the winter it is a very cold walk and there are often tears in my eyes when I arrive. The waitress usually gives a sympathetic little shiver and says, "Boy, it must be really cold out there; you got tears in your eyes."

"Yes," I say, "it sure is; it really is."

And then the three or four of us who are always in such places at such times make uninteresting little protective chit-chat until the dawn reluctantly arrives. Then I swallow the coffee which is always bitter and leave with a great busy rush because by that time I have to worry about being late and whether I have a clean shirt and whether my car will start and about all the other countless things one must worry about when he teaches at a great Midwestern university. And I know then that that day will go by as have all the days of the past ten years, for the call and the voices and the shapes and the boat were not really there in the early morning's darkness and I have all kinds of comforting reality to prove it. They are only shadows and echoes, the animals a child's hands make on the wall by lamplight, and the voices from the rain barrel; the cuttings from an old movie made in the black and white of long ago.

I first became conscious of the boat in the same way and at almost the same time that I became aware of the people it supported. My earliest recollection of my father is a view from the floor of gigantic rubber boots and then of being suddenly elevated and having my face pressed against the stubble of his cheek, and of how it tasted of salt and of how he smelled of salt from his red-soled rubber boots to the shaggy whiteness of his hair.

When I was very small, he took me for my first ride in the boat. I rode the half-mile from our house to the wharf on his shoulders and I remembered the sound of his rubber boots galumphing along the gravel beach, the tune of the indecent little song he used to sing, and the odour of the salt.

The floor of the boat was permeated with the same odour and in its constancy I was not aware of change. In the harbour we made our little circle and returned. He tied the boat by its painter, fastened the stern to its permanent anchor and lifted me high over his head to the solidity of the wharf. Then he climbed up the little iron ladder that led to the wharf's cap, placed me once more upon his shoulders and galumphed off again.

When we returned to the house everyone made a great fuss over my precocious excursion and asked, "How did you like the boat?" "Were you afraid in the boat?" "Did you cry in the boat?" They repeated "the boat" at the end of all their questions and I knew it must be very important to everyone.

My earliest recollection of my mother is of being alone with her in the mornings while my father was away in the boat. She seemed to be always repairing clothes that were "torn in the boat," preparing food "to be eaten in the boat" or looking for "the boat" through our kitchen window which faced upon the sea. When my father returned about noon, she would ask, "Well, how did things go in the boat today?" It was the first question I remember asking: "Well, how did things go in the boat today?" "Well, how did things go in the boat today?"

The boat in our lives was registered at Port Hawkesbury. She was what Nova Scotians called a Cape Island boat and was designed for small inshore fishermen who sought the lobsters of the spring and the mackerel of summer and later the cod and haddock and hake. She was thirty-two feet long and nine wide, and was powered by an engine from a Chevrolet truck. She had a marine clutch and a high speed reverse gear and was painted light green with the name *Jenny Lynn* stencilled in black letters on her bow and painted on an oblong plate across her stern. Jenny Lynn had been my mother's maiden name and the boat was called after her as another link in the chain of tradition. Most of the boats that berthed at the wharf bore the names of some female member of their owner's household.

I say this now as if I knew it all then. All at once, all about boat dimensions and engines, and as if on the day of my first childish voyage I noticed the difference between a stencilled name and a painted name. But of course it was not that way at all, for I learned it all very slowly and there was not time enough.

I learned first about our house which was one of about fifty which marched around the horseshoe of our harbour and the wharf which was its heart. Some of them were so close to the water that during a storm the sea spray splashed against their windows while others were built farther along the beach as was the case with ours. The houses and their people, like those of the neighbouring towns and villages, were the result of Ireland's discontent and Scotland's Highland Clearances and America's War of Independence. Impulsive emotional Catholic Celts who could not bear to live with England and shrewd determined Protestant Puritans who, in the years after 1776, could not bear to live without.

The most important room in our house was one of those oblong old-fashioned kitchens heated by a wood- and coal-burning stove. Behind the stove was a box of kindlings and beside it a coal scuttle. A heavy wooden table with leaves that expanded or reduced its dimensions stood in the middle of the floor. There were five wooden homemade chairs which had been chipped and hacked by a variety of knives. Against the east wall, opposite the stove, there was a couch which sagged in the middle and had a cushion for a pillow, and above it a shelf which contained matches, tobacco, pencils, odd fish-hooks, bits of twine, and a tin can filled with bills and receipts. The south wall was dominated by a window which faced the sea and on the north there was a five-foot board which bore a variety of clothes hooks and the burdens of each. Beneath the board there was a jumble of odd footwear, mostly of rubber. There was also, on this wall, a barometer, a map of the marine area and a shelf which held a tiny radio. The kitchen was shared by all of us and was a buffer zone between the immaculate order of ten other rooms and the disruptive chaos of the single room that was my father's.

My mother ran her house as her brothers ran their boats. Everything was clean and spotless and in order. She was tall and dark and powerfully energetic. In later years she reminded me of the women of Thomas Hardy, particularly Eustacia Vye, in a physical way. She fed and clothed a family of seven children, making all of the meals and most of the clothes. She grew miraculous gardens and magnificent flowers and raised broods of hens and ducks. She would walk miles on berry-picking expeditions and hoist her skirts to dig for clams when the tide was low. She was fourteen years younger than my father, whom she had married when she was twenty-six and had been a local beauty for a period of ten years. My mother was of the sea as were all of her people, and her horizons were the very literal ones she scanned with her dark and fearless eyes.

Between the kitchen clothes rack and barometer, a door opened into my father's bedroom. It was a room of disorder and disarray. It was as if the wind which so often clamoured about the house succeeded in entering this single room and after whipping it into turmoil stole quietly away to renew its knowing laughter from without.

My father's bed was against the south wall. It always looked rumpled and unmade because he lay on top of it more than he slept within any folds it might have had. Beside it, there was a little brown table. An archaic goose-necked reading light, a battered table radio, a mound of wooden matches, one or two packages of tobacco, a deck of cigarette papers and an overflowing ashtray cluttered its surface. The brown larvae of tobacco shreds and the grey flecks of ash covered both the table and the floor beneath it. The once-varnished surface of the table was disfigured by numerous black scars and gashes inflicted by the neglected burning cigarettes of many years. They had tumbled from the ashtray unnoticed and branded their statements permanently and quietly into the wood until the odour of their burning caused the snuffing out of their lives. At the bed's foot there was a single window which looked upon the sea.

Against the adjacent wall there was a battered bureau and beside it there was a closet which held his single ill-fitting serge suit, the two or three white shirts that strangled him and the square black shoes that pinched. When he took off his more friendly clothes, the heavy woolen sweaters, mitts and socks which my mother knitted for him and the woollen and doeskin shirts, he dumped them unceremoniously on a single chair. If a visitor entered the room while he was lying on the bed, he would be told to throw the clothes on the floor and take their place upon the chair.

Magazines and books covered the bureau and competed with the clothes for domination of the chair. They further overburdened the heroic little table and lay on top of the radio. They filled a baffling and unknowable cave beneath the bed, and in the corner by the bureau they spilled from the walls and grew up from the floor.

The magazines were the most conventional: *Time, Newsweek, Life, Maclean's Family Herald, Reader's Digest.* They were the result of various cut-rate subscriptions or of the gift subscriptions associated with Christmas, "the two whole years for only $3.50."

The books were more varied. There were a few hard-cover magnificents and bygone Book-of-the-Month wonders and some were Christmas or birthday gifts. The majority of them, however, were used paperbacks which came from those second-hand bookstores which advertise in the backs of magazines: "Miscellaneous Used Paperbacks 10¢ Each." At first he sent for them himself, although my mother resented the expense, but in later years they came more and more often from my sisters who had moved to the cities. Especially at first they were very weird and varied. Mickey Spillane and Ernest Haycox vied with Dostoyevsky and Faulkner, and the Penguin Poets edition of Gerard Manley Hopkins arrived in the same box as a little book on sex technique called *Getting the Most Out of Love.* The former had been assiduously annotated by a very fine hand using a very blue-inked fountain pen while the latter had been studied by someone with very large thumbs, the prints of which were still visible in the margins. At the slightest provocation it would open almost automatically to particularly graphic and well-smudged pages.

When he was not in the boat, my father spent most of his time lying on the bed in his socks, the top two buttons of his trousers undone, his discarded shirt on the ever-ready chair and the sleeves of the woollen Stanfield underwear, which he wore both summer and winter, drawn half way up to his elbows. The pillows propped up the whiteness of his head and the goose-necked lamp illuminated the pages in his hands. The cigarettes smoked and smouldered on the ashtray and on the table and the radio played constantly, sometimes low and sometimes loud. At midnight and at one, two, three and four, one could sometimes hear the radio, his occasional cough, the rustling thud of a completed book being tossed to the corner heap, or the movement necessitated by his sitting on the edge of the bed to roll the thousandth cigarette. He seemed never to sleep, only to doze, and the light shone constantly from his window to the sea.

My mother despised the room and all it stood for and she had stopped sleeping in it after I was born. She despised disorder in rooms and in houses and in hours and in lives, and she had not read a book since high school. There she had read *Ivanhoe* and considered it a colossal waste of time. Still the room remained, like a solid rock of opposition in the sparkling waters of a clear deep harbour, opening off the kitchen where we really lived our lives, with its door always open and its contents visible to all.

The daughters of the room and of the house were very beautiful. They were tall and willowy like my mother and had her fine facial features set off by the reddish copper-coloured hair that had apparently once been my father's before it turned to white. All of them were very clever in school and helped my mother a great deal about the house. When they were young they sang and were very happy and very nice to me because I was the youngest and the family's only boy.

My father never approved of their playing about the wharf like the other children, and they went there only when my mother sent them on an errand. At such times they almost always overstayed, playing screaming games of tag or hide-and-seek in and about the fishing shanties, the piled traps and tubs of trawl, shouting down to the perch that swam languidly about the wharf's algae-covered piles, or jumping in and out of the boats that tugged gently at their lines. My mother was never uneasy about them at such times, and when her husband criticized her she would say, "Nothing will happen to them there," or "They could be doing worse things in worse places."

By about the ninth or tenth grade my sisters one by one discovered my father's bedroom and then the change would begin. Each would go into the room one morning when he was out. She would go with the ideal hope of imposing order or with the more practical objective of emptying the ashtray, and later she would be found spell-bound by the volume in her hand. My mother's reaction was always abrupt, bordering on the angry. "Take your nose out of that trash and come and do your work," she would say, and once I saw her slap my youngest sister so hard that the point of her hand was scarletly emblazoned upon her daughter's cheek while the broken-spined paperback fluttered uselessly to the floor.

Thereafter my mother would launch a campaign against what she had discovered but could not understand. At times although she was not overly religious she would bring in God to bolster her arguments, saying, "In the next world God will see to those who waste their lives reading useless books when they should be about their work." Or without theological aid, "I would like to know how books help anyone to live a life." If my father were in, she would repeat the remarks louder than necessary, and her voice would carry into his room where he lay upon his bed. His usual reaction was to turn up the volume of the radio, although that action in itself betrayed the success of the initial thrust.

Shortly after my sisters began to read the books, they grew restless and lost interest in darning socks and baking bread, and all of them eventually went to work as summer waitresses in the Sea Food Restaurant. The restaurant was run by a big American concern from Boston and catered to the tourists that flooded the area during July and August. My mother despised the whole operation. She said the restaurant was not run by "our people," and "our people" did not eat there, and that it was run by outsiders for outsiders.

"Who are these people anyway?" she would ask, tossing back her dark hair, "and what do they, though they go about with their cameras for a hundred years, know about the way it is here, and what do they care about me and mine, and why should I care about them?"

She was angry that my sisters should even conceive of working in such a place and more angry when my father made no move to prevent it, and she was worried about herself and about her family and about her life. Sometimes she would say softly to her sisters, "I don't know what's the matter with my girls. It seems none of them are interested in any of the right things." And sometimes there would be bitter savage arguments. One afternoon I was coming in with three mackerel I'd been given at the wharf when I heard her say, "Well I hope you'll be satisfied when they come home knocked up and you'll have had your way."

It was the most savage thing I'd ever heard my mother say. Not just the words but the way she said them, and I stood there in the porch afraid to breathe for what seemed like the years from ten to fifteen, feeling the damp moist mackerel with their silver glassy eyes growing clammy against my leg.

Through the angle in the screen door I saw my father who had been walking into his room wheel around on one of his rubber-booted heels and look at her with his blue eyes flashing like clearest ice beneath the snow that was his hair. His usually ruddy face was drawn and grey, reflecting the exhaustion of a man of sixty-five who had been working in those rubber boots for eleven hours on an August day, and for a fleeting moment I wondered what I would do if he killed my mother while I stood there in the porch with those three foolish mackerel in my hand. Then he turned and went into his room and the radio blared forth the next day's weather forecast and I retreated under the noise and returned again, stamping my feet and slamming the door too loudly to signal my approach. My mother was busy at the stove when I came in, and did not raise her head when I threw the mackerel in a pan. As I looked into my father's room, I said, "Well how did things go in the boat today?" and he replied, "Oh not too badly, all things considered."

He was lying on his back and lighting the first cigarette and the radio was talking about the Virginia coast.

All of my sisters made good money on tips. They bought my father an electric razor which he tried to use for a while and they took out even more magazine subscriptions. They bought my mother a great many clothes of the type she was very fond of, the wide-brimmed hats and the brocaded dresses, but she locked them all in trunks and refused to wear any of them.

On one August day my sisters prevailed upon my father to take some of their restaurant customers for an afternoon ride in the boat. The tourists with their expensive clothes and cameras and sun glasses awkwardly backed down the iron ladder at the wharf's side to where my father waited below, holding the rocking *Jenny Lynn* in snug against the wharf with one hand on the iron ladder and steadying his descending passengers with the other. They tried to look both prim and wind-blown like the girls in the Pepsi-Cola ads and did the best they could, sitting on the thwarts where the newspapers were spread to cover the splattered blood and fish entrails, crowding to one side so that they were in danger of capsizing the boat, taking the inevitable pictures or merely trailing their fingers through the water of their dreams.

All of them liked my father very much and, after he'd brought them back from their circles in the harbour, they invited him to their rented cabins which were located high on a hill overlooking the village to which they were so alien. He proceeded to get very drunk up there with the beautiful view and the strange company and the abundant liquor, and late in the afternoon he began to sing.

I was just approaching the wharf to deliver my mother's summons when he began, and the familiar yet unfamiliar voice that rolled down from the cabins made me feel as I had never felt before in my young life or perhaps as I had always felt without really knowing it, and I was ashamed yet proud, young yet old and saved yet forever lost, and there was nothing I could do to control my legs which trembled nor my eyes which wept for what they could not tell.

The tourists were equipped with tape recorders and my father sang for more than three hours. His voice boomed down the hill and bounced off the surface of the harbour, which was an unearthly blue on that hot August day, and was then reflected to the wharf and the fishing shanties where it was absorbed amidst the men who were baiting their lines for the next day's haul.

He sang all the old sea chanties which had come across from the old world and by which men like him had pulled ropes for generations, and he sang the East Coast sea songs which celebrated the sealing vessels of Northumberland Strait and the long liners of the Grand Banks, and of Anticosti, Sable Island, Grand Manan, Boston Harbor, Nantucket and Block Island. Gradually he shifted to the seemingly unending Gaelic drinking songs with their twenty or more verses and inevitable refrains, and the men in the shanties smiled at the coarseness of some of the verses and at the thought that the singer's immediate audience did not know what they were applauding nor recording to take back to staid old Boston. Later as the sun was setting he switched to the laments and the wild and haunting Gaelic war songs of those spattered Highland ancestors he had never seen and when his voice ceased, the savage melancholy of three hundred years seemed to hang over the peaceful harbour and the quite boats and the men leaning in the doorways of their shanties with their cigarettes glowing in the dusk and the women looking to the sea from their open windows with their children in their arms.

When he came home he threw the money he had earned on the kitchen table as he did with all his earnings but my mother refused to touch it and the next day he went with the rest of the men to bait his trawl in the shanties. The tourists came to the door that evening and my mother met them there and told them that her husband was not in although he was lying on the bed only a few feet away with the radio playing and the cigarette upon his lips. She stood in the doorway until they reluctantly went away.

In the winter they sent him a picture which had been taken on the day of the singing. On the back it said, "To Our Ernest Hemingway" and the "Our" was underlined. There was also an accompanying letter telling how much they had enjoyed themselves, how popular the tape was proving and explaining who Ernest Hemingway was. In a way it almost did look like one of those unshaven taken-in-Cuba pictures of Hemingway. He looked both massive and incongruous in the setting. His bulky fisherman's clothes were too big for the green and white lawn chair in which he sat, and his rubber boots seemed to take up all of the well-clipped grass square. The beach umbrella jarred with his sun-burned face and because he had already been singing for some time, his lips which chapped in the winds of spring and burned in the water glare of summer had already cracked in several places, producing tiny flecks of blood at the corners and on the whiteness of his teeth. The bracelets of brass chain which he wore to protect his wrists from chafing seemed abnormally large and his broad leather belt had been slackened and his heavy shirt and underwear were open at the throat revealing an uncultivated wilderness of white chest hair bordering on the semi-controlled stubble of his neck and chin. His blue eyes had looked directly into the camera and his hair was whiter than the two tiny clouds which hung over his left shoulder. The sea was behind him and its immense blue flatness stretched out to touch the arching blueness of the sky. It seemed very far away from him or else he was so much in the fore-ground that he seemed too big for it.

Each year another of my sisters would read the books and work in the restaurant. Sometimes they would stay out quite late on the hot summer nights and when they came up the stairs my mother would ask them many long and involved questions which they resented and tried to avoid. Before ascending the stairs they would go into my father's room and those of us who waited above could hear them throwing his clothes off the chair before sitting on it or the squeak of the bed as they sat on its edge. Sometimes they would talk to him a long time, the murmur of their voices blending with the music of the radio into a mysterious vapour-like sound which floated softly up the stairs.

I say this again as if it all happened at once and as if all of my sisters were of identical ages and like so many lemmings going into another sea and, again, it was of course not that way at all. Yet go they did, to Boston, to Montreal, to New York with the young men they met during the summers and later married in those far-away cities. The young men were very articulate and handsome and wore fine clothes and drove expensive cars and my sisters, as I said, were very tall and beautiful with their copper-coloured hair and were tired of darning socks and baking bread.

One by one they went. My mother had each of her daughters for fifteen years, then lost them for two and finally forever. None married a fisherman. My mother never accepted any of the young men, for in her eyes they seemed always a combination of the lazy, the effeminate, the dishonest and the unknown. They never seemed to do any physical work and she could not comprehend their luxurious vacations and she did not know whence they came nor who they were. And in the end she did not really care, for they were not of her people and they were not of her sea.

I say this now with a sense of wonder at my own stupidity in thinking I was somehow free and would go on doing well in school and playing and helping in the boat and passing into my early teens while streaks of grey began to appear in my mother's dark hair and my father's rubber boots dragged sometimes on the pebbles of the beach as he trudged home from the wharf. And there were but three of us in the house that had at one time been so loud.

Then during the winter that I was fifteen he seemed to grow old and ill at once. Most of January he lay upon the bed, smoking and reading and listening to the radio while the wind howled about the house and the needle-like snow blistered off the ice-covered harbour and the doors flew out of people's hands if they did not cling to them like death.

In February when the men began overhauling their lobster traps he still did not move, and my mother and I began to knit lobster trap headings in the evenings. The twine was as always very sharp and harsh, and blisters formed upon our thumbs and little paths of blood snaked quietly down between our fingers while the seals that had drifted down from distant Labrador wept and moaned like human children on the ice-floes of the Gulf.

In the daytime my mother's brother who had been my father's partner as long as I could remember also came to work upon the gear. He was a year older than my mother and was tall and dark and the father of twelve children.

By March we were very far behind and although I began to work very hard in the evenings I knew it was not hard enough and that there were but eight weeks left before the opening of the season on May first. And I knew that my mother worried and my uncle was uneasy and that all of our very lives depended on the boat being ready with her gear and two men, by the date of May the first. And I knew then that *David Copperfield* and *The Tempest* and all of those friends I had dearly come to love must really go forever. So I bade them all good-bye.

The night after my first full day at home and after my mother had gone upstairs he called me into his room where I sat upon the chair beside his bed. "You will go back tomorrow" he said simply.

I refused then, saying I had made my decision and was satisfied.

"That is no way to make a decision," he said, "and if you are satisfied I am not. It is best that you go back." I was almost angry then and told him as all children do that I wished he would leave me alone and stop telling me what to do.

He looked at me a long time then, lying there on the same bed on which he had fathered me those sixteen years before, fathered me his only son, out of who knew what emotions when he was already fifty-six and his hair had turned to snow. Then he swung his legs over the edge of the squeaking bed and sat facing me and looked into my own dark eyes with his of crystal blue and placed his hand upon my knee. "I am not telling you to do anything," he said softly, "only asking you."

The next morning I returned to school. As I left, my mother followed me to the porch and said, "I never thought a son of mine would choose useless books over the parents that gave him life."

In the weeks that followed he got up rather miraculously and the gear was ready and the Jenny Lynn was freshly painted by the last two weeks of April when the ice began to break up and the lonely screaming gulls returned to haunt the silver herring as they flashed within the sea.

On the first day of May the boats raced out as they had always done, laden down almost to the gunwales with their heavy cargoes of traps. They were almost like living things as they plunged through the waters of the spring and manoeuvred between the still floating icebergs of crystal-white and emerald green on their way to the traditional grounds that they sought out every May. And those of us sat that day in the high school on the hill, discussing the water imagery of Tennyson, watched them as they passed back and forth beneath us until by afternoon the piles of traps which had been stacked upon the wharf were no longer visible but were spread about the bottoms of the sea. And the *Jenny Lynn* went too, all day, with my uncle tall and dark, like a latter-day Tashtego standing at the tiller with his legs wide apart and guiding her deftly between the floating pans of ice and my father in the stern standing in the same way with his hands upon the ropes that lashed the cargo to the deck. And at night my mother asked, "Well, how did things go in the boat today?"

And the spring wore on and the summer came and school ended in the third week of June and the lobster season on July first and I wished that the two things I loved so dearly did not exclude each other in a manner that was so blunt and too clear.

At the conclusion of the lobster season my uncle said he had been offered a berth on a deep sea dragger and had decided to accept. We all knew that he was leaving the *Jenny Lynn* forever and that before the next lobster season he would buy a boat of his own. He was expecting another child and would be supporting fifteen people by the next spring and could not chance my father against the family that he loved.

I joined my father then for the trawling season, and he made no protest and my mother was quite happy. Through the summer we baited the tubs of trawl in the afternoon and set them at sunset and revisited them in the darkness of the early morning. The men would come tramping by our house at four A.M. and we would join them and walk with them to the wharf and be on our way before the sun rose out of the ocean where it seemed to spend the night. If I was not up they would toss pebbles to my window and I would be very embarrassed and tumble downstairs to where my father lay fully clothed atop his bed, reading his book and listening to his radio and smoking his cigarette. When I appeared he would swing off his bed and put on his boots and be instantly ready and then we would take the lunches my mother had prepared the night before and walk off toward the sea. He would make no attempt to wake me himself.

It was in many ways a good summer. There were few storms and we were out almost every day and we lost a minimum of gear and seemed to land a maximum of fish and I tanned dark and brown after the manner of my uncles.

My father did not tan—he never tanned—because of his reddish complexion, and the salt water irritated his skin as it had for sixty years. He burned and reburned over and over again and his lips still cracked so that they bled when he smiled, and his arms, especially the left, still broke out into the oozing salt-water boils as they had ever since as a child I had first watched him soaking and bathing them in a variety of ineffectual solutions. The chafe-preventing bracelets of brass linked chain that all the men wore about their wrists in early spring were his the full season and he shaved but painfully and only once a week.

And I saw then, that summer, many things that I had seen all my life as if for the first time and I thought that perhaps my father had never been intended for a fisherman either physically or mentally. At least not in the manner of my uncles; he had never really loved it. And I remembered that, one evening in his room when we were talking about *David Copperfield*, he had said that he had always wanted to go to the university and I had dismissed it then in the way one dismisses his father's saying he would like to be a tight-rope walker, and we had gone on to talk about the Peggottys and how they loved the sea.

And I thought then to myself that there were many things wrong with all of us and all our lives and I wondered why my father, who was himself an only son, had not married before he was forty and then I wondered why he had. I even thought that perhaps he had had to marry my mother and checked the dates on the flyleaf of the Bible where I learned that my oldest sister had been born a prosaic eleven months after the marriage, and I felt myself then very dirty and debased for my lack of faith and for what I had thought and done.

And then there came into my heart a very great love for my father and I thought it was very much braver to spend a life doing what you really do not want rather than selfishly following forever your own dreams and inclinations. And I knew then that I could never leave him alone to suffer the iron-tipped harpoons which my mother would forever hurl into his soul because he was a failure as a husband and a father who had retained none of his own. And I felt that I had been very small in a little secret place within me and that even the completion of high school was for me a silly shallow selfish dream.

So I told him one night very resolutely and very powerfully that I would remain with him as long as he lived and we would fish the sea together. And he made no protests but only smiled through the cigarette smoke that wreathed his bed and replied, "I hope you will remember what you've said."

The room was now so filled with books as to be almost Dickensian, but he would not allow my mother to move or change them and he continued to read them, sometimes two or three a night. They came with great regularity now, and there were more hard covers, sent by my sisters who had gone so long ago and now seemed so distant and so prosperous, and sent also pictures of small red-haired grandchildren with baseball bats and dolls which he placed upon his bureau and which my mother gazed at wistfully when she thought no would see. Red-haired grandchildren with baseball bats and dolls who would never know the sea in hatred or in love.

And so we fished through the heat of August and into the cooler days of September when the water was so clear we could almost see the bottom and the white mists rose like delicate ghosts in the early morning dawn. And one day my mother said to me, "You have given added years to his life."

And we fished on into October when it began to roughen and we could no longer risk night sets but took our gear out each morning and returned at the first sign of the squalls; and on into November when we lost three tubs of trawl and the clear blue water turned to a sullen grey and the trochoidal waves rolled rough and high and washed across our bows and decks as we ran within their troughs. We wore heavy sweaters now and the awkward rubber slickers and the heavy woollen mitts which soaked and froze into masses of ice that hung from our wrists like the limbs of gigantic monsters until we thawed them against the exhaust pipe's heat. And almost every day we would leave for home before noon, driven by the blasts of the northwest wind, coating our eyebrows with ice and freezing our eyelids closed as we leaned into a visibility that was hardly there, charting our course from the compass and the sea, running with the waves and between them but never confronting their towering might.

And I stood at the tiller now, on these homeward lunges, stood in the place and in the manner of my uncle, turning to look at my father and to shout over the roar of the engine and the slop of the sea to where he stood in the stern, drenched and dripping with the snow and the salt and the spray and his bushy eyebrows caked in ice. But on November twenty-first, when it seemed we might be making the final run of the season, I turned and he was not there and I knew even in that instant that he would never be again.

On November twenty-first the waves of the grey Atlantic are very very high and the waters are very cold and there are no signposts on the surface of the sea. You cannot tell where you have been five minutes before and in the squalls of snow you cannot see. And it takes longer than you would believe to check a boat that has been running before a gale and turn her ever so carefully in a wide and stupid circle, with timbers creaking and straining, back into the face of storm. And you know that it is useless and that your voice does not carry the length of the boat and that even if you knew the original spot, the relentless waves would carry such a burden perhaps a mile or so by the time you could return. And you know also, the final irony, that your father like your uncles and all the men that form your past, cannot swim a stroke.

The lobster beds off the Cape Breton coast are still very rich and now, from May to July, their offerings are packed in crates of ice, and thundered by the gigantic transport trucks, day and night, through New Glasgow, Amherst, Saint John and Bangor and Portland and into Boston where they are tossed still living into boiling pots of water, their final home.

And though the prices are higher and the competition tighter, the grounds to which the *Jenny Lynn* once went remain untouched and unfished as they have for the last ten years. For if there are no signposts on the sea in storm there are certain ones in calm and the lobster bottoms were distributed in calm before any of us can remember and the grounds my father fished were those his father fished before him and there were others before and before and before. Twice the big boats have come from forty and fifty miles, lured by the promise of the grounds, and strewn the bottom with their traps and twice they have returned to find their buoys cut adrift and their gear lost and destroyed. Twice the Fisheries Officer and the Mounted Police have come and asked many long and involved questions and twice they have received no answers from the men leaning in the doors of their shanties and the women standing at their windows with their children in their arms. Twice they have gone away saying: "There are no legal boundaries in the Marine area"; "No one can own the sea"; "Those grounds don't wait for anyone."

But the men and the women, with my mother dark among them, do not care for what they say, for to them the grounds are sacred and they think they wait for me.

It is not an easy thing to know that your mother lives alone on an inadequate insurance policy and that she is too proud to accept any other aid. And that she looks through her lonely window onto the ice of winter and the hot flat calm of summer and the rolling waves of fall. And that she lies awake in the early morning's darkness when the rubber boots of the men scrunch upon the gravel as they pass beside her house on their way down to the wharf. And she knows that the footsteps never stop, because no man goes from her house, and she alone of all the Lynns has neither son nor son-in-law that walks toward the boat that will take him to the sea. And it is not an easy thing to know that your mother looks upon the sea with love and on you with bitterness because the one has been so constant and the other so untrue.

But neither is it easy to know that your father was found on November twenty-eighth, ten miles to the north and wedged between two boulders at the base of the rock-strewn cliffs where he had been hurled and slammed so many many times. His hands were shredded ribbons as were his feet which had lost their boots to the suction of the sea, and his shoulders came apart in our hands when we tried to move him from the rocks. And the fish had eaten his testicles and the gulls had pecked out his eyes and the white-green stubble of his whiskers had continued to grow in death, like the grass on graves, upon the purple, bloated mass that was his face. There was not much left of my father, physically, as he lay there with the brass chains on his wrists and the seaweed in his hair.

Topics for Discussion

1. How does MacLeod present the setting of the story? Is the ocean a place?

2. How does MacLeod achieve a sense of irony with the climax of the story?

3. What is the function of storytelling in "The Boat"?

4. How does MacLeod's style create ocean rhythms?

5. Do the choices we make really shape our lives?

Katherine Mansfield

About the Author

Katherine Mansfield was born Kathleen Beauchamp in Wellington, New Zealand, in 1888. Her father was a wealthy banker and businessman and she grew up in upper-class surroundings. She studied by "grand tour," by travelling throughout Europe, and was educated in art and music at Queen's College, London, before settling permanently in England in 1908. In 1909 she married George Bowden, but the marriage lasted only one day. After that she pursued a bohemian lifestyle among the artists and writers of London. Her most famous friendships include those with D. H. Lawrence and the editor and critic John Middleton Murry (whom she later took as her second husband). During this period in her life she began writing short stories and editing small literary magazines such as Murry's *Rhythm*. In 1915, shortly after the death of her favourite brother, Leslie, Mansfield developed a severe cough that deteriorated into tuberculosis. She died at Fontainbleau in France early in 1923.

Partly as a result of her incapacitating illness and partly owing to her incredible descriptive skills and powers of observation, Mansfield produced a large volume of work over a very short period. Dismissed as a writer in her own time as too "feminine" and "domestic" because of her sense of detail and her focus on the perspectives and concerns of female characters, Mansfield is today considered to be one of the finest writers of the modern short story. Her powers of observation, applied not only to the external world of the stories but to the internal lives of her characters, is expressed through the recurring use of "secret selves," the private insight into a character's psychology and personality that is usually hidden from public scrutiny.

Often associated with the "Imagist" movement, a group of writers who sought to convey their images as directly as possible without authorial exegesis or editorial "telling," Mansfield's clearly delineated images do most of the work of conveying the narrative information of her stories. Her desire to tell stories from the point of view of women has placed her at the core of feminist literature and thought.

Selected Works

In a German Pension (1911)
Bliss, and Other Stories (1920)
The Garden-Party, and Other Stories (1922)
The Doves' Nest, and Other Stories (1923)
Something Childish, and Other Stories (1924)
Collected Stories (1945)
Selected Stories (1953)

About the Story

"The Garden-Party," the title story from the collection of the same name, opens on the morning of a major social event on the Sheridan family's calendar. The story is set in New Zealand where Mansfield grew up, and has many biographical associations with her own life.

When reading the story, note Mansfield's use of flowers. These are more than just images for the sake of description—she is creating "still life" portraits, visual representations of static objects arranged and presented for purposes of aesthetic balance. Part of the way that Mansfield supports the visual dimension of her stories is through the use of colours, and the stories are often delicately detailed.

Also of note is her use of class distinctions, the differences between the very rich and the very poor. The juxtaposition of their lifestyles is a major source tension in the story.

The Garden-Party

And after all the weather was ideal. They could not have had a more perfect day for a garden-party if they had ordered it. Windless, warm, the sky without a cloud. Only the blue was veiled with a haze of light gold, as it is sometimes in early summer. The gardener had been up since dawn, mowing the lawns and sweeping them, until the grass and the dark flat rosettes where the daisy plants had been seemed to shine. As for the roses, you could not help feeling they understood that roses are the only flowers that impress people at garden-parties; the only flowers that everybody is certain of knowing. Hundreds, yes, literally hundreds, had come out in a single night; the green bushes bowed down as though they had been visited by archangels.

Breakfast was not yet over before the men came to put up the marquee.

"Where do you want the marquee put, mother?"

"My dear child, it's no use asking me. I'm determined to leave everything to you children this year. Forget I am your mother. Treat me as an honoured guest."

But Meg could not possibly go and supervise the men. She had washed her hair before breakfast, and she sat drinking her coffee in a green turban, with a dark wet curl stamped on each cheek. Jose, the butterfly, always came down in a silk petticoat and a kimono jacket.

"You'll have to go, Laura; you're the artistic one."

Away Laura flew, still holding her piece of bread-and-butter. It's so delicious to have an excuse for eating out of doors and, besides, she loved having to arrange things; she always felt she could do it so much better than anybody else.

Four men in their shirt-sleeves stood grouped together on the garden path. They carried staves covered with rolls of canvas and they had big tool-bags slung on their backs. They looked impressive. Laura wished now that she was not holding that piece of bread-and-butter, but there was nowhere to put it and she couldn't possibly throw it away. She blushed and tried to look severe and even a little bit short-sighted as she came up to them.

"Good morning," she said, copying her mother's voice. But that sounded so fearfully affected that she was ashamed, and stammered like a little girl, "Oh—er—have you come—is it about the marquee?"

"That's right, miss," said the tallest of the men, a lanky, freckled fellow, and he shifted his tool-bag, knocked back his straw hat and smiled down at her. "That's about it."

His smile was so easy, so friendly, that Laura recovered. What nice eyes he had, small, but such a dark blue! And now she looked at the others, they were smiling too. "Cheer up, we won't bite," their smile seemed to say. How very nice workmen were! And what a beautiful morning! She mustn't mention the morning; she must be business-like. The marquee.

"Well, what about the lily-lawn? Would that do?"

And she pointed to the lily-lawn with the hand that didn't hold the bread-and-butter. They turned, they stared in the direction. A little fat chap thrust out his underlip and the tall fellow frowned.

"I don't fancy it," said he. "Not conspicuous enough. You see, with a thing like a marquee"—and he turned to Laura in his easy way—"you want to put it somewhere where it'll give you a bang slap in the eye, if you follow me."

Laura's upbringing made her wonder for a moment whether it was quite respectful of a workman to talk to her of bangs slap in the eye. But she did quite follow him.

"A corner of the tennis-court," she suggested. "But the band's going to be in one corner."

"H'm, going to have a band, are you?" said another of the workmen. He was pale. He had a haggard look as his dark eyes scanned the tennis-court. What was he thinking?

"Only a very small band," said Laura gently. Perhaps he wouldn't mind so much if the band was quite small. But the tall fellow interrupted.

"Look here, miss, that's the place. Against those trees. Over there. That'll do fine."

Against the karakas. Then the karaka trees would be hidden. And they were so lovely, with their broad, gleaming leaves, and their clusters of yellow fruit. They were like trees you imagined growing on a desert island, proud, solitary, lifting their leaves and fruits to the sun in a kind of silent splendour. Must they be hidden by a marquee?

They must. Already the men had shouldered their staves and were making for the place. Only the tall fellow was left. He bent down, pinched a sprig of lavender, put his thumb and forefinger to his nose and snuffed up the smell. When Laura saw that gesture she forgot all about the karakas in her wonder at him caring for things like that—caring for the smell of lavender. How many men that she knew would have done such a thing. Oh, how extraordinarily nice workmen were, she thought. Why couldn't she have workmen for friends rather than the silly boys she danced with and who came to Sunday night supper? She would get on much better with men like these.

It's all the fault, she decided, as the tall fellow drew something on the back of an envelope, something that was to be looped up or left to hang, of these absurd class distinctions. Well, for her part, she didn't feel them. Not a bit, not an atom.... And now there came the chock-chock of wooden hammers. Someone whistled, someone sang out, "Are you right there, matey?" "Matey!" The friendliness of it, the—the—Just to prove how happy she was, just to show the tall fellow how at home she felt, and how she despised stupid conventions, Laura took a big bite of her bread-and-butter as she stared at the little drawing. She felt just like a work-girl.

"Laura, Laura, where are you? Telephone, Laura!" a voice cried from the house.

"Coming!" Away she skimmed, over the lawn, up the path, up the steps, across the veranda and into the porch. In the hall her father and Laurie were brushing their hats ready to go to the office.

"I say, Laura," said Laurie very fast, "you might just give a squiz at my coat before this afternoon. See if it wants pressing."

"I will," said she. Suddenly she couldn't stop herself. She ran at Laurie and gave him a small, quick squeeze. "Oh, I do love parties, don't you?" gasped Laura.

"Ra-ther," said Laurie's warm, boyish voice, and he squeezed his sister too and gave her a gentle push. "Dash off to the telephone, old girl."

The telephone. "Yes, yes; oh yes. Kitty? Good morning, dear. Come to lunch? Do, dear. Delighted, of course. It will only be a very scratch meal—just the sandwich crusts and broken meringue-shells and what's left over. Yes, isn't it a perfect morning? Your white? Oh, I certainly should. One moment—hold the line. Mother's calling." And Laura sat back. "What, mother? Can't hear."

Mrs. Sheridan's voice floated down the stairs. "Tell her to wear that sweet hat she had on last Sunday."

"Mother says you're to wear that *sweet* hat you had on last Sunday. Good. One o'clock. Bye-bye."

Laura put back the receiver, flung her arms over her head, took a deep breath, stretched and let them fall. "Huh," she sighed, and the moment after the sigh she sat up quickly. She was still, listening. All the doors in the house seemed to be open. The house was alive with soft, quick steps and running voices. The green baize door that led to the kitchen regions swung open and shut with a muffled thud. And now there came a long, chuckling absurd sound. It was the heavy piano being moved on its stiff castors. But the air! If you stopped to notice, was the air always like this? Little faint winds were playing chase in at the tops of the windows, out at the doors. And there were two tiny spots of sun, one on the inkpot, one on a silver photograph frame, playing too. Darling little spots. Especially the one on the inkpot lid. It was quite warm. A warm little silver star. She could have kissed it.

The front door bell pealed and there sounded the rustle of Sadie's print skirt on the stairs. A man's voice murmured; Sadie answered, careless, "I'm sure I don't know. Wait. I'll ask Mrs. Sheridan."

"What is it, Sadie?" Laura came into the hall.

"It's the florist, Miss Laura."

It was, indeed. There, just inside the door, stood a wide, shallow tray full of pots of pink lilies. No other kind. Nothing but lilies—canna lilies, big pink flowers, wide open, radiant, almost frighteningly alive on bright crimson stems.

"O-oh, Sadie!" said Laura, and the sound was like a little moan. She crouched down as if to warm herself at that blaze of lilies; she felt they were in her fingers, on her lips, growing in her breast.

"It's some mistake," she said faintly. "Nobody ever ordered so many. Sadie, go and find mother."

But at that moment Mrs. Sheridan joined them.

"It's quite right," she said calmly. "Yes, I ordered them. Aren't they lovely?" She pressed Laura's arm. "I was passing the shop yesterday, and I saw them in the window. And I suddenly thought for once in my life I shall have enough canna lilies. The garden-party will be a good excuse."

"But I thought you said you didn't mean to interfere," said Laura. Sadie had gone. The florist's man was still outside at his van. She put her arm round her mother's neck and gently, very gently, she bit her mother's ear.

"My darling child, you wouldn't like a logical mother, would you? Don't do that. Here's the man."

He carried more lilies still, another whole tray.

"Bank them up, just inside the door, on both sides of the porch, please," said Mrs. Sheridan. "Don't you agree, Laura?"

"Oh, I *do*, mother."

In the drawing-room Meg, Jose and good little Hans had at last succeeded in moving the piano.

"Now, if we put this chesterfield against the wall and move everything out of the room except the chairs, don't you think?"

"Quite."

"Hans, move these tables into the smoking-room, and bring a sweeper to take these marks off the carpet and—one moment, Hans—" Jose loved giving orders to the servants and they loved obeying her. She always made them feel they were taking part in some drama. "Tell mother and Miss Laura to come here at once."

"Very good, Miss Jose."

She turned to Meg. "I want to hear what the piano sounds like, just in case I'm asked to sing this afternoon. Let's try over 'This Life is Weary.'"

Pom! Ta-ta-ta *Tee*-ta! The piano burst out so passionately that Jose's face changed. She clasped her hands. She looked mournfully and enigmatically at her mother and Laura as they came in.

This Life is Wee-ary,
A Tear—a Sigh.
A Love that Chan-ges,
This Life is Wee-ary,
A Tear—a Sigh.
A Love that Chan-ges,
And then ... Good-bye!

But at the word "Good-bye," and although the piano sounded more desperate than ever, her face broke into a brilliant, dreadfully unsympathetic smile.

"Aren't I in good voice, mummy?" she beamed.

This Life is Wee-ary,
Hope comes to Die.
A Dream—a Wa-kening.

But now Sadie interrupted them. "What is it, Sadie?"

"If you please, m'm, cook says have you got the flags for the sandwiches?"

"The flags for the sandwiches, Sadie?" echoed Mrs. Sheridan dreamily. And the children knew by her face that she hadn't got them. "Let me see." And she said to Sadie firmly, "Tell cook I'll let her have them in ten minutes."

Sadie went.

"Now, Laura," said her mother quickly, "come with me into the smoking-room. I've got the names somewhere on the back of an envelope. You'll have to write them out for me. Meg, go upstairs this minute and take that wet thing off your head. Jose, run and finish dressing this instant. Do you hear me, children, or shall I have to tell your father when he comes home to-night? And—and, Jose, pacify cook if you do go into the kitchen, will you? I'm terrified of her this morning."

The envelope was found at last behind the dining-room clock, though how it had got there Mrs. Sheridan could not imagine.

"One of you children must have stolen it out of my bag, because I remember vividly—cream-cheese and lemon-curd. Have you done that?"

"Yes."

"Egg and—" Mrs. Sheridan held the envelope away from her. "It looks like mice. It can't be mice, can it?"

"Olive, pet," said Laura, looking over her shoulder.

"Yes, of course, olive. What a horrible combination it sounds. Egg and olive."

They were finished at last, and Laura took them off to the kitchen. She found Jose there pacifying the cook, who did not look at all terrifying.

"I have never seen such exquisite sandwiches," said Jose's rapturous voice. "How many kinds did you say there were, cook? Fifteen?"

"Fifteen, Miss Jose."

"Well, cook, I congratulate you."

Cook swept up crusts with the long sandwich knife, and smiled broadly.

"Godber's has come," announced Sadie, issuing out of the pantry. She had seen the man pass the window.

That meant the cream puffs had come. Godber's were famous for their cream puffs. Nobody ever thought of making them at home.

"Bring them in and put them on the table, my girl," ordered cook.

Sadie brought them in and went back to the door. Of course Laura and Jose were far too grown-up to really care about such things. All the same, they couldn't help agreeing that the puffs looked very attractive. Very. Cook began arranging them, shaking off the extra icing sugar.

"Don't they carry one back to all one's parties?" said Laura.

"I suppose they do," said practical Jose, who never liked to be carried back. "They look beautifully light and feathery, I must say."

"Have one each, my dears," said cook in her comfortable voice. "Yer ma won't know."

Oh, impossible. Fancy cream puffs so soon after breakfast. The very idea made one shudder. All the same, two minutes later Jose and Laura were licking their fingers with that absorbed inward look that only comes from whipped cream.

"Let's go into the garden, out by the back way," suggested Laura. "I want to see how the men are getting on with the marquee. They're such awfully nice men."

But the back door was blocked by cook, Sadie, Godber's man and Hans.

Something had happened.

"Tuk-tuk-tuk," clucked cook like an agitated hen. Sadie had her hand clapped to her cheek as though she had toothache. Han's face was screwed up in the effort to understand. Only Godber's man seemed to be enjoying himself; it was his story.

"What's the matter? What's happened?"

"There's been a horrible accident," said cook. "A man killed."

"A man killed! Where? How? When?"

But Godber's man wasn't going to have his story snatched from under his very nose.

"Know those little cottages just below here, miss?" Know them? Of course she knew them. "Well, there's a young chap living there, name of Scott, a carter. His horse shied at a traction-engine, corner of Hawke Street this morning, and he was thrown out on the back of his head. Killed."

"Dead!" Laura stared at Godber's man.

"Dead when they picked him up," said Godber's man with relish. "They were taking the body home as I come up here." And he said to the cook, "He's left a wife and five little ones."

"Jose, come here." Laura caught hold of her sister's sleeve and dragged her through the kitchen to the other side of the green baize door. There she paused and leaned against it. "Jose!" she said, horrified, "however are we going to stop everything?"

"Stop everything, Laura!" cried Jose in astonishment. "What do you mean?"

"Stop the garden-party, of course." Why did Jose pretend?

But Jose was still more amazed. "Stop the garden-party? My dear Laura, don't be so absurd. Of course we can't do anything of the kind. Nobody expects us to. Don't be so extravagant."

"But we can't possibly have a garden-party with a man dead just outside the front gate."

That really was extravagant, for the little cottages were in a lane to themselves at the very bottom of a steep rise that led up to the house. A broad road ran between. True, they were far too near. They were the greatest possible eyesore and they had no right to be in that neighbourhood at all. They were little mean dwellings painted a chocolate brown. In the garden patches there was nothing but cabbage stalks, sick hens and tomato cans. The very smoke coming out of their chimneys was poverty-stricken. Little rags and shreds of smoke, so unlike the great silvery plumes that uncurled from the Sheridans' chimneys. Washerwomen lived in the lane and sweeps and a cobbler and a man whose house-front was studded all over with minute bird-cages. Children swarmed. When the Sheridans were little they were forbidden to set foot there because of the revolting language and of what they might catch. But since they were grown up Laura and Laurie on their prowls sometimes walked through. It was disgusting and sordid. They came out with a shudder. But still one must go everywhere; one must see everything. So through they went.

"And just think of what the band would sound like to that poor woman," said Laura.

"Oh, Laura!" Jose began to be seriously annoyed. "If you're going to stop a band playing every time someone has an accident, you'll lead a very strenuous life. I'm every bit as sorry about it as you. I feel just as sympathetic." Her eyes hardened. She looked at her sister just as she used to when they were little and fighting together. "You won't bring a drunken workman back to life by being sentimental," she said softly.

"Drunk! Who said he was drunk?" Laura turned furiously on Jose. She said just as they had used to say on those occasions, "I'm going straight up to tell mother."

"Do, dear," cooed Jose.

"Mother, can I come into your room?" Laura turned the big glass door-knob.

"Of course, child. Why, what's the matter? What's given you such a colour?" And Mrs. Sheridan turned round from her dressing-table. She was trying on a new hat.

"Mother, a man's been killed," began Laura.

"*Not* in the garden?" interrupted her mother.

"No, no!"

"Oh, what a fright you gave me!" Mrs. Sheridan sighed with relief and took off the big hat and held it on her knees.

"But listen, mother," said Laura. Breathless, half choking, she told the dreadful story. "Of course, we can't have our party, can we?" she pleaded. "The band and everybody arriving. They'd hear us, mother; they're nearly neighbours!"

To Laura's astonishment her mother behaved just like Jose; it was harder to bear because she seemed amused. She refused to take Laura seriously.

"But, my dear child, use your common sense. It's only by accident we've heard of it. If someone had died there normally—and I can't understand how they keep alive in those poky little holes—we should still be having our party, shouldn't we?"

Laura had to say "yes" to that, but she felt it was all wrong. She sat down on her mother's sofa and pinched the cushion frill.

"Mother, isn't it really terribly heartless of us?" she asked.

"Darling!" Mrs. Sheridan got up and came over to her, carrying the hat. Before Laura could stop her she had popped it on. "My child!" said her mother, "the hat is yours. It's made for you. It's much too young for me. I have never seen you look such a picture. Look at yourself!" And she held up her hand-mirror.

"But, mother," Laura began again. She couldn't look at herself; she turned aside.

This time Mrs. Sheridan lost patience just as Jose had done.

"You are being very absurd, Laura," she said coldly. "People like that don't expect sacrifices from us. And it's not very sympathetic to spoil everybody's enjoyment as you're doing now."

"I don't understand," said Laura, and she walked quickly out of the room into her own bedroom. There, quite by chance, the first thing she saw was this charming girl in the mirror, in her black hat trimmed with gold daisies and a long black velvet ribbon. Never had she imagined she could look like that. Is mother right? she thought. And now she hoped her mother was right. Am I being extravagant? Perhaps it was extravagant. Just for a moment she had another glimpse of that poor woman and those little children and the body being carried into the house. But it all seemed blurred, unreal, like a picture in the newspaper. I'll remember it again after the party's over, she decided. And somehow that seemed quite the best plan....

Lunch was over by half-past one. By half-past two they were all ready for the fray. The green-coated band had arrived and was established in a corner of the tennis-court.

"My dear!" trilled Kitty Maitland, "aren't they too like frogs for words? You ought to have arranged them round the pond with the conductor in the middle on a leaf."

Laurie arrived and hailed them on his way to dress. At the sight of him Laura remembered the accident again. She wanted to tell him. If Laurie agreed with the others, then it was bound to be all right. And she followed him into the hall.

"Laurie!"

"Hallo!" He was half-way upstairs, but when he turned round and saw Laura he suddenly puffed out his cheeks and goggled his eyes at her. "My word, Laura! You do look stunning," said Laurie. "What an absolutely topping hat!"

Laura said faintly "Is it?" and smiled up at Laurie and didn't tell him after all.

Soon after that people began coming in streams. The band struck up; the hired waiters ran from the house to the marquee. Wherever you looked there were couples strolling, bending to the flowers, greeting, moving on over the lawn. They were like bright birds that had alighted in the Sheridans' garden for this one afternoon, on their way to— where? Ah, what happiness it is to be with people who all are happy, to press hands, press cheeks, smile into eyes.

"Darling Laura, how well you look!"

"What a becoming hat, child!"

"Laura, you look quite Spanish. I've never seen you look so striking."

And Laura, glowing, answered softly, "Have you had tea? Won't you have an ice? The passion-fruit ices really are rather special." She ran to her father and begged him: "Daddy darling, can't the band have something to drink?"

And the perfect afternoon slowly ripened, slowly faded, slowly its petals closed.

"Never a more delightful garden-party ..." "The greatest success ..." "Quite the most ..."

Laura helped her mother with the good-byes. They stood side by side in the porch till it was all over.

"All over, all over, thank heaven," said Mrs. Sheridan. "Round up the others, Laura. Let's go and have some fresh coffee. I'm exhausted. Yes, it's been very successful. But oh, these parties, these parties! Why will you children insist on giving parties!" And they all of them sat down in the deserted marquee.

"Have a sandwich, daddy dear. I wrote the flag."

"Thanks." Mr. Sheridan took a bite and the sandwich was gone. He took another. "I suppose you didn't hear of a beastly accident that happened to-day?" he said.

"My dear," said Mrs. Sheridan, holding up her hand, "we did. It nearly ruined the party. Laura insisted we should put it off."

"Oh, mother!" Laura didn't want to be teased about it.

"It was a horrible affair all the same," said Mr. Sheridan. "The chap was married too. Lived just below in the lane, and leaves a wife and half a dozen kiddies, so they say."

An awkward little silence fell. Mrs. Sheridan fidgeted with her cup. Really, it was very tactless of father....

Suddenly she looked up. There on the table were all those sandwiches, cakes, puffs, all uneaten, all going to be wasted. She had one of her brilliant ideas.

"I know," she said. "Let's make up a basket. Let's send that poor creature some of this perfectly good food. At any rate, it will be the greatest treat for the children. Don't you agree? And she's sure to have neighbours calling in and so on. What a point to have it all ready prepared. Laura!" She jumped up. "Get me the big basket out of the stairs cupboard."

"But, mother, do you really think it's a good idea?" said Laura.

Again, how curious, she seemed to be different from them all. To take scraps from their party. Would the poor woman really like that?

"Of course! What's the matter with you to-day? An hour or two ago you were insisting on us being sympathetic."

Oh well! Laura ran for the basket. It was filled, it was now heaped by her mother.

"Take it yourself, darling," said she. "Run down just as you are. No, wait, take the arum lilies too. People of that class are so impressed by arum lilies."

"The stems will ruin her lace frock," said practical Jose.

So they would. Just in time. "Only the basket, then. And, Laura!"— her mother followed her out of the marquee—"don't on any account—"

"What, mother?"

No, better not put such ideas into the child's head! "Nothing! Run along."

It was just growing dusky as Laura shut their garden gates. A big dog ran by like a shadow. The road gleamed white, and down below in the hollow the little cottages were in deep shade. How quiet it seemed after the afternoon. Here she was going down the hill to somewhere where a man lay dead, and she couldn't realise it. Why couldn't she? She stopped a minute. And it seemed to her that kisses, voices, tinkling spoons, laughter, the smell of crushed grass were somehow inside her. She had no room for anything else. How strange! She looked up at the pale sky, and all she thought was, "Yes, it was the most successful party."

Now the broad road was crossed. The lane began, smoky and dark. Women in shawls and men's tweed caps hurried by. Men hung over the palings; the children played in the doorways. A low hum came from the mean little cottages. In some of them there was a flicker of light, and a shadow, crab-like, moved across the window. Laura bent her head and hurried on. She wished now she had put on a coat. How her frock shone! And the big hat with the velvet streamer—if only it was another hat! Were the people looking at her? They must be. It was a mistake to have come; she knew all along it was a mistake. Should she go back even now?

No, too late. This was the house. It must be. A dark knot of people stood outside. Beside the gate an old, old woman with a crutch sat in a chair, watching. She had her feet on a newspaper. The voices stopped as Laura drew near. The group parted. It was as though she was expected, as though they had known she was coming here.

Laura was terribly nervous. Tossing the velvet ribbon over her shoulder, she said to a woman standing by, "Is this Mrs. Scott's house?" and the woman, smiling queerly, said, "It is, my lass."

Oh, to be away from this! She actually said, "Help me, God," as she walked up the tiny path and knocked. To be away from those staring eyes, or to be covered up in anything, one of those women's shawls even. I'll just leave the basket and go, she decided. I shan't even wait for it to be emptied.

Then the door opened. A little woman in black showed in the gloom.

Laura said, "Are you Mrs. Scott?" But to her horror the woman answered, "Walk in, please, miss," and she was shut in the passage.

"No," said Laura, "I don't want to come in. I only want to leave this basket. Mother sent—"

The little woman in the gloomy passage seemed not to have heard her. "Step this way, please, miss," she said in an oily voice, and Laura followed her.

She found herself in a wretched little low kitchen, lighted by a smoky lamp. There was a woman sitting before the fire.

"Em," said the little creature who had let her in. "Em! It's a young lady." She turned to Laura. She said meaningly, "I'm 'er sister, miss. You'll excuse 'er, won't you?"

"Oh, but of course!" said Laura. "Please, please don't disturb her. I—I only want to leave—"

But at that moment the woman at the fire turned round. Her face, puffed up, red, with swollen eyes and swollen lips, looked terrible. She seemed as though she couldn't understand why Laura was there. What did it mean? Why was this stranger standing in the kitchen with a basket? What was it all about? And the poor face puckered up again.

"All right, my dear," said the other. "I'll thenk the young lady."

And again she began, "You'll excuse her, miss, I'm sure," and her face, swollen too, tried an oily smile.

Laura only wanted to get out, to get away. She was back in the passage. The door opened. She walked straight through into the bedroom, where the dead man was lying.

"You'd like a look at 'im, wouldn't you?" said Em's sister, and she brushed past Laura over to the bed. "Don't be afraid, my lass"—and now her voice sounded fond and sly, and fondly she drew down the sheet—" 'e looks a picture. There's nothing to show. Come along, my dear."

Laura came.

There lay a young man, fast asleep—sleeping so soundly, so deeply, that he was far, far away from them both. Oh, so remote, so peaceful. He was dreaming. Never wake him up again. His head was sunk in the pillow, his eyes were closed; they were blind under the closed eyelids. He was given up to his dream. What did garden-parties and baskets and lace frocks matter to him? He was far from all those things. He was wonderful, beautiful. While they were laughing and while the band was playing, this marvel had come to the lane. Happy ... happy.... All is well, said that sleeping face. This is just as it should be. I am content.

But all the same you had to cry, and she couldn't go out of the room without saying something to him. Laura gave a loud childish sob.

"Forgive my hat," she said.

And this time she didn't wait for Em's sister. She found her way out of the door, down the path past all those dark people. At the corner of the lane she met Laurie.

He stepped out of the shadow. "Is that you, Laura?"

"Yes."

"Mother was getting anxious. Was it all right?"

"Yes, quite. Oh, Laurie!" She took his arm, she pressed up against him.

"I say, you're not crying, are you?" asked her brother.

Laura shook her head. She was.

Laurie put his arm round her shoulder. "Don't cry," he said in his warm, loving voice. "Was it awful?"

"No," sobbed Laura. "It was simply marvellous. But, Laurie—" She stopped, she looked at her brother. "Isn't life," she stammered, "isn't life—" But what life was she couldn't explain. No matter. He quite understood.

"*Isn't* it, darling?" said Laurie.

Topics for Discussion

1. How does Mansfield use plants and flowers in the story and how do they function as images?

2. What is the relationship between the upper and lower classes in the story, and how does Mansfield demarcate the boundaries and differences between the worlds of the upper and lower classes? What does this distinction say about the nature of her society?

3. How does Mansfield treat the issue of death in the story?

4. How is grief communicated in the story?

5. What is the purpose of the opening third of the story, when the domestic situation of the family throwing the party is examined?

6. As illustrated in the story, what are the challenges that an author faces in writing about happiness?

7. What tension results from the juxtaposing of the plentifulness of the Sheridan family and the poverty of the carter's family, especially as they are conveyed through Mansfield's descriptions?

8. How does Mansfield articulate or convey the inner life of her protagonist?

John Montague

About the Author

John Montague was born in Brooklyn, New York, in 1929 and grew up in Northern Ireland. He received his education at St. Patrick's College, Armagh, University College, Dublin, Yale University and the University of Iowa. He has worked as a film critic, journalist and educator, and has taught at University College, Cork, and State University of New York, Albany.

Well-known as a major Irish poet, Montague examines the relationship between the contemporary individual and his environment, particularly through the consciousness of ancient Celtic beliefs and motifs such as the Earth Mother goddess. He is also fascinated by the tension between sexuality and the puritanical social, religious and moral codes still embraced by contemporary Ireland. For Montague, the writer is, in Joycean terms, the articulate spokesperson for the "uncreated conscience of my race," a bard who observes the ambivalences manifested in society through the confrontation of desire and standard. His poems carry an air of nostalgia, and Montague has noted that "my effort to understand as much of the modern world as possible serves only to illuminate the destruction of the small area from which I initially came, and that theme is only part of the larger one of continually threatened love."

Selected Works

Death of a Chieftain (short stories, 1964)
A Chosen Light (poems, 1969)
The Rough Field (poems, 1972)
Selected Poems (1982)
The Lost Notebook (novella, 1987)
An Occasion of Sin (short stories, 1992)

About the Story

In his novel *A Portrait of the Artist as a Young Man* (1914), James Joyce described the Irish as "a priest-ridden race." Montague's story examines the tension between a free-spirited French woman, Françoise O'Meara, and the restrictive, puritanical society into which she gains unwelcome insight when she goes bathing on a beach south of Dublin.

A martello tower (examples can be found both in Ireland and Canada, and Joyce uses one in the opening scene of *Ulysses*) is a small, round fort built by the British during the Napoleonic Wars for defence against possible French invasion. Many martello towers are now used as houses or museums.

Dun Laoghaire (pronounced Dunn-lowry) is the port town for the city of Dublin. Cavan is a county in the north of the Republic, and the message on the mirror is directed against the county's soccer team, which participates in the Irish Football League.

An Occasion of Sin

About ten miles south of Dublin, not far from Blackrock, there is a small swimming place. You turn down a side road, cross a railway bridge, and there, below the wall, there is a little bay with a pier running out into the sea. The water is not deep, but much calmer and warmer than at many points further along the coast. When the tide comes in, it covers the expanse of green rocks on the right, lifting the seaweed like long hair. At its highest, one can dive from the edge of the Martello Tower, which stands partly concealed between the pier and the sea wall.

Françoise O'Meara started coming there shortly after Easter. A chubby, open-faced girl, at ease with herself and the world, she had arrived from France only six months before, after her marriage. At first she hated it: the damp mists of November seemed to eat into her spirit; but she kept quiet, for her husband's sake. And when winter began to wear into spring, and the days grew softer, she felt her heart expand; it was as simple as that.

Early in the new year, he bought her a car, to help her pass the time when he was at the office. It was nothing much, an old Austin, with wide running boards, and a rust-streaked roof, but she cleaned and polished it till it shone. With it, she explored all the villages around Dublin: Delgany, where a pack of beagles came streaming across the road; Howth, where she wandered for hours along the cliffs; the hilly roads above Rathfarnham. And Seacove, where she came to swim as soon as her husband would allow her.

"But nobody swims at this time of the year," he said, "except the madmen at Forty Foot!"

"But I want to!" she cried. "What does it matter what people do. I won't melt!"

She stretched her arms wide as she spoke, and he had to admit that she didn't look as if she would; her full breasts, her stocky, firm hips, her wide grey eyes—he had never seen anyone look so positive in his life.

At first it was marvellous being on her own, feeling the icy shock of the water as she plunged in. It brought back a period of her childhood, spent in Etretat, on the Normandy coast: she had bathed through November, running along the deserted beach afterwards, the water drying on her body in the sharp wind. She doubted if she could do that at Seacove, but she found a corner of the wall which trapped whatever sun there was, and when the rain spat she went into the Martello Tower Café and had a bar of chocolate and a cup of tea. Sometimes it was so cold that her skin goose-pimpled, but she loved it all; she felt she had never been so completely alive.

It was mid-May before anyone joined her along the sea wall. The earliest comer was a small man who unpeeled to show a paunch carpeted with white hair. He waved to her before diving off the pierhead, trundling straight out to sea. When he came back, his face was lobster-red with exertion, and he pummeled himself with a towel. He had surprisingly small, almost dainty feet, she noticed as he danced up and down on the stones blowing a white column of breath into the air. As he left, he always gave her a friendly wink or called: "That beats Banagher!"

She liked him a lot. She didn't feel as much at ease with the others. An English couple came down from the Stella Maris boarding house to eat a picnic lunch and read the *Daily Express*. Though sitting side by side, they rarely spoke, casting mournful glances at the sky which, even at its brightest, always had a threatening aspect, like a chemical solution at the point of precipitation. And more and more local men came, mainly on bicycles. They swung to a halt along the seawall, removing the clips from their trousers, removing their trunks from the carrier, and tramping down to the sea. One of them, who looked like a clerk (lean, bespectacled, his mouth cut into his face), carried equipment for underwater fishing, goggles, flippers and a spear.

What troubled her was their method of undressing: she had never seen anything like it. First they spread a newspaper on the ground. Then they squatted, unpeeling their outer garments. When they were down to shirt and trousers, they took a swift look round, and then gave a kind of convulsive wriggle, so that the lower half of the trousers hung limply. There was a brief glimpse of white before a towel was wrapped around the loins; gradually the full length of the trousers unwound in a series of convulsive shudders. Another lunge and the trunks went sliding up the thighs until they struck the outcrop of the hips. A second look round, a swift pull of the towel with the left hand, a jerk of the trunks with the right, and the job was done. Or nearly: creaking to their feet, they pulled their thigh-length shirts over their heads to reveal pallid torsos.

At the beginning this amused her: it looked like a comedy sequence, especially as it had to be performed in reverse when they came out of the water. But then it began to worry her: why were they doing it? Was it because there were women present? But there were none, apart from the Englishman's wife who sat gazing out to sea munching her sandwiches, and herself. She had seen men undressing on beaches ever since she was a child and hardly noticed it. In any case the division of the human race into male and female was an interesting fact with which she had come to terms long ago: she did not need to have her attention called to it in such an extraordinary way.

What troubled her even more was the way they watched her when she was undressing. She usually had her suit on under her dress, but when she hadn't, she sat on the edge of the sea wall, sliding it swiftly up her body, before jumping down to pull the dress over her head: the speed and cleanness of motion pleased her. But as she lifted the straps over her back she could feel eyes on her every move. It was not either curiosity or admiration, because when she raised her eyes, they all looked away. The man with the goggles was the worst: she caught him

staring, the black band pushed up around his ears like a racing motor-
ist's. She smiled to cover her embarrassment, but to her surprise he
turned his head with an angry snap. What was wrong with her? She
mentioned her doubts to her husband, who laughed and then grew
thoughtful.

"You're not very sympathetic," he pointed out. "After all, this is a
cold country."

"Rubbish," she replied. "It's as warm as Normandy. It's something
more than that."

"Maybe it's just modesty."

"Then why look at me like that? They're as lecherous as troopers,
but they won't admit it."

"You don't understand," he retreated.

It was mid-June when the clerical students appeared at Seacove. They
came along the coast road from Dun Laoghaire on bicycles, black as a
flock of crows. Their coats flapped in the sea-wind as they tried to pass
each other, rising on the pedals. Then they curved down the side-road
towards the Martello Tower, where they piled their machines into the
wooden racks, solemn rusted Raleighs and low-handled racers. Some
started undressing, taking off their coats and hard clerical collars as
they came. Most already had their trunks on, stepping out of their trousers on the beach to create a huddle of black shirts and shoes. The others undressed under the shadow of the sea wall, and then came racing
down; together they trooped towards the pierhead.

For the next quarter of an hour the sea was teeming with them,
dense as a shoal of mackerel. They plunged, they splashed, they turned
upside down. One who was timid kept retreating to shallow water, but
two others stole up and ducked him, only to be buffeted from behind in
their turn. The surface of the water was cut into clouds of spray. Far out
the arms of the three strongest flashed in a race to the lighthouse point.

When they came out of the sea to dry and lie down, they found a
space cleared around their clothes, people having withdrawn to give
them more room. But the students did not seem to observe or mind,
plumping themselves down in whatever space was offered. One or two
had brought books, but the rest lay on their backs, talking and laughing. At first their chatter disturbed Françoise from the novel she was
reading, but it soon sank into her consciousness, like a litany.

"But Pius always had a great cult of the Virgin. They say he saw her
in the Vatican gardens."

"If Cacan had banged in that penalty, they'd be in the final Sunday."

"Father Conroy says that after the second year in the bush you
nearly forget home exists."

While she was amused by their energy, Françoise would not have spoken to them if she hadn't fallen asleep one day with a yellow edition of Mauriac on her stomach. When she awoke, the students were settling around her. It was a warm day, and their usual place near the water had been taken by a group of English families with children, so they took the nearest free spot. Although they pretended indifference, she could feel a current of curiosity running through them at finding her so close; now and again she caught a shy look, or a chuckle, as one glanced at another. Among their white skins and long shorts, she became conscious of her blue and red-striped bathing suit, blazing like a flag in the sunshine. And of her already browning legs and arms.

"Is that French you're reading?" said one just back from a second plunge in the sea, towelling himself slowly, shaking drops of water over everyone. He had a coarse, friendly face, covered with blotches and a shock of carroty hair stuck up in wet tufts.

"Le Fleuve de Feu," she said, "the river of fire, one of Mauriac's novels."

"He's a Catholic writer, isn't he?" said another with sudden interest. The others turned to him, and he flushed brick-red, sitting his ground.

"Well," she grimaced, remembering episodes in the novel, "he is and he isn't. He's very bleak, in an old-fashioned sort of way. The river of fire is meant to be," she searched for the words, "the flood of human passion."

There was silence. "Are you French?" said a wondering voice.

"Yes, I am," she confessed. "But I'm married to an Irishman."

"We thought you couldn't be from here," said another voice. Everyone seemed more at ease now that her identity had been established. They talked idly for a few more minutes before the red-haired boy, who seemed to be in charge, looked at his watch and said it was time to go. They all dressed quickly, and as they sailed along the seawall on their bicycles (she could only see their heads, moving targets in a funfair) they waved to her.

"See you tomorrow," they called.

⚔️

By early July the meetings had become a daily affair. As they rode up they would call out, "Hello, Françoise." After they swam, they came clambering up the rocks to sit around her in a semi-circle. Usually the big red-haired boy (called "Ginger" by his companions) started the conversation with a staccato demand: "What part of France are you from?" or, "Do you like it here?" but the others soon took over, while he sank into a satisfied silence like a dog that had performed an expected trick.

Françoise felt like a teacher as they questioned her about her life in Paris. Whatever she told them seemed to take on an air of unreality, more like a lesson than real life. They liked to hear about the Louvre or Notre-Dame, but when she tried to tell them about the student life around the Latin Quarter, their attention slid away. It was not her fault, because when she questioned them about their own future (they were going on to the foreign missions), they were equally vague. Only what related to the present was real, and anything else was exotic. Such torpor angered her.

"But wouldn't you like to see Paris?"

They looked at each other. Yes, they would like to see Paris, and might, some day, on the way back from Africa. But what they really wanted was to learn French: all they got was a few lessons a week from Father Dundee.

Another day they spoke of the worker priests. When she had left her convent school, Françoise had plunged into social work around the Rue Belhomme and the fringes of Montmartre. She had come to know several worker priests. One had fallen in love with a prostitute and had to struggle to save his vocation: she thought him a wonderful man. But her story was received in silence.

"Things must be very lax in France," Ginger said.

She could have brained him.

Still, she enjoyed their company, and felt disappointed whenever (because of examinations or some religious ceremony) they did not show up. It was not just because she liked being surrounded by admiring men. Totally at ease with her, they offered no calculation of seduction or flattery, only a friendly teasing. It reminded her of when she had played with her brothers (she was the only girl) through the long summer holidays; that their relationship might not seem as innocent to others never crossed her mind.

She was lying on the seawall after a swim one afternoon, when she felt a shadow move across her vision. At first she thought it was one of the students, though they had told her the day before that they might not be coming. But no, it was the small fat man. She smiled up at him shielding her eyes against the sun. But he did not smile back, sitting down beside her, his usual cheery face solemn.

"Missing your little friends today?"

"Yes, a bit," she confessed. "I rather like them, they're very pleasant company."

He remained silent for a moment. "I'm not sure it's right for you to be talking to them."

"But what do you mean?"

"Lots of people on the beach"—he was obviously uncomfortable— "are talking."

"But they're only children!" Her shock was so deep that she was trembling: if such an inoffensive man believed this, what must the others be thinking?

"They're clerical students," he said. "They're going to be priests."

"But you can't," she searched for the word, "*isolate* them."

"That's not how we see it. You're giving a bad example."

"I'm giving what?"

"Bad example."

She felt tears prick the corners of her eyes. "Do you believe that?" she asked, trying to smile.

"I don't know," he said. "It's a matter for your conscience. But it's not right for a single girl to be making free with clerical students."

"But I'm not single!"

It was his turn to be shocked. "You're a married woman! And you come—"

He did not end the sentence, but she knew what he meant.

"Yes, I'm a married woman, and my husband lets me go to the beach on my own, and talk to whoever I like. You see, he trusts me."

He rose slowly. "Well, daughter," he said, with a baffled return to kindliness, "it's up to yourself. I only wanted to warn you."

As he padded away, she saw that the whole beach was watching her. She did not smile, but stared straight ahead. There was a procession of yachts making towards Dun Laoghaire harbor. Turning over, she hid her face against the concrete and began to cry.

As she drove back to Dublin, Françoise was so absorbed that she nearly got into an accident obeying a reflex to turn right into the Georgian street where they lived. An oncoming bus hooted and she swung her car up onto the pavement. She saw her husband's surprised face looking through the window: thank God he was home.

She did not mention the matter till several hours later, when she was no longer as upset as she had been at the beach. And when she did come round to it, she tried to tell it as lightly as possible hoping to distance it, to see it clearly. But though her husband laughed a little at the beginning, his face became more serious, and she felt her nervousness rising again.

"But what right had he to say that to me?"

Kieran O'Meara did not answer, but kept turning the pages of the *Evening Press*.

"Obviously he thought he was doing the right thing."

"But surely *you* don't think ..."

His face became a little red. "No, of course not. But I don't deny that in certain circumstances you might be classed as an occasion of sin."

She sat down with a bump in the armchair, a dishcloth in her hand. At first she felt like laughing, but after repeating the phrase "occasion of sin" she no longer found it funny. Did everyone in this country measure things like this? At a party, a few nights before, one of her husband's friends had told her that "sex was the worst sin because it was the most pleasant." Another had gripped her arm crossing the street: "Be careful." "But you're in danger too!" she laughed, only to hear his answer: "It's not myself I'm worried about, it's you. I'm in the state of grace." The face of the small fat man swam up before her, full of painful self-righteousness, as he told her she was "giving bad example." What in the name of God was she doing in this benighted place?

"Do you find me an occasion of sin?" she said.

"It's different for me," he said seriously. "After all, we're married."

He was surprised when she rose from the chair, threw the dishcloth on the table, and vanished from the room. He heard the front door bang and her running down the steps.

Hands in the pockets of her white raincoat, Françoise O'Meara strode along the bank of the Grand Canal. There was a thin rain falling, but she ignored it, glad if anything for its damp imprint upon her face. Trees swam up to her out of the haze: a pair of lovers were leaning against one. Neither of them had coats; they must be soaked through, but they did not seem to mind.

There was a pair enjoying themselves, anyway. But why did they have to choose the dampest place in all Dublin? What was this instinct to seek darkness and discomfort rather than the friendly light of day? She remembered the couples lying on the deck of the Holyhead boat when she had come over: she had to stumble over them in order to get down the stairs. It was like night-time in a bombed city, people hiding from the blows of fate; she had never had such a sense of desolation. And then when she had negotiated the noise and porter stains of the Saloon and got to the Ladies she'd found that someone had scrawled FUCK CAVAN in lipstick on the mirror.

Her husband had nearly split his sides laughing when she had asked what that meant. And yet, despite his education and travel, he was as odd as any of them. From the outside, he looked completely normal, especially when he left in the morning in his neat executive's suit. But inside he was a nest of superstition and stubbornness. It emerged in all kinds of small things: the way he avoided walking under ladders, the way he blessed himself during thunderstorms, the way he saluted every church he passed, a hand flying from the wheel to his forehead even in the thick of city traffic. And that wasn't the worst. One night she had woken to see him sitting bolt upright in bed, his face tense and white.

"Do you hear it?"

Faintly, on the wind, she heard a crying sound, a sort of wail. It sounded weird all right, but it was probably only some animal locked out, or in heat, the kind of cry one hears in any garden, magnified by the echo-chamber of the night.

"It's a banshee," he said. "They follow our family. Aunt Margaret must be going to die."

Aunt Margaret did die, but several weeks later, and from old age more than anything else: she was over eighty and could have toppled into the grave at any time. But all through the funeral Kieran had looked at Françoise as if to say *you see!* Now the disease was beginning to get to her, sending her to stalk through the night like a Mauriac heroine, melancholy eating at her heart. As she approached Leeson Street Bridge, she saw two swans, a cob and a pen, moving slowly down the current. Behind them, almost indistinguishable because of their grey feathers, came four young ones. The sight calmed her: it was time to go back. Though he deserved it, she did not want her husband worrying about her. In any case, she had decided what she was going to do.

The important thing was not to show that she was troubled by what they thought of her. Swinging her suit in her left hand, she sauntered down to the beach at Seacove. It was already full, but as though by design a little space had been left directly under the seawall where she usually sat. So she was to be ostracized as well! She would show them: with a delicious sense of audience she hoisted herself up on the concrete and began to undress. She was only halfway through changing when the students arrived. On an ordinary day she would have taken this in her stride, but she saw the people watching them as they tramped over, and the clasp of her bra stuck, so she was left to greet them half in half out of her dress. When she did get the bathing suit on she saw that, since they had all arrived more or less together, they were expecting her to join them for a swim. Laying his towel out carefully on the ground, like an altar-cloth, Ginger turned towards the sea: "Coming?"

Scarlet-faced she marched down with him to the pierhead. The tide was high, and just below the Martello Tower the man with the goggles broke surface, spluttering to stare at her. A little way out, clerical students were horse-playing. Without speaking, she struck out towards the Lighthouse Point, cutting the water with a swift breaststroke. But before she had gone far, Ginger was at her side and another boy on the other. They swam with her out to the point, and back again. Were they never to leave her alone?

And afterwards as they lay on the beach, they kept pestering her with questions. And not the usual ones, but much bolder, in an innocent way. The boy who had asked about Mauriac wanted to know if she had finished the book, whether she knew any people like that, and what she thought of Mauriac's view of love. And then another asked:

"What's it like, to be married?"

She rolled over on her stomach and looked at him. No, he was not being roguish, he was quite serious, gazing at her with interest, as were most of the others. But how could one answer such a question, before such an audience?

"Well, it's very important for a woman, naturally," she began, feeling as ripe with clichés as a Women's Page columnist. "And not just because people—society—imply that if a woman is not married that she's a failure: that's a terrible trap. And it is not merely living together, though—" She looked at them: they were still intent. "—that's pleasant enough. And that's the whole paradox, if it's a true marriage, since she feels freer, just because she has given."

"Freer?"

"Yes, freer after marriage. It's not like an affair where one knows that one can escape. The freedom in marriage is the freedom of committing oneself: at least that's true for the woman." Her remarks were received in silence, but a thoughtful one, as though while they could not quite understand what she meant, they were prepared to examine it.

"What made you ask me that?"

"Sure, it's well-known," Ginger said gathering his belongings, "that French women think of nothing but love."

He pronounced it "luve," with a deep curl in the vowel. Before she could think of a reply, they were half-way across the beach.

She was raging when she got home, all the more so since she knew she could not tell her husband about it. She was raging when she went to bed, shifting so much that she made her husband grunt. She was still raging when she woke up from a dream in which the experience lay curdled.

She dreamt that she was at Seacove in the early morning. The sea was a deep running green, with small waves hitting the pierhead. There was no one in sight so she took off her clothes and slipped into the water. She was half-way across to the Lighthouse Point when she sensed something beneath her: it was the man with the goggles, his black flippers beating the water soundlessly as he surged up towards her. His eyes roved over her naked body as he reached out for her leg. She felt herself being pulled under, and kicked out. She heard the glass of his goggles smash as she broke to the surface where her husband was drawing the blinds to let in the morning light.

Today, she decided, she must end the whole stupid affair: it had gone on too long, caused her too much worry. After all, the people who had protested were probably right: that the boys were getting fresh with her proved it. She toyed with the idea of not going back to the beach, but that seemed cowardly. Better to face the students directly and tell them that she could not see them again.

When the students arrived at the beach in mid-afternoon they found her sitting stiffly against the sea wall, a book on her knees. Saluting her with their usual friendliness, they got no reply. Lying on the beach after their swim they found her silence heavy and tried to coax her with questions. She cut them short each time, ostentatiously returning to her book.

"Is there anything wrong?"

Keeping her eyes fixed on the printed page she nodded, "More or less."

"It wouldn't have anything to do with us?"

"As a matter of fact, it has." Shy stiffness slowly giving way to relief, she told about her conversation with the little fat man. "But of course it's really my fault," she ended lamely. "I should have known better." To her surprise, they smiled at her, affectionately.

"Is that all?"

"Isn't that enough?"

"But sure we knew all that before."

"You knew it!"

"Somebody came to the College a few days ago and spoke to the Dean."

"And what did he say?"

"He asked us what you were like."

"And what did you say?"

"We said you were a better French teacher than Father Dundee."

The casual innocence of that remark restored their relationship and she shouted her laughter. Yet as her surprise wore off she could not resist picking at it, suspiciously, at least once more.

"But what about what the people said? Didn't it upset you?"

Ginger's gaze seemed to rest on her for a moment, and then moved away, bouncing like a rubber ball down the steps to the sea.

"Ach, sure some people would see bad in anything," Ginger said.

And that was all: no longer interested they turned to talk about something else. They were going on their holidays soon and wouldn't be seeing her again. They had enjoyed meeting her; maybe she would be there next year? She sat with her back against the warm sea wall, with Simone de Beauvoir's *Le Deuxiéme Sexe* at her side. A movement caught her eye down the beach: someone was trying to climb on to the ledge of the Martello Tower. First came the spear, then the black goggles, then the flippers like an emerging sea monster. Remembering her dream, she began to laugh again, so much that the students looked at her inquiringly.

"Yes," she said quickly, "I might be at Seacove next year."

Though in her heart, she knew that she wouldn't.

Topics for Discussion

1. How does Montague define temptation?
2. What is the relationship between the title and the content of the story?

3. Why does Montague make the protagonist French? What does her background say about the nature of Irish society?

4. Why are the local people concerned about the seminary students' being tempted? What are the local people afraid of?

5. How does Montague give the woman an air of mystery?

6. Why does the woman say in the final lines of the story that the following year she will not be back at Seacove?

7. What is the role of locality in the story?

Frank Moorhouse

About the Author
Frank Moorhouse was born in Nowra, New South Wales, Australia, in 1938. He has worked as a journalist, editor, labour organizer, screenwriter and full-time writer. Moorhouse's best-known screenplay is *The Coca-Cola Kid* (1985), about the relationship between Australian and American culture. He lives in Sydney, Australia.

    Critics have pointed out the relationship between Moorhouse's style, with its catchy titles and clipped prose style, and his background as a journalist. Early in his career, Moorhouse found difficulty getting his work accepted because of its frankness and sexual explicitness. He achieves much of his humour and poignancy by pointing out the absurdities of Australian life.

    "The Drover's Wife" is from his 1985 collection of short stories, *Room Service.*

Selected Works
Futility and Other Animals (short stories, 1969)
The Americans' Baby (short stories, 1972)
The Electrical Experience (short stories, 1974)
Conference-Ville (short stories, 1976)
Tales of Mystery and Romance (short stories, 1977)
The Everlasting Secret Family and Other Secrets (short stories, 1980)
Room Service (short stories, 1985)

About the Story
"The Drover's Wife," written in the form of an essay, examines, humorously, the problems and absurdities that ensue when a foreign critic only partially understands the culture and context of the work he is examining and the sexual innuendo that arise from the resulting misinterpretation.

The Drover's Wife

Memo Editor:
Chief, I picked this paper up while hanging out at the Conference on Commonwealth Writing in Milan. This Italian student, Franco Casamaggiore, seems to be onto something. As far as I know it's a scoop, me being the only press around. I'd go with it as the cover story if I were you. This study of Australian culture is a big deal here in Europe—twenty-six universities have courses on Australian writing. I'm hanging out angling for a professorship or something like that. This Casamaggiore has got a few of his facts wrong, but the subs can pick those up. Great stuff, eh! He could do for the Merino what Blainey did for Asians. (The inspired Suzanne Kiernan helped me with the translation.)

Conference Paper by Franco Casamaggiore

The writing of a story called *The Drover's Wife* by Henry Lawson in 1893, the painting of a picture called *The Drover's Wife* by Russell

Drysdale in 1945, and the writing of another story by the same name in 1975, by Murray Bail, draws our attention to what I will argue in this paper, is an elaborate example of a national culture joke, an "insider joke" for those who live in that country—in this example, the country of Australia. Each of these works has the status of an Australian classic and each of these works, I will show, contains a joking wink in the direction of the Australian people which they understand but which non-Australian people do not. The joke draws on the colloquial Australian humour surrounding the idea of a drover's "wife."

First, a few notations of background for those who are unfamiliar with Australian folklore and the occupation of a drover, which is corruption of the word "driver." The drover or driver of sheep literally drove the sheep to market. The sheep, because of health regulations governing strictly the towns and cities of Australia, were kept many kilometres inland from the seamarket towns. The sheep had then to be "driven" by the driver or drover from inland to the towns, often many thousands of kilometres, taking many months. I am told that this practice has ceased and the sheep are now housed in the cities in high-rise pens.

The method of driving the sheep was that each sheep individually was placed in a wicker basket on the backs of bullock-drawn wagons known as the woollen wagons. This preserved the sheep in good condition for the market. These bullocks, it is said, could pull the sheep to the coast without human guidance, if needed, being able, of course, to smell the sea. But the sheep had to be fed and the drover or driver would give water and seed to the sheep during the journey. The wagon in the Drysdale painting is horse-drawn, denoting a poorer peasant-class of drover. The wagon in the painting would probably hold a thousand sheep in wicker baskets.

Now the length of the journey and the harshness of conditions precluded the presence of women and the historical fact is that for a century or more there were no women in the pioneering country. This, understandably, led men to seek other solace in this strange new country. Australian historians acknowledge the closeness of men under this conditions of pioneering and have described it as mateship, or a pledging of unspoken alliance between two men, a marriage with vows unspoken.

Quite naturally too, with the drover or driver, a close and special relationship grew between him and his charges who became an object for emotional and physical drives, but this remains unacknowledged by historians for reasons of national shame, but is widely acknowledged by the folk culture of Australia. And now acknowledged by art. Interspecies reciprocity. Hence the joke implicit in the use of two writers and a painter of the title The Drover's Wife and the entry of this unacceptable historical truth from the oral culture to high culture via coded humour and until this paper (which I modestly consider a breakthrough study) absent from academic purview.

I elicited the first inkling of this from answers received to questions asked of Australian visitors to Italia about the sheep droving. First, I should explain. Unfortunately, I am a poor student living in a humble two-room tugurio. It is a necessity for me to work in the bar of the Hotel Principe e Savoia in Milano and for a time before that, in the Gritti Palace Hotel Venezia. If the authorities would provide more funds for education in this country maybe Italia would regain its rightful place at the forefront of world culture. But I wander from my point. This experience in the bar work gave me the opportunity on many occasions to talk and question visiting Australians, although almost always men.

There is an Australian humour of the coarse peasant type not unknown in Italia. Without becoming involved in these details it is necessary for me to document some of the information harvested from contact with the Australian, not having been to the country at first hand—thanks to the insufficiency of funds from the educational authorities in Italia—however, my brother Giovanni is living there in Adelaide, but is not any help in such matters, knowing nothing of the droving or culture and knowing only of the price of things and the Holden automobile. Knowing nothing of things of the spirit. You are wrong, Giovanni.

Yes, but to continue. A rubber shoe or boot used when hunting in wet weather called the gun boot was used by the drovers or drivers and found to be a natural love aid while at the same time a symbol used in a gesture of voluntary submission by the drover before his charge.

The boots were placed on the hind legs of the favoured sheep. The drover would be shoeless like the sheep and the sheep would "wear the boots" (cf. "wearing pants" in marriage). The toe of the boots would be turned towards the drover who would stand on the toes of the boot thus holding the loved sheep close to him in embrace. These details suffice.

According to my Australian informants the sheep often formed an emotional attachment to the drover who reciprocated. But the journey to the coast had its inherent romantic tragedy. The long journey and shared hardship, shared shelter, and kilometres of companionship, daily took them closer to the tragic conclusion with the inevitable death of the loved one through the workings of capitalist market forces. But also the return of the drover's natural drives to his own species as he re-entered the world of people. And the limited vision of the anti-life Church.

"Why not dogs?" comes the question. Close questioning of my Australian sources suggests that dogs as bed companions was characteristic of the Aboriginal and thus for reasons of racial prejudice considered beneath the Australian white man. The sheep from Europe was a link

with the homelands from whence he had migrated and further, I speculate, that the maternal bulk of the merino sheep, with its woolly coat
and large soft eyes, its comforting bleat, offered more feminine solace
than the lean dog with fleas. Again, on this and other matters, Giovanni is of no assistance being concerned only with his Holden automobile and the soccer football. The unimaginative reaction of the
educational authorities for research funding for this project indicts our
whole system of education in this country.

Returning now to the art works under study. In Henry Lawson's
story the woman character lives out her life *as if she were a sheep*. She is
not given a name—in English animal husbandry it is customary to give
cows names (from botany) and domestic pets are named, but not sheep.
The scholar Keith Thomas says that a shepherd however, could recog-
nise his sheep by their faces. She is penned up in her outback fold,
unable to go anywhere. Her routines of the day resemble closely the life
of a sheep and it can be taken that this is a literary transformation for
the sake of propriety. She tells in the story how she was taken to the
city a few times in a "compartment," as is the sheep. In the absence of
her drover husband she is looked after by a dog, as is a sheep. The climax of the Henry Lawson story is the "killing of the snake" which
needs no Doctor Freud, being the expression of a savage and guilt-rid-
den male detumescence (in Australia the male genitalia is referred to
in folklore, as the "one-eyed trouser snake." The Australian folk language is much richer than its European counterpart, which is in state of
decay). I am told that to this day, Australian men are forever killing
the snake. The drover is absent from the story, a point to be taken up
later.

In the Drysdale painting (1945) oddly and fascinatingly, there are
no sheep. Then we realize uneasily that it is as if they have been swept
up into a single image overwhelming the foreground—the second
drover's "wife." This unusually shaped woman is, on second glance, in
the form of a sheep, a merino sheep, the painter having given her the
same maternal physical bulk as the merino. Her shadow forms the
shape of a sheep. Again, the drover is all but absent. He is a background smudge. The snake, you ask? In the trees we find the serpents.
They writhe before our eyes.

Murray Bail is a modern Australian long removed from the days of
pioneering and droving. However, his biography reveals that his father
was a drover, but our discipline requires us to disregard this fact when
considering his work of art. In his contemporary story he pays homage
both to the Drysdale painting and the Lawson story. In the Bail story
the woman is referred to as having one defining characteristic, what
author Bail calls a "silly streak." This is a characteristic traditionally
ascribed to sheep (cf. "woolly minded"). The woman figure in this Bail
story, or precisely the "sheep figure," wanders in a motiveless way;

strays, as it were; away from the city and her dentist husband. Curious it is to note that she flees the man whose work it is to care for the teeth which are the instruments used to eat the sheep, and for the sheep, symbol of death. Recall: the journey from the inland paradise in the protection of a loving drover to the destination of death: the city and the slaughterhouse and finally the teeth of the hungry city. In the Bail story the woman goes from the arms of her natural predator, the one who cares for the predator's teeth—the dentist—into the arms of the natural protector, the drover or driver. The Bail story also has a "killing of the snake."

So, in all three works of High Art under discussion we have three women clearly substituting (for reasons of propriety) for sheep, but coded in such a way as to lead us, through the term "drover's wife" back into the folk culture and its joke. And we note that in the three works there is *no drover*. This is a reversal of situation, an inside-out-truth, for we know historically that *there was a drover* but there was historically *no wife*, not in any acceptable conventional sense.

The question comes, given that the drover has a thousand sheep in his care, how did the drover choose, from that thousand, just one mate? This question, intriguing and bizarre at the same time, was put to my Australian sources. Repeatedly I also ask Giovanni to ask the other men at GMH factory, but he has a head that is too full of materialism to concern himself with exploration of the mythology of this new culture.

How was the sheep chosen? But as in all matters of the human emotion the answer comes blindingly plain. It was explained to me that it is very much like being in a crowded lift, or in a prison, or on board a ship. In a situation of confinement it is instinctive for people to single out one another from the herd. There is communication by eye, an eye-mating, the search for firstly, mate, and then community. The same it is with sheep, my Australian sources tell me (thanks to educational authorities in Italia I have no chance to research this first hand). In the absence of human contact the eyes wander across species, the eyes meet, the eyes and ewes (that is English language pun).

Yes, and the question comes, was I being fooled about by these Australian visitors and their peasant humour after they had drunk perhaps too much? Was I being "taken in" as they, the Australians, say. I ask in return—were the Australian visitors telling more than they knew or wanted to tell? They were also, by joking with my questions, trying to make me look away from my enquiry. To joke away something that was too painfully serious. But they were also telling me what they did not wish me to know as outsider, for the confession is precisely this, and brings relief. They experience an undefined relief from their joking about such matters—that is, the relief of confession. I let them joke at me for it was a joke to which I listened not them. This is the manoeuvre of the national joke, the telling and the not telling at the same time. So yes, I was being "taken in" by my Australian sources—"taken in" to the secret. Taken in to their confidence.

We are told that humour has within it the three dialogues. The dialogue between the teller and the listener, where the teller is seeking approval and giving a gift at the same time. The dialogue between the teller's unconscious mind and his voice, to which the teller cannot always listen. The dialogue between the joker, teller, and the racial memory which is embodied in the language and the type of joke the teller chooses to tell, the well of humour from which the joker must draw his bucket of laughter. Humour is the underground route that taboo material—or material of national shame—must travel, and it is the costume it must wear.

Today such relations between sheep and men are, of course, rare in Australia. However, the racial memory of those stranger and more primitive days—days closer, can we say, to nature and a state of grace— still lingers. It is present in a number of ways. As illustrated, it is present in the elaborate cultural joke of High Art. The art which winks. It is there in the peasant humour of the male Australian, the joke which confesses. It is present, I would argue (here I work from photographs and cinema) in the weekly ritual called "mowing the lawn." On one afternoon of the weekend the Australian male takes off grass from his suburban garden which in earlier times would have been fodder for the sheep—this is an urban "hay-making ritual," Australian city man's last connection with agriculture. But, alas, his sheep is gone, and the grass, the hay, is burned, to a memory of an association all but forgotten. Finally, I am told that there is an Australian national artifact—the sheepskin with wool attached. It is used often as a seat cover in the automobile. That today the driver or drover of a car sits (or lies) with sheep, as it were, under him while driving not a flock of sheep but a family in a modern auto. It gives comfort through racial memory far exceeding the need for warmth in that temperate land. The car sheepskin covering is an emotional trophy from the sexual underworld of the Australian past. The artifact which remembers.

Naturally, all this is still not an open subject for academic explicitness in Australia and it is only here in Italia where such candour can be enjoyed with our perspective of centuries—and our knowledge of such things. But I say, Australia—be not ashamed of that which is bizarre, seek not always the genteel. Remember that we, the older cultures, have myths which also acknowledge such happenings of interspecies reciprocity (cf. Jason and Search for Golden Fleece). See in these happenings the beginnings of your own mythology. See it as an affirmation of the beautiful truth—that we share the planet with animals and we are partners, therefore in its destiny.

So, in Lawson, Drysdale and Bail, we see how High Art in this new culture, admits a message of unspeakable truth (albeit, in a coded and guilty way), this being the ploy of all great national cultures.

Thus is the magic of the imagination.

Topics for Discussion

1. How is Moorhouse parodying the essay form in this story? What is the relationship between form and content in "The Drover's Wife"?

2. What is the purpose of having a story comment on other works of literature? Is there a relationship between fiction and criticism?

3. What role does the absurd play in the story?

4. How does Franco Casamaggiore misinterpret the earlier stories and the painting called "The Drover's Wife"?

5. What does this story say about the problem of misreading a work of art?

6. What role does sex play in the story?

7. How does language contribute to the characterization of Franco Casamaggiore?

8. What role do digressions play in Casamaggiore's narrative?

Bharati Mukherjee

About the Author

Bharati Mukherjee was born in Calcutta, India, in 1940 and educated at the University of Calcutta, the University of Baroda, Gujarat, and the University of Iowa. She has taught at Marquette University in Wisconsin, the University of Wisconsin, McGill University in Montreal, Skidmore College in Saratoga, New York, and the City University of New York. She is married to Canadian novelist Clark Blaise and became a Canadian citizen in 1972. She has since returned to the United States and become a citizen there.

Mukherjee often writes of individuals who are caught between two worlds, who are seeking possibilities and desires that conflict with their pasts or their ideals. As a writer who has had to adjust to changes in circumstance and environment in her own life, Mukherjee has written about characters "in transition" with sensitivity and depth. *The Middleman and Other Stories*, from which "A Wife's Story" is taken, is an exemplary statement on the new "international person" who is attempting to balance heritage with new situations.

Selected Works

The Tiger's Daughter (novel, 1972)
Wife (novel, 1975)
Darkness (short stories, 1985)
The Middleman and Other Stories (short stories, 1988)
Jasmine (novel, 1989)

About the Story

"A Wife's Story" tells the narrative of a woman from India who has broken with tradition and convention to come to New York to do her Ph.D. While living in the United States, she adapts to the new culture and becomes distant from her roots—a process of transition that causes problems for her when her Indian husband comes to visit her in New York.

The play mentioned in the opening of the story, *Glengarry Glen Ross*, by American playwright David Mamet, deals with a group of real estate salesmen who are told that they will lose their jobs if they do not outsell their fellow workers. The play is written in frank, often prejudiced language against which Mukherjee's protagonist reacts vehemently.

Con Ed is the electric company for New York. Bonwit Teller is a fashionable American chain of department stores. Idi Amin was dictator of Uganda during the 1970s, who expelled from his country, with considerable violence, all residents (including those of Asian origins whose families had lived there for generations) not of African background. This expulsion left an indelible mark on South Asian communities all over the world.

A Wife's Story

Imre says forget it, but I'm going to write David Mamet. So Patels are hard to sell real estate to. You buy them a beer, whisper Glengarry Glen Ross, and they smell swamp instead of sun and surf. They work hard, eat cheap, live ten to a room, stash their savings under futons in Queens, and before you know it they own half of Hoboken. You say, where's the sweet gullibility that made this nation great?

Polish jokes, Patel jokes: that's not why I want to write Mamet.

Seen their women?

Everybody laughs. Imre laughs. The dozing fat man with the Barnes & Noble sack between his legs, the woman next to him, the usher, everybody. The theater isn't so dark that they can't see me. In my red silk sari I'm conspicuous. Plump, gold paisleys sparkle on my chest.

The actor is just warming up. *Seen their women?* He plays a salesman, he's had a bad day and now he's in a Chinese restaurant trying to loosen up. His face is pink. His wool-blend slacks are creased at the crotch. We bought our tickets at half-price, we're sitting in the front row, but at the edge, and we see things we shouldn't be seeing. At least I do, or think I do. Spittle, actors goosing each other, little winks, streaks of makeup.

Maybe they're improvising dialogue too. Maybe Mamet's provided them with insult kits, Thursdays for Chinese, Wednesdays for Hispanics, today for Indians. Maybe they get together before curtain time, see an Indian woman settling in the front row off to the side, and say to each other: "Hey, forget Friday. Let's get her today. See if she cries. See if she walks out." Maybe, like the salesmen they play, they have a little bet on.

Maybe I shouldn't feel betrayed.

Their women, he goes again. *They look like they've just been fucked by a dead cat.*

The fat man hoots so hard he nudges my elbow off our shared armrest.

"Imre. I'm going home." But Imre's hunched so far forward he doesn't hear. English isn't his best language. A refugee from Budapest, he has to listen hard. "I didn't pay eighteen dollars to be insulted."

I don't hate Mamet. It's the tyranny of the American dream that scares me. First, you don't exist. Then you're invisible. Then you're funny. Then you're disgusting. Insult, my American friends will tell me, is a kind of acceptance. No instant dignity here. A play like this, back home, would cause riots. Communal, racist, and antisocial. The actors wouldn't make it off stage. This play, and all these awful feelings, would be safely locked up.

I long, at times, for clear-cut answers. Offer me instant dignity, today, and I'll take it.

"What?" Imre moves toward me without taking his eyes off the actor. "Come again?"

Tears come. I want to stand, scream, make an awful scene. I long for ugly, nasty rage.

The actor is ranting, flinging spittle. *Give me a chance. I'm not finished, I can get back on the board. I tell that asshole, give me a real lead. And what does that asshole give me? Patels. Nothing but Patels.*

This time Imre works an arm around my shoulders. "Panna, what is Patel? Why are you taking it all so personally?"

I shrink from his touch, but I don't walk out. Expensive girls' schools in Lausanne and Bombay have trained me to behave well. My manners are exquisite, my feelings are delicate, my gestures refined, my moods undetectable. They have seen me through riots, uprootings, separation, my son's death.

"I'm not taking it personally."

The fat man looks at us. The woman looks too, and shushes.

I stare back at the two of them. Then I stare, mean and cool, at the man's elbow. Under the bright blue polyester Hawaiian shirt sleeve, the elbow looks soft and runny. "Excuse me," I say. My voice has the effortless meanness of well-bred displaced Third World women, though my rhetoric has been learned elsewhere. "You're exploiting my space."

Startled, the man snatches his arm away from me. He cradles it against his breast. By the time he's ready with comebacks, I've turned my back on him. I've probably ruined the first act for him. I know I've ruined it for Imre.

It's not my fault; it's the *situation*. Old colonies wear down. Patels— the new pioneers—have to be suspicious. Idi Amin's lesson is permanent. AT&T wires move good advice from continent to continent. Keep all assets liquid. Get into 7-11s, get out of condos and motels. I know how both sides feel, that's the trouble. The Patel sniffing out scams, the sad salesmen on the stage: postcolonialism has made me their referee. It's hate I long for; simple, brutish, partisan hate.

After the show Imre and I make our way toward Broadway. Sometimes he holds my hand; it doesn't mean anything more than that crazies and drunks are crouched in doorways. Imre's been here over two years, but he's stayed very old-world, very courtly, openly protective of women. I met him in a seminar on special ed. last semester. His wife is a nurse somewhere in the Hungarian countryside. There are two sons, and miles of petitions for their emigration. My husband manages a mill two hundred miles north of Bombay. There are no children.

"You make things tough on yourself," Imre says. He assumed Patel was a Jewish name or maybe Hispanic; everything makes equal sense to him. He found the play tasteless, he worried about the effect of vulgar language on my sensitive ears. "You have to let go a bit." And as though to show me how to let go, he breaks away from me, bounds ahead with his head ducked tight, then dances on amazingly jerky legs. He's a Magyar, he often tells me, and deep down, he's an Asian too. I catch glimpses of it, knife-blade Attila cheekbones, despite the blondish hair. In his faded jeans and leather jacket, he's a rock video star. I watch MTV for hours in the apartment when Charity's working the evening shift at Macy's. I listen to WPLJ on Charity's earphones. Why should I be ashamed? Television in India is so uplifting.

Imre stops as suddenly as he'd started. People walk around us. The summer sidewalk is full of theatergoers in seersucker suits; Imre's year-round jacket is out of place. European. Cops in twos and threes huddle, lightly tap their thighs with night sticks and smile at me with benevolence. I want to wink at them, get us all in trouble, tell them the crazy dancing man is from the Warsaw Pact. I'm too shy to break into dance on Broadway. So I hug Imre instead.

The hug takes him by surprise. He wants me to let go, but he doesn't really expect me to let go. He staggers, though I weigh no more than 104 pounds, and with him, I pitch forward slightly. Then he catches me, and we walk arm in arm to the bus stop. My husband would never dance or hug a woman on Broadway. Nor would my brothers. They aren't stuffy people, but they went to Anglican boarding schools and they have a well-developed sense of what's silly.

"Imre." I squeeze his big, rough hand. "I'm sorry I ruined the evening for you."

"You did nothing of the kind." He sounds tired. "Let's not wait for the bus. Let's splurge and take a cab instead."

Imre always has unexpected funds. The Network, he calls it, Class of '56.

In the back of the cab, without even trying, I feel light, almost free. Memories of Indian destitutes mix with the hordes of New York street people, and they float free, like astronauts, inside my head. I've made it. I'm making something of my life. I've left home, my husband, to get a Ph.D. in special ed. I have a multiple-entry visa and a small scholarship for two years. After that, we'll see. My mother was beaten by her mother-in-law, my grandmother, when she'd registered for French lessons at the Alliance Française. My grandmother, the eldest daughter of a rich zamindar, was illiterate.

Imre and the cabdriver talk away in Russian. I keep my eyes closed. That way I can feel the floaters better. I'll write Mamet tonight. I feel strong, reckless. Maybe I'll write Steven Spielberg too; tell him that Indians don't eat monkey brains.

We've made it. Patels must have made it. Mamet, Spielberg: they're not condescending to us. Maybe they're a little bit afraid.

Charity Chin, my roommate, is sitting on the floor drinking Chablis out of a plastic wineglass. She is five foot six, three inches taller than me, but weighs a kilo and a half less than I do. She is a "hands" model. Orientals are supposed to have a monopoly in the hands-modelling business, she says. She had her eyes fixed eight or nine months ago and out of gratitude sleeps with her plastic surgeon every third Wednesday.

"Oh, good," Charity says. "I'm glad you're back early. I need to talk."

She's been writing checks. MCI, Con Ed, Bonwit Teller. Envelopes, already stamped and sealed, form a pyramid between her shapely, knee-socked legs. The checkbook's cover is brown plastic, grained to look like cowhide. Each time Charity flips back the cover, white geese fly over sky-colored checks. She makes good money, but she's extravagant. The difference adds up to this shared, rent-controlled Chelsea one-bedroom.

"All right. Talk."

When I first moved in, she was seeing an analyst. Now she sees a nutritionist.

"Eric called. From Oregon."

"What did he want?"

"He wants me to pay half the rent on his loft for last spring. He asked me to move back, remember? He *begged* me."

Eric is Charity's estranged husband.

"What does your nutritionist say?" Eric now wears a red jumpsuit and tills the soil in Rajneeshpuram.

"You think Phil's a creep too, don't you? What else can he be when creeps are all I attract?"

Phil is a flutist with thinning hair. He's very touchy on the subject of *flautists* versus *flutists*. He's touchy on every subject, from music to books to foods to clothes. He teaches at a small college upstate, and Charity bought a used blue Datsun ("Nissan," Phil insists) last month so she could spend weekends with him. She returns every Sunday night, exhausted and exasperated. Phil and I don't have much to say to each other—he's the only musician I know; the men in my family are lawyers, engineers, or in business—but I like him. Around me, he loosens up. When he visits, he bakes us loaves of pumpernickel bread. He waxes our kitchen floor. Like many men in this country, he seems to me a displaced child, or even a woman, looking for something that passed him by, or for something that he can never have. If he thinks I'm not looking, he sneaks his hands under Charity's sweater, but there isn't too much there. Here, she's a model with high ambitions. In India, she'd be a flat-chested old maid.

I'm shy in front of the lovers. A darkness comes over me when I see them horsing around.

"It isn't the money," Charity says. Oh? I think. "He says he still loves me. Then he turns around and asks me for five hundred."

What's so strange about that, I want to ask. She still loves Eric, and Eric, red jumpsuit and all, is smart enough to know it. Love is a commodity, hoarded like any other. Mamet knows. But I say, "I'm not the person to ask about love." Charity knows that mine was a traditional Hindu marriage. My parents, with the help of a marriage broker, who was my mother's cousin, picked out a groom. All I had to do was get to know his taste in food.

It'll be a long evening, I'm afraid. Charity likes to confess. I unpleat my silk sari—it no longer looks too showy—wrap it in muslin cloth and put it away in a dresser drawer. Saris are hard to have laundered in Manhattan, though there's a good man in Jackson Heights. My next step will be to brew us a pot of chrysanthemum tea. It's a very special tea from the mainland. Charity's uncle gave it to us. I like him. He's a humpbacked, awkward, terrified man. He runs a gift store on Mott Street, and though he doesn't speak much English, he seems to have done well. Once upon a time he worked for the railways in Chengdu, Szechwan Province, and during the Wuchang Uprising, he was shot at. When I'm down, when I'm lonely for my husband, when I think of our son, or when I need to be held, I think of Charity's uncle. If I hadn't left home, I'd never have heard of the Wuchang Uprising. I've broadened my horizons.

Very late that night my husband calls me from Ahmadabad, a town of textile mills north of Bombay. My husband is a vice president at Lakshmi Cotton Mills. Lakshmi is the goddess of wealth, but LCM (Priv.), Ltd., is doing poorly. Lockouts, strikes, rock-throwings. My husband lives on digitalis, which he calls the food for our *yuga* of discontent.

"We had a bad mishap at the mill today." Then he says nothing for seconds.

The operator comes on. "Do you have the right party, sir? We're trying to reach Mrs. Butt."

"Bhatt," I insist. "B for Bombay, H for Haryana, A for Ahmadabad, double T for Tamil Nadu." It's a litany. "This is she."

"One of our lorries was firebombed today. Resulting in three deaths. The driver, old Karamchand, and his two children."

I know how my husband's eyes look this minute, how the eye rims sag and the yellow corneas shine and bulge with pain. He is not an emotional man—the Ahmadabad Institute of Management has trained him to cut losses, to look on the bright side of economic catastrophes—but tonight he's feeling low. I try to remember a driver named Karamchand, but can't. That part of my life is over, the way *trucks* have replaced *lorries* in my vocabulary, the way Charity Chin and her lurid love life have replaced inherited notions of marital duty. Tomorrow he'll come out of it. Soon he'll be eating again. He'll sleep like a baby. He's been trained to believe in turnovers. Every morning he rubs his scalp with cantharidine oil so his hair will grow back again.

"It could be your car next." Affection, love. Who can tell the difference in a traditional marriage in which a wife still doesn't call her husband by his first name?

"No. They know I'm a flunky, just like them. Well paid, maybe. No need for undue anxiety, please."

Then his voice breaks. He says he needs me, he misses me, he wants
me to come to him damp from my evening shower, smelling of sandalwood soap, my braid decorated with jasmines.

"I need you too."

"Not to worry, please," he says. "I am coming in a fortnight's time. I
have already made arrangements."

Outside my window, fire trucks whine, up Eighth Avenue. I wonder
if he can hear them, what he thinks of a life like mine, led amid disorder.

"I am thinking it'll be like a honeymoon. More or less."

When I was in college, waiting to be married, I imagined honey-
moons were only for the more fashionable girls, the girls who came
from slightly racy families, smoked Sobranies in the dorm lavatories
and put up posters of Kabir Bedi, who was supposed to have made it as
a big star in the West. My husband wants us to go to Niagara. I'm not
to worry about foreign exchange. He's arranged for extra dollars
through the Gujarati Network, with a cousin in San Jose. And he's
bought four hundred more on the black market. "Tell me you need me.
Panna, please tell me again."

I change out of the cotton pants and shirt I've been wearing all day and
put on a sari to meet my husband at JFK. I don't forget the jewelry; the
marriage necklace of *mangalsutra*, gold drop earrings, heavy gold bangles. I don't wear them every day. In this borough of vice and greed,
who knows when, or whom, desire will overwhelm.

My husband spots me in the crowd and waves. He has lost weight,
and changed his glasses. The arm, uplifted in a cheery wave, is bony,
frail, almost opalescent.

In the Carey Coach, we hold hands. He strokes my fingers one by
one. "How come you aren't wearing my mother's ring?"

"Because muggers know about Indian women," I say. They know with
us it's 24-karat. His mother's ring is showy, in ghastly taste anywhere but
India: a blood-red Burma ruby set in a gold frame of floral sprays. My
mother-in-law got her guru to bless the ring before I left for the States.

He looks disconcerted. He's used to a different role. He's the knowing, suspicious one in the family. He seems to be sulking, and finally he
comes out with it. "You've said nothing about my new glasses." I compliment him on the glasses, how chic and Western-executive they
make him look. But I can't help the other things, necessities until he
learns the ropes. I handle the money, buy the tickets. I don't know if
this makes me unhappy.

Charity drives her Nissan upstate, so for two weeks we are to have the
apartment to ourselves. This is more privacy than we ever had in India.

No parents, no servants, to keep us modest. We play at housekeeping. Imre has lent us a hibachi, and I grill saffron chicken breasts. My husband marvels at the size of the Perdue hens. "They're big like peacocks, no? These Americans, they're really something!" He tries out pizzas, burgers, McNuggets. He chews. He explores. He judges. He loves it all, fears nothing, feels at home in the summer odors, the clutter of Manhattan streets. Since he thinks that the American palate is bland, he carries a bottle of red peppers in his pocket. I wheel a shopping cart down the aisles of the neighborhood Grand Union, and he follows, swiftly, greedily. He picks up hair rinses and high-protein diet powders. There's so much I already take for granted.

One night, Imre stops by. He wants us to go with him to a movie. In his work shirt and red leather tie, he looks arty or strung out. It's only been a week, but I feel as though I am really seeing him for the first time. The yellow hair worn very short at the sides, the wide, narrow lips. He's a good-looking man, but self-conscious, almost arrogant. He's picked the movie we should see. He always tells me what to see, what to read. He buys the *Voice*. He's a natural avant-gardist. For tonight he's chosen *Numéro Deux*.

"Is it a musical?" my husband asks. The Radio City Music Hall is on his list of sights to see. He's read up on the history of the Rockettes. He doesn't catch Imre's sympathetic wink.

Guilt, shame, loyalty. I long to be ungracious, not ingratiate myself with both men.

That night my husband calculates in rupees the money we've wasted on Godard. "That refugee fellow, Nagy, must have a screw loose in his head. I paid very steep price for dollars on the black market."

Some afternoons we go shopping. Back home we hated shopping, but now it is a lovers' project. My husband's shopping list startles me. I feel I am just getting to know him. Maybe, like Imre, freed from the dignities of old-world culture, he too could get drunk and squirt Cheez Whiz on a guest. I watch him dart into stores in his gleaming leather shoes. Jockey shorts on sale in outdoor bins on Broadway entrance him. White tube socks with different bands of color delight him. He looks for microcassettes, for anything small and electronic and smuggleable. He needs a garment bag. He calls it a "wardrobe," and I have to translate.

"All of New York is having sales, no?"

My heart speeds watching him this happy. It's the third week in August, almost the end of summer, and the city smells ripe, it cannot bear more heat, more money, more energy.

"This is so smashing! The prices are so excellent!" Recklessly, my prudent husband signs away traveller's checks. How he intends to smuggle it all back I don't dare ask. With a microwave, he calculates, we could get rid of our cook.

This has to be love, I think. Charity, Eric, Phil: they may be experts on sex. My husband doesn't chase me around the sofa, but he pushes me down on Charity's battered cushions, and the man who has never entered the kitchen of our Ahmadabad house now comes toward me with a dish tub of steamy water to massage away the pavement heat.

Ten days into his vacation my husband checks out brochures for sight-seeing tours. Shortline, Grayline, Crossroads: his new vinyl briefcase is full of schedules and pamphlets. While I make pancakes out of a mix, he comparison-shops. Tour number one costs $10.95 and will give us the World Trade Center, Chinatown, and the United Nations. Tour number three would take us both uptown *and* downtown for $14.95, but my husband is absolutely sure he doesn't want to see Harlem. We settle for tour number four: Downtown and the Dame. It's offered by a new tour company with a small, dirty office at Eighth and Forty-eighth.

The sidewalk outside the office is colorful with tourists. My husband sends me in to buy the tickets because he has come to feel Americans don't understand his accent.

The dark man, Lebanese probably, behind the counter comes on too friendly. "Come on, doll, make my day!" He won't say which tour is his. "Number four? Honey, no! Look, you've wrecked me! Say you'll change your mind." He takes two twenties and gives back change. He holds the tickets, forcing me to pull. He leans closer. "I'm off after lunch."

My husband must have been watching me from the sidewalk. "What was the chap saying?" he demands. "I told you not to wear pants. He thinks you are Puerto Rican. He thinks he can treat you with disrespect."

The bus is crowded and we have to sit across the aisle from each other. The tour guide begins his patter on Forty-sixth. He looks like an actor, his hair bleached and blow-dried. Up close he must look middle-aged, but from where I sit his skin is smooth and his cheeks faintly red.

"Welcome to the Big Apple, folks." The guide uses a microphone. "Big Apple. That's what we native Manhattan degenerates call our city. Today we have guests from fifteen foreign countries and six states from this U.S. of A. That makes the Tourist Bureau real happy. And let me assure you that while we may be the richest city in the richest country in the world, it's okay to tip your charming and talented attendant." He laughs. Then he swings his hip out into the aisle and sings a song.

"And it's mighty fancy on old Delancey Street, you know...."

My husband looks irritable. The guide is, as expected, a good singer. "The bloody man should be giving us histories of buildings we are passing, no?" I pat his hand, the mood passes. He cranes his neck. Our window seats have both gone to Japanese. It's the tour of his life. Next to this, the quick business trips to Manchester and Glasgow pale.

"And tell me what street compares to Mott Street, in July...."

The guide wants applause. He manages a derisive laugh from the Americans up front. He's working the aisles now. "I coulda been somebody, right? I coulda been a star!" Two or three of us smile, those of us who recognize the parody. He catches my smile. The sun is on his harsh, bleached hair. "Right, your highness? Look, we gotta maharani with us! Couldn't I have been a star?"

"Right!" I say, my voice coming out a squeal. I've been trained to adapt; what else can I say?

We drive through traffic past landmark office buildings and churches. The guide flips his hands. "Art deco," he keeps saying. I hear him confide to one of the Americans: "Beats me. I went to a cheap guide's school." My husband wants to know more about this Art Deco, but the guide sings another song.

"We made a foolish choice," my husband grumbles. "We are sitting in the bus only. We're not going into famous buildings." He scrutinizes the pamphlets in his jacket pocket. I think, at least it's air-conditioned in here. I could sit here in the cool shadows of the city forever.

Only five of us appear to have opted for the "Downtown and the Dame" tour. The others will ride back uptown past the United Nations after we've been dropped off at the pier for the ferry to the Statue of Liberty.

An elderly European pulls a camera out of his wife's designer tote bag. He takes pictures of the boats in the harbor, the Japanese in kimonos eating popcorn, scavenging pigeons, me. Then, pushing his wife ahead of him, he climbs back on the bus and waves to us. For a second I feel terribly lost. I wish we were on the bus going back to the apartment. I know I'll not be able to describe any of this to Charity, or to Imre. I'm too proud to admit I went on a guided tour.

The view of the city from the Circle Line ferry is seductive, unreal. The skyline wavers out of reach, but never quite vanishes. The summer sun pushes through fluffy clouds and dapples the glass of office towers. My husband looks thrilled, even more than he had on the shopping trips down Broadway. Tourists and dreamers, we have spent our life's savings to see this skyline, this statue.

"Quick, take a picture of me!" my husband yells as he moves toward a gap of railings. A Japanese matron has given up her position in order to change film. "Before the Twin Towers disappear!"

I focus, I wait for a large Oriental family to walk out of my range. My husband holds his pose tight against the railing. He wants to look relaxed, an international businessman at home in all the financial markets.

A bearded man slides across the bench toward me. "Like this," he says and helps me get my husband in focus. "You want me to take the photo for you?" His name, he says, is Goran. He is Goran from Yugoslavia, as though that were enough for tracking him down. Imre from Hungary. Panna from India. He pulls the old Leica out of my hand, signaling the Orientals to beat it, and clicks away. "I'm a photographer," he says. He could have been a camera thief. That's what my husband would have assumed. Somehow, I trusted. "Get you a beer?" he asks.

"I don't. Drink, I mean. Thank you very much." I say those last words very loud, for everyone's benefit. The odd bottles of Soave with Imre don't count.

"Too bad." Goran gives back the camera.

"Take one more!" my husband shouts from the railing. "Just to be sure!"

The island itself disappoints. The Lady has brutal scaffolding holding her in. The museum is closed. The snack bar is dirty and expensive. My husband reads out the prices to me. He orders two french fries and two Cokes. We sit at picnic tables and wait for the ferry to take us back.

"What was that hippie chap saying?"

As if I could say. A day-care center has brought its kids, at least forty of them, to the island for the day. The kids, all wearing name tags, run around us. I can't help noticing how many are Indian. Even a Patel, probably a Bhatt if I looked hard enough. They toss hamburger bits at pigeons. They kick styrofoam cups. The pigeons are slow, greedy, persistent. I have to shoo one off the table top. I don't think my husband thinks about our son.

"What hippie?"

"The one on the boat. With the beard and the hair."

My husband doesn't look at me. He shakes out his paper napkin and tries to protect his french fries from pigeon feathers.

"Oh, him. He said he was from Dubrovnik." It isn't true, but I don't want trouble.

"What did he say about Dubrovnik?"

I know enough about Dubrovnik to get by. Imre's told me about it. And about Mostar and Zagreb. In Mostar white Muslims sing the call to prayer. I would like to see that before I die: white Muslims. Whole peoples have moved before me; they've adapted. The night Imre told me about Mostar was also the night I saw my first snow in Manhattan. We'd walked down to Chelsea from Columbia. We'd walked and talked and I hadn't felt tired at all.

"You're too innocent," my husband says. He reaches for my hand. "Panna," he cries with pain in his voice, and I am brought back from perfect, floating memories of snow, "I've come to take you back. I have seen how men watch you."

"What?"

"Come back, now. I have tickets. We have all the things we will ever need. I can't live without you."

A little girl with wiry braids kicks a bottle cap at his shoes. The pigeons wheel and scuttle around us. My husband covers his fries with spread-out fingers. "No kicking," he tells the girl. Her name, Beulah, is printed in green ink on a heart-shaped name tag. He forces a smile, and Beulah smiles back. Then she starts to flap her arms. She flaps, she hops. The pigeons go crazy for fries and scraps.

"Special ed. course is two years," I remind him. "I can't go back."

My husband picks up our trays and throws them into the garbage before I can stop him. He's carried disposability a little too far. "We've been taken," he says, moving toward the dock, though the ferry will not arrive for another twenty minutes. "The ferry costs only two dollars round-trip per person. We should have chosen tour number one for $10.95 instead of tour number four for $14.95."

With my Lebanese friend, I think. "But this way we don't have to worry about cabs. The bus will pick us up at the pier and take us back to midtown. Then we can walk home."

"New York is full of cheats and whatnot. Just like Bombay." He is not accusing me of infidelity. I feel dread all the same.

That night, after we've gone to bed, the phone rings. My husband listens, then hands the phone to me. "What is this woman saying?" He turns on the pink Macy's lamp by the bed. "I am not understanding these Negro people's accents."

The operator repeats the message. It's a cable from one of the directors of Lakshmi Cotton Mills. "Massive violent labor confrontation anticipated. Stop. Return posthaste. Stop. Cable flight details. Signed Kantilal Shah."

"It's not your factory," I say. "You're supposed to be on vacation."

"So, you are worrying about me? Yes? You reject my heartfelt wishes but you worry about me?" He pulls me close, slips the straps of my nightdress off my shoulder. "Wait a minute."

I wait, unclothed, for my husband to come back to me. The water is running in the bathroom. In the ten days he has been here he has learned American rites: deodorants, fragrances. Tomorrow morning he'll call Air India; tomorrow evening he'll be on his way back to Bombay. Tonight I should make up to him for my years away, the gutted trucks, the degree I'll never use in India. I want to pretend with him that nothing has changed.

In the mirror that hangs on the bathroom door, I watch my naked body turn, the breasts, the thighs glow. The body's beauty amazes. I stand here shameless, in ways he has never seen me. I am free, afloat, watching somebody else.

Topics for Discussion

1. What is the difference between Panna Bhatt's perceptions of New York and those of her husband? Why does Mukherjee portray this difference?

2. How does Mukherjee define culture in the story?

3. What is the impact of place upon the individual in the story and how does Mukherjee portray and convey that impact?

4. What is Mukherjee's view of the United States? Is it a homogeneous culture? What does America represent as a metaphor?

5. What problems does Panna Bhatt face in her attempts to gain an education? What is Mukherjee saying about the role of women in Indian society?

6. What does the story say about the nature of prejudice?

7. What implications does the title have on the way the story is read? Is Panna still married in the traditional sense?

8. How does Mukherjee portray women in the story, and what message does the story convey about the potential women have for education and advancement and the problems that confront them when they attempt to pursue their goals?

Alice Munro

About the Author

Considered by many to be Canada's finest short story writer, Alice Munro was born in Wingham, Ontario, in 1931 and was educated at the University of Western Ontario. She has lived in Vancouver, Victoria and London, Ontario. She has won the Governor General's Award for Fiction three times (in 1969, 1978 and 1987).

Munro's stories are direct and initially often deceptively simple; yet they work on large universal themes such as love, death, sex, growing up, aging, puberty and family relationships with deftness and delicacy. Many of her stories are set in southwestern Ontario, where her familiar landscape becomes a microcosm for all of human experience. For Munro, history is not simply the experience of the place, but the experience of the individual, the chronicle of growth and personal self-knowledge that is essential to each human being. "The Found Boat" is from her 1974 collection *Something I've Been Meaning to Tell You*.

Selected Works

Dance of the Happy Shades (short stories, 1968)
Lives of Girls and Women (novel, 1971)
Something I've Been Meaning to Tell You (short stories, 1974)
Who Do You Think You Are? (short stories, 1978)
The Moons of Jupiter (short stories, 1982)
The Progress of Love (short stories, 1986)
Friend of My Youth (short stories, 1990)
Open Secrets (short stories, 1994)

About the Story

In "The Found Boat," Munro tells a "rite of passage" story in which five children find a wrecked boat in a nearby river and decide to restore it. After fixing the vessel, they take it to a secluded spot in the countryside where they discover the mysteries of puberty in a game of Truth or Dare.

The Found Boat

At the end of Bell Street, McKay Street, Mayo Street, there was the Flood. It was the Wawanash River, which every spring overflowed its banks. Some springs, say one in every five, it covered the roads on that side of town and washed over the fields, creating a shallow choppy lake. Light reflected off the water made everything bright and cold, as it is in a lakeside town, and woke or revived in people certain vague hopes of disaster. Mostly during the late afternoon and early evening, there were people straggling out to look at it, and discuss whether it was still rising, and whether this time it might invade the town. In general, those under fifteen and over sixty-five were most certain that it would.

Eva and Carol rode out on their bicycles. They left the road—it was the end of Mayo Street, past any houses—and rode right into a field, over a wire fence entirely flattened by the weight of the winter's snow. They coasted a little way before the long grass stopped them, then left their bicycles lying down and went to the water.

"We have to find a log and ride on it," Eva said.

"Jesus, we'll freeze our legs off."

"Jesus, we'll freeze our legs off!" said one of the boys who were there too at the water's edge. He spoke in a sour whine, the ways boys imitated girls although it was nothing like the way girls talked. These boys—there were three of them—were all in the same class as Eva and Carol at school and were known to them by name (their names being Frank, Bud and Clayton), but Eva and Carol who had seen and recognized them from the road, had not spoken to them or looked at them or, even yet, given any sign of knowing they were there. The boys seemed to be trying to make a raft, from lumber they had salvaged from the water.

Eva and Carol took off their shoes and socks and waded in. The water was so cold it sent pains up their legs, like blue electric sparks shooting through their veins, but they went on, pulling their skirts high, tight behind and bunched so they could hold them in front.

"Look at the fat-assed ducks in wading."

"Fat-assed fucks."

Eva and Carol, of course, gave no sign of hearing this. They laid hold of a log and climbed on, taking a couple of boards floating in the water for paddles. There were always things floating around in the Flood—branches, fence-rails, logs, road signs, old lumber; sometimes boilers, washtubs, pots and pans, or even a car seat or stuffed chair, as if somewhere the Flood had got into a dump.

They paddled away from shore, heading out into the cold lake. The water was perfectly clear, they could see the brown grass swimming along the bottom. Suppose it was the sea, thought Eva. She thought of drowned cities and countries. Atlantis. Suppose they were riding in a Viking boat—Viking boats on the Atlantic were more frail and narrow than this log on the Flood—and they had miles of clear sea beneath them, then a spired city, intact as a jewel irretrievable on the ocean floor.

"This is a Viking boat," she said. "I am the carving on the front." She stuck her chest out and stretched her neck, trying to make a curve, and she made a face, putting out her tongue. Then she turned and for the first time took notice of the boys.

"Hey, you sucks!" she yelled at them. "You'd be scared to come out here, this water is ten feet deep!"

"Liar," they answered without interest, and she was.

They steered the log around a row of trees, avoiding floating barbed wire, and got into a little bay created by a natural hollow of the land. Where the bay was now, there would be a pond full of frogs later in the spring, and by the middle of summer there would be no water visible at all, just a low tangle of reeds and bushes, green, to show that mud was still wet around their roots. Larger bushes, willows, grew around the steep bank of this pond and were still partly out of the water. Eva and Carol let the log ride in. They saw a place where something was caught.

It was a boat, or part of one. An old rowboat with most of one side ripped out, the board that had been the seat just dangling. It was pushed up among the branches, lying on what would have been its side, if it had a side, the prow caught high.

Their idea came to them without consultation, at the same time:

"You guys! Hey, you guys!"

"We found your boat!"

"Stop building your stupid raft and come and look at the boat!"

What surprised them in the first place was that the boys really did come, scrambling overland, half running, half sliding down the bank, wanting to see.

"Hey, where?"

"Where is it, I don't see no boat."

What surprised them in the second place was that when the boys did actually see what boat was meant, this old flood-smashed wreck held up in the branches, they did not understand that they had been fooled, that a joke had been played on them. They did not show a moment's disappointment, but seemed as pleased at the discovery as if the boat had been whole and new. They were already barefoot, because they had been wading in the water to get lumber, and they waded in here without a stop, surrounding the boat and appraising it and paying no attention even of an insulting kind to Eva and Carol who bobbed up and down on their log. Eva and Carol had to call to them.

"How do you think you're going to get it off?"

"It won't float anyway."

"What makes you think it will float?"

"It'll sink. Glub-blub-blub, you'll all be drowned."

The boys did not answer, because they were too busy walking around the boat, pulling at it in a testing way to see how it could be got off with the least possible damage. Frank, who was the most literate, talkative and inept of the three, began referring to the boat as *she*, an affectation which Eva and Carol acknowledge with fish-mouths of contempt.

"She's caught two places. You got to be careful not to tear a hole in her bottom. She's heavier than you'd think."

It was Clayton who climbed up and freed the boat, and Bud, a tall fat boy, who got the weight of it on his back to turn it into the water so that they could half float, half carry it to shore. All this took some time. Eva and Carol abandoned their log and waded out of the water. They walked overland to get their shoes and socks and bicycles. They did not need to come back this way but they came. They stood at the top of the hill, leaning on their bicycles. They did not go home, but they did not sit down and frankly watch, either. They stood more or less facing each other, but glancing down at the water and at the boys struggling with the boat, as if they had just halted for a moment out of curiosity, and staying longer than they intended, to see what came of this unpromising project.

About nine o'clock, or when it was nearly dark—dark to people inside the houses, but not quite dark outside—they all returned to town, going along Mayo Street in a sort of procession. Frank and Bud and Clayton came carrying the boat, upside-down, and Eva and Carol walked behind, wheeling their bicycles. The boys' heads were almost hidden in the darkness of the overturned boat, with its smell of soaked wood, cold swampy water. The girls could look ahead and see the street lights in their tin reflectors, a necklace of lights climbing Mayo Street, reaching all the way up to the standpipe. They turned onto Burns Street heading for Clayton's house. the nearest house belonging to any of them. This was not the way home for Eva or for Carol either, but they followed along. The boys were perhaps too busy carrying the boat to tell them to go away. Some younger children were still out playing, playing hopscotch on the sidewalk though they could hardly see. At this time of year the bare sidewalk was still such a novelty and delight. These children cleared out of the way and watched the boat go by with unwilling respect; they shouted questions after it, wanting to know where it came from and what was going to be done with it. No one answered them. Eva and Carol as well as the boys refused to answer or even look at them.

The five of them entered Clayton's yard. The boys shifted weight, as if they were going to put the boat down.

"You better take it round to the back where nobody can see it," Carol said. That was the first thing any of them had said since they came into town.

The boys said nothing but went on, following a mud path between Clayton's house and a leaning board fence. They let the boat down in the back yard.

"It's a stolen boat, you know," said Eva, mainly for the effect. "It must've belonged to somebody. You stole it."

"You was the ones who stole it then," Bud said, short of breath. "It was you seen it first."

"It was you took it."

"It was all of us then. If one of us gets in trouble then all of us does."

"Are you going to tell anybody on them?" said Carol as she and Eva rode home, along the streets which were dark between the lights now and potholed from winter.

"It's up to you. I won't if you won't."

"I won't if you won't."

They rode in silence, relinquishing something, but not discontented.

The board fence in Clayton's back yard had every so often a post which supported it, or tried to, and it was on these posts that Eva and Carol spent several evenings sitting, jauntily but not very comfortably. Or else they just leaned against the fence while the boys worked on the boat. During the first couple of evenings neighborhood children attracted by the sound of hammering tried to get into the yard to see what was going on, but Eva and Carol blocked their way.

"Who said you could come in here?"

"Just us can come in this yard."

These evenings were getting longer, the air milder. Skipping was starting on the sidewalks. Further along the street there was a row of hard maples that had been tapped. Children drank the sap as fast as it could drip into the buckets. The old man and woman who owned the trees, and who hoped to make syrup, came running out of the house making noises as if they were trying to scare away crows. Finally, every spring, the old man would come out on his porch and fire his shotgun into the air, and then the thieving would stop.

None of those working on the boat bothered about stealing sap, though all had done so last year.

The lumber to repair the boat was picked up here and there, along back lanes. At this time of year things were lying around—old boards and branches, sodden mitts, spoons flung out with the dishwater, lids of pudding pots that had been set in the snow to cool, all the debris that can sift through and survive winter. The tools came from Clayton's cellar—left over, presumably, from the time when his father was alive—and though they had nobody to advise them the boys seemed to figure out more or less the manner in which boats are built, or rebuilt. Frank was the one who showed up with diagrams from books and *Popular Mechanics* magazines. Clayton looked at these diagrams and listened to Frank read the instructions and then went ahead and decided in his own way what was to be done. Bud was best at sawing. Eva and Carol watched everything from the fence and offered criticism and thought up names. The names of the boat that they thought of were: Water Lily, Sea Horse, Flood Queen, and Caro-Eve, after them because they found it. The boys did not say which, if any, of these names they found satisfactory.

The boat had to be tarred. Clayton heated up a pot of tar on the kitchen stove and brought it out and painted slowly, his thorough way, sitting astride the overturned boat. The other boys were sawing a board to make a new seat. As Clayton worked, the tar cooled and thickened so that finally he could not move the brush any more. He turned to Eva and held out the pot and said, "You can go in and heat this on the stove."

Eva took the pot and went up the back steps. The kitchen seemed black after outside, but it must be light enough to see in, because there was Clayton's mother standing at the ironing board, ironing. She did that for a living, took in wash and ironing.

"Please may I put the tar pot on the stove?" said Eva, who had been brought up to talk politely to parents, even wash-and-iron ladies, and who for some reason especially wanted to make a good impression on Clayton's mother.

"You'll have to poke up the fire then," said Clayton's mother, as if she doubted whether Eva would know how to do that. But Eva could see now, and she picked up the lid with the stove-lifter, and took the poker and poked up a flame. She stirred the tar as it softened. She felt privileged. Then and later. Before she went to sleep a picture of Clayton came to her mind; she saw him sitting astride the boat, tar-painting, with such concentration, delicacy, absorption. She thought of him speaking to her, out of his isolation, in such an ordinary peaceful taking-for-granted voice.

⚔

On the twenty-fourth of May, a school holiday in the middle of the week, the boat was carried out of town, a long way now, off the road over fields and fences that had been repaired, to where the river flowed between its normal banks. Eva and Carol, as well as the boys, took turns carrying it. It was launched in the water from a cow-trampled spot between willow bushes that were fresh out in leaf. The boys went first. They yelled with triumph when the boat did float, when it rode amazingly down the river current. The boat was painted black, and green inside, with yellow seats, and a strip of yellow all the way around the outside. There was no name on it, after all. The boys could not imagine that it needed any name to keep it separate from the other boats in the world.

Eva and Carol ran along the bank, carrying bags full of peanut butter-and-jam sandwiches, pickles, bananas, chocolate cake, potato chips, graham crackers stuck together with corn syrup and five bottles of pop to be cooled in the river water. The bottle bumped against their legs. They yelled for a turn.

"If they don't let us they're bastards," Carol said, and they yelled together, "We found it! We found it!"

The boys did not answer, but after a while they brought the boat in, and Carol and Eva came crashing, panting down the bank.

"Does it leak?"

"It don't leak yet."

"We forgot a bailing can," wailed Carol, but nevertheless she got in, with Eva, and Frank pushed them off, crying, "Here's to a Watery Grave!"

And the thing about being in a boat was that it was not solidly bobbing, like a log, but was cupped in the water, so that riding in it was not like being on something in the water, but like being in the water itself. Soon they were all going out in the boat in mixed-up turns, two boys and a girl, two girls and a boy, a girl and a boy, until things were so confused it was impossible to tell whose turn came next, and nobody cared anyway. They went down the river—those who weren't riding, running along the bank to keep up. They passed under two bridges, one iron, one cement. Once they saw a big carp just resting, it seemed to smile at them, in the bridge-shaded water. They did not know how far they had gone on the river, but things had changed—the water had got shallower, and the land flatter. Across an open field they saw a building that looked like a house, abandoned. They dragged the boat up on the bank and tied it and set out across the field.

"That's the old station," Frank said. "That's Pedder Station." The others had heard this name but he was the one who knew, because his father was the station agent in town. He said that this was a station on a branch line that had been torn up, and that there had been a sawmill here, but a long time ago.

Inside the station it was dark, cool. All the windows were broken. Glass lay in shards and in fairly big pieces on the floor. They walked around finding the larger pieces of glass and tramping on them, smashing them, it was like cracking ice on puddles. Some partitions were still in place, you could see where the ticket window had been. There was a bench lying on its side. People had been here, it looked as if people came here all the time, thought it was so far from anywhere. Beer bottles and pop bottles were lying around, also cigarette packages, gum and candy wrappers, the paper from a loaf of bread. The walls were covered with dim and fresh pencil and chalk writings and carved with knives.

I LOVE RONNIE COLES
I WANT TO FUCK
KILROY WAS HERE
RONNIE COLES IS AN ASS-HOLE
WHAT ARE YOU DOING HERE?
WAITING FOR A TRAIN
DAWNA MARY-LOU BARBARA JOANNE

It was exciting to be inside this large, dark, empty place, with the loud noise of breaking glass and their voices ringing back from the underside of the roof. They tipped the old beer bottles against their mouths. That reminded them that they were hungry and thirsty and they cleared a place in the middle of the floor and sat down and ate the

lunch. They drank the pop just as it was, lukewarm. They ate everything there was and licked the smears of peanut butter and jam off the
bread-paper in which the sandwiches had been wrapped.

They played Truth or Dare.

"I dare you to write on the wall, I am a Stupid Ass, and sign your
name."

"Tell the truth—what is the worst lie you ever told?"

"Did you ever wet the bed?"

"Did you ever dream you were walking down the street without any
clothes on?"

"I dare you to go outside and pee on the railway sign."

It was Frank who had to do that. They could not see him, even his
back, but they knew he did it, they heard the hissing sound of his pee.
They all sat still, amazed, unable to think of what the next dare would
be.

"I dare everybody," said Frank from the doorway, "I dare—Everybody."

"What?"

"Take off all our clothes."

Eva and Carol screamed.

"Anybody who won't do it has to walk—has to *crawl*—around this
floor on their hands and knees."

They were all quiet, till Eva said, almost complacently, "What
first?"

"Shoes and socks."

"Then we have to go outside, there's too much glass here."

They pulled off their shoes and socks in the doorway, in the sudden
blinding sun. The field before them was bright as water. They ran
across where the tracks used to go.

"That's enough, that's enough," said Carol. "Watch out for this-
tles!"

"Tops! Everybody take off their tops!"

"I won't! We won't, will we, Eva?"

But Eva was whirling round and round in the sun where the track
used to be. "I don't care, I don't care! Truth or Dare! Truth or Dare!"

She unbuttoned her blouse as she whirled, as if she didn't know
what her hand was doing, she flung it off.

Carol took off hers. "I wouldn't have done it, if you hadn't!"

"Bottoms!"

Nobody said a word this time, they all bent and stripped themselves. Eva, naked first, started running across the field, and then all
the others ran, all five of them running bare through the knee-high hot
grass, running towards the river. Not caring now about being caught
but in fact leaping and yelling to call attention to themselves, if there
was anybody to hear or see. They felt as if they were going to jump off a

cliff and fly. They felt that something was happening to them different from anything that had happened before, and it had to do with the boat, the water, the sunlight, the dark ruined station, and each other. They thought of each other now hardly as names or people but as echoing shrieks, reflections, all bold and white and loud and scandalous, and as fast as arrows. They went running without a break into the cold water and when it came almost to the tops of their legs they fell on it and swam. It stopped their noise. Silence, amazement, came over them in a rush. They dipped and floated and separated, sleek as mink.

Eva stood up in the water her hair dripping, water running down her face. She was waist deep. She stood on smooth stones, her feet fairly wide apart, water flowing between her legs. About a yard away from her Clayton also stood up, and they were blinking the water out of their eyes, looking at each other. Eva did not turn or try to hide; she was quivering from the cold of the water, but also with pride, shame, and exhilaration.

Clayton shook his head violently, as if he wanted to bang something out of it, then bent over a took a mouthful of river water. He stood up with his cheeks full and made a tight hole of his mouth and shot the water at her as if it was coming out of a hose, hitting her exactly, first one breast and then the other. Water from his mouth ran down her body. He hooted to see it, a loud self-conscious sound that nobody would have expected, from him. The others looked up from wherever they were in the water and closed in to see.

Eva crouched down and slid into the water, letting her head go right under. She swam, and when she let her head out, downstream, Carol was coming after her and the boys were already on the bank, already running into the grass, showing their skinny backs, their white, flat buttocks. They were laughing and saying things to each other but she couldn't hear, for the water in her ears.

"What did he do?" said Carol.

"Nothing."

They crept in to shore. "Let's stay in the bushes till they go," said Eva. "I hate them anyway. I really do. Don't you hate them?"

"Sure," said Carol, and they waited, not very long, until they heard the boys still noisy and excited coming down to the place a bit upriver where they had left the boat. They heard them jump in and start rowing.

"They've got all the hard part, going back," said Eva, hugging herself and shivering violently. "Who cares? Anyway, it never was our boat."

"What if they tell?" said Carol.

"We'll say it's all a lie."

Eva hadn't thought of this situation until she said it, but as soon as she did she felt almost light-hearted again. The ease and scornfulness of it did make them both giggle, and slapping themselves and splashing out of the water they set about developing one of those fits of laughter in which, as soon as one showed signs of exhaustion, the other would snort and start up again, and they would make helpless—soon genuinely helpless—faces at each other and bend over and grab themselves as if they had the worst pain.

Topics for Discussion

1. What is significant of the time of year the story is set?
2. What is the significance of the title of the story?
3. How is Munro using the image of the boat in the story?
4. What part does imagination play in the way the children perceive the boat?
5. How does Munro show the differences between boys and girls in the story and how do the characters become aware of these differences?
6. What roles do self-consciousness and guilt play in the story? How does Munro convey these ideas?
7. How does Munro define the transition from childhood to puberty in the story?
8. What makes the girls hide from the boys at the end of the story?

R.K. Narayan

About the Author

R(asipuram) K(rishnaswami) Narayan was born in Madras, India, in 1906 and educated at Maharaja's College, Mysore. He has worked as a teacher, journalist, publisher and a member of Parliament for India's upper house. Narayan is considered by many to be pre-eminent among Indian novelists of the twentieth century.

Narayan's work has been compared to that of William Faulkner in that both have created imaginary worlds from the material and history presented to them by their localities. Most of his work is set in the mythical southern Indian town of Malgudi, which functions as a metaphor and microcosm for India itself. The town of Malgudi functions as the setting for "Lawley Road," the title story of Narayan's 1956 collection of short stories.

Selected Works

The Dark Room (novel, 1938)
Malgudi Days (short stories, 1943)
The English Teacher (novel, 1945)
Waiting for the Mahatama (novel, 1955)
Lawley Road (short stories, 1956)
The Man-Eater of Malgudi (novel, 1962)
The Sweet-Vendor (novel, 1967)
A Tiger for Malgudi (novel, 1983)
Under the Banyan Tree and Other Stories (short stories, 1985)
Talkative Man (novel, 1987)
A Storyteller's World: Stories, Essays and Sketches (1989)
The World of Nagaraj (novel, 1990)

About the Story

Names define places. Narayan makes the point in his short story "Lawley Road" that if a place name is changed the entire ethos of the place changes with it. As in Irish playwright Brian Friel's drama *Translations*, place names carry connotations of history, mythology and identity as well as location.

The story takes place after Indian independence in 1947, when Indians were attempting to re-establish themselves politically, intellectually and spiritually over their own country in the wake of British withdrawal. As Narayan points out, part of this process entailed the dismantling of British history and iconography (such as the statue), which had become interwoven with the texture and meanings of locations throughout the country. Pay particular attention to the way that Narayan pursues the issue of conflicting histories, and the manner in which the history of the past can become misinterpreted or misused in the context of the present.

Mahatma Gandhi was the spiritual leader and political force behind the Indian independence movement. He was assassinated shortly after Independence. Niccolo Machiavelli was a Florentine political philosopher of the Renaissance who is best remembered for his work *The Prince* (1513) in which he advocated the use of bad means for good ends and the establishment of a tyrannical system of government led by a dictator.

Lawley Road

For years people were not aware of the existence of a Municipal Council in Malgudi. The town was none the worse for it. Diseases, if they started, ran their course and disappeared, for even diseases must end someday. Dust and rubbish were blown away by the wind out of sight; drains ebbed and flowed and generally looked after themselves. The Municipal Council kept itself in the background, and remained so till the country got its independence on the 15th of August, 1947. History holds few records of such jubilation as was witnessed on that day from the Himalayas to Cape Comorin. Our Municipal Council caught the inspiration. They swept the streets, cleaned the drains, and hoisted flags all over the place. Their hearts warmed up when processions with flags and music passed through their streets.

The Municipal Chairman looked down benignly from his balcony, muttering, "We have done our bit for this great occasion." I believe one or two members of the Council who were with him saw tears in his eyes. He was a man who had done himself well as a supplier of blankets to the army during the war, later spending a great deal of his gains in securing the chairmanship. That's an epic by itself and does not concern us now. My present story is different. The satisfaction the Chairman now felt was, however, short-lived. In about a week, when the bunting was torn off, he became quite dispirited. I used to visit him almost every day, trying to make a living out of news reports to an upcountry paper which paid me two rupees for every inch of published news. Every month, I could measure out about ten inches of news in that paper, which was mostly a somewhat idealized account of municipal affairs. This made me a great favorite there. I walked in and out of the Municipal Chairman's office constantly. Now he looked so unhappy that I was forced to ask, "What is wrong, Mr. Chairman?"

"I feel we have not done enough," he replied.

"Enough of what?" I asked.

"Nothing to mark off the great event." He sat brooding and then announced, "Come what may, I am going to do something great!" He called up an Extraordinary Meeting of the Council, and harangued them; and at once they decided to nationalize the names of all the streets and parks, in honor of the birth of independence. They made a start with the park at the Market Square. It used to be called the Coronation Park—whose coronation God alone knew; it might have been the coronation of Victoria or of Asoka. No one bothered about it. Now the old board was uprooted and lay on the lawn, and a brand-new sign stood up in its place, declaring it henceforth to be Hamara Hindusthan Park.

The other transformations, however, could not be so smoothly worked out. Mahatma Gandhi Road was the most sought-after name. Eight different Ward Councilors were after it. There were six others who wanted to call the roads in front of their houses Nehru Road or Netaji Subash Bose Road. Tempers were rising and I feared they might come to blows. There came a point when, I believe, the Council just went mad. It decided to give the same name to four different streets. Well, sir, even in the most democratic or patriotic town, it is not feasible to have two roads bearing the same name. The result was seen within a fortnight. The town became unrecognizable with new names. Gone were the Market Road, North Road, Chitra Road, Vinayak Mudali Street, and so on. In their place appeared the names, repeated in four different places, of all the ministers, deputy ministers, and members of the Congress Working Committee. Of course, it created a lot of hardship—letters went where they were not wanted, people were not able to say where they lived or direct others there. The town became a wilderness with all its landmarks gone.

The Chairman was gratified with his inspired work—but not for long. He became restless again and looked for fresh fields of action.

At the corner of Lawley Extension and Market there was a statue. People had got so used to it that they never bothered to ask whose it was or even look up. It was generally used by the birds as a perch. The Chairman suddenly remembered that it was the statue of Sir Frederick Lawley. The extension had been named after him. Now it was changed to Gandhi Nagar, and it seemed impossible to keep Lawley's statue any longer there. The Council unanimously resolved to remove it. The Council with the Chairman sallied forth triumphantly next morning and circumambulated the statue. They now realized their mistake. The statue towered twenty feet above them and seemed to arise from a pedestal of molten lead. In their imagination they had thought that a vigorous resolution would be enough to topple down the statue of this satrap, but now they found that it stood with the firmness of a mountain. They realized that Britain, when she was here, had attempted to raise herself on no mean foundation. But it made them only firmer in their resolve. If it was going to mean blasting up that part of the town for the purpose, they would do it. For they unearthed a lot of history about Sir Frederick Lawley. He was a combination of Attila, the scourge of Europe, and Nadir Shah, with the craftiness of a Machiavelli. He subjugated Indians with the sword and razed to the ground the villages from which he heard the slightest murmur of protest. He never countenanced Indians except when they approached him on their knees.

People dropped their normal occupations and loitered around the statue, wondering how they could have tolerated it for so many years. The gentleman seemed to smile derisively at the nation now, with his arms locked behind and sword dangling from his belt. There could be no doubt that he must have been the worst tyrant imaginable; the true picture—with breeches and wig and white waistcoat and that hard, determined look—of all that has been hatefully familiar in the British period of Indian history. They shuddered when they thought of the fate of their ancestors, who had had to bear the tyrannies of this man.

Next the Municipal Council called for tenders. A dozen contractors sent in their estimates, the lowest standing at fifty thousand rupees, for removing the statue and carting it to the Municipal office, where they were already worried about the housing of it. The Chairman thought it over and told me, "Why don't you take it yourself? I will give you the statue free if you do not charge us anything for removing it." I had thought till then that only my municipal friends were mad, but now I found I could be just as mad as they. I began to calculate the whole affair as a pure investment. Suppose it cost me five thousand rupees to dislodge and move the statue (I knew the contractors were overestimating), and I sold it as metal for six thousand. About three tons of metal might fetch anything. Or I could probably sell it to the British Museum or Westminster Abbey. I saw myself throwing up the upcountry paper job.

The Council had no difficulty in passing a resolution permitting me to take the statue away. I made elaborate arrangements for the task. I borrowed money from my father-in-law, promising him a fantastic rate of interest. I recruited a team of fifty coolies to hack the pedestal. I stood over them like a slave-driver and kept shouting instructions. They put down their implements at six in the evening, and returned to their attack early next day. They were specially recruited from Koppal, where the men's limbs were hardened by generations of teak-cutting in Mempi Forest.

We hacked for ten days. No doubt we succeeded in chipping the pedestal here and there, but that was all; the statue showed no sign of moving. At this rate I feared I might become bankrupt in a fortnight. I took permission from the District Magistrate to acquire a few sticks of dynamite, cordoned off the area, and lighted the fuse. I brought down the Knight from his pedestal without injuring any limb. Then it took me three days to reach the house with my booty. It was stretched out on a specially designed carriage drawn by several bullocks. The confusion brought about by my passage along Market Road, the crowd that followed, uttering jokes, the incessant shouting and instructions I had to be giving, the blinding heat of the day, Sir F.'s carriage coming to a halt at every inconvenient spot and angle, moving neither forward nor backward, holding up the traffic on all sides, and darkness coming on suddenly with the statue nowhere near my home—all this was a nightmare I wish to pass over. I mounted guard over him on the roadside at night. As he lay on his back, staring at the stars, I felt sorry for him and said, "Well, this is what you get for being such a haughty imperialist. It never pays." In due course, he was safely lodged in my small house. His head and shoulders were in my front hall and the rest of him stretched out into the street through the doorway. It was an obliging community there at Kabir Lane and nobody minded this obstruction.

The Municipal Council passed a resolution thanking me for my services. I wired this to my paper, tacking on to it a ten-inch story of the statue. A week later the Chairman came to my house in a state of agitation. I seated him on the chest of the tyrant. He said, "I have bad news for you. I wish you had not sent up that news item about the statue. See these." He held out a sheaf of telegrams. They were from every kind of historical society in India, all protesting against the removal of the statue. We had all been misled about Sir F. All the present history pertained to a different Lawley, of the time of Warren Hastings. This Frederick Lawley (of the statue) was a military governor who settled down here after the Mutiny. He cleared the jungles and almost built the town of Malgudi. He established here the first co-operative society for the whole of India, and the first canal system by which thousands of acres of land were irrigated from the Sarayu, which had been dissipating itself till then. He established this, he established that, and he died in the great Sarayu floods while attempting to save the lives of villagers living on its banks. He was the first Englishman to advise the British Parliament to associate more and more Indians in all Indian affairs. In one of his dispatches he was said to have declared, "Britain must quit India someday for her own good."

The Chairman said. "The Government have ordered us to reinstate the statue." "Impossible!" I cried. "This is my statue and I shall keep it. I like to collect statues of national heroes." This heroic sentiment impressed no one. Within a week all the newspapers in the country were full of Sir Frederick Lawley. The public caught the enthusiasm. They paraded in front of my house, shouting slogans. They demanded the statue back. I offered to abandon it if the Municipal Council at least paid my expenses in bringing it here. The public viewed me as their enemy. "This man is trying to black-market even a statue," they remarked. Stung by it, I wrote a placard and hung it on my door: "Statue for sale. Two and a half tons of excellent metal. Ideal gift for a patriotic friend. Offers above ten thousand will be considered." It infuriated them and made them want to kick me, but they had been brought up in a tradition of nonviolence and so they picketed my house; they lay across my door in relays, holding a flag and shouting slogans. I had sent away my wife and children to the village in order to make room for the statue in my house, and so this picketing did not bother me—only I had to use the back door a great deal. The Municipal Council sent me a notice of prosecution under the Ancient Monuments Act, which I repudiated in suitable terms. We were getting into bewildering legalities—a battle of wits between me and the municipal lawyer. The only nuisance about it was that an abnormal quantity of correspondence developed and choked up an already congested household.

I clung to my statue, secretly despairing how it was ever going to end. I longed to be able to stretch myself fully in my own house.

Six months later, relief came. The Government demanded a report from the Municipal Council on the question of the statue, and this together with other lapses on the part of the Council made them want to know why the existing Council should not be dissolved and re-elections ordered. I called on the Chairman and said, "You will have to do something grand now. Why not acquire my house as a National Trust?"

"Why should I?" he asked.

"Because," I said, "Sir F. is here. You will never be able to cart him to his old place. It'll be a waste of public money. Why not put him up where he is now? He has stayed in the other place too long. I'm prepared to give you my house for a reasonable price."

"But our funds don't permit it," he wailed.

"I'm sure you have enough funds of your own. Why should you depend upon the municipal funds? It'll indeed be a grand gesture on your part, unique in India." I suggested he ought to relieve himself of some of his old blanket gains. "After all, how much more you will have to spend if you have to fight another election!" It appealed to him. We arrived at a figure. He was very happy when he saw in the papers a few days later: "The Chairman of Malgudi Municipal Council has been able to buy back as a present for the nation the statue of Sir Frederick Lawley. He proposes to install it in a newly acquired property which is shortly to be converted into a park. The Municipal Council have resolved that Kabir Lane shall be changed to Lawley Road."

Topics for Discussion

1. What role do place names play in the story?
2. What role does history play in the story and which is more important: contemporary reality or past history?
3. How does Narayan portray politics?
4. According to the story, what is the significance of statues?
5. How does money—the greed for it or the lack of it—figure in the plot?
6. What role does fate play in the story?

Ben Okri

About the Author

Ben Okri, one of the leading lights of the new generation of Nigerian writers, was born in Minna, Nigeria, in 1959 and educated at the University of Essex in Colchester, England. He has worked as a broadcaster with "Network Africa" and the BBC World Service. He won the Booker Prize, England's prestigious award for the best novel of the year, for *The Famished Road* (1991). He has published three novels and two collections of short fiction.

Okri's work blends European literary traditions and conventions with African perceptions and mythologies. He looks at the world from oblique angles, often pointing out the inherent violence and political tensions of his country of birth. In the background of his writing is the tension between belief and the realities of the contemporary world. Okri believes that spirituality is still possible in the modern world, and uses the conventions of literature—images, symbols, narratives and metaphors—as a means of infusing the world of contemporary Africa with a sense of mystery.

Okri's sense of mystery, or at least the sense of mystery Western readers glean from his work, derives partly from the fact that he is writing out of an experience that is largely unfamiliar to most readers. This unfamiliarity is one of the chief attractions and chief drawbacks to contemporary postcolonial literature—the paradox of perceptual displacement where the familiar becomes strange and the strange becomes familiar.

Selected Works

Flowers and Shadows (novel, 1980)
The Landscape Within (novel, 1981)
Incidents at the Shrine (short stories, 1986)
Stars of the New Curfew (short stories, 1988)
The Famished Road (novel, 1991)

About the Story

This story deals with the curative powers of belief. The protagonist, Anderson, loses his job at a museum that houses the antiquities of an African nation—a place full of images, idols and masks that have been removed from their physical and spiritual contexts. Returning to his village, he is restored psychologically and spiritually.

The name given to masks and images such as those used in this story is *egungun*. These *egunguns* feature prominently in other stories from the collection *Incidents at the Shrine* because of their ability to act as unifying mediums. Reconciliation is an important message in Okri's work—most of the stories in this collection are set against the backdrop of the tribal, linguistic and political rifts that have caused great tensions in contemporary Nigerian history; the most tragic of these conflicts was the explosive and destructive war between the Ibos and the Biafrans in the early 1970s, a war Okri witnessed firsthand.

Incidents at the Shrine

Anderson had been waiting for something to fall on him. His anxiety was such that for the first time in several years he went late to work. It was just his luck that the Head of Department had chosen that day for an impromptu inspection. When he got to the museum he saw that his metal chair had been removed from its customary place. The little stool on which he rested his feet after running endless errands was also gone. His official messenger's uniform had been taken off the hook. He went to the main office and was told by one of the clerks that he had been sacked, and that the supervisor was not available. Anderson started to protest, but the clerk got up and pushed him out of the office.

He went aimlessly down the corridors of the Department of Antiquities. He stumbled past the visitors to the museum. He wandered amongst the hibiscus and bougainvillea. He didn't look at the ancestral stoneworks in the museum field. Then he went home, dazed, confused by objects, convinced that he saw many fingers pointing at him. He went down streets he had never seen in his life and he momentarily forgot where his compound was.

When he got home he found that he was trembling. He was hungry. He hadn't eaten that morning and the cupboard was empty of food. He couldn't stop thinking about the loss of his job. Anderson had suspected for some time that the supervisor had been planning to give his job to a distant relation. That was the reason why the supervisor was always berating him on the slightest pretext. Seven years in the city had begun to make Anderson feel powerless because he didn't belong to the important societies, and didn't have influential relatives. He spent the afternoon thinking about his condition in the world. He fell asleep and dreamt about his dead parents.

He woke up feeling bitter. It was late in the afternoon and he was hungry. He got out of bed and went to the market to get some beef and tripe for a pot of stew. Anderson slid through the noise of revving motors and shouting traders. He came to the goatsellers. The goats stood untethered in a small corral. As Anderson went past he had a queer feeling that the goats were staring at him. When he stopped and looked at them the animals panicked. They kicked and fought backwards. Anderson hurried on till he found himself at the meat stalls.

The air was full of flies and the stench was overpowering. He felt ill. There were intestines and bones in heaps on the floor. He was haggling the price of tripe when he heard confused howls from the section where they sold generators and videos. The meat-seller had just slapped the tripe down on the table and was telling him to go somewhere else for the price he offered, when the fire burst out with an explosion. Flames poured over the stalls. Waves of screaming people rushed in Anderson's direction. He saw the fire flowing behind them, he saw black smoke. He started to run before the people reached him.

He heard voices all around him. Dry palm fronds crackled in the air. Anderson ducked under the bare eaves of a stall, tripped over a fishmonger's basin of writhing eels, and fell into a mound of snailshells. He struggled back up. He ran past the fortune-tellers and the amulet traders. He was shouldering his way through the bamboo poles of the lace-sellers when it struck him with amazing clarity that the fire was intent upon him because he had no power to protect himself. And soon the fire was everywhere. Suddenly, from the midst of voices in the smoke, Anderson heard someone calling his names. Not just the one name, the ordinary one which made things easier in the city—Anderson; he heard all the others as well, even the ones he had forgotten: Jeremiah, Ofuegbu, Nutcracker, Azzi. He was so astonished that when he cut himself, by brushing his thigh against two rusted nails, he did not know how profusely he bled till he cleared out into the safety of the main road. When he got home he was still bleeding. When the bleeding ceased, he felt that an alien influence had insinuated itself into his body, and an illness took over.

He became so ill that most of the money he had saved in all the years of humiliation and sweat went into the hands of the quack chemists of the area. They bandaged his wound. They gave him tetanus injections with curved syringes. They gave him pills in squat, silvery bottles. Anderson was reduced to creeping about the compound, from room to toilet and back again, as though he were terrified of daylight. And then, three days into the illness, with the taste of alum stale in his mouth, he caught a glimpse of himself in the mirror. He saw the gaunt face of a complete stranger. Two days later, when he felt he had recovered sufficiently, Anderson packed his box and fled home to his village.

THE IMAGE-MAKER

Anderson hadn't been home for a long time. When the lorry driver dropped him at the village junction, the first things he noticed were the ferocity of the heat and the humid smell of rotting vegetation. He went down the dirt track that led to the village. A pack of dogs followed him for a short while and then disappeared. Cowhorns and the beating of drums sounded from the forest. He saw masks, eaten by insects, along the grass verge.

He was sweating when he got to the obeche tree where, during the war, soldiers had shot a woman thought to be a spy. Passing the well which used to mark the village boundary, he became aware of three rough forms running after him. They had flaming red eyes and they shouted his names.

"Anderson! Ofuegbu!"

He broke into a run. They bounded after him.

"Ofuegbu! Anderson!"

In his fear he ran so hard that his box flew open. Scattered behind him were his clothes, his medicines, and the modest gifts he had brought to show his people that he wasn't entirely a small man in the world. He discarded the box and sped on without looking back. Swirls of dust came towards him. And when he emerged from the dust, he saw the village.

It was sunset. Anderson didn't stop running till he was safely in the village. He went on till he came to the pool office with the signboard that read: MR. ABAS AND CO. LICENSED COLLECTOR. Outside the office, a man sat in a depressed cane chair. His eyes stared divergently at the road and he snored gently. Anderson stood panting. He wanted to ask directions to his uncle's place, but he didn't want to wake the owner of the pool office.

Anderson wasn't sure when the man woke up, for suddenly he said: "Why do you have to run into our village like a madman?"

Anderson struggled for words. He was sweating.

"You disturb my eyes when you come running into our village like that."

Anderson wiped his face. He was confused. He started to apologize, but the man looked him over once, and fell back into sleep, with his eyes still open. Anderson wasn't sure what to do. He was thirsty. With sweat dribbling down his face, Anderson tramped on through the village.

Things had changed since he'd been away. The buildings had lost their individual colours to that of the dust. Houses had moved several yards from where they used to be. Roads ran diagonally to how he remembered them. He felt he had arrived in a place he had almost never known.

Exhausted, Anderson sat on a bench outside the market. The roadside was full of ants. The heat mists made him sleepy. The market behind him was empty, but deep within it he heard celebrations and arguments. He listened to alien voices and languages from the farthest reaches of the world. Anderson fell asleep on the bench and dreamt that he was being carried through the village by the ants. He woke to find himself inside the pool office. His legs itched.

The man whom he had last seen sitting in the cane chair, was now behind the counter. He was mixing a potion of local gin and herbs. There was someone else in the office: a stocky man with a large forehead and a hardened face.

He stared at Anderson and then said: "Have you slept enough?"

Anderson nodded. The man behind the counter came round with a tumbler full of herbal mixtures.

Almost forcing the drink down Anderson's throat, he said: "Drink it down. Fast!"

Anderson drank most of the mixture in one gulp. It was very bitter and bile rushed up in his mouth.

"Swallow it down!"

Anderson swallowed. His head cleared a little and his legs stopped itching.

The man who had given him the drink said: "Good." Then he pointed to the other man and said: "That's your uncle. Our Image-maker. Don't you remember him?"

Anderson stared at the Image-maker's face. The lights shifted. The face was elusively familiar. Anderson had to subtract seven years from the awesome starkness of the Image-maker's features before he could recognize his own uncle.

Anderson said: "My uncle, you have changed!"

"Yes, my son, and so have you," his uncle said.

"I'm so happy to see you," said Anderson.

Smiling, his uncle moved into the light at the doorway. Anderson saw that his left arm was shrivelled.

"We've been expecting you," his uncle said.

Anderson didn't know what to say. He looked from one to the other. Then suddenly he recognized Mr. Abas, who used to take him fishing down the village stream.

"Mr. Abas! It's you!"

"Of course it's me. Who did you think I was?"

Anderson stood up.

"Greetings, my elders. Forgive me. So much has changed."

His uncle touched him benevolently on the shoulder and said: "That's all right. Now, let's go."

Anderson persisted with his greeting. Then he began to apologize for his bad memory. He told them that he had been pursued at the village boundary.

"They were strange people. They pursued me like a common criminal."

The Image-maker said: "Come on. Move. We don't speak of strange things in our village. We have no strange things here. Now, let's go."

Mr. Abas went outside and sat in his sunken cane chair. The Image-maker led Anderson out of the office.

They walked through the dry heat. The chanting of worshippers came from the forest. Drums and jangling bells sounded faintly in the somnolent air.

"The village is different," Anderson said.

The Image-maker was silent.

"What has happened here?"

"Don't ask questions. In our village we will provide you with answers before it is necessary to ask questions," the Image-maker said with some irritation.

Anderson kept quiet. As they went down the village Anderson kept looking at the Image-maker: the more he looked, the more raw and godlike the Image-maker seemed. It was as though he had achieved an independence from human agencies. He looked as if he had been cast in rock, and left to the wilds.

"The more you look, the less you see," the Image-maker said.

It sounded, to Anderson, like a cue. They had broken into a path. Ahead of them were irregular rows of soapstone monoliths. Embossed with abstract representations of the human figure, the monoliths ranged from the babies of their breed to the abnormally large ones. There were lit candles and varied offerings in front of them. There were frangipani and iroko trees in their midst. There were also red-painted poles which had burst into flower.

His uncle said: "The images were originally decorated with pearls, lapis lazuli, amethysts and magic glass which twinkled wonderful philosophies. But the pale ones from across the seas came and stole them. This was whispered to me in a dream."

Anderson gazed at the oddly elegant monoliths and said: "You resemble the gods you worship."

His uncle gripped him suddenly.

"We don't speak of resemblances in our village, you hear?"

Anderson nodded. His uncle relaxed his grip. They moved on.

After a while his uncle said: "The world is the shrine and the shrine is the world. Everything must have a centre. When you talk rubbish, bad things fly into your mouth."

They passed a cluster of huts. Suddenly the Image-maker bustled forward. They had arrived at the main entrance to a circular clay shrinehouse. The Image-maker went to the niche and brought out a piece of native chalk, a tumbler and a bottle of herbs. He made a mash which he smeared across Anderson's forehead. On a nail above the door, there was a bell which the Image-maker rang three times.

A voice called from within the hut.

The Image-maker sprayed himself forth in a list of his incredible names and titles. Then he requested permission to bring to the shrine an afflicted "son of the soil."

The voices asked if the "son of the soil" was ready to come in.

The Image-maker was silent.

A confusion of drums, bells, cowhorns, came suddenly from within. Anderson fainted.

Then the Image-maker said to the voices: "He is ready to enter!"

They came out and found that Anderson was light. They bundled him into the shrinehouse and laid him on a bed of congealed palm oil.

THE IMAGE

When Anderson came to he could smell burning candles, sweat and incense. Before him was the master Image, a hallucinatory warrior monolith decorated in its original splendour of precious stones and twinkling glass. At its base were roots, kola nuts and feathers. When Anderson gazed at the master Image he heard voices that were not spoken and he felt drowsiness come over him.

Candles burned in the mist of blue incense. A small crowd of worshippers danced and wove Anderson's names in songs. Down the corridors he could hear other supplicants crying out in prayer for their heart's desires, for their afflictions and problems. They prayed like people who are ill and who are never sure of recovering. It occurred to Anderson that it must be a cruel world to demand such intensity of prayer.

Anderson tried to get up from the bed, but couldn't. The master Image seemed to look upon him with a grotesque face. The ministrants closed in around him. They praised the master Image in songs. The Image-maker gave a sudden instruction and the ministrants rushed to Anderson. They spread out their multiplicity of arms and embraced Anderson in their hard compassions. But when they touched Anderson he screamed and shouted in hysteria. The ministrants embraced him with their remorseless arms and carried him through the corridors and out into the night. They rushed him past the monoliths outside. They took him past creeks and waterholes. When they came to a blooming frangipani tree, they dumped him on the ground. Then they retreated with flutters of their smocks, and disappeared as though the darkness were made of their own substance.

Anderson heard whispers in the forest. He heard things falling among the branches. Then he heard footsteps that seemed for ever approaching. He soon saw that it was Mr. Abas. He carried a bucket in one hand and a lamp in the other. He dropped the bucket near Anderson.

"Bathe of it," Mr. Abas said, and returned the way he had come.

Anderson washed himself with the treated water. When he finished the attendants came and brought him fresh clothes. Then they led him back to the shrinehouse.

The Image-maker was waiting for him. Bustling with urgency, his bad arm moving restlessly like the special instrument of his functions, the Image-maker grabbed Anderson and led him to an alcove.

He made Anderson sit in front of a door. There was a hole greased with palm oil at the bottom of the door. The Image-maker shouted an instruction and the attendants came upon Anderson and held him face down. They pushed him towards the hole; they forced his head and shoulders through it.

In the pain Anderson heard the Image-maker say: "Tell us what you see!"

Anderson couldn't see anything. All he could feel was the grinding pain. Then he saw a towering tree. There was a door on the tree trunk. Then he saw a thick blue pall. A woman emerged from the pall. She was painted over in native chalk. She had bangles all the way up her arms. Her stomach and waist were covered in beads.

"I see a woman," he cried.

Several voices asked: "Do you know her?"

"No."

"Is she following you?"

"I don't know."

"Is she dead?"

"I don't know."

"Is she dead?"

"No!"

There was the merriment of tinkling bells.

"What is she doing?"

She had come to the tree and opened the door. Anderson suffered a fresh agony. She opened a second door and tried the third one, but it didn't open. She tried again and when it gave way with a crash Anderson finally came through—but he lost consciousness.

✶

Afterwards, they fed him substantially. Then he was allowed the freedom to move round the village and visit some of his relations. In the morning the Image-maker sent for him. The attendants made him sit on a cowhide mat and they shaved off his hair. They lit red and green candles and made music around him. Then the Image-maker proceeded with the extraction of impurities from his body. He rubbed herbal juices into Anderson's shoulder. He bit into the flesh and pulled out a rusted little padlock which he spat into an enamel bowl. He inspected the padlock. After he had washed out his mouth, he bit into Anderson's shoulder again and pulled out a crooked needle. He continued like this till he had pulled out a piece of broken glass, a twisted nail, a cowrie, and a small key. There was some agitation as to whether the key would fit the padlock, but it didn't.

When the Image-maker had finished he picked up the bowl, jangled the objects, and said: "All these things, where do they come from? Who sent them into you?"

Anderson couldn't say anything.

The Image-maker went on to cut light razor strokes on Anderson's arm and he rubbed protective herbs into the bleeding marks. He washed his hands and went out of the alcove. He came back with a pouch, which he gave to Anderson with precise instructions of its usage.

Then he said: "You are going back to the city tomorrow. Go to your place of work, collect the money they are owing you, and look for another job. You will have no trouble. You understand?"

Anderson nodded.

"Now, listen. One day I went deep into the forest because my arm hurt. I injured it working in a factory. For three days I was in the forest praying to our ancestors. I ate leaves and fishes. On the fourth day I forgot how I came there. I was lost and everything was new to me. On the fifth day I found the Images. They were hidden amongst the trees and tall grasses. Snakes and tortoises were all around. My pain stopped. When I found my way back and told the elders of the village what I had seen they did not believe me. The Images had been talked about in the village for a long time but no one had actually seen them. That is why they made me the Image-maker."

He paused, then continued.

"Every year, around this time, spirits from all over the world come to our village. They meet at the marketplace and have heated discussions about everything under the sun. Sometimes they gather round our Images outside. On some evenings there are purple mists round the iroko tree. At night we listen to all the languages, all the philosophies, of the world. You must come home now and again. This is where you derive power. You hear?"

Anderson nodded. He hadn't heard most of what was said. He had been staring at the objects in the enamel bowl.

THE IMAGE-EATERS

Anderson ate little through the ceremonies that followed the purification of his body. After all the dancing and feasting to the music of cowhorns and tinkling bells, they made him lie down before the master Image. Then the strangest voice he had ever heard thundered the entire shrinehouse with its full volume.

"ANDERSON! OFUEGBU! YOU ARE A SMALL MAN. YOU CANNOT RUN FROM YOUR FUTURE. GOVERNMENTS CANNOT EXIST WITHOUT YOU. ALL THE DISASTERS OF THE WORLD REST ON YOU AND HAVE YOUR NAME. THIS IS YOUR POWER."

The ministrants gave thanks and wept for joy.

⟛⟨⟩⟛

Anderson spent the night in the presence of the master Image. He dreamt that he was dying of hunger and that there was nothing left in the world to eat. When Anderson ate of the master Image he was surprised at its sweetness. He was surprised also that the Image replenished itself.

In the morning Anderson's stomach was bloated with an imponderable weight. Shortly before his departure the Image-maker came to him and suggested that he contribute to the shrine fund. When Anderson made his donation, the Image-maker gave his blessing. The ministrants prayed for him and sang of his destiny.

Anderson had just enough money to get him back to the city. When he was ready to leave, Anderson felt a new heaviness come upon him. He thanked his uncle for everything and made his way through the village.

He stopped at the pool office. Mr. Abas was in his sunken cane chair, his eyes pursuing their separate lines of vision. Anderson wasn't sure if Mr. Abas was asleep.

He said: "I'm leaving now."

"Leaving us to our hunger, are you?"

"There is hunger where I am going," Anderson said.

Mr. Abas smiled and said: "Keep your heart pure. Have courage. Suffering cannot kill us. And travel well."

"Thank you."

Mr. Abas nodded and soon began to snore. Anderson went on towards the junction.

As he walked through the heated gravity of the village Anderson felt like an old man. He felt that his face had stiffened. He had crossed the rubber plantation, had crossed the boundary, and was approaching the junction, when the rough forms with blazing eyes fell upon him. He fought them off. He lashed out with his stiffened hands and legs. They could easily have torn him to pieces, because their ferocity was greater than his. There was a moment in which he saw himself dead. But they suddenly stopped and stared at him. Then they pawed him, as though he had become allied with them in some way. When they melted back into the heat mists, Anderson experienced the new simplicity of his life, and continued with his journey.

Topics for Discussion

1. What do the masks represent?

2. Why does Okri divide the story into three sections? What impact does this have on perspective and the development of the narrative?

3. How does Okri define what is sacred?

4. What does Okri mean when he states, "You resemble the gods you worship"?

5. How does Okri define community and what does the community do for the individual?

6. What does Okri mean by "hunger" in the final page of the story?

Sam Selvon

About the Author

Sam Selvon was born in Trinidad in 1923 and grew up in San Fernando, a small city on the island. During the Second World War he served in the British Royal Navy Reserve, but it was his work after the war as a journalist and his experience of the American presence on the island that convinced him to become a novelist. In 1950 he moved to England, where he did much of his writing before settling in Canada in 1978.

His early exposure to the cultures of the Indians on the land and the Africans in the oilfields piqued his interest in Creole Trinidad. A number of his works are concerned with the meeting of these two cultures.

Selected Works

A Brighter Sun (novel, 1952)
An Island Is a World (novel, 1955)
The Lonely Londoners (novel, 1956)
Moses Ascending (novel, 1975)
Foreday Morning: Selected Prose, 1946–1986 (essays and articles, 1986)

About the Story

The story examines the power of beliefs and stories and the impact they have on the way individuals lead their lives. Johnson, an Englishman, becomes fascinated by the folk beliefs and superstitions of the island of Trinidad, and in the process of embracing them transforms not only his life but the manner of his dying.

Selvon examines the way in which an outsider to a culture can become fascinated with what insiders take for granted. Through his depiction of an "exotic" landscape, Selvon leads the reader through the mystery of the place as seen from the perspective of the visiting Englishman.

As the story explains, a *cascadura* is a type of spiny fish found in the back streams of the island of Trinidad. An *immortelle* is a type of flower that maintains its original shape and colour when dried in the bloom. A *soucouyant* is an island name for an evil restless, wandering ghost or spirit.

Johnson and the Cascadura

Those who eat the cascadura, will the native legend says,
Wheresoever they may wander end in Trinidad their days.

—Allister MacMillan

If ever there was a man in love with life, it was Garry Johnson, the Englishman who came out to Trinidad in 1926 to spend a holiday at his friend Franklin's estate, in Sangre Grande. I knew Johnson well, because I was overseer of the estate, and he and I used to go around together often, and in the night Franklin invited me over to the house and we three sipped rum punches and yarned about the tropics.

This chap Johnson used to get up early mornings and breathe great gulps of air and say ah, it's good to be alive. The way he did that made you feel as if the wind blew only for him to swallow it greedily down his lungs. Johnson used to watch the buxom girls who came from the village to "dance" the cocoa seeds where they dried in the sun when the roof was rolled away, and a dreamy look would come into his eyes and he'd lick his lips and sigh. Down on the plantation when the young fruits were just coming out on the branches and trunks, he'd touch them with gentle hands and wonder at their growth, and when the rainy season set in and the crimson immortelles burst into splendid bloom, he called me and raved about the beauties of Nature, and talked about what a wonderful thing life was, and how he wished he could live forever.

Then, in the nights, I used to watch Johnson enjoy every second of existence as it ticked by, contemplatively sipping his rum punch and allowing the fiery liquid to course slowly down his throat, so you could tell his sense of taste was having a good time.

Franklin was a middle-aged man and a good manager. He was not prejudiced, and treated his labourers as fellow human beings. Even in the village he was respected for his kindness, for when the dry season lingered on, the villagers would come for water from the two huge concrete cisterns on the estate, carrying it away in barrels on donkey carts. He could have made them pay; they offered him money from the little they earned toiling in the canefields and in their gardens, but Franklin always shook his head and told them they could have anything they wanted on the plantation. So it was that he became godfather for many a ragged little child in the village, and no ceremony was held without an invitation to him.

I had to see that everything on the estate ran smoothly, get the cocoa ready for market, and keep an eye on the labour. So that when we got together in the night I would suggest to Franklin what should be done about the last trees we planted, or tell him we needed more immortelles to shade certain parts of the plantation.

At such times Johnson asked me to relate tales of local superstitions, and explain the customs of the natives. I told him about Papa Bois, who lurked in the forests and lured evil hunters away so that they were lost in the thick bush for days, and couldn't find their way out. He heard of soucouyants which sucked your blood while you slept, and which took the form of a ball of fire and scared the villagers in lonely paths in the night. You could only escape from a la diablesse by shooting it with a silver bullet, I explained as Johnson listened wide-eyed, or if you see it approaching, quickly draw the sign of the cross in the air in front of you, and that will keep the evil spirit away.

And Johnson swallowed the legends hook, line and sinker. Then Franklin would add his quota and say how he couldn't vouch for the authenticity of the stories, but that one night he was coming in late from inspecting some young orange trees at the other end of the plantation, and a flaming ball shot across the path and his horse got wild and galloped away, or else he didn't know what he would have done. Later, he thought there might be some logical explanation but he never worried about it.

When we waxed warm sometimes Franklin used to send for a labourer to get a firsthand account of some weird experience. Once Chanko, the old Indian watchman, came and told us how one night he heard a rattle of chains as if dragged by some powerful animal, but he couldn't see a thing. "All yuh wouldn't believe mah, chief, but day had ah man in de village, name Santogee, who used to wuk obeah and tun animal in de night, and go all 'bout de village fri'tenin' people. So wen we fine out is he who doin' all this businis, we make up a head and decide to chase 'im out, and since 'e gone all de noise and t'ing in de night did stop."

"Did you ever see a soucouyant?" Johnson asked him.

"Oh gawd Mister Johnson, don' call dat ting name. If ah ever see one! It had a time dong Icacos, wen ah was walking in de coconut one night, and de win' did blowin' strong, and wat ah cud see but dis piece ah light, like fire in de air, comin' at mi. So ah run out on de beach fo mi life, as a tort it wouldn't follow mi day. But ah see de ting still comin'. Ah fuss ah fri'ten! But ah stop an take mi cutlass and ah make de sine ah de cross in de san'. Ah bawl out, come now, leh we see who is man. But de light come rite up to dat cross and it cudn't pass it. It make two three circle in de air, and dis time ah only waiting to bus dut if it come any nearer; but it stay rite dey; it cudn't make ah note. Is really true, Mister Johnson, bad tings does run from de sine ah de cross."

And Johnson took in every word and sipped his punch with delight, and so the nights passed away.

So now, one evening Franklin calls me and says he is worried, that Johnson has gone out into the plantation since morning and has not returned. So I say he must have gone to the village, and there is nothing to worry about. But Franklin would have me make a search for his guest, so I get Chanko, who only works in the night guarding the plantation, and we set off.

The estate covers more than a hundred acres of land, and all of it isn't cleared, so you can imagine we have a good job looking for the Englishman. And so it is nearing dusk and we are thinking Johnson might have returned and we are only looking for a wild goose, when we hear a call from overhead and raising our heads, whom do we see but Johnson, in the fork of an immortelle tree, holding on for dear life.

I am so amazed that I can only ask him, foolishly, what he is doing up there, to which query he replies that we had better get him down quickly, as he is thirsty and hungry, and then maybe he could explain. So I tell him it is an easy matter, that he only has to hug the trunk with his arms and legs and slide down. But Johnson would not budge. Chanko appreciates that the situation excites mirth, and he grins so that his brown face is stretched and his strong white teeth gleam white, but at the same time he goes into all kinds of shapes illustrating to Johnson how easy it is. But all our coaxing and pleading is of no avail.

Then Chanko has an idea and he cuts a length of "supplejack" vine and tosses it up to the Englishman, telling him to make it fast to the branch and hold it in descending. Johnson is averse to the idea, but I encourage him, and in a few minutes he is resting firmly on the good earth.

But he is silent until much later when he and I are sitting with Franklin out on the verandah, it being moonlight and the trees all lighted up and casting weird shadows on the grounds, and the breeze scented with guava blossoms. Then Johnson tells us that a native told him if he got a corbeau's egg he'd be very lucky, as he would only have to ask it, and anything he wanted he would have. "He told me that I had to replace it with a hard-boiled egg," Johnson continues, "so I got one from the cook. Then the cook had his bit to say, and told me to be careful, as if the carrion saw me he'd pick out my eyes. So I went to look for a corbeau's nest. I thought I saw one in the immortelle tree, but it was only a broken branch with dead leaves, and I couldn't climb down."

We have a hearty laugh, but Johnson is very serious about the affair, I can tell you, so to humour him I explain that he'd have to search for the nest in holes in the ground, near bushy places, or in the trunks of dead trees.

Now I tell you all this because I want you to understand how this fellow Johnson had faith in these legends, or you'd never believe me when you hear about him and the cascaduras.

The time comes when he has to leave us, and the day before his departure he gets it into his head to eat cascaduras. So Franklin allows me to have the day off and Johnson and I get some simple fishing tackle, which is really not fishing gear at all, consisting of a basket and a cutlass, the latter always being carried around by country folk.

Now the cascadura is a small horny-scaled fish to be found in the muddy slushes of streams. You catch him by damming the spot where you know he is, and bailing out the water. But the method we adopt is different. When the rains fall and the streams are swollen, branches, twigs and old leaves float down, and where the water is calm they gather in little islands. Under these shelters the cascadura lays its eggs. All you have to do is to dip your bucket partly into the water, so that you cover the nest, and splash the water near the basket. When the fish hears the noise it leaps towards it, and you catch him in your basket, lift it and drain off the water, and you've landed your first cascadura.

So it being the rainy season, I figure this method may be more fruitful and we'd have better fun and we go to Mitan, which is a small village a few miles from Sangre Grande, where these fishes abound.

Well, you can imagine us wading in the muddy slushes in our leggings, and Johnson pausing to admire some tropical flower, and insisting once that I climb a tree to get him a wild orchid. Anyway, we come across a muddy stretch of water in which many of these nests are, and we have great fun catching the fishes as they leap from under the twigs and leaves. But many escape as we are not experts and it is the evening before we decide to return with a catch of eight. We string them on a piece of blacksage bark and walk back with them dangling in our hands, and Johnson mighty proud of his catch, admiring them with his usual vigour, and calling out to the villagers.

So that last night Franklin has a variety of tropical dishes prepared for his friend. There is crab and callalloo, boiled plantains and bananas, a "sancoche," which is a mixed pot of all the vegetables you can think of, and meat, peas, and rice cooked together with salted meat, rotis and Indian sweetmeats and, of course, the cascaduras curried in real "creole" fashion.

And just as Johnson swallows his first bite of a cascadura and comments favourably on its flavour and sweet taste, he looks around at Franklin and I and says solemnly:

Those who eat the cascadura the native legend says
Wheresoever they may wander end in Trinidad their days.

"I read that in a book," he says, "and I'll see how true it is."

But years pass by before these words echo forcefully in our minds. It happens that Franklin invites Johnson to come over to Trinidad, it being the Carnival season. Johnson replies thanking him and even inquires after my health and hopes the estate is flourishing, but says he is sure he will live forever if he keeps away from Trinidad.

Well, at first Franklin and I are highly amused at this, but then we remember it is a long time ago, and knowing Johnson as we do, get to thinking that he must have believed with all his heart that Trinidad legend about the cascadura.

But after the incident of the letter we forget about it, as there are many things to do, Franklin having bought another hundred acres of land as the price of cocoa has risen in the market and the plantation is prospering.

Then one day—it must have been a year or so after the letter—Franklin comes up to me when I am watching the girls "dance" the cocoa and he waves a sheet of paper in my face and asks if I remember Johnson. I nod and say yes, he must be getting on in his years now, and must be a wiser man. "Not only is he getting old," Franklin says, "but ill. His doctor in England has recommended that he spend a few months in the tropics and Johnson has written me saying that he'll be sailing by the next boat."

And it seems then that we both get the same idea, thinking that Johnson's number is up and he is impelled by some spirit to return to Trinidad, but we are silent. I can see that is what Franklin is thinking, though he feels ashamed to put his thoughts into words.

So that our enthusiasm is dampened and our welcome is not as cheerful as it should be, though we don't say a word and we are hoping he has forgotten all that nonsense about the fish.

As the days pass by we are careful not to drop a hint, and Johnson sits out on the verandah breathing the fresh country air and taking in the genial warmth of the sun. But for all that it is a great pity to see him so frail and weak, and remember how he used to be gay and laughing and bubbling with the joy of living. Not that he doesn't have that love for movement and animation, but we are sad that he cannot move around much, as his heart is weak. Sometimes his eyes glow strangely as if he remembers his youth and what a great part he'd taken in the drama, but for the most part he is melancholy and silent for days.

The villagers remember him and not a day passes but some gift is brought for him. He gets the choice oranges from the estate and the ripest bananas, and the old men in the village keep him company, telling stories, and the women bring their children to play with and amuse him.

But what happens one day than a grateful woman in the village remembers Johnson and decides to give him a gift, and what does it turn out to be but a string of cascaduras she offers him. As Johnson sees the fishes a fearful look comes into his eyes, and we know he is thinking back on that last night when he was full of vitality. It seems he realises he is getting old and cannot escape the inevitable, and as the realisation seeps slowly into his reluctant brain he sinks back in his chair with a gasp.

For all that, Franklin keeps his head on and does as if nothing has happened, and he even orders the cook to have the fishes done up for supper. Afterwards he calls me aside and says he thinks it is the best thing to do as if all of us have forgotten, and in a way I agree with him, though I am very much afraid of the outcome in my mind.

And sure enough Johnson, poor fellow, faints when he sees the cascaduras on the table, and we have to put him to bed right away.

That night he is pale and gasping for breath, and we send for the nearest doctor, who lives miles away in Arima. Franklin and I are helpless as we watch Johnson panting on the bed. He opens his eyes and he keeps muttering that legend about whoever eats the cascadura must die in Trinidad.

And then he is silent, and Franklin and I sit there thinking about that legend, too, and we wait for the doctor to arrive, though we know it will be too late as the Englishman, Johnson, has breathed his last.

Topics for Discussion

1. How does Selvon use the first person narrative voice in the story? How involved is the narrator in the action?

2. What role does superstition play in the story?

3. Why does Johnson think he will be immortal? What does this idea say about the nature of stories and their relationship to beliefs?

4. What role does the setting play in the story? How does Selvon define and evolve his "setting"?

5. What sort of comparison does Selvon establish between Johnson and the islanders?

6. Why does Johnson return to Trinidad? Why does he die?

7. How does Selvon convey the "exotic" and the "mysterious" in the story?

8. What role does specialized language play in the story and how does Selvon make the language accessible to his readers?

Olive Senior

About the Author

Olive Senior was born in Jamaica in 1943 and educated in Jamaica and Canada. She has worked as an editor, a journalist and a freelance writer. Her first collection of short stories, *Summer Lightning* (1987), won the Commonwealth Prize for Fiction. For several years she was editor of *Jamaica Journal*, a magazine about her native island. She now lives in Toronto.

Senior writes both mythically and metaphorically about the Jamaican experience. Her stories, which often carry the quality of fables and folk tales, are creative chronicles of the ways of life and the pressures confronting Jamaican society in the twentieth century.

"The Chocho Vine" is from *Discerner of Hearts* (1995).

Selected Works

Talking of Trees (poetry, 1986)
Summer Lightning (short stories, 1986)
Arrival of the Snake-Woman and Other Stories (short stories, 1989)
Gardening in the Tropics (poetry, 1994)
Discerner of Hearts and Other Stories (short stories, 1995)

About the Story

In "The Chocho Vine," Senior tells the story of an old widow, Miss Evadney. In the course of the narrative, Miss Evadney's life, her relationship with her neighbours and her children and her spirit of generosity are explored. Senior chronicles the social and spiritual history of Jamaica by metaphorically associating Miss Evadney and the changes in that character's life with the country itself. The departure of her children, her devotion to the land, her stubborn resistance to change and her determination to remain rooted and independent reflect the experience of her people in the twentieth century.

Bauxite, a mineral, is one of the chief exports of Jamaica and is an essential ingredient in the production of aluminum. Rastas (Rastafarians) are members of a Jamaican religion/philosophy that reveres the former Ethiopian Emperor Haile Selassie (1892–1974) as the Messiah, and uses *ganja* (marijuana) as a sacrament.

The Chocho Vine

The only thing that flourished in Miss Evadney's yard was her chocho vine. Her son had made her sell off all the property except for the square surrounding the house, and this piece of land, neglected like her, was nothing now but hard-packed red dirt trampled by so many feet over the years, sluiced so clean by the rain and by dirty water flung from kitchen and bedroom windows, that it had acquired a shiny red patina like the ox-blood shoes her husband used to wear. By the front step, a rusting yellow margarine tin held a sickly looking Wandering Jew, and even the Ram-goat-roses which peeked out from under the house did so nervously, as if ready to jerk their heads back at the first discordant note, for though it had grown increasingly feeble in volume, Miss Evadney's temper was legendary.

The chocho vine evidently felt no fear, for in the back right-hand corner, up against the property line, it had literally captured a whole quarter of the yard sweeping majestically over the arbour of split bamboo originally built and extended many times to hold it, clambering over the abandoned chicken coop, and then aiming upwards to almost completely smother the old Number Eleven mango tree which had after a while given up the battle and simply ceased bearing. It did put forth feeble blossoms each year on the few bits of branches which still retained the privilege of being exposed to the sun, but the tiny fruit which actually came seemed embarrassed to compete with the magnificent chochos and dried up from confusion when they were no bigger than plums. Meanwhile, the chocho vine from its high perch on the mango tree hurled itself into the air before bending down and attaching itself to a new branch, or anything else in its path, waving as if in triumph its probing tentacles and plump greeny-white offspring that were a source of unending bounty.

Miss Evadney derived great satisfaction from her splendidly robust chocho, for she was herself subject to the longest list of ailments imaginable, and any question to her about her health elicited a torrent of words, as if her infirmities, real and imagined, were now the only topic of conversation left to her. "Ai, my dear, the gas, the gas da kill me," she would commence, rubbing that part of her anatomy which was currently the locus of her pain, looking proud and surprised if she managed to produce a large belch. That greeting over, she had no trouble jumping to her "pressure," her "arthritis," her "heart," her "head," her "foot," in an endless recital which—if one didn't take care—might even include an exhibition of some afflicted part. Not that Miss Evadney had much of an audience these days since she had outlived all her contemporaries and most of the younger generation had migrated to more prosperous locations. It was really only Miss Vie and her family who paid her any mind.

Miss Vie lived up the road and had been vaguely related to Miss Evadney's husband. But that wasn't the reason why she took an interest in the old lady. The real reason was that somebody had to do it, as she often told her husband, and she saw it as her Christian duty. Besides, they were all fond of Miss Evadney, who, like so many people who tyrannized their own families and those who dared to cross them, was a perfectly benign and sociable being in her relationships with others. To them, she was almost mythical, she was so old, and could always be relied upon to give the "true version" of events whenever an argument arose or someone failed to remember things that had happened in the past. Despite her physical infirmities, Miss Evadney still had a wonderful memory.

She could remember when she had planted her first chocho vine. "It was the year I get married, Miss Vie. The said year. You see all them other girls there? All of them was busy a live common-law life. But not me, Miss Vie, not me. I had *standards*, you know." So when Mr. Shaw had the impertinence to "put question" to her, she told him she wasn't that kind of woman. "Is so I tell him," she was fond of saying, "I said, 'I am not that kind of woman. I have mother and father at my yard, so if you have anything to say, go and put question to them.'"

Mr. Shaw had just come back from the Great War, in which he had served as a volunteer. He had ten acres of land, was expecting to get his soldier's pension, and he wanted to settle down with someone. Though the white people had fixed him up in the hospital, his head still felt groggy and his chest wheezed sometimes, but he knew all this would go away once he got a good woman to look after him. He liked that Evadney Gordon, liked the cut of her jib, though he still couldn't believe this tall strapping young woman he came back to find was the skinny little pickney-gal he had left behind. That more than anything else made him conscious of how quickly time was passing, so he went to her parents and took off his hat and asked for her hand in marriage.

"Well, the other girls were so jealous afterwards!" Miss Evadney loved to say. "Here I was a married woman! And Mr. Shaw would never allow me to work again. Would never hear of his wife working. I never ever went to the ground like the other women and I never work in nobody's kitchen neither." She stayed home and looked after the house and Mr. Shaw and the three children. She kept chickens and sometimes rabbits and planted skellion and cabbages around the yard. And she planted her chocho. Mr. Shaw himself put up the arbour when the vine started to grow. Such a strong vine it was from the start.

"You have good hand with chocho," Mr. Shaw said, and she was pleased with the compliment. It was white-skin chocho, nice and fleshy inside and not too many prickles on the skin.

In those days she never sold the chochos, she gave them away, took pleasure in the fact that her vine was so bounteous she could afford to give chocho freely to all who came and asked and still have plenty left over to feed the babies on and to put in the soup or the stew. "That's the thing with chocho," she was given to saying. "It's not one of those things like pumpkin that you could get a good meal out of now. You could eat nothing but pumpkin if that was all you had and pumpkin would may yu stomach feel full. There is nothing to beat a good pumpkin soup, but chocho by itself is nothing much. Same like squash there; it's a tasteless kind of thing, you know. But to fill out the meal now, when things short, to stretch the codfish or the meat or the soup or the susumber—nothing to beat chocho."

The other good thing, Miss Evadney said, was that once you planted chocho, you didn't have to do anything but water it and give it something to climb on; the chocho would just carry on from there. Whenever her chocho vine started to look weak, she would set another one so that by the time the old one started to wear out, the young one would be flourishing.

Anyone who wanted chocho only had to come and ask; that was one rule she had. Nobody should just come into her yard and pick chocho as they liked. If they asked, they could have chocho by the dozen. But woe betide anyone who dared to take even one little vegetable without asking. Miss Evadney's tongue could blister.

When she was first married Miss Evadney wasn't at all quarrelsome. Mr. Shaw was at his ground all day and she sang as she went around doing her chores and she set his meal on the table the minute he came home. But then Mr. Shaw began to get sickly: it happened to a lot of people who had gone away to the war—"fighting for King and Country," he proudly used to say even on his sick-bed, though she was vexed that King and Country never knew anything about his coughing out his soul-case and having to take to his bed more and more. And that was the time the boys started to give trouble and back-answer her.

"Is three boy pickney I did have—Leroy, Everald, and Joseph—that is the one there we did call Mighty," she told anyone who asked. But it was only to Miss Vie or Miss Vie's daughter Hermione that she confided all. "Well, everybody know how boy pickney hard to raise from morning. And mine was no different. But you see me here, I wasn't going to let them get away with one single thing, they had to know who was boss. I let them know from morning I wasn't going to tolerate no force-ripe man at my yard. If their father couldn't chastise them anymore, they would still find out where water walk go a pumpkin belly, for I would take the strap to them myself. 'Spare the rod and spoil the child,' the Good Book says, but nobody could say I was guilty of that sin. I had *standards*, Miss Vie, *standards*. I wanted the world to know my children come from good home. All them other little pickney around could run wild and act like ragamuffin all they want. But not mine. They had to have standards, too."

When their father got too poorly to go to his ground any more, it was they who had to go. She had to take Leroy out of school before he even reached sixth standard to send him to the ground. "Leroy bawl every day because he was bright in school and had his heart set to become a teacher. Every year, every year I promise I would send him back to school, but there was no way he could go back, you almost had to say he was man-a-yard now, he had to take charge of the ground, and the two younger ones hardly ever had the chance to go to school at all for they had to help their brother. But nuh so life stay?"

Miss Evadney used to be upset about this, she often told Miss Vie: upset about the fact that her children had to drop out of school. "Because, my dear Miss Vie, if they didn't get an education, what was there for them but slaving on the land? The land wasn't a thing now that you could ever make money out of, you know. You can see for yourself that the land there never fat. Never fat. Pure hillside and rock-stone. No matter how hard Mr. Shaw work, it was barely enough to keep body and soul together." Mr. Shaw's pittance from the government there, well, that was something, but it wasn't enough to send the boys to school when Mr. Shaw had to go to doctor so often and buy medicine and tonic to build up his strength. Miss Evadney remembered how she used to curse the Germans every day for what they had done to Mr. Shaw, though what it was she wasn't sure. All she knew is that they had reduced her big strapping man to nothing but a skeleton, skin and bone there lying on the bed. When the boys saw their father help-less like that, no wonder they felt they could just do as they liked.

Whenever things got too much for Miss Evadney she would go into the yard and stand and gaze in admiration at her chocho vine; it made her feel good just to look at it. One thing in her life was flourishing exuberantly. She always thought that it was a pity some of those nayga round the place were so bad-minded that they had to come and steal her chocho, were too red-eye and ill-mannered to come and ask, the way people were supposed to. Like those Pettigrews and those Vernons. She had caught them red-handed several times and cursed them hog-rotten, them and all their generation.

When Mr. Shaw died, the pittance from the government stopped coming, and soon all the boys were gone. It was then that Miss Evad-ney started to sell her chocho.

"Miss Vie, I regret that I never had a daughter," she would often complain, "for I sure a daughter would stay faithful to her mother, a daughter would never, never abandon you in your old age. Daughters are always true to their mothers." Look at Miss Vie's children now, she thought to herself but didn't say out loud. Five children she has and which is the most loving to her, which one always coming to visit and bring her things? Who but the one girl pickney?

Of all Miss Vie's children, Miss Evadney loved Hermione the best. Hermione never ever came to visit her mother without bringing some-thing for Miss Evadney. If she didn't see the old lady at her mother's, she would often walk down the road to her house, calling out loudly in jest as she neared, "Miss Evadney, Miss Evadney. Hold dog!" for Miss Evadney had not even a cat to guard her house. On these occasions, Miss Evadney felt sorry that all her neighbours had died off or moved away, sorry that they couldn't see people of quality coming to visit her at her yard.

Whenever Hermione visited her parents in the country, she always left with some of Miss Evadney's chochos. It was now a family joke: Miss Evadney and her chochos. Hermione hated the squash-like vege-tables, regarding them as useless, tasteless things, and she always gave hers away. But she took the gift from Miss Evadney with many thanks, because she knew the old lady was proud to have something to give.

"Thank God for you and your mother every day, Miss H," she told her every visit, "for I don't know what I would do without you. You wouldn't believe is three boys I did birth? Three of them. Leroy the eldest. Everald the middle one, and Joseph who is the one we call Mighty for him did little but him lion-heart. And where the three of them now, eh? I ask you that. Why not a one to mind me?"

Hermione, like her mother, had heard Miss Evadney's stories so many times she didn't need to listen as the old woman talked.

"Leroy was the first one to leave home. Well I did hear some rumour there about Leroy and one of the Pettigrew girls, the one that did say she studying for nurse. But I couldn't believe it, Miss H, couldn't believe Leroy would do his mother such a thing, take up with the daughter of my enemy, those thieving red-eye people. And when I question that boy, he deny every word of it. Look me straight in mi face and tell me lie, and to think how I did try to beat the lying out of them. So how I could tell anybody to this day how I did feel when my son Leroy and that girl run away together, run off to Kingston without a word to his mother?"

Miss Evadney would stand there silent for a long, long time, contemplating her fate and the injustice of it all. "Well, maybe the girl's parents did know about it, that is the hurtful part. Maybe is them fix it up to tief away my good-good boy," she would finally say in a wondering tone, as if thinking about this for the first time. "For next thing I hear, Miss H, them nuh going off to Kingston to wedding?" She even heard long afterwards that Leroy went back to school and turned teacher after all. But not a word did Leroy ever send to her, leaving her with his sick father and the ground to look after. What did she ever do to make him treat her like that?

"Miss H, I cry over Leroy, I tell you, for nothing in life never hot me so. Not even when Mr. Shaw die and leave me." She told Hermione this standing up in the middle of the road, with tears welling up in her eyes.

Mr. Shaw didn't have long to go after that disappointment and there was barely enough to bury him. "We had was to sell the three goat, though Mr. Shaw always said that because he was an old soldier the government would give something toward the burial. Well, I send and ask the government about that, and I still waiting. Thirty years now and I still waiting. You think they get the letter yet?"

The case of Everald now: Everald didn't walk off and leave her like Leroy, he just brought a woman into the house. "That didn't last long, Miss H, for though I try, God know I try, me and the girl couldn't get on, just couldn't agree." So she gave Everald permission to build his own house next door. And Everald still continued to work his father's ground and bring her something—he used to look after he, she always said, you have to give Everald that.

"But is only afterward that I really get the full picture of what he was after, you know. For Everald is the one that make me sell off the land."

If Mighty had been around at the time, maybe she wouldn't have done it, Miss Evadney always said, but Mighty went away, too. "Mighty get to go away as farm worker, was earning good-good American dollar, turn into a fine young man, except the third time Mighty go away, he jump his contract and never come back, never send his mother another word."

So it was just she and Everald left and she was grateful to him for staying, for he looked after her and she had her grandchildren next door, in and out of her house all day. And even Cynthia, their mother, and she started to pull together. So everything was working well and she could afford to just give chocho away to anybody who came and asked.

It was the bauxite coming in that caused it, Miss Evadney always maintained, that caused everything to spoil. They brought in all these machines that were digging up the earth, pulling down the mountains even, clawing away at the red dirt to ship it to America, though she always wondered why they wanted to do that, if America didn't have its own dirt. But it was the biggest thing that had happened since the war, not the war Mr. Shaw was in, the other one, and all the men around were rushing there to get work. Everald went too. He got a job working with one of these machines that was mashing down the place, and he came home beaming all over his face. The money was so good and they were going to train him and everything; he could work his way up. Everald told her that for the first time in his life, he could see his future straight like an asphalt road out there in front of him. She thought of Leroy and Mighty and felt she was going to lose Everald, too, lose him to a place where he could earn proper money and feel like a big shot, just like the others.

At first it was all right, Everald came home every weekend and went over to the ground as usual; Jackie Davison, who was his playmate from morning, and his big boy Jason were keeping an eye on things during the week. Then he started to talk of moving his family to the town where he would be nearer his workplace and Cynthia could learn to drive and shop in a supermarket and the children could go to proper schools. She knew what was coming next but this time she prayed. She prayed like she never prayed for anything else in her life, prayed that Everald wouldn't leave her, too.

Miss Evadney always said she thought it was like the devil was dealing that deck there, for look what Everald turned around and did. She was so afraid of losing him that she gave no thought to the land, said yes when he came and asked her if she would sell the land and lend him the money. "Leave only the house spot, Ma," Everald told her, "for there is no point in your keeping this land that will just go to waste when you could make something off of it now when you need it. Because I cannot keep on looking after it. My life change now. And you know once my children get education they not coming back." The way he put it, it all made sense to her, and she agreed to sell the land and let Everald borrow the money, for he needed the down payment for a house in the town. How could she stand in his way when he said she should come and live with them, there would be plenty space for her? She said, no, she could never take to life in town. So he said all right, if she stayed in her house he would look after her. He would pay back the money as soon as he could, put it into the bank to mind her in her old age.

"Where is the money now, eh?" she asked Hermione, for about the hundredth time. "Once Mister Everald get his hand on it, never see hide or hair of it again. That Everald with his sweet mouth! Is when last I see him? Tell me nuh?" Once in a while Everald would come, she reported, or his grown-up children would breeze by and leave her a little something. All driving their flashy big cars. But if she was waiting on them to live, she would starve to death.

If it wasn't for Miss Vie and Hermione, God knows what would happen to her. She was glad she had chocho to give them, for her mother always told her, "Hand wash hand. Never take something for nothing." In all her born days, she had never stooped to begging. Every Thursday Miss Mae, who higgled in the market, would come by with her little boy and a long stick and the boy would climb up and pick all the ripe chochos he could reach, and Miss Mae would pay her for them and take them to the market to sell. That was how she lived. Anyone who came by and wanted chocho now had to pay, unless she knew they were poor like her; only then she would give.

⇥⫞⇤

At first, when the people moved into Everald's old house next door she paid them no mind, for she was at an age where she couldn't be bothered with anything new and to her they seemed orderly and manners-able enough. Something strange was happening in the whole country these last days anyway, Miss Evadney thought, changes were everywhere, all was topsy-turvy and confusion, it would stir up your brain to take it all in. New people were moving into the area every day. That wasn't too surprising, for all the young people had gone away; only the old people were left and the grandchildren that they had to mind.

With all the young people gone, so much of the land was idle, so many houses empty, that people from town or god-knows-where were simply coming and squatting. "Take my old land there," Miss Evadney said, "from Everald sell it to the people, they never come back once to even look at it, let it turn into wilderness, ruinate, let Everald good-good house fall to pieces, you almost have to say."

She didn't know what business these people next door had with the land and with Everald's old house, but she didn't pay them any mind at first. She heard them hammering and nailing, so she figured they were decent people who had come to fix up the house. "Is only when the renk ganja smell start to come from over there that I sit up straight and pay attention," she recounted later. "And more and more people were coming till I wonder how many of them planning to live in the house. Then I start to see some of those bearded fellows there, those Rastas. I never wanted any of those people living near to me. They never look good in the sight of God with their long beard and natty hair." But Miss Evadney didn't complain, for though she was too old to walk and see, people said they were clearing the whole of the land, and if they were hard-working, she said, who was she to pass judgement?

They could have got on all right, would have had no trouble at all, no trouble, Miss Evadney always said, if they hadn't started to pick her chocho. When she saw it, she couldn't believe it, for not even when her own son was living next door would he do such a thing. These people were standing in their yard and using a long stick to cross the property boundary and hook chocho of her vine. She never raised her voice, only called out to them nicely: "Young man. Young man," she said, "is my chocho that you picking, you know?" She expected that he would say, "Sorry," and she would say, "Is all right this time, I don't mind you take a few. But next time, if you want chocho, all you have to do is ask. I only sell them at twenty cents apiece." To her amazement, though, the young man laughed when she called out to him and continued pulling down chochos. "Mother, rest yuself. You have plenty chocho to spare."

She was so shocked, she was speechless for a moment. But not for long. As soon as she recovered, she let him have the full length of her tongue. Miss Evadney thought she still had the voice she had used in the past to stun her children and frighten chocho thieves. But it had got so trembling and thin, it sounded laughably frail to the young man next door. He just continued to pick chocho. "Mother," he called out, still laughing, "you nuh hear is Socialist time now? All a we must share. Nothing nuh belong to you one any more." And before she had a chance to marshal her thoughts, hurl at him the most crushing abuse, he had picked up the chochos, *her* chocho, and disappeared into the house. Every day they came to the fence and picked chocho and got so bare-faced they did it even when they could see her standing in her yard. She would hobble over to the arbour and shout and wave her arms, but they paid her not the slightest attention, the stick continuing its remorseless passage, stabbing away at chochos until the picker decided that he had reaped enough. Each scene would leave Miss Evadney with just enough strength to make it back to her doorstep where she would sit for a while and fan herself to cool down and try to recover her composure. At first, she would go from there to Miss Vie as soon as she could manage it, to complain about the latest assault, but she did this less and less because she was shocked to discover that Miss Vie was not wholeheartedly on her side.

"Miss Evadney, I know just how you feel," Miss Vie had said. "I know it's an aggravation. But it's not like first time, you know. You have to be careful how you deal with everybody these days. Those people not good people to quarrel with, from what I hear. It would be better if you just leave them to take the chocho."

Leave them to take the chocho! Miss Vie couldn't know what she saying. It was all right for her, for she had house and land and husband and pickney and car. Could afford to give away all kind of thing. But all she had was her chocho and nobody had any right to just come and take. No right at all. She told Miss Vie as much, shaking with anger and disappointment at her attitude.

"Miss Evadney, if you want me to put it straight: you know what those people planting on the land there? I hear that is pure ganja them a plant, you know. You don't want to tangle with those kind of people."

"Plant ganja! Everybody a plant ganja these days," Miss Evadney cried. "That is the only thing them young people farming. Them all a plant ganja. Mek them gwan. Them could plant the whole world in ganja for all I care. But that don't give them no right to take stick so pick my chocho. I bring up my boys to know right from wrong and to respect other people property. That is one thing I beat into them. Nobody could ever complain that any of my boys ever put hand on what don't belong to them. So why I should put up with other people tiefing from me?"

Miss Vie just sighed.

One day Miss Evadney came home and found some gungo peas laid out on a piece of plantain leaf on her doorstep. She cooked the gungo because she thought they were left there by one of the men around who sometimes brought her things from his ground. Another time it was a piece of pumpkin. Then one day she learned the truth. She'd heard a voice calling out, "Mother? Mother?" but she didn't answer because the only people who called her that were the thieving nayga boys next door. She peeked through a crack and sure enough it was one those dirty Rastas, bending down at her doorstep. She trembled in anger. What did he want? She couldn't quite see but was satisfied that he didn't stay. She watched him leave, made sure he got off her premises without stealing anything. When she opened her door and saw a piece of yam lying there on the plantain leaf, Miss Evadney's anger knew no bounds. Did they think she was the kind of person they could just sweeten up so that she would let them take chocho as they liked? All she wanted was for them to leave her chocho alone. She picked up the yam and plantain leaf and hobbled over to the fence where, cursing, she hurled them back into the Rastas' yard.

But Miss Evadney soon realized she would have to find other means of keeping the chocho thieves from off her vine, to let them know once and for all that she meant business. She began to keep watch on the arbour, sitting there silently hour after hour till her body got so cramped and stiff she could hardly move. When they came, she was ready for them. By her was a pile of stones which she had slowly and painfully collected. As soon as she saw the stick of the chocho thieves disturbing the foliage, she would hurl as many stones as she could over the fence, her strength so weakened that she was forced to stop and catch her breath after each throw. Though her range was short and the hail of stones ineffectual, they did cause the young men reaping the chocho to pause and even to jump to get out of range of the stronger throws. At first, they were more amused than anything and took to reasoning with her: Lawd, Mother. Behave yuself, nuh. Why you have to fight and quarrel so with the bredren? Nuh Jah send I-bredren so help you reap Jah blessing?"

Miss Evadney simply continued with her stone-throwing. Though she never managed to hit anyone, after a while the amused cajoling turned to curses and then to threats. Once, one of them rushed to the fence with a raised machete. But still she didn't give up, screaming at the men "Unno gwine stop pick mi chocho. Even if it kill me. Not one of you ever plant chocho over here." Now they had stopped laughing, they got in the habit of shouting words across the fence even when they weren't picking chocho. And every time Miss Evadney saw them with a stick, she hurled stones.

One day, as she sat under the arbour with her pile of stones as usual, she saw the young men moving around the yard, heard them talking, heard the bad words they flung about, caught the smell of ganja on the wind. But no one came near the fence. No one attempted to pick chocho. The next day it was the same. After the third day of this she felt she had won a victory and, confident that she had finally put the chocho thieves in their place, she slept soundly for the first time in weeks. Next morning she walked as fast as her legs could take her to tell Miss Vie the good news, so pleased with herself she forgot the usual recital of her ailments. Miss Vie gave her chicken soup with chocho— her favourite—to celebrate. That night, she again slept the whole night through.

It wasn't until late the following day that she walked down to her chocho vine and immediately noticed something strange. The vine was not looking good, it seemed droopy and disheartened. She rushed to water the root, carrying the margarine tin full of water back and forth. But for all the water she poured, the chocho didn't perk up as she expected. It continued to wilt. Alarmed, she rushed over to Miss Vie and begged her to come and see what she could make of the vine, why it was drying up so.

Miss Vie came and examined the chocho carefully, looking at the arbour from various angles, disturbed at the obviously dying leaves, the colourless exposed fruit which were already shrivelling. When she could find no explanation, she went and got Miss Evadney's rickety ladder and, leaning it against the mango tree, started to climb.

"You see anything, Miss Vie?" Miss Evadney called out anxiously before she was even halfway up. With great caution, Miss Vie moved steadily up the ladder until she reached a point where she had a good view of the vine. She held on to the tree with both hands and followed the main stem with her eyes. She almost shouted out then, but caught herself just in time, for she had seen where the chocho vine had been cut, sliced right through with a sharp machete. She stood very still, gazing on the arbour, wondering how on earth she was going to find the heart to come down and tell Miss Evadney the news.

Miss Evadney, using her hand to shield her eyes against the afternoon sun so she could better see Miss Vie's every move, had spent too many years scrutinizing potential chocho thieves and wayward children to miss the quick stiffening of Miss Vie's back, the droop of her neck, her sudden stillness. In that moment of recognition, Miss Evadney audibly caught her breath and felt the stillness enter and possess her own body, emptying her of anger, of memory, or desire. Cocooned in that unaccustomed softness, she experienced only the nagging thought that, for some reason, she needed to say something to cheer up Miss Vie, to get her down safely from the ladder. "Well, the thing about chocho now," Miss Evadney heard herself saying, "the thing about chocho now," she said again and kept on saying long after Miss Vie had climbed back down the ladder to find her trembling and wordless.

Topics for Discussion

1. What does the lushness of the chocho vine represent?
2. What is the relationship between the chocho vine and Miss Evadney's life?
3. In what ways does Senior use Jamaican *patois* to create characterization?
4. What role does generosity play in the story?
5. What part do parent/child relationships play in the story?
6. Why is Miss Evadney so protective of the chochos?
7. Is the ending of the story just?

Amy Tan

About the Author

Amy Tan was born in Oakland, California, in 1952 and educated at San Jose State University and the University of California at Berkeley. Her parents immigrated to the United States from Beijing, China, two years before her birth. She has worked as consultant to programs for disabled children and as a freelance writer. She lives in San Francisco.

In her first novel, *The Joy Luck Club* (a series of interconnected stories from which "Two Kinds" is taken), Tan explored the complexities of the Chinese-American experience and of relationships between mothers and daughters, themes she continued in her next book, *The Kitchen God's Wife*.

Selected Works

The Joy Luck Club (novel/short stories, 1989)
The Kitchen God's Wife (novel, 1991)
The Hundred Secret Senses (novel, 1995)

About the Story

"Two Kinds," a story about a mother/daughter relationship and the expectations and dreams that parents have for their children, is set in the Chinese-American community in California. Tan examines the relationship between the traditional Chinese ways of life and the new American modes of behaviour. Note Tan's use of humour and the absurd in the role of the deaf piano teacher, and the way in which the story confronts issues of guilt, betrayal, hurtfulness and stubbornness.

Two Kinds

My mother believed you could be anything you wanted to be in America. You could open a restaurant. You could work for the government and get good retirement. You could buy a house with almost no money down. You could become rich. You could become instantly famous.

"Of course you can be prodigy, too," my mother told me when I was nine. "You can be best anything. What does Auntie Lindo know? Her daughter, she is only best tricky."

America was where all my mother's hopes lay. She had come here in 1949 after losing everything in China: her mother and father, her family home, her first husband, and two daughters, twin baby girls. But she never looked back with regret. There were so many ways for things to get better.

We didn't immediately pick the right kind of prodigy. At first my mother thought I could be a Chinese Shirley Temple. We'd watch Shirley's old movies on TV as though they were training films. My mother would poke my arm and say, "*Ni kan*"—You watch. And I would see Shirley tapping her feet, or singing a sailor song, or pursing her lips into a very round O while saying, "Oh my goodness."

"*Ni kan,*" said my mother as Shirley's eyes flooded with tears. "You already know how. Don't need talent for crying!"

Soon after my mother got this idea about Shirley Temple, she took me to a beauty training school in the Mission district and put me in the hands of a student who could barely hold the scissors without shaking. Instead of getting big fat curls, I emerged with an uneven mass of crinkly black fuzz. My mother dragged me off to the bathroom and tried to wet down my hair.

"You look like Negro Chinese," she lamented, as if I had done this on purpose.

The instructor of the beauty training school had to lop off these soggy clumps to make my hair even again. "Peter Pan is very popular these days," the instructor assured my mother. I now had hair the length of a boy's, with straight-across bangs that hung at a slant two inches above my eyebrows. I liked the haircut and it made me actually look forward to my future fame.

In fact, in the beginning, I was just as excited as my mother, maybe even more so. I pictured this prodigy part of me as many different images, trying each one on for size. I was a dainty ballerina girl standing by the curtains, waiting to hear the right music that would send me floating on my tiptoes. I was like the Christ child lifted out of the straw manger, crying with holy indignity. I was Cinderella stepping from her pumpkin carriage with sparkly cartoon music filling the air.

In all of my imaginings, I was filled with a sense that I would soon become *perfect.* My mother and father would adore me. I would be beyond reproach. I would never feel the need to sulk for anything.

But sometimes the prodigy in me became impatient. "If you don't hurry up and get me out of here, I'm disappearing for good," it warned. "And then you'll always be nothing."

Every night after dinner, my mother and I would sit at the Formica kitchen table. She would present new tests, taking her examples from stories of amazing children she had read in *Ripley's Believe It or Not,* or *Good Housekeeping, Reader's Digest,* and a dozen other magazines she kept in a pile in our bathroom. My mother got these magazines from people whose houses she cleaned. And since she cleaned many houses each week, we had a great assortment. She would look through them all, searching for stories about remarkable children.

The first night she brought out a story about a three-year-old boy who knew the capitals of all the states and even most of the European countries. A teacher was quoted as saying the little boy could also pronounce the names of the foreign cities correctly.

"What's the capital of Finland?" my mother asked me, looking at the magazine story.

All I knew was the capital of California, because Sacramento was the name of the street we lived on in Chinatown. "Nairobi!" I guessed, saying the most foreign word I could think of. She checked to see if that was possibly one way to pronounce "Helsinki" before showing me the answer.

The tests got harder—multiplying numbers in my head, finding the queen of hearts in a deck of cards, trying to stand on my head without using my hands, predicting the daily temperatures in Los Angeles, New York, and London.

One night I had to look at a page from the Bible for three minutes and then report everything I could remember. "Now Jehoshaphat had riches and honor in abundance and ... that's all I remember, Ma," I said.

And after seeing my mother's disappointed face once again, something inside of me began to die. I hated the tests, the raised hopes and failed expectations. Before going to bed that night, I looked in the mirror above the bathroom sink and when I saw only my face staring back—and that it would always be this ordinary face—I began to cry. Such a sad, ugly girl! I made high-pitched noises like a crazed animal, trying to scratch out the face in the mirror.

And then I saw what seemed to be the prodigy side of me—because I had never seen that face before. I looked at my reflection, blinking so I could see more clearly. The girl staring back at me was angry, powerful. This girl and I were the same. I had new thoughts, willful thoughts, or rather thoughts filled with lots of won'ts. I won't let her change me, I promised myself. I won't be what I'm not.

So now on nights when my mother presented her tests, I performed listlessly, my head propped on one arm. I pretended to be bored. And I was. I got so bored I started counting the bellows of the foghorns out on the bay while my mother drilled me in other areas. The sound was comforting and reminded me of the cow jumping over the moon. And the next day, I played a game with myself, seeing if my mother would give up on me before eight bellows. After a while I usually counted only one, maybe two bellows at most. At last she was beginning to give up hope.

Two or three months had gone by without any mention of my being a prodigy again. And then one day my mother was watching *The Ed Sullivan Show* on TV. The TV was old and the sound kept shorting out. Every time my mother got halfway up from the sofa to adjust the set, the sound would go back on and Ed would be talking. As soon as she sat down, Ed would go silent again. She got up, the TV broke into loud piano music. She sat down. Silence. Up and down, back and forth, quiet and loud. It was like a stiff embraceless dance between her and the TV set. Finally she stood by the set with her hand on the sound dial.

She seemed entranced by the music, a little frenzied piano piece with this mesmerizing quality, sort of quick passages and then teasing lilting ones before it returned to the quick playful parts.

"Ni kan," my mother said, calling me over with hurried hand gestures. "Look here."

I could see why my mother was fascinated by the music. It was being pounded out by a little Chinese girl, about nine years old, with a Peter Pan haircut. The girl had the sauciness of a Shirley Temple. She was proudly modest like a proper Chinese child. And she also did this fancy sweep of a curtsy, so that the fluffy skirt of her white dress cascaded slowly to the floor like the petals of a large carnation.

In spite of these warning signs, I wasn't worried. Our family had no piano and we couldn't afford to buy one, let alone reams of sheet music and piano lessons. So I could be generous in my comments when my mother bad-mouthed the little girl on TV.

"Play note right, but doesn't sound good! No singing sound," complained my mother.

"What are you picking on her for?" I said carelessly. "She's pretty good. Maybe she's not the best, but she's trying hard." I knew almost immediately I would be sorry I said that.

"Just like you," she said. "Not the best. Because you not trying." She gave a little huff as she let go of the sound dial and sat down on the sofa.

The little Chinese girl sat down also to play an encore of "Anitra's Dance" by Grieg. I remember the song, because later on I had to learn how to play it.

✵

Three days after watching *The Ed Sullivan Show*, my mother told me what my schedule would be for piano lessons and piano practice. She had talked to Mr. Chong, who lived on the first floor of our apartment building. Mr. Chong was a retired piano teacher and my mother had traded housecleaning services for weekly lessons and a piano for me to practice on every day, two hours a day, from four until six.

When my mother told me this, I felt as though I had been sent to hell. I whined and then kicked my foot a little when I couldn't stand it anymore.

"Why don't you like me the way I am? I'm *not* a genius! I can't play the piano. And even if I could, I wouldn't go on TV if you paid me a million dollars!" I cried.

My mother slapped me. "Who ask you be genius?" she shouted. "Only ask you be your best. For you sake. You think I want you be genius? Hnnh! What for! Who ask you!"

"So ungrateful," I heard her mutter in Chinese. "If she had as much talent as she has temper, she would be famous now."

Mr. Chong, whom I secretly nicknamed Old Chong, was very strange, always tapping his fingers to the silent music of an invisible orchestra. He looked ancient in my eyes. He had lost most of the hair on top of his head and he wore thick glasses and had eyes that always looked tired and sleepy. But he must have been younger than I thought, since he lived with his mother and was not yet married.

I met Old Lady Chong once and that was enough. She had this peculiar smell like a baby that had done something in its pants. And her fingers felt like a dead person's, like an old peach I once found in the back of the refrigerator; the skin just slid off the meat when I picked it up.

I soon found out why Old Chong had retired from teaching piano. He was deaf. "Like Beethoven!" he shouted to me. "We're both listening only in our head!" And he would start to conduct his frantic silent sonatas.

Our lessons went like this. He would open the book and point to different things, explaining their purpose: "Key! Treble! Bass! No sharps or flats! So this is C major! Listen now and play after me!"

And then he would play the C scale a few times, a simple chord, and then, as if inspired by an old, unreachable itch, he gradually added more notes and running trills and a pounding bass until the music was really something quite grand.

I would play after him, the simple scale, the simple chord, and then I just played some nonsense that sounded like a cat running up and down on top of garbage cans. Old Chong smiled and applauded and then said, "Very good! But now you must learn to keep time!"

So that's how I discovered that Old Chong's eyes were too slow to keep up with the wrong notes I was playing. He went through the motions in half-time. To help me keep rhythm, he stood behind me, pushing down on my right shoulder for every beat. He balanced pennies on top of my wrists so I would keep them still as I slowly played scales and arpeggios. He had me curve my hand around an apple and keep that shape when playing chords. He marched stiffly to show me how to make each finger dance up and down, staccato like an obedient little soldier.

He taught me all these things, and that was how I also learned I could be lazy and get away with mistakes, lots of mistakes. If I hit the wrong notes because I hadn't practiced enough, I never corrected myself. I just kept playing in rhythm. And Old Chong kept conducting his own private reverie.

So maybe I never really gave myself a fair chance. I did pick up the basics pretty quickly, and I might have become a good pianist at that young age. But I was so determined not to try, not to be anybody different that I learned to play only the most ear-splitting preludes, the most discordant hymns.

Over the next year, I practiced like this, dutifully in my own way. And then one day I heard my mother and her friend Lindo Jong both talking in a loud bragging tone of voice so others could hear. It was after church, and I was leaning against the brick wall wearing a dress with stiff white petticoats. Auntie Lindo's daughter, Waverly, who was about my age, was standing farther down the wall about five feet away. We had grown up together and shared all the closeness of two sisters squabbling over crayons and dolls. In other words, for the most part, we hated each other. I thought she was snotty. Waverly Jong had gained a certain amount of fame as "Chinatown's Littlest Chinese Chess Champion."

"She bring home too many trophy," lamented Auntie Lindo that Sunday. "All day she play chess. All day I have no time do nothing but dust off her winnings." She threw a scolding look at Waverly, who pretended not to see her.

"You lucky you don't have this problem," said Auntie Lindo with a sigh to my mother.

And my mother squared her shoulders and bragged: "Our problem worser than yours. If we ask Jing-mei wash dish, she hear nothing but music. It's like you can't stop this natural talent."

And right then, I was determined to put a stop to her foolish pride.

A few weeks later, Old Chong and my mother conspired to have me play in a talent show which would be held in the church hall. By then, my parents had saved up enough to buy me a secondhand piano, a black Wurlitzer spinet with a scarred bench. It was the showpiece of our living room.

For the talent show, I was to play a piece called "Pleading Child" from Schumann's *Scenes from Childhood*. It was a simple, moody piece that sounded more difficult than it was. I was supposed to memorize the whole thing, playing the repeat parts twice to make the piece sound longer. But I dawdled over it, playing a few bars and then cheating, looking up to see what notes followed. I never really listened to what I was playing. I daydreamed about being somewhere else, about being someone else.

The part I liked to practice best was the fancy curtsy: right foot out, touch the rose on the carpet with a pointed foot, sweep to the side, left leg bends, look up and smile.

My parents invited all the couples from the Joy Luck Club to witness my debut. Auntie Lindo and Uncle Tin were there. Waverly and her two older brothers had also come. The first two rows were filled with children both younger and older than I was. The littlest ones got to go first. They recited simple nursery rhymes, squawked out tunes on miniature violins, twirled Hula Hoops, pranced in pink ballet tutus, and when they bowed or curtsied, the audience would sigh in unison, "Awww," and then clap enthusiastically.

When my turn came, I was very confident. I remember my childish excitement. It was as if I knew, without a doubt, that the prodigy side of me really did exist. I had no fear whatsoever, no nervousness. I remember thinking to myself, This is it! This is it! I looked out over the audience, at my mother's blank face, my father's yawn, Auntie Lindo's stiff-lipped smile, Waverly's sulky expression. I had on a white dress layered with sheets of lace, and a pink bow in my Peter Pan haircut. As I sat down I envisioned people jumping to their feet and Ed Sullivan rushing up to introduce me to everyone on TV.

And I started to play. It was so beautiful. I was so caught up in how lovely I looked that at first I didn't worry how I would sound. So it was a surprise to me when I hit the first wrong note and I realized something didn't sound quite right. And then I hit another and another followed that. A chill started at the top of my head and began to trickle down. Yet I couldn't stop playing, as though my hands were bewitched. I kept thinking my fingers would adjust themselves back, like a train switching to the right track. I played this strange jumble through two repeats, the sour notes staying with me all the way to the end.

When I stood up, I discovered my legs were shaking. Maybe I had just been nervous and the audience, like Old Chong, had seen me go through the right motions and had not heard anything wrong at all. I swept my right foot out, went down on my knee, looked up and smiled. The room was quiet, except for Old Chong, who was beaming and shouting, "Bravo! Bravo! Well done!" But then I saw my mother's face, her stricken face. The audience clapped weakly, and as I walked back to my chair, with my whole face quivering as I tried not to cry, I heard a little boy whisper loudly to his mother, "That was awful," and the mother whispered back, "Well, she certainly tried."

And now I realized how many people were in the audience, the whole world it seemed. I was aware of eyes burning into my back. I felt the shame of my mother and father as they sat stiffly throughout the rest of the show.

We could have escaped during intermission. Pride and some strange sense of honor must have anchored my parents to their chairs. And so we watched it all: the eighteen-year-old boy with a fake mustache who did a magic show and juggled flaming hoops while riding a unicycle. The breasted girl with white makeup who sang from *Madama Butterfly* and got honorable mention. And the eleven-year-old boy who won first prize playing a tricky violin song that sounded like a busy bee.

After the show, the Hsus, the Jongs, and the St. Clairs from the Joy Luck Club came up to my mother and father.

"Lots of talented kids," Auntie Lindo said vaguely, smiling broadly.

"That was somethin' else," said my father, and I wondered if he was referring to me in a humorous way, or whether he even remembered what I had done.

Waverly looked at me and shrugged her shoulders. "You aren't a genius like me," she said matter-of-factly. And if I hadn't felt so bad, I would have pulled her braids and punched her stomach.

But my mother's expression was what devastated me: a quiet, blank look that said she had lost everything. I felt the same way, and it seemed as if everybody were now coming up, like gawkers at the scene of an accident, to see what parts were actually missing. When we got on the bus to go home, my father was humming the busy-bee tune and my mother was silent. I kept thinking she wanted to wait until we got home before shouting at me. But when my father unlocked the door to our apartment, my mother walked in and then went to the back, into the bedroom. No accusations. No blame. And in a way, I felt disappointed. I had been waiting for her to start shouting, so I could shout back and cry and blame her for all my misery.

⌁

I assumed my talent-show fiasco meant I never had to play the piano again. But two days later, after school, my mother came out of the kitchen and saw me watching TV.

"Four clock," she reminded me as if it were any other day. I was stunned, as though she were asking me to go through the talent-show torture again. I wedged myself more tightly in front of the TV.

"Turn off TV," she called from the kitchen five minutes later.

I didn't budge. And then I decided. I didn't have to do what my mother said anymore. I wasn't her slave. This wasn't China. I had listened to her before and look what happened. She was the stupid one.

She came out from the kitchen and stood in the arched entryway of the living room. "Four clock," she said once again, louder.

"I'm not going to play anymore," I said nonchalantly. "Why should I? I'm not a genius."

She walked over and stood in front of the TV. I saw her chest was heaving up and down in an angry way.

"No!" I said, and I now felt stronger, as if my true self had finally emerged. So this was what had been inside me all along.

"No! I won't!" I screamed.

She yanked me by the arm, pulled me off the floor, snapped off the TV. She was frighteningly strong, half pulling, half carrying me toward the piano as I kicked the throw rugs under my feet. She lifted me up and onto the hard bench. I was sobbing by now, looking at her bitterly. Her chest was heaving even more and her mouth was open, smiling crazily as if she were pleased I was crying.

"You want me to be someone that I'm not!" I sobbed. "I'll never be the kind of daughter you want me to be!"

"Only two kinds of daughters," she shouted in Chinese. "Those who are obedient and those who follow their own mind! Only one kind of daughter can live in this house. Obedient daughter!"

"Then I wish I wasn't your daughter. I wish you weren't my mother," I shouted. As I said these things I got scared. It felt like worms and toads and slimy things crawling out of my chest, but it also felt good, as if this awful side of me had surfaced, at last.

"Too late change this," said my mother shrilly.

And I could sense her anger rising to its breaking point. I wanted to see it spill over. And that's when I remembered the babies she had lost in China, the ones we never talked about. "Then I wish I'd never been born!" I shouted. "I wish I were dead! Like them."

It was as if I had said the magic words. Alakazam!—and her face went blank, her mouth closed, her arms went slack, and she backed out of the room, stunned, as if she were blowing away like a small brown leaf, thin, brittle, lifeless.

It was not the only disappointment my mother felt in me. In the years that followed, I failed her so many times, each time asserting my own will, my right to fall short of expectations. I didn't get straight As. I didn't become class president. I didn't get into Stanford. I dropped out of college.

For unlike my mother, I did not believe I could be anything I wanted to be. I could only be me.

And for all those years, we never talked about the disaster at the recital or my terrible accusations afterward at the piano bench. All that remained unchecked, like a betrayal that was now unspeakable. So I never found a way to ask her why she had hoped for something so large that failure was inevitable.

And even worse, I never asked her what frightened me the most: Why had she given up hope?

For after our struggle at the piano, she never mentioned my playing again. The lessons stopped. The lid to the piano was closed, shutting out the dust, my misery, and her dreams.

So she surprised me. A few years ago, she offered to give me the piano, for my thirtieth birthday. I had not played in all those years. I saw the offer as a sign of forgiveness, a tremendous burden removed.

"Are you sure?" I asked shyly. "I mean, won't you and Dad miss it?"

"No, this your piano," she said firmly. "Always your piano. You only one can play."

"Well, I probably can't play anymore," I said. "It's been years."

"You pick up fast," said my mother, as if she knew this was certain. "You have natural talent. You could been genius if you want to."

"No I couldn't."

"You just not trying," said my mother. And she was neither angry nor sad. She said it as if to announce a fact that could never be disproved. "Take it," she said.

But I didn't at first. It was enough that she had offered it to me. And after that, every time I saw it in my parents' living room, standing in front of the bay windows, it made me feel proud, as if it were a shiny trophy I had won back.

Last week I sent a tuner over to my parents' apartment and had the piano reconditioned, for purely sentimental reasons. My mother had died a few months before and I had been getting things in order for my father, a little bit at a time. I put the jewelry in special silk pouches. The sweaters she had knitted in yellow, pink, bright orange—all the colors I hated—I put those in moth-proof boxes. I found some old Chinese silk dresses, the kind with little slits up the sides. I rubbed the old silk against my skin, then wrapped them in tissue and decided to take them home with me.

After I had the piano tuned, I opened the lid and touched the keys. It sounded even richer than I remembered. Really, it was a very good piano. Inside the bench were the same exercise notes with handwritten scales, the same secondhand music books with their covers held together with yellow tape.

I opened up the Schumann book to the dark little piece I had played at the recital. It was on the left-hand side of the page, "Pleading Child." It looked more difficult than I remembered. I played a few bars, surprised at how easily the notes came back to me.

And for the first time, or so it seemed, I noticed the piece on the right-hand side. It was called "Perfectly Contented." I tried to play this one as well. It had a lighter melody but the same flowing rhythm and turned out to be quite easy. "Pleading Child" was shorter but slower; "Perfectly Contented" was longer, but faster. And after I played them both a few times, I realized they were two halves of the same song.

Topics for Discussion

1. Why does the mother demand so much from her daughter? What is the basis for the mother/daughter relationship?

2. How are America and Americans defined in the story?

3. In what ways does the first person narrative form influence the reader's perception of the story?

4. What sort of childhood does the narrator have? How is childhood defined in the story?

5. What role does pride play in the story? How is pride in both the narrator and the mother defined?

6. What is the significance of the title in relation to the narrative of the story?

7. What role does silence or reticence play in the relationship between the narrator and her mother?

8. How is failure portrayed? What kinds of failure are conveyed in the story?

M.G. Vassanji

About the Author

M. G. Vassanji was born in Kenya in 1950 and grew up in Dar es Salaam in Tanzania. Before coming to Canada in 1978, he was educated at the Massachusetts Institute of Technology and earned a Ph.D. in Physics before becoming a full-time writer. He has also studied Indian history, philosophy and Sanskrit at the University of Pennsylvania. He has served as writer-in-residence at the Writer's Program of the University of Iowa. He currently lives in Toronto.

In his writings, Vassanji is interested in the differences and tensions between the experiences of the First World and the Third World and the manner in which the colonial past influences the ways in which postcolonial nations and nationals view themselves and their aspirations. His experience in Africa as a person of Indian background, and the cultural and physical displacement often associated with that situation, has found its way into his novels, especially *The Gunny Sack*, in which, as he has said, "the driving force" is "its African spirit." This sense of a culture within a culture, and the anxieties, tensions and concerns that result, are major themes to which Vassanji returns in his other works. He has been described as an "Afro-Asian," a term which he finds apt both for its physical description of his background and for his concerns as a writer attempting to articulate an experience caught between many worlds.

Selected Works

The Gunny Sack (novel, 1989)
No New Land (novel, 1991)
Uhuru Street (short stories, 1992)
The Book of Secrets (novel, 1994)

About the Story

"Leaving" deals with the struggle of students in emerging nations to obtain an education that will give them either a chance to leave their countries permanently for economic advantage or to return to their countries to be leaders. Set in the Indian community of Dar es Salaam in Tanzania, the story reflects on the personal as well as logistical issues that confront students from Third World nations in their attempts to better themselves and their people.

This story is taken from the collection *Uhuru Street*, all of whose stories are set in the same locale in order to create a narrative not only of individuals but of a community. This sense of community also reinforces the idea that the Indian culture in Tanzania is a world unto itself, surrounded yet vibrant.

Leaving

Kichwele Street was now Uhuru Street. My two sisters had completed school and got married and Mother missed them sometimes. Mehroon, after a succession of wooers, had settled for a former opening batsman of our school team and was in town. Razia was a wealthy housewife in Tanga, the coastal town north of Dar. Firoz dropped out in his last year at school, and everyone said that it was a wonder he had reached that far. He was assistant bookkeeper at Oriental Emporium, and brought home stationery sometimes.

Mother had placed her hopes on the youngest two of us, Aloo and me, and she didn't want us distracted by the chores that always needed doing around the store. One evening she secured for the last time the half a dozen assorted padlocks on the sturdy panelled doors and sold the store. This was exactly one week after the wedding party had driven off with a tearful Razia, leaving behind a distraught mother in the stirred-up dust of Uhuru Street.

We moved to the residential area of Upanga. After the bustle of Uhuru Street, our new neighbourhood seemed quiet. Instead of the racket of buses, bicycles and cars on the road, we now heard the croaking of frogs and the chirping of insects. Nights were haunting, lonely and desolate and took some getting used to. Upanga Road emptied after seven in the evening and the sidestreets became pitch dark, with no illumination. Much of the area was as yet uninhabited and behind the housing developments there were overgrown bushes, large, scary baobab trees, and mango and coconut groves.

Sometimes in the evenings, when Mother felt sad, Aloo and I would play two-three-five with her, a variation of whist for three people. I had entered the University by then and came back at weekends. Aloo was in his last year at school. He had turned out to be exceptionally bright in his studies—more so than we realised.

That year Mr. Datoo, a former teacher from our school who was also a former student, returned from America for a visit. Mr. Datoo had been a favourite with the boys. When he came he received a tumultuous welcome. For the next few days he toured the town like the Pied Piper followed by a horde of adulating students, one of whom was Aloo.

The exciting event inspired in Aloo the hope that not only might he be admitted to an American university, but he could also win a scholarship to go there. Throughout the rest of the year, therefore, he wrote to numerous universities, culling their names from books at the USIS, often simply at random or even only by the sounds of their names.

Mother's response to all these efforts was to humour him. She would smile. "Your uncles in America will pay thousands of shillings just to send you to college," she would say. Evidently she felt he was wasting his time, but he would never be able to say that he did not have all the support she could give him.

Responses to his enquiries started coming within weeks and a handful of them were guardedly encouraging. Gradually Aloo found out which were the better places, and which among them the truly famous.

Soon a few catalogues arrived, all looking impressive. It seemed that the more involved he became with the application process, the more tantalising was the prospect of going to an American university. Even the famous places did not discourage him. He learnt of subjects he had never heard of before: genetics, cosmology, artificial intelligence: a whole universe was out there waiting for him if only he could reach it. He was not sure if he could, if he was good enough. He suffered periods of intense hope and hopeless despair.

Of course, Aloo was entitled to a place at the local university. At the end of the year, when the selections were announced in the papers, his name was on the list. But some bureaucratic hand, probably also corrupt, dealt out a future prospect for him that came as a shock. He had applied to study medicine, he was given a place in agriculture. An agricultural officer in a rural district somewhere was not what he wanted to become however patriotic he felt. He had never left the city except to go to the national parks once on a school trip.

When Aloo received a letter from the California Institute of Technology offering him a place with a scholarship, he was stupefied at first. He read and reread the letter, not believing what it seemed to be saying, afraid that he might be reading something into it. He asked me to read it for him. When he was convinced there was no possibility of a mistake he became elated.

"The hell I'll do agriculture!" he grinned.

But first he had to contend with Mother.

Mother was incredulous. "Go, go," she said, "don't you eat my head, don't tease me!"

"But it's true!" he protested. "They're giving me a scholarship!"

We were at the table—the three of us—and had just poured tea from the thermos. Mother sitting across from me stared at her saucer for a while then she looked up.

"Is it true?" she asked me.

"Yes, it's true," I said. "All he needs is to take 400 dollars pocket money with him."

"How many shillings would that make?" she asked.

"About three thousand."

"And how are we going to raise this three thousand shillings? Have you bought a lottery? And what about the ticket? Are they going to send you a ticket too?"

As she said this Aloo's prospects seemed to get dimmer. She was right, it was not a little money that he needed.

"Can't we raise a loan?" he asked. "I'll work there. Yes, I'll work as a waiter. A waiter!—I know you can do it, I'll send the money back!"

"You may have uncles in America who would help you," Mother told him, "but no one here will."

Aloo's shoulders sagged and he sat there toying with his cup, close to tears. Mother sat drinking from her saucer and frowning. The evening light came in from the window behind me and gave a glint to her spectacles. Finally she set her saucer down. She was angry.

"And why do you want to go away, so far from us? Is this what I raised you for—so you could leave me to go away to a foreign place? Won't you miss us, where you want to go? Do we mean so little to you? If something happens . . ."

Aloo was crying. A tear fell into his cup, his nose was running. "So many kids go and return, and nothing happens to them . . . Why did you mislead me, then? Why did you let me apply if you didn't want me to go . . . why did you raise my hopes if only to dash them?" He had raised his voice to her, the first time I saw him do it, and he was shaking.

He did not bring up the question again and he prepared himself for the agricultural college, waiting for the term to begin. At home he would slump on the sofa putting away a novel a day.

If the unknown bureaucrat at the Ministry of Education had been less arbitrary, Aloo would not have been so broken and Mother would not have felt compelled to try and do something for him.

A few days later, on a Sunday morning, she looked up from her sewing machine and said to the two of us: "Let's go and show this letter to Mr. Velji. He is experienced in these matters. Let's take his advice."

Mr. Velji was a former administrator of our school. He had a large egg-shaped head and a small compact body. With his large forehead and big black spectacles he looked the caricature of the archetypal wise man. He also had the bearing of one. The three of us were settled in his sitting-room chairs staring about us and waiting expectantly when he walked in stiffly, like a toy soldier, to welcome us.

"How are you, sister?" he said. "What can I do for you?"

Aloo and I stood up respectfully as he sat down.

"We have come to you for advice . . ." Mother began.

"Speak, then," he said jovially and sat back, joining his hands behind his head.

She began by giving him her history. She told him which family she was born in, which she had married into, how she had raised her kids when our father died. Common relations were discovered between our families. "Now this one here," she pointed at me, "goes to university here, and *that* one wants to go to America. Show him the documents," she commanded Aloo.

As if with an effort, Aloo pushed himself out of the sofa and slowly made his way to place the documents in Mr. Velji's hands. Before he looked at them Mr. Velji asked Aloo his result in the final exam.

At Aloo's answer, his eyes widened. "Henh?" he said. "All A's?"

"Yes," replied Aloo, a little too meekly.

Mr. Velji flipped the papers one by one, cursorily at first. Then he went over them more carefully. He looked at the long visa form with the carbon copies neatly bound behind the original; he read over the friendly letter from the Foreign Student Adviser; he was charmed by the letters of invitation from the fraternities. Finally he looked up, a little humbled.

"The boy is right," he said. "The university is good, and they are giving him a bursary. I congratulate you."

"But what should I do?" asked Mother anxiously. "What is your advice? Tell us what we should do."

"Well," said Mr. Velji, "it would be good for his education." He raised his hand to clear his throat. Then he said, a little slowly: "But if you send him, you will lose your son.

"It's a far place, America," he concluded, wiping his hands briskly at the finished business. "Now what will you have—tea? orange squash?"

His wife appeared magically to take orders.

"All the rich kids go every year and they are not lost," muttered Aloo bitterly as we walked back home. Mother was silent.

That night she was at the sewing machine and Aloo was on the couch, reading. The radio was turned low and through the open front door a gentle breeze blew in to cool the sitting room. I was standing at the door. The banana tree and its offspring rustled outside, a car zoomed on the road, throwing shadows on neighbouring houses. A couple out for a stroll, murmuring, came into sight over the uneven hedge; groups of boys or girls chattered before dispersing for the night. The intermittent buzz of an electric motor escaped from Mother's sewing machine. It was a little darker where she sat at the other end of the room from us.

Presently she looked up and said a little nonchalantly, "At least show me what this university looks like—bring that book, will you?"

Mother had never seen the catalogue. She had always dismissed it, had never shown the least bit of curiosity about the place Aloo wanted so badly to visit. Now the three of us crowded around the glossy pages, pausing at pictures of the neoclassic façades and domes, columns towering over humans, students rushing about in a dither of activity, classes held on lush lawns in ample shade. It all looked so awesome and yet inviting.

"It's something, isn't it?" whispered Aloo, hardly able to hold back his excitement. "They teach hundreds of courses there," he said. "They send rockets into space . . . to other worlds . . . to the moon—"

"If you go away to the moon, my son, what will become of me?" she said humorously, her eyes gleaming as she looked up at us.

Aloo went back to his book and Mother to her sewing.

A little later I looked up and saw Mother deep in thought, brooding, and as she often did at such times she was picking her chin absent-mindedly. It was, I think, the first time I saw her as a person and not only as our mother. I thought of what she must be going through in her mind, what she had gone through in bringing us up. She had been thirty-three when Father died, and she had refused several offers of marriage because they would all have entailed one thing: sending us all to the "boarding"—the orphanage. Pictures of her before his death showed her smiling and in full bloom: plump but not excessively fat, hair puffed fashionably, wearing high heels and make-up. There was one picture, posed at a studio, which Father had had touched up and enhanced, which now hung beside his. In it she stood against a black background, holding a book stylishly, the nylon pachedi painted a light green, the folds falling gracefully down, the borders decorated with sequins. I had never seen her like that. All I had seen of her was the stern face getting sterner with time as the lines set permanently and the hair thinned, the body turned squat, the voice thickened.

I recalled how Aloo and I would take turns sleeping with her at night on her big bed; how she would squeeze me in her chubby arms, drawing me up closer to her breast until I could hardly breathe—and I would control myself and hope she would soon release me and let me breathe.

She looked at me looking at her and said, not to me, "Promise me . . . promise me that if I let you go, you will not marry a white woman."

"Oh Mother, you know I won't!" said Aloo.

"And promise me that you will not smoke or drink."

"You know I promise!" He was close to tears.

⊱≼⊁

Aloo's first letter came a week after he left, from London where he'd stopped over to see a former classmate. It flowed over with excitement. "How can I describe it," he wrote, "the sight from the plane . . . mile upon mile of carefully tilled fields, the earth divided into neat green squares . . . even the mountains are clean and civilized. And London . . . Oh London! It seemed that it would never end . . . blocks and blocks of houses, squares, parks, monuments . . . could any city be larger? . . . How many of our Dar es Salaams would fit here, in this one gorgeous city . . . ?"

A bird flapping its wings: Mr. Velji nodding wisely in his chair, Mother staring into the distance.

Topics for Discussion

1. What is the purpose of the final lines of the story and what statement is Vassanji making in that final image of the bird flapping its wings and the Mother staring off into the distance?

2. How does London contrast to Dar es Salaam?

3. Why is it important for Aloo to obtain a foreign education? What are the implications of this situation?

4. What role does money play in the story?

5. Why are the Mother's feelings so important and how does Vassanji convey these to the reader?

6. How does Vassanji establish and sustain suspense in the story?

7. What devices and techniques does Vassanji use to convey the idea of aspirations?

Archie Weller

About the Author

Archie Weller, who also writes under the pseudonyms R Chee, Kirk Weller and Irving Kirkwood, was born in 1957 near Katanning, in the southwestern part of Western Australia, and grew up on an isolated farm. He is of Nyoongah (Aboriginal) origin. Weller received much of his education in Perth and at the Western Australian Institute of Technology, where he studied film and creative writing before embarking on a number of jobs. He has worked as a farm labourer, a printer, a gardener, a stablehand, a dishwasher, a professional writer and as a university writer-in-residence.

The stories in the collection *Going Home*, whose title story is included here, are largely about the Nyoongah culture in Western Australia and the tensions and struggles of the minority Aboriginal community in Australia.

Selected Works

Day of the Dog (novel, 1988)
Going Home (short stories, 1986)
Chronicle of Blue Elves (novel, 1991)
Journey of the Stone People (novel, 1991)

About the Story

The story recounts the homecoming of a young Nyoongah man, Billy, who has received his education and found success among whites in the city, and who returns for a visit to his impoverished family home in the bush. He is welcomed by his family, but in the course of events he unjustly falls into trouble with the law.

Charley Pride, whose lyrics are mentioned in the opening of the story, is an American country music star who is very popular in Australia.

Going Home

I want to go home.
I want to go home.
Oh, Lord, I want to go home.

Charley Pride moans from a cassette, and his voice slips out of the crack the window makes. Out into the world of magpies' soothing carols, and parrots' cheeky whistles, of descending darkness and spirits.

The man doesn't know that world. His is the world of the sleek new Kingswood that speeds down the never-ending highway.

At last he can walk this earth with pride, as his ancestors did many years before him. He had his first exhibition of paintings a month ago. They sold well, and with the proceeds he bought the car.

The slender black hands swing the shiny black wheel around a corner. Blackness forms a unison of power.

For five years he has worked hard and saved and sacrificed. Now, on his twenty-first birthday, he is going home.

New car, new clothes, new life.

He plucks a cigarette from the packet beside him, and lights up.

His movements are elegant and delicate. His hair is well-groomed, and his clothes are clean.

Billy Woodward is coming home in all his might, in his shining armour.

Sixteen years old. Last year at school.

His little brother Carlton and his cousin Rennie Davis, down beside the river, on that last night before he went to the college in Perth, when all three had had a goodbye drink, with their girls beside them.

Frogs croaking into the silent hot air and some animal blundering in the bullrushes on the other side of the gentle river. Moonlight on the ruffled water. Nasal voices whispering and giggling. The clink of beer bottles.

That year at college, with all its schoolwork, and learning, and discipline, and uniformity, he stood out alone in the football carnival.

Black hands grab the ball. Black feet kick the ball. Black hopes go soaring with the ball to the pasty white sky.

No one can stop him now. He forgets about the river of his Dreaming and the people of his blood and the girl in his heart.

The year when he was eighteen, he was picked by a top city team as a rover. This was the year that he played for the state, where he was voted best and fairest on the field.

That was a year to remember.

He never went out to the park at Guildford, so he never saw his people: his dark, silent staring people, his rowdy, brawling, drunk people.

He was white now.

Once, in the middle of the night, one of his uncles had crept around the house he rented and fallen asleep on the verandah. A dirty pitiful carcase, encased in a black greatcoat that had smelt of stale drink and lonely, violent places. A withered black hand had clutched an almost-empty metho bottle.

In the morning, Billy had shouted at the old man and pushed him down the steps, where he stumbled and fell without pride. The old man had limped out of the creaking gate, not understanding.

The white neighbours, wakened by the noise, had peered out of their windows at the staggering old man stumbling down the street and the glowering youth muttering on the verandah. They had smirked in self-righteous knowledge.

Billy had moved on the next day.

William Jacob Woodward passed fifth year with flying colours. All the teachers were proud of him. He went to the West Australian Institute of Technology to further improve his painting, to gain fame that way as well.

He bought clean, bright clothes and cut off his long hair that all the camp girls had loved.

Billy Woodward was a handsome youth, with the features of his white grandfather and the quietness of his Aboriginal forebears. He stood tall and proud, with the sensitive lips of a dreamer and a faraway look in his serene amber eyes.

He went to the nightclubs regularly and lost his soul in the throbbing, writhing electrical music as the white tribe danced their corroboree to the good life.

He would sit alone at a darkened corner table, or with a painted-up white girl—but mostly alone. He would drink wine and look around the room at all the happy or desperate people.

He was walking home one night from a nightclub when a middle-aged Aboriginal woman stumbled out of a lane.

She grinned up at him like the Gorgon and her hands clutched at his body, like the lights from the nightclub.

"Billy! Ya Billy Woodward, unna!"

"Yes. What of it?" he snapped.

"Ya dunno me? I'm ya Auntie Rose, from down Koodup."

She cackled then. Ugly, oh, so ugly. Yellow and red eyes and broken teeth and a long, crooked, white scar across her temple. Dirty grey hair all awry.

His people.

His eyes clouded over in revulsion. He shoved her away and walked off quickly.

He remembered her face for many days afterwards whenever he tried to paint a picture. He felt ashamed to be related to a thing like that. He was bitter that she was of his blood.

That was his life: painting pictures and playing football and pretending. But his people knew. They always knew.

In his latest game of football he had a young part-Aboriginal opponent who stared at him the whole game with large, scornful black eyes seeing right through him.

After the game, the boy's family picked him up in an old battered station wagon.

Billy, surrounded by all his white friends, saw them from afar off. He saw the children kicking an old football about with yells and shouts of laughter and two lanky boys slumping against the door yarning to their hero, and a buxom girl leaning out the window and an old couple in the back. The three boys, glancing up, spotted debonair Billy. Their smiles faded for an instant and they speared him with their proud black eyes.

So Billy was going home, because he had been reminded of home (with all its carefree joys) at that last match.

It is raining now. The shafts slant down from the sky, in the glare of the headlights. Night-time, when woodarchis come out to kill, leaving no tracks: as though they are cloud shadows passing over the sun.

Grotesque trees twist in the half-light. Black tortured figures, with shaggy heads and pleading arms. Ancestors crying for remembrance. Voices shriek or whisper in tired chants: tired from the countless warnings that have not been heeded.

They twirl around the man, like the lights of the city he knows. But he cannot understand these trees. They drag him onwards, even when he thinks of turning back and not going on to where he vowed he never would go again.

A shape, immovable and impassive as the tree it is under, steps into the road on the Koodup turnoff.

An Aboriginal man.

Billy slews to a halt, or he will run the man over.

Door opens.

Wind and rain and coloured man get in.

"Ta, mate. It's bloody cold 'ere," the coloured man grates, then stares quizzically at Billy, with sharp black eyes. "Nyoongah, are ya, mate?"

"Yes."

The man sniffs noisily, and rubs a sleeve across his nose.

"Well, I'm Darcy Goodrich, any rate, bud."

He holds out a calloused hand. Yellow-brown, blunt scarred fingers, dirty nails. A lifetime of sorrow is held between the fingers.

Billy takes it limply.

"I'm William Woodward."

"Yeah?" Fathomless eyes scrutinise him again from behind the scraggly black hair that falls over his face.

"Ya goin' anywheres near Koodup, William?"

"Yes."

"Goodoh. This is a nice car ya got 'ere. Ya must 'ave plen'y of boya, unna?"

Silence from Billy.

He would rather not have this cold, wet man beside him, reminding him. He keeps his amber eyes on the lines of the road as they flash under his wheels.

White ... white ... white ...

"Ya got a smoke, William?"

"Certainly. Help yourself."

Black blunt fingers flick open his expensive cigarette case.

"Ya want one too, koordah?"

"Thanks."

"Ya wouldn't be Teddy Woodward's boy, would ya, William?"

"Yes, that's right. How are Mum and Dad—and everyone?"

Suddenly he has to know all about his family and become lost in their sea of brownness.

Darcy's craggy face flickers at him in surprise, then turns, impassive again, to the rain-streaked window. He puffs on his cigarette quietly.

"What, ya don't know?" he says softly. "Ya Dad was drinkin' metho. 'E was blind drunk, an' in the 'orrors, ya know? Well, this truck came out of nowhere when 'e was crossin' the road on a night like this. Never seen 'im. Never stopped or nothin'. Ya brother Carl found 'im next day an' was nothin' no one could do then. That was a couple of years back now."

Billy would have been nineteen then, at the peak of his football triumph. On one of those bright white nights, when he had celebrated his victories with wine and white women, Billy's father had been wiped off the face of his country—all alone.

He can remember his father as a small gentle man who was the best card cheat in the camp. He could make boats out of duck feathers and he and Carlton and Billy had had races by the muddy side of the water-hole, from where his people had come long ago, in the time of the beginning.

The lights of Koodup grin at him as he swings around a bend. Pinpricks of eyes, like a pack of foxes waiting for the blundering black rabbit.

"Tell ya what, buddy. Stop off at the hotel an' buy a carton of stubbies."

"All right, Darcy." Billy smiles and looks closely at the man for the first time. He desperately feels that he needs a friend as he goes back into the open mouth of his previous life. Darcy gives a gap-toothed grin.

"Bet ya can't wait to see ya people again."

His people: ugly Auntie Rose, the metho-drinking uncle, his dead forgotten father, his wild brother and cousin. Even this silent man. They are all his people.

He can never escape.

The car creeps in beside the red brick hotel.

The two Nyoongahs scurry through the rain and shadows and into the glare of the small hotel bar.

The barman is a long time coming, although the bar is almost empty. Just a few old cockies and young larrikins, right down the other end. Arrogant grey eyes stare at Billy. No feeling there at all.

"A carton of stubbies, please."

"Only if you bastards drink it down at the camp. Constable told me you mob are drinking in town and just causing trouble."

"We'll drink where we bloody like, thanks, mate."

"Will you, you cheeky bastard?" The barman looks at Billy, in surprise. "Well then, you're not gettin' nothin' from me. You can piss off, too, before I call the cops. They'll cool you down, you smart black bastard."

Something hits Billy deep inside with such force that it makes him want to clutch hold of the bar and spew up all his pride.

He is black and the barman is white, and nothing can ever change that.

All the time he had gulped in the wine and joy of the nightclubs and worn neat fashionable clothes and had white women admiring him, played the white man's game with more skill than most of the wadgulas and painted his country in white man colours to be gabbled over by the wadgulas: all this time he has ignored his mumbling, stumbling tribe and thought he was someone better.

Yet when it comes down to it all, he is just a black man.

Darcy sidles up to the fuming barman.

"Scuse me, Mr 'Owett, but William 'ere just come 'ome, see," he whines like a beaten dog. "We will be drinkin' in the camp, ya know."

"Just come home, eh? What was he inside for?"

Billy bites his reply back so it stays in his stomach, hard and hurtful as a gallstone.

"Well all right, Darcy. I'll forget about it this time. Just keep your friend out of my hair."

Good dog, Darcy. Have a bone, Darcy. Or will a carton of stubbies do?

Out into the rain again.

They drive away and turn down a track about a kilometre out of town.

Darcy tears off a bottle top, handing the bottle to Billy. He grins.

"Act stupid, buddy, an' ya go a lo—ong way in this town."

Billy takes a long draught of the bitter golden liquid. It pours down his throat and into his mind like a shaft of amber sunlight after a gale. He lets his anger subside.

"What ya reckon, Darcy? I'm twenty-one today."

Darcy thrusts out a hand, beaming.

"Tw'n'y-bloody-one, eh? 'Ow's it feel?"

"No different from yesterday."

Billy clasps the offered hand firmly.

They laugh and clink bottles together in a toast, just as they reach the camp.

Dark and wet, with a howling wind. Rain beating upon the shapeless humpies. Trees thrash around the circle of the clearing in a violent rhythm of sorrow and anger, like great monsters dancing around a carcase.

Darcy indicates a hut clinging to the edge of the clearing.

"That's where ya mum lives."

A rickety shape of nailed-down tin and sheets of iron. Two oatbags, sewn together, form a door. Floundering in a sea of tins and rags and parts of toys or cars. Mud everywhere.

Billy pulls up as close to the door as he can get. He had forgotten what his house really looked like.

"Come on, koordah. Come an' see ya ole mum. Ya might be lucky, too, an' catch ya brother."

Billy can't say anything. He gets slowly out of the car while the dereliction looms up around him.

The rain pricks at him, feeling him over.

He is one of the brotherhood.

A mouth organ's reedy notes slip in and out between the rain. It is at once a profoundly sorrowful yet carefree tune that goes on and on.

Billy's fanfare home.

He follows Darcy, ducking under the bag door. He feels unsure and out of place and terribly alone.

There are six people: two old women, an ancient man, two youths and a young, shy, pregnant woman.

The youth nearest the door glances up with a blank yellowish face, suspicion embedded deep in his black eyes. His long black hair that falls over his shoulders in gentle curls is kept from his face by a red calico headband. Red for the desert sands whence his ancestors came, red for the blood spilt by his ancestors when the white tribe came. Red, the only bright thing in these drab surroundings.

The youth gives a faint smile at Darcy and the beer.

"G'day, Darcy. Siddown 'ere. 'Oo ya mate is?"

"'Oo'd ya think, Carl, ya dopy prick? 'E's ya brother come 'ome."

Carlton stares at Billy incredulously, then his smile widens a little and he stands up, extending a slim hand.

They shake hands and stare deep into each other's faces, smiling. Brown-black and brown-yellow. They let their happiness soak silently into each other.

Then his cousin Rennie, also tall and slender like a young boomer, with bushy red-tinged hair and eager grey eyes, shakes hands. He introduces Billy to his young woman, Phyllis, and reminds him who old China Groves and Florrie Waters (his mother's parents) are.

His mother sits silently at the scarred kitchen table. Her wrinkled brown face has been battered around, and one of her eyes is sightless. The other stares at her son with a bleak pride of her own.

From that womb I came, Billy thinks, like a flower from the ground or a fledgling from the nest. From out of the reserve I flew.

Where is beauty now?

He remembers his mother as a laughing brown woman, with long black hair in plaits, singing soft songs as she cleaned the house or cooked food. Now she is old and stupid in the mourning of her man.

"So ya come back after all. Ya couldn't come back for ya Dad's funeral, but—unna? Ya too good for us mob, I s'pose," she whispers in a thin voice like a mouth organ before he even says hello, then turns her eyes back into her pain.

"It's my birthday, Mum. I wanted to see everybody. No one told me Dad was dead."

Carlton looks up at Billy.

"I make out ya twenty-one, Billy."

"Yes."

"Well, shit, we just gotta 'ave a party." Carlton half-smiles. "We gotta get more drink, but," he adds.

Carlton and Rennie drive off to town in Billy's car. When they leave, Billy feels unsure and alone. His mother just stares at him. Phyllis keeps her eyes glued on the mound of her womb and the grandparents crow to Darcy, camp talk he cannot understand.

The cousins burst through the door with a carton that Carlton drops on the table, then he turns to his brother. His smooth face holds the look of a small child who is about to show his father something he has achieved. His dark lips twitch as they try to keep from smiling.

" 'Appy birthday, Billy, ya ole cunt," Carlton says, and produces a shining gold watch from the ragged pocket of his black jeans.

"It even works, Billy," grins Rennie from beside his woman, so Darcy and China laugh.

The laughter swirls around the room like dead leaves from a tree.

They drink. They talk. Darcy goes home and the old people go to bed. His mother has not talked to Billy all night. In the morning he will buy her some pretty curtains for the windows and make a proper door and buy her the best dress in the shop.

They chew on the sweet cud of their past. The memories seep through Billy's skin so he isn't William Woodward the talented football player and artist, but Billy the wild, half-naked boy, with his shock of hair and carefree grin and a covey of girls fluttering around his honey body.

Here they are—all three together again, except now young Rennie is almost a father and Carlton has just come from three months' jail. And Billy? He is nowhere.

At last, Carlton yawns and stretches.

"I reckon I'll 'it that bed." Punches his strong brother gently on the shoulder. "See ya t'morrow, Billy, ole kid." He smiles.

Billy camps beside the dying fire. He rolls himself into a bundle of ragged blankets on the floor and stares into the fire. In his mind he can hear his father droning away, telling legends that he half-remembered, and his mother softly singing hymns. Voices and memories and woodsmoke drift around him. He sleeps.

He wakes to the sound of magpies carolling in the still trees. Rolls up off the floor and rubs the sleep from his eyes. Gets up and stacks the blankets in a corner, then creeps out to the door.

Carlton's eyes peep out from the blankets on his bed.

"Where ya goin'?" he whispers.

"Just for a walk."

"Catch ya up, Billy," he smiles sleepily. With his headband off, his long hair falls every way.

Billy gives a salutation and ducks outside.

A watery sun struggles up over the hills and reflects in the orange puddles that dot the camp. Broken glass winks white, like the bones of dead animals. Several children play with a drum, rolling it at each other and trying to balance on it. Several young men stand around looking at Billy's car. He nods at them and they nod back. Billy stumbles over to the ablution block: three bent and rusty showers and a toilet each for men and women. Names and slogans are scribbled on every available space. After washing away the staleness of the beer he heads for the waterhole, where memories of his father linger. He wants—a lot—to remember his father.

He squats there, watching the ripples the light rain makes on the serene green surface. The bird calls from the jumble of green-brown-black bush are sharp and clear, like the echoes of spirits calling to him.

He gets up and wanders back to the humpy. Smoke from fires wisps up into the grey sky.

Just as he slouches to the edge of the clearing, a police van noses its way through the mud and water and rubbish. A pale, hard, supercilious face peers out at him. The van stops.

"Hey, you! Come here!"

The people at the fires watch, from the corner of their eyes, as he idles over.

"That your car?"

Billy nods, staring at the heavy, blue-clothed sergeant. The driver growls, "What's your name, and where'd you get the car?"

"I just told you it's my car. My name's William Jacob Woodward, if it's any business of yours," Billy flares.

The sergeant's door opens with an ominous crack as he slowly gets out. He glances down at black Billy, who suddenly feels small and naked.

"You any relation to Carlton?"

"If you want to know—"

"I want to know, you black prick. I want to know everything about you."

"Yeah, like where you were last night when the store was broken into, as soon as you come home causing trouble in the pub," the driver snarls.

"I wasn't causing trouble, and I wasn't in any robbery. I like the way you come straight down here when there's trouble—"

"If you weren't in the robbery, what's this watch?" the sergeant rumbles triumphantly, and he grabs hold of Billy's hand that has marked so many beautiful marks and painted so many beautiful pictures for the wadgula people. He twists it up behind Billy's back and slams him against the blank blue side of the van. The golden watch dangles between the pink fingers, mocking the stunned man.

"Listen. I was here. You can ask my grandparents or Darcy Goodrich, even," he moans. But inside he knows it is no good.

"Don't give me that, Woodward. You bastards stick together like flies on a dunny wall," the driver sneers.

Nothing matters any more. Not the trees, flinging their scraggly arms wide in freedom. Not the people around their warm fires. Not the drizzle that drips down the back of his shirt onto his skin. Just this thickset, glowering man and the sleek oiled machine with POLICE stencilled on the sides neatly and indestructibly.

"You mongrel black bastard, I'm going to make you—and your fucking brother—jump. You could have killed old Peters last night," the huge man hisses dangerously. Then the driver is beside him, glaring from behind his sunglasses.

"You Woodwards are all the same, thieving boongs. If you think you're such a fighter, beating up old men, you can have a go at the sarge here when we get back to the station."

"Let's get the other one now, Morgan. Mrs. Riley said there were two of them."

He is shoved into the back, with a few jabs to hurry him on his way. Hunches miserably in the jolting iron belly as the van revs over to the humpy. Catches a glimpse of his new Kingswood standing in the filth. Darcy, a frightened Rennie and several others lean against it, watching with lifeless eyes. Billy returns their gaze with the look of a cornered dingo who does not understand how he was trapped yet who knows he is about to die. Catches a glimpse of his brother being pulled from the humpy, sad yet sullen, eyes downcast staring into the mud of his life— mud that no one can ever escape.

He is thrown into the back of the van.

The van starts up with a satisfied roar.

Carlton gives Billy a tired look as though he isn't even there, then gives his strange, faint smile.

"Welcome 'ome, brother," he mutters.

Topics for Discussion

1. How does Weller handle the issue of racial prejudice?

2. Why is the protagonist guilty by association? How does Weller portray the law in this story?

3. What roles do family and family relationships play in this story?

4. What differences does Weller articulate between the city and the country?

5. How does Weller treat the problem of alcohol abuse in the story?

6. Is there justice in this story? If not, what is the impact of the final situation on the reader?

7. What paradox is Weller creating with the term "home"?

Credits

Jean Arasanayagam. The story on page 15 from *All Is Burning* by Jean Arasanayagam is reproduced courtesy the publishers (Penguin Books India Pvt. Ltd.) and the author. • Margaret Atwood, "Death by Landscape." From *Wilderness Tips* by Margaret Atwood. Used by permission of the Canadian Publishers, McClelland & Stewart, Toronto. • James Baldwin. "Sonny's Blues" was originally published in The Partisan Review. Collected in GOING TO MEET THE MAN © 1965 by James Baldwin. Copyright renewed. Published by Vintage Books. Reprinted by arrangement with the James Baldwin estate. • Charles Baxter. "A Relative Stranger," from A RELATIVE STRANGER by Charles Baxter. Copyright © 1990 by Charles Baxter. Reprinted by permission of W.W. Norton & Company, Inc. • Neil Bissoondath. "The Cage" from *Digging Up the Mountains* by Neil Bissoondath © 1985. Reprinted by permission of Macmillan Canada. • Dionne Brand. By permission of the author, "Photograph" from *Sans Souci and Other Stories* (Women's Press, Toronto, 1989. • A.S. Byatt. "Rose Coloured Teacups" from *Sugar and Other Stories* reproduced with permission from Chatto and Windus. • Barry Callaghan, "Our Thirteenth Summer." From *A Kiss Is Still a Kiss and Other Stories*, 1995. Reprinted by permission of Little, Brown and Company. • Jose Y. Dalisay Jr., "Spy Story." Reprinted with permission by the author. • Anita Desai, "Pineapple Cake." Copyright © 1979 Anita Desai. Reproduced by permission of the author c/o Rogers, Coleridge & White Ltd., 20 Powis Mews, London W11 1JN. • Louise Erdrich, "Fleur." Copyright © 1986 by Louise Erdrich. Reprinted by permission of the author. • William Faulkner, "A Rose for Emily." From COLLECTED STORIES OF WILLIAM FAULKNER by William Faulkner. Copyright © 1930 and renewed 1958 by William Faulkner. Reprinted by permission of Random House, Inc. • Mavis Gallant, "The Moslem Wife." From FROM THE FIFTEENTH DISTRICT by Mavis Gallant © 1979. Reprinted by permission of Macmillan Canada. • Nadine Gordimer. "Six Feet of the Country, pp. 7-20," copyright © 1956 by Nadine Gordimer, from SIX FEET OF THE COUNTRY by Nadine Gordimer. Used by permission of Viking Penguin, a division of Penguin Books USA Inc. • Katherine Govier, "The Immaculate Conception Photography Gallery." From *The Immaculate Conception Photography Gallery*, 1994. Reprinted by permission of Little, Brown and Company. • Graham Greene. "The Innocent" from TWENTY-ONE SHORT STOES by Graham Greene, Reed Books. Reprinted with permission. • James Joyce, "Eveline." Reprinted with permission of the Estate of James Joyce. • Alex La Guma. "The Lemon Orchard" from A WALK IN THE NIGHT by Alex la Guma reprinted by permission of Heinemann Educational, a division of Reed Educational and Professional Publishing Ltd. • Margaret Laurence. "The Loons" from A BIRD IN THE HOUSE by Margaret Laurence. Used by permission of the Canadian Publishers, McClelland & Stewart, Toronto. • D.H. Lawrence. "Odour of Chrysanthemums" from THE COLLECTED SHORT STORIES OF D.H. LAWRENCE reprinted with permission of Laurence Pollinger Ltd. and the Estate of Frieda Lawrence Ravagli. • SKY Lee, "The Soong Sisters." Reprinted with permission from *Bellydancer*, by SKY Lee (Vancouver: Press Gang Publishers, 1994). • Doris Lessing. "CASUALTY" from THE REAL THING by DORIS LESSING. Copyright © 1987, 1988, 1989, 1990, 1991, 1992 by Doris Lessing. Reprinted by permission of HarperCollins Publishers, Inc. No abridgements, edits or adaptations without approval. • Catherine Lim, "The Jade Pendant." From *Little Ironies*, 1978. Reprinted with permission of Heinemann Southeast Asia. • Bernard MacLaverty. "Secrets," from SECRETS AND OTHER STORIES by Bernard MacLaverty. Coyright © 1977, 1979 by Bernard MacLaverty. Used by permission of Viking Penguin, a division of Penguin Books USA Inc. • Alistair MacLeod, "The Boat." From THE LOST SALT GIFT OF BLOOD by Alistair MacLeod. Used by permission of the Canadian Publishers, McClelland & Stewart, Toronto. • John Montague, "An Occasion of Sin." © Exile Editions Ltd. and John Montague. • Frank Moorhouse, "The Drover's Wife." From *Room Service*, 1985. With permission of the author. • Bharati Mukherjee, "A Wife's Story." From *The Middleman and Other Stories* by Bharati Mukherjee. Copyright © Bharati Mukherjee, 1988. Reprinted by permission of Penguin Books Canada Limited. • Alice Munro. "The Found Boat" from SOMETHING I'VE BEEN MEANING TO TELL YOU by Alice Munro. Copyright © 1974 by Alice Munro. Published by McGraw-Hill Ryerson Limited. Reprinted by arrangement with the Virginia Barber Literary Agency. All rights reserved. • R.K. Narayan, "Lawley Road," from MALGUDI DAYS by R.K. Narayan. Copyright © 1972, 1975, 1978, 1980, 1981, 1982 by R.K. Narayan. Used by permission of Viking Penguin, a division of Penguin Books USA Inc. • Ben Okri, "Incidents at the Shrine." Copyright Ben Okri 1986 Reproduced by kind permission of the author. • Sam Selvon, "Johnson and the Cascadura." Reprinted by permission of the Estate of the late Samuel Selvon. • Olive Senior, "The Chocho Vine." From DISCERNER OF HEARTS by Olive Senior. Used by permission of the Canadian Publishers, McClelland & Stewart, Toronto. • Amy Tan, "Two Kinds." Reprinted by permission of G. P. Putnam's Sons from "Two Kinds" from THE JOY LUCK CLUB by Amy Tan. Copyright © 1989 by Amy Tan. • M.G. Vassanji, "Leaving." From *Uhuru Street* by M.G. Vassanji. Used by permission of the Canadian Publishers McClelland & Stewart, Toronto. • Archie Weller, "Going Home." From *Going Home*, 1986. Reprinted with permission of Allen & Unwin Australia Pty Ltd.

Suggested Essay Topics

See Alternate Table of Contents for stories that are appropriate to the various topics listed here.)

1. Compare the ways in which two authors portray Africa. Is their reading political or cultural?

2. Discuss an author's treatment of alcohol abuse and explain how alcohol plays a part in shaping the events of the narrative.

3. Compare the ways in which two authors play with the concept of structure. How does the structure of the story influence the process of characterization?

4. What role does landscape play in two Canadian short stories? How do the authors depict their landscapes and what are they saying about life in Canada?

5. Discuss the ways in which two authors portray the Caribbean experience. To what extent do personal and public mythologies influence the Caribbean way of life?

6. How do two authors create and convey their characters? Do they give more weight to a character because he or she is sympathetic?

7. Discuss the relationship between protagonist and antagonists in two stories and compare the methods by which the authors enable their heroes to achieve resolution.

8. Compare the ways in which two authors define and convey childhood. What roles do innocence and naivete play in the children's lives?

9. Discuss the treatment of the theme of displacement in two stories and how the characters grapple with or overcome their isolation.

10. How do documents or documentary evidence influence either the plot or the structure of the stories of two authors?

11. In two stories, what role do family relationships play in the formation of various characters' perspectives and outlooks on life? In what way do family relationships affect the actions of the characters?

12. Compare the treatment of First Nations experience in two stories and discuss how the authors draw a relationship between the characters and their environments.

13. Compare the treatment of First Nations experience in two stories and discuss why it is necessary for authors to chronicle their culture and way of life.

14. In two stories, discuss the influence of first person narration on the plot. Are the narrators reliable? What makes them credible or unbelievable?

15. Discuss the role of the supernatural in two stories and examine how the author creates a sense of magic or mystery in the process of conveying his or her narrative.

16. What are two authors saying about the nature of their culture or society when they address the issue of prejudice? What solutions, if any, do they offer for the problems of their society? Are the stories themselves solutions or pointers to solutions?

17. How do two authors use imagery to convey their narratives? If the images are *leitmotifs*, do they unify the works and if so in what ways?

18. How does imagery assist in the telling of two stories? Does the imagery reflect the nature of the theme or the plot?

19. Discuss the role of love in two stories and compare the ways in which the authors define what love is. How do the characters in the stories respond to love?

20. Compare the treatment of mother/daughter relationships in two of the stories and examine how, if at all, the characters come to a sense of resolution in their conflicts.

21. Compare the treatment of the novella form in two novellas. How do the authors sustain their narratives and what devices do they employ to unify their works?

22. What role does setting play in two of the stories? How do the authors create their setting, what do they choose for the reader to see and what impact does this have on the course of the narrative?

23. Discuss the treatment of sex in two of the stories. How do the authors define sexuality? Does their treatment of sexuality shed any light on the nature of their societies?

24. Discuss the role of women in two of the stories and define how the authors perceive women's struggles. What solutions to the problems women face are offered by these authors?

25. How do women authors portray women? Compare the treatment of women by two women authors. Do the authors create sympathetic characters, and if so, how do they achieve this?

26. How do two authors define the United States? Are they sympathetic? What problems do these authors perceive as being inherent in the American experience?

Glossary of Terms

Allegory An extended metaphor in which the narrative of the story conveys a larger idea, usually of a moral nature.

Antagonist A primary character in a story who opposes the actions, ideas and intents of the protagonist. The antagonist often influences the protagonist's decisions and actions.

Background See Setting.

Character A participant in a narrative. Those who play important roles are *primary characters*; those of lesser importance are *secondary characters*; those who play very small roles in the dramatic action are *minor characters*. The central character of a story is called the *protagonist*.

Character development The ways in which a character changes, learns or grows during a narrative through the acquisition of knowledge that enriches his or her understanding of events.

Characterization The process by which an author gives individuality and depth to a character, building up a complete personality so that the reader gains the sense of a real person. Characterization is established through the accumulation of details relating to physical appearance, habits, movements, speech patterns and language usage, motives, psychology and personality.

Climax The critical moment in a plot when the conflict reaches its decisive point.

Collapsed time A technique used to propel the narrative forward in time by means of a short linking passage or segue. See Segue.

Comedy In classical drama, a play that ended with a happy resolution of opposing parties. The word is now applied to any narrative that evokes a humorous response in the reader or audience.

Comic See Comedy.

Conflict Tension created through interaction between characters with opposing ideas or motivations. Conflict is an essential element in the dramatic action of a story. See Plot.

Denouement The conclusion of a story, when the implications of the plot are studied, and the events placed in context and clarified for the characters and the readers.

Dialogue A conversation between two or more characters.

Diction An author's choice of words and vocabulary, and the manner in which the author applies linguistic devices such as imagery.

Dramatic action The events of the plot of a short story—essentially, the what happens in a story and the dynamics that result from the interaction of the characters. See Conflict.

Dramatic irony See Irony.

Dynamics In the specific sense used here, the interaction between characters

512

and the forces affecting their behaviour.

Exegesis   The explanation or interpretation of events or ideas by the author or a character in the process of a narrative. See Showing and telling.

Exposition   The narrative element in which the setting, characters and situations of the plot are presented. The exposition or "showing" of the key elements of the story is usually the first step in presenting the plot. See Plot.

Extended metaphor   See Metaphor, Allegory.

Fairy tale   A story that uses the supernatural or the mysterious in order to propel the narrative.

Fantasy   Any piece of literature that consciously deviates from reality or the boundaries of plausibility. Fantasy stories often contain elements of the supernatural and the imaginary in terms of character, plot and setting.

Field of vision   See Setting.

First person narrative   In a first person narrative, the story is told by a character who is an active participant or a witness to the events. The first person narrator, using the pronoun "I," conveys the events from a subjective, eyewitness or participatory perspective, and brings to the narrative a sense of emotional connectedness, though this subjectivity may contribute to a biased or limited point of view.

Foreground   See Setting.

Genre   The class or style of literature. The short story is a genre; drama, poetry, the novel and biography are others.

Hyperbole   A figure of speech using gross exaggeration for comic or observational purposes.

Image   In a literary sense, a verbal construct that creates a visual impression in the mind of the reader, often called a "word picture." See Imagery.

Imagery   A linguistic element that illustrates meaning figuratively through the use of images or word pictures. It can take various forms: an image or word picture that conveys meaning literally, such as "the red chair"; a *leitmotif* or an image repeated through a story to lend both verbal and metaphorical unity to the work; a symbol, which is an image with multiple meanings and readings; a metaphor, which is an image used in an associative relationship with another to establish a range of possible associations and readings; or a simile, which establishes a comparative relationship between two images to illustrate or clarify an idea.

Here is a simple way to remember the systems of imagery:

Image x = x (the thing itself)

Leitmotif   x,x,x,x,x   (repeated usage)

Metaphor x is y (association)

Simile x is like y (comparison)

Symbol x = a,b,c,... (multiple meanings)

See Image, Metaphor, Leitmotif, Simile, Symbol.

Irony Using irony, an author or character will say one thing while implying the opposite, often to draw attention to some incongruity. Irony can also be extended to the narrative of the story and is then called *dramatic irony*, through which the reader is able to see beyond the events of the plot and perceive another meaning that may or may not be known to the character.

Leitmotif A motif (image or theme) that is repeated, perhaps in varying forms, in the course of a narrative. This repetition serves to unify an extended work.

Literalism The misreading of a fictional narrative through the reader's belief that whatever he or she reads is true.

Metaphor A word picture in which one image is associated or equated with another. This imaginative association helps to illuminate meaning.

Modernism A movement among writers and artists in the early twentieth century that rejected the forms and structures established in previous eras. The modernists sought to rejuvenate art through a re-evaluation of basic principles such as form and language.

Narrative An account of a sequence of connected events. The word narrative is used synonymously with story.

Narrative voice The voice through which a story is told. All stories have a teller, whether identified or not. When the narrator is not a character in the story, it is assumed that the person telling the story is not the author, but a mask or persona adopted (much as an actor will adopt a role in order to convey a character in a drama) to assist in the narrative process. See First person narrative and Third person narrative.

Narrator The person who tells a story.

Novella An extended narrative of between 12,000 and 18,000 words in length that tends to be more ambitious in scope than a short story.

Omniscient narrator The third person narrative voice, or omniscient narrator, observes, relates and comments on the action from outside, from the point of view of complete knowledge of events and their implications.

Open ending An ending that leaves the reader to decide several outcomes rather than presenting one clear-cut resolution.

Oral history Historical events passed down by word of mouth, often in the form of stories.

Persona The character or "mask" assumed by the author as narrator in a story. See Narrative voice.

Plausibility The believability of the events in a story; Could they have happened? Do they seem real, logical and acceptable to the reader. Plausibility helps in establishing *verity* or the authenticity of a story.

Plot The sequence of events of a story, the what happens of the narrative. In conventional narratives, plot usually consists of the *exposition*, or the opening of the story; the *conflict*, in which characters confront and often oppose each other; the *climax*, where the conflict reaches a critical point and where the characters are committed to the actions and situations in which they have placed themselves; the *resolution*, where the outcome of the climax is worked through; and the *denouement*, or the aftermath of events where the complications of the plot are unravelled and examined in retrospect.

There are several types of plots: A *linear plot* follows the course of events from one moment to the next, without use of digression or backtracking, in a logical and chronological, a,b,c pattern. A *digressional plot* has a non-linear, non-chronological structure and may backtrack in time to provide information to the reader, following a sequence such as f,g,h,a,b,i,j, etc. A *reverse plot* is a story that is told from its end to its beginning in order to highlight the cause-and-effect relationship at work within the narrative, and usually follows a z,y,x,w sequence. See Exposition, Conflict, Resolution, Climax, Denouement.

Poetic justice An outcome that provides a satisfying and morally appropriate ending to a story. Most readers want a fair and just resolution of conflict in a story, which is said to be poetic because it often stretches plausibility in order to satisfy a reader's hopes or expectations.

Point of view The perspective of the narrator, which influences the interpretation of events. It therefore depends on the narrative voice, which may entail various limitations. A character or narrator who cannot determine all the events or their implications has a limited point of view. See Narrative voice, First person narrative, Third person narrative.

Postcolonial literature The body of literary works produced by former colonies. In the English-speaking world, many of these former colonies are still part of the British Commonwealth of which the Queen of England is the symbolic head.

Postcolonial literatures present significant challenges to readers used to reading from a Eurocentric point of view—that is, readers who are often unfamiliar with the culture, customs, geography, mythology and language of the country. This reaction to the unfamiliar or "exotic" is an essential part of the experience of reading works produced in these literatures.

Postcolonial literatures tend to express themes of cultural and political self-awareness and self-assertion in order to counter the enduring dominance of Eurocentric cultural expression during the colonial era, and to reflect the emergence of a new literary synthesis.

Protagonist   The central character in a narrative, often called the hero or "anti-hero," on whom the reader's attention, and often sympathies, are focused. See Character.

Realism   The portrayal of life as it is, in as direct and authentic a manner as possible. Stories using realism often contain a great deal of visual detail and dialogue that sounds as though it was transcribed rather than invented, and follows actual patterns and habits of speech.

Resolution   The juncture in the plot of a story during which the outcome of the events leading to the climax is traced. It may offer the way out of a difficult situation or the answer to a troubling question. See Plot.

Reverse plot   See Plot.

Segue   A bridge between two sections of a story or a link between two ideas.

Setting   The where and when of the story. Setting can be understood in physical terms (place, geography, interior or exterior situations) or temporal terms (when the story happens, present time or historical time). The emotional and cultural context of the events and the characters are other aspects of setting.

In physical terms, setting consists of the *foreground* (the focus of narrative attention) and the *background* (the narrative context of this focus). Readers should pay particular attention to the author's field of vision, or what the author chooses to describe in terms of the environment for the story.

Setting the scene   The description of situation and circumstance often found in the opening of a story. See Exposition.

Short story   A narrative in prose of more than 500 words and usually not more than 12,000 words in length. With its roots in the oral tradition, which sought both to entertain and to inform, the short story gained considerably in popularity in England during the nineteenth century with the rise in literacy and the cheap production and dissemination of printed matter.

Short short story   A prose narrative of less than 500 words. Sometimes referred to as a sketch or "postcard fiction," because it can be written in a very small space, the short short story often takes the form of a vignette that examines a brief situation or sketches an emotional response to an event.

Showing and telling   Showing and telling distinguishes between the two prime methods authors have at their disposal for conveying a narrative. In a *showing* story, the author dramatizes the information through dynamics, dialogue and imagery, with little narrative exegesis. By allowing the characters to convey the narrative information, the author communicates the information of the story from a dramatic rather than instructive stance.

In a *telling* story, the author or narrator describes and comments on the action, providing background information that enlarges the reader's interpretation of the action. It relies on a descriptive rather than dramatic approach to storytelling.

Simile A figure of speech in which one thing is likened to another in order to clarify an image.

Sketch See Short short story.

Story within a story A digression into a different thread of narrative in the course of a story.

Stream of consciousness A form of narrative that records the natural process of a mind at work, flowing from one thought to the next with no apparent logic.

Subnarrative See Subplot.

Subplot A story narrative of secondary importance, usually involving secondary characters.

Symbol An image that represents or is associated with something else. A symbol may become widely associated (through metaphor and simile) with an extended range of meanings and possible readings. For instance,

the image of the sun connotes life, growth, spring, goodness, warmth, knowledge, power, constancy, brightness; when it is mentioned in relation to a specific situation, character or setting, those connotations are implied.

Telling See Showing and telling.

Theme The prominent or recurring idea of a story, which may be invoked through imagery, plot, characterization or diction.

Third person narrative A story told by a detached observer who is usually outside the action and observes the events from a distance. The use of the third person pronouns *he* or *she* and the absence of the first person pronoun *I* is usually an indicator of this narrative form. A third person narrator is also called an omniscient narrator. See Narrative voice, First person narrative, Omniscient narrator.

Tone The emotional register of the narrative. The tone of a story can be happy, sad, serious, profound, humorous, etc.

Tragedy By convention, any literary work, but particularly drama, in which the protagonist, through circumstance and personal shortcoming, falls to disaster.

Understatement An expression that is excessively restrained, often for ironic effect.

Vignette See Short short story.